I0651918

TURNER'S RAGE

JAMES SEYMOUR

Copyright © 2022 James Seymour

ISBN: 978-1-922409-94-2
Published by Vivid Publishing
A division of Fontaine Publishing Group
P.O. Box 948, Fremantle
Western Australia 6959
www.vividpublishing.com.au

 A catalogue record for this
book is available from the
National Library of Australia

All characters – other than the obvious historical figures – in this publication are fictitious and any resemblance to real persons, living or dead, is purely coincidental. Some place names are fictitious and any resemblance to real places is purely coincidental.

Revised third edition. All rights reserved. No part of this publication may be reproduced, stored in a retrieval system or transmitted in any form or by any means, electronic, mechanical, photocopying, recording or otherwise, without the prior written permission of the copyright holder.

Books by James Seymour

Turner's Rage, first published 2020, Vivid Publishing
Third edition, published 2022, Vivid Publishing

Turner's Awakening, Vivid Publishing 2021

. . . .

Keep an eye out for the release date
for Book Three of the Turner series.

Published by Vivid Publishing,
a division of Fontaine Press.
www.vividpublishing.com.au

Dedicated to the memory of my dear friend
Alexander Pinkerton Crawford
1952 – 2017

We miss his wonderful humour, fellowship and fun.
He was a blessing to so many.
We will meet again.

Foreword

The language used in this story is modern English, with a few hints of the Georgian and Regency eras. The purpose here is to make the novel easy to read – helping everyone with their time management.

The novel is the first in a series of books primarily about William Turner and his adventures as he grows into manhood. While writing the first novel, I found the characters so interesting that there was a need to expand the series so that the Turner family's life runs in parallel with William. The focus will remain on William, but this first book also aims to fully introduce the characters who create the action and suspense. Each book contains a complete story, and the reader will gain a richer experience chronologically following the series.

In this first book, the period from July to November 1826 is covered. William's large family, which surrounds him, enriches his adventures. This allows exploring several family life issues in and around 1826, defining William's character and future. While this is a work of fiction, it draws heavily on the history of the early nineteenth century, the rapid expansion of technological change taking place, and the struggle against poverty that threatens all classes of English society.

The period of the novel is only eleven years since the end of the Napoleonic wars. The naval sequences provide an initial opportunity to explore what is happening across the Irish sea and the revolts to come. The initial discussion is from the English point of view; however, the future books restore the balance with some exciting developments.

The characters surrounding William give us a unique insight into a community that was still traditional despite the changes taking place around them.

I have added a detailed list of characters assisting readers with the large cast.

I hope you enjoy the first book in this series as much as I enjoyed writing it. Keep an eye out for the release date of Book 2 from the publisher.

James Seymour, October 2020

Prologue

In 1826 England was in the end years of the first industrial revolution, a time of increasing poverty as the country still felt the effects of the Napoleonic wars. History shows us that slavery was continuing and Catholic emancipation, while soon to be achieved, did little to help the plight of the Irish. Political unrest in the north of England and Ireland was spreading, and the government carefully guarded against any movements that would threaten the country's stability.

Members of the aristocracy in the House of Lords were more interested in maintaining their way of life than assisting social change. But change was coming, and many brilliant men in the British parliament worked tirelessly to achieve Catholic emancipation legislated, and the slave trade ended. The Corn Laws, not to be repealed for another twenty years, were a huge concern in the northern industrialised cities. Workers' families were starving because of low wages, excessive rents, and the high price of bread.

The Church of England remained a powerful force in England with many good-natured and well-meaning clergymen. The great evangelical movement commenced that saw so many missionary organisations founded, reforming the English conscience. The Church of England and the Methodists were the catalyst for much reform, charity, social justice, and the importance of the family.

Due to the miserable conditions in the industrialised cities, unrest was building. Various groups were fermenting for workers' rights, and massive rallies were held in the north of England. The government was determined to stamp out unrest, and it was before this time that the transportation of convicts was enacted. Magistrates were not slow in handing down harsh sentences, many for the slightest crimes.

It was a time when women were dependent on their husbands and were denied the vote. Women who did not marry usually ended up in the most difficult circumstances of poverty and isolation. In most cases, women who inherited property or money found their wealth transferred to their husbands in marriage. For good reason, we notice the growing disenchantment of women and the seeds of 'rights for women' developing.

Significant discoveries were being made in medicine, which was still primitive compared to today. Similarly, engineering advances saw experimentation with the refinement of cast iron into steel. The steam engine, which was transforming many industries, saw greater use of robust steel components rather than those made from wood. Companies scrambling for train line routes were changing England's transport infrastructure forever.

It was ten years before the reign of Queen Victoria, a coming time when the Victorians invented some of the most significant technological changes of all time.

In this setting, we find the Turner family, who, a generation before, was dependent on a small but successful Guildford bakery business in Surrey. Jonathan Turner, carrying on and expanding the family business, is determined his family will not slip into poverty, no matter what the cost.

William Turner, a perceptive and intelligent six-year-old, awakens from his dreams and faces challenges he will only understand in the distant future.

Turner's Rage
List of Characters
July 1826

The Turner Family of Guildford

Jonathan Turner	Father of William	Baker and Business Owner
Eleanora Turner	Mother of William	Wife of Jonathan Turner
Thomas Turner	Son of Jonathan & Eleanora	Baker
Bethany Charlotte Eleanora Turner (Beth)	Daughter of Jonathan & Eleanora	Governess
Anne Turner	Daughter of Jonathan & Eleanora	Business Assistant & Home help
Clementine Turner (Clemmie)	Daughter of Jonathan & Eleanora	Home help
Madeline Turner (Maddie)	Daughter of Jonathan & Eleanora	Child
Simeon Turner (Sim)	Son of Jonathan & Eleanora	Child
William Turner (Will)	Son of Jonathan & Eleanora	Child
Marcia Turner	Daughter of Jonathan & Eleanora	Child
Neville David Turner (Nev)	Son of Jonathan & Eleanora	Child

Service Staff

Mrs Jennings	Housekeeper
Miss Aggie Peters	Maid
Mrs Ethel Nibley	Mrs Turner's Maid
Miss Rosalind Nibley	Ethel's daughter

Huntley House, Greenwich

Mr Charles Boot	Butler
Miss Mary Troath	Lady's Maid
Mrs Eliza Smythe	Cook

Turner Family Dogs

Snups

Nosey

Family Doctors

Dr Jeremy Stephens

Dr Neville Bassington

Dr David Sopwith

The local Church, Guildford

Rev Andrew Taggart	Rector
Mrs Laura Taggart	The Rector's wife and church worker
Mrs Glossip	Church worker
Mr Jonathan Turner	Chairman, Parish Council
Mr Rupert Smith	Parish Council
Mr Blake Wood	Parish Council & Council Secretary & Solicitor
Dr Jeremy Stephens	Parish Council & Secretary
Mr James Stewart	Parish Council, Solicitor
Miss Ruby Bowers	Student – Church School
Miss Dawn Luckett	Student – Church School

The Church at Woking

Rev Charles Upton	Rector
Mrs Wendy Upton	Spouse of Charles Upton
Miss Bethany Turner	Governess

The Turner Bakery

Mr Jeb Hiscock	Bakery Manager
Mr Peter Hammer	Senior Foreman
Mr Aaron Hall	Baker
Miss Rose Bell	Baker
Miss Sophia Stanton	Pastry Baker
Miss Heather Gant	Bakers Assistant
Mr Ralph Fenn	Bakery Cart Driver
Miss Audrey Stern	Accounts Clerk

| Mr Robert Baxter | Stable Manager |
| Judd Hedge | Stable Man |

The Epsom Stables
| Mr Thomas Baxter | Stable Manager |

Hurst's Tailors and Seamstresses
Mrs Fiona Smith	Seamstress and Guildford Shop Manager
Mr Lionel Wall	Tailor and Manager Woking, and of the Store chain
Miss Fiona Handle	Seamstress, Guildford Shop
Mr Tom Mead	Tailor, Guildford Shop

The Steam-Powered Flour Mill
Mr Stanley Percival	Engineer, Watson's Steam Engineers
Mr Terence Spencer	Mill Manager
Mrs Lydia Spencer	Wife of Terence
Master Levi Spencer	Son of Terence and Lydia
Miss Andrea Spencer	Daughter of Terence and Lydia

Chimney Sweeps
Mr Jack Slope	Master Chimney Sweep
Reuben	Chimney Sweep
Tom	Chimney Sweep
Olivia Stepton	Chimney Sweep

Batton Place Manor
Mr Patrick Easton	Lord of the Manor
Mr Mark Stepton	Labourer
Mrs Alison Stepton	Spouse of Mark Stepton and Maid

The Guilford Community
Mr Rupert Smith	Mayor & Parish Council Member
Mrs Marjorie Smith	Wife of Rupert
Master Richard Smith	Son of Rupert & Marjorie
Mr Russel Elliot	Blacksmith

Master Caleb Elliot	Son of Russel
Mr Isiah Linton	Blacksmith
Mr Frederick Higgins	Storekeeper
Mr Daniel Tuesbury	Master of Abbot's Hospital

Guildford Constabulary

Mr Michael Rawlins	Parish Constable
Mr Daniel Cricks	Watchman

The Guildford Institute

Mr Henry Sharples	Institute Volunteer Officer

The Bassington Family of London

Mr David Bassington	Newspaper Owner and Bookseller
Mrs Jennifer Bassington	Wife of David
Doctor Neville Winston Bassington, RN	Son of David & Jennifer
Miss Megan Bassington	Daughter of David & Jennifer

The Bassington Family of Guildford

Doctor Neville Bassington	Son of David Bassington
Mrs Bethany Bassington	nee Turner

The McPherson Family of Greenwich

Mr Hamish McPherson	Brewer and Businessman	
Mrs Marjorie McPherson	Spouse of Hamish	
Mr Douglass McPherson	Son of Hamish	Brewery Manager Glasgow
Mr Archie McPherson	Son of Hamish	Brewery Manager Edinburgh
Mr Lachlan McPherson	Son of Hamish	Brewery Manager Edinburgh
Mr James McPherson	Son of Hamish	Brewery Manager & Businessman Glasgow
Jenkins	Butler	
Babcock	Coach Driver	
Handle	Footman	
Mrs Swiggins	Cook	
Miss Jones	Nanny	
Family Dogs	Red Socks, Boiler	

The Steele Family of Woolwich

Mr Alexander Steele	Engineer & Founder of Woods Artillery Foundry
Mrs Jennifer Steele	Wife of Alexander
Mr Mark Steele	Son of Alexander & Jennifer
Mr Andrew Steele	Son of Alexander & Jennifer
Mr Timothy Steele	Son of Alexander & Jennifer
Miss Marion Steele	Daughter of Alexander & Jennifer
Miss Nicole Stephens	Bridesmaid of Marion

The local Church at Greenwich

Archdeacon Rufus Handle	Rector and Rural Dean
Mrs Felicity Handle	Wife of Archdeacon Handle

The Turner Family of Ewell

Richard Turner	Brother of Jonathan	Pub Owner 'The Black Swan'
Sarah Turner	Wife of Richard	
Oliver Turner	Son of Richard & Sarah	Pub Manager, Epsom
Harry Turner	Son of Richard & Sarah	Pub Manager, Ewell
Katherine Turner	Daughter of Richard & Sarah	Child

The Racing Horse Pub, Epson

Oliver Turner	Manager, Racing Horse Pub	Epsom

The South Family of Fintelton Manor

The Right Honourable Sir David South	Earl of Fintelton, and Lord of the Manor
The Right Honourable Lady Jane South	Countess of Fintelton, and wife of Sir David
Sir Hugh South	Son and Entitled Heir of Sir David
Sir Robert South RN	Son of Sir David
Lady Emma South	Daughter of Sir David
Mr Malcolm Stem	Estate Manager
Mr Thomas Pike	Butler
Mrs Cora Walsh	Housekeeper
Mr Henry Barrett	Earls Valet

Mrs Judy Wapples	Cook
Miss Margaret Lane	Lady Jane's maid
Miss Jane Winston	Lady Emma's maid
Miss Sally Johnson	Maid

In-Laws of the South's

Sir John Philps	Brother of Lady Jane South
Lady Angela Philps	Sir John's wife

The South Family Attorneys

Manifold & Stout	Sir David's Attorneys.	
Mr Michael Manifold	Senior Partner, Manifold & Stout	Deceased
Mr Evan Finchley	Senior Partner, Manifold & Stout	

"Harting" House, St James's Square

Mr Matthew Staines	Butler
Mr Dennis Hopton	Previous Butler
Mrs Cora Walsh	Housekeeper
Mr Henry Barrett	Earls Valet
Mrs Judy Wapples	Cook
Miss Margaret Lane	Lady Jane's maid
Miss Jane Winston	Lady Emma's maid

Tenant Farmers of Fintelton

Mr Michael Merton	Tenant Farmer
Mrs Jenny Merton	Wife of Michael

The Crew of HMS Providence

Captain Mark Foster	Captain
Lieutenant Neville Bassington	Surgeon
Lieutenant Robert South	Officer of the Watch

The Crew of HMS Restless

Commander Sir Robert South	Captain
Sergeant Michael Swanton	Captains First Servant
AB Jonathon Bright	Captains Second Servant
Lieutenant Richard Small	First Officer (Mate)
Lieutenant Frederick Ham	First Officer (Mate)
Lieutenant Richard Brinkley	Second Officer
Warrant Officer Kevin Trotters	Master (Sailing Master)
Petty Officer Richard Door	Master at Arms
Petty Officer John Fulcher	Master at Arms
Mr William Collins	Midshipman
Mr Albert Kent	Midshipman
Petty Officer Richard Young	Quartermaster (Helmsman)
Captain Horace Coombes	Marine Commander
Lieutenant Stanley White	2IC to Captain Coombes
Sergeant Philip Wait	Marines Sergeant
Petty Officer Ian Dodds	Ships Carpenter

Admiralty

Admiral Sir Franklin Crouch	First Naval Lord
Lady Katherine Crouch	Wife of Admiral Crouch
The Right Honourable Sir Cecil Fowey	Earl of Dawlting, and Advisor to the Board of Navy
The Right Honourable Lady Hannah Fowey Countess of Dawlting	Countess of Dawlting, and wife of Sir Cecil
Mr Malcolm Smith	Comptroller
Mrs Robyn Smith	Wife of Malcolm Smith
Colonel Jonathan Scott	Admiralty Security Chief of Staff

Flagship, Commander in Chief, Blue Fleet, Portsmouth

Admiral Sir Tristan Sutherland	Commander in Chief, Portsmouth Blue Fleet
Lady Amanda Sutherland	Wife of Sir Tristan
Commodore Richard Jacobs	Secretary to Admiral Sutherland
Lieutenant Reginald Ludlam	Surgeon

The Guildford Medical Practice

Dr Neville Bassington	Founding Partner
Dr David Sopwith	Founding Partner

The Sopwith Family

Dr David Sopwith	Local Doctor	Estates at Cookstown and Coleraine in Ireland
Miss Victoria Sopwith	David's Sister	
Mrs Molly Lane	Housekeeper	

Lions Bank of Guildford

Mr Thomas Meyhew	Founder and Owner
Mr Lawrence Appleby	High Street Branch Manager
Mr John Short	Teller

Lions Bank of Petersfield

Miss Katherine Constance	Bank Teller

United Kingdom Investments

Mrs Janet Stubbington	Wife of Frank Stubbington – Deceased

PART 1

"With Age Comes Understanding"

July 1826, High Street, Guilford, England

Chapter 1

William pressed his nose against the small bedroom window far above High Street and noticed puffs of mist drifting across the Guildford meadows and disappearing behind the castle ruins. The house was quiet – almost too quiet. Rubbing the sleep from his eyes, he remembered the horrible scene he encountered last night. A chill came over the boy of six. He dropped back under the blanket stopping the shivers, hiding from the memory that was blazing on his mind.

Opening his eyes again, he noticed his big toe sticking out from under the crinkled blanket. He pulled it under quickly as if a fox chased it. What was his father doing? Why was he beating her? The memory put fear in his heart. He was sure his father saw him peeking around the bedroom door. Would he receive a belting again today?

From downstairs came a muffled cry of alarm. Then footsteps came running up the stairs. His sister, Anne, broke into the room and cried out, "Sim! Quick, run and fetch Doctor Stephens. Mother is very unwell!"

Simeon, waking from a deep sleep, turned over and faced her.

"Hurry! Once you have told Doctor Stephens, run to the bakery, and tell father that mother has taken ill. He should return home!"

She stood there, ensuring Simeon was awake. Anne Turner was a thoughtful, quiet girl of seventeen, helping in the house and working mornings at her father's bakery. Her elder sister Bethany excelled in education and found a position as governess with the Reverend Charles Upton at Woking. With Beth being away, Anne was now the eldest daughter at home and took on more domestic responsibilities. Her mother's health was slowly fading, worrying both sisters for some time. Anne would advise her sister of the home situation – sending a letter today! She ran back down the stairs.

The moaning cry came again. This time louder, and William was sure it was his mother. He heard Clementine's alarmed, loud voice, "Simeon, hurry, and fetch the Doctor."

Clementine was three years younger than Anne and of an age and nature where panic came too quickly. Her voice was loud and usually achieved a quick result, but never calming. This time it worked, with Simeon climbing out of bed half asleep. William's elder brother by two years was a calm and methodical boy, always sent on missions that needed someone reliable.

William watched as Simeon stumbled out of bed, pulled on his trousers, then shirt, and flew through the bedroom door, down two flights of stairs and out the front door. He heard Sim ask Anne, "What shall I tell the doctor if...". The voices trailed off, and someone quietly closed the front door.

Pulling on his clothes, William tip-toed down the stairs past the same door he peeped into last night. Sheets and towels covered in blood lay in the hallway. William gasped and suddenly felt sick. He became dizzy as he smelled the blood.

Mrs Jennings, coming through the bedroom door, almost colliding with the boy, noticed his face colour turning white. "Come with me, young William." The small thickset housekeeper grabbed him under one arm, the sheets and towels in the other, and struggled down the stairs. She pushed William into the kitchen, seating him beside Madeline.

"Have some breakfast before your father returns!" Mrs Jennings was sympathetic towards William knowing how unfair the treatment from his father usually was.

"Mrs Jennings, may I see Mother please?"

"Not now, William. She is unwell and needs rest. The doctor will be here soon, then we will know. Now eat your breakfast, please, as your chores are waiting before school. Reverend Taggart is very particular about the starting time."

William watched Madeline struggling with four-year-old Marcia Turner. The youngest of the Turner children also asked for her mother and became quite difficult about her food. Madeline, a calm girl who spoke softly, settled Marcia down for breakfast.

The young lad found that his stomach was not ready for breakfast due to the upstairs sights. Last night his father was angry when William peeped into their room. Safety in his mother's arms was no longer an option, and the pending return of his father was not a pleasant thought. At age six, he was astute; some would say 'street smart', having the perception of an older lad that now warned him of the danger lying ahead.

Pocketing a piece of bread, some cheese and an apple, he darted out the back door, calling Snups, the lolloping family dog who was his partner in adventure. Round the back of the neighbouring houses and down the garden slope towards the river, they galloped. William hated the continual suffering he endured from his father and the consequences that came with it. Whatever happened, father always blamed him and then the belting came. Being out of the line of fire was safer than staying at the table. He made himself scarce and headed for the river.

While sitting beside her mother, Anne glanced out the window and noticed the little head bobbing behind some hedges. She frowned, immediately recognising William's mop of dark brown hair and thinking, "This will not go well for William." As his head moved out of sight, she refocused on her mother and grimaced at the bruising showing on the cheeks and arms.

"Has he been beating you again, Mother?"

Anne's mother, Eleanora Turner, lay there with her eyes slightly closed, her body shaking. She was tense, exhausted, and in pain. She murmured, "Just call the Doctor, please." Anne gently held her hand and whispered, "Simeon has gone for the doctor – it won't be long now." Anne wiped her mother's brow with a damp clean cloth. She understood that a married couple would have disputes but never with results like this.

In her mind Eleanora was miles away – her body floated over the pain as she questioned why her husband was treating her so. 'I know he loves me dearly, but why does he need union every night. How do I explain that I am no longer able? How do I fulfil my marital duty for him? But I so much need rest.' Then she felt Anne's warm, steady hand holding hers and the comfort it brought. "Thank you, Anne, you are such a blessing ...." and she drifted back into sleep again.

Anne's father, Jonathan Turner, was an intelligent man but driven by passion and the need for success. His violent rage at times became all-consuming. On occasions, his wife and children felt its full force. He believed punishment for a misdemeanour was always warranted, which was the converse of his children's thoughts, particularly the girls.

Jonathan was a tough man, coping with volatile times in the early nineteenth century as Britain struggled with the reforms needed for an industrialised society. His business had generated some slight wealth, and the family was now benefiting. Through foresight and strong management, his bakery was successful. His children were gaining an education and the skills needed for this new century. It was essential for the family's future that his business continued to grow and build on the progress already achieved.

After alerting the Doctor, Simeon ran on towards the river. He was now tiring and running out of breath. At the bakery, he found his father and passed on the message. Jonathan was not pleased with being disturbed.

"Are you sure they need me?"

"Yes, Father, mother is very unwell – Anne insists! They also asked that I fetch the doctor."

Jonathan Turner stared at the boy, considering what action he should take. He was becoming agitated by this unnecessary interruption. His wife was sleeping perfectly well when he left for the bakery at three this morning. He stared at Simeon, who shuffled on his feet, uncomfortable that his father would doubt his word and being eager for some breakfast at home.

Jonathan knew that of all his children, Simeon was trustworthy and reliable – he would not overstate an issue. There was a mountain of work here, but there must be a problem if Anne insisted and had called the doctor.

"Come then, boy - this urgent call must be serious! William is not involved, is he?"

"No, Sir!"

Simeon knew well that William usually was blamed for everything. William, with boundless energy, needed activity all the time. He inherited the attributes of his father - strength, coordination, and a quick mind, but lacked concentration and sometimes displayed his father's temper. Simeon desired the coordination that William called on naturally, yet he must be happy with what the Lord gave him – as the Reverend Taggart had advised him. William, with his energy, was quite often the one left holding the stick. For this, he suffered greatly at the hands of his father, and Simeon was thankful for being spared this pain.

"Thomas, you best come too, as I might need you running messages. Jeb can take over. We have finished baking so he can handle the staff. Come on then, hurry up! Oh, please remind Jeb, the stable men must have all the delivery carts ready within the half-hour and the chimney sweeps attend the house once finished here."

Jonathan Turner moved off towards home with Simeon.

Thomas, Jonathan's eldest son, quickly searched for and found Jeb. "I must go with father….".

"I heard! I know the tasks. I'll get it all going!"

"Thanks, Jeb. Do not forget Slope, the Chimney Sweep!"

Having worked with the Turners for nearly six years, Jeb Hiscock, a tall, lean young man, was skilled at all the jobs in the bakery. He was steady, reliable and street smart, coming from a labourer's family in Batton Place. Jonathan Turner knew that Jeb would manage the bakery one day, while Thomas might manage another bakery in Woking. The baking business was thriving, the benefits lifting his children above the chains of poverty. Hardened men like Jeb saw the effects of poverty firsthand and desired a better life. Hard work was a quality he would instil in his children if he ever married.

The bakery and store buildings were beside the river near High Street. Jonathan Turner and Simeon walked quickly, and within minutes Thomas was following. The journey home was about fifteen minutes.

Earlier, William emerged from the back of the houses and ran through the long grass on the riverbank. This was an adventure land where his dreams came into being as he and his pirates sailed the seven seas. Here he would play with his mother, brothers and sisters. They would go on conquests and have picnics celebrating pirate victories and laugh in the sunshine as the river ran its silent course towards the ocean. It was a happy place for him.

William had suffered many a beating from his father. He understood that suppressing a situation was a better option than attracting attention. Unfortunately, being at such a tender age, sometimes the adventure far outweighed the risk assessment, and William landed on the wrong end of his father's outburst. He was now very wary, which made last night's scene even more of a burden. Should he confide in either his brother or sisters? Could he talk with his mother? Given the attention she was receiving, they would not let him see her, and even if they did, his father would be there.

Mother was always his confidant. She cuddled him close, reassured him, and never let his father touch him. But his mother was out of reach! He was near bursting point with the burden of what he had seen. Perhaps he should speak with Anne – she always protected him – perhaps!

Terrified of his predicament, he considered a possible escape. Unfortunately, his strategy was a bit lean on detail and might come undone later in the day.

'I must keep clear until father eats breakfast. Perhaps then he will not belt me!' William knew how much his father enjoyed a hearty breakfast. He always seemed more contented after this. A possible short delay before his return home may be prudent.

He sat down on the riverbank with Snups, watching the barges being loaded or untied from their berths and slowly heading off with cargoes for up and down the river Wey. William's dreams of pirates on the high seas and adventures of fame and fortune took over his thoughts. Picking up a stick, which became a sword, he started fencing and repelling the boarding pirates. Snups jumped up, barking and darting around him, occasionally jumping as his teeth grabbed at the sword. William quickly entered his imaginary world of safety with a little smile appearing on his face. Running around him, Snups yelped for joy.

A light rain was now falling, and as the southerly breeze increased, the temperature dropped a few degrees. Another pirate ship was approaching, but William was shivering from the wet and cold. Perhaps it was time for breakfast. He stood and slowly started walking home. Then, it occurred to him that his mother may be well now. He walked faster.

William was unaware that the footpath from the High Street offered an excellent view of the riverbank. Jonathan Turner glanced sideways and saw William dancing with his stick and a barking Snups darting around him as a barge passed. The tension tightened in Jonathan's chest as he felt his temper rising. He stopped and took a deep breath.

'What was Anne thinking letting William out at this time in the morning when he should be taking breakfast, finishing his chores and dressing for school? Why do I waste my hard-earned money on him?'

Jonathan took a deep breath, "Thomas, go and clip his ear and get him into the kitchen. I'll have some words with him there."

In Eleanora's bedroom, Anne continued watching over her mother. She was sleeping but not peacefully and exhibited all the signs of exhaustion. Anne was sure that their mother had been beaten by her father again last night. Unnoticed, Doctor Jeremy Stephens quietly moved into the room. Anne smiled in relief, welcoming their family doctor beside her.

Jeremy Stephens looked down at Eleanora and immediately saw the bruising that was obvious on her cheeks and arms. He frowned, "How did she come by this bruising Anne? It is very recent!"

Anne was aware of her predicament. She went to speak but then closed her mouth. As the emotion stirred within her, tears rolled down her cheeks. She dared not speak out!

Jeremy put his arm around the girl and reassured her that her mother would recover. He gently asked for a towel and hot water. As Anne left the room, Eleanora's eyes opened and focused on their old family doctor. She smiled in recognition and held out her hand to him.

Jeremy took her hand, giving it a gentle squeeze of affirmation and then said, "Now tell me, Eleanora, what has happened here?"[1]

---

[1] Domestic violence is a horrid and vile crime and must never be tolerated or left unreported. It has only been in the last fifty years that western countries have attempted combating and putting in place laws against this scourge. Unfortunately history demonstrates that domestic violence has been used as a method of control through the ages and continues to this day. If you or someone you know is suffering from domestic violence, seek help. In Australia call 1800 RESPECT. In other countries search 'Domestic Violence Help' on the web. Most western governments ensure support is available. Do not become a victim – seek help today!

Chapter 2

Jonathan and Thomas arrived at the house, finding the children at breakfast in the kitchen.

"Thomas, please check with Anne on your mother's condition while I take some breakfast! Ah, Marcia, what have you been doing here?"

Marcia looked up with a beaming smile of joy, yelling out, "Father, Father, look at this!" Jonathan walked around the table and admired the coloured crayon lines exploding across the page.

Madeline whispered, "It's a pirate ship!"

"Ah, perhaps down here it needs some blue for the sea?" Jonathan pointed, and Marcia found a blue crayon and started colouring urgently.

Jonathan kissed Marcia on her forehead and gave her a little hug which pleased her immensely.

Poking his head carefully around the door, William faced his father's glaring eyes. An apple fell out of William's pocket as he took a step backwards in fright. Jonathan Turner was of medium height, about five feet eight inches, but with a strong build and thick dark brown hair. His muscular body gave him an imposing presence. He was a foreboding sight sitting there, straight-backed and with a sour expression on his face.

Now glaring into his son's eyes, Jonathan was on the verge of beating the boy.

'If only William were the blessing Thomas was to the family!' Then he recalled the boy peering into the bedroom last night and the actions he may have observed. Worried if he beat the boy, it may all come out – he checked himself. For a man in Jonathan's position in society, he preferred his matrimonial details not to be discussed publicly. He decided on a softer approach.

William slowly walked around the kitchen door, facing his father; he straightened his back and gritted his teeth, ready for a belting.

"Where have you been, William? You know you have morning chores! Get about them, boy, before I strap you!" William's eyes opened in horror, and he ran from the room. Jonathan Turner smiled – he enjoyed handing out discipline. Better than that, he admired how quickly William reacted – the boy was quick – it reminded him of himself. His temper subsided slightly, with breakfast now becoming his focus.

William rushed up the stairs and ran straight into Anne, coming out of her mother's bedroom with paper in hand for a letter to Bethany. He put his arms around her waist and hugged her tightly. Anne stopped in surprise.

"Father will beat me again, and I'm scared for mother. Do not let him hurt mother or me, please, Anne? Can I see mother?"

By eleven years, Anne was William's elder sister and loved him with all her heart. She was a loving, gentle girl, but there was underlying steel in her armour and an intelligent mind that would help her stand up to her father. She loved playing pirates and 'hide and seek' with William and marvelled at his imagination. Wiping away the tears running down his face and folding her arms around the shuddering child, she knelt, kissed his cheek, and gave him a big hug.

"No one will hurt you, William. Doctor Stephens told us mother would be better soon, but we must not disturb her as the doctor is giving her a sleeping potion. Now come with me. We will draw a pirate."

The housekeeper was passing with various linens in her hands. "Ah - Mrs Jennings, I will be with William upstairs in the boys' bedroom."

Mrs Jennings turned, "I thought you and Clementine were with Mrs Turner, Miss Anne?"

"No. Doctor Stephens is with her now. Clementine is in the kitchen with Madeline and Marcia."

Anne pulled some chalk and a slate from a drawer in the boys' bedroom.

"How about you draw me a picture of a pirate, William?"

William toyed with the chalk as he was not presently interested in drawing. His mind was bursting with the images of what transpired last night and what the consequence would be for him. Anne, drafting a letter to her sister Eleanora, noticed William watching her.

"What is it, William?"

He looked down and moved backwards and forwards on his feet, considering his words. Then looking up again, he said, "Anne, if I told you something that was a secret, would you keep it a secret?"

"Of course, I would, William – I'm one of the pirate crew! So, it would remain a secret!"

William gave a slight shudder. "I was cold last night, and I woke up wanting mother. So, I tip-toed down the stairs. When I opened the door ever so little, I saw something I should not have seen!"

Anne was unsure she would welcome William's next words.

"Are you sure this was not a dream, William?"

"No, I got out of bed and went down!"

Anne leaned back on her chair and took a deep breath.

"Anne, you promise you won't tell anyone?"

"I promise!"

"Father was beating mother with his hand. I was so scared! He saw me at the door. I think he will beat me too."

William's comments now confirmed Anne's suspicions. She was aware of women's dependent position in a marriage relationship and how she was helpless to assist. But William was frightened – and with good reason!

"William, I think you may have been dreaming. I think it would be best if you forget this matter. We will keep this as a pirate's secret between you and me. If father asks, say you had a bad dream. This way, you will be safe, and it will stay a secret."

William shivered and looked straight into Anne's face. She reflected, 'What a handsome boy you are!' William saw the reassurance in her smile and collapsed into her arms for a big hug.

Jonathan Turner felt satisfied as he finished a good breakfast in the kitchen.

Thomas, Jonathan's eldest son, rushed in, "Father, Doctor Stephens has asked for you in the drawing-room. He asked for you alone!"

Jonathan scowled at his son, then moved through to the drawing-room where he found old Jeremy Stephens sitting at a table, looking down into a cup of tea.

"Jeremy?"

"Jonathan." Doctor Stephens knew this would be a difficult discussion and decided on the most diplomatic approach for Jonathan. They must agree on the medical outcome that Eleanora needed. Unfortunately, this would not please Jonathan. He paused, wiping his mouth. "Jonathan, let us talk a bit longer than last time. I need your help if Eleanora is to regain her health. She will recover, but she is weak and must rest! Undisturbed rest!"

"This she shall have, Doctor!" Jonathan stood aloof.

"I have given Anne and Clementine instructions on what is needed. They are both good smart girls and capable of nursing your wife. She will be recuperating for several weeks – I will call as often as possible."

Jeremy Stephens had served as the family Doctor for over forty years and delivered the eight Turner children. He was also a good friend of Jonathan's, serving with him on the church parish council. Jeremy was usually a happy fellow, always smiling, but not today. He looked up into Jonathan Turner's questioning eyes.

"Jonathan, I know you have a strong need for comfort from your wife. I also understand that you have been a faithful husband. Johnathan, it is time you understood that you might not expect repayment in kind!"

Jonathan's face tightened, and the colour in his temple slightly glowed. He stared directly into Jeremy's eyes, concerned about what might be said next.

"Jonathan, Eleanora has provided you with eight children. Praise God that they are healthy and beautiful. But childbirth has a major effect on a woman's health. With the number of births, there must be some consideration of the effects this has on Eleanora's body. You must be practical, Jonathan. It is in your interest that your relations with her are gentle."

"Jeremy, what are you telling me – that I cannot have union with my wife? That she cannot fulfil her role in our marriage?"

"No, I'm not saying that – what I'm saying is that you must master your enthusiasm for that union. Surely you understand that as a person grows older, they slow down and need more care. Take care and be gentle with her. That is not that hard for a fellow like you, who dearly loves his wife."

"I expect my wife to serve me as promised on our wedding day. However, at your request, I will curb my demands."

"Thank you, Jonathan – I'm sure you will both benefit from this. And it must be at least three months before you share her bed again. Even then, I will insist on examining her before one of these unions occurs."

"What!"

Jonathan stepped back. He was a man who expected his nightly comfort. This enforced abstinence would be most inconvenient. The anger welled up inside him.

Jeremy, expecting this reaction, led quickly to his next point.

"Now, there is just one other matter!"

"I thought you had said enough, Jeremy!"

"On examining Eleanora, I found bruises on her face, arms, and back as if someone beat her. These were not injuries that would have come from a union of loving partners, Jonathan. I'm not sure how these injuries were incurred or when, but I would ask that you protect your wife in future and ensure this does not happen again."

Jonathan Turner looked away from the Doctor. His mind flew into a panic. In his enthusiasm for union last night, he had beaten her into submission. He felt some guilt but reassured himself that this was what his wife's duty was – otherwise, the population would decrease. Then he shuddered at the memory of the door creaking open and William peeking through looking for his mother. The boy dashed away quickly on being discovered. However, Jonathan was not sure how much he had seen.

"I am not sure how she came by those bruises, but whoever caused them shall receive a beating if I catch them. I will talk with her once she is recovered and find out how this happened."

Jeremy looked long and hard at Jonathan in silence, then sipped his cup of tea.

"Jonathan, you hold an honoured place in our community as Chairman of the Parish Council. As a council member myself, I can assure you of my total support. I would advise that it might be prudent if your wife is confined until the bruises are well gone. Who knows what gossip may start if Eleanora appears in her present state?"

"Ah......I agree, Doctor. I understand. Thank you for the advice and your understanding. It is much appreciated."

Doctor Jeremy Stephens refrained from judgement but surmised what happened. He took a final sip of his cup of tea and took his leave. "I will show myself out, Jonathan."

Jonathan stood there silently, his anger rising as he knew he must not touch his wife again for some time. His knuckles grew white as the grasp of both hands gripped the mantelpiece. He steadied himself. But he must have comfort. How?

Before leaving, Jeremy made a final comment. "Ah, Jonathan .... Eleanora is with child!"

Jonathan turned in disbelief, "She never said that this was so last night."

"It may be between two and three months. She will need extra care during her confinement. You were fortunate she did not lose the child this morning – yet this may still occur. Good morning, Jonathan."

As Doctor Stephens was leaving, Anne quickly moved beside him and whispered, "Doctor, would you have time for William, as he has blood on him and is shaking awfully."

"Where is the boy, Anne?"

"In the kitchen with Simeon."

Doctor Stephens quickly moved into the kitchen, where Mrs Jennings talked with the chimney sweeps in harsh tones. He saw the boy cowering on a chair. Noticing a shirt sleeve covered in blood, Doctor Stephens quickly examined him and found no physical injuries. However, he was obviously either in shock or in a state of fear. Either way, he needed settling down. Mrs Jennings, turning from her conversation, looked at William and the doctor, eyeing the bloodied sleeve. "Why, Doctor Stephens, I thought you were gone; the sheets must have rubbed against his sleeve as I carried him downstairs." The doctor nodded.

"Anne, please get a blanket and wrap him up. Make sure he stays warm for the next few hours. No chores, no school; I will advise Reverend Taggart as I pass. Keep him warm and quiet. I will call again this afternoon and check on Mrs Turner and William."

"Thank you, Doctor."

Jeremy Stephens took his leave, walked down the hallway, and exited by the front door. He believed Jonathan Turner to be a sensible man who was well mannered and successful in business. He found it difficult to accept that Jonathan, a fellow member of the church parish council, would beat his wife. But it was common with those who had money. The more money, the more beatings it seemed. Stephens frowned – there was no other explanation – the bruising was fresh. He knew that Jonathan's wife would recover with a month's rest but better three months. After providing eight children and another on the way – surely she deserved a rest.

There were no money troubles – Jonathan could afford extra help around the house. Eleanora would recover, although, after last night, she might still lose the baby. Perhaps in her state, that may be the best thing. He was more concerned about William. What would have put the child into shock? There were no physical injuries – there must be some other cause! Jeremy Stephens thought hard as he walked away down High Street. 'Perhaps there was a witness!'

Jonathan Turner stood alone in the drawing-room. With his hands on the sideboard near the window, he gazed out, seeing nothing as he considered the implications of his conversation with Jeremy. His mind raced – the prospect of being without the comfort of a wife for the next three months was not acceptable. How would he cope with that? He pulled out his handkerchief and wiped his brow. Another child – God was blessing them with another child. How wonderful! Please let it be another boy. He must make sure Eleanora was carefully cared for over the next few months.

Clementine was already helping around the house, and she could do more. He would stop her finishing school lessons for three months and set her to work with Mrs Jennings. Perhaps Anne should not attend the bakery and stay home – no, she was too important now in managing the finances and the office staff. Johnathon decided he would increase Clementine's load – it would be good for her. This change may even save some money on her finishing school fees.

What troubled him was his desire for his wife. He was a man who needed a union often. He was a faithful husband and never touched another woman. He sighed. Perhaps now he must think along the lines as other men did - find an alternative. He needed advice on this.

Jonathan was due at a Bakers Guild meeting in London next Tuesday. It was Thursday now. He would consult his brother Richard, who ran a small tavern in Ewell – The Black Swan. By breaking his journey there, he would discuss the issues with his brother. Jonathan and Richard were close and shared similar outlooks on business. Richard was a risk-taker and left home early, not keen on becoming a baker.

He now rented a building in Ewell where he ran a prosperous tavern. The rental agreement with the local Manor Lord required a rental and the sharing of profits, which Richard found not to his liking as the pub's profits were growing nicely.

For the last few years, Richard had mounted a search for new business opportunities. A letter had come requesting a visit from Jonathan, when convenient, as Richard sought Jonathan's opinion on a new venture. The London trip would be a good opportunity for Jonathan to visit Richard and share his predicament.

Jonathan was satisfied with this strategy. His planning was always well thought out, ensuring thorough consideration of new ventures. The one failing was his rage which quickly heightened if anything went wrong. Sometimes deciding in haste would prove costly for him. At present, he must keep the family's situation stable, but more importantly, private! Now was the time to talk with his wife gently and then William. If William saw too much, then he must silence the boy somehow. That would be a challenge with a six-year-old.

He turned from the window, moved slowly up the stairs, and stopped at his wife's bedroom. Having considered what he should say, he entered and found Clementine sitting at her mother's side, stroking her hand and quietly talking with her.

"Where is Anne?" Jonathan asked – he wanted privacy in the next few minutes.

"She is at the bakery catching up on her work – caring for mother this morning took some time, and when she heard you and the doctor were here, she rushed off."

"Ah, she is a fine young lady—the same as you, Clementine, sitting here taking care of your mother. I am so thankful for you both. I will call you back when we finish talking. You might check with Mrs Jennings on the household duties and where William is?"

Clementine, at fourteen, was finished at the church school and undertaking finishing lessons three days a week. Outside of these lessons, she assisted her mother with running the house. Jonathan saw potential in Clementine with her energy, health, and adventurous spirit. She was well educated - could read and write and was gifted with some skill in mathematics but not as sound as Anne. He felt she would be capable of running a business for him in the coming years. The only problem was her loud booming voice, fit for a sergeant major rather than a sweet young girl. He was surprised at the softness in her voice today and found another quality in her, empathy.

"Certainly, Father. I shall wait for you to call."

Eleanora Turner gave a slight tremble and turned her head away from

Jonathan. She lay resting in a large double bed with soft pillows and a light bedspread. The sheets were white and crisp. She was a beautiful woman at forty-two, even after delivering eight children. Her white complexion was flawless, and her long golden hair draped down over her shoulders and covered her full breasts in a beautiful blue nightgown. She wore a slight amount of rouge on her cheeks, just enough to make her look radiant.

Jonathan loved this woman with all his heart and wanted her immediately, and yet he knew he must hold back – give her time to recover. He marvelled at how she became more beautiful as she matured in age.

He gently picked up her hand.

"How are you, my darling, Eleanora?"

Eleanora shook again and then slowly turned and looked at him. He could see the bruises on her cheeks and arms. Her eyes were tired and red, and from a closer look, he saw that under the rouge, she was pale, probably from loss of blood, and displayed signs of little energy.

"Jon, you beat me last night. You promised never to do that again, yet last night you did. Why? I asked you to stop, I pleaded with you, yet it was as if you were enjoying it. Then you forced yourself on me so violently, causing me to bleed!" She began sobbing.

"Jon, please, I am your wife, your helpmeet. I have always honoured you and served you well, but you must not treat me so."

Jonathan Turner sat in silence and knew what she said was true. He would not deny that he enjoyed the violent union. His lust drove the complete loss of control last night, and even now, Jonathan wanted more but knew he needed forgiveness for his acts. It frightened him that he unknowingly harmed his loving wife. What was at work within him that caused this? He could not speak. He just sat there in shame, looking into her moist eyes.

"The Doctor told me to remain in bed for some time. He will visit regularly and check on my recovery. He left potions with Anne and Clementine, who will take care of me. But I must have rest, Jonathan; you must let me rest. Come the time, we will have union again but never again like that, please, or you may not have me anymore."

The words slowly came from his trembling mouth.

"Please forgive me, Eleanora. I know I have acted wrongly, and I will plead my case with the Almighty in Church on Sunday. I will let you rest for as long as you need and consult the doctor regularly on your progress. Let me know of anything that you need."

He sat there, clutching for the right words.

"I love you so much, my Dear! I am ashamed of what happened last night. I lost control. Please forgive me!"

Eleanora slightly smiled in relief and placed her hand on his.

He leant over to kiss her, but she turned her head away.

"Why did you not tell me you were with child? I am so pleased for us. Another one for the family."

She turned slowly and looked at him again. "I was not sure, Jonathan - it is early, and I was not sure. But it might be lost – you must not abuse me anymore, or you will harm the child. Please let me rest now. And Jon, it will be best if you sleep in the guest room for the next few months."

"Yes, Dear. I will leave you now as much is happening in the house and the bakery. I will visit with you after dinner."

Jonathan left quietly, finding Clementine outside, waiting for him. She asked calmly, "Father, I am afraid for mother. She suffers greatly, and did you see the bruising on her arms and cheeks? It is as if she was in a fight..........!" She went silent as he stared at her.

"The Doctor advised me on all this, and we shall hear no more of it. Thank you for looking after your mother and please stay with her while she requires it. She must have a long rest, and when she recovers, we will take a holiday. There are bakeries and cake shops in London. I wish your's and Anne's opinion on them. Now, where is William?"

"He is in his room, Father – drawing pirates. Doctor Stephens said he must remain at home today and rest."

Jonathan nodded and climbed the stairs to the second-floor bedrooms. Wrapped tightly in a blanket, William sat on the floor, drawing on a slate. The young boy appeared relatively peaceful in his task.

For a few minutes, Johnathan considered his relationship with his son. William was hot and cold. The boy was full of energy and vigour and could do almost any physical activity at his young age, but he was also full of mischief, and there was a stubborn streak in him that clashed violently with Jonathan.

What did he see? What had he heard? He must find out.

"William, the Doctor, advised that you need rest - you may stay at home today and not attend school. However, I do not want you involved in mischief. Now, why are you unwell – did you not sleep well last night?"

William, at six years, had a sharp mind and could see his chance at an excuse.

"Nightmares, Father! Anne told me I was too hot in bed, and they were bad dreams that I would forget."

Jonathan Turner considered this response. He was not sure if the child thought he was sleepwalking? If so, he would encourage this belief of nightmares so it was no more an issue.

"Yes, William, I would say it was nightmares, and you will be over it soon."

Jonathan Turner knew he was safe. Thank goodness for Anne.

Mrs Jennings gently tapped him on the shoulder and beckoned him.

Jonathan followed but turned and took one last look at his son. William also looked up and gazed straight into his father's eyes - displaying a knowing well beyond his years. Jonathan Turner knew at that moment William saw everything.

He turned and went without saying a word.

"The chimney sweep, Mr Jack Slope, is demanding a meeting with you, Mr Turner, about the pay for his work. He says he won't send his boys up until you see him and settle it." Mrs Jennings would usually manage these things without him, but Slope was angling for more money today, and Mrs Jennings was a bit rattled by the morning events.

Jonathan mused - Slope knew the rates were the same as his business. Damn the man for the trouble he was causing!

"Come, Mrs Jennings – let us see Jack Slope and solve his problem."

William peered around the corner, making sure the coast was clear. His father was downstairs, meaning William was free for a while. He loved watching the chimney sweeps do their job. Some of the boys were younger than him but could crawl up amazingly thin chimneys and clean them quickly. It was also fun watching Mrs Jennings curse about all the soot coming down and out over the floors.

A loud conversation took place in the kitchen, where his father was giving the chimney sweep, Jack Slope, a good roasting. Quietly, William crept along the hallway, stopping at the stairwell window to see his father walking down the path. Hopefully, it would be soon before the chimney sweeps started work.

Chapter 3

The Turner Bakery, Guilford ...

Jeb Hiscock and Thomas Turner stood at the front of the Turner bakery, looking towards the new mill that was almost complete beside the River Wey. Jeb understood how well-placed Guilford was on the canal for purchasing flour from the various local mills. Given this proximity, he was undecided if the new mill was needed.

"Thomas, why is your father building such a large mill?"

"You remember the Albion Flour Mills near Blackfriars Bridge in London?"

"No, never heard of it. Never been to London!"

"Yes, it was a bit before our time. It was the first steam-powered flour mill in England. There was an uprising against it because of its high productivity and excellent flour quality. Put all the other mills in London out of business. There were suggestions that the out of work mill workers were responsible for the fire that destroyed it in 1791." Thomas lifted his eyebrows.

"You mean the workers burnt it down?"

"The investigation found no evidence backing the suspicions. But all the closed mills reopened and employed their staff again as soon as the Albion mill was gone."

"Well, should we expect that to happen here?"

"It's been thirty-five years since that occurred, and steam engines have become far more refined. All the components are now made of iron and last far longer. Others are now experimenting with the concept, so if we ignore steam power, we may lose any advantage we presently have here in Guildford. Yes, it will eventually put the other mills out of business but not straight away. We intend a gradual introduction, so there is no uprising here. But it will mean that we produce flour at half the cost we currently purchase it at."

"I see!"

"Jeb, we should know by October if it works. Do not worry; your job is safe. If anything, your role will become more important as we will need far more grain."

Jeb was amazed at all the other innovations that Jonathan Turner was implementing and the amount of change happening.

"I'm glad I work here, Thomas. The new ovens your father is installing are amazing. They are far better than the old earthen ones, and the three levels allow far more products baked each day. I wonder what he will come up with next."

"Not sure, Jeb, but we can discuss those new biscuits we produce while you have a minute. Let's go down and look at that oven. I feel they will be in high demand, and we may need a production line. Have you got time now? We should discuss the design."

"Let me pick up the orders from the office first, and then we can start."

Meeting at the rear of the bakery, they spent an hour discussing a reorganisation for higher output.

Later in the morning, Jeb ensured the last of the day's production was off on carts from the dispatch area, then made his way into the office where Anne was working. The business was expanding, and Jeb always checked the next day's orders before starting tomorrow's preparations.

The office held all the paperwork and was becoming central to the business operations. One of the benefits of visiting the office was spending some time with Anne. Of all the girls in town, he found her the most pleasant and sensible. She respected him as an equal and always gave helpful suggestions – he was amazed at how smart she was for a girl! Jeb was a man of perception and realised that Anne's role was growing in importance in the Turner businesses. He was careful in how he managed this relationship.

As Jeb entered the office, he noticed Mr Turner was not in, and most of the staff were across in the counting room concentrating on the banking.

"Good morning, Anne. I have come for the dispatches and orders. Would you pass them over, please?"

Anne did not reply but just sat there, pen in hand, looking out the window towards the river.

"Miss Anne?"

Suddenly seeing Jeb there, she realised he must have said something, "Jeb, sorry, I was thinking of my mother; she is so unwell!"

Jeb saw the look of concern on her face and was troubled. "I thought something must be wrong – how is your mother?"

"Not well at all – I have never seen her so low. Father is with her now and the Doctor. I think I will be spending more time at home looking after her."

"I'm sorry! I was not aware that she was that sick. Will she recover?"

"Thank you for your concern – yes – in time and given good care. I am sure Clementine and I will be spending much time nursing her soon. If you would excuse me, this letter for Bethany is quite urgent. I must advise her that mother is unwell."

Jeb was disturbed that Anne would be away more in the future. He was eager not to waste this opportunity.

"I hope your mother recovers soon as I enjoy our conversations. I would miss talking with you, Miss Anne."

"Jeb ….I enjoy talking with you too, but I must help my mother. There will be plenty of time ahead for discussion. I will still be working here. I'm glad you enjoy our conversations."

Jeb was embarrassed. He blushed slightly and looked down at his feet. He was not as well educated as Anne and lacked the gift of easy conversation.

"Will you be at Church on Sunday?"

"Why Jeb – anyone would think you were making opportunities for us to meet. You best not let my father know about this – he may not understand. But yes, I will be at church, and I shall see you there!" She smiled at him and then continued her writing.

Jeb was elated knowing that Anne thought well of him. Her kind words were a step forward - she was not against their acquaintance growing, this giving him some hope. He remembered the documents were still not checked.

"Miss Anne. Would you pass me those documents, please?"

"What documents, Jeb?"

"The dispatch notices for today and the orders for tomorrow. Thank you."

At the Turner Household …

Jonathan Turner walked into the kitchen and glared at the head chimney sweeper, Jack Slope.

"What's this about, Sweep? We set the terms at the bakery, and I want no more of this disturbing my household with your loud arguments."

"Ah, Mr Turner, it's just that these chimneys are far smaller than at the bakery, around 9 inches by 12 inches, and it will be difficult for my boys without getting stuck. They must strip right off and move very carefully and slowly. I paid dearly for them, so I want 'em surviving! The bakery has far wider chimneys, 12 inches by 14 inches, allowing ample room. I will need an extra shilling here per chimney. That is five shillings for the five chimneys, Sir."

"You're a thief, Slope, but you're right. The chimneys are narrower but not by that much! Three shillings for the five chimneys, and now get on with it."

"Thank you, Sir - we can do the job for that!"

With the issue settled and breakfast finished, Jonathan Turner left for the bakery. It was a freezing morning for July, but now, the clouds were gliding to the north with a southerly blowing, and the mid-summer temperature was rising. He enjoyed a quick moment of warm sunlight as he walked down the familiar path towards the bakery, unaware of the beauty around him.

Jonathan could not shift his focus from the issues with William. After hearing the advice Anne gave William, he was sure the boy would remain quiet. Recalling the work still waiting for him today, Jonathan took a deep breath and picked up his walking pace. Meeting with the builders of the new mill was now a priority before leaving on his Ewell and London trip. The next few months needed to be problem-free and the weather fine. Also, Thomas and Jeb must brief him on the production and store situation. He would determine which customers they needed to visit, ensuring their orders grew. Overcome by his business demands, Jonathan soon lost his focus on the home situation.

William saw his father striding down the street towards the bakery from a hallway window. He let out a sigh of relief. The coast was clear for venturing downstairs and watching the chimney sweeps. He threw off the blanket, jolted down the four stairs, and burst into the kitchen. Mrs Jennings turned and frowned but said nothing.

William immediately saw the Master Chimney Sweep, Mr Jack Slope, a thin and dirty looking man, peering up the chimney on his knees in the fireplace. He poked a long stick up and around the inside of the chimney. Standing in the kitchen corner were three children, all about William's age but shorter in height.

Slope shouted at the children, "Stay here while I check the other chimneys! Don't you move or touch anything, or there will be trouble! You see? You see?"

The children dutifully answered, "Yes, Mr Slope."

"That's better. Now, Mrs Jennings, if you would show me the other chimneys, please?"

Mrs Jennings breathed deeply and led Jack Slope out into the hallway and across to the drawing-room, saying, "Tell me when you are doing Mrs Turner's room as I must be present."

William noticed that the children were small and thin. One of them was a girl. Their clothes were black with soot, and their faces were grey as if they were dry wiped. They stood quite still with no interest in anything except the fireplace, which was out and cooling.

William approached the girl and asked her name. She turned her gaze up at him and then said her name was Olivia. There was no life in her voice, just a kind of croaking. He noticed that she was a good six inches shorter than him. Her hair was black and cut very short, and she smelt very foul. He took a step backwards.

"How old are you, Olivia?"

"Who's asking?" said one of the other boys looking him up and down.

"Sorry!"

Olivia very quietly murmured out of the side of her mouth, "I'm five – I think!"

The boy who spoke previously turned and cracked her across the face. "Don't you talk, or you'll get us all belted by Jack!" He then turned and glared at William warning him off.

William moved away. He noticed white streaks running down Olivia's cheeks and felt guilty for causing her trouble.

Suddenly Jack Slope was back with Mrs Jennings. "Right, Reuben, up this one as it is a bit bigger than the others and clean it out. Olivia and Tom with me. The drawing room is next."

William watched as the boy who warned him off quickly put a mat over the fireplace, put on his cap and, holding his brush above his head, promptly scaled up the chimney and out of sight. A steady flow of soot started coming down the chimney onto the mat covering the hearth. Seeing that this chimney sweeper was out of sight, he followed the others into the drawing-room. Not noticing William at the rear near the doorway, Jack talked sternly with Olivia.

"You're the only one who can get up this chimney. So up you go, my girl."

The fireplace in the drawing-room seemed a reasonable size, but when William looked hard, he could see that Jack Slope was right. The chimney vent was much smaller than the one in the kitchen. Olivia was looking up the chimney but hesitating. The head Chimney Sweep could see she was afraid.

He quietly demanded her, "Get up that chimney, or I'll push you up there, you little brat."

She began whimpering, saying it was too narrow. Jack Slope grabbed her and pushed her head and shoulders up the chimney. She stood there, shaking.

"Tom! Light the fire." William felt a chill over his body as he imagined being up that chimney. He was horrified as Tom lit the fire with Olivia's feet still in the fireplace.

Tom edged back past Jack Slope. Sparks surrounded the girl's feet, and she screamed and then quickly moved up the chimney. Tom covered the fire and put it out. As in the kitchen, a flow of soot fell onto the mat that now covered the fireplace.

"Stupid little brat, she should have finished by now!"

The soot flow continued for a minute or two and then stopped.

Jack Slope cautiously looked up the chimney but could see nothing as it was pitch black. He knew there was no bend in the flue, so either Olivia was refusing, or she was stuck. He called up the chimney, "Olivia, get to work! No soot is coming down. Get a move on, girl! What's holding you up?"

There was no reply.

Reuben came into the room and stood beside Jack.

"Ah, good boy. Tom, you keep calling Olivia and get her going. If she don't answer, light the fire again, that'll get her going. Reuben, come with me upstairs."

Jack Slope left the room, and Tom moved towards the fire. Horrified, William said, "Hey, don't light that. Olivia's up there!".

Tom shrugged and yelled up the chimney, "Olivia - what's happening up there? Are you stuck or something? Olivia, what's happening?"

There was no answer.

Jack came back into the room and confronted Tom. He belted him twice around the head. "Why ain't that fire going. We gotta get her moving!"

He removed the mat and lit the fire, which crackled into life but subsided as there was no draft in the chimney. It appeared solidly blocked as a small cloud of smoke filled the room. Slope quickly opened a window hoping the smoke would clear. He was becoming worried - this was all taking too long – he needed Olivia finished and in the next chimney.

"Tom, up you go and put pins in her feet. "

Tom reluctantly moved onto the fireplace, which was still partially alight. He squeezed into the narrow chimney. Being a slightly larger boy than Reuben or Olivia, he was not more than three feet up the chimney before he became stuck. His feet were still showing in the fireplace.

Jack Slope belted the boy's feet until they bled in a final effort at moving Tom. William watched this whole episode with horror, imagining Olivia's plight. Tom cried out that he was stuck. Slope pulled Tom down and belted him again.

The young lad hid his face in his arms as he suffered his master's anger. Mrs Jennings entered the room and, on seeing the mess, hurled abuse at Slope with no mercy. Soot was all over the parlour floor, walked in by the chimney sweeps in their chaos to solve the situation. The smoke continued building up in the room, adding to the melee.

Slope gestured at the chimney and said, "One of me chimney sweeps is stuck up there - it is a very narrow chimney and…." His voice trailed off as the smoke thickened. "Stop that fire, Tom!"

There was still no response from Olivia.

William moved slowly back towards the hallway door – he stood behind a chair and watched the panic unfolding in the room. He thought in terror about the little girl. Was she stuck in the chimney? How would they get her out? William heard Mrs Jennings calling Clementine.

"Quick, get your father from the Bakery – we need the builders! A chimney sweep is stuck."

William panicked – he knew that calling his father home a second time would be a disaster. There would be fireworks; he must remain hidden in case there were any repercussions. William backed out of the room, through the kitchen, along the hall and up the stairs. He would have a good view from the top step of what was happening when the builders came.

It was early afternoon before Jonathan Turner arrived. The Master Chimney Sweep was out of ideas, and there was still no response from the girl. Jonathan Turner was infuriated as this was the second time his work arrangements had been disturbed today; he was running out of time before his trip. Although he knew he had started the mess, the day was developing into a disaster. A shade of pink was forming on his brow as the rage inside him verged on erupting.

"What has happened, Slope?"

"Ah! it seems one of my Sweeps has become stuck in your chimney Mr Turner and we can't get her down."

"Her? You told me you had boys!"

"Yes, the girl was the right size for the chimney, and we sent her up."

"Why use a girl? She would not be strong enough!"

Jack slope just shrugged his shoulders and looked away. Jonathan Turner got down on his knees and peered up the chimney. It was pitch black – he usually could see the light at the top.

"It appears your chimney sweep has completely blocked the flue. There may be a large amount of soot falling on her. What are you doing to rescue her?"

Jonathan didn't wait for an answer. He knew time was critical.

"Where are the builders? Clementine. Find Clementine and see where the builders are. Damn you, Slope. Now I must take apart my chimney! I doubt the chimney sweep girl will survive this."

Slope grunted, "It ain't no matter, Mr Turner, they are queuing up from the poor house for indentures. They are cheap and plenty of em!"

Recalling his wife's suffering from his treatment and the guilt he now blocked out caused his reflection on the fragility of life during the day. He was thankful that his wife was recovering and for his daughters, who now looked after her. This little chimney sweep was someone's daughter – a child who either was orphaned or sold into an indenture for a life of misery. He was startled by Slope's complete ignorance of the value of human life. He stared at him as his inner tremblings took over his self-control. The rage that was growing erupted. He lost perception and could focus only on this man that treated human life with disdain.

Jonathan grabbed the scruff of his neck and dragged him through the house, across the rear veranda, and into the backyard. Slope's protests had no effect. In the backyard, out of sight of the neighbours, his rage, which grew in intensity, overcame him. He threw Slope on the ground, with one foot on either side of the sweep. Jonathan was a well-built, medium height man, strong from a life of manual labour. With fists of iron clenched and the strength of an ox, Jonathan glared down at this protesting, ignorant fellow. His rage drove him – he lost perspective; his anger took over, and the world around him disappeared as he punished this sinner. The belting was savage.

He stood above Jack Slope's chest and yelled down at him, "You sent a little girl up my chimney. God damn you, man! Have you no sense?" The Chimney Sweep was beyond answering.

If it were not for Doctor Jeremy Stephens arriving in the next few moments, Jonathan might have beaten the man senseless. Jeremy Stephens stopped him.

"Jonathan. Jonathan stop. Stop, Jonathan!"

Suddenly aware of his surroundings, Jonathan Turner stopped and noticed Jeremy's presence. It was as if he was surfacing from a deep dive in the ocean. He took a great breath.

"There is a chimney sweep stuck in my drawing room chimney. A little girl! This idiot sent a little girl up the chimney to clean it!"

Jeremy put his arm around Jonathan's shoulders and led him away. "Some chimney sweeps use girls now, as they are smaller and can scale the smaller chimney vents. But I agree they would not have the strength of a boy."

Jonathan's fist started relaxing and unclenched. His perception returned, and he realised he was in the back garden. He glanced over his shoulder.

Jack Slope lay groaning on the ground. His face was a bloodied mess. He cringed as he saw Turner looking at him.

Soon the builders arrived with Jeb, who pointed out the critical chimney. Thomas and Anne joined the growing crowd of concerned onlookers.

Jeremy sat Jonathan down, requesting a cup of water. Sipping the water Jonathan now appeared under control. Jeremy then attended Slope. The chimney sweep would not work again this day.

Mr Robinson, the head builder, asked Jeb, "Have you got a long rope, Jeb?"

Jeb nodded and darted off to the garden shed, grabbed a rope, and returned to the builder in a minute.

"Climb up on the roof and drop the rope down the chimney until it reaches the girl. Before taking out the bricks, we must find out how far down she is." Jeb darted back into the back shed and tied a weight onto the rope's end. He also took a ladder and scaled the roof at the back of the house. Carefully traversing the roof ridges, he reached the drawing-room chimney.

There was a large crowd of bystanders on the footpath by this time.

As he peered down the chimney, Jeb could see pitch dark about ten feet down. He dropped the rope until it stopped, further down than the darkness indicated. Quickly knotting the rope, he pulled it out and lowered it down the outside of the chimney by the same length. Robinson and his men rapidly positioned ladders, climbed up and slowly started removing the bricks, shoring up the chimney and avoiding the possibility of a collapse.

It took about half an hour before the hole was large enough to extract the chimney sweep. Robinson lifted the limp little body out. Gently carrying her down, he placed Olivia on the ground on some linen Anne thoughtfully brought from the house. Robinson's eyes filled with tears as he put the lifeless warm body on the sheet. Jeremy Stephens examined her and found no pulse. Her eyes were open, with a look of horror on her face. He checked her mouth, which was full of soot. The falling mass encasing her resulted in suffocation. The sight sadly moved the Doctor as he noticed each of the soles of Olivia's feet showed signs of burns.

William crept down from his bedroom and, peeping out the drawing-room window, saw the helpless body on the linen sheet. He was horrified at what he saw and the events of this afternoon. Tears rushed down his cheeks.

"Olivia!" he thought.

Jeremy Stephens knelt and gently closed the dead girl's eyes. "Sleep peacefully, little one. You are safe now. God will keep you in his care."

Standing, he shared with the group around the body, "It's a real pity, but I often see it. It will be called accidental death. Nothing you could have done, Jonathan. Do we know where her family is?"

Jonathan Turner, overcome by emotion, could not speak. Regaining his thoughts, 'There should be a law against idiots like Jack Slope. There must be a better way than this.'

Jeb was standing beside the girl's body. He looked up at Doctor Stephens. Quietly in his deep voice, he said, "I know her family – Stepton! Her father was a labourer up at Batton Place until he became sick. I think they have a cottage on the estate, but they let go some of the children. Couldn't afford to keep them! Mark Stepton and his wife, Alison."

Thomas moved up beside his father. "Mother must be disturbed by all this noise. You should be with her. I will take care of this accident now. Constable Rawlings has been informed and will be here soon. We shall discuss it all at dinner."

Jonathan Turner looked at Thomas and felt some relief. His first-born son was becoming a good manager, a person he was proud of, "Thank you, Thomas. I will visit your mother directly. No, no. Jeremy, you go first and complete your check on her. Ah, Thomas, this little one shall have a good funeral, poor thing. Someone must tell her family what has happened. It is a sad business."

Jeb moved closer. "Mr Turner, if I may please, may I tell them? There will be others in the community who will want to know as well as my own family. My mother will come and comfort Mrs Stepton."

"Yes. Yes, Jeb, good fellow. Thank you, and take one of the bakery carts, please. Tell them we will arrange the return home of the body as soon as the Constable finishes. Please tell Mr Stepton that we will pay for all the funeral costs and attend. Thomas will make the arrangements. And Jeb, would you call at the Manor House and advise Squire Easton of what has happened."

Thomas quietly said, "Father, you know the Eastons are recusant[2]. Is this wise?"

"No time for these views now, Thomas – we have no quarrel with them!"

Jonathan stared at the dead child for a further few minutes. He knew well the desperation from poverty that many parents faced. Without an income and many mouths to feed, they would sell their children into an indenture with the chimney sweeps. Jonathan Turner was a tough businessman, but he was also a man who had empathy for the people around him. A family losing a child was a tragedy, but it should not be allowed in such circumstances as this. He muttered that he would never see his children in such a state. There must be a better way – he was aware of a man using a mechanical sweep. He must find him and never let this happen again. He turned and went into the house.

Sleep for William that night did not come easily. Visions of Olivia's body being taken away on a cart kept flashing in his mind. He continually imagined soot filling his mouth and his body wedged up a chimney with a fire coming from underneath. What Reverend Taggart said about hell was true. Chimney sweeping was like visiting hell.

The room was pitch dark – it was cold, and William feared the dark. He could hear Thomas and Simeon softly breathing as they slept. Getting out of bed, he knelt beside Simeon's bed and shook him. There was no response. William shook him again. Simeon opened one eye.

"What?" he said.

Thomas rolled over in his sleep. William froze until the soft breathing started again. He very quietly said,

"I'm scared of death!"

Simeon looked at him and then grunted, "You won't be scared for long if you don't stop shaking me!"

William whimpered, "I'm cold!"

Simeon sighed and rolled over in his bed. William slid in and put his back against his brother. He was quickly asleep, feeling warm and safe.

---

[2] In the early 1800s dealing with Roman Catholics was socially unacceptable until the Roman Catholic Relief Act 1829 which removed most of the barriers for catholic emancipation. Even so the stigma remained and was slow to change.

At Reverend Andrew Taggart's church school, the next day, the big topic of conversation amongst the children was the death of the chimney sweep at the Turner's house. Reverend Taggart could see that the children needed an understanding of the events. He explained that as chimneys filled with soot, they must be cleaned. A consequence of not cleaning chimney flues were house fires – William shuddered at the thought of family members burning.

This description was a new thought of terror for William – yes, chimneys must fill up with soot, so that is why they needed cleaning. But why would parents let their children become chimney sweeps?

The good Reverend explained that the Master Chimney Sweeps would find young children from the Poor House or from low-income families, who would indenture their children as chimney sweeps. The money was essential for the family's survival. He said that the chimney sweep who accidentally died was from the Poor House, without relatives. William thought about this as Jeb said she was from a family at Batton Place.

William opened his mouth but thought better of it and stayed quiet. She had a mother; she had a father; he was unsure about brothers and sisters. She was part of a family but sold into chimney sweeping. How could any family do this to a little girl? Then he thought about how his father often found fault with him. Would his father sell him to a Master Chimney Sweep? He shuddered. Olivia was dead. What would become of him? Reverend Taggart said that she was in heaven and safe with the Lord. William was not so sure!

During lunch, Richard Smith and Caleb Elliot, both five years older than William, suggested who cares anyway as it was just a chimney sweep. They were the poorest and lowest parts of the community, and who cared. William felt slight anger rising in his heart.

"They are dirty, grubby little moles and should be kept in the chimneys." Caleb laughed.

"Yes, up the chimneys and on fire!" They both laughed.

William was incensed that these boys, older than himself, would be laughing about a little girl who was dead. William inherited two things from his father: a sense of justice and his rage. He took a deep breath and fronted Richard and Caleb.

"Hey. Olivia was a nice girl and from a family. You shouldn't laugh at her!"

Caleb smirked and nudged Richard, "I think young Will here had feelings for little Olivia? Eh Will? You liked the smelly little brat!"

The rage inside William was now heating up.

Sitting close by with friends, Simeon saw the frown come over his brother's face. He quietly kept an eye on William, standing near Richard and Caleb. Simeon knew how Will was deeply affected by the little girl's death and bothered in his sleep last night.

Richard continued degrading the chimney sweeps, and the boys started baiting William. "Will loved Olivia! Ha, Ha Ha."

William clenched his fists, his rage boiling when Simeon grabbed him by the scruff of his neck and dragged him away.

"Ignore it, Will. They are fools."

William could not ignore it but understood he must calm down so his brother would release his grip.

Simeon felt William relaxing, "Ok, then. You will leave them alone?"

William nodded.

Simeon let him go. "We can talk about this after school on the way home. Just stay away from them. "

Mrs Taggart rang the bell calling the children into class. Some of the children started moving back into the church.

William walked in the other direction, not saying a word. Unlike Jonathan Turner, William masked his rage far better than his father. He found an old axe handle in the church shed near the vegetable garden without the head. William smiled. Reinforcements!

After all the other students were in class, Richard and Caleb remained sitting outside.

Caleb laughed so hard he did not see Richard tumble off the seat. As he turned, he found Richard on the ground, shaking. The smile vanished from his lips as the axe handle crashed into his mouth, knocking out both front teeth with a gush of blood. Caleb went white for a moment seeing stars.

On that day, all three boys learnt some profound lessons. Fortunately, at six years old, William was without the strength to seriously hurt Richard, but Caleb's injuries were severe. The Reverend Taggart, who found the boys, looked in disbelief at the screaming eleven-year-olds lying on the ground and the fierce six-year-old standing behind them with an axe handle in his hand. For Reverend Taggart, this was a first.

Being a man of peace, the Reverend knew that if the details of this incident reached the parents, three of his most worthwhile families might take punitive action. But what could be done? Rather than taking the axe handle off William, he asked politely, "William return the axe handle to where it came from, please." Best keep William was away from the scene altogether. Once he was satisfied all the other children were in the classroom, Mrs Glossip was called and assisted Caleb. The Reverend Taggart saw a large bump on Richard's head and checked if the lad was steady. Richard was unaware of what had happened, except for an immense pain in the back of the head. He slowly walked back into class, feeling a little giddy and rubbing the rear of his head.

Caleb was also unsteady on his feet and could not remember what had happened. Reverend Taggart explained, "Somehow, Richard lost his footing and fell over. He must have bumped you, and you hit your head on the seat, and out came your front teeth. We think that's what happened, as nobody saw it. Now just hold that cloth against your mouth while we send for your mother."

Coming back from the shed, William was interested in why Reverend Taggart would tell Caleb this story of the events. Without being noticed, he took his seat in the class.

The Reverend Taggart sent Caleb off with his mother, who was stuttering, "You stupid boy, now look what you've done". Andrew Taggart thought this was working out well but then remembered William. Before he spoke with the boy, he must consult Simeon, who he believed might know how this all came about. This line of enquiry proved most helpful.

When it was William's turn, Reverend Taggart sat the nervous boy down and gave him a stern look.

William said, "Please don't tell my parents, Reverend Taggart. My father will beat me as he does, mother! He may even sell me to a chimney sweep!"

The good Reverend was shocked when he heard these comments but quickly focused on the present situation.

"Ah. And, so your father might if he finds out, young William. However, only Simeon knows what happened, and he tells me that someone provoked you. So, I think that we can make a pact."

William said, "What is a pact?"

"It means that we both agree this will remain a secret, and as long as it does, the pact remains in place."

William said, "I don't understand."

"William, I am encouraging your good behaviour and hard work at school. This way, you will become a good reader and writer. I would most appreciate it if you would do this for me, and in return, we will not mention Caleb and Richard's injuries. This way, you will not be beaten or sold as a chimney sweep! What do you say? Do we have a Pact?"

William looked in amazement at the good Reverend. He was not expecting this.

William gave a slight grin. He looked up thankfully at the Reverend Taggart. "I like you, Reverend Taggart. I agree to a pact!" This agreement gave reading and writing a new meaning for William.

"Good boy William - now back into class and remember, no more of this."

The Reverend Taggart was astounded. This child of six going on seven displayed street smartness well beyond his years. He now wondered if his approach might be slightly misguided. However, he would not jeopardise the future of the school. Richard was the son of the mayor, who was a member of the parish council. Caleb's father was the local blacksmith and a strong supporter of the church, and William's father was a prominent businessman and the Chairman of the Parish Council. There was no need for disagreement between these men. He would visit both Richard and Caleb's families tonight, reinforce the story, and check on the boys' welfare. He might miss the Turner house - better left alone at this stage. 'It is like being a politician being a clergyman. What was it that his wife said? Ah, yes! Just keep smiling, Andrew, keep smiling?' It was now late morning, and already Reverend Taggart longed for his afternoon glass of sherry.

After school, William pestered Simeon about playing pirates by the river. Simeon, while not opposed, said they should return home and invite the girls along as well.

"Who knows, mother may be recovered and wanting a walk!"

William agreed with this readily as he missed seeing his mother. Having the girls there would be super for a pirate game. William began striding out for home, and Simeon scampered behind him. Bursting into the kitchen, William spied Clementine and asked if she, Anne and mother would enjoy a pirate game at the river.

"I will come, but I'm not sure if Anne and Mother will agree. I would like a game of hide-and-seek, and mother needs some fresh air. How about you go and ask them?"

William looked at Clementine with a question on his face. Having been banned from seeing his mother for the last two days, he questioned Clementine's saying, he was free to ask her.

Noticing the confusion on William's face, Clementine smiled. "Go on then. They are in the drawing-room!"

William, finally understanding, just bolted. Simeon coming into the kitchen, said, "Me too?"

Clementine smiled. "Yes – Go on!"

William burst into the drawing-room and saw his mother sitting with Marcia at her feet and Anne pouring a cup of tea. Eleanora looked up and smiled when she saw William.

"How's my big boy, William?" she said.

Not waiting for any further invitation, William threw himself into his mother's arms and buried his head against her chest. For William, his mother was the symbol of security and happiness. She was his confessor and his mentor. William found himself lost without her, and now they were together again.

"Mother, please come and play pirates with us at the river today?"

Eleanora hugged him tightly. She saw Simeon enter the room and beckoned him over – he too ran and gave her a warm hug. Anne moved the tea table back a bit, given these awkward males were disturbing the balance of the teacups.

"Hey, Boys! William and Simeon, watch your feet. I have Mother's tea here!"

The boys sat on either side of Marcia, who continued gabbling at everyone – she was excited that they were all together again. William quickly lifted a biscuit into his mouth and chomped it down. Anne gave him a gentle kick, saying, "The biscuits are for mother!"

Eleanora looked at the children, glowing in her matronly pride. What a blessing these wonderful little people were. She contrasted the position she found herself in with a husband, whose carnal needs dictated his behaviour, and these beautiful children so full of life and attentiveness.

"I'm not sure your father would like me outside yet. Doctor Stephens wants me inside for at least a week before I venture out, but this does not mean you children should stay inside. It is a perfect summer's day for some fun, and I will be happy here with Mrs Jennings and this lovely afternoon tea that Anne made."

The children cheered for joy at the prospect of a pirate game at the riverbank. William stayed hugging his mother. "I thought you wanted a pirate game, William?"

William released his grip on her and sat back down. He looked up at her face and noticed the bruises below the makeup on her cheeks.

"Mother, I missed you so much. Why are you sick? Will it last long?"

Eleanora flinched, remembering the beating she took from Jonathan. She also remembered seeing, out of the corner of her eye, a little head peering around the corner of her bedroom door.

"I fell over William and hit my head – I will be better soon, and then I will be at the river with you."

William heard the excited talk in the kitchen with Clementine bawling out pirate commands as if she were Captain Blood, and much laughter followed. Seeing that they were alone and out of earshot, William took the opportunity.

"I have bad dreams, Mother. I told Anne, and she said they would go away."

"What have you been dreaming, William?"

"I dreamed I woke up at night, walked downstairs, and called you. But when I peeped into your bedroom, father was beating you. Father turned and saw me, so I ran back upstairs and hid. Anne said it was a nightmare and I should forget about it."

Eleanora could see that the child was asking for either confirmation of the story or acceptance that it was a nightmare. She was not sure she wanted the truth known, and she resisted placing her woes on this six-year-old boy. She was unsure whether to smile or cry – she became overwhelmed for a moment by her anxiety, and then she hugged him again.

She whispered in his ear, "It was just a nightmare, William. Your father loves me very much, and he would never hurt me. It was just a nightmare!"

William stepped back and saw that tears ran down his mother's cheeks. The makeup was running, and the bruises on her cheeks were obvious.

Anne came in and stood beside William, gently nudging him.

William took hold of Anne's hand, "I will think of it as a nightmare, Mother!"

In his mind, he understood what she wanted. She was telling him to disregard what he saw and believe something else more fitting. William could not understand why she wanted this, but he would do this for her as he loved his mother more than anyone else in the world.

"Come on, Mr Pirate; Captain Blackbeard is waiting down at the river."

William continued looking at his mother as Anne led him out, holding his hand, which gripped hers tightly.

Eleanora smiled at him as he left. She realised now that William was at the door on that terrible night and witnessed her beating. She shivered, knowing the terror it must have planted in the child. Yet William seemed to cope with her suggestion that it was a nightmare.

That day her intuition told her there was something different about William. He was a thinker as well as having all his gifted physical abilities. It was as if the child understood her predicament; his thinking seemed unrestricted by his age. He was still young and innocent, but this would not last long as he grew. Jonathan's rage was present in him but different from his father's. It appeared well under control, but would it stay that way.

Some said that mothers sometimes had visions of their children's future. Feeling a cold chill, she wrapped a shawl around her. In her dream, she saw him crossing vast seas, far away and in danger. Then the skies cleared, and the sun came out over another land where he was building a life and a family of his own. Eleanora saw him with a swarm of children around him, his gentle hand quietly slipping out of her grip. She shuddered. The room was quiet – the children were gone.

Her memory recalled that night. Jonathan must have seen the lad. What would he be thinking? Eleanora knew she must protect William. What had Anne and William shared? She must talk with Anne soon. Anne was aware of Jonathan's beating her, but Anne was an adult and would maintain secrecy. With William, this would prove more difficult. She sighed and took a sip of warm tea.

Chapter 4

The Turner Household, Guildford ...

Sunday morning was an important day for the Turner family, being the Sabbath and a convenient opportunity for meetings with influential community members and friends. Aside from spiritual issues, the cost of grain was always high on the discussion list. The Corn (grain) Laws[3] were a significant issue for landholders and the community, and Jonathan Turner delicately managed both parties.

Jonathan was a shrewd businessman and understood the importance of good relationships with the landowners, grain suppliers, his customers, the business owners, and Guildford citizens. The future of his baking and other businesses depended on developing new markets, which both classes of society would support. Grain contracts with a fair price were essential for keeping his products at a reasonable cost. Church provided the opportunity to further relationships with suppliers and customers, ensuring their support.

Waking early, he lay in bed, thinking through his marital predicament. Being in the guest room was not his preferred option. Eleanora remained quite cold towards him, despite his talking with her several times since the incident. He now realised his abuse of her was inexcusable. At times Jonathan's behaviour was beyond his understanding. His problem with rage was unresolved, and somehow he must find a cure.

Now fully awake, he enjoyed the warmth of the early morning summer sun coming in the easterly facing window. England was a beautiful place in mid-summer. His bed was now warm from the sunlight, and he felt a sense of

---

[3] The Corn Laws related to grains such as wheat, corn, and sorghum. The Corn Laws were legislated as a method of protection for British grain farming after the end of the Napoleonic wars in 1815. It kept the price of bread high. There was much opposition from the industrial workers in northern cities on limited wages. The corn laws suited the Aristocracy well. Being landholders, it maintained their income from corn harvests and allowed the maintenance of their worker's wages. However, workers in the industrial cities were demanding the Corn Laws be repealed. This would result in a lower price for bread. Wikipedia.

energy and happiness. Being thankful for all the blessings his family enjoyed, Jonathan decided it was time to solve the situation with his wife. Jumping out of bed in his nightgown, he went downstairs to the kitchen, made two cups of tea, and found two crisp bread rolls and butter. With the offerings on a tray, he climbed the stairs and entered Eleanora's bedroom.

"Morning, my love!"

Eleanora slowly rolled over, noticing the cups of tea, bread rolls and the pleading look on Jonathan's face. His stay in the guest bedroom was having the right effect. She sat up in bed, brushed her long blonde hair back across her shoulders and waited for his next move.

"I brought you up a cup of tea so we could talk before the day begins." He sat the tray down on the bedside table and passed across a full cup. Waking fully, she rubbed her eyes and looked at him. Was this the same man who beat her into submission the other night? She was pleased by his warm smile and the offering of an early morning tea and rolls.

Eleanora took the cup, "Thank you, Jonathan. I think this is the first time in our twenty-four years of marriage that you have made me a cup of tea. Is there something that you want to say?"

"Eleanora, my Dear, I have thought deeply about my actions the other night. I realised that I was wrong in what I did. My passion for you overcame me, and I lost control. I know I should have shown more control and failed you, but I am truly sorry and plead for your forgiveness. I truly love you and will always cherish you. Please forgive me and let us put this behind us?"

"Forgiveness now, Jon, requires change on your part. Firstly, I must be sure that this will not happen again, and secondly, I must believe I can trust you. Will you assure me it will never happen again? Should I trust you?" Eleanora took a sip of the tea.

Jonathan Turner was not a man of great vocabulary. He struggled to find the right words that would win his case. So, he kept it simple.

"Eleanora, you are the only woman I have ever loved and will always be the only woman I love. I will never let this happen again. I am ashamed of my actions and ask your forgiveness."

Eleanora was amazed that Jonathan was so repentant and wondered what had influenced this. She was still unsure he was genuine but would give him the benefit of the doubt. She, too, wanted this episode over and was quite content with his repentant state.

"Jon, as you know, I am with child, and I am bruised and battered from your beating the other night. I am afraid of you and that you will turn on me. I will forgive you, but it will take time. You must give me more time."

Jonathan breathed a deep sigh of relief and lent forward and kissed her gently on the forehead. She leaned back on the pillows and watched him.

"You shall have all the time you require, Eleanora. Now, here is a buttered roll for you and one for me."

Eleanora took the roll, and for the first time since the incident, she felt a sense of relaxation come over her. She realised the cup of tea and the roll was a peace offering. It was more important than anything else could be at this time. Jonathan's repentance this morning had restored her husband and her marriage. There was a future again and another child on the way. A slight look of contentment came over her face.

"The children will attend church with me this morning. Anne, Clementine, and Marcia will remain here with you. Mrs Jennings will bring your breakfast soon. Anne will keep you company while Clementine looks after Marcia until we return home. I will pray for forgiveness from the Almighty and a steady hand in the future. You have my commitment to this, Eleanora. Your welfare is my first concern, and regaining your trust is everything. We will make this work, Eleanora. We will make this work!"

"Thank you, Jonathan,"

"I will also be attending the Guild meeting in London this week. Brother Richard has requested I stop at Ewell on my way for discussions on some business matters. I will be gone on Tuesday, returning on Friday. Thomas will look after the bakery, and Anne will watch over the household while I am away."

"Jonathan, please give my apologies at church as the ladies will notice I am missing."

"Of course, my Dear."

Jonathan made his exit from the room, and Eleanora watched him as he left. As the door closed, Eleanora lay back on the pillows and smiled as the warm sunlight seeped into her room. The commitment made by Johnathan now assured her of a secure future. She felt a growing sense of calm, and a tear ran down her face – there would be a relationship for them again. Having lived with this man for twenty-four years, she knew him backwards. She now believed he was genuine and would make a change for the better. She closed her eyes and quietly gave thanks while she felt her stomach for signs of the baby.

At breakfast, Jonathan looked around the kitchen. Mrs Jennings and Anne were busy serving, and Clementine shouted instructions at them all. William was teasing Marcia, who was becoming agitated. Simeon was quietly thinking and eating, probably still half asleep. He was a slow starter that one. Thomas, already finished breakfast, was upstairs dressing for church.

"William, leave Marcia alone!"

"But Father, she loves it!" William cried out.

Jonathan glared at William, and the boy took the hint that he should stop immediately. As the room calmed down, Jonathan thought through how he would handle the issues at church today.

"Anne and Clementine. You will remain home with your mother today. She will require company and assistance while we are at Church. I will need Thomas with me as there will be an important visitor and his wife who we must attend on."

Clementine was happy with this, as she was not fond of the hour and a half at church on a Sunday morning. However, Sunday was the only time Anne met with friends and acquaintances. Missing this would be a disappointment indeed. Anne quickly assessed the situation – this must be diplomatically put and not arouse any suspicion.

"Father! Mother will not be attending! The ladies will ask after her, and it would be better if one of us answered their inquiries. Given you will be busy with the menfolk and introducing Thomas, might it be better if I come and fend off any questions?"

Anne was very respectful, ensuring her father would not become suspicious. Surely, he would understand that dealing with the lady's questions was better left in her hands. It was in his interest that they presented a unified and consistent approach at church. She was not sure that her father knew of her knowledge of the incident, but she suspected he was quick on the uptake once hearing from William of her suggestion that it was a bad dream.

"And what shall you tell the womenfolk, Anne?"

"That mother fell on the stairs, and she suffers severe bruising, and Doctor Stephens insists she remains home resting this week."

Jonathan Turner was acutely aware, just as at any other church, that the gossip chain here was quick. He needed a counter against any rumours spreading. Anne's suggestions sounded far more plausible. She was gifted at speech and would add creditability by giving a simple answer. Working together, they could dispel any rumours that might surface.

"And if one of the ladies requests a visit, what shall you tell them?"

"Simply that Mother is embarrassed by the bruising and that it should have subsided by next Friday, and she would welcome visits then?"

Jonathan was pleased with this. It was a better plan than his. His daughter had a sound mind, and he must not ignore it.

"Certainly, Anne, I think your plan is an excellent one. You shall attend Church and manage the ladies' enquiries. I will confirm your comments if required. Let us be off soon then."

William watched as Anne breathed a sigh of relief. He smiled at Anne as she walked past, and Anne stuck her tongue out at William but then smiled. Together, they were thieves of the truth but protecting their mother and father. Surely this could not be wrong.

The family house was not far from the church. As they walked along the street, William suddenly remembered his exploits with Richard Smith and Caleb Elliot. Simeon and William were last in the family line. Jonathan Turner led with Thomas at his side. They were busily talking about the corn laws reflecting on what Jenkinson's[4] next move would be in parliament. Anne and Madeline followed them. Much to Marcia's disgust, Clementine and Marcia remained at home as she doted on being with her father. William nudged Simeon.

He whispered, "You don't suppose Richard and Caleb will be there?"

"Of course, they will! Perhaps not Caleb. "

"Oh!"

Simeon whispered back, "Just keep the pact."

"Did Reverend Taggart tell you about it?"

"Yes, he did, and I agreed too, as I was the only other witness. If you say nothing, things will remain calm. If you say the wrong thing and others become aware, father will beat us miserably, and I don't want that." Simeon was now speaking in an urgent but hushed voice.

William nodded eagerly in agreement.

As the family reached the church stairs, the Smith family were ahead of them. Jonathan Turner greeted the mayor warmly, who in turn reciprocated. Moving down the aisle towards their family pew, Jonathan nodded a friendly greeting at several gentlemen.

The lady folk noticed that Eleanora was not present, and a ripple of side glances followed the Turner procession. Anne was correct in her predictions. As they moved down the aisle, Anne noticed the ladies passing hushed but concerned comments. Eleanora's absence would be the hot topic of gossip after the service. Jonathan appeared very relaxed and smiled at one and all. He mouthed sideways, "I am glad you are ready for this, Anne, as I may have underestimated the concern!" Anne gave her father a reassuring smile, giving him some confidence.

Four rows back on the other side of the Church, Jeb sat by himself in his Sunday best. Anne glanced around, smiling at friends; suddenly, seeing Jeb, she smiled at him. Jeb was so overcome he nodded back without any change in expression. As the congregation stood, Anne's quick return to looking forward was a good move, as Jonathan Turner faced the entering procession, followed by Reverend Andrew Taggart. Jonathan quickly looked back at Anne, who now gazed forward with a nondescript look. Jonathan, noting this, thought no more of it. Anne relaxed.

William and Simeon saw Richard Smith scowling at them in the pew directly opposite. Simeon ignored Richard, but William was petrified and

---

[4] The Right Honourable Robert Jenkinson 2nd Earl of Liverpool, Prime Minister of the UK. Wikipedia.

looked down at his clasped hands as if he was praying. He remained that way for most of the service.

The Reverend Andrew Taggart was a friendly ordained man who loved his job. He was of the liberal tradition, which suited the congregation very well. His Church was a church of faith and an important social centre for the community. Bearing in mind the death of the chimney sweep, Olivia Stepton, and her funeral, Andrew Taggart searched the scriptures for comfort and was encouraged by what he found. Many of his congregation attended the funeral, including friends of the Easton family from Batton Place and associated tenants. This morning he knew they would be questioning why this accident occurred. Some may even be casting blame. He, too, wondered at times about sad incidents.

For the Reverend Andrew, his sermon preparation increased the number of personal questions he was considering about his faith. He was unsure of where it was leading, but the question of why these accidents happened needed answering. His sermon today was fragmented, confused and not very convincing. Each member of the Turner family had different expectations. Simeon had expected a lesson on love, and Anne thought an appeal for forgiveness might be appropriate. Jonathan's mind dwelt on his upcoming conversations with customers, and Thomas was worried about being involved with Catholics. Madeline was starting to take notice of the boys about a year or two older than her.

But Reverend Andrew Taggart surprised them all. His sermon was about 'Sin'. He said he would develop this theme over the next few weeks and explain it as best he could each time. Unfortunately for the good Reverend Taggart, who had little theological training and far less in sermon giving, he made quite a mess of his first sermon on sin.

By the end of the sermon, everyone was confused about the aim of his message. However, the longer he talked, the more relaxed he became. Most were thankful when the sermon finished and the familiar prayer book liturgy for the eucharist commenced.

At the time of communion, they all went forward in order of pews in two queues to the communion rails. William and Madeline remained seated as Anne quietly but firmly told Madeline not to move from her seat. As Anne followed her father forward, she noticed that Jeb was on the other side of the aisle in the other queue. As Jonathan Turner passed him, he took Jeb's hand and shook it, smiled and then patted Jeb on the back. He quietly said, "Thank you, Jeb, for all you did at the funeral."

Jeb smiled back at him, "It was my pleasure, Mr Turner."

Anne was surprised at how human her father could be. She looked at them both and thought how handsome they were, but then checked herself, realising that any sign of familiarity might lead Jeb on unfairly and spoil their working relationship.

Following the other family members, Simeon suddenly found Richard Smith standing beside him. Richard whispered in his ear, "Turner, meet me at the back of the Church after the service; bring little William with you!" Simeon swallowed backwards and nodded, wondering what this bully wanted. Richard was the typical spoilt brat who must have his way. Simeon was sure this would involve the events on Friday when he accidentally fell!

After the service, as they exited the church, Mrs Smith, the Mayor's wife, grasped Jonathan Turner's hand.

"Jonathan, where is Eleanora? I intended to invite her for afternoon tea on Tuesday, but she is not here. Is she unwell?"

Jonathan smiled, "She is a little battered as the result of a fall, and at the request of Doctor Jeremy Stephens, she will remain resting at home till next Friday. But perhaps, Marjorie, you could discuss it with Anne, as I must catch up with the McPhersons while they are still here. Anne, come and talk with Mrs Smith about your mother, please."

Anne was quick in attendance and produced a lovely warm smile for Mrs Smith.

"Certainly. Now Dear Anne, do tell me all?"

"Mrs Smith, I have been attending Mother since Tuesday last, and the swelling and bruising from the fall is slowly fading, but she is most reluctant about appearing in public or having visitors until the swelling goes down. But she is coping well and …."

Jonathan Turner left the two in deep conversation as the pair soon became a swarm of women discussing the topic. Pleased that Anne handled the situation so well, he searched through the crowd for the McPhersons to introduce Thomas before they departed. Thomas followed reluctantly, knowing his duty.

"Good day, Hamish and Mrs McPherson. I am delighted you are attending our little church here. Please, may I introduce my son Thomas, who manages the bakery!" Thomas was surprised to hear of his promotion but took it in his stride.

Hamish McPherson owned four Scottish breweries, two in Glasgow and two in Edinburgh, and a string of pubs around the Scottish countryside. He recently built a brewery in Woolwich, invested in a pub in London and was now negotiating for a large hotel in Guildford. Jonathan Turner could see a significant future trade with Hamish if he settled here and built a chain of businesses in the accommodation and hotel industry.

"Jonathan, good to see you, and I am pleased to make your acquaintance, Thomas. Let me introduce my niece, Miss Marion Steele, who is with us for the next few weeks. She is from Woolwich, near London, and enjoys your country town very much!"

Not expecting an introduction, Thomas was pleasantly surprised by the young lady. Marion was quite attractive and of a similar age, if not slightly older than Anne.

"A pleasure Miss Marion. Are you enjoying your stay in Guildford?"

Marion, overjoyed about meeting someone around her age, was full of interest in Thomas and his sisters.

"Yes, the fresh air out here away from London is lovely. I understand you have sisters, Mr Turner. Are they here today?"

"Miss Steele, please call me Thomas. We are a little less formal out here at Guilford."

"Then please call me Marion."

Thomas nodded in agreement. He was most taken with the young lady and was unsure why Miss Steele was so friendly.

"Please let me introduce my sisters – I have five, but today you must be content with the two who attend, Anne and Madeline. My oldest sister, Bethany, is a governess at Woking and attends church there. Clementine is caring for my indisposed mother at home, and Marcia, the youngest, is also there today."

Thomas beckoned his sisters. Madeline acknowledged Thomas's call and advised Anne politely, who made her apologies and followed Madeline across to meet Marion. It was apparent from the smiles and good wishes following Anne that she had settled the congregation's women. The gossip network was well and truly under control.

"Miss Marion Steele, may I present my sisters, Anne and Madeline."

"Delighted Miss Anne and Miss Madeline. It is so nice meeting some folk my age."

Anne twigged that this may be a significant introduction and was also impressed at how beautiful Miss Steele appeared. She could see that Thomas was also quite impressed with Miss Steele, quick thoughts of a future sister-in-law flashing through her mind.

Anne was familiar with most resident families in the town and realised that Miss Steele must be visiting. She would enjoy making a new friend. "Miss Steele, it is a pleasure. I do hope you are enjoying a lovely stay."

"Yes. I accompany Mr McPherson and his wife, my Auntie, who are currently talking with your father. It appears they have much in common. We are staying at the Black Moon Inn on Quarry Street, and perhaps you would join me for tea there later in the week."

Anne happily accepted this invitation, but another thought crossed her mind.

"Why Miss Steele, on a Sunday afternoon, we often stroll beside the river and enjoy the view. We also play a pirate game with the children. Father often supplies some biscuits for a picnic, which is most pleasant. If you have nothing planned, perhaps you would join our family for this outing today."

Thomas was astounded that things were moving this fast. What was Anne doing?

"That is kind, Miss Anne – I would enjoy that very much. I must first check with Mr and Mrs McPherson; however, I am unaware of any appointments this afternoon, and it would be so refreshing joining with you and your family."

Marion quickly confirmed the arrangements with her aunt and uncle. Thomas and Anne found they were due at the Black Moon Inn at three in the afternoon and would escort Miss Steele down the High Street, meeting the others at the riverbank.

Behind the church, Simeon and William looked for Richard. He dramatically appeared without warning from behind a gravestone. Standing menacingly above them, the Turner boys took a step backwards. He was a big lad for his age and stood a foot above them. Simeon knew he used his size as a weapon; however, he also knew that Richard was lazy and moved and reacted slowly.

"Hey, Sim – I think your little brother here might have hit me from behind last Friday. I don't fall over and hit my head – that has never happened!"

"That's what Reverend Taggart told us happened. Anyway, William was in class with me." Simeon thought a little white lie would not hurt at this time and especially against a bully like Richard. Simeon wanted this line of questioning stopped before it went too far. He was not sure if William could hold his tongue.

"You are lying. Liar, liar, liar!" Richard commenced his bullying tactics.

Simeon did not want this to continue, worrying that William would say the wrong thing.

"Why not tell Reverend Taggart he is a liar? We're only saying what he told us happened!"

William was impressed with Simeon's quick thinking under pressure. He knew Sim would not be hurried in anything and was calm and calculated, but this deflection was clever. Richard, unable to counter this fact, found whichever way he answered, he lost. Being a bully, losing was not an option. He decided on action rather than reason.

Richard rushed William, punching him hard in the eye with his right fist. The six-year-old went down like a sack of oats holding his head in his hands. Simeon knew his turn would be next, so he backed up against a rather large but flat gravestone. Richard turned on Simeon and ran towards him with fists clenched. Simeon stood quite still, watching for the punch. He ducked sideways from the right-hand fist, inches away from his face.

His observation of Richard's processing information slowly proved correct. Simeon noticed that Richard closed his eyes before his punch hit William's eye socket. The pattern was similar in the schoolyard, where he bullied other children. Simeon assumed that once Richard's arm commenced the punch, he would have his eyes closed and follow through.

The timing of Simeon's evasive action was perfect, but it was close. As he ducked sideways, he felt the rush of air against his cheek as the fist flew past and then collided heavily with the gravestone. It shuddered with the force of the punch. There was a loud crack of a breaking bone and then silence.

Richard opened his eyes, seeing his hand hanging limply, and then the pain struck him. He screamed in agony and sat on the soft thick grass. Tears ran down his cheeks as he sat there, sobbing and holding his wrist. Simeon knew it was now time for action.

"William, quick, help me lift him."

William was still rolling around and quite giddy. Thinking, 'Are you kidding, Sim, I can hardly stand up, and this big brute will have another go at me!'

"Quickly, William! Grab his arm, and let's find his parents."

William begrudgingly pulled himself up and staggered towards Richard but tripped and fell on him. Richard screamed again in agony.

"Oops. Sorry, Richard!" William exclaimed. Richard howled.

Under Simeon's instruction, they both took one of Richard's arms and lifted him onto his feet as best they could. The three of them were a bit lopsided as William was slightly shorter than his brother. They staggered towards the front of the church and approached the mayor's wife. Marjorie Smith noticed her son in agony, and she immediately rushed over and consoled him.

"Thank you, Simeon and William. Whatever happened, Richard? Oh, poor little fellow!"

Simeon was careful with his words and produced a brief explanation.

"We were playing hide and seek in the graveyard when Richard came out from behind a gravestone, and William ran into him. As Richard fell, he put out his hand and struck it on the gravestone."

"Oh, poor little Dear – we must find Doctor Stephens and have him look at you. Probably a sprain. Quick now, Simeon, please tell Mayor Smith that I need him. That would be so helpful. And William looks like he is hurt as well."

"It's nothing, Mrs Smith – just a slight knock. He will be fine." William grinned at her gingerly with more of a grimace than a smile. However, Marjorie Smith now lost her focus on William and attended to her howling son.

Simeon dutifully collected the mayor, and the Smith family set off with Doctor Stephens towards his surgery.

The Reverend Andrew Taggart watched the complete discussion between Mrs Smith and Simeon Turner with some trepidation. Jonathan Turner saw the look on Andrew's face and found himself becoming suspicious but felt there were more pressing matters at hand.

Anne and Marion Steele, chatting and becoming acquainted, stood beside Simeon and William.

Anne mouthed at Simeon, "I don't want to know!"

Sim cultivating a concerned expression for both Richard and William, found he could not contain a slight smile on his face. Jonathan Turner seeing all this, and having completed his discussions, decided it was time for the family's return home for lunch.

Approaching Miss Steele, "I understand that you will be meeting for a walk with Thomas and Anne this afternoon. The weather looks fine, so I am sure you will have a lovely time. Please take care on the riverbank as it can be rather steep. I hope we shall see more of you, Miss Steele."

Having grown fond of both Thomas and Anne far quicker than she expected, Marion replied, "Thank you, Mr Turner. That is kind of you, and I will heed your advice."

Anne lifted her eyebrows and thought that the morning events were taking a turn for the better. She wondered what might develop from this.

The Turners and the McPhersons were among the last families leaving the church. Simeon Turner gave Reverend Taggart a confident wave acknowledging everything was fine. Reverend Taggart waved back with a smile and then wiped his brow with a handkerchief. He turned and escorted Mrs Taggart into the Rectory for luncheon.

At lunch, Jonathan Turner looked at Simeon and wondered what happened at church to cause Richard's injury. The mayor's son was a fine specimen of a boy, and Jonathan doubted that Richard's injury resulted from a game of 'hide and seek'.

"Simeon, how exactly did Richard injure his wrist?"

"Just as I told Mrs Smith, Father. He bashed it at an awkward angle on a gravestone. I have never seen anything like it before. He shuts his eyes when he throws his arms around. I heard the bone crack as he did it. It was a bit sickening."

Jonathan Turner considered this for a while and said, "It must have been a freak accident – how unlucky! Was it broken?"

"I'm not sure, Father, but I would say it probably was by the sound of the crack we heard!"

William could not contain himself and let out a little laugh.

Jonathan, dismayed by William's laugh, said, "It is not a laughing matter, William, and your eye socket is turning blue. It looks like someone gave you a good bruiser! Have you an explanation?"

Simeon quickly answered, "Richard's elbow knocked William in the eye quite hard as he fell."

"Is that what happened, William?"

"Yes, Father!"

"I also heard that Caleb Steele knocked his front teeth out at school on Friday. Did you boys hear anything about this?"

Simeon sensed that this question was more of an interrogation than a mere passing comment. He felt danger. William quickly said, "We were in class at the time, but Reverend Taggart told us what happened."

Eleanora broke into the conversation before Jonathan could dig any further.

"You boys should take more care when you play around the back of the church. I was pleased that Anne and Thomas have acquainted Miss Marion Steele, and she will attend the river walk this afternoon. I, too, need a walk in the cool beside the river, Jonathan. If I wore a veil, that would sufficiently cover my bruising."

Simeon and William looked at each other in relief. They knew their father suspected foul play, but mother had cleverly diverted him.

"I'm not sure that is wise, my Dear, as it is still Sunday, and we explained at church that you would not receive visitors until next Friday."

"Jonathan, I will not be receiving visitors, just regaining my strength on a sunny afternoon walk. I will cover-up, and as usual, all the families we know will probably be up at the castle grounds where the band is playing today. We will not be disturbed at the river, and I will make sure that my face and body are covered. I would like a walk in the sun with the children and rest down by the river."

Jonathan was terrified but held his voice. He had no choice and must agree.

"I shall join you then, Ma'am. Mrs Jennings? If you would pack a basket of biscuits, some rolls and a rug. We can make a little picnic afternoon feast."

"Splendid Jonathan, what a wonderful idea. Now you boys and girls, run upstairs and put on your play clothes."

The boys and Marcia needed no more encouragement and were gone in a second; the other girls finished their lunch and quietly went upstairs. Eleanora then spoke softly.

"Jonathan, the opportunity for Thomas with Miss Steele may be fortunate. Anne tells me she has a sweet personality and is quite pleased with Thomas. He is of marriageable age. From what Anne tells me, she would be a good match."

Jonathan enjoyed a conversation with his wife again on a subject other than the incident. He quickly replied, "It took me by surprise – I was talking with Mr McPherson, and he introduced his niece. She is charming. However, I am not sure why she would prefer our family. Surely coming from London, there must be a finer catch there. If a match eventuates, it will be a good alliance for the family. Now Eleanora, are you sure about this walk?"

"Yes, Jonathan, I have been shut up all this week, and I would welcome some fresh air. I will be very gentle with myself and enjoy walking with you."

Jonathan was quite pleased with this comment, and it lessened his fear of a chance meeting with friends.

The Picnic Beside the River Wey, Guildford ...

At the time appointed, Thomas and Anne set out for the Black Moon Inn with high hopes for their new friend. The afternoon became quite warm, requiring light clothing. Eleanora worked hard on disguising her bruising with a full-length sleeved dress, hat and veil. She felt more alive today than for a week and eagerly awaited watching her children play beside the river.

As they set out, Jonathan took her arm and waited attentively on her. He was concerned about any contact with other friends and neighbours. While Eleanora enjoyed the walk in the warm sunshine, the experience outdoors would also emphasise to Jonathan that he must fulfil his promise about change. She noticed how rigidly he walked, which must be from his stress over the whole situation.

William loved these excursions where the family played games beside the river. He ran ahead, full of energy and excitement, leaving everything behind until he reached the riverbank first.

They found a pleasant spot where the bank was mainly gently sloping, covered in deep green grass and, in some places, little grassed mounds and trees on each side of the river. The calm brown water drifted past slowly and moved the branches of weeping willows, so they looked like ghosts walking on water. William found a stick and waved it madly, scattering the ducks and swans away from the riverbank. His imagination took him into the pirate world, where adventure reigned supreme. He jumped onto a mound near the water's edge and imagined himself on his ship's quarter deck. Soon commands could be heard as he issued orders to the crew.

"Hoist the sails me lads, and cast off. There be a treasure for the taking!"

Turning, he found himself facing Simeon, who also held a stick.

"Surrender, Captain of the pirates! I, Captain Turner, arrest you in the name of the King. Yield and stand down."

"Never!" cried William, "We will fight to the death!"

"Then prepare pirate captain for the hereafter. My crew will take your ship!"

Clementine and Marcia soon joined Simeon's crew, ready for the boarding. Clementine yelled, "Aye, Aye, Captain," Marcia gave little shrills of excitement as she ran back and forth, and Maddie jumped in, joining pirate Captain Will.

The two boys started jousting, and the imaginary pirate swords struck and waved as the boys danced around the mound.

As Anne, Thomas and Marion Steele approached the riverbank, they laughed as they saw the small boys and girls battling with sticks.

"It is the age they are at, Marion. Pirates are a great romance in their lives now. We have a lot of fun as a family this way. I hope you don't mind?" Thomas was concerned that she was comfortable with this informal behaviour.

"Thomas, I am honoured and privileged by your family's hospitality. I have three elder brothers at home, and I can see myself some years ago doing just as Marcia is. She is so cute. Let us join in!"

"Aye, Aye, Captain," Anne yelled, and the two girls were off in a run joining the melee.

Thomas stood there with his mouth open. He was amazed that this polished young lady from the city would run and join in with these childish antics. Perhaps, he thought, he was taking himself too seriously. An excellent old pirate battle would be fun, especially with Marion. He launched himself into the yelling frenzy on the quarter deck.

Any bystander would have been confused by the running and yelling of this small swarm of young folk. But these free spirits knew precisely what they were doing. The difficulties of this world disappeared for a time, and they revelled in the energy of youth under a warm summer sun.

Jonathan and Eleanora, nearing the riverbank, stopped in amazement, seeing Thomas fencing with Marion, obviously as an opponent, and laughing and giggling as the others wrestled and ran around them.

"My, I haven't seen Thomas enjoying himself so much in ages, Jonathan. They do make a good match, don't they?"

"I'm not sure what Mr and Mrs McPherson would think if they saw this!" Jonathan shuddered at the thought. His striking a deal with Hamish McPherson could be a clincher for a much larger business in Guildford. It would also possibly involve Richard in Ewell with a new pub. He was keen that these possibilities were not spoilt.

"I think I might just calm them down a bit."

Eleanora smiled as Jonathan walked towards the pirate brawl on the bank.

As the numbers increased on the poop deck, William, leading the pirates, broke his first sword and now held a fiercely thick branch as a landing hook. He twirled the branch around at anyone he could. As Jonathan approached for a word with William, the young boy missed seeing his father nearby. As Jonathan came into range, William, unawares and facing the other direction, took a mighty swing at Sim, the King's man, and missed. The momentum of his large branch twirled him around, striking Jonathan a beauty right across the forehead.

When Jonathan regained consciousness, he found himself lying on the ground peacefully with his head in his wife's lap. She looked down at him with a gentle smile as she delicately wiped his face with a wet cloth. Jonathan smiled back, thinking, 'This was nice!' Until the pain started. Suddenly he remembered what happened. His body went rigid. He wrestled with sitting up, but Eleanora held him back. She whispered in his ear, "Let it go, Jonathan – it was an accident. Let it go!"

Jonathan stopped and realised, 'That wretched William belted me one!'

Eleanora could see the rage growing. "Jonathan, listen, please! The children and Marion are most concerned for you. There is much going on here, Jonathan. Remember Thomas and Marion. Do not spoil this, Jonathan. Please relax."

Jonathan Turner was not in the mood to listen, but for Eleanora, he complied. He would prefer thrashing William, as the boy was too volatile. Perhaps the events at the church school involved William. Perhaps not. If his suspicions were correct, then he would lose business for sure. But the deal with the McPhersons was more critical. The goodwill of Marion could be a significant influence. His wife was right; he must control his temper.

Jonathan lay his head back on his wife's lap and closed his eyes. He relaxed and said, "More, please."

Eleanora smiled, "Now, that's the boy." She wiped his face again softly.

William slowly came near his father and knelt beside him. "I'm sorry, Father! It was an accident."

Jonathan said back, "Thank you, William." He opened his eyes, seeing William kneeling close and a shadowy figure behind his head. He shut his eyes and opened them again, this time achieving a better focus – it was Hamish McPherson grinning at him from behind William's shoulder.

"My, he clocked you a beauty, Jonathan. Such entertainment I have not seen since my children were young. Ha, Ha. You were out for a while, but Eleanora was very calm and told us how tough you were and that you would be conscious soon. A fine wife, you have, Sir."

Jonathan lay there with his mouth open. Hamish laughed.

"Eleanora told us a bit about the children while you rested. I must also say these biscuits are delicious. We need them in my hotels, Jonathan. We can speak about this tomorrow at our meeting before you leave for London. Just take it easy – I must re-join the pirate game!"

Hamish saluted with a stick and rushed off after William shouting pirate type words.

Eleanora wiped Jonathan's face and smiled, saying, "Such a nice man!" Jonathan closed his eyes again and let the rage leave his body. The sun was warm. The tension was gone.

Anne, Marion, and Thomas laughed about the day as they walked home up the High Street. Anne was keen to know more about this girl, now a new friend from Greenwich.

"Marion. Do you have brothers and sisters at home in Woolwich?" Anne was curious about Miss Steele's family and why she would be visiting with her uncle rather than her mother and father.

Marion looked down and swallowed deeply. Blushing, she struggled with her words.

Anne immediately felt worried Marion was upset by the question. But then Marion spoke up before Anne could apologise.

"It is difficult discussing my family at this time. We are going through some deeply personal issues."

Anne spoke forthrightly, "I am sorry, Marion. Pray, forgive me if I caused you any sorrow."

Marion slowly looked up. Anne could see the moisture in her eyes – as tears appeared.

"No, no …it does not cause me sorrow – it has been so wonderful being included in your family fun today. I have felt more alive today than I have been for months."

Her sentiment touched Thomas, and noticing her tears, he handed her a handkerchief.

"Please, Marion, do not let us press you."

"No, Thomas, I must explain. My mother is unwell. Father has placed her in a hospital for her care, and we visit often. She has lost her memory. One day she knows us, then the next there is nothing!

I have three brothers, and they all work with my father in the cannon casting business. They make cannon shafts for the army. My brothers and father have disagreed over my mother entering care. My brothers want her home; however, father feels that she is at a stage now where we cannot meet her care needs. I love my family dearly and hate this disagreement destroying our happiness.

Mr McPherson and Mrs McPherson, being my mother's sister, have been such a tremendous help. They are such kind people. You would never know it of Mr McPherson as he is a tough businessman and has made a fortune. They have taken me under their wing. Mrs McPherson has replaced my mother over the last year, and I cannot thank them enough for their generosity.

Our family is like yours. We are tradespeople who have done well. That is why it was so much fun being with you today. Being part of some family fun again was so good!"

Thomas felt sympathy for her situation but found himself wordless. Anne was impressed that Marion would be so open. She felt a close bond growing with this girl.

"Marion, while you are here in Guildford, please spend as much time with us as you wish. Perhaps we could have tea tomorrow afternoon – you will not see much of Thomas for the rest of the week, as he will be running the bakery while Father is away, and Thomas rises early in the morning – about three. I, too, work at the bakery for a few hours in the morning, but I am free in the afternoons. Perhaps you and Mrs McPherson would join us for afternoon tea?"

Marion wiped the tears from her eyes, "I would like nothing more!"

The two girls took each other's hands and hugged. Then each taking one of Thomas' arms, they strolled up High Street, letting the warm summer afternoon soak into this growing friendship.

Chapter 5

The Black Swan Pub, Ewell …

The Coach from Guilford arrived in Ewell late in the afternoon. Having been cramped up in the coach for several hours, Jonathan Turner was tired and hungry, anxious for a good meal and a long talk with his brother Richard. Since his meeting with Hamish McPherson early this morning, there were some urgent issues for their discussion.

Hamish had grand plans for the south of England, and he would establish a pub near the Epsom Downs racecourse. A calendar of regular race meetings, including some of the national race days, indicated growing crowds and patronage. When Jonathan mentioned his brother in Ewell, who ran a pub, Hamish's curiosity was aroused. Hamish suggested that Richard might be interested in the management of the new pub.

Jonathan turned this proposal over and over all day, and by the time he arrived, he was keen for dinner and their discussion.

Richard's pub, The Black Swan, was ahead down the street. A hired man followed with Jonathan's bags. The establishment was three floors high with a grand entrance that appeared a little run down. Richard must improve the external appearance of the pub before Hamish visited. Jonathan would include this on the agenda for tonight.

In the lobby, Jonathan recognised Oliver, Richard's eldest son.

"Uncle Jonathan! Welcome. Father said you were coming today. We have a fine room ready for you."

"Oliver. Good to see you again. The coach was cramped, and I am thankful for a good stretch. Some dinner and a soft bed will be my desire tonight."

"You travel on to London tomorrow?"

"Yes, I do!"

"We will make sure you have a good night's rest."

Later that evening, the two brothers sat in Richard's small but well decorated private dining room, having a hot meal and wine as they caught up on family and business matters. Sarah, Richard's wife, joined them for the main course but now left them to their business discussions. Jonathan did not hide his excitement about his new business acquaintance, Hamish McPherson.

"You see, Richard, he is planning three or four pubs in strategic locations south of London, and Epsom has the attraction of some well-known races."

Richard broke in, "Pity he was not more flexible and would consider Ewell!"

"Your arrangement with the Lord of the Manor is distressing you. Why not consider cancelling that arrangement and taking on the management role at Epsom? Start afresh with some significant backing. Both Hamish and I would invest in the new pub. We need someone like you who understands the pub business." Jonathan was hoping for Richard's commitment.

"Yes, I could, but an owner would still constrain me. I aim to control my own business! I envy you, Jonathan, in that you control your interests. Having never achieved this, it is time I did. I have been giving it a great deal of thought over the past two years, and if I don't move soon, then I may be too old for such a move."

Jonathan was encouraged by what he heard.

"However, it is more than just changing pubs. My need is more capital. The business here will not generate this. A friend recently informed me that the government is offering land, free title, for those who will settle in South Africa[5]. A grant of land free of charge may be the opportunity to open the future for me. I could go out there for five years, set it up, then sell and return with some capital in my pocket. Who knows what other opportunities might arise? There is gold in South Africa, and many have gone there prospecting."

Jonathan sat back and rubbed his hand across his chin. This proposed change in direction by Richard took him by surprise. Moving countries was a more significant challenge than what he was suggesting. But that was Richard – he was a risk-taker.

His brother continued. "If I can keep the pub going here and settle in South Africa, this will work. Oliver is now twenty-six and quite capable of running the pub. His brother, Harry, is a bit younger and well acquainted with the business. I would free up Oliver for what you are suggesting in Epsom. It is unlikely that I will leave until next year, so I would keep an eye on Oliver and assist with the new pub. I would also train Harry for Ewell before I go. McPherson could join us and show us any new ideas he desires implemented. The training should all be complete by the time we leave for South Africa."

"Surely!" Jonathan interrupted, "You would take Oliver and Harry with you? You would need their help."

---

[5] British Settlers were encouraged to take land grants near Grahamstown (Makhanda) west of Port Elizabeth (Gqeberha) in the early part of the nineteenth century. Many failed and the land was either transferred or sold on. Wikipedia.

"In the first few years, we will be grazing cattle and sheep, and plenty of locals are available for work on farms. I will hire supervisors who know the local customs and hiring of staff. My boys will be better off here, developing the business. England is their home, and they have no desire to leave. It is a funny thing, but they have been growing apart from me for some time now. I think they would prefer me out of the business so they can make their mark. Young men need their turn just as I did. You will recall how I stepped out in faith many years ago and set this business up. That is me. I like a challenge.

I will take Sarah and Katherine. Firstly, we will set up the farm and then build a farmhouse. During the first six months, I will become acquainted with the locals. I hear there is a growing community of English farmers."

Jonathan was surprised by this move and considered the implications of what Richard was suggesting—making Oliver the manager might well work. Hamish would like this as Oliver would be young and searching for new ideas – having his father there as a backup would also mean a mentor on-site for some time. Jonathan would make sure Richard remained in England for at least a year, if not more. Hopefully, it would be 1828 before Richard went overseas and not 1827.

The brothers talked about the new Epson pub until Jonathan changed the subject.

"Discuss this venture with your boys tonight, Richard, as I must go tomorrow morning and give Hamish an answer. I will return from London on Thursday and advise you of the outcome. However, there is another matter where I seek your advice. A matter of great confidentiality!"

Jonathan described the incident with Eleanora and how she banished him to the guest room. He explained how he was addressing the situation but could find no satisfactory solution. Richard drank a glass of red wine as he listened with interest.

"Jonathan, you have landed yourself in a pickle with your wife!"

Jonathan leaning forward in his chair, agreed. "Yes, well, it was my fault! As you know, I have a problem with rage. When she refused me, I lost control! It should never have happened, but I succumbed to my desires. The restraint needed last week has been terrible, and I struggle with my need for comfort."

Richard had a sparkle in his eye. "Jonathan. You are not the first man with this problem. Many a man in our society takes a mistress not only for satisfaction but also for the company."

"I have pondered this thought, and it does not sit well with me. Yet I am in great want of satisfaction. My life has changed overnight, and it is because I cannot control my rage. The thought of a mistress is greatly tempting, but I have resisted this so far. The problem is that I find it difficult reconciling the taking of a mistress, firstly due to my beliefs and secondly, it would be a breach of my trust relationship with my wife."

Richard smiled, "Father taught you well about the church. Pity he missed me on that count. I struggle with belief in God. I never accepted the faith you have – I have tried but not found any divine inspiration or answers. For me, life is simple - there is no struggle. I do not envy your struggle with Christian principles. However, with your wife, if you have beaten her, then I am surprised she trusts you at all, Jonathan!"

"I have apologised and vowed that it will never happen again. Eleanora has accepted this, and I am indeed fortunate, but it does not solve my problem."

"Why if I tried that with Sarah, she would have beaten me and thrown me out of the pub. You are fortunate that Eleanora is so understanding." Richard took another sip of red wine and sank deep into thought.

"I am. I am!"

"And returning to William, you say the boy saw you beating her?"

"Yes, I looked up and saw him peeking around the corner of the bedroom door."

"I told you about having children long ago, Jonathan. You should have listened. Did you give him a beating too?"

"I should have, but I had other reasons for avoiding this. William is six and a half, and a slip of the tongue could be dangerous for my reputation. He has a will of his own, and I am afraid he might inadvertently expose me, which could be humiliating in the community. For now, I have convinced him that it was a bad dream."

"Are you and he close, Jonathan? Can he be reasoned with?"

"Not really - he dotes on his mother and has strong desires. I think it fair to say he and I irritate each other."

Richard pondered this and then said in jest, "This really could become a problem then! Perhaps South Africa is a solution. He may come in handy given Oliver and Harry are not coming."

While Richard was not seriously suggesting this, Jonathan looked interested in the idea and mused, "This might become necessary!"

Jonathan took a last sip of wine, "Let me know tomorrow morning of your discussion with your sons. I shall join you at breakfast."

Richard stood up, "I will think about your satisfaction problem and consider alternatives."

Jonathan shook hands with Richard and then proceeded to his room. The hallways of the pub were attractive and well kept – far better than the exterior. It was a well-furnished and comfortable hotel with soft carpets that made little noise as you walked down the hallways.

Jonathan Turner was thinking of snuffing the candle flame when a soft knock came at his door. Not expecting anyone, he was surprised by the interruption. Being tired and needing sleep, he was in two minds but decided to answer the knock. Moving from his bed, he opened the door. In front of him, there stood a well-dressed, attractive young woman.

She asked in a low, calm voice, "Jonathan Turner?"

"Yes."

She walked past him in a saucy way and sat on the end of his bed.

Jonathan closed the door, wondering if this woman was who he thought she was. He may have been tired, but his brain was now running fast. He suddenly shuddered, realising this was his brother's solution for his lust - arranging a woman for him! In the doorway, the light was low and restricted his vision. Now she sat on his bed; he admired her detail. She was young, around twenty-five, with a beautiful figure if not a little plump in some areas. The heightened colour of her cheeks was perfect, her hair was long and blonde as his wife's, and her perfume was light but intoxicating.

She was there for the taking – handed to him on a platter - a gift from the establishment. No questions asked.

Jonathan felt himself becoming aroused and walked back and got into the bed. He sat there, considering her.

"My name is Francene. I am yours for the night, Jonathan." She stood up and slowly unfastened her dress, revealing her lingerie and moved up the bed and sat in front of him. "Well?"

He remained silent. For Jonathan Turner, this was a defining moment. His marriage was a faithful one for twenty-four years. Now he found himself with a delicious woman sitting nearly on his lap, offering him everything he wanted for the night – no questions asked.

What kept ringing in his brain was his promise, 'Eleanora, you are the only woman I have ever loved and will always be the only woman I love.' Was he faithful to this? Of course, he meant this, but love and lust were two different things. Surely, he was assisting his wife by using another woman for his desire, saving her from this action. But then he recalled Reverend Taggart's sermon on sin. 'Sin not only affects ourselves, but it affects all those around us. We can pretend that it is confined and justify it that way, but it hurts the ones we love as well.' Jonathan thought, 'Damn, Taggart and his preaching!'

After loosening her corset, she put her hands on his shoulders and slowly leaned forward, exposing her soft, firm breasts. He wanted this so badly. He put his hands on her waist, so she could not move further forward. She felt soft and wonderful. He breathed in her perfume which was like rose petals all around him. Surely if no one knew, no one would be hurt! He wanted her lingerie off so he could join with her. Her touch aroused him so much that beads of sweat were forming on his forehead. She smiled and gently licked his lips with her tongue. He felt himself submerging under this harlot's spell. He pulled the covers away to roll this dream into his bed. She smiled again and kissed his chest, rubbing her hair across his face. He pulled her closer, so her nipples were on his chest. It felt so good.

From inside his mind, Eleanora's soft voice came, 'I must learn to trust you. Can you assure me it will never happen again? Can I trust you?' The voice was quiet but determined.

Jonathan Turner was well educated for his time, attending a Christian church with good preaching each Sunday. There was no escaping his understanding of the responsibilities of marriage. He was a man whose word was his bond. He had a conscience. Horrors such as little Olivia being suffocated in his chimney deeply angered him. He loved his wife.

Then in a flashback, he saw the little boy peeping into his bedroom. His face showed confusion, and then he scampered away. His mind was awash with shame as he heard Anne calling him, 'Wake up, Father, Wake Up!' He looked up and only saw a ceiling. There was no one there except this half-dressed woman lying on his chest and kissing him madly. He took a deep breath.

"Stand up, put your dress on and leave, please." He gently pushed her into a sitting position.

"Come on, big boy; it is yours for the taking. All free, no strings attached." Francene was about to move forward and kiss him when he pushed her aside and looked her in the eye. "Don't make me get out of bed, or you will be sorry!"

Francene stood up and looked at him for a minute. "Your wife is a lucky woman, Jonathan Turner!"

Jonathan replied, "No, I am a lucky man having her trust and love!"

Francene smiled, dressed, and quietly closed the door behind her.

The Turner Household, Guildford ...

Eleanora was retiring for the night and was about to snuff the candle as Anne knocked and entered her room. Giving her mother a gentle hug, she seated herself on the bed.

"Mother, it is not easy finding a time when we can talk. There has been so much happening that the chance has not appeared until now. While father is away, there is an opportunity for both of us. The boys and girls are in bed, and the house is quiet, and I desperately need your advice on some things. I know you are tired, but perhaps we could spend a few minutes, Mother?"

Eleanora smiled at her daughter. These must be pressing issues if Anne was so insistent. How much Anne reminded her of Beth, now nineteen and a governess at Woking. Bethany bloomed early, with long brown hair, the colour of her father's. Jonathan found her the work with Reverend Upton, and the reports back from the good Reverend were very pleasing. Indeed, it would not be long before some eligible young bachelor asked for her hand. She wondered how Jonathan would cope with that. He would probably ask the young man about his wealth and connections! Ah, Beth – how much she missed her. But Anne, with her long locks of golden blonde hair, was now blooming too, and in more ways than just beauty. While Eleanora suffered ill health, Anne took over responsibilities for the house and proved most competent. She managed with confidence the inquiries of women twice her age at church and helped cement the friendship between Marion and Thomas. Who knew where that might lead? She was becoming an accomplished woman at seventeen without a finishing school – a daughter, any family, would appreciate.

"Anne, let us talk, darling. Come sit beside me." They sat on the large bed that Eleanora shared with Jonathan for so many happy years.

Anne moved along the bed but then looked down as if she was gaining courage before speaking. She hesitated.

"What is it, child? You know this is a mother and daughter talk, and it will go no further."

Anne's eyes became watery, and a tear rolled down her left cheek. "Mother, I think Jeb at the bakery is taking an interest in me, and I'm not sure if I should respond. I like him but not romance; he is a friend, and it must stay that way. I know that if I become familiar with him, then father will be very aggravated. I do not want Jeb hurt. You know father; he is always saying he will find someone worthwhile who will marry me. But I am not ready to marry. I am happy at home, but home has been full of sadness and pain these last few days. I fear the future. I was so afraid when you were injured – we must not lose you, Mother! I am so scared of what's happening around me."

She burst into tears, clinging to her mother. Eleanora held her tight as she violently sobbed against her chest. Her mother whispered in her ear, "There, there, Anne, you are safe here. There, there."

Slowly, Anne regained her calm, drew back, and wiped her dripping nose and red eyes on a handkerchief given by her mother.

"Anne, there has been so much you have dealt with over the last week. You have done it well and earned great respect, especially from your father. You are deeply loved by all of us and deserve some rest from those responsibilities. I am growing stronger by the day and will soon order Mrs Jennings around as before."

They both laughed as Anne said, "She needs it – she has become a little bossy lately!".

"She is working hard too. All these issues are new ground for her as well."

"Mother, what about Jeb? He is a fine man, and I am sure he is looking for a wife. But I am not ready for marriage – I am not even interested in considering marriage at present. I would never hurt his feelings, but I am not in love with him. There is so much I still wish to achieve. Visiting London, perhaps one day Paris, and see the sights. There is a world out there that I have never seen. Must I be married before this happens?"

"No, not at all. But you will need a good chaperone. Perhaps your father and I can organise something like that for you next year. Perhaps Beth could go as well – you would enjoy that?"

"Yes, Mother - Beth and I with a nice chaperone. It would be such fun. Why could you not come with us, Mother?"

"Because I am with child, Anne!"

Anne drew back in amazement, "But we have not been made aware! Mother, in your condition, is it wise? What has Doctor Stephens said?"

"He says the baby is fine, but the doctor has warned your father that he must leave me alone for several months. It will all be fine, Anne, and I will discuss with him about a trip next year for you and Bethany. Beth will be ready for a break and welcome the suggestion. That is if she is not married by then."

"Why, Mother, have you heard something we do not know?"

"No. No. But Bethany is such a beautiful girl, just like you! There are bound to be eligible men lining up for her hand."

"Not if they know our father!"

"Now Anne, your father, is a good man, and he means well by all of us. Certainly, he makes mistakes at times but don't we all? When some young man calls upon him, we will draw our conclusions. It may not be a suitable match, as many issues must be considered."

"What do you mean by that, mother?"

"We, women, live in a predicament where we mostly do not own property. Our husbands usually take possession of any property coming with us in marriage. We do not have occupations; the vote is withheld from us, and we have little education. The men control everything. There are some women of wealth, and that is because their fathers were rich outside the aristocracy, and they legally willed it fairly for their children. But in most cases, the eldest son receives the lot.

In families such as ours, there is some opportunity for the daughters. Where a business is grown, generating wealth, there will be an inheritance for the daughters. You have learned much of the baking trade without indentures! You have also attended the church school, but unfortunately, we could not find you a suitable finishing school. But Anne, you are well educated, and you shall have more as we send you on a trip with a chaperone.

We, women, must depend on our husbands' love and generosity. So, when it comes to marriage, your spouse must have a suitable position and means. We do not want you in servitude, Anne. We want a better life for you - better than ours!"

Anne nodded in agreement but then put the question that had bothered her since last week.

"Mother, after the beating you received from father, are you not afraid about the future?"

"Why, Anne, you should not judge that I received a beating. You must understand that perhaps the wrong was not only your father's but also mine. Perhaps I should have been more accommodating."

Anne's eyes widened, and she put her hand across her mouth, "Mother, No! It must have been so humiliating for you."

"Anne, Anne, now calm down. You must understand that when your father and I were married, it was not a marriage made in heaven. My parents selected him as they sought opportunities for me, but I needed convincing. I am sure Jonathan thinks it was all his charm, but there was far more involved than charm. My parents loved me very much, and they desired that the man who won my hand would provide a comfortable living for me. They succeeded more than they could have ever imagined. My parents never knew the luxuries that we afford now."

"If this is so, Mother – tell me – do you love father? And does he love you?"

Eleanora looked at the painting on her bedroom wall of herself and her husband posing as newlyweds. She sighed.

"Anne, the issue is, what is love? At first, I could not stand your father as he was insistent on union every night, and he did not have the manners of our family. He even resisted church-going, not understanding its impor- tance for spiritual belief and business acquaintants. I often cried on my mother's shoulder, but she also reminded me of a woman's insecurity without a husband. She encouraged me to always look for the good things in him, and there were many. I'm sure he found me tiresome in the early years of our marriage as I bent him into shape."

Anne smiled and then threw herself backwards on the bed, giggling, "Bent him into shape – how I wish I had seen that."

Eleanora smiled and giggled too. "There were many funny little things that happened!"

She lay down beside Anne and took Anne's hand in hers. "You would be surprised, but it is from those little things that love springs."

They gazed into each other's eyes – mother and daughter.

'You mean you love him?"

"Yes, marriage has bound us together, and we have made a life that I would never swap with anyone. Certainly, the romance was lacking to start with, but the man has devoted his life to our family. He is tough and can be wicked, but he can also be outstanding. I have not been the model wife, but we have been fortunate in childbirth, seeing some of our children become adults. We have shared these joys. We have laughed together, and we have cried together. On Sunday morning, before everyone was up, he made me a cup of tea and buttered rolls and brought them upstairs for the first time in our marriage. So out of bad can come good. If you asked me if I love him, I would say I do. If you ask me if he loves me, I would say yes, I do. But perhaps you should ask him that, Anne. But not now!" She smiled, and Anne giggled.

"Mother, what do I do about Jeb?" They sat up.

"From what you are telling me, you are not interested in a relationship yet. Anne, you show a lot of wisdom for someone your age. Friendship is ample, and if he wants more, you must make him understand it is friendship only, and he must keep his distance. Jeb is no fool and will heed your advice."

"Thank you, Mother. I have been so confused. I so much love talking with you. Do you think I will ever find happiness like you?"

"Let us see what develops in the next few years, shall we?"

"Mother. I nearly forgot. I have invited Marion and Mrs McPherson for afternoon tea tomorrow. Mr McPherson returns to London tomorrow for some business, so some company for them will be welcome while he is away. If you are unsure of your health, then I will look after them myself, but it would be good if you could attend."

"Now Anne, perhaps next time you should consult me before handing out invitations, but in this case, I will attend indeed! Now it's time for bed."

In the morning, Anne made sure that Mrs Jennings understood the arrangements for the afternoon tea. When a knock came at the front door, Anne frowned as she was not expecting anyone.

Mrs Jennings returned and announced that Miss Marion Steele was waiting upon Anne in the drawing-room.

Madeline, Simeon, and William were packing their bags before leaving for school. Clementine was checking that everyone had their lunch.

"Your sandwiches, William, are they in your bag?"

"Yes".

"Are you sure as there are some sandwiches here on the table? Let me see." Clementine opened his bag.

"Brother, you must concentrate - there are no sandwiches in your bag – now put these in and catch up with Sim. Madeline, I will walk with you as Mrs Jennings needs some items from the grocer. Now, where is the money jar?"

Anne left the organising and found Marion waiting in the drawing-room.

"Anne, please excuse me for visiting so early, but I was so bored as Mrs

McPherson calls on the mayor's wife this morning. Mr McPherson is at Dapdune Wharf, where he takes the Weybridge barge. For some reason, he loves barges and will also inspect the canal network between here and London.

I wondered if I could come with you today for a few hours and see what you do at work? I am curious as I have never been allowed into a workplace – you know, the 'Lady thing' in London, and this is my opportunity. I do so admire you and the freedom your father gives you."

Anne was amazed. Usually, it was the other way around; people disliked work.

"It would be a pleasure, Marion, but you can't come in those fine clothes. Come upstairs, and we will change you into some old clothes of mine. I will find you a smock. Are you sure about this?"

"Yes. You probably think me a romantic, but I am so bored and fascinated by what you must do there. Also, perhaps we might meet Thomas!"

"Ah!" Anne said, giving a little smile and thinking that Marion must be keen on Thomas! As she pulled out the best old clothes in her wardrobe, Anne wondered whether Marion was more interested in work or Thomas.

"Now try these on – we must be quick, or I will be late. Father loves punctuality – even though he is away, I can feel him watching me."

Eleanora carrying Marcia, walked in as Marion's head popped out of the top of the smock. "What are you girls doing?"

"Marion asked if she could join me at work for a few hours, and I thought it would be fun. Mr & Mrs McPherson are engaged this morning, so Marion is all alone. But we must not let her ruin all her beautiful clothes at the bakery!"

"Yes, yes, I agree. Have fun, girls."

"Thank you, Mrs Turner – my mother is most excited about the afternoon tea."

The Church School, Guildford ...

Simeon, William, and Madeline crossed the busy street between horses, carts and other pedestrians and made their way into the Church school. William immediately dropped his bag and darted off towards the game of cricket on the other side of the graveyard. Simeon picked up William's bag and dropped it near the church's back door at the bag stand.

Madeline slowly walked into school and sighed. She was not interested in school and would prefer staying home even if she was doing housework. The sight of her friends, Ruby Bowers and Dawn Luckett, cheered her up as they went into a huddle, talking and giggling about minutiae.

Just before Reverend Taggart called the children in, Ruby whispered in Madeline's ear that Richard and Caleb were plotting a fight with Simeon and

William for today. She heard that it was because Caleb's teeth were knocked out, but she was unsure of the whole story. A frown came over Madeline's face, and she dashed and warned Simeon.

Simeon groaned, wondering whether this would ever end. There was nothing for it. He must ask for Reverend Taggart's protection and quickly.

The good Reverend was a man of action and sent William and Simeon on an errand while he thought out a strategy on hearing about the plot. When they returned an hour later with the goods requested, he ushered them into his office.

"Now, boys, you know how we have been learning about gravity? A day at home will allow you enough time to prepare an example. Tomorrow morning you may demonstrate what you have prepared. Perhaps you could discuss the project with Anne and Thomas at the bakery this morning. Simeon, you can take care of William – I'm sure your parents will be happy with your supervision. When you get home, please explain why you are home early and the task I have given you." He gave Simeon a wink.

William was unsure what gravity was, but before he could ask Reverend Taggart, Simeon cut across him, "Certainly, Sir. We will come up with something." Grabbing William's collar, he dragged him off towards home.

The Reverend Taggart thought, 'Good, those two are out of danger. Now for some straight talking with Richard and Caleb.'

William and Simeon grabbed their bags and set off for home.

It was a beautiful day with a cloudless blue sky and a slight breeze from the west. William breathed in the summer air and felt the exhilaration of a perfect day for an outing. He wanted an adventure.

"Simeon! Why should we go home? We could go on a hike in the forest. We could be knights in shining armour. I've always wanted to see what was over that hill across the river there." William pointed at the highest part of the forest across the river Wey.

The King's hunting forest extended from Windsor to Guildford. It was a vast forest full of deer and other game that regularly entertained royalty and their guests.

Simeon was not so keen. "I'm not sure we are allowed into that forest. At least not by ourselves."

"Then we shall never see it! Father will never take us. It would only be half an hour up to the top of the hill."

Simeon thought, 'Maybe I could find a hollow log and a round stone that would roll down it. That would be a good example for the Reverend tomorrow.'

"Ok, then. I have an idea for the example we might find up there." Simeon's interest was rising as he wondered what was over that hill. The two boys set off down High Street on their adventure. Once across the bridge, they walked along the Portsmouth Road up to the first corner. They ducked through the fence into the trees and climbed upwards over the pine-covered earth and rocks.

The hill proved higher than expected, and it was a good hour before they reached the top, by which time it was nearly midday.

"I can't see Guildford at all; the forest is too thick," William said as he peered around the trees.

Simeon was scouting the terrain for a better vantage point.

"Will, over there. I can see a rocky outcrop one hundred yards along the ridge."

The two boys set out at a run for the vantage point. William got there first and broke into song. "Sim, look at this. I can see the whole town. Wahooooo......"

Simeon arrived and set his pack down. "Wow. What a view!"

Feeling hunger pangs, the boys decided on lunch.

"It's a good thing Clementine remembered your sandwiches, Will. They taste nice."

William turned and found Sim eating his lunch. "Hey, they are mine."

"You can have mine. Look in my bag."

William searched Simeon's bag and found it empty of food except for about ten biscuits.

Simeon grinned and said, "I ate mine at morning tea!"

William was about to scream at Simeon when he stopped, dead still, and slowly sat down. His face went white. Simeon, enjoying a thick sandwich, expected a reaction from his little brother but noticed William was white and silent. "What's wrong?"

William whispered, "Don't…. Do not move, Sim. Just peek a look over your shoulder."

Simeon slowly turned his head. There, not more than five steps behind him, was a huge stag, nearly fifteen hands high before adding the antlers. William was sitting facing the deer head-on. He could see that it was twitching its nose, smelling the sandwich and slowly waving its antlers.

William whispered, "Throw the sandwich over your head. I think it fancies it."

Sim gently took hold of another sandwich and threw it quickly over his shoulder, landing at the deer's feet. The stag started waving its antlers in rage. Then, three arrows flashed past the boys from the right, striking the deer's side in a second. Thud, Thud, Thud. The deer, in fright, raised its front hooves high in the air and crashed onto the ground, falling behind Simeon. Its antlers fell across his arm, breaking it.

Simeon looked in horror as he felt the warmth of the deer's breath expiring on his back. It did not move. William stood up and, from two feet away, watched as the deer's eyes blinked madly and then just opened and became still.

"Good shot, Horace!" came a shout from fifty yards down the hill.

A hunting party of ten horsemen came out from the forest further down the ridge. They shouted to each other in high spirits as they galloped up to where the boys were sitting. Simeon was crying out in pain as his arm hung limply by his side. Every movement increased his pain, and blood was streaming from a nasty gash.

One horseman dismounted and ran up the rocks to the injured boy.

"Good thing we turned up, or that stag would have cut you, boys, into pieces." The horseman then noticed Simeon's arm limp by his side with blood pouring from it. He could see the boy was in agony but keeping a straight face. "Let me have a look at that arm."

Simeon could not move. He noticed the horseman had a brilliant blue tunic and a quiver over his shoulder. An even larger man then approached and stood on the rock towering above the boys.

He said, "What are you boys doing here?" William, frightened to speak, sat there with his mouth open.

The large man thought the boys were poaching. He questioned, looking in William's bag, "What have you got here? Ah, some biscuits – let me have a taste. I am a bit hungry." He crunched onto one of the Turner bakery biscuits. "My, that's good – where did you get these?"

The first man looked up and yelled at the large man, "Horace, snap out of it, man! We have a serious injury here." Horace, enjoying an exceptional biscuit made even better due to his hunger, turned quickly, "Yes, Sire."

Taking a quick look at Simeon, he bellowed at the party below, "Neville, quickly bring some bandages and splints up here. On the move, man! Now! Sir Cuthbert – you too, please. We could use help from your gentle hands."

Below, a horseman dismounted quickly, dived his hands into his saddlebags, and pulled out some cloth and sticks. He raced up the rock face as if it were flat and put them beside the younger man tending Simeon.

The man in the blue tunic asked, "What's your name, boy?"

"Simeon, Sir."

The larger man looked at Simeon and said, "You call him Sire, Simeon!"

William said, "Yes, Sir."

In a rage, the man called Horace yelled at William, "Sire!"

He yelled so loudly that William, in fright, started falling off the rock ledge. Horace leaned over and grabbed William with one hand in a flash, and placed him back down safely. He breathed a sigh of relief and said, "We nearly had another casualty!"

Quietly he mouthed at William, "Sire!"

"Yes, Sire", William trembled.

The man named Horace said, "Where did you get these delicious crunchy biscuits, lad? I have not tasted anything as good before."

Feeling some friendship in the question, William said proudly, "From our kitchen, Sire!"

Horace and the man with the blue tunic looked at each other and laughed. Not understanding the humour, William caught the joviality and laughed as well. The smaller man said, "By the look of you two, you are brothers. And what might your name be, brother of Simeon?"

"William Turner, Sire." William noticed that the smaller man had a magnificent blue uniform and could not have been more than a few years older than Anne. He also saw that all the men obeyed his commands.

"Horace, give me one of those biscuits if there are any left! I'm hungry!"

"Why Sire, I don't think there are any left!" Horace grinned.

William was surprised at this and looked in his bag.

"Yes, there is, Sire! Please have one."

The small man thumbed his nose at Horace and took a bite of the biscuit. "My goodness, you're right, Horace. These are good! I think we must visit this kitchen."

While this was going on, the other men, Neville and Sir Cuthbert, were very gently splinting and binding up Simeon's arm.

Neville spoke softly, "Careful, Robert, this little chap is in a bad way. We must return him home quickly and have a doctor called."

"I'm aware of that! Now, William, you can ride with me, and Horace, you will carefully carry Simeon."

Neville placed a soft jacket under Simeon's head. In a very gentle voice, he quietly instructed Simeon, "Hold still as we bind these splints on. The more relaxed you are, the less it will hurt!"

Simeon gritted his teeth, but the pain was too great. He started screaming but then saw white and passed out. The next thing he knew was waking and staring into the kind eyes of Doctor Jeremy Stephens.

The "Sire" sent a man in advance for Doctor Stephens, requesting his services at the Turner's house. The hunting party slowly headed off down the hill towards the township. Directed by William, they made their way up North Street behind the houses and shops, the large number of horsemen being careful not to attract attention. The 'Sire', Horace carrying Simeon, and Neville, followed William's directions across High Street, through an alley and around a corner at the rear of the Turner house, and entered along the back veranda and into the kitchen. The other party members stabled the horses at the Fox & Hound and decided on a hearty lunch as they waited.

Anne and Mrs Jennings, who were preparing the afternoon tea, were surprised as the three men in brilliant tunics entered the kitchen led by William, while the largest man, Horace, carried an unconscious Simeon.

They stood there for a second or two in silence, looking at each other.

The appearance of the men dumfounded Mrs Jennings. Anne was astonished that possibly three knights stood in the kitchen facing them. Then she saw Simeon held gently in the arms of the larger man.

William broke the ice, "Anne, Mrs Jennings, Is Doctor Jeremy here yet?"

Anne replied, "Why no! What has happened to Simeon? My Goodness!"

The man with the blue tunic said, "Our apologies, maids, for entering your kitchen, but the situation's urgency demanded this. Master Simeon and Master William have been hunting with us, and Master Simeon was in an altercation with a rather large stag. The deer's antlers have damaged his arm, and he is in much pain and passed out. He requires his bed. If you would lead us, please? "

Mrs Jennings continued standing there with her mouth open. Anne immediately reacted.

"Of course – please follow me."

She quickly led the way up the flights of stairs, Horace bending down carefully, avoiding the low doorways.

The young man in the blue tunic quietly whispered, "William! Is Anne Mrs Jennings's daughter or a servant girl?"

"No, Sire, she is my sister!"

"Ah!"

Horace laid Simeon gently on the bed and withdrew backwards. As Neville knelt beside Simeon, checking his wound, the man in the blue tunic asked, "I am sorry young maid, what is your name?"

"Anne, Sir."

Horace called, "Call him Sire, young Anne!"

Neville, turning and looking up with a smile, asked Anne for cloth and water and another blanket till the doctor arrived. Anne called Mrs Jennings and requested the required items.

The man in the blue tunic then stood back as Neville continued his monitoring of the boy.

"Is he a doctor, Sire?" Anne asked.

"Yes, he is my physician. He is an excellent surgeon and will explain the exact symptoms and treatment required when the doctor comes."

He turned and looked at Anne. He found her most attractive. There was something special about this girl – she was full of life, and her beauty glowed from her. But there was something more that he struggled to understand. It was as if he knew her from somewhere else.

Anne looked at him. She had never seen someone in such a magnificent uniform. The blue tunic must have been new as it was without blemish.

The man in the blue tunic was amazed by the beauty of this girl called Anne. He could not take his eyes off her.

Horace could see what was developing, so he mentioned the need for biscuits.

The 'Sire' nodded his head out of a trance and said, "Yes. William was so good as to give us a biscuit each. We have never tasted a finer biscuit and learned they came from your kitchen. Might we sample some more, Anne? Neville will remain with Simeon."

"Certainly, Sire. However, I would rather remain with my brother until the doctor arrives."

The young man quietly said, "Anne, I would trust Neville with my life. He will be at Simeon's side till the doctor comes. Your devotion to your brother is admirable, but he is in safe hands and rests comfortably. Neville will call us if required."

Anne nodded and reluctantly agreed and led the way. They passed the doctor rushing up the stairs. He stopped abruptly on a landing, allowing them past.

"Thank you, Doctor Jeremy, for coming so quickly. Simeon is in his room with this gentleman's doctor. They are waiting for you."

Jeremy Stephens's eyes opened wide when he saw who was standing beside Anne on the landing.

The 'Sire' said, "We are going downstairs for some biscuits. Should we send some up?"

"No, thank you, Sire." Jeremy Stephens hurried on.

They entered the kitchen, where Mrs Jennings continued preparing the afternoon tea. Horace looked at the spread in pleasure but took note of the stern look from his friend.

Anne took a deep breath and, steadying herself, asked, "Sire, I am sorry, but we have not been introduced. May I ask your name?"

The man in the blue tunic looked up, and his eyes opened wide, "My apologies, Anne. In all the rush with Simeon, I forgot the introductions. I am Robert South, and this gentleman is Sir Horace Coombes from Cornwall. Please call me Robert."

Anne smiled, "I am pleased to make your acquaintance, Robert. How did you come across William and Simeon?"

"Ah?" Robert said. "Let me tell you the whole story while we have a biscuit at your kitchen table. Come join us, Horace."

Horace came from the doorway and gently parked his massive frame on one of the kitchen chairs. With a charming voice, he asked, "Any chance of a cup of tea, Mrs Jennings?"

Mrs Jennings looked sternly at Horace and retorted, "I suppose you will want some of these cakes next!"

Horace's face broke into a begging smile, hoping for sympathy.

Robert and Anne looked at each other, enjoying the banter, and began laughing.

Chapter 6

In the faint candlelight, William woke early and noticed Thomas dressing for work. Simeon was sleeping in the next bed, softly breathing, and appeared normal. Anne lay fast asleep across the end of his bed. She was fully clothed and held a washing cloth in her limp left hand. Her golden hair lay draped across her face, and she breathed slowly in a deep sleep.

William thought, 'She must have been here all night looking after Simeon! If I broke my arm, I wonder if she would do that for me.'

Thomas noticed William's eyes were open and darting around. He approached the bed and quietly but firmly told him, "Stay in bed, William and keep watch on Simeon. Anne and I watched him all night; it was a bad night for him! He needs rest. I will lift Anne onto my bed. If Simeon wakes, go down and fetch Mrs Jennings; she knows what he needs. Dr Stephens will be here around eight o'clock."

William whispered, "What time is it?"

"About three-thirty. Because of your little adventure yesterday, I am late! Father will not be pleased when he returns. You will need a good excuse!"

William shivered at the thought of another beating, despite the new friends he had made from the hunting party and Reverend Taggart sending them home from school early. Father would be furious when he found that they had explored the forest. Someone would receive a belting, and as Simeon was injured, William expected the worst.

Thomas gently shifted Anne onto his bed and covered her with a sheet and blanket. She groaned and moved around a bit, settling in the comfort of the bed and was soon in a deep slumber. Now fully dressed and ready for work, Thomas tiptoed across the room but turned to check on William. He signalled by waving his finger and whispered, "Shush........ Will!". Then he was gone.

William quietly watched the candle flame flicker in the early morning darkness. It danced around, casting moving shadows on the walls. Strange that Thomas did not snuff the candle before he went! Father always told them, 'Put out all the candles before bedtime, please!' William quietly got up and snuffed out the candle. Hopping under the covers, he gazed through the window and saw some stars appear in a gap in the clouds. The boy imagined Robert South sleeping at the hunting party's camp, out in the forest somewhere above the township. He wished he could be with them. William was entranced by the thought of racing his mount through the woods chasing down the deer. What excitement – all those friends with their magnificent coloured tunics and the different weapons. He hoped Robert would return one day and tell him more stories of the forest.

William's eyelids drooped and slowly closed. Suddenly he was on a quest with Robert in the forest, but this time William was in the lead, riding a stallion who boomed through the thicket keeping him well above the brush. The stag was just ahead, ducking and weaving and seemed almost flying as he jumped this way and the other. Robert shouted, "Will, take your shot before he darts away!" But the deer had other intentions. It thundered far ahead, then stopped facing William. Its eyes focused directly on him with a look so terrifying that William reigned in his mount and stopped. The stag grew enormous in front of him, and the intensity of its eyes penetrated William's mind. It was as if the deer was speaking.

"How dare you invade my forest, my home. You have killed my brother, and now I will kill you!"

They stood and gazed at each other from fifty yards, gathering their strength as they prepared for battle. The stag's eyes were full of fury, alerting William of the mortal danger he now faced.

Robert, from further behind, screamed at him, "Take your shot, Will! Take your shot!" It seemed as if Robert was further and further away. The battle would be between William and the stag.

As the deer charged, he desperately tried threading the arrow but fumbled. He tried repeatedly, but the string would not fit the arrow nock. The deer was now on him. His stallion jumped in terror, throwing him down into the long soft grass. The stag towered over him – so close he felt its hot breath on his face. Will gritted his teeth as the stag's antlers slashed down.

William sat up, waking in a sweat. Taking a great breath of relief, he realised it was a dream. It seemed so real, but he was safe in his bed. His tense little body relaxed and becoming calm, William lay back down.

"Did you know you whimper when you're dreaming?" came a sorrowful voice from the next bed.

A dull morning glow was entering through the window.

"Sim – are you feeling better?"

"It still hurts a lot, but I think I am."

"Thomas said you need sleep. The Doctor will be here at around eight o'clock. So, you should sleep or just rest now. Is there anything you want?" There was no response.

Saying it louder, he repeated, "Sim is there anything you want?"

No answer came. William sat up and peered across at Sim in the faint light. He was fast asleep again.

The King's Hunting Forest above Guildford ...

Not five miles away from Guildford, Robert South awoke at the hunting party's camp and heard the men making breakfast outside. He was hungry and wanted some food before the final day of the hunt. This morning was their last opportunity before returning via Sandhurst and then Portsmouth. The events of yesterday came across his mind. William, Simeon, and Anne Turner. That girl - something was special about her in many ways – different from any girl he had met before. But she was not of his class, and he must put her out of his mind. He refocused on the last day of the hunt.

Robert threw on his tunic and britches and stretched. Sir Roger Duffield struggled with a pan of some bacon and eggs over an open fire. Before setting out from Sandhurst, the steward had carefully packed the provisions. Sir Roger had drawn the short straw and was appointed cook.

"Roger, do you need a hand? Smells good!"

"Give me a minute, and you will have some fried eggs and bacon once I find the room on this small skillet, Sire!"

"Good, good! If you were born a pauper, Roger, you could have become a great cook."

"Next time, Sire. You might consider bringing a cook!"

"Where is your sense of adventure, Roger? Hunting parties do not take cooks. Consider this as in-service training!"

Sir Roger smiled as he fiddled with the frying pan, "Sire, I hope you enjoy your eggs. I will enjoy the mess at Sandhurst tonight with a well-cooked meal prepared by a real cook and served on a warm china plate!"

"Probably Horace is thinking the same. More than you, Roger, Eh!"

The men were stirring, and Sir Roger passed over a plate with some fried eggs and a tiny strip of bacon. Robert took the plate and sat on a log outside his tent.

"Yum!" he said as he started eating.

Neville came over and sat beside him.

"Robert, about yesterday, I am still concerned about that boy in Guildford. That was a nasty break, and I am not sure old Doctor Stephens is up to date in the treatment of breaks. He is a country doctor, and I have more recent experience at sea. I'm not sure he understood the need for complete immobilisation of the arm."

Robert sat back and scratched the back of his head. "Are you saying we should check on the boy again today, Neville?"

"Yes. I would not normally make this request, but something else is bothering me!"

Robert knew that Neville was a deep thinker. He was seven years older than Robert and had studied medicine at the Royal College as a sponsored navy officer. Neville was an experienced surgeon serving for several years in the navy before Robert met him five years ago. He found that Neville never overstated a situation. If Neville was worried, there was a good reason for it.

"And what else would be bothering you, Neville?"

Lowering his voice, Neville leaned a little closer. Robert paid close attention.

"After you went downstairs with Horace on the biscuit tasting expedition…."

"And fine biscuits they were, Neville, we brought a sack of them back for the Manor. I think the Earl will be quite impressed."

"Robert, while you were at the tasting downstairs, William's mother appeared in the bedroom. The lady was sleeping when we arrived but awoke from the noise of conversation coming from the bedroom upstairs. It was clear that she was surprised by what she found. I think you must have been downstairs when she appeared."

"Neville?"

"She was a handsome lady, having very fair skin and long blonde hair. Mrs Turner looked much like the daughter you met."

"Ah, Neville. You are sweet on this woman! If she is married, then I think you should withdraw from any romantic attraction."

"No, nothing like that. Mrs Turner appeared in Simeon's room only in a nightgown – as if she were startled. Doctor Stephens explained the details of Simeon's accident and then introduced me. As I explained the treatment, I noticed quite easily because of her fair skin, some bad bruising on the rear of her cheeks and her arms. She blushed and quickly withdrew when she saw me looking at her bruising."

Robert cut in, "So is this the sign of some bad disease or injury, Neville?"

"I conferred with Doctor Stephens, and he explained it resulted from a fall on the stairs. He requested I disregard it as the lady is most sensitive about the bruising. But Sire, bruising like that cannot come from a fall. The marks were apparent on both cheeks. Bruising from a fall usually is only on one side, not both, and is on the forepart of the cheek. It has faded but not that much, which means it was far worse a week and a half ago. She must have been beaten severely by someone."

Robert raised his eyebrows.

"You are saying that someone has beaten William and Simeon's mother. You think she may be in danger?"

"I am not sure, but I have seen that bruising before, and it is more common from an assault. In most cases, it is from an angry husband!"

"There are many husbands who demand from their wives what they want, Neville. Especially those who do not care for their wives!"

"Precisely."

"Ah!"

Robert looked down and had another piece of egg. As he chewed, he turned and looked at Neville, still thinking about his friend's suggestion. He noticed Neville seemed edgy and impatient.

"There is more, isn't there, Neville?"

"Yes, there is."

"You're saying that if this husband beats his beautiful wife, he may beat William or even Simeon."

"That's correct."

"Neville, we cannot interfere between a man and his wife and what they do behind closed doors. It is their business. However, if it were my mother or your mother, I would be greatly concerned."

"Robert, young Simeon and William are our friends!"

Robert now remembered Anne's beautiful face, with her long golden hair. She was enchanting, and he found himself often thinking of her. As she was not of his social status, his family would not appreciate him meeting with a baker's daughter, but she was an angel. There seemed an attraction between them that was unsettling but quietly pleased him. He would never wish any of her family any harm.

Robert took a deep breath – this was the last day with his friends. They were keen on a hunt this morning before heading for Sandhurst. He was soon due back on his ship at Portsmouth. 'Damn this interruption, but there would be further hunts, and who knew what they would find in Guildford!' In the back of his mind, he knew he would enjoy seeing Anne again, despite what they might find in the workings of this house.

"Neville, it appears that we might revisit Guildford this morning. This time we shall be a bit more formal. Please tell Horace he will join us. We will rejoin the party either at lunch or dinner at Sandhurst."

The Turner Household, Guildford ...

Breakfast, lunches packed, and dressing for the day was complete. Anne talked with William and Madeline as they walked towards the church school further down High Street. She left them at the church and then hurried on towards the bakery, noting the time on the Guildhall clock. Anne smiled as she saw crowds already forming along the street. Weaving her way through the crowd, she thought, 'This will be good for business.'

William strolled into the school area as Madeline rushed off with her friends. Mrs Taggart welcomed the children as they arrived, deliberately speaking with William.

"William, I have been told by a message about Simeon's broken arm. How is he today?"

"He told me this morning, Mrs Taggart, that he felt much better."

"Good, good, now off you go and play with the others."

Reverend Taggart was glad of some good news from his wife as he was still dealing with Richard Smith and Caleb Elliot, who once again were airing their suspicions about Caleb's accident. After explaining the outcome of his investigation, the boys still were insistent on suggesting otherwise. Ensuring a quick settlement of the matter, he counselled the boys that continuing their objections would result in discussions with their parents about their previous indiscretions. He listed some in detail, soon noticing that the boys eagerly accepted his explanation of events. Reverend Taggart, from experience, made sure he held something up his sleeve on each child just in case bargaining was required.

Considering his strategy, Reverend Taggart thought recruiting the services of Jonathan Turner might be in his interest, ensuring this went no further. He trusted the Chairman of the Parish Council and would speak with Jonathan at next Monday night's council meeting. They usually spent fifteen minutes together after each session, going through the outcomes of the agenda items. One more item would not hurt.

Before he met with Jonathan Turner, he would need to prepare carefully. For this, he would need some inside information. Perhaps he and Mrs Taggart would pay a call on Mrs Turner and enquire on her recovery before Jonathan returned from London.

Soon after nine in the morning, there was a knock on the door of the Turner household, which Mrs Jennings answered. She found two of the gentlemen who visited yesterday standing there.

"Good morning Mrs Jennings," said Robert. "We enquire on Simeon's recovery! Might we meet with Mrs Turner if it is convenient?"

"Why, Sir, excuse me, I mean Sire. She was not expecting anyone today, but please come in, and I will advise her you are here."

When Eleanora Turner heard who was waiting on her downstairs, she immediately commenced dressing carefully before receiving her guests. She organised with Mrs Jennings some tea and cake for the gentlemen while they waited. She began work on her camouflage.

In the meantime, Horace tied up the horses at the back of the house and quietly visited Mrs Jennings in the kitchen. He sat at the kitchen table with a smile, crunching biscuits and drinking tea.

Robert and Neville were being entertained by Clementine and Marcia when Mrs Turner entered.

"Gentlemen, I am honoured by your visit. I hope Clementine and Marcia have been on their best behaviour. Please, for what reason do I owe this pleasure?"

Robert could immediately see that Mrs Turner cleverly covered the areas of bruising with heavy makeup and a scarf. Given the day's warmth, the scarf did look a little out of place. Neville was correct. She was a beautiful woman with all the graces of the upper class. Robert quickly provided an answer.

"Mrs Turner, unfortunately, yesterday I did not meet with you as I was downstairs. I understand you have not been well, so I did not press the matter, but I thought I should remedy this and make our introduction today. I am Sir Robert South, son of the Earl of Fintelton. I understand you have met my physician, Dr Neville Bassington. Neville has served in the navy with me for years and gained much battle experience. He is quite an expert in broken bones, and I would trust him with my life."

Eleanora Turner immediately realised that this young man was from one of the leading families in the land. He was probably doing himself a disservice by visiting their home. She was impressed that they had returned.

"Sir Robert, we are greatly honoured by your acquaintance and you too, Doctor Bassington. I am a little overwhelmed that you take such an interest in our boys."

"Please, Mrs Turner – we have now been introduced, and I insist you call us by our first names; otherwise, we would be uncomfortable. "

"Very well, gentlemen!"

"Mrs Turner, we intend to monitor Simeon's recovery and ensure Doctor Stephens employed Neville's instructions."

"Gentlemen, Doctor Stephens has served this family for forty years, and I'm sure he knows what is best. He called this morning, checked the boy's bandages, and bled him, relieving the pressure."

Neville looked back at Eleanora Turner in horror. "He bled him when he lost so much blood yesterday? Ma'am, may I see the boy? I have some medical supplies with me and will explain upstairs if I may?" Neville was quite concerned and did not hide this.

Eleanora Turner looked at the gentlemen – their concern was slightly alarming. At the time, she did wonder why the Doctor bled the boy given his injuries. Eleanora had dismissed her doubts trusting in the Doctor's judgement and assuming it was a standard medical precaution. Now she became worried.

"Certainly, Doctor Bassington. I mean Neville."

Neville smiled, "Please, Mrs Turner, feel at ease using my Christian name. Given what Simeon and I went through yesterday, I think a first name basis is best."

Robert added, "Please call me Robert, Mrs Turner."

"Gentlemen, you take me by surprise with your generosity. I will comply with your request, but certainly, in public, I must call you by your titles. Please call me Eleanora."

Arriving at Simeon's bed, Neville found the boy fast asleep and with a slight fever. Since yesterday, the bandages were unchanged, and he checked the incisions where Doctor Stephens bled him. Of more concern were the loose bandages and splints incorrectly fastened.

Robert realised that Neville's concerns were correct again. Perhaps Doctor Stephens was getting on and missing things. Maybe his eyesight was failing, or he was overworked. Robert felt unqualified for criticism as he was not a medical man, but the look of concern on Neville's face was unmistakable.

"Mrs Turner, Simeon has a slight fever. That is normal but keeping him calm for the next few days is essential. He will require care; regularly wiping his brow with cold water will help. Also, the bandages need changing, and the arm must be firmly dressed around the splints, so the forearm cannot move for at least six weeks or more. I have brought new bandages, but I will require some assistance. Perhaps Mrs Jennings could help?

Forgive me for suggesting this, but I have learned from Doctor Stephens that you are recovering from a fall and not at full strength yet. Perhaps, Anne would look after the boy for the next few days until the fever passes. Where might we find her?"

Eleanora was now alarmed. She always regarded Doctor Jeremy Stephens as competent, but perhaps he did miss something. Eleanora became dizzy and suddenly sat down on the end of William's bed. Her scarf fell off, and out of habit, she pulled her long blonde hair behind her neck. Robert immediately saw the bruises on her cheeks. He looked away.

"She is at the bakery. I will send for her."

Robert could see that Mrs Turner was now unsteady on her feet. Neville would certainly require Mrs Jennings's assistance. Better that he should find Anne and bring her home quickly.

"Let me fetch her, Mrs Turner! Where is the bakery?"

Neville noticed that as Eleanora looked up, there was a puzzled look on her face. He realised this woman was near collapse. The situation was becoming complicated. From the doorway, he called for Mrs Jennings.

Eleanora whimpered, "At the end of the High Street near the wharf."

"Sire, if you would please. I think Mrs Turner may also require assistance soon."

Robert jumped into action.

Neville was becoming concerned for Eleanora Turner. He noticed how she was quickly losing her strength and sat crouched over. He knelt beside her and asked, "Eleanora, are you well?"

"I think you can see I am struggling, Neville. I think I need more rest – much more rest. I am so tired."

"Eleanora. Are you with child?"

She looked up at him in alarm. All she saw was a kind, understanding face.

"How did you know, Neville?"

"I am a doctor, Eleanora - a doctor with much experience. I agree with you about your needing more rest. Mrs Jennings will assist you downstairs. Do not be alarmed; Simeon will have the best care, and Clementine may assist me until Anne arrives. I will visit you once I have finished here with Simeon."

Robert rushed down the stairs passing Mrs Jennings on the way up. He flew out the back door and nearly collided with Horace. "Ride with me, Sir Horace. Make haste!"

They mounted their horses and cantered down the High Street towards the River Wey.

"We are looking for the Turner bakery. It is near the river and the wharf at the end of the High Street."

They found the building quickly with a Turner's Bakery sign above the entrance. It was far more extensive than Robert expected. There was a building site nearby where it appeared a warehouse and mill were under construction.

"Horace, find the hunting party and tell them we will join them when we can. If we are not back by lunch, they should head off for Sandhurst. Kindly arrange the packing of our things, and we will join them tonight. Once done, I would value your presence here again."

"Keep safe, Squire. I don't like leaving you here alone. I shall return soon!"

Robert watched as Horace turned his horse and cantered off towards the Portsmouth Road. He dismounted and secured his mount. Walking into the bakery, he found a hive of activity with men and women in aprons and smocks hard at work. It appeared baking was in high demand.

A young man approached him. "May I be of help, Sir?"

"Yes, of course. I am Sir Robert South from Fintelton Manor. I have come from the Turner home and must find Miss Anne Turner as quickly as possible."

Jeb took a good look at the visitor, who, from his dress standards, was from the upper class. Despite his attire and manners backing his introduction, Jeb was still suspicious.

"What is your business with Miss Anne, Sir?"

Robert checked himself and refrained from reprimanding the man for insolence. Understanding this employee was careful. He swallowed his pride and remained calm.

"Simeon is unwell and needs care, and Mrs Turner has fallen ill!"

Jeb then realised the urgency, "If you would follow me, Sir Robert."

They moved quickly through the rows of ovens and tables. Towards the rear of the building, there were offices on a platform overlooking the bakery work floor. Jeb entered a door with Robert following. Anne was sprawled over a sloping clerk's desk, fast asleep.

Jeb said gently, "Anne, Sir Robert is here for you!"

Anne slowly lifted her head. Rubbing her eyes, and then some dribble from her mouth as she looked up. Pulling the long hair away from her face, she saw a smiling Robert standing directly in front of her desk.

"Robert ......Robert, where did you come from? I'm sorry – I was with Simeon all night. I hardly slept at all."

Robert admired the girl as she regained her countenance. She just oozed beauty, manners, and intelligence. He liked her more with her ruffled hair and crinkled work clothes. She talked with such gentility; it was a pleasure being with her.

Robert explained the situation and offered a ride on his horse as time was of the essence. She agreed without hesitation, and they set off, Jeb watching with a frown as the couple walked away.

"Do you always work, Anne?"

"Just a few hours each morning helping Father with the paperwork. I find the work challenging, and I am interested in accounting and business."

"You must meet my sister, Emma – she needs occupying! I'm sure she is bored living on the estate." Robert knew of no other employed female of his acquaintance. He liked the idea.

They found Neville and Clementine hard at work on Simeon's arm on returning. They had changed the bandages and washed the arm. Neville was now demonstrating how to starch a dressing.

"You see, Clementine, we use starched bandages that will immobilise the arm for a long period, probably around eight weeks. These bandages must be changed and starched every week from now. There is a new procedure where a cast of plaster is applied, but I have no gypsum here. Perhaps if I can procure some at Sandhurst or Portsmouth, I will return and make a cast."

Clementine brushed the starch onto the tight dressing around the splints, but not so firm that it affected the circulation.

"Simeon, it is essential that your arm remains still. When you feel capable of walking around, the arm must be in a sling, so you maintain this position." Neville demonstrated this by holding his arm in the position required. "I will make a sling up for you before I leave. It is important that once your fever is gone, you get up and exercise. The movement will help you regain your strength. Now Clementine, while you finish with the starch, I will attend your mother."

Neville stood and could see that Anne heard all that he said.

"Anne, I think Clementine is quite competent with the bandages. However, Simeon has a fever and should remain in bed for two days. I will leave some potions that will help him rest. From what I hear, you will need some rest tonight, so having Simeon sleep through will be a blessing!"

"Amen, Doctor."

Neville followed Mrs Jennings downstairs. They found Eleanora lying on the bed facing the window. Neville knocked and entered.

Eleanora said, "You may assist Clementine now, Mrs Jennings."

Neville sat beside the bed and opened the small case he was carrying. "Eleanora – the best thing you can do is rest. I will give you a potion that will help. When does your husband return?"

"He should be home from London on Saturday by coach. Mrs Jennings and the children are such good help! I will be well cared for till then."

Neville commenced the examination.

"From what I observe, I think you will require more care. Mr Turner will need to employ an additional maid. My observation is that you are about two or three months with child. Your fall would not have helped, and the confinement will be very taxing. I also note that you are pale and you have little energy. At this stage of pregnancy, this is unusual."

"You are right, Doctor. I have never felt this way before with a child. I am afraid something is wrong."

"Time will tell, but the key, for now, is rest." He looked at her bruising. There was more than he first thought. "Eleanora, might I ask that you sit up and then cough for me?"

She sat up slowly and coughed lightly. Neville requested a stronger cough as he felt her back. She gave a hard cough but then collapsed onto the bed. Her nightgown was loose and revealed the top of her back, where Neville saw some more bruising, probably the result of body blows. She rolled onto her back with her eyes closed in embarrassment.

Neville sat back and waited until she opened her eyes.

"You are short of breath – have you any chest pain?"

Eleanora turned and looked him in the eye. She knew he noticed the bruising and needed his guarantee of confidentiality.

"No. ……. Doctor Neville?"

Neville was quite wise from many years of patient care. Before she spoke, he cut in, "Eleanora. I will talk with Mrs Jennings about some special food for you. You need more iron in your diet. More fresh vegetables. You also need regular exercise and fresh air, but not until you have rested and only gradually."

She was about to answer, but he spoke again, "Eleanora, your secret is safe with me!.............. Please excuse me now as I discuss your diet with Mrs Jennings. I will leave a letter for Mr Turner, recommending the employment of an additional maid until this baby is born and probably for some time after that."

Eleanora was alarmed that Neville was aware of her circumstances. His intuition was uncanny. But she saw the gentle face and kind smile as he withdrew. His professional curiosity was satisfied; he would not say anything untoward. She was now comfortable that she could trust him.

"Thank you, Neville." She whispered as he backed out through the bedroom door as if she were a queen.

Neville made a final check on Simeon's bandaging and then descended to the kitchen, where he would brief Mrs Jennings. Also, he decided to write separate letters to Mr Turner and Doctor Stephens advising of his diagnosis and recommended treatment for both patients. The message would include mention of his return in two weeks – this might act as an insurance clause delaying any more beatings. He found Robert and Anne sitting at the kitchen table, eating biscuits.

"I must write letters for Mr Turner and Doctor Stephens, Sire, before we leave."

Robert nodded in agreement. He was in no hurry, given his enjoyable conversation with Anne.

"Would you like a biscuit Neville?"

"Thank you, Sire. The biscuits are fresh, tasty, and far better than what we find onboard. Perhaps we could order some before our next voyage."

"The thought had crossed my mind too! Anne, is this possible? Would your father consider baking a batch of fifty dozen biscuits for provisions on our next voyage? Neville and I will pay for them."

Anne was delighted. "Certainly, Robert. We have special airtight tins that you may want as well. It keeps the biscuits fresh."

While Neville wrote his letters in the drawing-room, Robert enjoyed this last opportunity of conversing with Anne.

"I'm afraid we must leave soon as Neville and I are due back at Portsmouth by early next week."

"It has been a pleasure making your acquaintance Robert. Thank you for saving William and Simeon's lives in the park. They are beautiful boys each in their way, except William can be a bit adventurous."

Robert blushed, "It was a bit of a coincidence. Our hunting party had been stalking the stag for some time. I think we drove it towards its final position.

It was a happy coincidence with a good outcome. Simeon may disagree with that!"

They both smiled.

"So, you are in the navy. What do you do?"

"I am a lieutenant on the frigate *Providence*. Neville is the ship's surgeon. He outranks me on board the vessel in terms of seniority. I think we will sail for Greenwich next week to install some new canons. My father intended that I would become a man by being at sea. So, I went at age twelve as a midshipman, and as you probably know, class has its connections, so now I am a lieutenant and may gain a command next year."

Anne enquired, "If Neville is your senior, why does he call you Sire?"

"It is a class thing. For me, it is of no significance, but my friends keep it up. Perhaps they think it is good manners. I am not sure, but do not be concerned about it. Neville mostly calls me Robert in private."

"I see." Anne wondered if she would ever see Robert again, "How long will you be away?"

"Now, that is an excellent question. It all depends on the Admiralty. Who knows – perhaps three months or maybe six? I am not sure. We will be in Greenwich for several weeks testing the new canons. I will write and advise you."

"May I also write and find out how the biscuits go at sea?"

"I would like that. I receive very few letters."

Anne thought for a moment. "I have never seen the sea. I have been told about it at school and seen paintings. But we have never ventured further than Woking, or Ewell, on trips with father. The biggest ship I have ever seen is a coal barge down in the canal."

"We must remedy that. As soon as I am back, I will send an invitation and show you the sea and my ship. You should bring the boys as well and perhaps your father."

"That would create great excitement in our family Robert. I'm not so sure about father – I think he feels safer on land."

Robert saw his opportunity, "I have not had the pleasure of meeting your father – perhaps on my next trip, this way you could introduce me. I think Neville will return before we disembark and review Simeon's arm. He is a very caring doctor. He is always helping people – he should have been a missionary.

The boys will not be in trouble with your father, will they? You and your mother will be safe, Anne, won't you?"

Anne was surprised by this comment, "Yes, Father is very protective of our family. He would enjoy meeting you."

She thought about his comment on safety. First, she was surprised that he would let slip that he cared about their safety. The comment almost signalled a kind of attachment. Could it be that he cared for her? It was not until much later that Anne put other facts together and realised Robert and Neville were aware of her mother's bruising. Delicately he revealed their suspicions that her father might have abused her mother. Anne shuddered. What must they think of her father?

Jonathan Turner returned late Saturday afternoon, the coach stopping at the Fox and Hound Inn. There was much news for the family, and as far as he was concerned, it was all good news. He hired a porter for his bags and proceeded up the street towards home in good spirits.

Once inside, he found the drawing-room empty. Climbing the stairs and entering his wife's room, he found Eleanora asleep. Quietly sitting beside where she slept, he gently took hold of her hand, "Eleanora, I am back and with much good news!"

She opened her eyes and saw him. She opened her arms with a warm smile, giving him a great hug, "Jonathan, how much you were missed. There is also so much news for you here. The children have made such a wonderful new acquaintance – I'm not sure where I should begin."

Jonathan Turner, receiving such a welcome, felt a new feeling of belonging, something he had not experienced for some time. A broad happy smile appeared on his face. He was home and loved.

Chapter 7

The Reverend Andrew Taggart sat at a small table in the back corner of a coffee house on High Street near the Turner bakery. It was a beautiful Monday morning, and visitors were already streaming into Guildford's High Street, enjoying the delights of this growing town. He sipped at his coffee, deciding upon the key points he must make in the coming conversation. Jonathan Turner was a fair and honest man; however, he did have a temper. Not wanting an escalation of the situation or the possibility of consequences later at home, he thought carefully about which calming words he would employ. Wives and children paid the price for many a successful man's achievements. He could write a book on the dark pasts of many men whose families he helped over the years through counselling or charitable help.

Andrew Taggart loved his ministry and found himself gifted in explaining the human condition. As his church was full each week, he felt no urgency in evangelism as the Wesleyans did. His major struggle was balancing the social needs of his congregation with its maturity in spirituality. Despite being a man with a gentle heart and always offering genuine hospitality, the realities of life had hardened him; some would say it made him street smart. The church establishment in England was highly political, and a position such as his, being Rector of a notable church, could be put in jeopardy by poor leadership. 'Good Governance!' He mulled this over, 'There are some risks that must be taken, but not too many!' He would need to take care as he addressed his parish council chair this morning.

"Reverend Taggart. What a fine morning we see today!" Jonathan smiled heartily and shook the Reverend's hand. Andrew was surprised by the warmth of his greeting.

"I have brought some small gifts for Mrs Taggart's larder and some biscuits for your study. We can share the biscuits at some time over a cup of tea." Jonathan Turner was thankful for one of Andrew Taggart's recent sermons, which gave him strength in an incredibly tempting situation. He was keen that Andrew should be encouraged by this news.

"Jonathan, this is far too much! Your generosity honours me. We shall share them and soon." Reverend Taggart placed the bag of bread and the small tin of biscuits beside his chair. "Now, shall you have coffee or tea?"

The orders quickly arrived, and Jonathan thanked Andrew for the home visit he and Mrs Taggart made to Eleanora the previous Friday. Being burdened and anxious about the coming conversation, Andrew silently made a quick prayer.

Jonathan noticed the hesitation, "Out with it, please, Andrew. The coffee is good, and I am ready for discussion, whatever the issue is!"

Andrew relaxed.

"Ah, Jonathan, there is a delicate matter I must brief you on, and I hope my explanation will be adequate. I am sure you understand that being a clergyman is like being a politician. Keeping the members of the congregation content is not an easy task."

Jonathan nodded and said, "Ah yes, it is a hard path that you must find that keeps everyone at peace but also declaring the truths of the Bible. Why, I think, most folks would prefer giving God some advice rather than obeying His word. I don't envy your position."

"Yes, Jonathan. It is not easy, and, in this instance, it concerns you. I think you will understand. But it is better if you hear the confidential details from me."

Jonathan nodded in agreement. He wondered what the issue could be.

"You will recall the recent incident at school when Richard Smith collapsed and accidentally knocked out Caleb Elliot's front teeth."

Jonathan nodded.

"It was more complicated than this. My first thoughts were for the safety of the children. Then for reasons of church unity, I slightly changed the details. I aimed to avoid ill will developing between families. These slight changes have achieved their purpose!"

Jonathan was already thinking, 'I am sure this involves William. I had my suspicions.' He regained his concentration and continued listening.

"The families involved were Mayor Smith's family and our blacksmiths family, the Elliots. However, another family was not mentioned, and this will continue, given your blessing. That family is yours!"

Jonathan sat back in his chair and took a good swig of his coffee. He always suspected William's involvement. He now needed the details. "How are we involved?"

"You remember the death of little Olivia Stepton, the chimney sweep?"

"I will never forget!"

"The day after the funeral, Richard and Caleb made rather sordid remarks about Olivia and her family. William, standing close by, was not impressed and politely rebuked them. When he did this, they set upon him with their unkind remarks. Now, as you understand, William has a high regard for justice. Fortunately, Simeon witnessing the growing tensions, prevented William from attacking them before Mrs Taggard rang the bell for class."

"This seems innocent enough?" Jonathan questioned.

"Yes, it was, but when William reappeared with an axe handle and bashed Richard on the head, knocking him out cold, things became more serious. He then targeted Caleb. Unfortunately, Caleb turned at the wrong moment, and the full force of the next swing hit Caleb in the mouth. Hence the injuries he suffered."

Jonathan sat there in shock. In a few seconds, William might have destroyed the Turner's long-term relationships with the mayor and the town's leading blacksmith. Becoming agitated, he felt the emotion stirring within his head. Andrew noticed the colour change on his forehead.

"But do not worry, all is not lost! You will understand that I saw the implications of this hostile event and set about quickly changing the real story. I strongly believed there was no need for acrimonious disputes between families. For the good of the school, I maintained calm. After all, Richard and Caleb will finish school here at the end of the term. Hence the explanation of the events that you first heard still stands. The one complication is that Richard and Caleb are now aware of the real events. They have their suspicions and have questioned my explanation. At present, I have, through various means, contained the situation and kept them off the trail. We may have avoided further incidents now that we are on term break. But it might come out in the future. I desired the opportunity of confidentially advising you of this in advance."

Jonathan sat there, stunned. This wicked little boy, who was probably oblivious of the implications, had interfered in his life again. If this surfaced in the congregation or the marketplace, it would seriously affect his business in the town. Of all people, why the mayor's son? Andrew's swift action avoided a significant dispute developing. Jonathan's concern subsided slightly.

"Thank you, Andrew, for telling me about this. I must admit I was concerned that it involved the boys when I first heard of the incident. But you are correct; we must keep this quiet. I am most thankful for your skilful management of this situation and must apologise for my boy taking justice into his own hands when he should have referred the matter to you. But surely, Andrew, you took a great risk in handling it this way?"

Andrew smiled nervously, "Richard and Caleb are not little angels either! There are indiscretions they have committed and kept quiet with the agreement of their parents. I think we can maintain confidentiality if I remind them regularly. My first consideration was harmony in the running of the church school. But now, thankfully, with the mid-term recess upon us, they will both attend the Free School next term. There will still be the church service on Sunday, which will need watching. With most of these issues, I find that the problems soon disappear once the children are separated."

"Well done, Andrew. We will meet any problem when it arrives."

Andrew continued, "I know you are fully aware of the events of Simeon's injury. We are praying for his speedy recovery. He is a fine boy and very sensible. I feel some guilt for the injury he received."

"How can that be, Reverend?"

"On that day, we learned of Richard and Caleb's plan of publicly exposing the events. Simeon, who was tipped off by a friend, advised me in advance. So, I gave them some projects outside the classroom, including an errand, and then sent them home. Unfortunately, being young adventurous boys, they decided on an expedition. I must admit I did not ask them to go directly home, so they acted within my directions."

Jonathan Turner smiled, "You have supported my family and I with great kindness, Andrew, and I was unaware. I am greatly thankful and in your debt." Jonathan added this indiscretion of William's activities into his mental ledger. He seemed incapable of thinking of the boy as a six-year-old but as an adversary who would destroy him if he was not careful.

Andrew Taggart felt a heavy burden fall from his shoulders. He felt relieved from his discussion and that Jonathan received it with thanks. Charles Simeon[6] was right, "God's grace was unmeasurable and life-enriching!"

Jonathan sipped again from his cup and said, "Perhaps, if possible, the details should remain between us?"

Andrew Taggart nodded his agreement, "It seems Simeon's current injury, while being most unfortunate, is a blessing in disguise. The longer he is kept away from the others, the better. These boys will forget the issues in time, and it will all settle. But the only other issue is containing William."

Jonathan agreed with this, "Yes, managing William is a challenge." They both sighed, and there was a short silence.

"Andrew, you will recall your first sermon on 'Sin'!"

"I'm afraid it was not the most polished performance, but it was well-meant."

"No, no! I must encourage you. I was recently in an unpleasant situation where the words of your sermon were of significant help. Your indirect

---

[6] Rev Charles Simeon, Curate in Charge of Holy Trinity Church Cambridge. His lectures on sermon composition and his own evangelical theology were widely read by Church of England ministers in the 1820s. He is regarded as one of the most influential church leaders of his time. Simeon Association and Mathew Hale Public Library.

guidance assisted me greatly under considerable pressure, and I know I made the right decision! It may be that I may not have reached the correct conclusion if not for that sermon. I will not go into details, but you must have my thanks. The parish is fortunate that a man of your calibre ministers here."

Andrew was overwhelmed. He smiled, and the flow of thankful emotion overcame him. Rarely did the Reverend receive positive feedback. He opened his mouth, but Jonathan spoke first.

"We should meet more often, Andrew. Now I must be off - a lot on today." Jonathan shook hands with Andrew and left him sitting in the coffee shop.

Jonathan Turner knew that Simeon would be out of harm's way as he recovered at home. It was William now that he must manage. Jonathan needed a plan. William, at age six, was still naïve and could have a slip of the tongue at any time in the future. Richard's glib comment about visiting Africa may not be far from the truth!

Most of the day's business at the bakery was complete before Jonathan met Reverend Taggart. He decided to return home as there were issues that still required consideration. Thomas, Anne and Jeb would be quite capable of managing the daily business, and the meeting with the mill builders was not until the coming Saturday. He needed some quiet space to think through these issues, including the revelations about William and Simeon. He was not annoyed about what transpired in his absence, but planning the future was the challenge.

Walking along the street, he enjoyed the warmth of this bright summer's day. Guildford was bustling with traders, visitors, and both town and country folk actively moving up and down the High Street. He was content as he saw many of his bakery carts transacting brisk business in the streets and the corn market. As he passed his family's church, he remembered the rear wall repair project he intended but forgot, discussing with Andrew Taggart. He must advise the Rector that he would make a significant contribution to the project on its announcement.

Arriving home, he strolled through the hallway and into the kitchen, letting Mrs Jennings know he would be in his study. He collected a letter from Doctor Bassington and called upon his wife upstairs. Jonathan found her fast asleep, still in her nightclothes. He thought she should be up by now but considered the rest would be beneficial. Quietly sitting beside her bed, he reread Doctor Bassington's letter.

"Mr Jonathan Turner   *July 1826*

My apologies, Sir, I am writing without an introduction. However, the emergency with your son Simeon required immediate medical action.

I look forward to making your acquaintance in person soon. I intend that this will occur towards the end of July, depending on the Navy's requirements for me.

No doubt, by now, you have a full explanation of the events. Simeon's injury was quite severe, with a deep laceration on the upper arm and a break of the radius, one of the bones between the wrist and the elbow.

The laceration has been cleaned and stitched. The bandaging for this will need to be changed regularly, and the wound cleaned each time the bandages are replaced. Given the number of stitches used on the laceration, I suggest that the dressing be renewed daily for the first week and then twice a week. I noticed that Simeon suffered from a slight fever when I last examined him. A fever is consistent with a laceration of this type. I have left instructions with Anne and Clementine for managing this. If the fever is not gone by the time you return, please call Doctor Jeremy Stephens for a further examination. Please Note, Sir, that the process of bleeding Simeon should not be undertaken at present. He lost much blood in the accident and should be drinking plenty of milk, ensuring his blood supply increases.

Eleanora stirred and rolled over. Jonathan looked up and then refocused on the letter. He thought it strange that Doctor Stephens would bleed Simeon after considerable blood loss. He continued reading.

The broken bone will require around eight weeks of healing time. The arm should remain immobile during this healing process. I have used a method of splints and bandaging where starch is used and stiffens the bandages. Please renew the dressings at least weekly. Once again, I have left the appropriate instructions with your daughters.

I will return near the end of July and review Simeon's recovery.

You may not understand why we show such interest in your son, Simeon. My good friend, Sir Robert South, who I have served with these last few years on His Majesty's Ship Providence takes a personal interest in the boy. He feels responsible that his bow shot did not kill the stag earlier and protect your son. My view is that Sir Robert, Sir Horace Combes and Sir Roger Duffield saved the lives of both your sons, Sir.

Sir Robert is the youngest son of the Earl of Fintelton, and a lieutenant on the HMS Providence docked at Portsmouth. Both Sir Horace and Sir Roger are good friends of Sir Robert. Sir Horace holds the rank of Captain and is an Assistant Adjutant at Sandhurst, and Sir Roger is a Major in the Royal Artillery stationed at Woolwich Common.

Sir Robert requested that I take an interest in this case until the boy is quite well again. There will be no cost for this treatment.

Yours sincerely
Lieutenant Neville Bassington RN
Surgeon
HMS Providence

Jonathan considered the boys' exploits. What were they doing in the forest in the first place? He must discuss this with them. Thank goodness for Sir Robert and his friends. He noted there was more in the letter.

PS: While treating your son Sir, your wife took ill. I attended to her and found that she was fragile and suffered from some bruising and slight yellowing of the eyes. You should look deeply into her eyes in a place of adequate sunlight and see the yellow colour. It may be that your family doctor missed this in his last examination of Mrs Turner. While I am concerned that there is a more serious underlying cause, the best treatment for this condition is a regular healthy diet of fresh fruit and vegetables. I will confer with you more on this when I return.

I would say that your wife is not gaining in strength and will need nursing in the coming months, particularly given that she is with a child. I suggest you employ a lady's maid for your wife over the coming twelve months.

It may be prudent that Doctor Stephens attends to your wife regularly. I would welcome an opportunity to discuss your wife's condition with Doctor Stephens when I return.

I have left some limited potions with Anne until we meet in late July."

Jonathan Turner sat in silence for some time, going over the letter several times. He was most grateful that Sir Robert took such an interest in Simeon. Indeed, his interest was very generous, and the man must be a true gentleman with a good heart. He was more worried about the comments on Eleanora's condition. Jeremy Stephens warned him that Eleanora was weak, but he assumed she was recovering. It appeared his assumption was incorrect! What was this underlying cause the Doctor mentioned? Jonathan's guilt returned – the mismanagement of his emotions had led him astray, and now his wife suffered. Would he ever find peace of mind again?

Glancing out of the window, he noticed the differing patterns of the leaves as the wind gently blew the waving branches. He was a tough businessman and rarely considered nature or beauty. His was a life of action, setting a goal and achieving it. His thoughts now reflected on the fragility of life and how unfair it could be.

He watched a yellow leaf drop from a branch and float in the breeze. Light as a feather, it slowly glided out of sight. It was silent, with only him noticing its downfall. It was gone forever.

A chill came over him as he turned and looked down at his wife quietly sleeping. What was this undiagnosed disease ailing her? He could not manage his family or business on his own. There must be a cure.

Jonathan's mind was near panic, breaking out in a cold sweat.

Then he felt Eleanora's warm hand gently fall on his. "Jonathan, you are back. I am so excited about Thomas and Anne visiting the McPhersons in Greenwich. I feel that Thomas and Marion may have found a partner in each other."

"It is a very generous invitation, indeed. Perhaps if requested, they might extend an invitation to William as well. This way, Anne would spend more time with William. It may be providential for Thomas and Marion." Jonathan suggested this with more than one strategy in mind.

"Jonathan, do you think they would agree?"

"I'm not sure, but William should see more of the world. He may appreciate what he has here more. It may calm his wild spirits. I'm sure he would enjoy catching up with his Uncle Richard on the way and his cousins as well."

Eleanora was thinking about this as Jonathan continued.

"Eleanora, I find you need rest, and I understand this with the child coming. I wonder if it would be helpful if we employed an additional maid. She would also assist with cleaning, washing, and cooking. Mrs Jennings would welcome the help. I cannot spare Anne, and Clementine will soon work in the bakery. Would you consider this, please? "

"Can we afford it, Jonathan?"

"Yes, money is not a problem. The business grows stronger and stronger every day. Do you remember Mark and Alison Stepton, Olivia's parents? They have two elder daughters, one being fourteen and are still at home. I was thinking of offering her a job as a new maid. Mrs Jennings could train her, and the Steptons could use the money. I will have the builders put another room onto Mrs Jennings's quarters, perhaps a larger room. Who knows, we may need more maids in the future."

Eleanora wondered at this change in Jonathan. He seemed most concerned with the family suddenly. She was surprised, but she welcomed it.

Jonathan rose, "I will be in my study."

Eleanora noticed the letter he was carrying, "Who is that letter from Jonathan?"

"Nothing of worry! Just business." He moved off, knowing change was already happening, and this was just the start.

Greenwich – Some days later …

Hamish McPherson sat in his office reading the morning mail. There was a letter from Jonathan and Eleanora Turner sending their best wishes and accepting the kind invitation for Thomas and Anne to visit in early August. Jonathan also requested that William might be included. He was keen that his son should see the Naval College – Jonathan intimated that a naval career for William might be a fair calling.

A letter was soon dispatched with a cheerful request that William join the party and that Mrs Marjorie McPherson was thrilled about his coming. Hamish noted that William would be in luck as many naval ships were presently arriving at the Woolwich wharves. Mrs McPherson missed her children in Scotland and promised not to spoil the boy.

At dinner, Hamish McPherson informed Marion of the visit. Marion, who was now living with the McPherson's permanently, was thrilled and looked forward to the company. She was pleased about Thomas attending.

"I have missed Anne and Thomas so much since we were in Guildford. I would love a return visit soon, but this is better. Oh! Aunty Marjorie, they have never visited London before – there is so much they need to see. We will have a wonderful time."

Marjorie was of a generous disposition. When Marion was excited, Marjorie was excited and would do anything for this girl's happiness. They treated her as if she were their own.

"Yes, Marion, and we shall have a merry time doing this!"

"Should we have a dinner party so they meet my father and brothers? I have already explained my mother's difficulties but not the other issues. How will we manage these, Uncle?"

Mr McPherson was a mature and experienced Scottish man who believed if there were any skeletons in the closet, they were best brought out and dusted off. If Anne and Thomas suspected any such issues, these questions would have arisen during their Guildford visit. On the contrary, he felt that the Turner family shared similar values with no presumptions of greatness but were down to earth good citizens. He admired Jonathan Turner's achievements and his planning for expansion. Business success was where the future lay, not in the landholdings of the aristocracy. These people would be brushed aside as their control of parliament and their outdated practices became apparent. It was creative thinkers like Jonathan Turner and himself who would change the world in the future. He saw significant advantages in Marion marrying into such a family.

Hamish looked over at Marion and thoughtfully said, "I think your father, Alexander, will manage this, my Dear! It is probably best that I talk with him beforehand. It will be fine."

"But you know what happens when they drink, Uncle. They become brash, and the arguments start. Anne and Thomas will think I have a terrible family!"

"Marion, we cannot hide the real situation. They must be asking why you reside here instead of your home. The dinner will answer all their questions. Dear, we have known you since you were a child. Jennifer, before her illness, was a wonderful mother. You have all the graces of any great lady. Your parents are extremely proud of you, just as we are. I am confident that Anne and Thomas will see your goodness and not the problems that your family experiences."

"I hope so, Uncle, as I do like Thomas ever so much!"

Marjorie joined in, "And so do we. From all that I have seen of them, I have every confidence that they have already made their decisions about you, Marion. Why would they visit if not?"

"Uncle Hamish and Auntie Marjorie, you have been so kind. I thank you from the bottom of my heart. Tonight, I will not sleep a wink thinking about this visit." She jumped up and gave them each a hug and kiss. Marion said goodnight and rushed away with various plans already brewing.

Hamish was delighted with Marion's excitement. He thought, 'You will never know the happiness you have brought for myself and my wife, Marion.' Marjorie was also beaming and becoming a little teary.

"Now, Marjorie, I may be incorrect on this, but I'm not sure if the Turners will be aware of the latest fashions in London. Anne and Marion are similar in size, perhaps you and Marion should purchase some fashionable dresses tomorrow. I am sure Thomas will have the appropriate outfits, as Jonathan also has this tailor's business. Anne is such a fine young lady – we must not see her embarrassed!"

"I was thinking the same thing. Hamish, for a tough businessman, you are an old darling, aren't you? No wonder I married you. I'll just go up, sit with Marion for a while and plan the shopping."

Hamish McPherson was a shrewd businessman. He and Jonathan had signed the contract for the Epsom pub. His advisers assured him of this being an excellent investment with a handsome return. As for Thomas, the plan was that he would become a brewer and join the McPherson Brewing Company. The question Hamish now considered was the best approach to convince him of such a move. Friendship with this boy would reveal what made him tick. Hamish saw great promise in Thomas – the question was whether he should be in Guilford or Woolwich. Time would tell.

"Jenkins! Another brandy, please. Tell Babcock that I will require the small coach at six, first thing in the morning. Also, Mrs McPherson and Marion will require the large coach all day tomorrow – say from ten in the morning."

"Certainly, Sir."

"Tell me, Jenkins! I hear a small fleet of Royal Navy frigates is arriving at Woolwich. Do you know which ships they are? Their names."

"No, Sir, but our cook will know. She has a boy in the navy. She usually knows all about them before anyone else. Let me check with her, Sir."

Hamish McPherson enjoyed the brandy as it soothed his throat at each sip. Over the past twenty years, he had developed partnerships with many men, only one or two of whom he liked. The Turners reminded him of his own family about ten years ago. Both Jonathan and Thomas were likeable fellows. They were good company with similar interests. Young Thomas would develop well with the right mentoring.

"Mr McPherson – the cook was not sure about the first four that came into port. One is *Hampshire*, and another is *Nottingham*, but she is unsure of the others. But she does know the name of the last ship which came in this evening."

"Spit it out, man?"

"HMS *Providence*, Sir."

Hamish's homework was correct. His contact in Guildford informed him of certain notable gentlemens' visits, particularly the Earl of Fintelton's son.

"Good, Jenkins. Please advise Mrs Swiggins that there will be a need for more provisions in early August. We will be entertaining that week. I will see that Mrs McPherson sees her about this tomorrow morning."

At Guildford – Late July …

Anne finished yesterday's accounts as Jeb entered the office. He lingered a bit before asking, "That man the other day, Sir Robert South. I was surprised he came here. I understand he is involved in some way with Simeon's broken arm. Have you known this Sir Robert long?"

Jeb knew he could never compete with such a man after meeting Sir Robert. The knight's appearance changed his plans entirely and put Anne on a pedestal far out of his reach. He also associated the order for biscuits was from this gentleman's meeting with Anne.

Taken aback by this question, Anne carefully considered her reply. She was now sure that Jeb thought their relationship more than friendship. It was becoming uncomfortable, and the thought of needing an explanation for every man she met did not sit well with her. It was time to set the boundaries. Still, she liked Jeb and must be gentle and ensure their long-term working relationship remained harmonious.

"Ah, I only met him the day before when they brought William and Simeon home from the forest. He is quite a good conversationalist, but I know little about him. We may never see him again, I expect. But we are grateful for his saving William and Simeon from that stag."

Jeb was relieved that it was a passing acquaintance. He was keen on advancing his relationship with Anne. "Yes, it may have been far worse. Simeon was fortunate." Jeb paused and then asked, "Anne, the church fair is in August. Will you be going?"

"Jeb, that was my intention, but the McPhersons have invited us to Greenwich around that date, so I will not be here. Thomas is going as well, so you and father will be looking after the bakery for a few days."

Jeb planned to spend time with Anne at the fair. Letting her see him in the tug of war and perhaps teaming up in the three-legged race would further his cause. Her absence would be disappointing, as there were few opportunities besides sitting in the church. Anne noticed the frustration on his face. She had dreaded this moment.

She gently said, "Jeb, come over here and sit down."

"I really must be getting back, Miss Anne."

"Jeb, it will only take a few minutes."

Jeb appeared reluctant but then shrugged, moved across, and took a seat beside her desk.

"Jeb, it is nice that you take an interest in me, and I enjoy talking with you. But you must understand that it is friendship only."

There was an awkward silence between them.

"Jeb, do you understand what I am saying?"

He moved in his seat and then looked up, "Friendship is a start, is it not, Anne?"

"Yes, it is Jeb, but that is where it ends for us. I like you, Jeb. I enjoy talking with you, and my wish is that our friendship continues. Any relationship besides friendship may destroy that. We work together well here, Jeb, and I think of you as a friend, but that is as far as it goes. I have the highest respect for your work, and I know you are an upstanding community member. But I have other dreams, Jeb. I want other experiences outside Guildford. My life here is just the beginning for me, and I must not encourage any hopes you have that might spoil your life. I hope you will understand this."

Jeb's smile became a frown of concern. "You mean you do not desire my companionship?"

"No, Jeb, many women, I am sure, would desire your attention. But I cannot control the beliefs, likes, and dreams that I have. I am happy at present as my parents need me, but I long for more in life, the chance to travel and seeing new lands. I want some adventure in my life before I settle down."

"I could wait, Anne!"

"That's not it, Jeb. I don't want you waiting. You need your freedom to find the girl who is right for you. I am sure many girls out there would love you courting them. Let us just remain friends. Please, Jeb?"

Jeb looked down in embarrassment. "I see. I must apologise for making my feelings known. I have been too eager. I must go. Sorry."

He stood up, smiled and walked out slowly. Anne felt a low pain in her heart. She knew Jeb as a kind man, but he was not the man for her. If she married him, she would not grow – she would feel trapped and frustrated. It was better that he knew now. Then she thought again. Perhaps she was mistaken. It may be that she may never receive an offer of romance again! She shuddered. She wanted marriage and children as her mother had accomplished, but Jeb was not the one for her. Was she too selective? Was she missing an opportunity? She was unsure of the answers. Perhaps a talk with mother might clarify her fears.

That afternoon the Turner's eldest daughter, Bethany, arrived by coach from Woking. Since receiving Anne's letter, thoughts of home were uppermost in her mind. The Reverend Charles and Mrs Wendy Upton were quite understanding and arranged a week off for a visit. A temporary governess would look after the children while she was away.

Bethany Turner, nineteen years of age, was the second eldest of the Turner children. Although gaining most of the better attributes of her mother, some would not have considered her as attractive as Anne. What Bethany may have slightly lacked in beauty, she made up for with an amazingly warm personality.

Alighting from the coach, she cried with excitement, "Anne, let me hug you and see you are real!" Snups was whining and shaking with excitement. "Snups – down, boy! Let me organise a man for my bags, and then we will walk home and talk."

Anne was astonished at how worn and tired Beth looked.

They set off on foot for the Turner home with a hired man carrying the bags.

"Thank you for your letter, Anne. I was shocked by the news. Reverend Upton was kind in allowing me this time off. Now, what else can you tell me about the situation?"

Anne and Bethany were close, still sharing that sisterly love of unconditionally supporting each other. Anne gave a brief outline of recent events. She ended with the news that Doctor Neville Bassington would arrive tomorrow to examine Simeon and her mother. Bethany was pleased to hear her mother was resting more and improving in energy.

"Now, Beth, it's time for your bath and a rest before dinner!" They both agreed.

At dinner that night, Jonathan Turner announced some news. He waited until everyone finished their meals and then asked for their attention.

"As you all know, Thomas and Anne will be visiting the McPherson's in Greenwich the week after next. I received a letter today that contained an invitation for William as well. Mrs McPherson is much excited by the idea of William's attendance."

William beamed with joy, saying, "I'm going too, Anne and Thomas, I am going too!"

Mrs Turner was pleased for William but also felt a little jealous of losing her son for this time. She would have preferred accompanying her children, but that was out of the question in her current state of health.

Jonathan continued, "William, I have asked Mrs McPherson if she would arrange visits to both the dockyard and the Naval College. It may be that you take an interest in the Navy. I have been advised they take on boys between the ages of eight and twelve."

Suddenly, silence came over the gathering, and Simeon blurted out, "But father William is only six and a half. He is far too young at present. Why am I not invited?"

"It will do William no harm. These things may inspire him in the future. At present, Simeon, you will be better off remaining at home due to your broken arm."

Simeon was not convinced but said no more.

"I also announce that Lieutenant Neville Bassington will be returning tomorrow, intending to re-examine you, Simeon and possibly try a new treatment on your arm. He will take a room at the Fox and Hound and attend you here.

Also, I have conferred with your mother, and we will be hiring an additional maid over the next twelve months. We have not told all of you yet, but your mother is with child, so we shall need the extra help. With that in mind, Robinsons' builders will extend the maid's quarters, increasing our staff accommodation."

Marcia did not understand, "What does it mean, Mama, that you are with child?"

Eleanora smiled and bent down low and said, "Mama is going to have another baby. A little sister or brother for you. "

Marcia's face lit up, "Yoweee – when will it come, Mama?"

"Soon! Too soon."

Anne looked at her sister Beth with a slight frown. They both thought about the dangers for their mother, given her delicate state.

Later in the evening, a knock came on the front door. Mrs Jennings informed Mr Turner that the Reverend Andrew asked for an interview. Jonathan immediately answered the request, apologising profusely about Andrew being left outside and ushered him quickly into his study.

"Mrs Jennings – tea, please."

The minister slumped down in an armchair. He seemed a little tired and ruffled.

Andrew sadly said, "Jonathan, I have just come from Jeremy Stephens' home. Jeremy has passed away tonight!"

Jonathan looked in utter disbelief, "No!"

"I'm afraid so. Dorothy told me of his hard, long day visiting patients and then arriving home looking exhausted. They decided he should have a rest before dinner. She went up thirty minutes later calling him – he did not respond. She then noticed that his eyes were open."

Jonathan sat in silence. The man was almost part of their family for over forty years. His death was a tragic loss. Jonathan commented, "He just drifted off?"

"Dorothy related how lately he was becoming worn out and thinking of retiring. Now, I think he must have been over sixty years of age. He was also becoming forgetful, but I did not notice this. They decided on taking a holiday where he could decide on retirement, but it all came too late."

They both sat in silence, remembering a good friend.

"Jonathan, as he was on the parish council for so many years, it would be good if you would give the eulogy. I know he was a close friend of yours, and I am sure Dorothy would agree with this. He has no other family here in Guildford, with his children living in London. A local person who knew him well, someone such as yourself, should take on this responsibility."

Mrs Jennings brought in the tea.

"Laura is with her now – Dorothy is naturally most upset. I called in Doctor Sopwith, and he informed the Constable. They will take care of her tonight. Andrew informs me some of the children will come down from London and comfort her."

"Yes, of course, I am honoured to be asked. I will call on Dorothy in the morning and pay my condolences."

"Thank you, Jonathan. I knew I could count on you. Jeremy's passing leaves a vacancy on the Parish Council. Unfortunately, this will cause an election. Do you recall how many applied the last time there was a vacancy? It would be good to find someone interested in the church rather than status this time. Not that Jeremy was ever inclined that way, but some of our council members seem too proud of their positions. You understand what I am saying, Jonathan, don't you?"

"Yes! We probably have until the weekend before questions start being asked, so why don't we both think about possible new members. We can talk again later in the week and compare lists."

Andrew was scratching his head. "It would be convenient if the Council could appoint an interim person until next year's vestry meeting, saving the heartache of an election."

"Good idea, Andrew. Why not consult with the bishop tomorrow? Perhaps write a message tonight and have a rider deliver it tomorrow. We must not break any canon laws when we act.

By the way, Andrew, I am looking for an extra maid for the housekeeping. I tried the Stepton family, but I received a message from Patrick Easton that the Stepton girls work for the manor house. Would you let me know if you think of anyone, please?"

"There are a few around - let me talk with Laura and see if she knows anyone good. Leave it with me!"

The two men chatted for some time, recalling good times spent with Jeremy and all the work he did for the poor at no charge. They both agreed it would be a big funeral; they would need a plan developed in advance. Hopefully, the undertaker would maintain the corpse for a little longer than usual, allowing time for the preparations.

Andrew then rushed home, thinking about service details and the bishop's letter.

Jonathan sat there, sipping on his tea. He was thinking about his family's medical needs. Which Doctor would the family employ now? He was not fond of Doctor Sopwith, as the man was like an aristocrat and would look down on them. Thank goodness this Neville Bassington was coming on Thursday. They had not met yet, but he liked the tone of his letter. The man was a more comfortable fit for Jonathan. Perhaps Guildford would attract him? Probably a long shot – but what attraction did Guildford have to attract a young navy doctor? Jonathan sighed.

In the girl's bedroom on the first floor, Bethany Turner was enjoying the comfort of being at home. She and Anne had the first long sisterly talk in over a year.

"I love being home and back in our room – you would not know how much I missed this place and you, Anne."

Anne grinned with joy – having her elder sister back was just what she needed. A confidant, someone she could discuss issues with and advise her on the wisdom of her decisions. Mother was wise, but a sister gave a whole new perspective on so many matters.

"I know Woking is not that far away, but it seems on the other side of the world when you are there. How is it working at the rectory? You seem tired, Beth."

"Looking after five children is somewhat demanding – even with the housekeeper helping. They are good children, but they are active and always have demands. Take my advice Anne – resist becoming a governess at all costs. Perhaps avoid marrying – children are too demanding. I'm hoping for a quiet stay with a few sleep-ins that will refresh my strength."

"It sounds demanding, but you must meet lots of different people. There must be many young men interested in you at Woking."

"You would think so, but no one ever appears at the rectory. Well, not often, except for the cleaners and contractors. It is quite lonely. My only opportunity for meetings is on Sunday at church. Then only farmer's sons appear, who are looking for a wife to feed them, provide them with satisfaction and have children. Not that exciting or romantic! I fear I will end up on some farm with ten children and a hungry husband who chases me to bed each night. I feel life slipping away from me."

"You are tired, Beth. Things will improve. But it is good having you home again."

"Now tell me about my mother."

Anne licked her top lip, "There is much I have not explained yet!"

The two sisters chattered well into the evening before finally snuffing the last candle alight in the house.

In the morning …

After being at the bakery for some hours with Thomas, Jonathan Turner returned home for breakfast with his wife. Eleanora was in the parlour with Marcia.

"Ah, Eleanora, you are looking much better this morning. Have you rested well?"

"I think it is the extra rest and good food. I still lack the energy for more exercise, but I am sure that will come again soon."

"Andrew Taggart visited last night and advised me that Doctor Jeremy Stephens died late yesterday afternoon. Such a pity, as he was a good friend. We will miss him as our family Doctor."

Eleanora was shocked at this news. "There was no warning that his health was declining. My goodness, this is sad, especially for Dorothy."

Jonathan replied that he would be visiting Dorothy Stephens later in the morning and would pass on their condolences and ask if they could do anything.

"We will need a new family doctor, my Dear! I know Doctor Sopwith is available, yet I am reticent about him – he is a bit arrogant. Do you have anyone in mind? Given your current state and our often need for family medical advice, I think we must make a decision soon!"

Eleanora looked puzzled. "There is a new doctor I have heard of practising on the western side of town. Some of the ladies at our church are using him. I think his name is Chenning. Perhaps you could talk with him, Jonathan."

"Yes, I will do that. Now Dr Neville Bassington will arrive tomorrow, and I believe he is taking rooms at the Fox and Hound. I thought that given the good service he affords us, the least we could do would be a dinner invitation tomorrow evening. I am looking forward to finally meeting him, and I am sure he would enjoy meeting the rest of the family."

"Jonathan, I agree, and I think you will find him a most pleasant gentleman. It is a pity he is in the navy and not a practising doctor in these parts." Eleanora thought for a moment and then asked, "Do you know if he is a married man? He must not be, or he would be bringing his wife with him. Perhaps Bethany might show him Guildford if he is staying longer."

"Ah, Eleanora, I see what you are saying, but let us see how the dinner goes first. We should meet him before planning any adventures, especially involving Bethany. Now I must tell you of my discussion with Andrew Taggart yesterday. You will be amazed!"

Jonathan then explained the full story of William and Simeon's exploits at school and how they hiked up the mountain. He ensured she understood it must remain confidential as the details, if revealed, might cause disputes between families.

"So, it may be advisable for William to remain around the home, keeping Simeon company until he departs with the others for Greenwich the weekend following. I think things will have settled enough by the time he returns."

Eleanora sat back in her chair. She agreed with Jonathan that this could have consequences if not handled carefully. Indeed, the Reverend Taggart had protected their family by his skilful management of the situation.

"Jon? For dinner, why not invite Andrew and Laura Taggart as well? They would be good company, and, in a way, it would be an indirect thank you for all he has done for us. It would also be a meeting opportunity for William and Simeon as they are not attending school."

"Eleanora, that is a grand idea as I was somewhat nervous about meeting Dr Bassington on my own. I will write notes this morning and have them delivered. If you would plan the dinner with Mrs Jennings and advise the children, we shall have an enjoyable evening."

"Now, Jonathan, you recall you suggested another maid. I have consulted Marjorie Smith on this, and she gave me the name of an agency that provides maids. The agency is in London; however, they can now place maids with Guilford expanding. I contacted their office, and they will be sending someone for a trial starting next Monday."

"That is a relief, Eleanora. I was wondering how I would find the time for this. Let us meet this new maid and review her references on Monday when she arrives."

Jonathan stood silently for a few moments, "Firstly, I must write these notes, and then it is time I visited Dorothy Stephens and offered assistance."

"Yes, he was such a kind, understanding man. But Jonathan, when Doctor Bassington visited Simeon on the second day, he was most concerned when I mentioned that Jeremy bled him. It also struck me as being strange, given Simeon had already lost so much blood. Doctor Bassington advised against bleeding. He also commented on Jeremy not renewing the dressings and ensuring their tightness."

Eleanora stopped talking as if she was considering this.

"When you said that Dorothy commented on his memory, I thought that perhaps there was something wrong even when he visited Simeon. While it is a sad loss for Dorothy, maybe it was time for Jeremy."

Jonathan was listening intently.

"Eleanora, there is a warning in this for us all!"

Chapter 8

Neville Bassington arrived in Guilford late on Friday afternoon. Receiving the invitation at the tavern's lobby desk, he quickly replied, advising he would join the Turner family for dinner. His ship, HMS *Providence*, had docked at the Woolwich naval yards on Thursday. Usually, the Guildford coach journey from this location on the Thames would be of two days duration. Neville was not wasting time and arranged the coach's departure well before first light on Friday morning. With a horse change at Ewell, he was confident of arriving at Guildford around four in the afternoon. Although the coach ride was long, bumpy, and tiring, the sight of Guildford again was welcome and refreshing, a town he found quite enchanting from his last visit.

Robert South's Father, the Earl of Fintelton, had dispatched the coach for his son's use during the planned port stay of four weeks. On hearing of Neville's journey plans, Robert insisted his friend use the coach. Neville protested, saying he would ride a horse. Still, understanding the distance involved, Robert would not hear of it and sent Neville off on Friday morning, promising to accompany him on the next visit.

The naval doctor arriving at his room in the Fox and Hound quickly ordered a bath. A relaxing soak for ten minutes would satisfy his yearning for rest before attending the dinner. As he relaxed in the warm water, his eyes began drooping. The water soothed his body, and any tension he felt drifted away. Breathing deeply, he was not aware as he fell asleep.

A knock on the door woke Neville, who found himself in a cold bath. Some considerable time had passed. The knock came again, and he heard a soft voice from the door.

"Lieutenant Bassington, are you all right? It is Anne and Bethany Turner. Doctor Bassington, are you all right?"

Neville jumped out of the bath, threw a towel around his midriff, and answered the knocking. Opening the door, he stood there, dripping water over the carpet, mouth open in an apologetic stance.

"I must have fallen asleep in the bath. I am sorry! What time is it? Golly, I'm so sorry!"

Anne and Bethany looked at each other and giggled. Anne laughed as she said, "All is redeemable, Doctor. You are only twenty minutes late – no hurry! My parents are busy entertaining the Rector and his wife. Now pop some clothes on, and we will escort you."

He grinned in relief, "My apologies, ladies – I must change – pray, what is the dress standard tonight?"

Bethany said, "A suit will be fine – we are not the aristocracy!"

Neville looked at Bethany with some puzzlement. Suddenly remembering his lack of clothing, he grabbed the towel around his waist, his eyes opening wide.

Anne, realising the need for a quick introduction, "Sorry, Doctor Bassington, let me introduce my elder sister, Bethany."

Neville smiled, still holding his towel tightly, "Good evening, Bethany. Please excuse my appearance!"

Bethany smiled.

Anne quickly said, "We will wait for you downstairs in the lobby."

Neville, understanding the message, nodded and ducked back inside, closing the door gently. The girls looked at each other with a smirk. They moved towards the lobby, but they covered their mouths laughing before taking more than five paces.

Arriving at the Turner house, Anne asked Neville, "Now, am I correct – your rank is Lieutenant, and your ship is HMS *Providence*?'

"That's correct. But Neville Bassington would do!"

"No, no, Doctor, we are honoured by your presence – let me do this correctly, please."

Neville nodded, allowing the two girls entry before following. Anne proudly announced, "Mother, Father, and Friends! May I introduce Lieutenant Neville Bassington of His Majesty's Ship *Providence*?"

Jonathan Turner walked forward and shook Neville's hand, saying, "Sir, you honour us with your presence this evening."

Neville sheepishly looked at Jonathan, "My Dear Mr Turner, I must apologise for being late. I fell asleep in my warm bath – the ride from Woolwich was long, and I fear the tiredness overcame my eyes. My apologies again, but I am now well-rested and glad of your company."

"Wonderful, Lieutenant. Please come through."

They found a magnificent setting laid out for them in the dining room. The family and guests enjoyed a beautiful dinner with lively conversation. After the first course, Neville passed on a message, "Sir Robert South sends his best wishes and says he would have joined me if it were not for some vital work this week. They will be settling in the new canons on *Providence* on Saturday and Sunday as the testing voyage is possibly Tuesday or Wednesday next."

Eleanora was pleased, "Please thank him, Neville, for his kind words."

"Does this mean that your ship will be in port over the next few weeks?" Anne was excited, given her pending trip.

"Yes, it appears the Admiralty are keen on full testing before we see Portsmouth again. I am not an expert on the process, but usually, it takes far longer than is planned. However, if it gives us an advantage, we must take it."

Anne was excited by the coincidence that Robert's ship would be at Woolwich at the same time as their visit. Now she would have three friends in London. She must tell Neville.

"Lieutenant Bassington! Thomas, William, and I will arrive in Greenwich Thursday next and remain for the week. We stay with Mr and Mrs McPherson and Marion Steele. The timing is perfect. Perhaps we might arrange a dinner, and we all meet. It would be wonderful if you and Sir Robert could join us. You both have been so kind over the last few weeks."

"That is amazing. What a coincidence! By the way, everyone, please call me Neville as I prefer my first name. Our sailing date for Gibraltar was changed as one of the ships tasked for canon refit developed a hull problem, so we were reassigned for Woolwich. That's why Robert is working now. *Providence* was the only ship not prepared, so we are now playing catch up. Woolwich is close to Greenwich, so only a short carriage trip. I would certainly attend, and Robert should have some free nights by then. Please send us a message about the arrangements."

Anne was uncertain whether she should have suggested this, but she was relieved to receive this favourable reaction from Neville. She found Robert's company most enjoyable – his conversation was lively and exciting with a good sense of humour. Anne found Robert's descriptions of his travels abroad fascinating, opening a window for her to the outside world.

Neville was pleasantly surprised by this development; recalling their previous encounter, he pondered whether Robert and Anne were a bit more than friends. The more she spoke of him, the more he suspected a relationship. As Robert was the son of an aristocrat, he would be interested in how Robert managed this.

On the other side of the table, Mrs Turner was aware of Neville's continuing glances at Bethany and she at him. A tiny candle flame of hope ignited in her imagination that there may be some prospect in this young gentleman. Perhaps his bride was not the Navy, and he may enjoy life in the country - if you could still call Guildford the country.

"Miss Turner, I don't recall you being here the last time I attended Simeon. Are you normally at home, or are you visiting?'

Beth quickly swallowed some dessert and looked up. She found his conversation welcome. "You are quite right, Doctor Bassington. I am visiting for the week. I am a governess at the home of Reverend and Mrs Charles Upton in Woking. They have five children and require a full-time governess. It is a very convenient position, Guildford being so close."

"Please call me Neville – we are already introduced, and I am a family friend. There is no need for titles. I prefer being addressed by my first name. In the navy, everything is by rank and surname. The use of Christian names is far more comfortable. Tell me then, are you on vacation?"

"It is a special visit. Anne's recent letter informed me that my mother was unwell, so a week off from my position in Woking was agreed. Reverend Upton and his wife are lovely people and were concerned that I should come home and see mother."

Jonathan Turner nearly choked on a piece of cake as he became aware of Anne's letter and the revelations about his wife's health. He excused himself and drank some water. Then he gave a few more slight coughs.

"My, my, Father! Neville, we are glad you are present tonight. Are you ill, Father?" Anne appeared sweetly concerned. Eleanora ended these antics by giving Anne a frown.

"I'm fine – just a bit of cake down the wrong way." Cough, cough.

Reverend Taggart, keen on hearing more about this young man, entered the conversation, "Neville, now tell me why you joined the navy? And pray from there, I understand, you became a doctor?"

"It is a long story Reverend, and I hope you will not find it boring. My Father, David Bassington, has a small printing business and publishing company in Fleet Street. He calls it Bass Printers and Booksellers. He also prints some local rags and does some articles for newspapers. You might not have heard of some of the papers, as their circulations are relatively small with the increased paper tax[7]. We have lodgings at Chandos Place near Trafalgar Square. Our family attended a magnificent church there, and my schooling was nearby. Anatomy always interested me, and I would spend hours reading about physiology and anatomy in my father's book shop. My Father worried that I was not engaging in enough exercise, so I commenced my career in the navy at twelve.

The first few years were challenging; however, with my reasonable level of intelligence, I raced through the naval exams and found myself as a Lieutenant by the age of seventeen. My captain noticed my interest in medicine – he probably could not miss it as I was always helping the surgeon on our

---

[7] The Tax on newspapers was introduced early in the eighteenth century to control the press. The tax was substantially increased in the early years of the nineteenth century and resulted in much dissention. Wikipedia.

ship. I learned a great deal from this – it was like an apprenticeship. So, he recommended me for training as a surgeon. The navy sponsored me to a medical college, and three years later, I was recognised as a doctor and found myself on active duty again. Robert and I met on HMS *Northumberland*. He was a midshipman then. Despite my being five years his elder, we became good friends and have served on the same ships together. Although I think Robert's father may have influenced this with his good connections."

Reverend Taggart was impressed, "I think I know the church you mean. A magnificent example of classical architecture, Sir. I hope you have kept up with your church practices?'

"Yes, Reverend Taggart. When I get the chance, I attend church and propose attending on Sunday with the Turner family, if I may be so bold?"

Jonathan Turner was most pleased to hear this and did not hold back, "It would be our honour, Sir! Yes, it would indeed!"

"Reverend Taggart, have you read any of the Reverend Simeon's sermons[8] or papers? I find his writing inspiring." Neville recently came across some of Simeon's printed extracts and was grateful to include them in his conversation.

"Yes, they are edifying indeed. You will understand I am an orthodox minister with a liberal persuasion, but I have found some of his sermons most useful and used some of his thoughts in my preaching. As you will find on Sunday!"

"I will enjoy that, Reverend."

Having satisfied Reverend Taggart's curiosity, Neville sought permission for a slight adjournment, "Mrs Turner, I wonder if you would excuse me for ten minutes before tea and coffee. I might go upstairs and quickly check Simeon's bandages with your permission. I have brought all I need for the plaster cast tomorrow, but perhaps I might avoid its use. I will return quickly."

Eleanora grasping the opportunity for her eldest daughter was quick to reply, "Certainly Neville. Bethany will show you the way. He may be asleep by now!"

"That is fine. Checking the tightness of the bandage will be easier if Simeon is relaxed."

Bethany took a candle and led the way for Neville. The house seemed far more extensive this time than previously. He was unsure if it was the candle-light or the calm of fewer people present. The stairs seemed higher as they climbed towards the first floor.

---

[8] Rev Charles Simeon 1759 – 1836, published hundreds of sermons distributed throughout England. He is regarded as a great supporter of the evangelical tradition in the Church of England. His legacy continues to this day through the Charles Simeon Trust. Simeon Association and Mathew Hale Public Library.

"You must be good with children, Bethany? Your role as a governess seems a success?"

"Thank you – I try - but I'm not sure that I'm that good. It is a very demanding job, and I recently told Anne how tiring it is. But it also has its benefits, especially once the children are in bed at night. I find time for reading and sometimes write a bit."

"And what do you read?"

"A bit of literature and a bit of poetry."

Neville scratched his head as he searched his mind for a poetry quote, "Ah, I am sure you are fond of the romantics[9]. What is your favourite? I will suggest it is the one about 'Daffodils.'"

"Yes, I love that poem, but the one I like best is the sonnet about Westminster Bridge. You see, the furthest I have ever been from home is Woking. I know there is a big world out there, and I dream of seeing London one day. The towers, domes, and temples must be magnificent. I am very jealous of Anne visiting Greenwich!"

"I would not worry about that. London has some pretty spots, but mostly it is crowded, dirty and smelly. I am sure you would find it interesting, and you should see it, but the country, in my opinion, is far better. After I have attended Simeon and your mother tomorrow morning, perhaps you could spare an hour or two and show me the sights of Guildford?"

Bethany swallowed backwards and gave a slight cough as she led Neville towards the next flight of stairs. She was not ready for this, especially so quickly. Yet, she liked the idea.

"I thought being in the navy and coming from the city, you would prefer to remain there?"

Neville looked at her with a grin, "The world! I understand your wish, but I have already seen the Americas and the Caribbean, India, and Africa. From what I have seen so far, Guildford seems more attractive."

Beth stopped on the first step, turned, and looked at him. In the candle's light, she could see his face quite clearly. It was a look of quiet contentment. She liked this – something was interesting about this man she had only met a few hours ago. He, too, quietly admired her as if he was breathing oxygen for the first time, and then he looked down in embarrassment.

"Yes! I will show you the town. But on one condition."

He looked up, "What might that be, Bethany?"

"That you might at some time guide me around London!"

He laughed, "You are not backward, Miss Bethany!"

---

[9] William Wordsworth, 1770 – 1850, was an English romantic poet, who with Samuel Taylor Coleridge, helped launch the Romantic Age in English literature with their joint publication Lyrical Ballads (1789). Wikipedia.

"I am certainly serious, Doctor Neville. I have been a governess for nearly two years, and I feel like the world has passed me by."

Neville drew in a breath and looked deep into her eyes. They were pleading with him. This young woman was telling him something not expected, something he was unsure he desired. Yet she attracted him in a way he could not explain.

"You have an agreement! – I shall enjoy your company, but I must advise that it may not be as exciting as you expect."

"Let me be the judge of that!" she giggled, "What time do you think you would be ready in the morning?"

"I plan on sleeping in a bit, as it has been a long journey and a hard week, but I should appear by ten-thirty. I shall probably need an hour with Simeon and then your mother and father. So, let us say eleven-thirty. Let me offer you lunch during our tour. I like the country; it is pristine and cleaner than the city. Also, the food is better in the pubs."

Bethany did not hold back – she was excited by this invitation, "I would not refuse such a kind invitation. Now here is Simeon's room."

After the guests departed, the girls went off together upstairs, talking and laughing about what had transpired. Eleanora took Jonathan's arm and led him back into the drawing-room, where they both sat and relaxed together.

"So much is happening, my Darling. I find it hard keeping up!"

"What do you mean, Eleanora?"

"Did you not recognise the attraction between your eldest daughter and Neville? There is a spark there that I believe will build into a fire. Mothers see these things, Jonathan!"

Jonathan sat back and thumbed his chin. He was not aware of any attraction, but he was not against it.

"With the possibility of Thomas and Marion's attachment and possibly Bethany finding a partner, well! Who knows what will happen? Life will change considerably for us, will it not? We shall need a larger house!"

"Jonathan, they will live elsewhere! Not with us."

"But how will I communicate with Thomas? It is so easy if he lives here!"

Eleanora leaned forward and faced Jonathan. The man was quite intelligent, yet considering the implications of his son and daughters' marriages was not an issue he had ever considered.

"Jonathan, Thomas is twenty-three. He is more than ready for marriage, finding his own home and having a family. There are issues here that you have not thought through. It may be that Thomas prefers another business besides bakeries. Who knows? These are issues for discussion with him. It is certain that if he does move on, you will need another man who will replace him. Family members cannot do it all."

"Has he expressed these desires?"

"No, but have you discussed them with him?"

Jonathan knew Eleanora was right. Planning for these possibilities was becoming a priority. With Thomas away next week, he would have the opportunity of working with Jeb in the bakery for the first time in many months. He would ask Jeb if he would take on more responsibility. Unlike Eleanora, Jonathan did not expect Thomas to move on, but he should prepare in case Thomas did declare his hand. He knew that there was a need for more supervisory staff with the business expanding. Perhaps Jeb could nominate someone from among the factory hands.

"Jonathan, Jonathan, are you listening?"

"Yes – sorry, I was just thinking about the staff!"

"I thought you were, but remember Thomas needs his final suit fittings tomorrow, so please remind him at nine in the morning. Also, Anne must have new dresses for this visit, so she and I will attend Hursts tomorrow morning. Mrs Smith is up to date with the latest fashions and will find something pretty for her. Is transport arranged for their visit?'

"Yes, Dear. I arranged the coach for Wednesday next. On the first day, I will join them. We will remain the night at Richard's pub in Ewell and have fellowship with his family. Also, Richard and I must discuss plans for the new pub at Epsom. Hopefully, this new maid will have settled in by my return on Thursday."

"Thank you, Jonathan. It has been a wonderful evening, but I am tired. I will retire now." She walked over, bending and kissing him on the cheek. "Good night."

"Eleanora, William will join me at the bakery tomorrow morning. He will be interested in what the builders are doing at the new mill. Thomas should be back by eleven, so I will be home with him around that time and hopefully meet with Doctor Neville."

Turner household, Saturday morning ...

Breakfast was the meal that Jonathon Turner enjoyed the most. William and Simeon were always amazed at their father's appetite in the mornings. They tried but could not match him.

Not aware of the competition, Jonathan said, "William, you will be coming with me this morning. I will inspect the progress on the new mill, and you can assist me. Before we go, make sure you feed Snups. Now get a move on as Thomas will be expecting us."

At the mention of his name, the dog wagged his tail and nudged Jonathan's leg looking for a pat. Jonathan gave him a rub around the ears, and then William filled his feeding bowl and led him outside.

Once all the morning chores were complete, Jonathan, William, and Snups set off for the bakery. As they passed the church, Reverend Taggert strode over, coming down the side alley steps. He appeared more relaxed today.

"Morning, Jonathan, Morning William." He gave the dog a stern look. Snups sat down and looked the other way.

Jonathan stopped and turned, "Morning, Reverend."

"Jonathan, I have had word from Dorothy Stephens. She has agreed with our format for the funeral proceedings. So, all is in place for Tuesday morning around eleven. The Stephens family will be arriving from London tomorrow, and I will comfort them. It will be a busy day. I would be most thankful if you were there a little before the service."

William was intrigued – he knew of Doctor Stephens' death but not that his father was involved with the funeral service.

"What are you doing at the funeral, Father?"

Jonathan ignored William and replied, "I will ensure the family is there fifteen minutes before the service."

Andrew looked first at William and then Jonathan, "Thank you. It will be good for your children as they knew Doctor Stephens well. The Mayor and Blacksmith Elliot, with their families, will be attending. I am sure you understand what I am saying? How is Simeon? I assume he needs company and will remain at home. I must be off, Jonathan. Good day."

Jonathan nodded in agreement and then smiled, "Good day, Rector."

William tugged his father's arm, "What are you doing at the funeral, Father?"

Jonathan looked down at William and could see the curious little mind working overtime. "I am giving the eulogy!"

"What is a eulogy, Father?"

"It is a talk, usually celebrating the achievements of a person's life. The eulogy is like Reverend Andrew giving his sermon. Giving the eulogy is an honour, as usually it is given by a son or daughter or a family member. In this case, Mrs Stephens asked that I do it because I knew Doctor Jeremy for such a long time."

"When did you first meet Doctor Stephens, Father?"

"He was a young doctor when I was born in 1777. So that is when I met him, and he was there when you were born, William, in 1820. Some people say he was close to sixty years in age, but I think seventy was closer. His was a good long life."

Jonathan could see William's mind ticking over. The boy was quick. If only he possessed more self-control, but he was only six and a half. Perhaps his expectations of William were too great. Jonathan thought back to his child-hood – it was a long time ago – but he was probably the same.

They walked down the High Street towards the river and docks beside the new mill. The day's temperature was good with a clear blue sky, but Jonathan felt that it would be hot later. He was keen on the shelter of the bakery building.

"Why do people die, Father?"

Jonathan was not ready for that question. Considering death was not on his list for this morning.

"They get old, William and their bodies wear out."

"But.."

"Not now, William! I have business at the bakery and then the mill. Make sure you hold Snups' leash tight while we go through the bakery. Don't let him sniff or start eating anything."

They entered the bakery, past the rows of ovens and entered the office where Anne sat at her desk. Snups rushed across and put his head on her lap.

"Hello, Snups! Aren't you lucky, going for a walk?"

Jonathan ignoring the dog, said, "How are the figures looking? I thought you were shopping for new dresses."

Still rubbing Snups, she said, "I am, but I wanted these figures out of the way first."

Anne turned away from the admiring dog and looked at her expectant father. Understanding he was requesting the sales figures, she held up the ledger for inspection. "Father, the sales are up again. Sales for the week are a little over three thousand five hundred pounds. There must be more people in town! Our flour store is nearly empty, so we need an urgent resupply."

Thomas entered the office, taking off his baker's apron, "Must be off! Suit fitting time – I'll be back as soon as I can."

"Thomas, have you talked with Jeb about the flour situation?"

"Yes, Father, he was waiting for your approval. Because it will be short notice, we will pay a hefty price. That new mill of ours is needed. Also, Father, if you would, please have a look at oven number seven, where the new pastries are baking. They look quite special. The new girl, Sophia, has a rare talent. I think she would make a good pastry cook, given time."

"Yes, I will. Off you go, Thomas, you are late! William tie up the dog and find oven number seven. Ask this Sophia for three pastries, no four pastries, for a tasting. Quick boy."

Jonathan scratched his head. He knew the church fair was coming up, but surely that would not bring so many people into town. Guilford must be growing more than he thought. Maybe that's why Hamish McPherson was interested. Hamish must know something that Jonathan had missed.

"Anne, talk with the cart operators and check through the orders. See if there is something that is not normal. Sales do not increase without a good reason. If we order additional flour, we might not require it if sales decrease."

Anne looked up from her books, "Father, I suggest a small order till we understand the increase."

"You are right! It may be a one-off occurrence and not continue."

"I'm not sure, but you can't make bread without flour!"

Anne went off towards the market searching for the cart drivers – she would be a while. Jonathan sat down, patting Snups, whose tail started waving madly. But Jonathan was far away, wondering about the origin of the increased sales.

Jonathan snapped out of it as William returned with the pastries. Thomas was right – this Sophia must be a magician – the pastries were quite different, almost French. The design was elegant, with rich crusty pastry scattered with almond slices and sultanas. They each tasted one and found them delicious.

The banking clerks were busy on the other side of the hallway in the larger office room, counting and bagging money. Jonathan took the opportunity while William was close and out of earshot of the others.

William was busily devouring his pastry, "Tastes good too!"

"William, I had a talk with Reverend Taggart on Monday last, and he told me about the incident with Richard and Caleb."

William suddenly frowned and watched his father as he continued eating. The pastry was rapidly disappearing into his mouth.

"Now, normally, I would give you a beating for this, William, but I must say I was very proud of your standing up for Olivia and her family."

William stopped eating.

"Reverend Taggart tells me you and Simeon have a pact about this incident." William nodded.

"It is important that you keep this pact. We don't want anyone knowing our private business, do we?" Jonathan kept the conversation as simple as possible. He knew William could take this in if it were kept simple. The boy looked as if he understood.

William took another bite of the half-finished pastry, then spoke as he ate, "You mean, like hitting Mama?" William, being six, did not realise the implications of such a statement.

Jonathan Turner's hands gripped the desk until his knuckles turned white. He found it difficult to contain himself, "Yes, that's right. But remember that was a dream, wasn't it?"

"I think so .....it's a long time ago now. Father, could I have another pastry, please?"

"Yes, William, go ahead. Sophia will appreciate hearing how much you enjoyed them. Stay here with Snups while I go down into the factory."

Snups followed Jonathan but the tied leash stopped him. William quickly slipped him the remaining part of his first pastry. The dog settled immediately and chewed up the portion. As he gently lifted his second pastry, William smiled. He was learning that silence had its benefits.

Jonathan Turner strolled down the stairs into the baking area of the building and stopped at the bottom step. He stretched and relaxed, calming his body down. He pondered, was that a threat that his young son had just given him? Surely a child of his age could not think that deeply. Jonathan leaned against the rail and slowly relaxed. William would keep quiet for now. He was glad the lad would be in Greenwich next week. Hopefully, the navy ships would fill his mind.

At the Turner Household ...

Neville Bassington arrived at ten-thirty as promised and finished off the plaster on Simeon's lower arm. Both Eleanora and Beth were fascinated by this cast – it was amazing how it turned from a paste into a rigid material. The plaster turned white and solidified, making Simeon's arm immobile.

He explained, "The cast will dry quickly and appears very tight. But as it dries, it slightly contracts and will loosen. As the plaster contracts, it gives the arm breathing space. Immobilising the arm is the first purpose, but it also protects the arm from injury while healing. This cast will do the trick, and he should recover fully now in about six weeks."

Simeon kept looking at the cast and found that movement of the complete arm was now possible without hurting. "It is so much better than the bandage."

"That's right – I think you will see a lot more of this treatment in the coming years. Now Bethany, please, if you would fetch me some cloth, I will make a sling for Simeon, so he rests the arm while walking around. Before I see you next time Simeon, I want your strength built up. So, plenty of exercise."

Mrs Turner was impressed but a bit unsure how they would remove it. "Neville, how does it come off?"

"In about eight weeks, either I or someone else will come, and we will remove the cast. It is a little tricky, but no harm will be done if we take it slowly. Now, Eleanora, I will wash up, and then I will examine you."

Jonathan Turner arrived home at eleven thirty and heard talking coming from the kitchen. There he found Bethany and Neville waiting for him.

"Bethany, if you would excuse me for a short time, I will discuss my examination of Mrs Turner with your father. We might then set off." Beth smiled as Jonathan led Neville into his study.

"Doctor Bassington, what have you discovered?"

Neville paused as he quickly refocused on the details, "Mr Turner, thank you for the warm welcome yesterday evening. I enjoyed dinner greatly, and it is very generous of Bethany taking time for our tour of Guildford today. If this meets your approval, I have ordered lunch for Bethany and myself at the Fox and Hound."

"That is welcome, Neville!"

"Thank you, Sir! I have examined Mrs Turner, and I find the same symptoms. I still detected some slight jaundice, and she suffers from a lack of strength. The better food over the last week has made a difference, and she has slightly more energy, but that may not last.

I have no diagnosis for her complaint yet, but I have my suspicions. I have seen it in women before, they can go on for years, becoming weaker, or they surrender very quickly. Sometimes the disease is aggressive. Eleanora seems strong enough and will deliver the baby – that is, reach the full term of the pregnancy, but the actual birth may be devastating for her. It may be fatal, and it may not. These predictions are difficult. I must advise you that the disease will have its way in the long term."

Jonathan looked up in alarm.

"It is better that you know now and remember this is only my opinion. I would encourage a second opinion. I have not discussed this with Eleanora, but I have explained that she is weak and needs plenty of good food, some exercise and rest. The employment of an additional maid is welcome, as this will take much stress off her. I would suggest an undercook as well, assisting Mrs Jennings.

I will visit and assist when I am in port, Sir. With your family doctor's death, I suggest you commence seeking a replacement. She will need regular medical attention from now on. By the way, I have not told any of your children."

Jonathan was wrestling with what Neville told him, "When you say you expect the disease will have its way! Do you mean she will die?"

"I'm afraid so. I might be wrong, but I have seen the same symptoms before, and there is little we can do."

"How much time will I have with her?"

"It seems that she will reach the forecast date of the birth, but after that, things could happen far quicker. I would not expect her to last more than six months after giving birth. I am sorry, Jonathan, that I cannot do more - this must be very distressing for you. I think your wife shouldn't know the issues here until after the birth, Sir. We must keep her in the best spirits possible. I know you will wish for privacy now, and consider this yourself. Perhaps there will be further questions. May I suggest we talk again after church tomorrow if that is convenient?"

"Thank you, Neville, you have provided much information. If you would excuse me as I need time for contemplation now."

Neville found Bethany in the kitchen, "Shall we go?"

As they walked down the High Street, Beth noticed that Neville was deep in thought. He was far away. She stopped in front of him and said, "Now Neville, if I show you Guildford, I must have your full attention."

He shook himself, "Sorry, I was miles away. Now, where were we?"

"In Guilford!"

Bethany took Neville along High Street towards the river for the first part of their tour. They passed the family's church, not entering as he would be there tomorrow. Then down past the Guildhall with its bracket clock and through the Tunsgate corn market in front of the tavern, where several of Turner's bakery carts conducted a busy trade. She purchased a small pastry for him, so he tasted her father's product. They continued down the High Street past many shop windows towards the river.

Neville said, "Before we go past the Fox and Hound, how about we have lunch?"

Bethany thought this a good idea, so they visited the hotel's dining room.

"Tell me, Bethany! Last night, you seemed very definite that you don't enjoy being a governess?"

"Please, Neville, don't misunderstand what I said. An unmarried woman must do something, and being a governess is a good occupation. I love the children, but they are not my own, so there is only so much that I can do for them. But it is a full-time job, and there is nothing left of the day once the children are in bed.

I certainly read and write, but it is not the same as being here with my family. If it were possible, I would remain here. I am sure that would not make my father happy."

"Why is that?"

"He has these romantic visions that by being with the Uptons at Woking, I will be meeting all the eligible young men in town. I can assure you it is entirely the reverse. I am the babysitter who must keep the children out of sight when visitors come. I have hardly met a soul in nearly two years except for the local shopkeepers.

Before I was a governess, I was like Anne and thought I would see much of the world before settling down. But now, I am faced with the prospect of living in Woking for some time. But that is not my dream. I will take you into my confidence. As I have not advised my parents, will you promise not to inform them?"

"I promise!"

"I have been making enquiries about positions in London. Now I have some experience and references. I think I stand a good chance."

"Have you any offers yet?"

"No, not yet! But my agent tells me that it will not be long as parents start looking in July, ensuring they are ready for the next school year."

"So, you may be in London soon. I must prepare for your tour. It will occur sooner than I thought."

"You mean you will keep our agreement and show me around London?"

"Bethany, there was never any doubt. It will be my pleasure!"

Neville enjoyed the sunlight coming through the window and shining on her long brown hair. Her smile was delightful, and her personality so warm. She was genteel and would be presentable at any level of society. Bethany was an unnoticed jewel hidden in a rectory at Woking.

There was this growing feeling of attraction for her that he found pleasant. It was as if they fitted each other, yet they had only met yesterday. Her smiling face, radiant complexion and flowing hair were now becoming a part of him. He would be content in her presence forever. Then it struck him – this attraction he felt for her was love!

Could it be that there was such a thing as love at first sight?

For a moment, he wrestled with this idea. He was a man of science, and his diagnosis could not be correct. Was it possible that one could become so acquainted with a woman this quickly! Many years ago, he asked his father how he would know who he should marry. His father told him, "The explanation is difficult. But you will know when you meet her!" He was right. None of the hundreds of women introduced during his travels affected him like Beth. She was the girl for him. But what could be done?

"Neville, I think you have drifted off again!"

Neville was smiling at her conversation, not noticing his long silence.

"Ah, yes! It is a thing we doctor types do! We drift off into a dream, distracted from the present. Please excuse me. We should order."

Bethany began giggling.

"What is it, Beth?"

"I was thinking of last night. My first meeting with you was when you were dripping wet from your bath, and there was only a towel around you. It was so funny." Her giggle turned into laughter.

At first, he sat there and blushed. But then he saw that the laugh was not of derision but affection. He chuckled himself, recalling the scene. They both laughed until the tears ran down their cheeks.

The rest of the tour took in the River Wey and its canal and locks. They walked in the summer sunshine across the cricket green and past Dapdune wharf, then back past another remarkable church and up Castle Street, where there was a magnificent view of the ruins of Guilford castle and the valley. Then they strolled through the market and past Tunsgate and up High Street towards the Turner home.

All the time, they talked and shared their life experiences. They shared in growing confidence their childhood adventures, their parents, their dreams and aspirations, their downfalls and the little mundane things that sometimes were so funny. Bethany felt free in his company. Talking so freely with a man was never possible for her before, but with Neville, it seemed natural.

As they neared the house, he asked her, "If you married, would you wish to stay in Guildford?"

Bethany stopped walking. She thought this was a very personal question. He must be thinking of marriage. Is he thinking of me?

"I always thought that I would as the family is important, but it depends on the man. If I was truly in love, and the right man proposed, I would follow wherever he led me, perhaps the ends of the earth if he asked!"

Bethany was amazed at how easily her words flowed out. They taught her that being forward was not ladylike at her finishing school. She was surprised at herself, at being so open. It was as if she felt comfortable trusting Neville with any secret. Was it just his doctor's bedside manner, or was this the man she would find a life with forever?

They both looked down, and there was a short embarrassing silence. Neville contemplated that if she left for London, some other young gentleman would discover and marry her. He would be away at sea and miss his chance. The time was right for him to end his life in the navy. If he went to sea again, he would miss his chance with this wonderful girl. He would not let this happen. He must find a way of telling her of his love for her.

Neville seemed about to say something, but then he hesitated. She knew then that he was on the verge of saying something important. Could it be that he might propose? She blushed and looked down again.

She must encourage him. "But surely Neville, this is a funny question as it has not happened, so I may never know what I may answer?"

Bethany's response spurred him into action.

"Bethany, tomorrow I am looking forward to attending church with your family. I know there will be many people and much socialising afterwards, and we may not have much time together. So, might I ask that you see me after lunch, say at three o'clock? There is an important question that I must ask you!"

She looked him straight in the face with a knowing expression. She blushed, but then it subsided. She looked down and then up at this tall, handsome man. His kind face carried a worried expression.

He waited for her answer, praying that she would see him.

Her expression changed into a determined look.

"Neville, if it is so important, why can't you ask me now while we are alone and free from any disturbance?"

Neville was surprised by this demand but welcomed it. "I have only known you for a day, Bethany, but I feel as if I have searched for you all my life. I have never enjoyed someone's company so much. I just thought perhaps I should think again tonight, so it is two days that I have known you before I ask this question." Neville felt a little perplexed as she seemed very keen on hearing the question.

"Neville, another night will not make any difference in how I answer?"

This statement hit Neville like a broadside of forty-eight canons. It was as if she could read his mind. It was uncanny. Neville swallowed. He smiled, then looked serious again; he took a breath, then another and opened his mouth when she said, "Neville, I should be sitting down for this. You understand the routine!" There were some steps beside the entrance to the church. They walked over, and he assisted her onto the third step.

Thomas Turner wandered up the street towards home, saw them and went over. He said, 'Hello Neville and Beth, how was your walk by the river?" There was no answer.

Neville and Beth could not hear anything; they were so focused on each other as Neville went down on one knee and held her hands in his.

"Miss Bethany Turner, would you do me the honour of becoming my wife?"

Beth cried with tears in her eyes, "Yes, Neville, Yes! I have been waiting for you all my life also."

Some other people stopped and watched.

They stood, and they kissed.

Thomas mused, 'I guess the walk went pretty well then!'

Neville and Beth then saw Thomas and the bystanders watching. They welcomed Thomas into their embrace.

Thomas said, "Let my congratulations be the first. My instinct told me something might be up last night. I am so glad for you both. I will not say anything until you have time with my parents. God bless you both!"

They said together, "Thank you, Thomas."

He laughed, gave them both a hug and then walked off for home.

Neville walked Bethany to the front door of the Turner house. As before, the conversation just flowed continuously. The joy of romance just radiated from them.

"I will come and see your father tomorrow after church, Beth. I must let you go in now, as it has been a wonderful day."

"Neville, I can't keep this a secret all night. You must come in now and face the music. This afternoon you have made me the happiest girl in the world. Becoming engaged is the biggest moment of my life. We will see them together."

Neville swallowed, smiled, and nodded in agreement, and they went in.

Chapter 9

Jonathan and Eleanora Turner sat in amazement as Neville Bassington, accompanied by their daughter Bethany, announced, "Mr and Mrs Turner! This announcement will come as a surprise, but we hope it is pleasant. We know it is sudden but may be explained by our circumstances." Neville took in a deep breath before he continued. "Mr and Mrs Turner, I have, a few minutes ago, asked your daughter Bethany for her hand in marriage, and she has accepted. I am now asking for your approval of this marriage?"

There was a stunned silence. Then Eleanora Turner could remain silent no longer, "Beth, this is so wonderful!" and she hugged her daughter joyfully.

Jonathan Turner stood in silence, taking in what Neville had said and watching his wife and daughter laughing and hugging. He smiled and asked, "Sir, you honour my family, and I would have no objection, but as a precaution, I must first be sure that my daughter Bethany is in total agreement with this proposal. I wonder if you would excuse us for a short time while we discuss this?"

"Certainly, Sir. That would be most appropriate as I understand this must be unexpected, given we had only met last night. I will wait in the kitchen if that is suitable."

"Certainly not, Sir, you will be welcome here in the drawing-room, and we will withdraw. We will return soon. Thank you for allowing us this time with our daughter."

Bethany squeezed Neville's hand and beamed up at him with happiness. "Thank you for doing this, Neville; I could not have waited till tomorrow." She turned and followed her parents.

Neville smiled and sat down. He was feeling a little lightheaded as he suddenly thought how important this day was in his life. Yet, Neville was deeply in love with this girl and would do anything she asked to secure her as his future partner in life. He was tired of being alone, and now, having found her, he would never let her go. He closed his eyes and relaxed his muscles to calm himself.

A slight tugging at his sleeve required the opening of his left eye, revealing William standing beside him. The boy wore a big smile on his face.

"I'm glad you're back, Neville. You can tell me about the sea now. I have never seen the sea – just rivers. Next Wednesday we will be in Greenwich. Would you tell me about navy ships and the sea before we get there? But why are you back – I thought you were staying at the Fox and Hound?"

"I am, but Bethany and I returned with a question for your mother and father."

"What was the question?"

"I have asked Bethany for her hand in marriage, and now I need your parent's permission."

"Why do you want to marry Bethany, Neville?"

Neville felt his agitation growing again but focused on William's face realising the child's question was innocent.

"William, today I realised that I love your sister more than anything else in the world, and she loves me that way too. So, we thought it would be a good idea if we married each other. Also, it means that I will be your brother-in-law!"

William thought for a moment. "What does it mean, brother-in-law?"

"It means that through marriage, we are related, and I will be your brother-in-law."

William thought about that for a minute while he looked at Neville. Then he said, "That's good, isn't it because you will visit here more often? I like seeing you, Neville. I hope you come again soon!"

"I'll try William, and by the way, I like you too!"

The comment pleased William immensely. Mr and Mrs Turner and Bethany returned, interrupting William's interrogation of Neville.

Jonathan Turner at first seemed a little ill at ease but then smiled, "Neville, we are very thankful for the honour you bestow on our daughter, and we give our most heartfelt blessing for this marriage. I think you will make an excellent son in law. Please join us for dinner as I am sure there will be much discussion tonight."

Bethany and Neville hugged each other before Eleanora Turner embraced Neville with a hug, and Jonathan shook Neville's hand, saying, "I would never have predicted this, Neville. You gave us a delightful surprise. Now let us celebrate at dinner."

William, who was listening carefully, was working out if Neville was a 'son-in-law' or a 'brother-in-law'. With the question on William's lips, his father said, "Not now, please, William. If you would please keep this secret for an hour, I will announce it at dinner."

The Farewell …

Neville Bassington set off mid-morning on Monday for Woolwich after saying his goodbyes and discussing plans for a return visit when they might set the wedding date. At last night's dinner, he asked Jonathan Turner if Bethany might remain at home rather than take up her governess position again. Given that the new maid would need settling in and Anne, Thomas and William would leave Wednesday on their visit, Jonathan readily agreed. Bethany's presence would be an unexpected blessing.

Later that morning, Jonathan Turner sat down in his office and wrote to the Reverend Charles Upton advising him that Bethany would return on the following Monday, but only long enough for their recruitment of a new governess. He was pleased to announce that Bethany had accepted a proposal of marriage. He thanked the Reverend Upton for his kindness in employing her and sent a gift of pastry and biscuits as a goodwill offering. Jeb arranged the speedy delivery of the letter and basket by one of his cart drivers. Jonathan Turner also noted in the letter that a wedding invitation would follow once the couple confirmed the wedding arrangements.

Neville would also visit his parents during the return trip, advising them of the engagement and suggesting a meeting of the Turners and Bassingtons in London. Given Mrs Turner's state of health, probably an earlier date would be preferable.

The attendance at the Tuesday funeral for Jeremy Stephens was far more extensive than anticipated, with a host of visitors coming from far and wide. Jeremy Stephens was a well-loved community member, giving outstanding service over a lifetime of work. So, they came in their hundreds. Reverend Taggart was glad the parish school was in recess as the church became crowded to overflowing with attendees in the graveyard and along the High Street.

Strategically, Jonathan Turner made sure William stayed at home with Simeon following the suggestion from Andrew Taggart. He agreed there was a risk of William mingling with the other boys and tempers flaring.

Johnathan stood at the front of the church, eulogy notes in hand, ready for Andrew Taggart's introduction following the conclusion of a hymn. Spending several hours over the past two days, the story of Jeremy Stephens's life had come together. He was now looking out over the vast sea of faces packed into the church, but his solemn gaze concentrated on another subject. He struggled with his thoughts, recalling Doctor Bassington's advice. 'I do not expect she will last more than six months after the baby is born.' Jonathan Turner was a tough man. His business survived many years of adversity following the wars[10], and he was now seeing the fruits of his work. The community knew

---

[10] The post-Napoleonic depression was an economic depression in Europe and the United States after the end of the Napoleonic Wars in 1815. Wikipedia

him as a stern but kind man.

Standing at the lectern, he gazed down at the coffin draped in flowers. His thoughts were not with Jeremy Stephens but with Eleanora. The tears flowed. His guilt became so great it took control of him. He lost focus and wept.

As were many in the congregation, Andrew Taggart was amazed, not realising how much Jonathan admired Doctor Jeremy. But only Jonathan knew why he wept. Andrew moved forward, put his arm around Jonathan's shoulder, and asked him if he should take over reading the Eulogy.

"No, I can handle this. Thank you, Andrew."

Jonathan looked up and, wiping the tears from his eyes, saw the vast crowd in front of him come back into focus. Some were weeping too. Some were giving him smiles of encouragement, and some were praying. Then he saw Eleanora a few rows from the front of the church looking at the coffin. She looked up and smiled at him with a look of confidence that pierced his soul. She was beautiful and full of life, his wife, whom he had beaten. He knew from her smile that she had forgiven him, and they were one again. From her joyous face, he heard the message of encouragement, 'Speak up loud and clear, Jonathan.'

He gazed out across the assembled company focusing his thoughts, and with a smile and a robust and respectful voice, he commenced. "Friends, today, we have come together with heavy hearts to bid farewell to one of our brothers. Jeremy Stephens was a greatly loved gentleman, and so many of us have benefited from his service and dear friendship. But be of good cheer as we will all meet again on the return of our Lord Jesus!" And so, he continued giving, as some said, one of the finest eulogies ever delivered at his family's church.

The McPherson Household, Greenwich ...

Late on Thursday afternoon, the Turner coach pulled up outside the McPherson's house in Greenwich. Due to the family's rising late, they delayed their departure from Ewell until mid-morning. The dinner that Uncle Richard put on for his niece and nephews the previous night was extensive. The extended family members made a wonderful evening of it, catching up on all the news, especially the engagement of Bethany Turner and Neville Bassington.

Richard quickly offered the hotel in Ewell as a venue for the wedding reception, but Jonathan politely declined, indicating they were looking for a function venue in Guildford. With Eleanora's declining health Jonathan would avoid travel if possible. Richard gave a concerned glance at Jonathan, and the two brothers talked well into the night about various matters.

Jonathan was on a coach for Guildford at first light, as there was pressing business at the bakery. He left knowing the others would enjoy a leisurely morning at Ewell before travelling on. Richard found the opportunity with

William most enjoyable. He could not understand Jonathan's displeasure with the boy as he was polite and full of fun.

Following a beautiful family breakfast, the party boarded the coach and travelled into unfamiliar territory for the Turner children. William spent the day gazing out the window, continually talking about everything he saw, which his brother and sister would then explain.

As they entered the outskirts of London, both Thomas and Anne were unprepared for what greeted them. The sky darkened as smoke poured from the outlying factories, causing a smoky mist. With Anne placing a handkerchief across her nose and mouth, breathing became difficult.

The pollution was vast, blocking out the sun at times and leaving the factories in half-darkness. Row after row of shoddy tiny houses stood blackened by the smog, and rubbish littered every street. Children, dirty and sparsely dressed, were running wildly together in packs of twenty or more. The population seemed immense, as well-dressed people and those in rags mingled together, moving through the sidewalk stalls lining the streets. It was a place of misery and contrasted greatly with the comfortable life they enjoyed in Guildford.

Children ran behind the coach, yelling out for money. Thomas, a man with a kind heart, made the mistake of taking some coins from his purse and throwing them onto the road. Through his action, Thomas inadvertently caused mayhem in the street. The crowd following the coach quickly trebled in size, the coachman whipping the horses into a canter, leaving the disturbance behind.

Finally, they travelled along Queens Road approaching Greenwich and were pleasantly surprised by the views from Blackheath Hill down across the Thames and onwards towards the city. The air seemed cleaner here despite significant industry further south towards Woolwich. It was a relief as they pulled up outside the McPherson's house, opened the carriage door and descended into the arms of an eagerly awaiting Marion and Mrs Marjorie McPherson.

Anne received the first hug from Marion, who then folded her arms around Thomas, giving him a gentle hug and a very precious kiss on the cheek. She then welcomed William patting the boy on the head and said, "My, what a handsome party you all are. I have been excited all day, waiting for your arrival, and now you are here. We shall have such a marvellous week."

Mrs McPherson followed Marion, hugging all the visitors, including a reluctant William. Marjorie McPherson directed the footmen with the luggage as the butler directed the coachmen towards the stables at the rear of the house.

Thomas, Anne and William were quite impressed as they stared up at the three-storey Georgian house. It seemed immense, and they were now eager to explore the interior. Marion took Thomas by the hand and led him in. Anne lifted her eyebrows at William and followed. William spied two dogs and a handler beside the house and thought of patting them when Anne called him to follow. It was clear already that Marion had eyes only for Thomas. She hoped there would be time for developing her new friendship with Marion but wondered if she was only playing the chaperone.

As Marjorie McPherson followed, she dished out directions in a good-hearted manner. William noticed the servants' prompt and smiling responses. It appeared to be a happy household. William liked this and took note of each of the servants' names.

"Now Jenkins, we will be in the parlour and, please, a lemonade for Master William. He must be very thirsty after that long hot journey. I know how I needed one when I returned from Guildford. Now, shall the rest of us take tea? I'm sorry - would anyone else like lemonade as well?"

Anne liked the sound of lemonade and accepted the offer.

They entered the parlour, amazed at the large size of the room and took a seat. Marion inquired about their trip and the visit last night at Ewell.

Anne replied, "As you know, I have never been further than Woking, so it was a surprise as we entered London and saw the smoke and poverty of the people living there. But this area seems lovely and has views of the Thames."

Marjorie McPherson spoke up, "My Dear, you should see it in Scotland – it is far worse. The people work and live in terrible conditions. Hamish and I have always ensured that the people who work for us have a decent roof over their heads and plenty of fuel for keeping warm at night. We always make sure the children have a school, keeping them off the streets. Our workers are the envy of others. There is always competition for work at our breweries."

William burst forth with a comment, "Mrs McPherson, we saw some ships from the hill. They had big masts and looked huge. Do you think we could see them tomorrow?"

Marjorie beamed with excitement, "Yes, William, we will. Now I hear some news that there has been an engagement. Is this true?"

Anne was amazed. How could news of Bethany's engagement be in London so quickly, and how could Mrs McPherson relate this to the navy ships.

Thomas said, "That is true, Mrs McPherson. Our sister Bethany announced her engagement last Saturday. She will wed Doctor Neville Bassington, or should I say Lieutenant Neville Bassington."

William blurted out, "He is a surgeon on HMS *Providence*. He will also be my son in law when they are married!"

Marjorie McPherson laughed. "That is sweet, William! I think you mean brother-in-law?"

William nodded in agreement as he sipped his lemonade.

"It is so exciting. We are so pleased for your family. I must send a message of congratulations to your mother at once. Please excuse me as now I know it is true, I must write. What a wonderful thing. But before I go, a special surprise for William!"

Everyone turned and wondered what this could be.

"Marion, please accompany the party and show them the roof deck and the view. You can see the Woolwich wharves and all the ships, William! We even have a telescope up there. HMS *Providence* is also in port. Perhaps you will pick her out."

Once again, Anne wondered at Mrs McPherson's reliable information. She did not dare ask. Being of tender age and not reliable in his etiquette, William asked, "How did you know the name of Neville's ship Mrs McPherson?"

Marjorie looked at William and blushed. She realised her mistake as soon as she commented. Unfortunately, Marjorie mentioned the ship's name in her excitement with the visitors. Now she needed an acceptable explanation.

"Mr McPherson told me - he is such a darling – he is very well informed. Now up you go, children and have a look at the ships. Jenkins will be available when you require your room directions. Dinner will be at half-past seven, everyone. We shall meet here before dinner."

Marjorie smiled and left the room. She had used Hamish as an excuse and realised her mistake. When the next engagement was announced, she might be more candid. For now, it was time for a congratulatory letter to Eleanora Turner. She was keen on receiving a wedding invitation – she did hope so!

The party of young people climbed up the winding staircase with William racing ahead. By the time they managed two flights of stairs, William was standing at the top, gazing out the doorway onto the roof.

He shouted down, "Marion, may I go on the roof?" Without waiting for a response, he was out the door.

"Yes, William, just stay behind the rails. You may also use the telescope."

They found William perched on a chair gazing through the telescope as the party arrived. He was most excited and announced, "I think I can see the ship!"

Anne gazing at the beautiful view from the balcony, replied, "Yes, you can, William, there are lots of them. They are huge! There must be seven or eight ships."

"No, Anne!" William said, "I mean HMS *Providence*!"

"Where?"

"Just look in here." William moved aside from the telescope allowing Anne access.

She put her eye on the telescope, at first finding it was a maze of light and distorted images; then, as she moved it backward and forward, it came into focus. On the stern of the ship was a group of officers. She was unsure that it was the correct ship, but two officers looked familiar. They were laughing and enjoying the late afternoon sunshine.

One of the men was like Neville. It was hard to tell, but as she wrestled with the focus, he came perfectly into view. It was him. Then as she watched, another officer came behind him and patted him on the shoulder. She would know that smile anywhere – it was Robert. She blushed and stood back from the telescope.

Marion, watching, saw Anne blush. She was right that Anne was most interested in this ship. She looked away, talking with Thomas and pointing out various landmarks.

Anne was impressed with the balcony and the view. She was also excited that there was Robert in her first glimpse through the telescope. He looked so handsome in his uniform. As usual, he was having a good conversation with his close friend. Perhaps she might ask Mrs McPherson to extend a dinner invitation for tomorrow night?

Onboard HMS Providence, Woolwich Naval Yard ...

Neville and Robert stood with a group of Officers on the poop deck of HMS *Providence*, watching the sailors complete their duties before the next watch commenced.

With a wide grin on his face, Robert said, "You mean that after meeting her for the first time last Friday, you proposed on Saturday? That is less than a day, Neville. Do you think that was wise?"

"I think it was the wisest decision I have ever made. You have not met Bethany, Robert, but you will agree with me when you do. She is the most wonderful person I have ever met. Also, I offered her a tour of London – all the sights. I thought if we were married, it would make the task far simpler and far more pleasurable. No need for a chaperone."

He grinned back at Robert.

"Well done, old salt. There's life in the old Neville yet. I wish you both well." Robert was pleased for Neville, yet he was still surprised at how quickly this had occurred.

Robert reconfirmed the arrangements for the evening. "Now about this dinner tonight. I have the carriage arranged for seven fifteen; that should get us there on time. You are sure they expect me as well?"

"Yes – Anne will be there, and she will be surprised when you appear. She is not aware that we are coming. Marion was keen on a surprise. It will be a pleasant meeting, indeed, for them!"

Robert mused on this comment. He looked forward towards the bow and watched some seagulls lift and glide in the breeze.

Neville saw the thoughtful look on Robert's face. He was probably wrestling with the class problem and how he should approach this issue with Anne. Neville raised the subject.

"Anne is seventeen and a half, Robert. She is young but intelligent. You are twenty-one and very handsome in your uniform. She is likely to be easily led. May I ask precisely what your feelings for her are?"

Neville was a good friend of Roberts; otherwise, he would never dare raise this issue. He also knew that as Robert and his father were not close, he needed a mentor for advice. Being the second son, Robert would not inherit the title or the estate and must make his own way in the world. Yet, the expectation from his father was that he should marry into the aristocracy.

"Neville, I have never indicated any romantic attraction; she is a good friend, and that is all at this stage. The age difference is less than you and Bethany – so let us not put that as a problem. Yes, I am interested in her as a person, but you are correct; she is too young at present, and I must keep my career advancing. My Father advises me of a captain's position coming up on a topsail schooner called *Restless*. It would give me command status, which my father desires while his connections are still warm. He is ageing, and keeping up with acquaintances is becoming more difficult. As for Anne, any relationship must wait for a couple of years. That is probably for the best – as you know, friendships and trust take me a while. How long did it take me with you, Neville, eh? Two years or a bit more. It is early days, but I will tell you right now. I would not let anything hurt Anne for the world. You have my pledge on that."

"Your pledge is good enough for me, Robert. More than good enough, young friend."

They rested against the back rail of the poop deck, enjoying their discussion when Captain Foster climbing from the quarter-deck, addressed them. They quickly both stood at attention.

'Ah, South and Bassington – All well?"

"Yes, Captain!" Robert spoke with a clear voice. Neville saluted.

"Good, Good. I understand you two are attending a dinner tonight with some friends. Behave yourselves, as the Admiral has informed me that the three of us are invited tomorrow night at the McPherson's house for a formal dinner party."

The two young officers were surprised.

"It seems the McPhersons have invited Admiral Sutherland and his wife and that engineer chap designing these new canons, Alexander Steele. Steele is a grumpy type, but Sutherland is good company – the association will assist your careers. Now Bassington, I hear a rumour that you have become engaged. Is this true?"

"Yes, Sir!"

"Congratulations! Now tell me the details. I hope you will remain in the navy, Sir, as we need good surgeons."

"Thank you, Captain. We have not made any arrangements for the wedding yet, so it is early days. You will be the first informed of any decisions I make about my navy career."

"Good, Good. I hope your time is enjoyable tonight, Gentlemen."

The McPherson's Residence, Greenwich ...

William was fed early and then met his temporary Nanny, who Mrs McPherson employed for the week. Much to William's disgust, he was under observation from dinner until he was asleep. Soon the effects of a long and exciting day overcame him, and by seven o'clock, he was fast asleep.

Anne checked on him before she went down. She found Nanny Jones sitting quietly in the room, reading by candle across from William. Anne made sure he was asleep as she knew the antics he might try. The boy was not disturbed by a small pinch, which convinced Anne that he was in a deep sleep.

Anne spoke softly, "You need care with this one, as he can be a bit naughty if left unchecked. But he is asleep! Good, now I can enjoy the evening. I will talk with you in the morning Nanny Jones, and please call me if anything is needed." Anne's voice was friendly and reassuring as she smiled at the Nanny.

"Yes, Miss Anne! My room is beside this one, so I will hear if he gets up. I will check him before I retire."

Anne wished the Nanny a pleasant evening. She was unaccustomed to this level of formality, but she was strangely enjoying the experience. Anne closed the door of the bedroom and walked off down the hallway. Here she was in London, with a brand-new dress on, all done up and feeling beautiful and living the luxury she never dreamed of before. With a slight smile on her face, she headed downstairs.

Joining the others in the parlour, Anne saw that Thomas and Mr McPherson were deep in conversation. She walked over and joined Marion and Mrs McPherson.

Thomas was a very down to earth fellow. Intelligent, fit, good looking with a short crop of brown hair and not pretentious. He was interested in what Mr McPherson was telling him.

"Now, Thomas, I can assure you that both baking and brewing have a great future. The difference is that baking has a limited market, whereas the brewing market is unlimited." Hamish continued with a lengthy explanation of why the brewing industry would expand in the future.

As he concluded, he said, "You see, the market is unlimited!"

"So, what you are saying is that the market for brewed products is ten, no, one hundred times the size of the baking market. So, we may make far more profit in this industry?"

"Bang on, Thomas. Particularly the brewing. Most think the money is in the alehouse, but the real wealth is brewing. Let me give you a tour of the Woolwich brewery we have built. At this stage, it is small, but production will increase over time. It only makes around 20 quarters a day but has a daily capacity of 150 quarters. What will interest you is the process. You, being a baking man, will easily understand. I think you will enjoy this."

"I would indeed, Mr McPherson. But pray, what is a quarter?"

"Are sorry, Thomas – just a bit of brewing terminology. A quarter is approximately one hundred and fifty gallons of beer."

"I see – that is a lot of beer! I will join you for the tour."

"Good, we start early at eight in the morning, but it is not that far from here. I ensure my housing is always close, as travelling time is a waste. I enjoy being on the spot and keeping an eye on progress. The ladies and William will tour the Woolwich naval yard wharves later in the morning. Hopefully, I will have you back here in time to join them. There will be breakfast available in the dining room from about six if you are interested."

"I'll be there, Mr McPherson – I usually start work at about three-thirty each morning, so six is sleeping in for me."

Anne noticed through the window that a carriage was pulling up outside the house.

"Marion, are you expecting anyone as there is a carriage outside?"

Marion, seeming surprised, addressed her uncle, "Now, Uncle, who have you invited?"

Mr McPherson turned and smiled, "It is a surprise for Thomas and Anne. Ah, Anne, you have joined us, and you look radiant, my Dear. My, what a lovely dress you have chosen."

Marjorie McPherson whispered that this was a dress Anne brought with her from Guildford. Hamish was even more pleased knowing this.

Anne felt very flattered after such a lovely comment.

"Now excuse me as I welcome our other guests."

Anne thought, 'Surely it could not be – but they did know about the engagement!'. She heard Mr McPherson welcoming the guests into the entrance room and ushering them in.

Neville Bassington entered the room first, followed by Robert South and Mr McPherson conversing. Hamish beamed as he saw the expression on the Turner children's faces.

Thomas rushed over and shook Neville's hand. "Good evening, Neville. Your timing is impeccable – what a marvellous surprise."

"And you to Thomas - it is only three days since we dined together in Guilford. Ah, Anne, good evening. How you remind me of Bethany. What a pity she is not here with us." Neville kissed Anne on the cheek and admired her. "Now you do look so lovely and grown-up tonight?"

"Neville, I am so surprised. No one told us you would be here. Your presence is a wonderful surprise!"

"Anne, you will remember Robert. Our ship is docked near the Woolwich dockyard, and Mr McPherson was kind enough to extend an invitation." Neville carefully looked at Anne, expecting a reaction. But he was disappointed as Anne adjusted in a flash and was her polished self.

"Robert, so good of you to join us. We missed your accompanying Neville over the weekend, and mother was so pleased that you sent your greetings."

Robert stood there, admiring Anne, not even noticing Thomas or Marion. He was mesmerised by this girl who changed from a sweet, intelligent country girl into a very presentable young city lady. She was beautiful with her long golden hair draped over her shoulders, with a low-cut bodice on a shining silk dress. He sheepishly approached Anne, took her hand and kissed it. In his officer's uniform, he appeared a little larger than life.

"My Anne! Are you the same young lady I met in Guildford? You look all grown up and beautiful."

"Thank you, Robert, you look very handsome in your uniform. Now I'm not sure, but have you met Miss Marion Steele and my brother Thomas?"

As he took Marion's hand, he said, "So glad to meet you, Miss Steele. It is a great pleasure attending dinner here tonight and making your acquaintance. It is most opportune that we are all here in Greenwich." He shook Thomas' hand. "Glad you are here, Thomas. We had so little time talking in Guildford. Perhaps we might spend some time together this evening?"

"Yes, Robert, that would be a pleasure." Thomas was interested in formally meeting Robert. He was curious, given his sister's comments about him. Thomas thought, 'At least she has known him longer than one day!'

Marion also moved forward and was introduced. "It is so good to meet you. I have heard much about you, Robert. Perhaps you would tell us more over dinner."

"Certainly, but first, I must thank your aunt for inviting us both. Ah, Mrs McPherson, thank you for your kind invitation tonight. I was not aware you knew our ship was in port. Pray, how did you manage such intelligence? It is better than the British Navy, Ma'am."

Mrs McPherson held her husband's hand and cheerfully said, "One of Mr McPherson's friends in Guildford sent us a letter, noting the engagement between Anne's sister Bethany and Neville. It also mentioned that your ship would be here in Woolwich for at least a month. So, I thought the least we could do was bring together all the young people. Marion is keen on having young people around her."

The butler announced dinner, politely informing the guests that each seat had a place name.

Thomas was seated between Mrs McPherson and Marion, and Anne, on the other side of the table, between Robert and Neville. Mr McPherson sat at the head of the table and gave an exceptional grace.

Robert addressed Thomas and Anne, "I am pleasantly surprised that you are both here. I was wondering when we might meet again. I understand William attends also?"

"Yes, he is upstairs and hopefully well asleep by now." Thomas chuckled and gave Robert a wink. "He can be a handful, that one."

"I checked on him before I came down. He is asleep – the excitement of the trip wore him out. Nanny Jones is with him, and she will let us know if anything is needed. I must thank you, Mrs McPherson, for providing the Nanny. It is a kind gesture."

"Thank you, Anne, I have four sons, and I know how demanding they are. I need a good rest at night at my age, so I thought a Nanny would be just the thing."

They all laughed, and Mr McPherson said, "Marvellous Marjorie, marvellous."

"Now, Robert, I hear you saved William and Simeon's lives up there in the forest some time back." Marion was interested in the story.

"I think that might be an overstatement, Marion, but we did intervene at an appropriate moment. It may have been Horace, a good friend of mine, who saved the day. You see, there were about ten of us keen on some fellowship. All good friends and we decided on a hunting party. The royal hunting forest is not often used due to the king's health. We gained permission, and off we went."

All enjoyed the descriptions given by the two young gentlemen of the events in the forest.

"My, that is an exciting story, gentlemen. I think we are all grateful that you intervened." Hamish McPherson was quite genuine in his compliments. "But tell me, Sir? Why not use guns? Why the bows and arrows?"

"We allowed the animals more of a chance, Sir. Also, bows do not scare away other animals as musket shots do. It gives more opportunity for hunting."

"I see – very sporting of you. Dear me, I almost forgot! Thomas and Anne, we are having a formal dinner here tomorrow night. Robert and Neville will come, your father Marion, Admiral Sutherland, and his wife, Amanda. I have also invited Captain Foster from HMS *Providence* and another friend from the admiralty. Jenkins! Is all ready for tomorrow night?"

"Yes, Sir. All is in order. However, if acceptable, I would request some time with Mrs McPherson on the menu. After dinner, Sir, it will not take long at all."

"Excellent, Jenkins!"

Great excitement broke out with much thanks directed towards Hamish McPherson for his hospitality. The dinner proceeded well, and as the conversation flowed, Robert took the opportunity of speaking with Anne. He spoke softly.

"You look delightful, Anne. I am impressed!"

"Thank you, Robert. Your comment is kind."

"So, you are in London. I hear William spotted the ships from the roof. If you come tomorrow with him, I will invite your party on board my ship. I might even take William up the mast, depending on the breeze. He should enjoy that."

Robert then added humorously, "But I will need Neville with you all the time. Otherwise, you will run off with one of the Officers."

"I shall do no such thing, Robert!" Anne failed to find the humour in Robert's comment.

"I meant that you are beautiful, and the officers will all be attracted. I meant no offence."

"I see. That is kind of you. Do you think I look beautiful or are you just humouring me?"

"I mean, what I say!" He turned and looked straight at her and smiled as he enjoyed her beautiful blue eyes. She blushed and looked down at her food.

Marion noticed the quiet conversation and said, "Now, what are you two plotting over there? You are discussing something very quietly."

Thomas, who was now feeling the effects of the champagne, spoke up, "Probably organising a picnic somewhere so William can play pirates."

Quick as a wink, Robert added, "Quite right. How about Sunday lunch after church? We could take the carriages and find somewhere nice and have a lot of fun."

"Splendid!" Neville said, "Sunday would be a good day, as I travel to Woking the following Sunday. I will see Bethany. The Reverend Upton has issued me an invitation for the weekend. He must be a splendid fellow offering this, given I am taking away his governess."

Anne spoke up, "He is a very charitable and lovely man!"

As the guests agreed on the plans for the picnic – Marion quietly said to Thomas, "I must speak with you, Thomas. I will visit your room later when all is quiet."

Thomas obediently nodded.

As the hour approached eleven, Neville and Robert again thanked Mr and

Mrs McPherson and said their goodbyes. They both tumbled into the coach, which carried them quickly towards Woolwich. Robert was very quiet, and Neville said, "A penny for your thoughts, Robert?"

"I am greatly attracted by her, Neville. You saw tonight how well we get on. She is so young. How can I justify my feelings?"

"I have known many a man who has married his childhood sweetheart!"

"Yes, but how would I ever persuade my mother and father that she is acceptable? You understand their views on class. The only middle-class people they have ever spoken with would be their servants. They would be most upset by the whole thing."

"Robert, you are young, and you will soon be a ship's captain. You are the second son, so your parents will not pass you a title, and you have already told me that your brother will inherit the estate. Surely you are free from their judgement. You have time on your side. She will be twenty in two years, and you will be a commander by then. You need not make any commitments before then but keep in contact."

"You are correct, Neville. Much can change in a few years. A visit to Fintelton would allow an introduction, but not yet. Neville, once you are married, perhaps you and Bethany would act as chaperones for Anne. That would work. I am afraid the reception may not be that warm from the family."

"Preparation ahead of time will be essential. Anne will require our protection. I would wait at least a year before you make the invitation. Given a year, she will handle it better. Your parents will need time also. The Earl and Countess will accept her once they understand your situation. Indeed, it would be hard to find anyone who did not admire your friend!"

Robert looked around at Neville, "Thank you, Neville. In many ways, you are the big brother I always wanted. Your advice is very welcome. By the way, I hope I receive an invitation to your wedding. It will be an opportunity for me with Anne again."

Neville looked sternly at Robert and quickly said, "You better be at the wedding. I want you as my best man."

"It would be an honour, Sir."

McPherson Residence, Later that night ...

Thomas was tired with his eyelids drooping when a soft knocking disturbed him. He jumped up and opened the door. Marion swished past him into the room, and after having a quick look outside, he gently closed the door. Thomas suddenly noticed that she was wearing a dressing gown and slippers in the candlelight.

"Is this wise Marion, you here at this time and in my bedroom?"

"It's probably not proper, but how else shall we ever find time together alone? During the day, Mrs McPherson continually watches me – she is very protective, bless her heart, and I love her so much."

"They are very generous and nice people."

"Now, Thomas, the time has come to plan our future. Tomorrow morning Mr McPherson will show you the brewery. He intends to persuade you to become a brewer!"

"I quite like that idea, but it will depend on what is required." Thomas was interested in a career change and felt that brewing would be better than baking, particularly the money and working hours.

"Thomas, it will all depend on another question."

"What is that, Marion?"

Marion was a bit put back by this answer, and she realised that Thomas would need a bit of help here grasping the facts.

"Thomas, for me, Mr and Mrs McPherson have become a father and mother. I have explained that before. They are very dear people who want what is best for me. They like you and feel you have the potential for a good husband. Do you understand, Thomas?"

Once explained, Thomas was quick on the uptake. "Yes. What you are saying is that it is a package deal."

"That's right. For which you will receive substantial compensation. But more than that, Thomas, I love you so much, and I know you love me."

"Yes, so much, Marion." Thomas moved towards her and placed his hands on her hips.

Marion did not waste the opportunity, putting her hands around his neck and kissing him with as much passion as she could generate. The one thing the Turner men had in abundance was sex drive, and Thomas needed no further encouragement. However, once he had sampled the goods, Marion withdrew and pried him off, despite being happy with his response.

"Thomas, there will be plenty more of that when we are married. But it is essential that you ask for Mr McPherson's permission by the end of the week and my father's. But first, you must ask me. Now down on your knee Thomas."

Having had a taste of what was to come, Thomas would have agreed to anything. He was down on one knee quickly, took her hand and said, "Marion, will you do me the honour of becoming my wife?"

Marion smiled down at him and said, "Yes, Thomas, with all my heart."

He rose, and they kissed again. Thomas was enjoying this kissing immensely.

Marion moved back a step, gently untangling herself from him. "I must be off to bed, Thomas. On your early trip tomorrow, you may tell Mr McPherson that we are engaged and you would like his permission. Also, ask his advice on how you should approach my father. Mr McPherson is clever at organising things like that. Thomas, we will be so happy. See you in the morning, Darling."

Marion quietly returned along the hallway where Mrs McPherson was waiting in her room. The suspense was making Marjorie McPherson tense.

"I am engaged!"

"Wonderful, Dear. I am so happy for you. Now not a word with anyone until the time is right. By Monday, perhaps! Good night, Darling, and I am so pleased for you."

Mrs McPherson quietly slipped out the door. Marion settled back in bed and thought, 'I love Thomas so much, but he can be slow at times. He will need some managing. It will take time. Once he is in management, it will not matter that much. It is all sorted – as long as he convinces Mr McPherson tomorrow.'

In the morning ...

Thomas' timeclock would not allow him more than four hours of sleep, and he was awake at three in the morning. He had become a baker at fourteen years of age, and his natural alarm clock would now stir him at that time every day. At six o'clock, he was craving breakfast and made his way down-stairs. Sitting in the breakfast room, he chatted with some of the footmen as they set up. The smell of freshly cooked bacon and eggs stirred his gastric juices, and there was no hesitation when Jenkins said, "All is ready, Sir."

Hamish McPherson found Thomas finishing as he entered the breakfast room. He was pleased as he liked a man who made an early start.

"I will be with you in half an hour, Thomas, and then we will set off."

"Thank you, Mr McPherson. I will be ready."

Hamish was delighted with the delicious breakfast, particularly enjoying the fruit compote before he tucked into some scrambled eggs and bacon. He considered the best approach for his discussions with Thomas as he ate. Advised that the proposal was made and accepted, all were ready for this final discussion before meeting with Alexander Steele. The meeting would be tricky, as Alexander was shrewd and, at times, not very pleasant. The safety and security of his daughter would be uppermost on his mind. Hamish knew that Thomas was a good man and would make Marion a fine husband, but it was wealth where Thomas would not meet the bill. The conversations this morning were critical for setting Thomas up for the future.

Hamish's sons were already well placed for life as brewers in Scotland. Thomas would be Hamish's first protégé in England, so this must go well. From what he knew of Thomas, the lad was not slow and caught on quickly once briefed. Perhaps this was the approach that was needed. If Thomas could not grasp the offer, there was a backup plan, but Hamish was not keen on this option.

As Thomas was leaving his room upstairs, Marion suddenly appeared in front of him. She was fully dressed and a picture of beauty. She wore a stunning red dress with a light shawl around her shoulders. She had arranged her hair beautifully, hanging down long over her back. As he gazed into her clear yet misty eyes and breathed in the intoxicating perfume, he found his desire aroused.

She approached and gently kissed him, "Thomas, while you are with Mr McPherson, listen carefully. At the end of your tour, please tell him about your proposal last night, that it was accepted and ask about the best way forward with my father."

Thomas was generally a happy soul, but today he found himself excited about the new developments in his life. He was feeling unusually confident.

"I want to tell the world, but as you say, we must go through the correct steps first. I must advise my family – I shall write soon. Tonight, we shall celebrate at dinner. What a surprise we will spring on them!"

Thomas was very much in love with Marion and in high spirits for the tour this morning.

"We will talk when you return, my Darling, then we may plan the meeting with my father! Now off you go and enjoy your tour."

The coach was ready, and Mr McPherson was already seated with the carriage door open. Thomas hopped in and sat down opposite him. With a tap on the ceiling, the carriage set off towards Woolwich.

"What I will show you this morning is one of my small breweries. I think you will be impressed, Thomas. But more than this, I am keen that you understand the processes involved. You are a process man, as you know, baking backwards. I want your impressions of the brewery and your suggestions for any improvements you would make?"

Thomas was interested, "How far away is the brewery Mr McPherson? While I am interested in seeing it, I am not sure I am qualified to suggest improvements. As this is the first time I have seen a brewery, my thoughts will be very uneducated, but I will do my best for you."

"Good boy, Thomas. I think you will see enough for a very fruitful discussion between the two of us. It's not far – about five minutes now. How are you enjoying London?"

At the McPherson house, Nanny Jones struggled as William bounded away from her down the stairs. William raced into the breakfast room, stopping abruptly in front of the butler.

"Morning, Master William. If you would take your place at the table, I will serve your breakfast!"

William could smell the delicious aroma from the serving vessels and licked his lips. He walked slowly past them taking note of the contents of each tray, and then sat at the chair Jenkins indicated. Nanny Jones, puffing, sat beside him.

William, eyeing off a large serving of bacon and eggs, became quiet as Nanny Jones ordered, "Please, Jenkins, William may start with some prunes and pear, thank you!"

"Yes, Ma'am." As the butler looked at William, he lifted his eyebrows. William smiled back and knew there was a kindred spirit in Jenkins.

A plate of prunes and pears appeared, and William ate a small mouthful. As Nanny Jones stood up and inspected the breakfast serving area, the butler whisked William's plate away and asked what he would like now. A large plate of scrambled eggs and bacon was soon placed before him, and he did not hold back. Nanny Jones, thinking William had finished his pears, was not worried. William was impressed. This Jenkins was a smart fellow indeed!

"When you have finished, William, you will be walking the dogs with Jenkins. There are two hounds, one called 'Red Socks' and the other, 'Boiler'. They have been fed and are ready for their walk. They usually go out on the common where they can run free for a while." Nanny Jones pointed at the two dogs through the window.

William looked up from his plate, which was his only interest, and glanced through the window. There outside stood a groomsman with two of the most beautiful dogs he had ever seen. They were a light brown to orange colour, beautifully groomed and standing still with their tails straight up in the air. Their eyes gleamed as they watched him through the window.

William forgot his food and told Jenkins, "I have a dog, and his name is Snups".

Jenkins replied, "Now, how did he get that name, Master William?"

"He was always doing naughty things when he was little, so we always said, 'Nup'. After a while, he realised that 'Nup' meant to stop. We said it so often that we called him 'Snups'. He is well behaved now."

"If you finish your meal William, Jenkins will take you outside and introduce you. Remember, their names are Red Socks and Boiler."

William nodded and then started shovelling food into his mouth. Leaning towards him, Nanny Jones advised, "Slow down, William, before you choke yourself. The dogs will wait. Eat slowly, please." She laughed.

Once William finished, Jenkins led him outside onto the patio, and they approached the dogs. Red Socks and Boiler sat there motionless, but William noticed their eyes following him as he neared them. William became apprehensive as he moved toward them.

Jenkins said, "Red Socks and Boiler, this is William. He and I will walk you today. Go!"

On the word 'Go', the two dogs immediately started wagging their tails and jumped up on William, licking him on the face, neck, and hands. It was love at first sight between William and the dogs. He patted them on their head and bellies and rubbed their ears.

Jenkins said, "They know you love dogs, William. You have now found two more friends for life. They never forget!"

William enjoyed being part of this household. They were friendly people, and the dogs were beautiful. He walked around the little courtyard outside the kitchen. The dogs walked beside him, jumping up and still licking him from time to time. Then Jenkins said, "Sit".

The dogs immediately sat facing Jenkins and became motionless again. The control was impressive.

"How do you teach them that?"

"A lot of training, William. As you will see in a minute." He attached each dog's leash and placed them in William's hand. "Let's go!"

Exiting via the courtyard gate, they strolled along the drive towards the rear of the house near the stables and then towards the back of the property. Here there was another gate that opened onto the common. The area they emerged into was vast, some of which were wooded and some cleared.

"We will head toward the trees. The army uses the open area for shooting, so we remain clear of their range. The woods are quite safe, and the dogs will chase rabbits. They are Hungarian hunting hounds, and that's what they live for – hunting!"

Jenkins and William set off at a brisk walk with the dogs obediently scampering at their side.

William looked up at Jenkins, "This is great fun. I like these dogs. Can we do this each day, Jenkins?"

"I think so, Master William. The others will not be up for some time yet. So, tell me, how did you meet Sir Robert South? He is such a nice man. And Lieutenant Neville Bassington? I believe he is a doctor."

William was pleased to oblige his new friend Jenkins with everything he could think of, as a six or seven-year-old will do.

Mrs Marjorie McPherson from the staircase window watched the two of them and the dogs scampering off towards the wooded area. She smiled as she saw William release the dogs from their leashes and then run after them quickly. He stumbled and fell over in the lumpy green grass. The dogs promptly doubled back and started licking him again. Jenkins would report back later in the morning. She continued writing her letter.

At the McPherson's Woolwich Brewery ...

Thomas and Hamish McPherson were now on their tour. Thomas was familiar with the bakery setup but was surprised by the sheer scale of a brewery. He listened closely as Mr McPherson ran him through the brewing process and then pointed out the first building.

"Thomas, this is the barley store." Thomas gazed up at the vast store and considered how much larger this operation was than their bakery.

"It is a huge store, Mr McPherson. Are you not worried about the loss if it caught fire?"

"Good point, Thomas. That is a risk I have sometimes considered. I will note it down."

From here, they walked, climbed and explored the factory. Through the malting house, over the malting floors, covering their ears as they went through the mashing house and watched as the Jacobs ladder carried the steaming wort up into the cooling tower. Thomas asked intelligent questions at each process point and commented on improving the process.

Thomas comments pleasantly surprised Hamish. On his first morning, the boy suggested some changes that none of Hamish's engineers had put forward. Their thoughts were within the design of the present system. Thomas was thinking of reengineering the system outside of the current factory design - a thought pattern he probably gained from his father's mentoring. Hamish continued writing up the list as they both talked.

Once again, Thomas was impressed when he entered the fermentation room, which was spotless with a clean tiled floor and large copper vats from wall to wall for the room's length.

"The yeast is added here once the wort is cooled. The beer finally appears here!"

Hamish lifted the lid of one of the fermentation vats, and Thomas could see a thick yeasty foam covering the surface. Facing Hamish, he inquired, "I suppose you skim that foam off and turn it into some kind of yeast product?"

"That's correct – how did you know that?"

"I thought yeast came from somewhere. We use it in our baking as well."

Hamish nodded and pointed towards the stairs, "Let's finish in the Conditioning-room and then go to my office where we can talk further." They walked down and found the room was immaculately clean and had a delightful smell of the brewed product. Thomas could see that the brew was then fed into casks and deposited in the racking plant. Thomas counted at least forty men busily carpentering casks in the cooperage as they walked past this store.

"Thomas, what is your impression?"

"My first impression is that it is ten times larger than the new complex my father is building and employs far more staff. I was impressed. But as I said earlier, I think now, with the invention of the steam engine, the process needs reengineering."

"Would you like a go at reengineering it?"

"I'm not sure I understand. I am a baker, not an engineer."

"You don't need to be an engineer or a mechanic – I can employ plenty of them. You have sound ideas that concur with what I have been thinking. My engineers have not come up with the ideas you have suggested. Thomas, there is a place for you in my brewing company. You are manager material."

Thomas shuffled in his chair and thought about this for a while, taking sips of tea.

"I would like the change, but I would not leave my father short of trained men just when we are developing a new plant."

Hamish smiled again. He liked this young man – he was loyal, which spoke well of him, but he was also looking for advancement.

"Let me tell you about my plans, Thomas. I have secured enough land in Guildford near the river on the southern side, away from the town, where I can build a brewery. I will need a manager for this new plant. My sons are all managing the four breweries in Scotland that I have. Two in Glasgow and two in Edinburgh. At this stage of my company's development, I only like employing men I know. I know you are a reliable, good man. But better than that, I think you will have a natural flair for the brewery business that others are trying to develop.

You see this chair! It is for the manager of the brewery. The brewery in Guildford will have the same office and chair. Thomas, I would like you in that chair. We can work together and design a brewery with the things you talked about today. It could become the most efficient brewery in this country, an exciting challenge.

I know you would not leave your father short, so I propose that you work for him for the next three months while the land for the new brewery settles. The lawyers are working hard, making sure the contracts are proper. Your father and I have some other business together, so I am not opposed to my engineers assisting him in his new mill. The knowledge they will gain from the steam engine will also help the new brewery. So, we all win together. We will make sure he does not go short of men. We will be a team."

Thomas liked the sound of this, "Mr McPherson. Firstly, thank you for the trust you are putting in me. Secondly, I will accept your most generous offer.

There is a slight issue that we must discuss before proceeding any further. It is best, you know, and that you give me some advice!"

Hamish remained calm as if he knew nothing of this news, "Thomas, what can it be?"

"Mr McPherson, last night, I proposed marriage to your niece, Marion, and she accepted!"

"Thomas, I am delighted. Let me offer my congratulations. This news is splendid! Mrs McPherson and I were hoping something like this would happen, and I can think of no better partner for Marion than you."

"Thank you, Sir. There is one matter on which I would appreciate your advice. Marion has told me about her father, and it appears I may not fit the requirements he has for his daughter. I am afraid he has very grand ambitions for her."

"It should not be a problem, Thomas. Let me think about that today. I will meet with you late this afternoon, and we shall discuss strategy. Probably, I think I will meet privately with him before dinner and set the scene. Then after dinner, perhaps you and I shall meet with him seeking his approval. I think he will agree."

"Thank you, Sir. You have been most kind. I am very encouraged by your assistance."

Thomas finished his tea and said his goodbyes. Hamish waved as the coach sped off with an excited Thomas onboard, eager to share his excellent news with Marion. It seemed this was a momentous day in their lives.

At the McPherson House, Greenwich …

William returned from a long dog walk and found the others starting breakfast. He thought of having seconds as Nanny Jones spied him and his dirty clothes.

"William! Upstairs please and change before meeting with the others. Your clothes are not fit for the breakfast room now, so let us go upstairs, and we will dress you for the trip."

William was not pleased with this command but saw Anne watching from the breakfast table. Anne nodded in agreement with Nanny Jones's directions. Before leaving Guildford, Anne carefully briefed William on his manners, but the spell was wearing off. He reluctantly turned with his head down and walked towards the stairwell.

Nanny Jones recognised the boy's hunger and said, "William, if we are quick, you may return here for some more breakfast!"

With that, the boy was off running up the stairs. Nanny Jones sighed and duly followed him at a more sedate pace.

Marion stood by the window, eager for Thomas' return and the outcome of his discussions with her uncle. Marion was becoming impatient, given she expected him back nearly half an hour ago. Then the coach came into sight.

"Ah, here is Thomas, back from his tour." She hurried towards the front door.

Anne and Mrs McPherson continued their breakfast together. Marjorie looked up at Anne, "I should have asked you yesterday, Anne. How is your mother's health? She appeared quite well by the time we left Guildford."

"Yes, she was recovering well. Those little bits of exercise and sunshine seem to be doing the trick. She is even regaining some of her colours now, which is always a good sign."

"Yes, I walk each day for my health – just being out there in nature is refreshing. Not that the London landscape can ever compare with Scotland, but this area is quite uplifting."

Anne could not resist asking, "I know you have come to London for business reasons, and your sons remain in Scotland. Would you be thinking of returning there one day once the businesses are all set up?"

"That is a good question. I have asked myself this also! I think this is a question you must ask Mr McPherson as I am not sure what his intentions are. But of course, I would prefer being near my sons and their families if possible."

Anne nodded politely, considering her comment. She must have grand-children by now. Her sons must be older than Thomas and my age. "Mrs McPherson, please forgive me asking, but how old are your sons in Scotland?"

"Anne, the youngest, James, is Thomas's age, and he will be joining us towards the end of the week. Hamish keeps in close contact with each of the boys. They are always discussing how their breweries fare. Mind you, what they discuss, I don't know."

Having experience working for her father, Anne suggested, "I suppose it would be production and sales figures and the maintenance schedules. I work for my father in the mornings; I find a never-ending amount of paperwork. Fortunately, I am handy at maths and can write well, so he now depends on me. There will be lots of catch-up work when we return."

Marjorie sat up straight and looked at her, "Why Anne, I did not know that! That is very impressive as most young girls would not have any idea of what goes on in a business. You must tell Marion about that."

Anne stood up and looked out the window seeing the coach pull in. While continuing her conversation with Mrs McPherson, she watched with interest, "Better than that, and I'm not sure if Marion told you of this, but she came with me one morning to the bakery. Marion arrived early at our house, and we found her a smock rather than wearing her good clothes. She spent a few hours working with me. We both thoroughly enjoyed the time together."

Marjorie sat there with her mouth open, "I never! Isn't that grand!"

Anne noticed Thomas getting out of the carriage and Marion flying into his arms. She thought these two were becoming quite close.

"Did you tell him, Thomas?" Marion was excited.

"Yes, and all is arranged for a meeting with your father tonight."

She kissed him on the lips, and they both walked hand in hand up the front steps.

Anne suddenly understood that there was quite an understanding between these two. She must talk with Thomas privately when a chance arose.

Marjorie McPherson looked up from her breakfast, "Anne, I noticed that you are good friends with Robert South. He is a fine young gentleman and comes from a very distinguished family. I am sure he has swept many a young lady off her feet. My Dear, do not be in too much of a hurry. You are a most beautiful and attractive young lady, but it is too early for you to make any romantic decisions. I mean this most sensitively, and I hope you will not mind my raising this. Especially as you are away from your mother."

Anne gently sat again. She sipped her tea and smiled, "You are too kind, Mrs McPherson. I am missing my mother, and you are so much like her. Thank you for your care."

Anne smiled as she thought, 'Ah, the next movement. Let me see where this will play! Where will this lady try to lead me?'

Marjorie was encouraged by Anne's response. "Yes, I understand. But do not fear, child, you may confide in me. Now let me tell you that many men in London are of great appearance, but you must handle them carefully. Take your time and see what is on offer. Why, who knows, my son James will be here Thursday. He is twenty-three and still unmarried. Let me have the pleasure of introducing you. So, Anne, please understand I am not saying anything about Robert South – he is a fine young man, but do not be in too much of a hurry as these things will take their course over time. And you have plenty of time. Hopefully, we will see much more of you in the future."

"Thank you, Mrs McPherson. I have been wondering about these things. Yes, Robert is a nice young man, but as you say, he is not the only fish in the sea. I will take your advice and take my time. And I will confide in you if that is acceptable. Now I must ready myself for our trip."

"Certainly, My Dear. I'm so glad we had this little chat!"

Marjorie McPherson imagined Anne's confidence was now won and was content with the conversation's outcome.

Anne politely moved out of the breakfast room and up the stairs. She sensed danger. In what direction was she trying to steer her? Was there a marriage plan for this son of hers? Was it a coincidence he would arrive on Thursday? What was happening between Thomas and Marion? Slowly things were becoming linked. Seeds of doubt crept into her mind. Perhaps this house was not the friendly household everyone made it out to be. Did she imagine this, or was it real? She must remain calm and see how things played out.

William was passing her on the way down in a rush. She grabbed him and said, "Where are you going, young man?"

"The breakfast room – I'm going for some more sausage before we go out. Anne, they have got two big dogs. Jenkins and I walked them this morning, and Jenkins and I are now good friends. He is such a nice man. He gave me lollies."

"Did he?"

"Yes, and we talked and talked, and I told him all about our family in Guildford."

"What did he ask William?"

"He asked why Mother was sick."

"And what did you tell him?"

William looked at her in surprise and then became silent.

"What did you tell him, William?"

"Just how someone beat Mother, and she had bruises everywhere, and she bled a lot, and I felt sick!"

"Did you tell him it was a dream, William? Did you tell him that she had a fall?"

"No."

"If anyone here asks again, that's what you must say. Remember our agreement William; it is between you and me! Make sure you tell them that it was a dream. Understand?"

"Yes."

"Now off you go and get your sausage!"

She watched him go. Anne was now sure that there was much at play here. She must talk with Thomas – leaving here next Wednesday before this James arrived was becoming a priority. Suddenly, she felt very unsettled.

Chapter 10

The McPherson Household, Greenwich ...

Alexander Steele, dressed in an evening suit, sat in Hamish McPherson's study, admiring the fine book collection housed around the walls. The door was closed, and they sipped scotch while seated on comfortable leather chairs. Now early August, the sun was still high, and the room was light and warm. A slight wind blew in from the southeast, up the Thames, drifting in through the open window.

"You say this Thomas will manage your new brewery in Guildford? But what are his connections, Hamish? What kind of a family does he come from?"

"You sound like the aristocrats, Alex! His connections do not matter! He is a sound thinker with ideas well ahead of his time. These are the sorts of young people who will transform our country. This morning I took him on a tour of the brewery. A newcomer, never seen a brewery before, and with ideas I have never considered. That is why he will become the manager. Once a business reaches a certain size, introducing non-family members into management is essential for business improvement and development. There are advantages of new people coming on board, progressive young people who can further develop the company. Thomas is perfect for that."

"So, who is his family?"

"Thomas's father, Jonathan, is a baker and inherited the family business. Jonathan has a brother who runs an alehouse in Ewell. I am uncertain of Jonathan's other siblings. I have met Jonathan's brother, Richard, who has two sons, Oliver and Harry. One of his sons, Oliver, who has substantial pub experience, will be running the new pub in Epping. Jonathan is investing significant amounts in that venture.

I believe Jonathan's baking business is quite profitable and extensive. It is also experiencing rapid growth, as is Guildford and the whole area southwest of London. They not only do bread but pastry and biscuits. I have a tin of the biscuits here – just try one. The quality is the best I have ever tasted, and I know many others who have the same opinion.

Thomas's sister, Anne, and one of his younger brothers stay with us for the week. You won't meet William as we have a Nanny looking after him. He is far too young for dinner parties – despite his protestations, but you will meet Anne. She is an attractive young lady, but don't underestimate her. She is knowledgeable and a match for any woman in London. The children are impressive indeed and indicate the quality of the family."

Alexander Steele looked out the window. Frowning, he took a bite of the biscuit offered. Surprised by its crisp quality and pleasant favour, Alexander smiled. He then took another sip of Hamish's enjoyable scotch whisky, rolling it around his mouth. His life was suffering from dramatic changes since his wife's health failed. Now that Jenny was in full-time care, he felt very alone. His three sons bitterly resented his decision. But he was thankful for the quality care she now received, something his sons refused to understand. Anyway, Jenny no longer recognised them. It was tragic.

"The biscuit is quite tasty." He took another sip of the whisky. "This is also a fine Scotch!"

"Of course, Alex. It is genuine scotch malt from the Isle of Islay. You can taste the peat!"

"You say that this young fellow will be the manager. Will he have the means Marion requires for her lifestyle?"

"I believe so, Alex. I will provide a substantial manager's house for them in Guildford. He will receive a good retainer. Given time, I expect he will progress well, and I will reward him with some equity in the company. He is also the manager of the bakery in Guildford. He will transition over time into brewing, but I expect he will inherit a fair share of the family businesses."

"Does Marion love this young man?"

"From what I can determine, she does. There is a willingness on her part that appears quite genuine. Marion found delight in being involved with them when we were in Guildford."

"Hamish, I'm not sure about this. Why not look for a better catch with one of the grand families."

"Alex, remember that we are the working class. They accept our existence but not our company. The world is changing quickly, but their natural reaction is to cling to their old traditions. Their reaction is understandable, but they do it at their financial peril. The class system will slowly defeat itself! The rise of industry will do this for us. The future of this country, our country, will depend on people like us."

Alexander Steele was also a business owner, forming his own company supported by various investors. He understood Hamish's argument but still seemed unconvinced.

"Believe me! I have done my research. I have found nothing wrong here. They have their hiccups, and so do we, but this Jonathan Turner is successful because he works hard and has bright ideas he implements. Thomas is just as smart, if not more innovative and has learned from his father. How many young people learn from their elders and build on it? Thomas does. He is a good catch, Alex! And I will make sure he prospers. You have my word on this.

My friend, we are ageing. I am planning my transition out of management. May I be bold and suggest you are in the same position. Marion will soon commence the next stage of her life. With Jenny now ill, your support will be vital for her."

Alexander Steele sat still and then took another sip of whisky. He rubbed his red eyes and then inside his collar. The sun was still hot despite the cool breeze.

"You are right! We are getting on. This thing with Jenny has aged me more than I admit. It has left me desolate, Hamish. I miss her company so much. The boys will only understand in time. It all takes time."

He took another sip. Alexander sat there for a few minutes, thinking deeply. Hamish was about to speak when Alex turned with a smile and said, "Thank you for looking after Marion. I could not have provided for her emotionally at this time as you and Marjorie have. It appears she has found a good partner in life!"

Hamish breathed out gently in relief. The explanation succeeded. Alexander Steele had agreed and was primed for the meeting later that night. It was delicate there for a while, and Hamish was pleased that his gentle persuasion succeeded. He took a large gulp of scotch and finished his glass with a warm feeling in his stomach.

"Another?" Hamish raised his empty glass.

"Yes, Hamish, thanks."

"I was thinking, Alex. While this is fresh in your mind, why not ask Thomas in here and discuss it now. It will save a meeting after dinner, and you can invite Thomas and Marion for dinner at your house in a few days before he leaves for Guildford. It is a good opportunity. Introducing the family will help build the acquaintance."

"Yes - that is the way. I am glad we have decided!"

Hamish made for the door, "Jenkins. Would you please locate Mr Turner and ask if we might have the pleasure of his company in the study here? Mr Thomas Turner, please."

The dinner would be a very formal affair, and Mr McPherson agreed that Jenkins hire two additional footmen for the night. Much preparation was going on inside the house, and soon everyone would begin dressing for dinner.

Anne finally found a free moment, with Nanny Jones occupying William, and Marion was discussing dinner arrangements with Mrs McPherson. She moved down the hallway quietly lest she attracted any attention and entered her brother's room. Thomas was dressed and waiting for dinner.

Anne looked Thomas up and down, noting his smart dinner suit, "You meet approval, Thomas! Very handsome. Mother and Father would be proud of you."

Thomas sat there, thinking. He had not been aware Anne was in the room. He looked up, "Thank you, Anne. I was thinking about how much has happened since we arrived here. It was a splendid visit with Robert today, wasn't it?"

"Yes, Thomas. The masts, rigging, and sails entranced William. It was as if he was born with it in his blood. I think he may be heading towards the Navy. Did you see the smile on his face? I enjoyed it, as well. But it must be a lonely life, all those long days at sea."

Thomas nodded in agreement and sighed, "Not the life I would choose!"

"Thomas, I need a private talk with you. I was becoming a little uncomfortable here and wondered how you were feeling?"

"What do you mean by uncomfortable?"

"My feeling is that the McPhersons are influencing us in our decisions for the future."

"Ah. I know what you mean. However, it may be a good thing. A wake-up call!"

"What do you mean by 'A wake-up call', Thomas?"

"As you know, I have grown very fond of Marion. At first, I thought it strange that she would fancy me, a baker from Guildford. Then as she explained her life and that her family was like ours, I understood she was not looking for someone grand but someone who shared the same values and lifestyle. I'm sure her family are not as well off as the McPhersons."

"Yes, I think you are correct on that."

"We have been exchanging letters, and our relationship has grown. So, when the invitation came for this trip, I thought that perhaps I would propose while I was here."

"You want to marry her?" Anne was alarmed. She felt she was already losing a sister, and now a beloved brother might be lost as well. "But I will be left alone at home, Thomas!"

"At some stage, Anne, I must marry, and you know me – there's not much on the horizon in terms of matrimonial stakes. You will not be losing a brother but gaining a sister and a wonderful one. Clementine, Madeline and Marcia will still be at home with William and Simeon."

"Sorry, Thomas, I was thinking of only myself. You and Beth are the ones I can confide in at home. But you are correct; Marion would be a good sister-in-law."

"The funny thing is that when Marion heard about Bethany's engagement, it must have spurred her on. She came to see me the night we arrived. We kissed and then I knew she was the girl for me. So, I proposed, and she accepted."

Anne sat there in stunned silence. She looked at Thomas in disbelief. "You are engaged?"

"Yes, Anne! Are not congratulations in order?"

"Does Father know?"

"I am my own man, Anne! I will advise mother and father on our return."

"Thomas, this is a big step. You will need a substantial income as Marion will have expectations. Have you thought this through?"

"I am glad you mention this, Anne. Do you recall my tour with Mr McPherson this morning? He offered me employment as manager of the new brewery in Guilford. I understand that I will be well remunerated and that there will be a manager's house that will be quite substantial. All these things happening at once is quite amazing!"

Anne stood up and gazed out the window. Her mind was buzzing. The tops of the ship masts at the wharf were visible, and the breeze was strengthening with the brightly coloured flags now fully extending like beacons. It was as if the breeze was blowing the past away. Her security, stability, and confidence all came from the past, but now, it was all changing in front of her eyes.

She was sure the McPhersons planned this well ahead of their visit. There were several ways of looking at it. Perhaps it was an innocent situation where this marriage would happily intertwine the McPhersons with the Turners, or it revolved around money and influence. She was not sure if she was over-cautious in suspecting these people of ill will towards her family. Maybe she imagined this, and the situation was genuine. Time would tell.

"Anne?"

Thomas looked over at her standing beside the window, gazing at the view, and he wondered what she was thinking.

"Will you not congratulate me on my good fortune in winning Marion's hand and the job in brewing?"

Anne's mind was moving her out over the ships as if she were a bird flying high in the gusts of wind. She felt as if the other birds were flying away, and there she was, alone, looking down at the waving flags. What would her future be? Where would it lead her?

Thomas could see she was struggling with it all. She needed reassurance. "Anne, you will always be my sister. You will always be welcome wherever I am. But I do love Marion so much. She and I will be so happy. Please, I need your blessing on this as you are my closest friend."

Unaware of a knocking, Anne looked around as Thomas opened the door to find Jenkins there. "Mr McPherson wonders if you would join him in his study, Mr Turner?"

"Yes, certainly, I will be right down."

"Thank you, Sir."

"Anne, I shall meet you at dinner. Must go now; the boss calls!"

Anne followed Thomas out of his room into the hallway. She stopped him kissing him on his cheek.

"God bless you and Marion, Thomas. I'm sure you will be most happy. I'll congratulate Marion at dinner!"

"Thank you, sister!" He gave her a hug and a kiss back. "Your blessing means a great deal to me!" Smiling at her, he rushed off down the stairs.

At Dinner ...

Anne was late as the conversation with Thomas was longer than expected. As she dressed, she gained courage from the beautiful new dress selected for tonight. Her mother had supplied Anne with some delicate jewellery that would perfect her costume.

She quickly looked in on William on the way down, finding him standing on a chair having a sword fight with Nanny Jones. It appeared all was well with William, so knowing she was running late, she smiled, waved and closed the door. As Anne arrived in the drawing-room, the party was moving into dinner. The McPhersons were unaware that Guildford was so contemporary with the London fashions, and they were astounded at her lovely dress and beauty.

The table was set another way tonight and extended, providing enough room for twelve places. What Anne considered a lavish setting last night did not compare with the glitter of this occasion. The chandeliers over the table sparkled light down on a magnificent flower setting of yellow and deep red roses, augmenting the shine of the beautiful crockery and shining silver cutlery. Jenkins had excelled tonight and bore a pleasant smile as they all entered admiring the dining room. Several footmen assisted in finding their seats designated by place names.

Mr McPherson stood behind his chair at the centre of the table. Beside him sat Admiral Sir Tristan Sutherland's wife, Amanda, and on the other side Miss Marion Steele. An unknown gentleman stood beside Mrs McPherson with a well-dressed lady joining their conversation. Anne later learned this was Mrs Felicity Handle, wife of Archdeacon Rufus Handle. The Archdeacon sat opposite Neville Bassington at the end of the table.

As Anne came through the dining room doorway, Mr McPherson noticed her and warmly welcomed her in a loud voice.

"Anne, you look positively beautiful tonight. As always! Let me introduce you to Admiral Sir Tristan Sutherland."

Anne was unsure of the protocol, having never met an Admiral before. She slightly blushed, which enhanced her complexion, and she put out her hand.

The Admiral taking her hand, said, "My, Miss Turner, Hamish did not tell me we would have such charming ladies with us tonight." He turned and gave Marion a nod, ensuring he included Hamish's niece. "Miss Anne, I am glad to make your acquaintance."

Marion was relieved by this comment, as while she felt outdone by Anne's beauty, she believed the statement included all the ladies.

"I am greatly honoured to meet you, Admiral Sutherland."

"Now tell me, Anne – you must be the daughter of Mr Jonathan Turner, whose biscuits I have heard so much, and I hear that I will finally taste some tonight."

"Yes, Sir Tristan, I am one of Mr Turner's five daughters. Lieutenant Neville Bassington and my sister Bethany have recently announced their engagement, so I am pleased he is here. I do hope you enjoy the biscuits. I was not aware there would be a tasting, but I am excited that it will occur. If I may be of assistance, it would be my pleasure."

The Admiral, who was much impressed by this young lady, said, "Miss Turner, thank you. I shall rely on your advice."

Standing at the end of the table, Captain Mark Foster whispered in Robert South's ear, "My, if her sister is only half as beautiful as this girl, then I wonder why it took Bassington a whole day before he proposed!"

Robert smiled and quietly replied, "Captain Foster, you and I both know that Neville sometimes procrastinates!"

"Ha! Well said, Lieutenant South."

They both chuckled as Anne moved on from the Admiral and walked their way, searching for her name place.

Captain Foster said, "And now, Sir Robert, you must introduce me."

Anne raised her eyes and found Robert straight in front of her. She broke into a beautiful smile, "Hello, Robert."

Robert winked, and she grinned, "Anne, let me introduce you. Captain Mark Foster of His Majesty's Ship *Providence*, may I introduce Miss Anne Turner."

Mark Foster was not retiring and valued mixed company, given he missed his absent wife. "Delighted to meet you, Miss Turner. I am sorry I was not there today when you and your party toured the ship with Sir Robert. I was with Admiral Sutherland on a pressing matter."

"Captain, thank you so much for your permission. The tour was a fascinating moment for me, and it greatly inspired my young brother William. I think you may have a new Midshipman tomorrow – so you will know where you may send him home if he suddenly appears."

They all had a good laugh at this.

"Ah, I heard that William enjoyed himself. Sir Robert assures me he will be a good Midshipman once he is twelve. Pray, where is he tonight?"

"When I last saw him some minutes ago, he was upstairs with Nanny Jones playing pirates. I think Nanny Jones will retire with bruises and aches. Poor thing!"

"Capital, Capital. The boy sounds like he has a spirit. That's what we want!"

Anne found her place between Captain Foster and Mr Malcolm Smith. Captain Foster introduced Mr Smith, "Now, Miss Anne Turner. May I introduce Mr Malcolm Smith of the Admiralty."

Mr Smith's suit was similar to the one worn by Thomas, and he was not a Navy man. Malcolm was quite tall and appeared to be mid-forties in his age. His smile was friendly, and he seemed somewhat reserved.

"Delighted, Miss Turner."

Anne was curious why this gentleman was there, "It is a pleasure meeting you, Mr Smith. I see you are not in uniform, so I assume you have a connection with these fine gentlemen?"

Robert was again impressed by Anne. At seventeen and a half, she handled these men like a sophisticated aristocrat twice her age. Her conversation was not pretentious but quite genuine and well-meaning, and they appreciated her like a breath of fresh air. She held them all in the palm of her hand. He marvelled at the girl's natural skills.

He looked up and winked at Neville, sitting at the other end of the table. He was thinking the same, and with a nod, he grinned back.

"Miss Anne, I work in the Admiralty Procurements Office – we buy supplies for the Navy."

Admiral Sutherland, enjoying these introductions, could not contain himself, saying, "Don't underrate yourself, Malcolm. Anne, he runs the place. A most important man."

Anne broke out into a beautiful smile and said, "In that case, I will be on my best behaviour tonight, Mr Smith."

Malcolm Smith was a shy and gentle soul who was exceptionally knowledgeable about procurements. His appointment as Comptroller was purely on merit, as the Admiralty, as with all organisations, put in place stringent rules ensuring the goods procured fulfilled the navy requirements. The Admirals found him the kind of man they enjoyed working with, as he was always obliging, listened carefully, and ensured quality when fulfilling their demands. These attributes had won their respect and assisted in his advancement!

Malcolm Smith blushed a little, and after Anne took her place, he sat down looking sideways, giving her a polite smile of thanks.

At the other end of the table sat Archdeacon Rufus Handle, Rector of the local church, which the McPhersons attended. His wife Felicity sat between Alexander Steele and Neville Bassington. After moving to Greenwich, the McPhersons decided to make the local Church of England their home church and became good friends with the Archdeacon and his wife. Thomas was particularly interested in meeting with this minister as he imagined that he would be the celebrant for his upcoming, yet unannounced, wedding.

Having only the slightest time before dinner, Thomas briefly shared with Marion the details of the pre-dinner meeting. The best news, of course, was Mr Steele's blessing for their marriage. Marion felt that it was a miracle and was on top of the world. She pleaded with Mr McPherson that he announce the engagement at dinner. Hamish agreed this would be an appropriate occasion for the announcement but understood that he should immediately send some notification to the Turners. He had no desire to offend his business partner and would send a rider tonight.

In between conversations at her end of the table, Anne noticed Marion and Thomas sitting side-by-side in their own world. They were conversing at a rapid rate and deep in concentration. Marion appeared excited and was continuously smiling. 'She looks radiant tonight,' Anne thought. 'Perhaps this is all genuine. My fears must be imaginary.'

Then Mr McPherson stood up and said, "Ladies and gentlemen! Before I presume on Archdeacon Handle for grace, there is a need for a couple of announcements. Thank you, everyone, for joining us here tonight as our guests. It gives myself and Marjorie (he indicated Mrs McPherson) great pleasure having you here in our home this evening, and I'm sure there will be much lively conversation."

"Here, here!" Several of the guests appreciated Hamish's comment.

"Please excuse me, Alexander, but I know I have your permission. There is great anticipation between these two young people beside me. So, I will now make this announcement, so we all might share in their excitement."

Anne thought, "No! Mother and father are unaware!"

Hamish continued, "It gives me great pleasure in announcing the engagement between my niece Marion, the daughter of Mr Alexander and Mrs Jennifer Steele, and the eligible and fine young man, Mr Thomas Turner, son of Mr Jonathan and Mrs Eleanora Turner of Guildford."

There was a loud commotion of congratulations and much joy around the table. Robert noticed that Anne was not surprised and showed little excitement. However, he displayed good manners and joined in the congratulations heartily. Mrs McPherson ran around the table and hugged and kissed them both. Alexander Steele reached across the table and shook hands with Thomas in a moving gesture of friendship. Mr McPherson then called for quiet, and Archdeacon Handle said a spectacular grace, duly noting thanks for the newly engaged couple, followed by a loud "Amen" by all. With the prayer complete, the footmen distributed the champagne for a toast.

"Ladies and Gentlemen, please charge your glasses. I give you the newly engaged couple, Marion and Thomas."

All followed, "Marion and Thomas!"

"Thank you all, and now let the dinner begin."

As the guests enjoyed the first course, Anne felt a slight tug on the side of her dress. There beside her was William in his pyjamas. Captain Foster said, "Ah, this must be my new midshipman, William?"

"Yes, Captain Foster, this is William."

William turned and politely said hello, then, turning to Anne in some urgency, said, "There's something wrong with Nanny Jones."

"What do you mean, William?"

"She is just lying on the floor with her eyes closed. She is not moving!"

Anne politely excused herself, stood and requested Neville's assistance. Robert also jumped up and followed.

Neville in a deep conversation with Felicity Handle and Alexander Steele about Mrs Steel's illness, looked up when called by Anne. "Please excuse me, Felicity and Alexander, as I must attend to the request of my future sister-in-law. It seems the Nanny requires medical assistance. The luck of a Surgeon!" They politely nodded, and Neville moved away, following Anne, William, and Robert up the stairs.

In William's bedroom, they found Nanny Jones lying flat out on the floor with a large bump on the forehead. She was unconscious and quite still. Neville knelt beside her, felt for a pulse, and found a strong one. He made a quick examination.

"Robert, would you please ask for a couple of footmen and a maid. We must carefully reposition Nanny Jones into her bedroom and ask the maid to fetch me some cloth and cool water. I think she will recover soon, but it appears she has been knocked unconscious."

Robert darted off for the help required.

"Anne, where is her bedroom?"

"Next door."

"Which side?"

"I'll show you as we move her."

Neville gently rolled Nany Jones onto her side, so she breathed more easily. Soon the footmen arrived, and Neville supervised the transfer, following as they carefully carried Nanny Jones out of the room. Robert looked around at

William, who quietly put himself into bed.

"William, what happened?"

"I like Nanny Jones. She is terrific fun. I didn't mean to hit her!"

Anne's eyes blazed at William, "What do you mean you hit her?"

"We were playing pirates, and she chased me around the ship. I jumped up on the poop deck, which is that chair, and I was waving this broom handle through the air. She turned and ran into it just like father did by the river that time. It was an accident. It hit her head, and she fell straight down on the floor."

Robert opened his mouth to laugh but covered it quickly as he saw Anne's anger.

"William, you will remain in bed now and sleep. It is now well past your bedtime. Nanny Jones will have a very sore head tomorrow and will need rest. I will be replacing Nanny Jones tomorrow. I don't want you to move from this bed again tonight."

William replied, "I am in bed, but what if I need the toilet?"

"You have your bedpan, you may use that, but that is it. I will arrange for a maid tonight who will check on you regularly. Good night."

Robert was amused but suppressed it as best he could. "I will see you for the picnic on Sunday, William. Good night."

William glared at them and pulled the covers over his chin as Anne blew out the candle.

As they went down the stairs, Robert could no longer contain himself and roared with laughter.

"He took out the Nanny with a broomstick. That's classic." He continued laughing.

"Robert, it is not funny. William might have severely injured the poor girl. She will probably leave for home tomorrow, and it will be our family's fault."

Robert was still shaking with laughter, "Come on, Anne, you must see the funny side of the event. He came and got us as soon as it happened. Neville will take good care of her. But it is just so funny!"

Anne calmed herself. She was disgusted with Robert's lack of sensitivity but then realised she might be overreacting. Slowly a glimmer of a smirk came upon her face, "You men! What we women put up with!"

They approached the dining room. Anne smiled at Robert and said, "I'll let you explain what occurred with William and Nanny Jones, the nanny Mrs McPherson hired."

Robert stopped laughing immediately and stood with his mouth open, "But, but......Anne!"

Anne glided silently into the dining room and sat down on her chair, smiling sweetly.

The dinner was a pleasant affair. All the better when Neville returned and announced that Nanny Jones was now conscious and laughing about the whole episode. Mrs McPherson was much relieved and put the hiring of another nanny out of her mind. Anne assured Marjorie that she would care for William tomorrow.

Admiral Sutherland and Captain Foster talked with Alexander Steele about the advantages of the new canons they were installing on *Providence*. Malcolm Smith and Archdeacon Handle seemed entangled on some theological point while Marjorie and Amanda Sutherland contemplated the newly engaged couple. Anne found an opportunity, congratulated Thomas and Marion, and then sat beside Robert and enjoyed some time with him. She was finally with Robert again. At last, they could talk.

At the end of the meal, there was a tasting of the Turner biscuits, which were well received. Captain Foster assured all present that the biscuits were now the favourite of his crew, and he should be pleased if Malcolm would make them standard navy provisions. Admiral Sutherland lent his support, "Let us test both the canons and the biscuits at sea next week. I would welcome the gentlemen and the crew eating them." Malcolm Smith would be sailing as well, and he made encouraging comments about the biscuits and the airtight storage tin boxes they came in.

Anne thought how pleased her father would be to hear these comments. Hamish McPherson was also pleased with the reaction from the navy officers, as he forecast a large standing order going Jonathan Turner's way. Good for friendship and good for business.

"Anne – now choose a destination for our picnic on Sunday." As the time was getting late, Robert wished to confirm the arrangements before leaving. The picnic would be his last meeting with Anne before they met again at the wedding, so he was determined the event would be pleasurable for her.

"I will have my carriage available, so we shall have options."

"Perhaps the sea or a view of London. But we must include the others before we decide!"

Robert agreed, then stood and announced the proposition, "Ladies and Gentlemen, we are proposing a picnic for Sunday lunch and afternoon. Miss Turner here desires either a seascape or a view of London; however, we thought we would canvass the ideas of anyone joining us."

Mrs McPherson and Marion were thrilled with the idea and had several suggestions. They concluded that the sea was too far away for a Sunday picnic, so the guests canvassed various sites.

Neville spoke up, "I say, may I suggest Shooters Hill as there is a splendid view from the top? There is a little common there and a good place for a picnic."

Admiral Sutherland then joined in, "Given the kind invitation, how about the whole party join us at Severndroog Castle. I am friends with the owner and am sure he would allow us the privilege of using the grounds. From the top of the Castle, London and the Thames have splendid aspects. On one condition, of course – that Amanda and I may bring the grandchildren?"

There was unanimous agreement with this proposal, and all was settled for a picnic at the Castle.

"William should be pleased with this! An adventure at the castle. We shall pick you up at eleven-thirty. It is only a fifteen-minute drive up there. I'm sure the McPhersons will provide a hamper for all of us." Robert was quite excited at the prospect of a pleasant afternoon with Anne and her new extended family of in-laws. "As we shall be playing pirates, I will be keeping a careful watch on William and his broomstick."

Anne laughed as she remembered poor Nanny Jones and her sore head, "Thank you, Robert. It is kind of you to devote such time to William and me. I hope we can return these favours in the future."

"Think nothing of it, Anne. It is nice having some friends in London. I do not have many acquaintances here."

"I thought that with your position, you would have many."

"Not really. I have been at sea since I was twelve years old. Most of my shore leave was overseas or at Fintelton Manor, my parents' home. I like to scramble home and catch up with my brother and sister if leave is possible. I am a bit of a stickler for home life. So, developing friendships here is rare."

"Then we friends must stick together. But I must warn you that playing pirates in our family can become a bit rough."

"So, I hear, as your father found out. William's antics will not detract from our friendship. If anything, they will enrich it. I hope we shall be friends for a long time."

Anne was surprised by this last comment. Robert was not the type who talked about relationships and clearly would not let anyone enquire into his feelings. Perhaps the navy life made him cautious. But he was a charming conversationalist. She and he never stopped talking when they were together.

"I hope so too, Robert."

The guests said their goodbyes and departed. Mrs McPherson was still running around congratulating and talking about the engagement. It was a happy and eventful evening, and there was a sense of joy as all retired. When Anne finally rested on her pillow that night, she could not put Robert out of her mind and his words, 'I hope we shall be friends for a long time.' Why would they not be friends? What could ever destroy their friendship? Was that what he meant? What did he mean?

Robert sat with Captain Foster and Neville as the coach bumped towards the Woolwich wharves.

"A fine evening. Lovely people, eh South?"

"Yes, Sir, that they are!"

Captain Foster could see the pleasant expression on Lieutenant South's face. It was almost identical to Neville Bassington's one. Foster was not a Captain by favour or chance – he was a wise leader of men and read their moods well. He was pleased when first told Lieutenant South was posted aboard *Providence*. Usually, a favourable recommendation was a two-edged sword. However, he was aware of South's fine exploits, and he was an excellent officer. His service on *Providence* was exemplary, and his admiration for the young lieutenant grew without reservation. The Admiral, the previous week in Portsmouth, briefed Foster that Lieutenant South would be leaving him. He would command a large topsail schooner named *Restless*. Foster considered it an honour mentoring and serving with a man like South. He now regarded him as a friend, as well as one of his officers.

"Robert?"

Neville was surprised to hear Captain Foster address Lieutenant South by his first name. In terms of intimacy for the Navy, this was quite a step. Robert, who was far away in his thoughts, looked up and straight at his Captain.

"Robert. She is too young yet. Wait for a year at least. I do not want you doing a Neville on me. You also must consider how your parents will react. It may be quite difficult."

Robert smiled. Foster, as usual, was reading his thoughts. Robert knew he was no poker player. His face was too transparent.

"I shall follow your recommendations with pleasure, Sir. I agree, and I might also say, Sir, that I have received similar advice from my most excellent fellow officer here, which entirely mirrors yours. I am very thankful for the friendship you both extend to me, Sir."

Neville grinned as he heard the comments. There was no need for further talk. The three friends sped off towards their ship at Woolwich, now eager for their warm bunks on board.

Greenwich – Sunday – the Picnic Day ...

William ran into the dining room with a great appetite. The activity of walking the dogs with Jenkins always aroused his hunger. The family and guests were already at breakfast, and they warmly received William.

"Did they catch any rabbits today, William?" Thomas asked.

"Red Socks got one, but there were not many out today. Jenkins said it was because of the fine weather with the sun rising early, and perhaps we were a bit late in the morning. Boiler was too busy chasing birds and following Red Socks. Jenkins said if we go late one afternoon, there might be more rabbits out. Thomas, can we go this afternoon just before dark? That's when the rabbits come out."

Thomas gobbled a piece of sausage and replied, "I don't see why not. We should be home by four in the afternoon, and dinner is usually not till eight o'clock, so why not? I would like to see these dogs in action. Mr McPherson, will you join us?"

Hamish was pouring a cup of coffee, "I'll see how me legs hold out, Thomas. Not getting any younger, you know. But if I am able, I will join you."

Marion changed the subject, "William, we will see a castle today after church. I hear it is four stories high and has lookouts at the top. That is nearly as high as the masts on Robert's ship. What an adventure awaits us today!"

William's eyes opened wide at the mention of the castle. "Who owns the castle – is it Blackbeard the pirate?"

"No. Admiral Sutherland knows a wealthy gentleman who owns the castle. I understand that it was originally built as a folly commemorating Commodore Sir William James[11] by his wife in 1784, some forty-one years ago."

"What is a folly, Marion?"

"It is a place of tranquillity where you remember someone."

The explanation was too complicated for William, so he returned to his favourite subject of pirates. "We can play pirates and find some treasure!"

"I'm told that there may be some hidden treasure at the bottom of the folly! Isn't that right, Mr McPherson?"

"I think so, and William, you and Admiral Sutherland's grandchildren, may search for it! Now get a good feed on board, young man, as you will need all your energy today."

William needed no more of an invitation, and he went straight for the scrambled eggs and sausages. Jenkins kindly served him a big helping. Anne raised her eyebrows when she saw how much was on the plate and wondered if William would develop a stomachache before they reached the church.

After attending holy communion at the McPherson's parish church at Greenwich, the party returned home for morning tea, changing their clothes and preparing for the picnic. Jenkins and a couple of footmen journeyed ahead and set up camp on the lawn in front of the castle.

Robert and Captain Foster arrived from Woolwich in a large carriage at around eleven o'clock, joining the party of excited participants in the drawing-room. Robert gave Neville's apology as an accident involving a seaman on one of the other vessels would prevent his attending.

"Admiral Sutherland sends his compliments, Mr McPherson, and says he will join us at the Castle at around twelve if not earlier. He fears it will take a little while to gather his party, some five or six ladies and children. Mr

---

[11] Severndroog Castle, is a folly at Shooter's Hill, built in 1784, by Lady James of Eltham, as a memorial to her husband, Commodore Sir William James, famous for his naval service in India. Wikipedia.

Malcolm Smith and his wife, Robyn, will travel behind the Admiral and join us there."

"Excellent, Robert. It sounds like you have arranged the timing with naval precision." Hamish laughed.

"Thank you, Sir. I propose that Thomas and Marion join you in your carriage, and Anne, William and Nany Jones join Captain Foster and me. If that is satisfactory, Sir."

"That will be very suitable, Sir. However, Captain Foster, we would be pleased if you could join us in our carriage so I might enquire about the navy brewed beer if that is not a navy secret, Sir?"

"Certainly, Sir, it is the least I can do for you. Please excuse me, Robert. I will ride with Mr McPherson and his party."

With the arrangements made, the party set off for the castle, a short journey of around fifteen minutes. At Shooters Hill, they followed the road winding through woods and the open castle gates. The carriage pulled up beside a large marquee erected with chairs, tables, and a fine selection for lunch already in place.

The McPhersons were the third carriage to arrive, and Hamish bounded out and shook hands happily with Archdeacon Handle and his wife, Felicity. Admiral Sutherland and his wife were also present and introduced their grandchildren.

The setting looked splendid, and the guests had no hesitation participating in a cold drink, given the day's warmth. Most now present were keen on climbing the castle and beholding the battlement's famous view. Hamish led them off on a tour of the four floors and the lookouts. The outlook was magnificent on this fine day, with Captain Foster pointing out HMS *Providence* moored at the Woolwich docks in all its splendour.

William requested their carriage drive past the docks on the way as he pleaded for another view of the navy ships again. Robert obliged as it would only take an additional twenty minutes and was happy spending the extra time in the coach with his guests. Hamish McPherson pointed out Robert's coach approaching the castle from the lookout.

A small group of the men gathered on the tallest vantage point and surveyed the green forest cap stretching out beyond them down Shooter's Hill. It was quite thick except for a long narrow track that included the castle's driveway.

Hamish asked, "Tell me, Captain Foster, how is it that you have a lieutenant serving on your ship who has a carriage?"

"That is a fair question, Sir. First, Sir Robert South is an excellent officer; I am proud of having him serve with me on *Providence*. His knighthood came as a reward from the King for a successful skirmish with Portuguese pirates in

- 161 -

the Mediterranean some years ago. The ship was caught by surprise by pirates at sunset and suffered a broadside that killed the captain and half the officers. South was a junior lieutenant and found himself the most senior officer left alive, so he took command. He rallied the crew together, no mean feat given half of them were either dead or injured. They kept the ship underway, making enough headway and avoiding boarding by the pirates. Then he urgently organised several gun crews, returning fire with broadsides until the pirate ship surrendered. Some of his crew were severely injured but not unhappy, as the captured ship resulted in each crew member receiving a pretty penny from the prize money.

It was a heroic action and indicated the quality of the fellow. The King knighted South, but there was little publicity for political reasons. But, as I said before, I would have him under my command at any time. He is a fine fellow.

His father is the Earl of Fintelton, and the coach comes from that great estate. Robert is the second son, so he will not inherit the title and must make his way in the world. I believe he also has a brother and sister. I think we shall see him rise far higher in the navy."

"Most impressive, Captain Foster. I had no idea that such a young officer would have seen so much action and served his country so well. You have all the fun, you navy fellows!" Hamish was quite impressed.

Admiral Sutherland commented, "We don't call it fun at the time, but it is exciting. In very desperate circumstances, South did an excellent job and probably saved his crew from either a bloody end or long captivity. He is a quick thinker, and he will go far. Quite fitting, we are here at a folly remembering another great Navy commander."

The account thoroughly convinced the party, and the Admiral's comment confirmed Sir Robert's bravery.

"Gentlemen, I think it is time we descended for lunch. I have it on good account that we have some fine Scottish beer on tap that will please you very well." The guests required no further encouragement from Hamish McPherson, and there was a quick movement towards the steps.

Approaching the castle, Robert leaned towards William and said, "Now when we play pirates, William, please no waving a pole around your head today."

Nanny Jones agreed and suggested, "Perhaps use something soft like a jumper or a hat."

They all laughed at this as the coach halted. In a flash, William was out through the carriage door and heading for the castle.

Admiral and Mrs Sutherland brought four grandchildren and a nanny with them. Being of a similar age, the children soon became friends and rushed after Mr McPherson looking for buried treasure. With two nannies watching over the children, the adults relaxed in the idyllic surroundings.

The lunch was a splendid affair, with Hamish and Marjorie McPherson generously over providing with two long tables, ample seating, and various dishes from the McPherson kitchen. As the sun grew warmer, there was plenty of demand for the cold lemonade, wine, and beer on call. Jenkins was quite satisfied with the setting he provided, and the guests were not complaining. The picnic was a great success with a perfect summer's day and these beautiful surroundings.

After lunch, Robert sat relaxing against a tree trunk away from the marquee. The shade was pleasant in the warm afternoon breeze. As he sipped a glass of cold beer, enjoying the calming effect, Anne walked across and joined him.

"A penny for your thoughts, Robert."

He was pleased she came before William demanded more pirate games.

"I was having a quick rest before the next round of Captain Blood. I say, sit here on this cloak, so you don't spoil your dress."

"Thank you. Yes, the children can be a bit much at times, can't they?"

"Yes and no. I am very fond of children. I have fond memories of many good times with my brother and sister at Fintelton. I quite often miss them. But life goes on, and we must make our way in this world. "

"Do you have brothers and sisters as I do?"

"Not the clan that you have, but yes. I have an older brother, Hugh, and a younger sister, Emma."

"I love the name, Emma. It just sounds so sweet."

"She is sweet, and we write often. She is just a year older than you, Anne."

"Do you return home and see them?"

"Yes, when I can, but that will not often be in the coming year. Between you and me, Anne, and please don't tell anyone yet – the Admiralty have appointed me captain of a schooner. The Navy board posted the captain ashore for some reason, and the command is now mine. That means I will be away quite a bit for at least the next year."

"Of course, congratulations Robert, but I will miss you!"

"I will be there for Neville and Bethany's wedding. I'm the best man, after all, Anne. I hope you will be a bridesmaid."

"I am sure Bethany will arrange that. Have they set a date yet?"

"I think that is the purpose of his Woking visit this coming weekend - so we shall know soon enough."

"I will miss you, Robert. You have been a good friend."

"Anne, don't forget me just yet. I will be home by next July, and by that time, Neville and Bethany will be well married. I have discussed a proposal with Neville, and if you also agree, the plan is this. That you, with Neville and Beth as chaperones, will visit Fintelton in July next year for two weeks and meet my parents. I will join you there as soon as my voyage is complete. Would you be willing to come?"

"I would be honoured. I do not usually plan for more than two or three weeks ahead, so this will be a new lesson for me. There will be much work assisting my father this year in the baking business now that Thomas will be working for Mr McPherson. So, time will fly."

"That was a bit of a surprise – he must have made his mind up quickly?"

"I think someone made his mind up for him!" She looked away with a frown on her face.

"Anne, I noticed that you did not over-react when Mr McPherson announced the engagement. Do you not approve?"

Anne ran her hand over the thick grass as she struggled to find the right words. Thinking her throat must be dry, Robert offered her a sip of his beer. She took a sip and passed it back to him.

"Thank you. How can I say this without appearing ungrateful? Since visiting the McPhersons, I have become uncomfortable and fear many of the events are orchestrated. As you have a secret, you must keep mine. I am afraid that the McPhersons are using Thomas and my father for their purposes. I am not sure what they are planning, but I hope they will benefit our family. I would hate it if they hoodwinked my father in some way. I have been questioning if I am becoming paranoid, but many of these events appear staged. They are nice people and kind, but it is also strange."

"May I ask what kind of things?"

"Thomas's engagement, the butler taking William for walks, Thomas offered a job as Brewery Manager, Mrs McPherson treating me as a daughter and giving me matrimonial advice."

"Are you sure?"

"Yes. James McPherson, their youngest son, is arriving on Thursday and Mrs McPherson almost offered him as a partner. I was not that impressed but thanked her for her advice."

"She is very forward!"

"But what a coincidence that we are here in Greenwich, and now this James is turning up."

Robert considered this as he took several sips of his beer. Anne sat with her hands on the grass, leaning backwards. She pushed her bonnet a little back, her face soaking up some of the sunshine. Her golden blonde hair fell across her shoulder and waved in the breeze. Robert took great pleasure in observing her beauty. Sitting back, he gazed at her.

Anne slowly turned and noticed him watching. She smiled and said, "What?"

"Just taking in a magnificent sight. Such beauty I have never before enjoyed!"

"It must be the beer!" she giggled.

Robert could see that some of the party were stirring. The mention of this James McPherson worried him. An attractive young lady such as Anne would receive other offers from young gentlemen. He must give her a clear understanding of their attachment and explain that he needed more time. He would meet the difficulties that would arise from his family next year, but at present, he must openly declare his attachment before he lost her.

"Anne, we may not have this opportunity again, so forgive me if this seems forward, but I must ask you. Please promise me two things, but only if you feel these are fair. You will join me at Fintelton next July, and you will not accept any other proposals offered before then. There is no rush, and we will both employ our time well in the next twelve months. You are free from these promises if I am lost at sea." He took another sip of beer and looked earnestly at her.

Anne was not sure how she should respond. This young man who she worshipped was now advancing an understanding that was not quite a proposal of marriage but perhaps an agreement of a proposal that might follow. She blushed as this was the first time he had declared his attachment to her. She was overjoyed at this but still unsure of her relationship with him.

"Why Robert, these promises you ask of me are almost a proposal! If I accept, does this mean you will complete the proposal next July?"

"Anne, you understand I am a navy man. My career depends on my masters at the Admiralty. My captain's role will be all-consuming in the next twelve months. By next July I will be free. We will find out if you would wait and join me at Fintelton next year!"

The smile slowly disappeared, but happiness remained on his face. Anne could see that there was much on Robert's mind, but he appeared very content just now. She thought, 'I will look at you now and remember your smile till next July.'

"Then, you will come?" Robert could see in her softening beautiful blue eyes that she would come.

"Yes. I will come! In July 1827!"

Thomas walked across with a large ball in his hand. "Come on, you two. Enough sipping beer. It's time we exhausted William, so he sleeps tonight."

At the Turner Bakery Guildford …

Jonathan Turner sat in the bakery office and poured over the figures. Sales growth continued, his bakery now working at one hundred per cent capacity. Of necessity, one of the pastry ovens would be used as a bread oven to keep up with demand. Jonathan was quite pleased with the increase in cash flow but still was confused about why sales were so far up.

Jeb came in and asked, "Mr Turner, may I go through the order sheets for tomorrow, please?"

"Jeb, if I had finished them, it would be a pleasure. Unfortunately, I am not as fast as Anne. I will need another two hours before I complete them. She must be a whiz, that girl. I'm not sure how she does it so quickly each morning."

"She is clever. Might I work through the orders, Mr Turner? I have done it before. It's just that it will be holding up the prepping if we don't have them soon!"

"Thank you, Jeb – I did not realise you understood the system. Take a seat and join me. I'll continue with the other figures."

The two of them toiled at their desks for the next hour without even sharing a comment. Jeb finished first and lifted his head. "That is the orders complete, Mr Turner. Now I'll start the prepping for tomorrow in the bakery."

Jonathan Turner suddenly realised Jeb had spoken. He looked up as he was walking out the door. "Jeb! Thanks for that. Tomorrow let's talk. I want your advice on a few things."

"Pleasure, Mr Turner."

Jonathan was surprised that Jeb had finished the orders so quickly. There must be a trick that only Anne and Jeb knew. 'I must find out how they complete that so quickly,' he thought. Jonathan spent another two hours going through the figures. He did find one difference in the trends. In the last two weeks, the supply of bread to the Chilworth gunpowder factory was steadily growing. Perhaps they were no longer baking their bread and using his bakery as a supplier, or maybe the owners were increasing staff. He would visit the facility soon and see the manager.

Jonathan Turner decided it was time for lunch. Several of the staff were closing the bakery for the day. Jeb was in the store, checking the stocks for the next morning's bake. Jonathan gathered a couple of loaves of bread and a bag of pastries and set off. The town was buzzing with people cramming the High Street. Shoppers filled the various retail outlets, and as it was lunchtime, the coffee houses and alehouses were full. He smiled as he saw the extent of business going on in the town. 'Good for Guilford and good for business,' he thought.

On arriving home, he was met by Eleanora, waving a message in her hand. She seemed very excited. "Jonathan, a rider delivered a message this morning. Thomas and Marion have announced their engagement!"

"What!"

This news took Jonathan by surprise.

"Let me see that. I can't believe Thomas would announce that without telling us first."

Eleanora was excited, "Jon, all I can say is good on him! He has done it himself and has found himself a wife. He is twenty-three, and I think we could have expected this after what we saw during the McPherson's visit. I think it is grand. Marion will be an excellent wife."

Jonathan stood there reading the letter and taking in Eleanora's comments.

"It is from Hamish McPherson – he says he thought he should write as soon as they announced it. He was sure we would be disappointed at not being there. The letter was sent by express late on Friday night. He sends us his hearty congratulations and may visit possibly next Thursday.

Hamish is leaving London on Tuesday morning. He has business in Guildford and asks if he might join us for dinner on Wednesday evening. He apologises again that the announcement was sudden but says he will explain the details on Wednesday. As a side note, Hamish mentions that Neville Bassington will be spending this weekend with Bethany and the Upton's at Woking. He says that we may expect Neville on his return journey on Sunday afternoon."

"Jon, it is all so wonderful. Like a dream come true. We will see Neville and perhaps Bethany this weekend. Thomas, Anne, and William will return on Thursday so that we will hear all their news. Thank goodness Aggie is assisting Mrs Jennings now – our lives are becoming very busy with the comings and goings of all these young people."

"I think we need a larger home, Eleanora. It would be an advantage if we could offer some of these people accommodation. But I am as amazed at the news as you are. First Neville and Bethany and now Thomas and Marion. Such excitement we have not seen in a long time!"

Chapter 11

Hamish McPherson arrived in Guildford late on Wednesday afternoon. He spent some time with his attorneys before joining the Turners for dinner. The occasion was full of excitement for Eleanora, with two of her children soon to be married. The conversation ebbed and flowed between the engagement, what happened during the children's stay with the McPhersons and how Marjorie enjoyed having William there.

Once dinner was over, the two men adjourned with a bottle of port, sitting down together in Jonathan's study for a quiet discussion on business plans.

"I see that Eleanora is most excited, as we are Jonathan, about the weddings. Once you have visited the Bassingtons in London, you must come and stay with us at Greenwich. Not fair that young people should have all the fun, eh?"

"That is kind of you, Hamish. We will be there the first weekend in September, so would Monday and Tuesday be a good time?"

"Certainly, Jonathan, I shall put it in my diary, and we shall do a tour of the brewery."

"Now, speaking of breweries, Hamish, I understand someone acquired a couple of acres on the south side of the river for a construction site. Would this be associated with yourself?"

"Jonathan, that was part of why I came today. I have been planning the expansion of my business for the last couple of years. There is a lot of synergy between your business and mine. People will always need food and drink, which occurs at least three times a day. So, your bread will never go out of fashion. Neither will my beer. The question is, how do we expand our marketplace?

The population is increasing rapidly in England – far faster than in Scotland. So, I am here where the market is growing. There are ten sites across southern England where I shall build or purchase pubs. I would like you as an investor in this project. Your part will be the production of bread, pastries and biscuits. My role will be the production of beer. Now the most significant obstacle standing in our way at present is distribution. Transport!

I propose that we need breweries and bakeries near the population growth centres! Probably more bakeries than breweries as my product has a longer shelf life."

"I agree. There is no other transport than canal barge, wagon, or coach. I have thought about this same problem for some time, and a fast cart can solve it for a distance of fifteen miles. Once beyond this, you need a horse change, which means a stable."

"Yes, that's right, Jonathan, but remember the pub at Epsom will be established soon, and there is also Richards at Ewell. If we have a stable at Epsom, we could map out a circumference of, say, twenty miles around either Ewell or Epsom. That would reach London."

"Ewell is eighteen miles from London and then from Ewell..." Jonathan scratched his head. "I would say Guildford would be another twenty miles!"

"You see what I mean? We can open the London market with a cart or coach and stables halfway. Turner's bread might become a household name!"

Jonathan sat there thinking – this would be a bold move. He now understood why the contract with Richard at Ewell was so important. With the developments that would follow, the investment in Epsom should be very sound.

Hamish took another sip of port and smiled gently at Jonathan. "A long-term strategy always pays off, Jonathan. I have three pubs already that I deal with in London. My aim is for twenty-five in the next three or four years. What would the supply of twenty-five pubs with fresh bread and extras do for your sales?"

Jonathan quickly did a calculation in his head. "It would mean at least another thousand pounds a week, Hamish. That is just for the bread, and there would be more for the pastries and biscuits. I see what you mean."

Hamish nodded and went on, "The fast carts will do for the early stage, but in time you need a plan for a bakery somewhere in London. When you visit, we might inspect a few sites within easy distance of the pubs I am targeting. Once the cash flow starts from the pub in Epsom, we can talk about finance. Until then, we plan for fast carts."

Hamish poured another glass of port for Jonathan, who sat back in his chair while his mind counted the money. Hamish McPherson knew he had convinced Jonathan, and now was the time to approach him about Thomas.

"Jonathan, you are building a steam-driven mill for a good reason. In May of this year, I watched an extraordinary event, a carriage powered by a new engine, driven up Shooters Hill carrying two people[12]. No horses required! Also, last September, I went down from Edinburgh to Darlington

---

[12] Samuel Brown, English engineer and inventor, demonstrated his internal combustion engine propelling a vehicle up Shooters Hill on 27 May 1826. Wikipedia.

and witnessed the opening of what they call a rail line[13]. A steam engine pulled the carts – there were almost six hundred people loaded on, and the train transported them to Stockton on Tees. Jonathan, it was incredible, and this is just the start. The fast carts or coaches pulled by horses will, in time, disappear, and trains and horseless carts will replace them. Mark my words – the steam engine will revolutionise the world. There will be trains between Guilford and London one day, and the travel time will be less than an hour. We must plan for this."

"Surely, it will never be as quick as an hour. If it were, I agree it would be a revolution."

Jonathan was amazed by the number of people transported by this steam engine thing.

"I will build my brewery over the next two years and employ a large work-force. It will be good for Guildford and create jobs. This investment will also assist your business. You are building a mill. We can share resources with mechanics and engineers. We can combine stables and carts for haulage. Jonathan, together our progress can be combined, taking great strides before our competitors understand our strategy."

Jonathan agreed, "Yes! Yes, we must stay ahead of them, ensuring we stay in business. Once I start milling, I expect much opposition from the smaller mills up and down the river. Do you recall what happened at the Albion Mill in London?[14] Being mindful of that outcome, I have been cautious about promoting the mill. It will only be a matter of time before the other mills realise they cannot compete on price. Then there is the price of corn. Over time, despite the corn laws, the landowners must see reason. The government must repeal the Corn Laws and reduce the price of grain."

"It's a pity we can't bring the corn in from France, which would cut our costs by twenty-five per cent. Barley is particularly cheap over there!" Hamish was thinking aloud.

"I wouldn't dwell on that. The Whigs and landholders maintain the corn laws for their benefit and ignore the people of England. It's criminal when you think that people are starving in the northern cities. I fear that it may end in revolution."

"When will the Mill commence operations, Jonathan?"

---

[13] The Stockton to Darlington Railway was opened on27 September 1825, with one locomotive hauling wagons carrying between 450 and 600 people. The railway line was surveyed and built by George Stephenson. Wikipedia.

[14] The Albion Mills, Southwark, London was completed in 1786 and was one of the first steam powered flour mills in England. It was highly efficient for the time, with local mills closing, unable to match its productivity and costs. It was gutted by fire in 1791. The cause of the fire was unknown. However, resentment against the changes being created by the advent of steam power, low wages, and the social effects of the industrial revolution in large cities such as London may have influenced the culprits. Wikipedia.

"I'm hoping for final testing in November and then have the mill in full operation from the start of the new year."

"So, soon! An exciting time for you?"

"It is! We will be installing the boiler and gears next month."

"Jonathan, we must talk about Thomas. I took him on a tour of the Woolwich brewery, and he expressed much interest in the process. You understand I am looking for good people?"

Jonathan sat forward. He immediately knew what was coming, "Hamish, presently Thomas is my right-hand man. I cannot do without him, and he will probably inherit the business."

Hamish sat back and took a sip of port. "Jonathan, he wants to become a brewer!"

Jonathan was stunned. Thomas must have discussed this in detail with Hamish – who knew what they had agreed?

"Johnathan, it will be around two years before the brewery is complete. In that time, could you take on a trainee manager and release Thomas say in six months or a year?"

Jonathan was not comfortable with this suggestion, but the comment suddenly reminded him of Eleanora's advice, 'Jonathan, Thomas may move on. Build a house of his own. Work somewhere else.' He calmed a bit – after all, with Hamish as a mentor, there would be benefits for them all.

"I think that could work, Hamish. Please, another glass of port? My nerves need steadying!"

Hamish poured him a full glass. They toasted Thomas's good fortune. Then Hamish said, "Jonathan, Thomas will develop far more skills and may run both businesses in time. He will be quite important in the future for both of us. Thomas will outgrow the brewery job, and we may put him in charge of wider operations."

Jonathan found merit in this suggestion. Moving from an awful dread that Thomas had deserted him to Thomas being an ally in developing the business long term. In a few minutes, Jonathan realised that he was not losing but gaining a valuable partner.

"Hamish, the idea of Thomas working for you has come as a surprise. But you have opened a new vision for my business. My business plans are parochial at best, and I now understand the reasons for the pub at Epsom. I started experimenting with steam power purely for productivity, but you have explained the changes steam power will make in our lives. It is frightening but also exciting. I agree that we will miss a huge opportunity if we do not start planning now. Thomas has my blessing for his move, but you must assure me that our companies will work together. I will be relying on you heavily in this expansion, so I must have your commitment."

"Jonathan, you have my commitment. After all, our bond is by the marriage of our younger ones. We will see this through together. Along the way, there will be others who will join our company. Our first challenge will be establishing Epsom quickly. The cash flow from Epsom will allow the launching of other pubs."

"I agree, and some stables there for the cart operations until these so-called steam-powered trains appear. They run on plateways, do they?"

"No, they run on rails of cast iron. The carts have wheels with flanges that run on the inside of the rail. It is quite ingenious and will mean far greater speed as the engine develops. The Stockton engine reached speeds of fifteen miles an hour. Can you imagine a train taking six hundred people between London and Epsom in a little over an hour! I tell you, Jonathan, the race is on for these things – it will change the world!"

"Hamish, if they could lay a track from Guildford to London, we could finish the bake at four in the morning and have it fresh in London by six. The faster the engine, the earlier the delivery. Distance does not become a barrier anymore. But what about this horseless carriage you saw at Shooters Hill. Surely that would be even better than engines on rails?"

"It was most impressive, but the cost is prohibitive. It will never be viable. Imagine the panic if horses met one of these things on the road. No, they will never catch on! Never!"

"Perhaps not Hamish, but who knows what will happen in the future? But you're right; we need young people like Thomas exploring and integrating these ideas."

"I am glad we have settled this. I will tell Thomas that he may start with me next year and that between now and then, you will be training staff, so he is not missed." Then Hamish changed the subject. "Eleanora will be happy with this, Jonathan?"

"She will indeed. She was wondering how Thomas would be supporting a wife."

"They will be fine, and Marion will have an allowance, so she shall lack nothing. I will arrange the building of a manager's house in Guildford. Now tell me, Jonathan, how is Eleanora? I recall when we were here last time, she suffered a fall and being with a child, this could have been quite serious?"

"She is recovering well, and all the good news has excited her and given her new vigour."

Hamish thoughtfully took another sip of port, "That is good. Both you and I would not want her injured again, would we?" Hamish gave Jonathan a knowing glance.

"No, Hamish!" A cold shiver ran down Jonathan's spine. This man knew of his secret. But how? All the suppressed guilt he was managing re-emerged.

His mind flashed back to the incident. He saw himself raising his hand against his loving wife. It was an action he would never repeat, yet he was guilty. He could not forgive himself, the guilt making him shiver.

From the change in facial expression, Hamish detected that Jonathan understood that he was referring to his secret. He changed the subject.

"Jonathan, I must tell you about Marion's mother before you meet the prospective in-laws. Jennifer Steele's health has been failing for some time. Her memory has gone, and she does not recognise anyone. It is a sad situation with the disease slowly decreasing her strength. Alexander is Marion's father, and he is not coping well. He misses Jennifer now that she is in care. It is not sympathy that he needs but more like fellowship. Alex has three sons, and they have turned on him, wanting their mother cared for at home. He does not have the resources for this and could not cope with the emotional drain. You may find him hard and a little strange at times. If you allow some patience with him, you will find him good company. During your stay, we will have dinner with Alexander and his family. Thomas will enjoy meeting with them again."

"Thank you, Hamish, for forewarning me. It sounds like a sad situation. Will Jennifer be attending the dinner?"

"I don't think so, but she will probably attend the wedding. It may prove difficult as she can become violent at times. I believe they keep her sedated. Marion will want her there if possible."

"It would be good for Marion, but perhaps we will need a special place for her mother. Tomorrow, Hamish, I have booked an appointment for you and myself with Mayor Smith at eleven in the morning. Having Thomas as the brewery manager will certainly smooth your entry as a member of the Guild."

The revelation that Thomas would be the brewery manager in Guildford changed Jonathan's plan to assist Hamish with his Guild membership application. The Guild seldom accepted non-residents. With Thomas being a long-term resident, this should ease the task. As he sipped his port, he quietly reflected on how shrewd an operator Hamish McPherson was. Thomas's proposal convinced Jonathan that Thomas was head over heels in love with Marion. But was he? Perhaps Hamish signed Thomas up, knowing it would assist his entry into commerce at Guildford. He was unsure and required more reflection on this possibility, but time was the one thing he was short of these days.

The Return of the Young People to Guildford ...
Thomas, Anne, and William left Greenwich early on Thursday morning as Anne insisted they finish the journey in one day. Their departure planned for Wednesday was delayed, placating Marion and Mrs McPherson, who

insisted they remain an additional day. Anne was relieved, keen on avoiding James McPherson, soon due. The farewells were long and sorrowful, with Marion begging Thomas for another visit, he willing to fulfil her request. Mrs McPherson shared kisses and hugs, and William cuddled the dogs who rushed around him with much tail wagging and licking.

Mrs McPherson made a point of taking Anne aside and giving her a special hug and some more words of advice. "Anne, Marion thinks of you as a sister now, so you will always be welcome here. Remember, Dear, do not hurry into any relationship with some young man. You are young and free, and there is plenty of time yet. What a pity James did not arrive earlier. He will be here tonight and disappointed that you are gone."

Anne sighed with an understanding smile and said, "Thank you, Mrs McPherson. You have been most kind!"

Standing beside Nanny Jones, William felt sad about leaving Red Socks and Boiler but then remembered Snups and grinned as he imagined how excited the dog would be at their reunion. He took a breath and, in a big voice, said, "I am sorry for knocking you out, Nanny, but it was an accident. It seems I come from a family that has accidents. They turn out all right in the end, though. My father accidentally hit my mother, but she has recovered now. Just like you. Thank you for being my friend while we were here."

Nanny Jones was quite surprised by the comment, "I have enjoyed your company, William. I hope we see you again soon. Be good on the trip and do all those drawings I have made for you. Anne will write and tell me your progress once you are home."

William smiled. He had no intention of doing drawings – he would be watching the scenery outside the coach window. He shook her hand and bounded into the coach.

With that, the others boarded. There was much waving as the coach rounded the corner, and then the McPhersons were gone. Anne leaned back against the seat and gave a long deep breath of relief. She smiled at Thomas and said, "I am very pleased for you, Thomas, but I am thankful we will be home soon."

William chirped up, "I will miss Red Socks and Boiler, but Snups will be excited and Mother and Father!"

"Perhaps Mother but not Father!" Thomas thought as he wondered how he would explain his decision to become a brewer.

The carriage quickly exited Greenwich and progressed along Queens Road and London. Throughout the day, each of them shut their eyes, even William! Anne imagined standing alongside Captain South on the quarter-deck, wind in their hair, the sea spray from the bow and the shouts of the crew as they handled the sails above, their ship ploughing out into the Atlantic. William dreamed he was hanging from the rigging, bandana on his head, sword in one hand, waving it fiercely at the pirates they were chasing. Thomas shut his eyes and saw himself tasting a batch of his own brewed beer – it tasted good. He woke in a start, feeling thirsty.

Despite protests from William about seeing Uncle Richard, they stopped for a late lunch at Epsom and changed the horses. They avoided Ewell, sure that visiting Uncle Richard's family would involve a long delay – time they could not afford. Finally, at about seven in the evening, the coach headed into Guildford, down High Street and pulled up outside the Turner house.

William jumped from the carriage, and as the front door burst open and his mother came out, he flew into her welcoming arms.

"Mother, Mother, I saw a real sailing ship. It was huge!" William closed his eyes as he felt the warmth and love of his mother.

"My little boy, I have missed you so much!" She kissed him on the cheek and gave him another hug. Jonathan Turner patted his son on the back, then walked down the stairs and assisted Anne with her cases. Thomas approached his father, and they shook hands.

"Congratulations, Thomas. We are pleased for you and Marion."

"Thank you, Father. How did you hear? I was sorry you and mother were not there when Mr McPherson made the announcement, but I thought perhaps Marion could come and stay, and we would have a special dinner here and announce it again."

"Splendid Thomas! Now go and greet your mother. It has given her a new lease on life."

Anne kissed Jonathan, "It is good to be home, Father. I was surprised by how large London was and majestic the navy ships were. But I did miss you all!"

"We missed you, Anne. You must explain how you do those figures each day so quickly. I struggled with them while you were away. I am glad you have returned. The figures are all yours now."

Anne beamed – this was a lovely greeting, and she felt their relationship was closer now than for a long time. He seemed changed, and she liked it. She bounded up the stairs, carrying a bag in each hand and hugged her mother, "Mother, there is so much to tell."

"Please tell me all, and I will tell you our news. Welcome home, darling. So much news and Beth will return home on Saturday afternoon. The Uptons have hired a new governess that took over while Beth was here. We shall all be together again! I think Neville is coming as well."

It was an evening of stories and excitement as they shared the tales of London. Thomas and William were in bed by eight o'clock as William was exhausted and some urgent work demanded Thomas at the bakery early the following day. Jonathan left Anne alone with her mother in the parlour and tackled the paperwork on his desk.

"Now Anne, from what you have said, you saw Robert twice, or was it three times? What a coincidence. Was he well?"

"I know what you are asking, Mother! Yes, he was well, and we had many talks. He is a wonderful young man, and I enjoyed meeting his Captain and the Admiral. The dinners were a great surprise, and I have never met so many people of such high rank. I am sure Robert likes me a lot, but at times it is hard understanding his thinking. Sometimes, he seems miles away."

"And what about you, Anne, do you like him?"

"I love him so much, Mother. If he asked, I would fall into his arms and never leave him. But there is some problem. I am unsure of what it is. But he said we were both young and should meet again next year. He plans to meet at Fintelton Manor next July with Bethany and Neville as chaperones. Robert seems very worried about his family and how they meet me."

"Anne, I think I understand the problem. You see, he is the son of an aristocrat. Even though he is the second son and will not inherit the estate, his family will still expect a marriage of advantage for him. That means a young lady with breeding and money. Robert has planned a slow introduction so his parents become familiar with you before showing his hand."

"But mother, Robert is not like that. He is practical, like us. There is no display of the pride that aristocrats have. He likes me as a person. I am sure he will marry someone he loves and not for money. He is doing very well in the navy, so he will have the freedom of marrying whom he likes."

"I am not sure about that, my Dear. The sacrifice forced upon Robert may be significant if he marries beneath his family's expectations. I am sure he loves his family and desires their continuing support. Mind you, plenty of men marry for money and then have a mistress they love."

Anne was not pleased with her mother's comment. "Mother, I will never be a mistress!"

"I would not suggest that, and I am glad you are totally against it. The consideration of your position is quite correct. You are a gentleman's daughter, and you shall have a gentleman for your husband."

Anne relaxed, glad that she had misunderstood her mother. She sighed, "I miss him already!"

Eleanora could see that Anne was madly in love with this young man, Robert, and there would be no happiness for her until he settled it. What concerned her was whether Robert felt for Anne or not. He would not be the first aristocrat who misused a young lady. She was glad that Bethany's wedding was coming up, giving Anne a different outlet.

"Neville and Beth were here last Sunday afternoon. They will be married soon after mid-October. The ceremony will be here in Guildford and the reception at the Fox and Hound. It will be a fine wedding, Anne, and I would expect that Bethany will want you as a bridesmaid."

"I was wondering when the wedding would be. Robert is the best man!"

"They must be close those two, Anne?"

"Yes, they served together for many years. Robert also seems very friendly with Captain Foster, who joined us for dinner one night. I think it is likely that it will be a large guest list. Perhaps father will serve Turner's bread and water; otherwise, father will go broke."

They laughed and talked about the preparations, dresses, and guests. Finally, Anne said, "Mother, at times, while staying at the McPherson's house, I felt as if they were manipulating us. I was uneasy, but then perhaps I imagined it."

While Anne spoke, Jonathan Turner entered the room and sat down. He heard the comment but said nothing.

Eleanora being quite surprised, inquired, "How did you arrive at this conclusion, Anne?"

"Thomas and Marion announced their engagement so quickly. It seemed prearranged! Then, later, Mrs McPherson started giving me marital advice and then described her son James, who was arriving from Scotland today. It appeared as if she was matchmaking."

Jonathan became interested, "And did this, James appear?"

"No, we left before he arrived."

Jonathan sat there, thinking while the women talked about the McPherson family and their achievements. Jonathan remained worried about Hamish's comment on Eleanora's health. Somewhere there was a source feeding him information.

"Anne, who looked after William while you were there?"

"He was with Nanny Jones and me most of the time."

Eleanora looked up, "Nanny Jones?"

"Yes, Mrs McPherson hired a nanny for William. At her age, she felt the need for assistance. It was a good idea. The Nanny was a nice young lady and suited William well. They played games in the bedroom before bed each night. It pleased me, as I was left free for the evenings."

Jonathan thought about this and then asked, "Did William become friendly with anyone else?"

"Besides Mr and Mrs McPherson, no. They did have a couple of dogs, Red Socks and Boiler, that he played with. They became great friends."

Jonathan agreed that this was harmless enough. Strangely he also shared Anne's feelings. He deferred any discussion on the subject as he desired this union between Thomas and Marion. The business benefits flowing from it would be significant for both families.

"Look at the hour! I think you should be in bed, my Dear."

Eleanora was becoming quite tired, but she was enjoying the reunion with Anne immensely. "Just a few more minutes Jonathan and then I will go up. I need a little more time with Anne." Jonathan was tired himself and wished them a good night.

"I am glad you are back, Anne and that you will take over the figures again tomorrow. Sleep well. I will talk with you at the bakery in the morning."

Anne grinned at him, "Perhaps Father, if you pay me a little more?"

"Yes, I probably should, but remember, I am also saving for your dowry!" They laughed. He kissed them both, excused himself and trudged off upstairs.

"Now, mother, tell me about your health and the baby?"

In the morning ...

William woke early, noticing Thomas was gone, and Simeon was sleeping peacefully. Snups wagged his tail as soon as he saw movement on William's bed.

"Good boy, Snups! You would love Red Socks and Boiler."

Snups rushed and jumped on William, giving him a lick on the cheek in exchange for a rub around the ears. "Would you like a walk, boy?" Snups knew what this meant and ran to the door and back. "Ok! Wait till I find my clothes."

In the kitchen, William found his father having breakfast. The enticing aromas of eggs and sausage garnished with parsley from the garden tempted him. William desired a run with Snups but now had second thoughts. Jonathan Turner looked closely at him.

"Where are you going, William?"

"Just taking Snups for a walk, Father."

"That is good, but have some breakfast with me before you go. Aggie, would you serve William some sausage and eggs, please? A sausage for Snups as well, please, Aggie!"

William licked his lips. He was a growing lad, and food was always welcome.

Aggie nodded and darted off for the eggs. The sausages were already cooked and stored in a bain-marie on a side table in the kitchen. While Aggie readied William's breakfast, Jonathan made the most of his opportunity.

"So, what did you do while in Greenwich, William? It looks like you have grown a bit taller."

"We saw the navy ships and went on a picnic at a castle. There was shopping in London and walking along the riverbank. The Wey is a far cleaner river than the Thames, Father."

"Yes, it is! The Thames is dirty because of all the people who live there. So, when you were at home, what did you do?"

"I stayed most of the time with Nanny Jones. Most days, we went up onto the roof. They have a viewing platform up there with a telescope. Sometimes, we played pirates, and Nanny Jones would read pirate stories. I saw Robert and Neville there one night, and at the picnic, Robert had races with me. He can run so fast."

"Did anyone else do anything with you – Like Mr McPherson or Mrs McPherson?"

William swallowed his first egg and sausage and thought about this, "I didn't see much of Mr McPherson at all, but Mrs McPherson went with us on most of the London trips. She is funny and talks about everything. We did walk the dogs one day with Mr McPherson and Thomas, and Jenkins came as well. But Mr McPherson was slow and had trouble keeping up. I think he is older than he looks."

"Ah huh, and who is this Jenkins fellow?"

"He is the Butler and takes care of Red Socks and Boiler. He was nice – we were good friends."

"Hmm, Jenkins was the butler, eh! Did you go out with him with the dogs more than once?"

"Yes, we went out every morning for an hour walking them. The dogs are so fast, Father; they are Hungarian hunting hounds. You would love them. Jenkins told me about his childhood and how he always had dogs and much about his life in London."

"I see. Did this Jenkins fellow ask about our family William?"

"Yes, every day, he was so interested. We had lots of conversations. He asked all about bakeries and what we did. He asked about Guildford also, as he has never been here. He let me hold the dogs' leashes every day, and I let them loose for their runs."

"Thank you, William. When you finish your breakfast, you may walk Snups, but don't be too long. Sim will be glad of your company today."

William cleaned his plate and said, 'Thank you, Father.' Then he dashed out with the dog, who carried a sausage in its mouth.

Jonathan Turner sat back in his chair and thought about Jenkins, the butler. Perhaps Anne was correct; there was more than coincidence involved here.

Aggie said, "Would you like more breakfast, Mr Turner?"

"No thanks, Aggie, that was ample, thank you."

"Mr Turner, pardon me, Sir, but I couldn't help overhearing the conversation with William. Sorry Sir, but it seems like this Jenkins fellow knows everything about this family now!"

"I think you're right, Aggie; I think you are right! I will be with Thomas at the bakery if I am needed."

"Yes, Mr Turner."

Jonathan Turner grabbed his coat and made his way down High Street towards the bakery. As he passed the corn market, he saw his bakery carts were already in place, and his bakery shops further down the street were opening. He walked on, thinking about what William might have told Jenkins. A skilled butler would easily milk a young boy. At his age, William would blurt out information without thinking.

He walked on, nodding to the occasional acquaintance. The shopkeepers were arranging their displays for another busy day in this growing town. He also noticed a contingent of red uniformed soldiers down by the docks. They must have come up from the Chilworth powder factory. He wondered why the army was here in strength.

Anne's comment last night worried him, but he had limited time for discussion this morning. Walking towards the bakery entrance Mr Stanley Percival, one of the engineers installing the new mill boiler, appeared, waved, and walked over.

"Mr Turner, we must talk urgently. It is about the foundations for the boiler. One section needs a slight adjustment, and it affects the levels. Would you have time for an inspection? I need a quick decision so we don't delay today's work."

"Certainly, Mr Percival. Just let me drop my coat into the office, and I shall come straight down."

Jonathan knew today would be busy. His discussions with both Anne and Thomas must wait until tonight.

The Turner Household, Guildford ...

Clementine's voice boomed out instructions towards the boys at breakfast, ensuring they cleared their plates before finishing. She hated cleaning up after them. Madeline carefully managed Marcia, restricting the spreading of egg and sausage everywhere. Aggie was busy washing up the breakfast dishes and equipment in the scullery as Mrs Jennings returned with Mrs Turner's tray.

Seeing the housekeeper return, Aggie said with a loud voice, "Do you think Mrs Jennings that Mr Turner will hire a Nanny for Marcia? Perhaps the one that looked after William in Greenwich?"

"Aggie, why don't you ask him yourself? I'm sure he would be happy with your advice!" She laughed and made for the pantry to check what was needed. Clementine would often pick up items for the household after breakfast on her morning walk, taking the children to school.

Putting down her list Mrs Jennings responded to a knock at the front door.

List in hand, she walked along the hallway and opened the front door. A rider presented a special delivery note for Mrs Eleanora Turner. She thanked the rider and gave him a penny for his troubles. He winked and was off.

Mrs Jennings looked closely at the letter and saw it was from Mrs Marjorie McPherson. As it arrived by a rider, she assumed it was important and took it straight upstairs. Eleanora Turner was still asleep. In the last few weeks, she suffered again from a lack of energy, and the tiredness increased each day. It was now usual that she rose late in the morning.

Gently covering Mrs Turner's arms and shoulders, Mrs Jennings ensured she would remain warm. Despite the sun shining in the window from the east, the room was colder than usual this morning; it seemed that autumn might be coming a bit early this year. Mrs Jennings left the note on Mrs Turner's bedside table. She noticed it was dated yesterday when the children left the McPhersons in Greenwich. Mrs Jennings was now in her twentieth year of service with the Turner family and understood this might indicate a visit.

She caught Clementine's eye on entering the kitchen, "Don't worry about the store this morning. I feel we may be having visitors soon, so that I might give you a larger order later. You may take Simeon, William, and Madeline for a walk when you go."

Clementine nodded in agreement and walked off quickly, eager to finish some chores before the errand later.

At the Turner Bakery ...
Jonathan Turner finished with the builders around nine thirty and was now in his office. He found Anne sitting at her desk, sorting out all the paperwork. There was no one else in the office, so a confidential talk was possible.

"Anne, you will recall last night you mentioned being uncomfortable at the McPhersons. Would you tell me more about this?"

"It's just that everything seemed arranged in advance. Even Thomas agreed it was Marion proposing to him rather than Thomas popping the question. Also, Mr McPherson offered him a job as a brewer the day after – why would he do that? Thomas knows nothing about brewing. He must have considered and decided this beforehand!"

Jonathan listened carefully. He knew from experience that Anne's perception was better than most realised. She sensed danger when others ignored it. Considering this, he was unsure if the threat was real or if they were both imagining something sinister?

"Father, I know you have made business arrangements with Mr McPherson, but all I would say is be careful. I feel uneasy about the relationship!"

"Did William spend much time with this butler, Jenkins?"

"Yes, every day they were walking the dogs. They seemed good friends by the end of our stay. Jenkins was out on the front steps as we left, waving goodbye. I know I am not familiar with servants, but I thought it strange that the butler waved goodbye."

"Perhaps it is the way that the McPhersons treat their staff. I hear they are very fair to them. They make sure all the children of their staff have good schooling. Certainly, it is a generous attitude for today. They seem such good people, but yes, I, too, at times, have my doubts. However, there is a hefty investment made in this relationship, so we must take care not to judge them too quickly."

Anne smiled in agreement and waited for her father's next words. There was nothing further, and she saw his thoughts were now elsewhere. She recommenced working on the figures and smiled as she saw the sales were still increasing. If this continued, they would be rich indeed.

Thomas spent the remainder of the day rearranging the bakery supervisors. Jeb Hiscock was thankful for his promotion. Thomas worked with the new bakery manager on the other appointments.

Later in the afternoon, Jonathan explained the importance of starting this transition. Thomas agreed, understanding how his role was already changing.

"This must work for us, Thomas! With our business sharing resources with McPherson Brewing, we may achieve some significant cost savings. Also, the access they allow you will help us understand their operations. I am sure James McPherson will be doing the same thing.

Meet with James soon and find out where he sits in their network. I am sure Hamish will only trust people he knows well, so I want you in Greenwich, developing that trust relationship."

Thomas listened and asked, "So I should spend more time there? But what about training Jeb?"

"Yes, I want you in Greenwich. I only gave Jeb the job because I already knew he was across everything. He can easily handle the bakery. What we need is an engineer for the mill. The enquiries will be both my job and yours until we can find someone. There is an engineering firm in London that specialise in breweries. Our new mill will be using similar machines so that they might find us an engineer. I have a few other options but let us wait and see - we have a bit of time up our sleeves. A discussion with Hamish about engineers will not hurt either."

"Perhaps I might find an engineer for you in Greenwich or Woolwich. Marion's father has in-depth knowledge in this area. We should consult him as well."

"Only if you consider it wise!"

"This will suit me well, father, as it means more time spent with Marion before we marry. One of my concerns is if Marion will adapt to living in

Guildford. It will be quite a change for her."

"There is an easy answer, my boy. Children!"

"Ah……...!" Thomas was more than willing with this proposal.

"Now, Thomas, there is another issue. It seems the McPhersons are confident in you and want you with Marion. However, the comments from Anne have disturbed me. I am investing a lot of money in these ventures, so I need more information on what they do in Scotland.

Befriending Hamish's son James is now a priority. Do not go in too hard; take it easily. Invite him out drinking and buy the drinks. Let him get tipsy and then quietly ask some interesting questions. You know the process – you have seen me do it enough. Now it is your turn.

I enjoy you being here, son, but I now think it would be advisable if you were beside Marion in Greenwich very soon."

"I agree, Father. I have been wondering how they have made so much money. It will be a pleasure, and I shall do it quietly. You shall have your information before you know it."

"Thank you, Thomas!" Jonathan chose his next words carefully.

"Thomas, one final piece of advice. When you return, Mrs McPherson will set a date for the wedding. Encourage her on a date as soon as possible. You see, women can be a bit fickle. It may be time that you cemented the relationship. I am sure you know what I mean. Find a time and place where the family or servants will not discover you. It will be difficult to unwind the marriage once this is complete."

Thomas looked at his father with a puzzled expression. Then he said, "Father, I am marrying Marion because I love her. There is no need for this suggestion. I would prefer doing this the right way!"

"Thomas, I applaud your sentiments and agree with you. However, I think you may find the suggestion may come from Marion sooner than you think. All I am saying is that if it does, play the game! There is much at stake here. Let this remain between you and me. Please come and discuss it with me in the future if there is a need. Whichever way, I will be happy for you both."

Thomas stood up, "I will keep it in mind, Father!"

At the Turner Household ...

Eleanora sat in the parlour with a cup of afternoon tea as Jonathan arrived home.

"Jonathan, this note arrived by express from Marjorie McPherson after you left this morning. She advises that Neville will visit the Uptons in Woking on Friday evening and return with Bethany here on Saturday. Marjorie asks if it would be acceptable if Marion came with them and then stayed for a week. They will arrange a coach for her return the following Sunday. She says Marion misses Thomas something terrible, and the week here would be most beneficial. There is no need for a reply as Marjorie has made the arrangements, and Neville will drop her off on Friday afternoon. Neville will be staying at the Fox and Hound."

Jonathan was surprised but not upset. After all, they would soon be in-laws and Marion their daughter-in-law.

"It seems Marjorie decided for us. We must send an express post back confirming the arrangements. Of course, she will arrive this afternoon, so the message will not arrive in time, but it will comfort Marjorie that the arrangements are well received. I wonder who else travels with Neville as it says 'them'?"

"Perhaps it is Robert! But say nothing Jonathan; otherwise, Anne will be most disappointed if he does not arrive."

Eleanora was pleased with this but then became alarmed, "Where will we put Marion? She will need a room. Perhaps we could put her in with Anne. It will only be a week. But Jonathan, this may happen again in the future."

"Yes – we need a bigger house until we can marry some of them off. I think I will get Robinson in and have an extra two bedrooms put in on the first floor. There is plenty of room out the back, and it will allow for additional servant rooms underneath. I will call on him as I visit the post office. Would you write the letter, Dear? Then I will be off?"

"Thomas will be so happy that Marion is coming. This time I will become better acquainted as well. Perhaps they will set the wedding date."

"The visit may prove very timely, indeed! Eleanora, I think you may find Marjorie has a date in mind already, and it will only require our confirmation! I suspect the McPhersons are excellent at planning!" Recalling the conversation just past, he considered the possibility of a return visit for Thomas.

"My Dear, given it is only a short time, perhaps I could move back with you for the week, and Marion might have the guest room. You have my word that I am a reformed man."

"I will take you on your word Jonathan, but only for a week and on the condition that you bring me an early morning cup of tea each day. But only for a week, Jonathan – I want those extra bedrooms built soon."

Jonathan was happy with that, "I will let you talk with the staff and arrange the bedding. Now the note, and I will be off."

Once Jonathan was armed with the note, he headed for the kitchen. "Mrs Jennings, from Sunday onwards, I would like an early morning cup of tea for Mrs Turner, please, at seven. Make that two please, as I will join her."

Walking out into the bright August sun, he noticed a chilly breeze blowing from the west. Pulling on his coat, he strode off towards the builder's office. Indeed, the last two weeks saw events that were changing their lives. This next week coming might prove even more eventful.

"Marion, Dear! Let us have a little talk before Neville's carriage arrives."

"Yes, Mrs McPherson, I am excited about staying with the Turners."

"Marion, you are now officially engaged, and we are pleased about this. As you know, Mr McPherson has become a business partner with Mr Turner. There is a lot of investment committed here, and you will benefit greatly." Marjorie then spoke slowly, making it clear.

"It is important that this marriage goes ahead. Thomas is a good catch, Marion, and he must be kept secure!"

"Why Mrs McPherson, Thomas and I are so in love. Why should I lose him now?"

"Sometimes these things can go wrong - not by your own doing, but who knows, things happen."

"Oh!"

"There will probably be tender moments while you are at Guildford, and opportunities might arise when you are alone together. Perhaps even the chance of cementing the alliance. You understand what I mean, Dear?"

Marion was not slow on romance and was immediately aware of her aunty's suggestion, "I thought we should wait until after the wedding. Wouldn't this be the proper way?"

"Yes, Dear – that's correct. But once you have cemented the alliance, there will be no going back, will there? And we do so want the two families connected. No one will be disappointed, as they will not know, will they?'

Marion was becoming a bit uncomfortable with this situation. She nodded obediently in agreement.

"Good girl! I will confirm the wedding date with the Archdeacon for the third weekend in November. If we hold off further, we may miss out on booking until after Christmas. It will be such a wonderful occasion. Now off you go and get ready. That's a good girl."

Marion was amazed her Auntie would ever suggest such a thing. Was this what happened when people married, and business arrangements were involved? Relieved that she would spend the next week in Guildford, she set her mind at rest about her aunt's comments. After all, Thomas was the one with who she would be spending the rest of her life, not Marjorie McPherson.

Chapter 12

The carriage pulled up at around six-thirty on Friday evening. Recognising Robert's carriage, Anne assumed he must have insisted on Neville using it again. That was Robert. He would do anything for a close friend – and close friends Robert and Neville were. She wished Robert was here too.

Johnathan and the family excitedly descended the steps and welcomed their visitors. There was joy on Marion's face as she hugged Thomas and then the others.

Neville, gentle and as friendly as ever, promising they would be back tomorrow early in the afternoon with Bethany and her belongings, "We have Robert's carriage and some footmen, so Bethany should be most pleased with the assistance."

Anne saw William peering into the carriage with a confused expression. She thought it strange that William was not already in the coach investigating. Perhaps he was worried about a reaction from his father.

"What do you mean 'We', Neville?" Anne asked.

"I have a surprise guest with me, but he fell asleep just short of Guildford."

Anne rushed around and climbed into the carriage. On the rear seat, fast asleep and covered in a blanket, was Robert with a very peaceful expression on his face. Anne sat across from him and gazed upon the man she loved without him knowing. Quietly she backed out of the coach and smiled at Neville.

"I thought you would be happily surprised by this. It was a big week for Robert as he takes command of HMS *Restless* next Wednesday. We both worked Tuesday and Wednesday nights, setting off early Thursday afternoon. We picked up Marion in Greenwich and spent the night with Robert's uncle and aunt, Sir John and Lady Angela Philps, in Wimbledon. Robert and I will assist Beth with her packing and return tomorrow afternoon. On Monday morning, we head off for Portsmouth. There is paperwork for both of us at the fleet headquarters. If it is not too much trouble, Mr Turner, Robert and I will join you for dinner tomorrow and Sunday night. I must apologise for the lack of notice, but I assumed you would be pleased. If time permits, I would value your advice on property here in Guildford."

Jonathan Turner was not reluctant. "Neville, I would be most disappointed if you and Robert did not attend our house in the evenings. I apologise that I cannot offer you accommodation. We shall take pleasure in your visit. Come back as soon as you can!"

"Thank you, Sir! The accommodation is not a problem. We will be in my favourite room, down High Street here, at the Fox and Hound. I promise there will be no sleeping in the bath this time. Alas, given the time, we must depart for Woking now. Bethany awaits our arrival! We will return tomorrow afternoon early with your wonderful daughter."

Jonathan said, "Please convey my best regards to Reverend Upton, Sir." He waved them goodbye as the coach gently pulled away up the High Street.

Marion finally released Thomas and hugged Anne tightly, "Anne, Anne, Anne, I have missed you so much. Just think, we have a week of fun awaiting us. I must come and do some more work with you. Mr Turner, you won't mind if I help Anne, will you? I must not become a useless lady sitting around all the time. Anne has inspired me!"

"I think you will need permission from the Bakery Manager. But he may allow you. Eh, Thomas?" Jonathan turned and smiled at Thomas.

"It might be possible, Sir!" Thomas seemed as excited as Jonathan could remember.

Marion and Anne joined arms and danced up the stairs. They were both in relatively high spirits. Mrs Turner hugged them at the landing, and the conversations continued.

William lingered at the bottom of the stairs watching after the coach.

"Upstairs now, William, dinner will be soon. I'm sure Snups would enjoy a walk." William did not look up but slowly walked up the stairs. Jonathan noticed the unusual lack of energy in the boy.

On arriving at her room, Marion was thrilled, "Thomas. The room is lovely; I shall be comfortable here. I was not expecting a room of my own. Why sharing with Anne would have been quite adequate! Thank you, Mr Turner, this is so considerate!" Marion hugged Thomas, and they began talking softly.

Jonathan nodded and quietly withdrew. He enjoyed seeing them so comfortable together – it must be true love. Quite amazing.

Marion looked into Thomas's eyes and gently said, "Darling, we must marry soon. I am so lonely without you in Greenwich."

The comment moved Thomas as he, too, missed Marion. "As soon as I am in Greenwich again, we shall fix the date. I suspect Bethany and Neville will announce their wedding date tomorrow. Let us hope so!" As he held her close, her perfume aroused him. He wanted this girl now, but he knew this was not the time.

"Marion, you should unpack and come down before dinner, and we shall talk. I'm sure it was a long day in the coach?"

Marion relaxed and sat down on the bed, "Yes, I am tired. Perhaps one of the servants might attend me before dinner?"

"I'll have Aggie come up." With that, Thomas kissed her again and then excused himself.

Marion was pleased with the room, and she lay down, finding the bed very comfortable. Soon she was fast asleep. Around six, Aggie met Anne at the top of the stairs.

"No need, Aggie. I will attend Marion. Please, you continue with Mrs Jennings." Finding Marion fast asleep on the big double bed, Anne gently covered her up and left her for a little longer.

The house was strangely quiet. Anne softly walked down the hall and peeked into her mother's room, finding her fast asleep. She noticed that her mother had less energy today. Despite being pregnant, when a woman usually looked a picture of health, she was fading. Anne noticed that her breathing was not peaceful but strained. She must ask Neville about this tomorrow if the chance arose.

Moving out into the hallway, she listened for any noise from the boys' room above. All was quiet – then she remembered that Simeon, Clementine, Madeline, and William took Marcia as they walked Snups. They were probably playing pirates and other games. She prayed that William did not injure anyone. Taking hold of the railing, she considered the beautiful woodwork. It was reliable, firm and stable. This house was a refuge for her family from the outside world, where they all felt safe. She looked at the paintings of her grandfather and grandmother from both sides of the family and other relatives. The wall was a reminder of her family's history. As she slowly went down the stairs breathing in the tranquillity of her surroundings, she felt protected and secure. This home was what she knew and understood. Perhaps one day, her painting would be on the wall with her children around her.

With so much happening in the last few months, she relished the stability the house provided. She was glad that Robert needed more time. It would be a year before she visited his home – he was a planner! She was eager but knew there was a good reason for his planning. The Fintelton visit may be a turning point in her life – marriage would mean leaving her family. It would be a new life without any support. Would she have the strength for this? But there would also be her darling, Robert!

She heard the drifting voices of Aggie and Mrs Jennings coming up the stairwell, talking and laughing together as they prepared dinner. She smiled, thinking about the amount of work that went into cooking the family meals. Aggie fitted in well and made no complaints about the poor accommodation. Thankfully, the builders would soon finish the extension for the maids. It would be just in time, as her mother already required a lady's maid. Anne knew her mother would resist the assistance. It would drive her mad having a servant looking over her shoulder all the time – her mother prefered looking after herself.

Anne walked down the hallway towards the parlour, seeking her father and Thomas. On reaching the parlour, she found no one there but heard them in the study. Thomas and her father shared a whisky as they sat near Jonathan's desk. They both looked severe and in deep conversation.

"Find this information out if possible. We have invested heavily in this project, and I am not confident in proceeding further if the risk increases. We could be left with nothing if anything underhand goes on!" Jonathan seemed concerned but then looked up and saw Anne. He beckoned, and Anne moved across the room and took a seat.

Thomas took Anne's hand in his and gently said, 'We will investigate your concerns, Anne. Father and I discuss how we might gain more information about the McPhersons. I believe they are a blessing for us, but Father is concerned. I agree we should be cautious. Marion may assist us in this."

Anne was amazed – they were taking her concerns seriously! But what if they were right. What would then become of Marion and Thomas? Would she have spoiled their happiness forever?

"I'm not sure if I imagined it all or if it was real. It was a feeling that came over me when we were staying there. I may have been wrong!"

Jonathan smiled at her. He knew she was struggling with this issue. It may be an incorrect suspicion, but Jonathan trusted Anne's perception. If she was concerned, then it was worth investigating.

"Do not distress yourself, Anne. As a businessman, I must minimise the risk involved before we decide. I am sure the McPhersons are genuine. I know your concerns, so having Thomas attend Greenwich soon will benefit us. There will be no difficulties in having our attorneys make enquiries before we sign the contract. Let us hope Hamish is the blessing we imagine him to be."

Anne was relieved that Thomas and her father were thankful for her contribution. Then she remembered Marion.

"I must go up and wake Marion; she has fallen asleep. Mother too. I will attend them. Thomas, perhaps you would ask Mrs Jennings if dinner might be half an hour later." Thomas agreed, and Anne withdrew from their conversation.

Bethany Returns …

Neville, Robert, and Bethany returned early on Saturday afternoon. Anne was thrilled that her older sister and long-term confidant were home again. The prospect of much reflection together was appealing. Knowing also that Robert was coming, she spent much time dressing and arranging her hair. William came into her room as she finished her powders. As he stood beside her, she noticed that he seemed listless.

He said, "You are beautiful, Anne, much more than anyone else. When I grow up, will I meet someone like you?"

Anne was surprised firstly by his statement and then his question. "Why William, I'm sure one day when you grow up, there will be the most beautiful lady for you."

He quietly said, "I thought Olivia was beautiful, but now she is dead! Where do people go when they are dead?"

"Why I believe that they live with God forever in heaven. Just as Reverend Taggart tells us, they are very safe there. Now William, why these sad thoughts?"

William shrugged his shoulders and bent over with his hands on Anne's bedroom table. She kept working on her face. William then lay down on the floor. For a boy who was always super active, Anne realised something was wrong. She leaned down and stroked his hair. William just lay there with his eyes open.

"William, what is the matter? Are you not feeling well?"

William closed his eyes and did not answer.

Since Eleanora Turner's health failed, Anne was almost the default mother. Being the eldest girl in the house, she naturally took on the role. With her perceptive skills, Anne quickly spotted any developing symptoms in the children. Looking down at William, she was becoming concerned.

She knelt beside him and tried sitting him up. He was very listless and unsteady.

He murmured, "I'm hot."

Anne felt his brow and immediately knew he suffered from a sweaty fever.

"I think we might lie you down for a while, and I will fetch a wet cloth for your forehead." Anne took the boy slowly upstairs and lay him on his bed. She opened the window, letting in some cooler air, and quickly retrieved a washer and pail of water from the kitchen. On returning, she found him fast asleep.

When she wiped his brow with the damp washer, it was then that she saw the rash on his neck. She gently lifted his shirt, finding no rash there. That was a relief. He seemed very warm when she felt his forehead – too warm even with a washer wiping his face.

Alarmed, Anne thought something was very wrong with William. William needed medical help. But the family Doctor was dead.

Then Clementine, in her earth-shattering voice, let out a cry from below, "The carriage is coming up the street!"

Anne looked at William – he was peacefully sleeping. She decided the closest medical help was now on that coach. She must summon Neville. Anne washed her face and hands, then bounded down the stairs and out the front door, making sure her hair was rearranged and straightened her dress. She joined the others as the carriage arrived.

Anne moved beside her mother, "Mother, William is not well. I think we need Neville quickly. He is asleep upstairs and has a rash on his neck."

Eleanora turned in alarm, "I must attend him at once!"

"No, Mother, he is sleeping, and Neville will deal with it. William may be contagious, and this may be dangerous in your condition. You should welcome our guests! I will take care of William."

Eleanora was reluctant and annoyed that Anne was so forceful. She swallowed her pride as she saw the wisdom in Anne's advice.

"Anne, remember that William is my son! Let me know what is wrong with him as soon as Neville has seen him."

Anne was surprised at the reprimand, "I am sorry, Mother! I meant no harm."

They both turned as the carriage pulled up.

Bethany was first out into the arms of her mother and father, then Neville, followed by a sheepish Robert. Anne flew down the steps and gave Robert a huge hug and a kiss. Robert was not upset by this at all. With Anne beside him, they approached her parents, where she made the introductions.

"Father, please may I introduce Sir Robert South."

Jonathan Turner was curious to meet this young man, "Sir Robert, you honour us with your visit. I have heard only great things mentioned about you."

"It is a pleasure, Mr and Mrs Turner." Robert gave a respectful nod of his head toward Eleanora. "It has been too long since I visited Guildford! Mr Turner, please call me Robert. I prefer that, Sir. I am not one for titles."

Eleanora Turner smiled and gave Robert a welcome kiss. She liked this young man and thought he would be a good match for Anne. He was intelligent, handsome, a quick thinker and very polite. Why he may even keep Anne on her toes, but she doubted this! Then after looking at him again and with a mother's intuition, she thought, 'Yes, he probably could match Anne's abilities if he was quick.' It was pleasing that he was here again, even if only for a short visit.

Jonathan Turner said, "I believe congratulations are in order. You now have a command I understand?"

"Yes! Yes, the commission came well before I expected it. I will be commanding the schooner, HMS *Restless*, and sail on Wednesday from Portsmouth. So, we must make the best of our time here, Mr Turner. Dinner, tonight with your family, will be most welcome, and I shall ensure that Neville is awake on time."

"Come in and have some tea, Robert."

"Thank you, Mr Turner. Please, let me assist with carrying some of Bethany's luggage upstairs with Neville, Sir, and then join you."

Jonathan Turner liked this young man – there was none of the aristocratic standoffishness. He was open and fitted in well. More impressive was his determined assistance with Beth's luggage. No wonder he was given a command so early.

As Robert spoke with her father, Anne moved around and hugged Neville and whispered in his ear, "Neville, please would you come and look at William before they unpack. He is complaining of a fever, and I have just found a rash on his neck."

Neville stood back and looked at Anne and saw the concern on her face. He realised that a fever could be severe and might need immediate attention. He retrieved his medical bag from the coach and followed Anne into the house after providing a quick explanation.

The remaining gentlemen followed Beth's instructions depositing her belongings as directed. Once unpacked, Robert dispatched the coach down High Street to the Fox and Hound stables.

At William's bedside, Neville knelt and examined the boy. There was a fever, and William was fast asleep, strange for an active boy like him. Neville pried open the mouth, turning William's head towards the window for an examination of the throat. Whatever the cause, it had inflamed the tonsils area and the surrounding skin. Neville asked for Anne's assistance in rolling William onto his side. On William's back, he found a blotchy red rash.

Neville carefully looked at his armpits and then his fingers and toes. He pulled out an instrument from his doctor's case, which surprised Anne. It was a glass cylinder around a foot long with a bulb at one end. He gently placed the bulb under William's armpit and sat back, watching the instrument.

Anne was curious, "What is that thing, Neville?"

"It is what we call a thermometer[15]. It measures a person's temperature. I picked this one up when we were in Holland last. The benefits of being a navy surgeon. They are not available in England yet, but I am sure they will soon appear. The normal body temperature is between 36.5 and 37.5 degrees Celsius. If the patient measures over 37.5 Celsius, you know they have a severe fever. We will know in ten minutes. Let me put that another way – I know he

---

[15] In 1714, the Dutch Scientist, Daniel Fahrenheit invented the first reliable thermometer using mercury. Wikipedia.

has a fever but is it a dangerous fever or not? The thermometer tells us the exact temperature. From the reading, it assists in giving a far more accurate diagnosis, which is helpful."

Anne nodded – she was amazed by this new looking instrument. She watched the black line extending as it edged up above the 37-degree mark.

After another five minutes, Neville removed the thermometer and washed it in the hand bowl nearby. He sat back and thought about the symptoms.

"He certainly has a sore throat and temperature. It is just above 37 degrees but not that far to be dangerous. Further than that, it is a bit unclear. I'm sure it is not measles as the rash is wrong. So, it may be scarlet fever. But if it is, we will not know for another two days. It may be a common sore throat – let's hope so. But I think it points more towards scarlet fever.

We need to isolate the room in case the fever is contagious. Sorry Anne, but as you have been attending to the boy, you're the nurse for the next few days. Wash your hands and face before you leave and return to this area. If convenient, Simeon and Thomas can sleep with us at the Fox and Hound. I will now go and brief the others. You should join me as he will probably sleep for the next few days. You can check him every few hours."

"Is there nothing you can give him to bring the fever down?'

"Unfortunately, not. The best we can do is keep William cool. Having that window open is a good idea as today is a bit cooler than the past week. Also, he needs a washer wiped over him regularly. Keep him drinking water regularly and give him some honey for the sore throat. Anne, you should sleep up here for the next few days as you are a close contact. Make sure you wash your hands thoroughly before you come down."

Neville left with his medical case, slowly walking downstairs. Anne sat and looked at William's fevered face. She wiped his brow again. 'These things never happen at the right time. Just when I was going to see Robert again!'

Dinner was a grand affair. The Turner's large family were well trained in organising sizeable gatherings.

Aggie, who contracted scarlet fever as a child, relieved Anne during dinner. Anne amicably accepted the offer as Aggie would have some resistance.

So, the family gathered with the adults having pre-dinner drinks while the younger children, Marcia, Madeline, Simeon and Clementine, were fed in the kitchen. Eleanora Turner enjoyed Neville and Bethany's company, and they discussed the wedding and the preparations. Marion and Thomas were most anxious that Neville and Bethany set a date allowing enough time for their wedding this year. So, the decision on a date was now becoming urgent.

Neville and Bethany seemed most content together as Marion talked with Mrs Turner. Thomas, Jonathan Turner, and Robert talked about politics and the corn laws, the hot topic of the time. With unrest growing among the factory workers in the north and public rallies becoming more organised, there was community concern.

Jonathan said, "We understand that the price of bread is difficult for workers. That is why we negotiate the lowest prices we can with the landholders. Our new mill requires far more grain, increasing our negotiating power on grain prices. Lower costs will reduce the price of bread while still keeping our margins at the same level."

Robert scratched his head. "I thought you must pay a specific price of eighty shillings per quarter[16]. My understanding was the Government set a minimum price so farmers could afford competitive wages for their workers and keep them on the farms."

Thomas answered, "Not quite. The corn laws restrict the importation of corn unless the cost of British corn reaches the minimum price as you quoted. However, the millers may still negotiate the price of English corn. Jenkinson's party made sure the corn law minimum price was high, restricting the entry of French and Spanish corn. We could buy French corn at half the cost we pay for British corn without the corn laws. So, by centralising milling, we will cut out the little mills and negotiate directly with the farmers. At first, the cost reductions will be small, but as the small mills go out of business, the farmers will have no other option. Unless other mills convert to steam and increase production, the landholders will have no other local market for their grain."

Robert looked worried, "Mr Turner, surely this is unfair on the smaller millers. Won't they lose their living?"

"Some will and some might work for us. I'm afraid the age of steam is upon us. The world is changing, Robert! Steam power has created the manufacturing industry in the midlands, spreading everywhere. Guildford will see it soon! Why even the Navy is experimenting with steam. The days of the sail will come to an end and in your lifetime, Robert. We all must adapt, as there will be no turning back!"

Robert pondered this suggestion – "The days of the sail will come to an end!" He must discuss this at Portsmouth. It was fascinating thinking about a ship that no longer required the wind. Perhaps steam could be a huge strategic advantage for Britain.

Neville clinked a spoon against a glass, gathering everyone's attention.

"Mr & Mrs Turner! A couple of quick announcements, if I might, before we go in for dinner. Firstly, thank you for your hospitality this evening. It is most kind of you, and I hope that we can repay that hospitality tenfold once Beth and I are married."

Everyone cheered this and agreed with the sentiment.

---

[16] A quarter of wheat in 1826 was equivalent to 8 bushels. A bushel was an old imperial measure of volume being at that time 8 dry gallons. 1 cubic foot equals 6.43 dry gallons.

"Secondly, I felt an explanation was necessary about why I am travelling to Portsmouth. I have served many years in the Navy now. After much consideration and discussion with my friend Robert here." Robert smiled and nodded in agreement. "I have decided to resign my commission from the Navy and establish a medical practice here in Guildford. This town has much attraction for me!"

There was a stunned silence for about five seconds before some clapping, cheering, and smiling broke out.

Eleanora Turner was delighted, "Neville. The news is wonderful. It means you and Beth will be living here in Guildford, and we will see much more of you. Such good news indeed!" And with tears in her eyes, she gave Bethany and Neville a great hug. There was much discussion until Neville held his hand up for silence again, "Now that brings me to the last point. Bethany and I have been discussing the date for the wedding."

Marion gripped Thomas's arm very tightly. Thomas feeling Marion's strength for the first time, became slightly excited. She whispered in Thomas' ear, "Mrs McPherson has asked if Saturday, November the eighteenth, would be a good day for our wedding."

Thomas raised his eyebrows and replied, "November will be suitable."

Neville commenced again, "As you all know, Beth and I fell in love at first sight. We have talked at length and feel there is no use in delaying the wedding, so we propose the date of Saturday, October the fourteenth. We will finalise the arrangements with Reverend Taggart tomorrow. This date will allow three weeks for the banns to be read and then a little time before the wedding."

Jonathan and Eleanora Turner applauded the news but then considered how quickly this date would arrive. They must start the preparations immediately, leaving for London to see the Bassingtons the following Thursday. Marion and Thomas looked at each other, and both agreed that the October date would fit well with their plans as it was another five weeks till their date. Mrs McPherson would be pleased, now having some certainty.

There was so much discussion about both weddings during dinner that Mr Turner supplied paper and pencils so Beth and Marion could take notes. Jonathan Turner also welcomed conversation with Neville about Guildford properties for sale or lease. Neville was keen on acquiring a home and a separate building for his medical practice. Jonathan was surprised when Neville advised him that he would also open a practice in London. Neville aimed to specialise in the treatment of major injuries. The navy experience he had gained in this area would prove invaluable. Being in London two days a fortnight would allow discussion with other colleagues and ensure his knowledge was up to date with current medical science. However, he reassured

Jonathan that his Guildford practice would be a partnership providing for a doctor always available.

Anne was finishing her dessert as Robert sat beside her. It was their first opportunity together during the evening.

"How is William?"

"Neville thinks he has scarlet fever! He is listless and will need a lot of care this week. Between Aggie and myself, we should manage. I do hope Neville will return soon!"

"I think it will only be a few days before he returns. I have never seen him like this before. Besotted might best describe it."

"They will make a beautiful couple. Beth loves him so much."

Robert thought and quietly said, "Just a question, Anne, without any implications. If you and I tied the knot, do you think I would fit in with your family?"

Anne looked at him in surprise. Robert posed a most personal question, but he had prefaced it with "without implications". It was as if some hurdle was holding him back. She wondered where their relationship was going.

"Robert, you keep mentioning marriage, but I don't understand your meaning. Sometimes you make me confused."

"I am sorry, Anne – I was asking if your family approve of me?"

"Yes, Robert, they love you. Everyone here accepts you now as a close family friend. My concern is what your family will think of me next July. I know you have kindly invited me, but in what context? As your friend? As Beth's sister? I must understand your intentions."

"I am working on that. I have written advising my father of your visit. Once they have the letter, they will make assumptions and start inquiries. So, you might expect a letter from them. I hope it will be polite and warm, but just in case it is a matter of fact, you should know that's how they are. I think that's where some of my personality problems arise from – I find it hard to make real friends and trust people. I appear confident, but deep down, I am quite shy."

"Do you think they will approve of my visiting?"

"Yes. My mother and father are not rude, but it will be difficult until they become acquainted with you. Once they know you as I do, they will accept you as one of the family. They are close, and the introduction needs working on."

"I see!'

"Yes, I have considered this long and hard. I have an idea that may make the process far more comfortable. I have told you of my younger sister Emma. She is Beth's age. Could she be included on the guestlist for Bethany and Neville's wedding and my invitation?"

"Yes, but would it not be a bit strange? She does not know anyone in our family! She would be uncomfortable."

"Yes, yes – that is true. But Emma is a long-term friend of Neville. So are my mother, father and brother! If an opportunity arose from a meeting before the wedding, she would also be your friend!"

"But Robert, there is so little time – she would need to visit Guildford. Mother, father, and Beth will meet Neville's parents next weekend in London and then stay with the McPhersons before returning. I will remain here managing William's recovery and keeping an eye on the business. I must also work at the bakery, and my father is concerned about the new mill, the bakery carts and the stables. I will be run off my feet."

"That is what I admire about you, Anne. You are so accomplished. You will handle all these tasks with ease!"

"Next week, you might see me fail, Robert! Things are moving too quickly. I'm not sure I will cope!"

"Hear me out, please, Anne. Emma and my mother often visit London for shopping trips. They will be travelling next Friday and return the week after. Fintelton is just outside Petersfield, and for a London trip, Guildford is an ideal stopping point. If Emma requests that mother explore the shopping here in Guildford, they will stay the night at the Fox and Hound.

On Monday, Neville and I will stay overnight at Fintelton on our way back to Portsmouth. I will brief Emma on taking the opportunity of a meeting with you. Perhaps a nice dinner at the Fox and Hound. It would be next Friday night. That is all I ask. Once I have made the preparations, I will arrange for Neville to deliver the invitation from Emma. The plan will work, Anne, and you will gain a new friend!"

"And should I give her a tour of the bakery? I'm sure she will be appalled when she sees I am a baker's daughter!"

"Anne, you are far more than that. Your father runs a huge bakery and various businesses, including a new steam-powered mill and a chain of tailor's shops. With his investment in breweries, he is one of England's new entrepreneurs. Anne, you know far more about business than any of my family. I have the highest admiration for your skills."

From this perspective, Anne agreed that the breadth of her father's businesses was increasing, but others would not realise this. Also, she was so young! Could she carry this off? Robert saw the fear on Anne's face.

"Anne, I know Emma. She will not judge you! Emma has a heart of gold. Far different from my elder brother Hugh who is cold and callous. You will be delighted with Emma, and it will give you an ally for next July. If they stay the Saturday, include them in the river walk with William and the other children. My mother and father will enjoy seeing them play pirates. Emma will love it."

Anne looked at Robert, who was pleading with her. He broke out into a great smile. "It will be a lovely evening at the Fox and Hound. Aggie and Mrs Jennings will look after the children, and I will send a footman with Emma. He will escort you in the evening and ensure your safety."

"I can arrive at the Fox and Hound by myself, Robert!"

"I know you can, but it would be preferable if you arrived escorted and were safely delivered home. Please, Anne – this will work?"

Anne could see that Robert saw this as an opportunity for them. He knew his family, and he thought Emma was the key. Anne hesitated, as she was worried that Emma, being of the upper class, might be opposed and resent this meeting.

"I'm still not sure forcing Emma is a good idea. What if she objects? What if she does not like me? Then it will be twice as hard next year at Finteton."

"It's Fintelton – Fin – tel – ton. And she will like you just as I do."

"Robert, I am afraid of this, and you won't be there with me. What if your mother comes as well?"

"I will arrange it, so it is Emma alone. My mother will require an early night. She is getting on!"

Anne put her head down and thought about it. The plan was complicated, and so much was already happening. She was afraid it would all go wrong. She was fearful of being with aristocrats alone.

"Anne – please?"

"Let me think about it until tomorrow!" She looked up and noticed that dazed look again as if he were miles away. Then he focused and smiled at her, "She will like you. It is impossible not to!"

Anne remembered it was time she checked on William again. "I must check on William."

"May I come?"

"No, you must not be near him. He may be contagious."

"That is alright. I contracted scarlet fever when I was a boy, and I have been subjected to far worse in the Navy. If we keep washing our hands, we should be safe enough."

"If you would fetch a pail of water from the kitchen. We must change the water in William's bedroom. I'll meet you up there."

Robert was off in a flash. He enjoyed this household where there were not many servants. It was like being on board a ship – never a spare moment.

Anne glided up the stairs and was soon beside William, who remained fast asleep. The fever was still there, but he slept soundly. Anne wiped his face with a wet cloth. He shook his head but did not wake. Then both Neville and Robert appeared in the doorway.

Neville sat down beside William's bed and gave him another check, including his temperature. Anne signalled at Robert and pointed out the bucket of water in the corner of the room. Robert nodded and took the pail, opened the window and threw the water out the window. He then filled the empty bucket with fresh water. Neville and Anne looked at him in surprise.

"What?"

"Is that how you change the water at home?" Anne said.

"It seemed logical!"

Anne started giggling, and Neville also raised his eyebrows.

"I hope there wasn't anyone below! Robert, the new bucket replaces the old bucket. We take the old bucket back downstairs."

"Oh!"

"That's why he has a servant on his ship, Anne!" Neville said out of the side of his mouth.

"I'm glad of that. Robert needs one!"

Robert leaned against the wall beside the door and slid down, sitting on the floor. A candle flickered on the chest of drawers near the doorway. Anne came and sat beside him.

"Thank you, Robert. I know you meant well. It was just a bit funny." She giggled again.

Robert looked at her and saw how beautiful she looked in the candlelight. He felt so relaxed with her beside him here. His mind was full of conversation, waiting to pour out. It must be something about this big old beautiful house. It must have affected Neville the same way.

Anne watched Neville as he checked William. He stood up and came over, "He is still feverish, but the rash has subsided slightly. I think he will recover in a couple of days. I will recheck him in the morning. Now, Robert, it has been a long day – ten minutes - and then we must be off. I find I require a night of good sleep. I will wait for you downstairs."

"Yes, Sir!" Robert replied.

Neville walked down the four flights of stairs and joined the others, who continued in excited conversation. Anne and Robert sat there together.

Robert asked her again, "Will you meet Emma? Please?"

Anne took a large breath and watched William, "Yes, I will meet Emma. If it works, we will send Emma her invitation to the wedding."

She shuffled and said, "Robert, why have you invited me to Fin-tel -ton?"

He smiled and looked down. Robert knew this was a defining moment, and his answer must be what she needed, or he might lose this girl. She did not understand the demands of class distinction and the problems it caused. He searched for a way of keeping his parents happy and preparing the ground so he could marry the girl he loved. He was desperate; she had an ally at Fintelton. But he was afraid she might not like his suggestion – he must be very gentle.

"Anne, I …….. I will introduce you to my family as the woman I will spend the rest of my life with!"

Anne took a deep breath as her heart jumped. Tears formed in her eyes as she heard the words that finally confirmed his love for her. Anne continued watching William in the candlelight and said, "Are you sure?"

"Yes."

He saw her eyes sparkling in the candlelight. Robert also needed confirmation, "How about you? Are you sure?"

"Yes."

He leaned over very slowly and kissed her gently on the cheek. She blinked and wiped away a tear and said with a smile, "Then I think I should like to visit Fin – tel – ton, very much!"

Sunday morning …

Waking early on Sunday morning, William found Aggie wiping his brow with a wet cloth.

"Good morning, young William!"

William felt very weak, but his thoughts were far ahead of his tired body. He was still unfamiliar with Aggie, and he was a bit confused finding her sitting at his bedside looking after him. He looked at her with wide eyes.

"Where is Anne?"

"She is catching up on some well-deserved sleep. She watched over you until three in the morning when I came up and took over. You have not been well at all, William!"

"I feel so tired!" He closed his eyes again and moved his hand over, holding hers. Aggie was surprised and heartened that this little fellow would want the comfort of her hand. She gave his hand a gentle squeeze reassuring him. Then she saw the eyes close, and he was asleep again.

"You rest, Master William. You will come through this and become strong again!" she whispered, wiping his brow. Aggie stood up, washed her hands, and then headed for the laundry with a pail of water. The house was still quiet, and she tiptoed down the stairs making sure she did not wake anyone.

Jonathan Turner woke beside his wife, realising he was back where he belonged. He looked over at Eleanora, who still slept, breathing easier this morning. Jonathan savoured the comfort of this beautiful bed and its clean sheets and soft pillows. He thought this was far better than the guest room bed he had occupied for several weeks.

As he lay there, his thinking shifted towards his business. Issues rushed through his mind: building the mill, finding a mill manager, expanding the bakery, stables at Epsom, designing the fast carts, and the biscuit production line. He sighed.

The morning light was slowly seeping into the room. Jonathan remembered it was Sunday and the events ahead of them today. The family would attend church except for William. He would check on his son and then fetch a cup of tea for Eleanora and himself. Jonathan also remembered checking with Reverend Taggart this morning on the wedding dates.

Surely the guest list would not be more than sixty. Jonathan rubbed his forehead – this would cost him a fortune. But Beth was worth it – she was a wonderful daughter and now blessed Guildford with a new doctor in town. He smiled as he thought about the blessing Bethany was.

He slipped out of bed quietly, put on his dressing-gown and went downstairs.

At the church, Neville, Robert and Simeon joined them before moving inside. The congregation seemed more than usual, with people greeting each other throughout the church. The Turners entered their pew and were welcomed by Reverend Taggart, who warmly greeted Sir Robert as a visiting dignitary. There were also some kind words for Neville and Bethany. Andrew Taggart advised that he had locked in the dates for the wedding and confirmed that the church arrangements were complete. He intended to announce the banns of marriage for the first time at today's service and prepared them for the many hearty congratulations they would receive afterwards.

Eleanora Turner beamed as the conversations took place around her. She gripped Clementine's hand as if to protect her from all the romances that were now taking place. Clementine wriggled a bit but then took comfort in her mother's wish. She smiled and rested her head on Eleanora's shoulder. Jonathan Turner edged closer and gently said, "Go to bed earlier, Clemmie!"

Eleanora nudged him away, enjoying the bond between mother and daughter. Clementine putting her hand on her mother's stomach, felt the baby move. She went, "Ooooh!" Eleanora and her daughter beamed at each other. The feeling of a new life was a miraculous thing. They sat there in awe, enjoying the intimate moment.

William was now sitting up at the Turner home with his eyes half-open. Aggie felt his brow and considered that he still had a slight fever. She put a couple of pillows behind his back, making him more comfortable.

"Here, William, have some water as it will help. My mother always told me to keep my liquids up when I had a fever. That way, it keeps the body clean."

"I have a headache!"

"That is the fever – it will be gone in a few days. But if you drink the water and keep drinking it regularly, then the headache will go away faster."

William thought about this. What Aggie suggested was not that difficult. So, he drank the complete cupful.

"Where is your mother, Aggie?"

"She is in Woking with my father."

"What does your father do?"

"He was in the army and spent a lot of time away. He was injured in India and came home with a slight limp, but he is fine. He works in a blacksmith shop at Woking, and he is one of the bell ringers at the church."

"Did he kill anyone while he was in India?"

"He fought in many battles, but he doesn't speak much about it. I think he might have, but I'm not sure."

"Wow! I want to be in the Navy like Robert when I grow up. I will fire the canons and chase pirates."

"You will need good health before you do that, so make sure you rest for a while. I will be back up in an hour, and we can talk some more then."

"What colour is your hair Aggie? You always keep a scarf over your head."

"I think it is brown, William. I will show you when I come back up, but right now, Mrs Jennings needs me downstairs preparing morning tea and then lunch. We have guests coming."

"I think your hair is brown but maybe black! Mine is dark brown. It is so different from Anne's. Hers is blonde, but I think it is more of a golden blonde. She has beautiful hair."

"Yes, Anne is beautiful. I like Anne. She is so sweet and gentle."

"She is not sweet all the time – she can fight like a tiger, and she has often whipped me in a wrestle. But when I get bigger, I will whip her back."

"Dear me, brothers and sisters! When you get bigger, you will miss her a lot when she is married and moves away."

"Is she going to get married like Bethany?"

"She is beautiful, so I think it may happen soon. But let us wait and see. I must go now. You just relax and watch the birds out the window here. Look over at that vine on the wall. There are some little finches there flying around. Aren't they beautiful?"

William looked out the window and saw around five or six rose finches with brilliant colours on their feathers. He turned around to say something else, but she was gone. William liked Aggie – she was friendly and told him exciting things. He closed his eyes again and thought about hunting tigers in India. He wondered if there were any tigers in England – he must ask Aggie. The sun shining through the open window warmed his room. Slowly his eyes closed, and soon he was fast asleep.

After the church service, there was much greeting and news as they met their friends outside. With Neville and Bethany's banns now read, the couple met with an endless procession of congratulations. Neville was amazed at the number of families he was meeting. One elderly gent eagerly said he wanted an appointment as soon as Neville set up practice. He was a past patient of

Doctor Jeremy Stephens and was looking for a new doctor. Neville was most encouraged.

Jonathan Turner made the most of the opportunity, with many of the land-holders at church today agreeing on appointments in the coming weeks. There was a need to establish an increased grain supply required for the new mill. Access to the production from the next harvest would be critical. Reverend Taggart suddenly appeared at his side, jolting him from his thoughts.

"Jonathan, forgive me for making this observation, but Sir Robert South and Anne seem particularly attentive to each other?"

"Yes, Andrew, they are now good friends. Robert retrieved Simeon from the King's forest some weeks ago, and they met that day, believe it or not, in our kitchen. He seems a very nice young man."

Andrew agreed and then stood there, silently gathering the right words.

"Jonathan, I'm not sure you understand who he is!"

"He is a captain in the navy, at a young age, and with a good career ahead of him."

"Jonathan, Sir Robert's Father, is Sir David South, the Earl of Fintelton. Their estate is near the Harting[17] area, just past Petersfield. The family goes back centuries, and they were prominent in the Royal court circles some years ago. I just advise you of this as Anne may find it somewhat difficult with the family if the attachment develops. I am aware of all this as I know several of the clergy in that area."

"So, what are you recommending, Andrew?"

"Well……. Well, I am not recommending anything, Jonathan. I thought I should let you know who this young gentleman is. His family may have great ambitions for him, and I would not want Anne disappointed or hurt."

"I see!"

Andrew then said, "It is a great honour having Sir Robert worshipping with us today."

Andrew and Jonathan stood there in embarrassing silence. Jonathan Turner felt his rage rising from the pit of his stomach. How dare this cler-gyman suggest that his daughter was not good enough for this young man. Jonathan clenched his teeth, quelling the rage. He understood that Andrew Taggart was a good friend and had protected Jonathan's reputation on several occasions. He must repress this anger, understanding that Andrew meant well. However, the silence continued. The comment by Andrew reinforced how unfair this world was. The aristocracy would never accept the middle class. The world was changing, and he decided then and there that he would

---

[17] Author's Note: 'Fintelton' is a fictional estate in Harting created for the story. For those wishing to visit Harting I recommend it. I think it is one of the most beautiful parts of England. Petersfield is also a delightful town.

succeed in his new ventures. Perhaps he could forgive Hamish even if he had duped William into sharing private family business. Hamish was right. There was no alternative except that people in industry succeed. They must work together and change this world for the better.

Andrew now feared he might have overstepped the mark. What he said may have been misinterpreted, and he must clarify the situation quickly with Jonathan. The good Reverend was about to speak when

Jonathan suggested, "When they are young, Andrew, nothing is a problem. I'm sure time will solve any problems that might emerge."

"If I can help, please let me know. I have seen many a lovely young lady destroyed by aristocrats, and I'm sure I won't let it happen to your daughter."

"Thank you, Andrew. Your sentiment does you credit. However, I think you will have the honour of Sir Robert returning soon as he will be Neville's best man."

"Ah! I shall be more circumspect in my statements then. Thank you for letting me know about this."

"I would also say that since we have met, I have found him quite different from what we expect of those of his rank, and I have a high opinion of him."

Andrew nodded in agreement. They continued standing together in silence, watching and nodding to their friends.

Andrew then said to Jonathan, "Jonathan, you understand my friendship with you is important to me. I would never intentionally offend you!"

"Why, thank you, Andrew. I think we both value our friendship greatly. It allows us the freedom to speak frankly in a peaceful way. I appreciate this, and I welcome your advice."

They both stepped back from the mark, thankful that their friendship was strong and respectful. The mayor approached, and Jonathan spoke up, "Ah, Rupert, how are you? Reverend Taggart and I were just commenting together on our healthy congregation."

Rupert Smith's face opened into a broad smile, and he shook both their hands, "Capital, Capital, I too was thinking the same thing."

Fintelton Manor, Harting ...

Neville and Robert left Guildford early on Monday morning, aiming for arrival at Fintelton by midafternoon. Robert allowed for a stop at Petersfield, purchasing flowers for his mother and sister. Before leaving Guildford, he briefed Neville and Bethany on the plan for a meeting between Emma and Anne. On first hearing of the plan, Neville thought it might be simpler if the invitation came from himself as Neville was a good friend of the South family. However, given the time already spent by Robert with Anne arranging the meeting, he was reluctant to suggest any change and pledged his support.

Bethany's knowledge of the plan would provide Anne with a confidant in the coming two days before Neville and she left for London. Beth would do her sisterly best to bolster Anne's confidence.

As the coach passed through the Fintelton Estate gates, Neville noticed Robert sitting up and breathing in the air of his home country. He took several deep breaths and sat wide-eyed, looking at the estate.

Neville suggested, "Good to be home?"

Robert thought about it and chewed over his answer for a few minutes. He left home when he was all of twelve and only returned on port stays ever since. There were long periods when the fleet was in port over Christmas. Even so, he was now becoming a stranger and thought of this estate as his boyhood home.

"When I was young, this was my world before I entered the Navy. I never considered anything else but this place, except for school, which was also relatively protected. I was unprepared for the Navy. I felt as if my parents had abandoned me. I never cried publicly, but I did silently in my hammock for the first two years. Being bullied, shouted at, wet, given poor food, never getting enough sleep and the constant fear of not meeting my parent's expectations. But by God's grace, I survived.

Is this my home? No, it is not. It is my parent's home, and my brother will inherit the lot. My father had made it quite clear that he would leave me a small allowance, but that was it. Even that depended on my marrying well. My parents left me with no doubt that I must make my way in the world as that was what the law required. Father said he would help where he had contacts and influence, but that was all he could do.

I'm not sure about your relationship with your father, Neville, but I struggled for my father's affection. He is a kind benefactor whom I seldom see. My mother is similar and has moments of intimacy, but not many. I was always looked after by nannies, and speaking was forbidden in front of my mother and father. We were seen but not heard. Then they would be gone because they were entertaining or there was a show. You know, the high society circles.

I will not emulate them. When I have a son, daughter or both, I will be an essential part of their life. We will run and play together and consider the world's great questions. I will tell them bedtime stories and answer their stupidest question with respect. We will laugh together until it hurts and share our sorrows with tears. I will be their father, not just an acquaintance.

So, is this my home? No, it is my parent's home, but this is where my boyhood was and where my boyhood dreams began. So, it has a special place in my heart. Do you understand what I am saying?"

Neville was not aware of how deeply Robert thought about his question. He looked up with a chuckle and said, "A yes or no would have sufficed!"

They both broke out into laughter as the coach came into sight of the manor house, which was quite grand indeed.

"I understand what you mean. My experiences with my father were quite different. He was a man who kept feeding me knowledge from an early age. There were no bedtime stories, but he always left me a book. He took me on excursions to museums and literature recitals. The worst thing was sitting still during a long recital from some of these old bats who just looked and sounded frightful. I remember at one recital falling asleep and waking up with my head on my father's lap. We went to museums, mainly after that!

But I do have good memories of home. My mother is a kind, gentle soul. They are happily married, and they gave me a very loving upbringing. I was fortunate – I have good memories. I would like the same for my children."

Robert nodded his agreement, looked ahead of the carriage, and spied the courtyard entrance.

"Ah, as I expected, just a servant to welcome us. They will be waiting for us and do the formal thing in the drawing-room. Neville, do you notice the difference?"

"What difference – looks the same to me?"

"No, no, I mean at the Turner's, you turn up, expected, of course, there is always a welcoming party, there is joy and hugs and kisses, and it is full of life."

"I see what you mean, and I agree that family has much joy. But Robert, do not be too hard on your own family; they are doing what they have always done. They probably think they are showing quite enough emotion."

"I will make sure Emma experiences real life by meeting the Turners. Praise God for them, they have shown me a different world, and I prefer theirs to this one."

With that, Robert jumped out of the carriage and shook the hand of Thomas Pike, the butler, and then to the butler's surprise, hugged him.

"Pike, Thank you for your welcome. How are you, my old friend?"

The butler was overwhelmed by this greeting and was unsure whether he should show a straight face or a smile. So, he tried an in-between grimace and a soft cough into his fist, "I am well, Sir, and you look very fit and well yourself."

"Thank you, Pike. You remember Neville."

Neville thought he would play along with this fun. Robert forgot the flowers, so Neville picked them up and alighted from the carriage, shook the butler's hand, flowers and all, and then gave him a quick hug. Pike stood there like a statue, unsure how he should respond.

Neville quietly whispered out of the side of his mouth. "Don't worry, Pike, it's the new fad in London, hugging servants!"

The butler quietly mouthed back, "My Goodness!"

With that, they proceeded up the front steps and inside.

The Parlour, Fintelton Manor, Harting ...

Robert's first chance of speaking alone with Emma came after dinner and the traditional port and pipe smoking. Lord Fintelton and his son, Sir Hugh, Robert's older brother, withdrew to discuss estate business. Lady Jane South decided to retire early, and Neville found some medical reading that interested him.

"Neville, I must meet this Bethany who has won your heart. I thought you were waiting for me, but now I must suffer in silence," Emma said with a cheeky smile.

"Emma Dear, I have always admired you but more as a little sister, so I must apologise if I have upset you with this announcement. She has won my heart, and I am the happiest man in the world for it. But Emma, I hope that we will always be the best friends?"

"Always, Neville."

"I must excuse myself as I have quite a deal of medical reading outstanding. The interpretation of thermometer readings! So, I will leave you and find a quiet spot as I understand Robert desires your ear." With that, Neville took his papers and quietly excused himself.

"Robert, what is it that you require my attention on?"

The drawing-room was theirs alone. Robert sat beside Emma and spoke in a soft voice. Emma was all ears as she was not familiar with Robert whispering. He usually spoke in a reasonably strong voice and a confident tone. Here, it was as if he was in conspiratorial mode.

"Emma, you will know that I am shy underneath. It takes a great deal of courage for me to speak about matters of my own heart."

She sat up. Robert was serious; she could tell by his furrowed brow.

"I need your help. I need it desperately, and you are the only one who can help me!"

"Why Robert, I am your little sister. I would do anything for you. Of course, as long as you are not misleading me!"

"That is the problem. You may not consider this correct or entirely proper!"

She looked at him and raised her eyebrows, "If you do not tell me, how may I decide. Out with-it, brother!"

"Emma, I have met this wonderful girl called Anne!"

"Ah-ha! Now, this is getting interesting! Tell me all."

They sat there like conspirators as Robert poured his heart out. He spoke freely and explained how he understood his mother and father's expectations for him but contrasted this with the reality of the Navy world. She would appreciate this as she would either marry well or become the aunt, dependent on her brother's charity for the rest of her life.

He gently said, "You will face a similar problem if you marry for love. It may be that your future partner has little wealth!"

"I will marry well."

Robert looked at her, "What about love?"

"For me, as a woman, love may play second fiddle – otherwise, the future might look quite bleak."

Robert continued and explained why she should meet with Anne. As Emma heard more of the proposal, Robert felt she was becoming reluctant.

"What if mother finds out? She will be very cross with me. I do not usually associate in those circles. You never know who will see me."

Once Robert explained the plan in full, he sat back and said, 'There you have it. I need your help, Emma. If Anne comes here without a friend, it may destroy her. You know how difficult our parents can be. They will discount her before they truly know her. You would love her if you could meet her."

"But she is a nobody, Robert. How do I justify that to our parents?"

"Emma, have you forgotten all you learned at church. She is a person created by God in the same light as you and I. This world blesses some with position and money, and others fight for survival. You have been highly blessed. You enjoy your situation in life because you were born into this family and have known nothing else. But I have enjoyed the company of Anne's family. They are good people, and they understand a joy that we have never experienced in this home. Our family is …. is … what do you call it? …. Sterile!

If you cannot help me, you may never experience this joy. It is better than all the mansions in England. And Emma, you may think our family is well off, but change is coming. New businesses are developing out there that will be far greater than our fortunes. Anne's father is a businessman building a company that will be ten times as big as this estate. So, do not underestimate who they are. Remember that the world is changing, and we must change and adjust also. If Fintelton does not change, it may not be here in twenty years."

"Come now, Robert, this estate will be here forever. We have land and produce here at Fintelton, in Scotland and Ireland, and father has investments in the Indies. The future is firm."

'Perhaps, but will you help me, Emma?"

"Your plan is like an old naval ship. It is full of holes. You should have let a woman plan it. You men, it is objective and outcome. You don't think that much about what is in between."

Robert became crestfallen as he thought Emma was turning away from him. But she loved her brother and gave him the benefit of her doubt.

"If I do this for you, please don't force friendship upon me with this baker's daughter, but I shall endure her for your benefit. She must have some good points if you are so keen on her, except I am bewildered how someone of such low birth could have the graces of our society. But I will try for you on one condition."

Robert bit his lip. He was disgusted with his sister's attitude. He thought about how his initiation into the Navy had changed his life. Over years of naval service, his youthful arrogance was beaten out of him. His education in the real world had made him equal with any man. However, he understood that this was his only chance for Anne's survival while visiting this household. So, he agreed.

"I will abide by your condition, whatever it may be."

"Let me plan how we might achieve this."

Robert knew he had no choice but to agree. He must have Emma's help, and she would extract a favour for it. He sat back and realised that she was right. If anyone could play his mother and father, it would be Emma.

"I agree. You may plan the exercise."

"Good. I will take your plan and change it, so mother and myself are protected. Now let me see. Firstly, a good reason why we must stop in Guildford next Friday. I have it! Neville is a close friend of yours and the family. As he will be leaving the Navy and setting up a practice in Guildford, he could offer us an inspection of his surgery. We are looking for a good doctor in this area, rather than visiting London. So, we will stay overnight and visit the proposed site of his practice. Robert, will you please call Neville?"

Robert jumped up and rushed off for Neville.

Emma kept thinking about the plan. Neville would invite them and tell them about the girl he was marrying, Bethany, and her sister Anne, both respectable girls whom the family should meet.

That would do nicely. She and her mother could also stay on Saturday and inspect the baker's mill and operations. In particular, the tailors' shop might provide them with some new ideas, but she doubted it very much. They would continue their trip on Sunday morning and depart for London.

The wedding invitation would come from Neville's family as their guests, this being consistent as they were acquainted with the family at Fintelton. Neville must include all her family in the invitation. This way, the family would know Anne and the Turners before she arrived at Fintelton next July. This plan avoided any chance of disapproval by society, and her mother and father would not suspect, until after the wedding, any attachment between Robert and Anne.

Robert returned with Neville.

"Neville, would you please invite me this Friday coming for an inspection of your new practice at Guildford?"

"But I won't be there!"

"Neville, you are like Robert. You cannot disregard the facts! It does not matter. Now I suppose this Mr Turner has recommended some sites for you?"

"Yes!"

"How convenient!"

"The site I have selected is excellent and will allow an expansion of the practice over time. My plan includes practising two days a fortnight in London also."

"Wonderful, this fits into the plan perfectly."

"What plan?"

"Robert and Neville, do be good boys and sit down and listen."

Emma explained the plan in detail, and they both agreed that it was the better plan. She smiled. There were still but two problems.

"Robert, you said you posted a letter asking permission for Anne's visit. Did you send it?"

"No, I have it here."

"Good, pass it over, please." She tore it up.

"There will be no need for a letter until after the wedding – well after the wedding."

"Yes, I can see that now."

"Also, it must be I who invites Anne to Fintelton. Otherwise, the invitation will never come. You understand mother and father's expectations. Their acceptance of Anne will take time, and I cannot promise my affection for this young lady. You must allow me to make up my mind. Surely this is fair, Robert?"

"That is fair. But I must have the same agreement from you. That I have free will on having affection for your husband or not!"

"Touché, Robert, that is also fair, and I agree. But do you think I will like this girl?"

"I am certain of it!"

"Neville, do you think I will like this, Anne?"

"Emma, would you have liked a sister?"

"Yes – someone to talk with and confide in!"

"Then, in Anne, you would not find a better sister in England! "

Emma sat up, speechless. She respected Neville's opinion. From his comment, it appeared this girl had his admiration. How interesting.

"Then I shall look forward to visiting Guildford this Friday and Saturday."

Robert smiled, "Please, Neville, if you would brief Anne when you return. Also include Bethany, so she is aware. I will send a rider tonight with a message advising that we have decided on a plan. I think this will work!"

Turner Household, Guildford ...

That same evening William sat in bed playing a game of draughts with Aggie. Jonathan Turner came into the boys' bedroom and felt his forehead checking his temperature.

"The fever appears gone, William. How are you feeling? Any better?"

"Yes, far better, Father. The headache is almost gone, but I am still tired!"

"We will see how you are in the morning. Let this be the last game of draughts Aggie, and then he may sleep. Thomas and Simeon will welcome their beds again tomorrow night."

"Yes, Mr Turner. Sir, have you considered the storeroom next to this one? I know you are seeking more accommodation in the house. The storeroom is almost as large as this room. A bit of carpentry and painting would make a good bedroom. It may solve some of the accommodation problems!"

Jonathan considered Aggie for a few seconds absorbing her suggestion. The thought never occurred to him about this alternative. He turned, went out and walked down the hallway. Opening the door, he found it dark inside. He returned, collected a candle, and inspected the room. As Aggie said, it was quite a large area full of old family items. It was dry and well built.

He came back and said, "You are correct, Aggie. It is very suitable. I will need an alternate space for the items stored there. A fine suggestion, Aggie. I will discuss this with Mrs Turner tomorrow."

With that, Jonathan turned and went off downstairs.

William looked up at Aggie, "Do you think it might be my room when they have built it?"

Aggie frowned at William, "I'm not sure about that, William. I think your parents need more room for guests. So, they will probably move the girls up here!"

William was not impressed with that idea at all. He slumped down in disappointment and focused again on the game of draughts.

Aggie noticed Jonathan Turner's failure to wish William a good night. It was as if the child was not necessary - just a duty. Mr Turner treated his other children far kindlier. She felt sorry for William, noticing his disappointment not so much about the room but that his father did not care for him. She thought, 'What a mistake not loving your son. How precious this child is!'

Aggie finished the game with William and wished him a good night. William said, "May we play tomorrow night again?"

Smiling, she replied, "Certainly, William, but only if you let me win!"

She tucked him in and blew out the candle.

PART 2

"Living by the Truth Requires Sacrifice."

September 1826, Portsmouth

Chapter 13

Admiral Sir Tristram Sutherland sat at a large desk in a comfortable office at Blue Fleet Headquarters, Portsmouth. Writing notes for the discussion with his next guest, he looked up as a cold gust of wind blew some papers off his desk.

"Jacobs, close that window for me, please."

Finishing his notes, he stood up and peered out the window. There were white caps on the bay from the rising northwesterly.

"When South arrives, hold him out there for a minute, please."

"Yes, Sir!" Commodore Jacobs placed a file on the Admiral's desk and exited the room.

The Admiral frowned. It was a bit early for a cold northwesterly, so perhaps they were in for a severe winter this year. He opened the window again and braced himself, breathing in. A career navy man of forty years, he missed standing on the quarter-deck, the ship twisting and turning, wrestling against the waves as the wind drove the sails hard above him. He longed for sea duty, but with the end of the Napoleonic Wars, the government reduced the navy budget. He shook his head. 'We must keep the navy strong! It is in the national interest.' He looked out across the harbour and enjoyed the sight of a frigate racing past Gosport, making full use of the stiff breeze. 'Lucky dogs – I wish!'

"Sir Tristram, your next guest has arrived."

"Give me a few more minutes, Jacobs, please," he enjoyed watching how the crew handled a frigate returning to port. They were nearly through the channel and should turn any time now. The captain would be aware of the many eyes watching. The sky and royals were already down. "Ah, there he goes," the Admiral murmured, and then the topgallants and topsails were quickly being furled, the fore and mizzen gallants followed, leaving just the courses, staysails, jibs and spanker up as she turned across the wind. "Good, Good!" the admiral murmured again. Then in sleek precision, the crew furled the courses as she used the breeze and glided toward the quay before finding her position, turning into the wind and letting down the anchor. "Well done!" the Admiral was pleased with this fine display of seamanship and smiled. Captain Mark Foster was no slouch and made no mistakes as he maneuvered HMS *Providence* beautifully into port.

"Jacobs!" the Admiral raised his voice slightly.

The door opened, and Commodore Jacobs announced the next guest.

"Sir Tristram, Commander Sir Robert South."

"Thank you, Jacobs. Come in, Sir Robert. Have you come direct from Fintelton?"

"Yes, Sir. We ventured down for some business of Lieutenant Bassington in Guildford, then on to Fintelton for the night. I arrived here as fast as I could. I am at your service, Sir."

"Good, good, South. Now let me congratulate you on your promotion to Commander and the Captain of *Restless*. You are a lucky fellow. There are plenty of captains without a ship, so the Admiralty has been kind to you. Make sure you take care of *Restless*, as that ship is your next career step, and you should build on this for the future."

"I was quite surprised at the honour bestowed on me, Sir. My great thanks for your trust in me."

"Now, now, Robert. The Board promoted you on merit. Foster gave you a splendid recommendation, and you have already distinguished yourself. We need young fellows like you commanding our ships. There are looming challenges on the horizon, so we must ensure the navy is kept strong despite the government cuts. Promotions like yours give me confidence that we can maintain a strong fleet."

"I noticed Captain Foster bringing in *Providence*, Sir. A splendid bit of seamanship!"

"Yes, I too was admiring it. I would not mind being back out there again, but duty calls here. While my flagship is under refit, the blue fleet headquarters will remain ashore. I am afraid, probably for some time. Blast it; the world is changing. Eh! Would you like a glass of sherry, Sir?"

"Yes, Sir, Thank you."

"Damned shame about Bassington giving the navy away! He is a fine surgeon. Do you think we might entice him back, Sir?"

Robert thought for a moment and then said, tongue in cheek with a smile, "Perhaps an invitation a few months after the first child is born, Sir!"

They both had a great laugh at this. Sir Tristram spluttered, "Well said, Sir. Well said! I will keep that in mind. Ha, Ha."

The Admiral sat down at his desk and offered Robert a chair. He called in Commander Jacobs, who entered and sat down with a large brown package on his lap.

"I will include Jacobs here as part of the interview, as he has prepared the documents for your mission."

"Very good, Sir."

The Admiral cleared his voice.

"Let me tell you what you will be doing over the next six months. Firstly, sail *Restless* hard up the coast and dock at the navy yards in Woolwich. Alexander Steele will install two of those new canons he makes in the bow of your schooner. Your ship is larger than the normal schooner and will easily handle these bow chasers' weight. You will need these canons for your first mission. Let me make it clear, Robert, you will see action. I'm sorry about sending you into this again, but the situation is serious."

"What situation is this. Sir?"

"Once your canons are on board, set sail quickly for Portsmouth. I believe you are the best man at Neville's wedding. He has sent me an invitation and Foster as well. So, our wives and we will be travelling up together. I will let you make your arrangements as I am sure you youngsters will organise some shenanigans before the day. Once the wedding is over, return here as soon as possible, and I will give you the latest briefing."

"Yes, Sir."

Admiral Sutherland thought for a moment, then looked at Robert again.

"After the war with Napoleon ended[18], we paid off a lot of the captains and crews downsizing the navy. Damn shame that was. But smuggling between France and England has increased dramatically, creating employment for paid off sailors. Knowing that smuggling was on the rise and with a reduced navy, the government decided to upsize coastal vigilance. Many seamen have now become either blockade men or joined the customs service. But the point is, with many ex-navy sailors making up the smuggler crews, they present a more significant challenge with their excellent seamanship skills.

On the east coast, we have a substantial preventative service established. There is a significant land presence but not many quality ships. This service extends as far as Bristol, but the west coast preventive measures are a bit sparse with no customs ships, and this area now provides a better opportunity for the smugglers. We have heard that with the corn laws keeping the price of grain high, there is some smuggling in of French grain on larger ships that use the Scottish west coast. The usual contraband of liquor and other high-priced items is also present. We do not have much intelligence on this, and your job will be challenging ships, boarding and checking cargo for smuggled goods.

Robert, these smugglers have been violent in the past. They have no morals

---

[18] The Napoleonic Wars finally ended in June 1815 with the defeat of the French army by the Allies (Seventh coalition) at Waterloo. Wikipedia.

– their game is making money. You should not trust anyone and always have soldiers with you. I will be assigning a double squad of marines for your voyage over the next six months. Your good friend Horace Coombes will be commanding the marines and working with you to gather intelligence."

The Admiral took a long breath and then refocused.

"Commander Jacobs, please give Captain South his orders."

Jacobs handed over the large brown paper packet.

"Thank you, Sir."

The Admiral then said, "Thank you, Jacobs. You may go now."

Jacobs stood and withdrew. The Admiral waited until he heard the door shut.

"Robert, what you have just heard is your cover story, and now I will tell you what your real mission is! Of course, if you find any smugglers, catch them and let the Customs men deal with them!"

Robert looked up from the brown paper packet with his name on it. He was now intrigued by what the Admiral was saying.

"The previous Captain of *Restless* is now in the navy hospital at Gosport. Hughes suffered terrible injuries from Irish nationalists who boarded and attempted to take over his ship. Many of the crew were seriously injured, including six dead. Hughes did a splendid job and luckily survived. The ship's crew is now at full strength again. We have dealt very quietly with this for obvious reasons.

You will recall the Irish Rebellion in ninety-eight and the more recent uprising involving Emmet. We have information about continuing unrest in Ireland. A new, more violent movement has emerged, seeking support from the French and Americans. We believe the nationalists are smuggling arms through the Irish sea. Once they reach the Irish shore, they are safe as movements against British rule are popular.

The government requires these ships to be intercepted, boarded, and their origin and destination discovered. This new movement has already demonstrated how dangerous it is. You will not take prisoners. These ships and their crews will be destroyed and sunk out of sight of land! No survivors - that is an order. There must be no contact between these ships and the enemy.

Robert, this is a bad business. As captain of *Restless*, you will remain onboard your ship. I have assigned Lieutenant Small as your senior supporting officer. Let Small and Coombes do any required boarding. The only trustworthy crew members will be Small and Coombes. Jacobs has briefed them, so do not trust anyone else, Sir. Make sure you find a trustworthy servant. As I said, *Restless* is larger than your normal schooner, and there is room for a servant. Brief him that he is your bodyguard, especially while Coombes and Small are off the ship."

Robert was becoming concerned about the amount of specific detail the Admiral was giving on security.

"We do not know how Captain Hughes was discovered or boarded, but we can only assume someone in the crew passed on that information. That person we believe will still be there. There may also be others. A few Irish are in the crew, but no facts link them to the previous mutiny attempt. It may be the Scottish who have fallen in with them. Investigate the background of every crew member Robert."

"You think they will try again, Admiral?"

"I do indeed, Sir! My advice is to work the crew hard. Do not give them time for scheming and regularly have crew counts completed by the men on watch. The responsibility is yours, Sir. By the way, if you discover the traitors in the crew, you as captain should have them executed immediately. You have the authority, so 'Hang Them High' in front of the crew as a lesson. Robert, you must get rid of them quickly. If you keep them as prisoners, they will infect the crew. Now, Commander South, I understand you are a fine fellow and would not recklessly destroy life. But this movement is a deadly one. They are already responsible for killing six of our men and nearly killing Captain Hughes; they will have no hesitation in killing you if they get the chance. It appears they aim to take your ship and use it against King and country. You will take no prisoners and show no mercy. We must destroy this movement quickly. Good hunting."

The Admiral stood up, and Robert immediately rose.

"Here is an additional set of orders, coming from a higher authority that Jacobs has not seen. You should return here by October eighteenth for your final Irish sea briefing, when we may have more intelligence. Horace will have his men here on the seventeenth and board that day. The Irish Sea will be performing by then, so you best make sure plenty of oilskins are aboard. Use Douglas in the Isle of Man as your station port. I have included some details for intelligence contacts there for you.

Foster will be patrolling the Irish west coast, so you need only cover the east coast. He knows of your mission and will be using an alternate home port. You should only meet with Foster at sea and out of sight of land. Put into some Scottish ports, so your cover story stays intact. I would like this business cleared up by the new year if possible.

Now, young man! Sail that ship of yours hard. Have Steele install those canons and return them here. Keep your mission confidential, Robert – indeed, the fewer people who know, the better. Do not delay there for testing – you can do that on your return journey. I will be expecting reports monthly, and I will have a packet coming through Douglas at the end of each month. It is all in the orders.

I shall meet you at the wedding before you depart for the Irish sea. Good luck and God Bless."

They shook hands.

Before Robert opened the door, Sir Tristram came around his desk and quietly said, "Robert, I know you think your father might have influenced your promotion, but let me put your mind at rest on this matter. The Admiralty decided on your promotion purely on merit. Your father's influence did not affect the outcome. You will be an excellent captain. By the way, that commander's epaulette looks most handsome. Now off you go."

"Thank you, Sir Tristram."

Robert left the room, closing the door quietly behind him. He saluted Commodore Jacobs and exited fleet headquarters. Walking quickly towards the quay, he thought, "This will be some first command!"

The Turner Household, Guilford ...

Later in the afternoon, a small coach with two horses drew up outside the Turner house. The Coachman dismounted and opened the door for a short well-dressed man who hopped down, straightened his attire and checked the address. William, who was feeling far better today, was on the front landing of the house and watched this gentleman's movements.

The gentleman did not smile and moved forward and up the stairs till he came face to face with William.

William addressed the man in his usual precocious manner, "Who are you?"

The man looked down at the young boy and breathed in.

"I am seeking Miss Anne Turner, young man, as I have a message and invitation for her! Would I be at the correct address?"

"You would be!" William said in reply, not assisting the situation.

They both stood in silence, looking at each other.

Breathing in again, the man said, "Who am I addressing, young man?"

"I am William Turner, one of Anne's brothers!"

"Then, young William, would you please call her?"

"I can take the message for you."

The man was about to snarl at William but checked himself, "The message must be delivered in person by myself. I have come a long way, and the message requires a meeting in person. Please fetch Miss Anne, William."

William understood that he dared not continue this situation any further, so he darted into the house, searching for Anne. The gentleman moved away from the front stairs onto the portico. He looked up at the two floors above and then turned and looked down at the coach waiting for him. He mused, 'At least it is a respectably sized house! Young William seems somewhat difficult for a small lad. Perhaps he did not sleep well!'

Anne, home from clothes shopping in preparation for her mother's London trip and the wedding, was in the parlour. Still dressed in a bright blue gown with her hair done with some matching ribbons, she, as usual, looked magnificent. William burst upon the group of women admiring the new clothes.

Clementine was most impressed with a hat Marion had bought, "Mother, could I have a hat like this one, please? It would match my best dress beautifully, and I am old enough for a hat like that now!"

William blurted out, "Anne, quick, a gentleman at the front door is asking for you."

They all turned and wondered who it could be. Anne put down the blouse she held and followed William outside.

As Anne appeared at the front door, Mr Stem took a step back, overcome by this young lady's beauty. For a moment, he lost his voice.

"Good day, Sir. I am Anne Turner. How may I be of assistance?"

"Miss Turner, please let me introduce myself. I am Malcolm Stem, the Estate Manager from Fintelton Manor."

Anne noticed the coach below waiting for the gentleman. "Good day Mr Stem. Would you come in and take some tea with us?"

"Excuse me, Miss Turner, it would be best if I remain here. I have some business in Guildford and have instructions from Lady Emma South to deliver this invitation by hand. Here is the invitation. I am also instructed with a message for you once you have read the invitation."

"Thank you." Anne took the invitation and noticed the 'Fintelton' symbol stamped on the seal. She opened it and read it aloud,

Lady Emma South and the Lady Jane South
The Countess of Fintelton
Request the pleasure and company of
Miss Anne Turner
At dinner at the Fox and Hound
High Street, Guildford
At 8.00 pm
On Friday, September Ninth, 1826
RSVP to the bearer of this letter.

Anne took a deep breath and then covered her mouth with her hand. The gentleman saw she was quite overcome by the invitation.

He gently asked. "Are you well, Miss Turner?"

She steadied herself and replied, "Yes, I am in good health. I did not expect the invitation so soon and in this manner."

"I am sorry, Miss Turner. Lady Emma advised me that she is excited to make your acquaintance. She indicated she welcomes the meeting as Doctor Neville Bassington and Sir Robert have told her much about you. Lady Fintelton also sends her warm greetings. She explains that at her age, she may retire early. It will depend on her health. However, she also welcomes your acquaintance and the inspection of the tailor's shop.

Lady Emma also requested that I call in the morning and take your reply with me on my return. I shall call at nine in the morning and pick up your response. Lady Emma sends her apologies for the short notice but was keen on not missing the opportunity of meeting you here in Guildford. She understands that Doctor Neville Bassington, whom she regards as a good friend, has advised you of the address of the residence he is purchasing and the building which will house his forthcoming medical practice.

Lady Emma also noted that your father owns a Tailor's chain of stores. They would be pleased if you would show them the Guilford store, as they are always in search of a good tailor closer than London."

"Thank you, Mr Stem. Certainly, I will accept the kind invitation. I will have the reply ready in the morning."

Mr Stem noticed that Anne remained nervous about the invitation. He understood that she was not of the aristocracy and would be overwhelmed by such an event. Mindful of his position, Malcolm Stem thought he might give this young lady some additional assurance. He suspected she was receiving this sudden invitation for some good reason. That reason, Lady Emma had not confided in him.

"Miss Turner, I see you are a little troubled by this invitation. I am not aware of the circumstances, but I would reassure you that the Earl and the Countess are fine people. I have worked for them for nearly twenty years, and they have always treated me fairly. This invitation is one of friendship. Lady Emma and Lady Jane desire your company. You need not be worried – they will accept you as a friend and an equal."

Anne once again breathed in and felt the tear in her eye. She did what she could to hide it and looked Malcolm Stem straight in the face, 'Thank you, Mr Stem. That is most comforting. In your message, Lady Jane indicates that because of her age, she may retire early. Pray, what age is she? You see, I have never met them before."

"Ah, the Lady would be nearly sixty, and the Earl is in his early seventies. They married late, with the children coming even later. Lady Emma was born about a year after I commenced my employment there. The two brothers were born before I commenced. Hugh the elder brother is now firmly in control of the estate, and the Earl now spends most of his time catching up with friends and family."

"I see!"

"Thank you, Miss Turner. I shall call for your reply at nine tomorrow morning!" Her sparkling blue eyes impressed him.

"Mr Stem. Would it be possible for you to call on me at Turner's bakery, at the offices there? I will have a reply ready for you. We are extremely busy at present, and I will have been at work for nearly two hours by then, so I will not be home."

"You work, My Lady?"

"Yes, Mr Stem, I assist my father in managing the bakery operations. I will expect you there." Anne thought she might give herself a slight promotion as it may improve the report this fellow gave Emma.

Mr Stem was quite surprised by this. He wondered how her father could employ such a well-dressed and refined young lady. Still, it was her father's business, so that would be something interesting in his report.

"Certainly, Miss Anne, I shall call there at nine in the morning and ask for you." He raised his eyebrows.

"The world is changing, Mr Stem, is it not?" She smiled.

"Yes, Miss Turner! I must now be about the estate business. Good day!"

"Good day, Sir. I shall not forget your kindness."

"And a good day to you, Master William." He gave William a wink.

William, who stood beside Anne during the conversation, looked up and said, "Good Day, Mr Stem." He tried winking back with his left eye and smiling at the same time but found the eye stayed shut. Anne put her arm around his shoulders.

Mr Stem smiled, looked up from William, nodded, and went down the stairs. Anne returned inside, finding Bethany, Clementine and Mrs Turner standing inside the open door. William stayed on the portico and watched the carriage clatter off down the High Street.

Looking a little sheepish, Anne said, "I would presume that you heard the conversation?"

"Yes," said Mrs Turner. "How exciting – may I look at the invitation?" She scanned it and looked up at Anne. "Dear, we will be going shopping for clothes again tomorrow. This news is excellent. Also, Mrs Smith will need her most elegant garments and fabrics on display for Saturday morning as she may have some new customers! "

Thomas Turner arrived home keen on a pre-dinner walk with Marion. He ventured in, attracted by the sounds of the excited conversation taking place in the parlour.

"Ah, Thomas – just look at all these lovely clothes we have purchased today," Mrs Turner said as he appeared. "And if you are looking for Marion, she is upstairs trying on some new garments."

"I will see her soon, but first, I must wash and change my clothes. I think we will take a walk before dinner." Moving off upstairs, he was glad they were now back again with William, who appeared recovered.

William tugged on his mother's sleeve, pleading to accompany Simeon as he walked Snups.

"Certainly, William – you seem recovered but take it slowly. Not too much excitement. Go slowly, please!"

William was delighted with this and was off in an instant.

Jonathan Turner finished the day satisfied the new staff arrangements were in place. Now everything was ready for the London trip! They would set out this coming Thursday morning. He was excited about making the acquaintance of the Bassingtons. The stay with the McPhersons should be straightforward.

Thomas knocked on Marion's door and, as the door opened, found her excited and radiant in a new dress.

"What a picture you are, Marion! That is a lovely dress. Did you purchase it today?"

"Thank you, Thomas. Yes, I found it at Hursts. They have some lovely fashions there, and Mrs Smith is so helpful, I could not resist. I thought you would like it."

"It is splendid!"

"By the way, Thomas, is it your father or your mother who owns Hursts?"

"It is mother's, but father appointed a manager who runs the chain. He lives in Woking. It would be fair to say both mother and father control the business, but it is legally mother's."

Marion was satisfied with this answer, and before ducking back through the door, she said, "Give me five minutes, and I will change." And the door closed.

Thomas leaned back on the railing and breathed in the atmosphere, which was a mixture of Marion's perfume and the usual smells of the well-polished wood of the house. He was a happy man. His love from Greenwich was in the next room, and his career was about to leap forward into a new industry. He now thought of brewing as far more exciting than baking. What more could a man want? Aggie passed him with a pail of water in her hand. She noticed his pleasant demeanour, "You look happy, Master Thomas."

"I am indeed Aggie, indeed! And what is Mrs Jennings preparing for our dinner tonight, may I ask?"

"It is a surprise, Sir, but I think it may contain some duck!"

"Good – I like the crispy duck she does!"

Marion reappeared from her room in a completely different outfit, more suitable for walking.

Thomas was impressed again, "I'm not sure how you ladies change your clothes so quickly!"

"Shall we go, Thomas, as I have a question that has been on my mind all day? I am so happy when I am here with you, but I shudder about Greenwich and returning without you. When will you visit next?"

They went down the stairs together, out the front door and off along the High Street.

"Marion. Let me tell you some good news. Father and I spent the day working out all the new staffing arrangements, and they are now in place. As a result, I may now change my role, and I am free to return with you to Greenwich. So, we can work on the wedding arrangements together."

"Thomas. The news is wonderful as the thought of the return journey on Thursday without you worries me. Your mother and father will travel to London on Thursday and Friday. I will accompany them. Now there is no reason why you cannot come. The trip will be perfect."

She hugged him with a kiss on the cheek. The good news gave Marion's confidence a boost.

"We shall enjoy the journey together. Now, shall we walk along the riverbank for a while? It is a cool and quiet place in the late afternoon. We may even see some swans. They are such regal birds – the white ones, I mean."

Marion was miles away, already planning the wedding day.

"Thomas, I'm sure Mr and Mrs McPherson will be planning a huge wedding for us. You don't mind if the guest list is rather large?"

"Not if they are paying and happy with a large list. No, I don't mind at all."

"The McPhersons have a great deal of money, and they and my father are close. I'm sure the money will not be a problem. If I know Mrs McPherson, she will be planning this as one of the year's social events. It will be good for both Mr McPherson and our fathers' businesses."

"The McPhersons appear quite wealthy. Was it always this way?"

"I understand they were poor when they were first married, but they have worked hard in Scotland and built up their brewing business over the years. In Glasgow, they have some ships they use for importing goods. The business regularly trades in France, Spain and the American states – mostly New York and Boston. I'm not clear how it started, but my father tells me it came from another brother of Mr McPherson, now deceased. I gather that my uncle inherited the business some twenty years ago. It was sad that he lost a brother but a nice surprise gaining a viable business for free."

"I'm sure it was! I wish someone would give me a shipping business!"

"I hear it is quite tricky, Thomas. James McPherson and his elder brother Lachlan are away most of the time on voyages. They often travel on the ships and run the Glasgow office. But it must be most lucrative as they are never short of money."

"I thought they each ran breweries."

"They do, but that is not all they do."

"It will be interesting meeting James when we are in Greenwich."

"He is a charming young man. I have known him most of my life, and he treats me like the little sister he never had. I think you two will get on well."

"Good, good! We have probably walked far enough along the bank here. Best if we now turn and head for home. We should be in plenty of time for dinner."

"Now, Thomas. We must talk tonight. After dinner...... "

They continued with an animated conversation while walking home.

There was much discussion about the coming weddings at dinner, and Thomas suggested joining Marion on the Thursday London trip. Jonathan Turner readily agreed as he was now satisfied that the new staff structure was complete. So, the travelling party would now be six. Jonathan, mindful that Eleanora was with child, decided the number was too many for the one coach. He announced he would hire an additional coach for Marion and Thomas on the condition they travelled in a convoy and stopped with them at Ewell. It would be a good opportunity for Uncle Richard and Auntie Sarah to meet Marion. She beamed at the thought of them having their coach. Thomas joked, saying that the coach would probably be one of his father's baker's carts. A quick explanation was necessary as Marion was perplexed at the thought. She was much relieved to find the comment was in jest.

Anne and Bethany talked a little about the coming occasions while sitting side by side.

"I'm sure you are looking forward to Neville returning tomorrow. I hope he makes it on time for the London trip."

"Yes, Anne. That has worried me, but he seems very punctual except when in the bath!" They both smiled.

"I understand that the paperwork was not about resigning his commission but some medical records that needed completing from his last ship. I hope he does not regret leaving the navy!"

"I think there is little prospect of that. It is a demanding career, and I am sure he will prefer the prospect of land-based life. It must take special men being cooped up on a ship like that for so long. They say the voyage to Sydney Cove takes at least four to six months by sail and twelve months if the winds are not right. You would lose all track of time."

"A life here will be very different for him!"

"Now, Bethany. Tomorrow, you must show me your new residence and the building Neville has purchased for his practice. Emma and Lady Jane have requested a viewing on Saturday. Perhaps before work tomorrow if you are free?"

"Yes, but I have written it all down and informed the agent. Surely you know these addresses?"

"I do, but I want your commentary on them, so I am prepared when talking with the ladies. They will surely have objections, and I need prepared answers ready. I must not be tongue-tied and look limited."

"Anne, with your gift of the word, I think it unlikely that you will appear limited, but I will give you the grand tour tomorrow morning early. I have the keys and will leave them with you. Are you prepared for the dinner on Friday night?"

"I should never have let Robert talk me into this, as I am petrified that it will all go wrong. These are aristocrats, and they must look down on me. It will only be their generosity that will allow any friendship at all. I should have thought of this when I first met Robert, but I did not. I now understand that the possibility of any attachment is almost impossible."

"That's not true, Anne. You are a gentleman's daughter and are their equal. Why the way father's businesses are growing, we may have more money than they, in the future."

Anne was not convinced and carried a troubled frown on her face.

"Anne, I am disappointed that I will not accompany you on Friday night. If I had my way, I would, but we must travel to London! There is no room for a delay with our mother's condition!"

"Beth, you are so sweet. Just the thought of your good wishes gives me some hope that the dinner will go well. Tell me, has Neville discussed mother's condition with you?"

Bethany looked concerned and said, "Not now, Anne, perhaps tonight in our room."

Dinner was now over, and Marion approached Beth, requesting help explaining the third chapter of a complex book. Bethany gladly obliged, taking the opportunity to understand Marion better. As they moved into the parlour, Thomas sat beside Anne.

He quietly said, "Marion told me a little about the McPhersons. They also have a shipping company working out of Glasgow, Scotland. They inherited it lock, stock and barrel. One of Mr McPherson's brothers passed away and left it to him. Father will have his attorneys enquire about it discreetly, of course. When I have more information, I will share it with you. Perhaps you would discuss with Robert what he knows about the shipping line?"

"You should not involve Robert! Anyway, we will not meet until Beth's wedding. He has enough responsibility in his life without our worries."

"He is already involved! During his last visit, I took the opportunity for a long private talk with him. He was wondering the same thing. How did they accumulate so much so quickly? He assumed it was just because of the successful breweries they own."

"You should not have involved him, Thomas. That is not fair."

"Nothing is fair in this world, Anne. Anyway, I hope he may be my brother-in-law one day."

It seemed that her secret was well and truly out. She wondered if Robert's family was aware.

The Evening before the Trip to London ...

Neville sat with the two boys in their room upstairs. Arriving back after Wednesday lunch, he announced he was now out of the navy unless there was a war. The government could call upon him if hostilities broke out. With no signs of a war on the horizon, there was little prospect of them calling upon him.

"It appears, William, the rash is gone, and your throat seems clear. I see you have your energy back. I think you will be ready for school once Reverend Taggart starts again."

William thought about school. Perhaps if he told Neville he was tired, school would not be an option. Neville, being quite perceptive, raised the issue, "Of course, if you're feeling tired, then I should bleed you again. How are you feeling?"

William instantly said, "I'm feeling fine. Let me run around the house and show you!"

"Really! Off you go and show me." William darted off, nearly knocking over his father as Jonathan entered the room.

"Damn boy!"

Neville frowned and directed his next comment at Simeon, "I think it is time we removed that cast so we can have a good look at the arm. It has been several weeks now. Let me see if the break has mended cleanly. I will put another cast on if needed."

"I think it is fine!" Simeon moved away from Neville up the bed.

"You will be far more comfortable with it off, and it won't hurt. I'll show you how."

Neville opened his medical bag and pulled out a massive pair of shears. "These will cut right through the plaster. You won't feel a thing."

Simeon's eyes grew quite large as he saw the long scissors.

Jonathan Turner said, "This, I must see!"

Bethany and Anne retired together upstairs after taking their leave.

Anne worried about her mother's health and wanted an update, "What does Neville think about mother's condition?"

"He feels the baby is fine, but he is concerned about the outcome for her after the delivery. He thinks there is some underlying health problem that he cannot easily diagnose. He has discussed this with his father but will not tell me the detail of those discussions. From the look on his face, I would say it is quite serious."

"Perhaps that explains why father is outlaying so much for her comfort on this trip?" Anne suspected there might be another reason.

"I think so – he takes such good care of our mother."

Anne was amazed. Beth seemed oblivious of her father's beating her mother.

"At times, Beth, but he has also been cruel. Father is presently very loving and kind, but that is possibly from guilt!"

"We are family Anne, so we must remain united – it is our strength in society. You should not criticise our father!"

The rage within Anne erupted, "Even if it means men may beat women into submission? You were away for two years, Beth. You have not seen what I have. I would rather run away than be beaten by a husband."

Beth thought about this and sighed, "It's not that I approve of it, but how do we deal with reality? A woman is completely dependent on her family or husband. I am lucky that I have found a kind gentleman who is so in love with me. I cannot foretell what will happen in twenty years! Should I find myself in our mother's position, I would probably do as she has done. Let it settle down and make the best of it."

Anne could not accept this, "No, Beth, we are all born equal and should plan for our future. Married or not, we need our independence. I have saved all my wages from my work at the bakery, and in time I will make investments that will grow. I will discuss it with father and mother, ensuring each of us gains a fair share of the business. This will allow us all to be independent. I fear being reliant on any man. If I marry, I want the option of independence if the need should ever arise."

"And if you marry Robert, would you think the same?"

"Of course, but he is making his career as his family's estate is entailed on the older brother. So, I'm sure he would encourage me in what I am doing. He will do the same thing. And if I am so lucky that we marry, I would enjoy a long, happy life with an Admiral and equally pass on all my wealth. None of this entailment nonsense for me."

"I am impressed with your aims Anne. I just pray you are not disappointed if it does not work out that way. But I will always be your friend and sister, whatever happens."

"And I yours."

Later that night, Thomas knocked lightly on Marion's door. He heard footsteps then the door slightly opened, revealing a dark room.

"Sorry, Marion, were you asleep?"

The door opened a bit more, and Marion pulled him quickly into the room and closed the door. Thomas found the room pitch dark. Then he felt her beside him. She guided him over towards the bed. As his eyes adjusted, he noticed her standing very close in a nightgown.

"Thomas, put your arms around me and kiss me."

Thomas was always one for a good kiss, and there was no hesitation in joining lips with her and enjoying the experience. Then Marion opened the nightgown, and he found her naked. He pulled her against him and said, "Are you cold?"

"A bit, but you can warm me up."

She pulled him onto the bed and started kissing his face madly.

Thomas was a bit surprised as he was expecting only a quick conversation. This action seemed a little desperate on her part and could be dangerous. But he found her perfume intoxicating, and his hands moved onto her breasts which were small and firm just as he had imagined. As he kissed them, she jumped as they were very tender. She whispered, "Gently darling, gently."

Following her instructions, he commenced exploring her body, but he thought better. 'Somehow, I must stop this now without upsetting Marion. I do not want a pregnant wife on our wedding day.'

Marion was thinking about Mrs McPherson's discussion with her before leaving Greenwich. In this household, she felt insecure, being the newcomer in the family. She needed affirmation of Thomas's full support. Her Aunt's advice was, 'If given a chance, you should cement the alliance.' Did Aunty Marjorie have doubts about Thomas or the Turner family? The daughters were all so beautiful, and the sons were handsome. Was she saying catch him while you can?

Pregnancy was not in her plan for the first year of marriage, but she was petrified of being left on the shelf. That would be a disaster. If Thomas found her pregnant, would he resent it? She must find a way of understanding his thoughts. This might be risky, but she must allow him the opportunity.

He rolled her onto her side and started kissing her back. He found it exquisite. She enjoyed his touch as he kissed her slowly from the top of her shoulders and down her spine. Slowly, he rolled her over, kissing her right around and onto her stomach. Lifting his head with her hands, she kissed his lips and wrapped her legs around his thighs.

"This is wonderful, Marion, but should we not stop here? If we go any further, I may not control myself. I want you so much, but we should do this correctly. I am sure we should wait until our wedding night!"

Marion was content with this comment. She was sure of him now as a lesser man would have taken advantage. She was not as innocent as Thomas might think and, unfortunately, had experienced men taking advantage of her before. She was amazed by the control he was showing. "Yes, darling, we should stop but let us just lie in each other's arms for a moment more, so we can think of this till the wedding day."

Thomas was not sure that this was a good idea but remembered his father's advice, 'If the opportunity arises, cement the alliance!' Perhaps his father was speaking from experience. His mother related that he was born premature, but there were no side effects. He was a happy and healthy baby. Thomas frowned – his father must have made sure of his mother well before the marriage. It was clear now in his mind - he was born full term.

"Marion, darling. There is nothing else I would rather do than what we are doing now. I want you forever lying in my arms. You are the sweetest, most beautiful young lady, and you will make a wonderful wife. But if I do this now, I will not honour you as I should. We should consummate our union in marriage and with God's blessing. I think we will need time as a couple before we have children. Enjoying the honeymoon would be difficult if you are pregnant, darling."

He was right. The honeymoon would be in France in winter. There would be plenty of time in bed, keeping warm. Marion was satisfied that she had offered him the opportunity. A lesser man would have taken her without even thinking. Thomas could think quite rationally, even in a stressful situation. He honoured her and valued chastity before marriage – Marion felt she liked this. She wasn't that worried about what God thought or what the church taught. Faith was something Marion rarely considered, but this man she loved held high ideals. This self-control must come from belief and faith – virtues she had always struggled with. Thomas was the right man for her, and perhaps he would teach her much as their relationship grew. She gently kissed his lips again and said, "You are right."

They kissed and hugged each other again, and then she said, "Good night. Off you go."

Thomas slowly moved off the bed and towards the door. He listened at the door for any movement. Nothing! Opening the door onto a dark landing, he faced his father. He froze, nearly jumping out of his skin.

Jonathan Turner winked at him and quietly said, "That's my boy!" His father tiptoed away down the hall. Thomas, in his surprise, said nothing, and then his father was gone. He wondered as he stood there what his father was thinking. Having done the honourable thing, he hoped his father thought the same. Somehow, he suspected his father thought differently. Thomas rationalised, "If that is what he believed, so be it. His problem, not mine."

Thomas tiptoed upstairs, making sure not to wake Simeon and William, who he thought were fast asleep! Once in bed, he was drifting off pleasantly when he felt a tugging on his sleeve. William was kneeling on the floor beside his bed with his eyes inches away from Thomas's face.

"He was standing at Marion's door, listening for about ten minutes. It was a bit spooky. I'm glad you were in there with her!"

Thomas opened his eyes and thought about it, then said, "Calm down, William. I have spoken to him. It is all explained. Go back to bed!"

The Turner Bakery, Guildford ...

Mr Malcolm Stem arrived at precisely nine in the morning. Entering the bakery, he asked for directions. His first impressions were of a far more extensive operation than he expected. Jeb led him past tables where staff mixed and kneaded dough, trays of products, storage racks and rows of ovens generating a heat well above the outside temperature. As he climbed up the stairs, he noticed several baker's carts with staff loading them with bread and various other products through a side door. The aroma of freshly baked bread pleasantly aroused his senses. Jeb stopped at the back of the office at the front of a desk where Anne Turner, wearing a grey smock, worked on a ledger full of figures. As usual, Anne lost herself in the calculations.

"Excuse me, Anne, Mr Malcolm Stem has an appointment with you?"

Raising her eyes, she recognised her visitor, "Ah, Mr Stem, thank you for coming."

The Fintelton estate manager feeling more comfortable in a working environment and the company of a man, asked Jeb, "Is she good at the figures, Mr Hiscock?"

"Ah, she is a genius! So quick and accurate. And better than that, she understands what they mean!"

Malcolm Stem looked impressed.

"Thank you, Jeb. You may go. I will look after Mr Stem."

The new bakery manager was pleased to leave them as there was a mountain of work waiting. Mr Stem considered Anne differently today. He now saw her in working clothes. She was just as attractive, but now he recognised that this girl was cleverer than anyone perceived. She would be a challenge for any of the ladies at Fintelton.

"Miss Anne, if you ever visit Fintelton, might I be so bold and request your assistance in giving me some instruction on the Estate figures. I can add up, subtract and divide, but I find it difficult understanding what they mean."

Anne smiled and quickly said, "Mr Stem, it would be an honour if I am ever fortunate enough to receive an invitation. Now here is the response for Lady Emma, and I wish you a pleasant journey."

Understanding that this young lady did not waste time, Mr Stem checked himself and said no more on the subject. He was unsure what he was dealing with here, but he thought if the ladies of Fintelton would be visiting, then there was a high probability she would soon appear at the estate. Unaware of what the connection was, he felt safer being careful.

"Thank you, Miss Anne." He made a respectful nod and went.

Anne breathed out a sigh of relief and recommenced her calculations. Sales continued increasing. The only explanation must be that Guildford was expanding. She would discuss this with her father on his return from London. Then she thought about the coming dinner, wondering how the ladies at Fintelton would receive her acceptance. It was all organised now. There was no turning back.

She was due at ten for a fitting at Hursts with Mrs Smith. Her mother and Beth would be gone by now, so only herself and Mrs Smith would be there. She preferred having her mother or Beth advise her on selections, but this would not be possible today. It was time she packed up, as time was running out for the two new dresses she ordered. Mrs Smith must complete them today, so there was no panic before Friday evening. Once the fitting was over, she would return and discuss the figures with Jeb.

At Ewell …

By mid-afternoon, the travelling party were keen for the comforts of brother Richard's hotel in Ewell. Eleanora, although uncomfortable in her gentle condition, handled the trip well. The conversation between Beth and Eleanora was endless, with Neville making comments occasionally. Jonathan wondered how so much discussion could be continually generated, and quickly lost interest. As they reached the outskirts of Ewell, he was ready for a quiet drink and some dinner.

The first chance for business discussion between Jonathan and Richard was later that evening. They were seated in Richard's private study, enjoying a scotch and quietly talking about business.

"Jonathan, I must tell you! My application for land in South Africa has been successful."

Jonathan looked up in surprise.

"It appears that some of the first farmers who took up land grants have given up their holdings and gone off looking for either gold or diamonds. Fortune hunters! To my advantage, they have lost their land grants, and the government has allocated to me five adjoining properties not more than twenty miles from Grahamstown[19] (Makhanda). Just up from Port Elizabeth[20] (Gqeberha)."

---

[19] The town's name change from Grahamstown to Makhanda was officially Gazetted on 29 June 2018. The town was officially renamed to Makhanda in memory of Xhosa warrior and prophet Makhanda ka Nxele. Wikipedia

[20] In 2019, the Eastern Cape Geographical Names Committee recommended that Port Elizabeth be renamed Gqeberha, after the Xhosa and Southern Khoe name for the Baakens River that flows through the city. The city's name change was officially gazette on 23 Febraury 2021. Wikipedia

"Congratulations, Richard. How much land would this be?"

"The normal grant is around one hundred acres, but it might be up to one hundred acres per member if it was a cooperative. In this case, it is a combination of two cooperatives and three individual holdings of two thousand five hundred acres. Interestingly, there are more holdings on offer, and some of the settlers have done so poorly that they are offering to indenture themselves for five years. I am negotiating for some of these."

"Wouldn't that mean the land is not good for farming?"

"That's precisely correct, Jonathan. But I have done my research and know that the native people, the land's original inhabitants, used it for cattle grazing, not farming. My feeling is that the locals might understand the country a bit better than the British governor out there. I plan to graze cattle and sheep, mostly sheep, and try for more land grants."

Jonathan was surprised Richard's plans had progressed so quickly and worried he would be leaving sooner than expected.

"Richard, when will you take up these land holdings?"

"I have already accepted them. Now I am arranging the transport of sheep and cattle out there for a breeding program. With the English appetite for wool these days, I should begin receiving income from wool clips by the middle of next year. There is a growing population in South Africa, so there will also be a market for beef and lamb."

"So, when is your departure date?

"If all goes well, it should be about February or March next year. Oliver is now fully trained at Epsom and will grow the business quickly. Harry understands the ropes here, and I am confident he will manage well. If you come down, let us say one day a month, have a discussion and a tour of the establishment, that should be enough. My attorneys have some accountants who will be doing the figures, so you might involve Anne in checking them. She will brief you on progress financially. I will depend on your assistance Johnathan. The boys will still need a mentor."

"I am not that familiar with the books of a pub, Richard. I have no experience in this."

"Jonathan, I do, and tonight will be your first lesson. If we can meet several times before I depart, you will become familiar with them. You will know from your business that cash flow is everything. In a pub, if you keep your margins correct and maintain your regular clientele, stable cash flow will result, and you cannot go wrong. Here, you may start with these ledgers."

"Perhaps I should bring Anne next time, so she is also familiar with the books? Do you have a bookkeeper?"

"Yes, Harry manages the bookkeeper. And yes, please bring Anne. She is a magician with the figures, Jonathan! You best make sure she does not marry!

Without her, you would be lost."

The two brothers worked long into the night. Around one in the morning, Jonathan cried for mercy, "Richard, that is enough, my head is spinning. Time for bed."

Richard smiled as he understood the difficulties of grappling with a new set of books.

"At our next meeting, say in October, I will have both Oliver and Harry here so you can question them. That will make it much easier. Oliver has found you a good 'stable manager'. He is an older fellow who was a trainer at the Epsom course but wants a more regular job. His name is Thomas Baxter, a single gentleman; he seems like a nice chap. You should meet with him if you can stop at Epsom on your return journey."

"Sounds promising, Richard, but I must retire now. Please have Oliver hire this Thomas Baxter. I trust his judgement. We need the stables operating for the fast carts. I am too tired now for any more figures, and it will be another long day tomorrow. Good night."

Jonathan did not linger, and within a few minutes of his head hitting the pillow, he was fast asleep.

At Fintelton Manor ...

Malcolm Stem worked on several estate issues needing priority, and it was not until around five in the evening when he met with Lady Emma and reported back.

"Mr Stem, how was your Guildford trip?"

"Most interesting, Milady. Most interesting. I have a reply from Miss Anne Turner for you here."

Mr Stem passed the envelope over. She took it with interest, taking a glance and then looked up.

"What did you think of the young lady, Mr Stem? You see, I have not met her myself!"

"Milady, it is strange that you say this as she said a similar thing about you. She welcomes the meeting, but I would say she is also nervous about the occasion." Before speaking, Malcolm Stem considered his next comment, "I found her very presentable, Milady. She is intelligent, and I think you will find her good company. She dresses well!"

"Mr Stem, I am relieved. It sounds as if her conversation is lively. You say she was well dressed. Do you mean she lacked in looks, and the dress made up for it? A plain girl, Mr Stem?" Emma hoped this might be the case.

"Far from it, Milady. I would call her handsome, indeed. Her sense of dress matches well with her good looks. I was impressed, and I think you will find her acceptable, Milady."

Emma was not without insight and understood that Stem was careful in what he said. There was no advantage in him becoming offside with the daughter of his master. But Emma knew Stem, and he meant what he said. By this account, Anne must be presentable indeed. Perhaps she should review her dressing plans for tomorrow night. She was determined that a baker's daughter would not outdo her.

"You were impressed, Mr Stem. I am intrigued. And the family?"

"I only met her younger brother, as I did not enter the house. However, it seems a very respectable house in Guildford, Milady."

The report was more than what Emma expected. This girl sounded interesting. Surely this baker's daughter could not have the manners of a well-educated lady such as herself and the circles she moved in! Of course not! Tomorrow would tell.

"Thank you for carrying out this task, Mr Stem – I appreciate your assistance. Now, I understand that you will be accompanying my mother to Guildford. You will collect Miss Turner from her home, escort her to the hotel and return her home at the end of the evening. I take it these arrangements are suitable?"

"They are Milady, and it will be my pleasure! Milady, might I inquire how this meeting with Miss Turner came about?"

Emma quickly thought about her response and decided not to mention Robert's name.

"Doctor Neville Bassington, a good family friend, has announced his engagement. He will marry Miss Turner's older sister, Bethany. We will break our London journey at Guildford and take the opportunity of meeting with her."

Emma thought this was ample explanation, and it satisfied the Estate Manager.

Mr Stem nodded and mused as he walked off, 'Lady Emma may be quite surprised when she meets Miss Anne Turner!'

After dinner, Emma found her mother reading in the parlour. She opened the letter from Anne and found the writing was of a high standard.

High Street, Guildford
Wednesday, 6 September 1826

Dear Lady Emma and Lady Jane South
Thank you for your kind invitation for dinner this coming Friday evening at the Fox and Hound. It gives me great pleasure to accept your invitation. I look forward to meeting you both and, on the

Saturday following, showing you the properties at Guilford that our mutual friend Doctor Neville Bassington has selected.

Yours sincerely
Miss Anne Turner.

"Mother, this young Miss Anne Turner displays a fair hand. Here is her reply."

Emma passed the letter across. Lady Jane South quickly read the letter and handed it back.

"She must have some education then. Most unusual for the daughter of a tradesman. But as you say, if we receive a wedding invitation, the acquaintance of at least one friendly face will be welcome. And, of course, Neville. Why is his fiancée not meeting with us for dinner as well?"

"As I told you, Mother, they are in London, where she and her parents meet with Neville's family for the first time."

"That should be amusing – the baker meeting the newspaper mogul!" Lady Fintelton gave a slight giggle.

"Now, Mother, sometimes we must keep an open mind. I am fond of Neville's parents. They are fine people, and I hope this young lady is a good match for him. And...... "

She was about to include Robert in her answer but stopped herself. Including Robert at this time would not be helpful.

"And what, Dear?"

"Nothing, Mother – it seems a good match. As the Curate says, we are fortunate in life, and we should not judge!"

"Judge who?" Hugh was interested.

Lord Fintelton and his son, Sir Hugh, came back into the parlour as their estate work was complete. Emma turned and smiled at them though she was a bit unsettled now as mentioning the meeting, particularly with Hugh, was certainly not part of their plan. Unfortunately, Hugh picked up on the last part of the sentence.

"Neville requested we call on the younger sister of his fiancée in Guildford as we travel up to London. Their family owns a chain of tailor's shops, and mother and I will visit the shop on Saturday morning. We will also inspect Neville's new residence and the building he will practice from."

The Earl standing beside his wife's chair, spluttered, "But has anyone formally introduced you? Surely not, my Dear. Go straight to London."

"Neville Bassington has introduced us, a long term and good friend of the family, my Dear, and the arrangements are complete. Anyway, the discovery of a decent tailor a bit closer than London would be welcome. We would no longer require these long trips so often. I am becoming too ancient for all this travel. Emma and I will go, and we will be pleased to make Miss Turner's acquaintance."

Emma said under her breath, 'Bravo, mother!'

"Where will you be staying, Mother?" Hugh's interest continued.

"The Fox and Hound is a very respectable hotel and is quite central and close to Miss Turner's family home."

Hugh sat in a chair beside his mother, putting his hands on his thighs as he leaned back, stretching the leather. He would not object as he was interested in a tailor in closer proximity. He agreed that the London trip was long, and he enjoyed Guilford. There were a few good wenches there that would satisfy his appetite. Perhaps this friend of Neville's might be a fair prospect. He had no plans for this coming Saturday.

"Mother, I have some business in Guildford. Perhaps I shall join your party for dinner on Saturday?"

Emma was petrified. She knew Robert would be against such a plan, as he and Hugh held quite different views. Robert was a true gentleman. On the other hand, Hugh rarely displayed the qualities of his class despite his heritage. Fortunately for him, his parents were not aware of his antics. They never inquired, and Emma had no wish of bringing a message that would ruin her relationship with her parents. Hugh was the apple of their eye, the next Earl of Fintelton.

"Yes, definitely, I will meet you there. What time on Friday do you dine?"

Lady Jane smiled and said, "Eight o'clock. That is kind of you, Hugh. I shall feel safe with you there!"

In a gruff voice, the Earl said, "No need at all. But good boy – keep the women protected, especially when mixing with the lower classes. I am for bed. Goodnight all! Come, Jane, I will walk you upstairs."

"Thank you, David."

The Earl and Lady Jane slowly moved out of the parlour.

Emma's heart sank. She had promised Robert a faultless plan. With Hugh coming, it could turn into a disaster. Anne would need protection from Hugh. Emma was aware of how he used women for his gratification. Sometimes she felt she disliked Hugh as much as Robert did. She must meet with Anne before dinner. Also, she would need Stem in town again for assistance as a backup against any improper advance Hugh might make. Emma sighed; this was turning into a major exercise.

Hugh walked over to the sideboard, grabbed a large whiskey bottle and two glasses, and came back to join her.

"Have a drink with me, Em?"

"No, thank you, Hugh. I have a headache and will turn in. Sorry, but I am also tired. Good night."

Hugh did not answer as he was too busy pouring the first glass of scotch down his throat. Then he looked around and, in a deep, loud voice, screamed out, "Pike! Where are you, man? Get me some pastries. I am hungry! Pike!"

Chapter 14

At Guildford ...

Snups' nose rested on the bed near Simeon's ear. He gently licked the ear until Sim turned over. The dog was persistent, turning his attention to William and nudging his shoulder. Sitting up, William stroked the dog's head and watched as he ran over and scratched at the closed door. Simeon's eyes were now open, and he wondered why his ear was wet.

"Sim, I think he needs a walk!"

Simeon sat up and rubbed his eyes. Opening the window, he could see the mist clearing towards the river. He turned and patted an increasingly agitated Snups.

"Yep, let's go." The boys pulled on their clothes and opened the door, releasing Snups into the second-floor hallway.

With their parents in London and only Anne in charge, they felt more freedom than usual. Creeping downstairs through the quiet house, the boys told Mrs Jennings they were taking Snups for a walk. A yawning housekeeper counselled that a return before breakfast would be advisable.

Making their way along the empty High Street, they felt the morning chill of early autumn. As they crossed the River Wey at the High Street bridge, they stopped and looked downstream towards the wharf, where several men were unloading three barges. A dog on the closest barge rushed among the men unloading the cargo. Snups saw the dog and started barking wildly.

"Quiet Snups, that's enough!" Simeon sternly said and then looked back at the wharf. The other dog barked back but soon lost interest and continued darting between the men.

Once across the bridge, they headed up the river where weeping willows dipped into the water, making a wonderland of greenery and small islands. Here was a place where imaginations could run wild.

"Here, boy, catch this!"

Willian threw a large stick out into the water. Snups watched the small branch fly over his head and, without hesitation, jumped into the water after it. Grabbing it in his mouth, the dog swam back, scrambled out of the water and ran to William, dropping the stick. Snups then shook himself, splattering water all over the lad. Simeon laughed as he saw William jump.

"You should know by now that he would do that!"

Wiping the water off as best he could, William turned towards Simeon. "I forgot, Sim! At least there is not much mud in it. But Anne will notice for sure."

"She won't mind. She has bigger things on her mind."

The boys started moving further up the river, where a walking bridge crossed the water, meeting a track below the castle ruins. Calling Snups, they ran up the slope imagining they were Norman invaders taking the castle. Snups, lingering at the riverbank, looked up, barked, and then flashed after them up the hill. At the top, breathing heavily, they sat on a log.

"What bigger things has Anne on her mind, Sim?"

"She is having dinner with Robert's sister and mother tonight, and I think she is a bit worried about it."

"Why is she worried?"

"Think about it, William! She hasn't met them before, and she likes Robert and needs to impress them."

William blinked as he thought about this.

"You mean she wants to marry Robert, so she needs to be good friends with the sister and mother, so he gets permission."

"You are not as dumb as you look, Will!"

"Why are they all getting married? They should stay here at home and have fun like we always have. If they get married and move away, then father concentrates more on us, and I am the one who usually gets belted."

"The bigger we get, the less he will belt us, Will."

"I'm not getting big enough, fast enough!"

"You are as tall as me and two years younger. I think you will be quite tall when you grow up."

"Growing up. It never happens. Each morning I wake up, and I'm the same. One day when I'm big, I will give father a belting."

"We better get home soon before Anne is awake, or she will give us a belting."

They both jumped up and started running down Market Street, dashing between the arriving stallholders and following the High Street towards home. Snups barked as he caught up with them, running past and onto the house.

Anne opened one eye to the sound of Snups barking as the three of them bounded up the street. She looked at the clock, and it was six-fifteen, time she was up and about. Today would be long and busy. She sighed. So much work at the bakery and then the dinner tonight. The new gowns would be ready, and she must pick them up at some time during the morning. She liked getting dressed up and having dinner out but not on her own without support. She shuddered at what might happen tonight and recalled how Robert had convinced her. She should never have agreed.

The Black Swann, Ewell …

Jonathon Turner was pleased with their progress after a good breakfast at Ewell and some quick farewells. It was now twelve-thirty as they approached Lewisham, having completed most of the trip. The plan was a stop at the McPherson's for luncheon, where they would leave Marion and Thomas and then head off for London. Jonathon was concerned for his wife, who was now approaching mid-term in her pregnancy. A long trip by coach such as this would not help her condition.

Neville Bassington saw the look on Jonathon's face and reassured him, "Jonathon, she is fine. A good break at Greenwich and some lunch will give her plenty of energy for the final few miles into London."

"Thank you, Neville. I have been worried about this trip for some time. While I understand we must make the journey, I also know that Eleanora's health must come first. She will need an early evening tonight."

"Perhaps a good rest this afternoon for a couple of hours. I'm sure my parents will wish for her presence at dinner. My sister, Megan, will be attending as well."

"Of course, Neville, of course."

Jonathon sat back, looking worried. Eleanora patted him on the knee.

"I am fine, Jonathon. We are close now, and the McPhersons will be expecting us."

Neville smiled as he saw them talking and Jonathon showing some slight signs of relief. On the other hand, Bethany was taking in everything outside the carriage.

"I have kept my promise!"

Bethany was surprised, "What promise?"

"To show you London!"

"Neville, this is Lewisham, not London!" She laughed, "Yes, you have kept your promise, but we are only just beginning. I want to see everything!" Having never travelled any further than Woking, Bethany relished each site as it passed by. The big world out there was proving fascinating for her.

"Perhaps not everything – time will determine what we see this time."

"Saint James Palace would be a good start, and then the Palace of Westminster. Harley Street, where you will set up your London practice, would also be good!"

"The first two are close by; perhaps we could take a stroll this afternoon while your mother is resting. Harley Street, probably tomorrow. We will need the carriage for that."

The coach moved on towards Greenwich.

In Guildford ...

Anne spent two hours working in the bakery when she realised it was ten o'clock. Rushing off to Hurst's, she picked up her new gowns and took them home. After laying them out on her bed and quickly admiring them, it was time to hurry back down the High Street through the crowds and into the bakery. Soon she was deep in thought, reviewing the figures. Jeb knocked on the wood of her desk.

"Miss Anne?"

Anne was miles away, considering the trends for this week. She rubbed her eyes and sat up straight, focusing on Jeb.

"You have a visitor!"

Anne peered around Jeb and saw a handsome young lady, about her age or perhaps a year older and close to her height, holding William's hand. The boy had a cheeky grin on his face. Anne stood up with a half-smile and a look of curiosity. She was wondering who this young woman could be.

"William, who is this?"

In a fine voice, the young lady said, "Now, William, you may officially introduce us."

William stood as straight as he could, took a big breath, and looked at the young lady for reassurance.

"Go on! Just as we practised, William." She encouraged him.

In a small child's voice, he said, "Miss Anne Turner, may I introduce Lady Emma South."

Anne gasped in surprise. This meeting took Anne entirely by surprise. Here was Anne in her work smock, no powdered face and looking like an office clerk, meeting one of the most important ladies in the neighbourhood. Anne steadied herself, straightened her smock, and brushed the hair out of her face. Her mouth was still open as Emma started the conversation.

"My Dear Anne, I must ask your forgiveness for meeting you unannounced, but as I will explain, there are some good reasons for this. I am so glad to meet you."

"It is a pleasure to make your acquaintance Lady Emma. I was not expecting you until this evening. If I had known, I would have dressed more respectfully. Please forgive my appearance. My father is in London, leaving me with much responsibility. But it is a pleasure meeting you."

Anne saw that Emma's warm smile was the same as Robert's, but she was more focused and wore very fashionable clothes. Her travelling suit was well-tailored and smart indeed, matching her soft brown hair tied in a bun. Anne assumed she had full-length hair that would be let out tonight.

Emma thought as she smiled at Anne, 'What can he see in this girl? Wearing a smock and working in her father's factory or bakery!' Emma was happy that she had caught Anne off-guard, but she recalled Robert's comments about her class. She felt a little ashamed of her pride. Despite the smock and ruffled hair, she did see a glimmer of the beauty that Neville had mentioned.

"Anne, I understand you are on a first-name basis with my brother Robert, so I would ask that I be on a first-name basis with you if that is acceptable?"

"Certainly Lady .... I mean Emma."

"I called at your home but only found the servants there and, of course, William. So, William and I have become acquainted, and he told me how Robert came across your family. Fascinating. So, I asked William to escort me down here and formally introduce us. Time is short, and I wished for a meeting with you before my mother arrives. We must discuss some unforeseen changes in our plan. Would you be taking lunch soon, as I will join you for a chat if that is acceptable?"

"Certainly, Milady.....sorry, I mean Emma! When I first met Robert, I had no idea who he was, and we became acquainted as equals. Now that I am informed, there is far more formality involved."

"I understand, Anne. Let us be friends, shall we?"

"Yes, I would like that. William, find Jeb and ask him for a packet of pastries, please."

"Enough for me too?" William looked up in hope.

"You did an excellent job of introducing Lady Emma, so yes, enough for you as well."

William needed no encouragement, lunchtime was close, and he was hungry. Emma smiled as he bustled off looking for Jeb, "I did a bit of coaching with him on the way down – he was unsure of the correct words for an introduction. He did very well! He seems a very energetic little man and knowledgeable for his age."

"Yes, Emma, he is street smart and a handful at times, but he is also a deep thinker when we can slow him down. Perhaps you would join me on the walk home and have some lunch? We will talk privately there."

"That would be lovely, Anne. I will ask Mr Stem to drive William home with the pastries."

"Mr Stem is back! He was very courteous when we met earlier in the week."

"He is a fine man, and we shall both require his protection tonight. But firstly, you may show me some of the sights of Guildford as we walk."

Anne tidied up her desk, handing Audrey Stern some papers and issuing some instructions quickly. She passed across a box of documents and re-checked her desk. Having advised where she would be, they set off.

Emma noticed the size of the bakery when she entered. There were people everywhere – it was quite an operation.

"So, your father leaves you in control of all this?"

"Not exactly – we have a bakery manager, Jeb, who showed you in. He is not so involved in the figures. I take care of the accounting and the money. The bakery is experiencing significant growth, and I was searching the records for the origin. There is an increased presence of the military visiting Chilton, and we supply the bread there, so that must contribute some of it. The unexplained increase is around five hundred pounds a week. Not that anyone is complaining."

"An extra five hundred pounds a month. That is a lot of money!"

"A week! Yes, it is a lot. The population of Guildford and the surrounding area is rapidly increasing, and we have a large range of products. It is not only bread but also pastries, cakes and biscuits. Our accounting problem is recording the sales and not having it directly connected with the invoices and costs. Cash flow is up, and debtors are also up, which is inconsistent. So, there is probably more money somewhere in the system that we have missed. I need the system changed, so it is clearer."

Emma was quite impressed. The detail was already confusing, and this girl was one year younger than her. She spoke confidently and with poise. Her posture was perfect, and she communicated explicitly but in a gentle, friendly way that made Emma feel at ease. Her father trusted her with the management of large amounts of money far greater than the Fintelton estate would see in a month. She was already noticing there was something different about Anne Turner.

As they approached Hurst's, Anne said, "That is a beautiful travelling suit you are wearing. Would you mind if we stopped for a few minutes so Mrs Smith may see it?"

"Thank you, Anne, I usually only receive praise like that from my mother. It would be a pleasure. Now, who is Mrs Smith?"

"She is our senior seamstress and manager of the family's Tailor's shop in Guildford. Mr Wall is the manager of the chain in Woking and sometimes visits. Mrs Smith is a darling – you will like her – she loves new ideas."

Emma saw Malcolm Stem passing in the carriage with William on the seat beside him. As she looked at him, she raised her eyebrows. He gave her a knowing smile and respectful nod, continuing his talk with William as they passed by. William waved, and Emma and Anne waved back. 'Such a friendly and refined family,' Emma thought.

Once at the Turner household, Emma and Anne sat in the dining room and took some tea, sandwiches and a pastry. Mrs Jennings made sure there was sufficient before leaving them.

Emma sipping her tea, said, "My apologies again for arriving early, Anne, but there are complications for our dinner tonight, and I thought I must forewarn you, so events do not take you by surprise."

"That is very kind of you, Emma, though I am slightly worried about what this involves. Robert's idea was dinner for you and me alone, but it seems now I shall meet your mother as well. I'm not sure what you or your mother will think of me in meeting this way."

Emma smiled at Anne, "From what Robert tells me, I understand that the two of you are close friends. He has the highest regard for you and desires friends for you at Fintelton when you visit next year."

Anne found this consistent with Robert's plan.

Emma continued, "Anne, I love my brother, Robert, dearly and will assist as best as possible, as long as it does not put me at odds with my family. You will understand that a girl's security comes from her family."

"Yes," Anne thought of Bethany's same words on Wednesday night.

"Robert's initial plan was most dangerous, as it would put both of us at risk of annoying my parents. So, I changed the plan. This way, you would become my friend, and the invitation to Fintelton would come from me. Robert is keen for proper introductions with my parents and some association before any attachment becomes known. He believes this path will assist as they are class conscious and seldom meet people out of their circles. They follow a strict rule of association. This Guilford visit is quite out of step, and I must praise my mother for agreeing to come. I was surprised when she readily agreed."

"But surely Emma, you too must move in these circles?"

"Yes and no. In London we do, but in the country not so much anymore. You see, politics and the economy are forcing change on the aristocracy. They struggle with this, especially with finances. The increase in the window tax[21] is not helping. I am sure people like my parents will find life vastly different in the next decade. Why? Because they find it difficult to understand the changes occurring in our country. But that is beside the point. Let us talk about our plan. We planned the dinner tonight for yourself, my mother and me. Unfortunately, my brother, Sir Hugh, is joining us."

"Robert has mentioned him."

"I must explain about Sir Hugh. He is six years older than Robert and will become the next Earl of Fintelton. Due to the entailment law, he will inherit the estate. He is not interested in detail, and he maintains the same old

---

[21] The Window Tax was a property tax based on the number of windows in a house. It was increased in 1825. Wikipedia.

farming practices. It is more complicated than I relate, but we shall discuss this later. My father is aging and has placed the estate management in his hands. Thankfully Mr Stem, a very honourable man, keeps things in order. My brother lives a dangerous life and craves alcohol and women. He spends most of his time at alehouses and houses of ill repute. Of course, I tell you this in absolute confidence and for your protection. My mother and father would not entertain such tales and are unaware of Sir Hugh's pursuits."

"I am surprised, Emma, as Robert is such a gentleman. He did tell me that Hugh was a bit cold!"

"My father and mother arranged a good marriage partner for him some years ago. From a very honourable and wealthy family, the young lady broke it all off after she found him most disagreeable. Unfortunately, he became drunk and attempted beating her into bed, but she was saved by a servant who heard the commotion. She and her family left the house that night, ending any chance of an attachment. My parents have not tried again since then. Hugh never apologised for the incident, and his behaviour has become worse."

These comments made Anne shudder. She thought of her father's actions against her mother. If Emma ever found out, what would she think of her? What would Robert think? Being the lone guardian of the Turner home while her parents were away, Anne was becoming agitated.

"And you say he is coming tonight?"

"Unfortunately, yes. There was nothing I could do about it. Father, in his mindlessness, was pleased as he felt Hugh would provide we ladies with some protection. However, I have sought protection and ensured that Mr Stem guards us against Hugh. He will be outside the hotel on call tonight if Hugh does not behave. It is the best I can do with such short notice."

"That will be sufficient, Emma. If he is a gentleman of any sort, he will behave for Mr Stem."

"Yes, that was my thought too, so I think we are safe. May I say that it may not be the most agreeable conversation at dinner tonight? I know the importance Robert places on this dinner, so I would plead that you do not judge my family on Hugh's behaviour. If I know Hugh, he will be getting drunk at the White Rabbit in Petersfield; then, he will ride here in time for dinner. Hopefully, some of the drink will have worn off by dinner time."

Anne sat there silently, petrified about the looming danger. It all seemed so possible when she was with Robert. What faced her now was a horror story that she would rather avoid. Why should she expose herself in this way? Indeed, a more prudent approach would be to cancel.

Emma recognised Anne was tense and thinking hard. Perhaps her explanation overstepped the mark. Yet, given the information Robert entrusted her with, she must protect this girl. It would be a tragedy if Anne mistook Hugh's compliments as those of a gentleman. She knew what would happen. It sickened her that she must warn young women about her brother's evil pursuits.

"Anne, it will be alright. You will be protected, and I will guarantee your safety. The only thing I cannot protect you from is Hugh's vulgar comments. However, from what I have seen of you today, I think you are a very mature young lady and that you will handle this situation well."

Anne was not so sure. "Perhaps we could call the dinner off and just meet in the morning. That would be far easier. I am not keen on being involved in a situation tonight."

Emma now realised she had overstepped the mark. Anne was showing good sense in avoiding any vulgar meetings. There must be some other way of eliminating the threat from the evening. The more guests who attended the dinner, the less chance Hugh would have of embarrassing his family, so she suggested this.

"Anne, is there anyone else we might invite tonight? Friends or acquaintances! If some friends were with you at dinner, this would help balance the situation and give you more confidence."

Anne readily agreed with this. She started thinking of the best person who would provide her with protection. "The Reverend Andrew Taggart and his wife Laura are good family friends. They are a respectable company, and your mother will find them acceptable."

Emma saw that Anne felt immediately more confident about the evening.

"Anne, I think we should pay the good Reverend a visit straight after lunch."

Anne was impressed by how quickly Emma made decisions.

"I think so too. Why, even the most difficult man would behave in the presence of a minister of religion, and we both must behave as well!" The girls smiled at each other and started giggling.

At Greenwich …

Hamish and Marjorie McPherson waved the party goodbye, thanking them for the hand-delivered wedding invitation, which they verbally accepted. Marjorie was still talking with Eleanora as the coach pulled out, her last words trailing away, "We will discuss it on Tuesday when you return, my Dear. Bye now ….."

Following Marion and Thomas inside, Marjorie said, "Quickly, children, Archdeacon Handle expects us this afternoon, and we will lock in the date. I have already two hundred and fifty on the guest list, and we must mail the invitations quickly so guests may reserve the date. For dinner on Tuesday, I will invite the Archdeacon and his wife so that they can meet your parents, Thomas."

"Splendid!" said Thomas. "Let's go!"

Hamish stood there smiling, watching the performance. He was not worried about the cost, as his main concern was the date. He thought, 'What a great day it will be.' The wedding will be an occasion where his success and business would be displayed. He entrusted Marjorie with most of the guests invited but occasionally suggested appropriate additions. Hamish wanted his brewery here in Greenwich, figuring prominently at the wedding. He was still thinking about how he would achieve this.

During lunch, Thomas met James McPherson, who was visiting from the north. James would visit Greenwich several times during the rest of the year, and Hamish was keen that Thomas and James review the systems at the Woolwich brewery. Thomas readily agreed, eager to learn from James, especially now that breweries were his future, and the opportunity with James, now opening for him

At Guildford …

Sitting on the portico, William was throwing a ball up and catching it. Snups occasionally would jump for the ball, but William was too quick for him, grabbing it before the dog. The young lad, being behind the portico rail, was partially obscured from the street view. However, the dog barking and jumping made it evident that he was there. He noticed some way down High Street on the other side, an older man seated behind the fence in front of their church. The man was relaxed, but occasionally he would sit up straight and peer in William's direction. It was almost as if he was keeping the house under observation.

William scratched his head and remembered seeing the man the day before. He thought nothing of it as many people sometimes rested there and then moved on. Sometimes Mrs Taggart would give them some water or talk with them. The man slowly moved towards the end of the fence and sat down again where there was a better view of the Turner home.

William was suspicious. Followed by Snups, he went inside, up the two flights of stairs and found Simeon reading a novel left by Anne from the library. Simeon was always reading and sometimes needed stirring into action.

William moved close, interrupting Simeon's reading. "Sim, come to the front window and have a look at this."

Sim, annoyed at being disturbed, said, "Look at what?"

"An old man is watching our house from across the street."

"Oh, all right."

Simeon followed William out, and they both peered through the hallway window.

"Where?'

William screwed up his eyes and peered down, searching the opposite side of the street. The man was gone.

"A man was sitting there watching our place, but he is gone now. I'm sure I saw him there yesterday."

"There probably was, but he was watching everything else too. He was resting there as all the other people do. I think your imagination got the better of you."

William was disappointed. He was uneasy about this. But perhaps Sim was correct, and he dismissed it.

"Let's take Snups for a walk, Sim."

'Not now. I am reading this book. Maybe later."

William shrugged his shoulders, went back downstairs, and told Mrs Jennings he and Snups were going for a walk.

"Don't go too far, please. Anne is going out tonight, and dinner will be early!" Mrs Jennings wanted everything done before Anne left. Aggie was upstairs helping Anne with her dressing.

William darted out the front door onto the portico, where he put Snups on a leash. The two of them headed off down High Street towards the river. As they approached Abbot's Hospital[22], Snups slowed down and started a low growl. William, sensing danger, quickly glanced in the direction of Snups line of sight. Everything looked normal.

"What's wrong, Snups? There's nothing wrong, boy, come on."

Snups charged toward the Abbot's Hospital low fence. William saw the same older man behind the fence before being dragged over by Snups' leaping forward. William knew he must never let go of the leash in the township. Snups yelped as the leash tightened and yanked William down. He picked himself up and searched for the man, but there was no one there. He was gone again!

William walked along the fence with Snups and saw the open front door of Abbot's Hospital. He sneaked into the alcove and peeked inside. The court-yard was empty.

From behind him, a deep voice said, "What do you want, William?'

William turned and found himself looking at Mr Tuesbury, the Master of Abbots, standing in an open doorway.

"I was looking for an old man, Mr Tuesbury."

"You will find plenty of them here, son. But not now! They are probably all

---

[22] Abbot's Hospital was founded by George Abbot, the Archbishop of Canterbury (1611-1633), in 1619 to provide homes for the elderly of Guildford. By permission AH 2020.

getting ready for dinner – they eat at five."

William took another look through the cloister gate and saw pathways leading off everywhere. If someone came quickly through here, they would disappear in seconds.

"Well, lad!"

"Thank you, Sir. I should be going."

William pulled on Snups' leash, and they set off towards the river.

At Petersfield ...

Sir Hugh South had spent the late morning hours upstairs at the White Rabbit hotel in the intimate company of a buxom wench. Having satisfied his desires for the half-dressed wench, he yelled at her for more scotch whisky. Since being kicked out of bed, she had ensured a supply of drinks continued as he sank into a loud drunken stupor.

Rosemary was the local madam that Hugh called on regularly when in town. She always gave him a good time and usually came out of it very well herself. Often, she was paid more than once, as Sir Hugh could not keep count of his money once drunk and could never remember the day after. Being Fintelton's heir, he always carried a large purse. Rosemary would put up with his antics, knowing she received at least a week's worth of client payments in exchange for a drunken session with Sir Hugh. She always stopped drinking once Hugh finished his first bottle as the alcohol would take its effect by then.

Hugh was now stone drunk and screaming for more scotch. Rosemary approached him, "Hey Dearie, ain't you expected in Guilford tonight?"

"Who wants to know?"

"You better get moving, Dearie, or you ain't going to make it."

"Where's that other bottle of scotch, Rosy, you fat bitch! Where is it?"

"It's down in carriage waiting for the gentleman going Guildford way, Dearie."

"No, I want it here. Now, Bitch."

With that, Rosemary opened the door, and two muscular men came in and bundled up Hugh, his clothes and bag, carting him downstairs. They threw him into the carriage and supplied a bottle of scotch and a glass. Sir Hugh was pleased and sucked the top of the bottle without removing the cork. Rosemary was glad he was gone, as she had a busy Friday night ahead of her, and she knew Sir Hugh would not remember a thing tomorrow.

"Take him, the Fox and Hound, Guilford, my good men!"

The coach moved off with the horses breaking into a quick canter.

In the carriage, Hugh used his teeth and pulled the cork out. He took an almighty swig of the scotch and sat back. Happy as a jester, he broke into song with much gusto. A considerable bump threw him from one seat to the other.

Losing his grip, he rolled onto the floor, with the bottle of whisky falling from his hands and pouring all over him. Hugh was so drunk he was unaware of what was going on, and he kept singing on the coach floor until he fell asleep.

At Charing Cross, London …

The Turner's coach trotted through Trafalgar Square, past St Martin in the Fields, down the Strand and around into Chandos Place. Bethany was in awe of all she was seeing. So many buildings four and five stories high for mile upon mile. She marvelled at how many people must live here in London.

Eleanora was showing signs of fatigue, and even Neville was hoping they would arrive soon, as she required rest. The coach stopped outside a large sandstone building around four stories high with a double door entrance onto the street. Neville dropped onto the ground, not waiting for the footman, rushed across the footpath and pulled the doorbell. He then doubled back, assisting Eleanora from the carriage.

By the time they were all out, Mr & Mrs Bassington welcomed them. Neville made the introductions, "Mr Jonathon and Mrs Eleanora Turner, please let me introduce my parents, Mr David and Mrs Jennifer Bassington."

There was much handshaking and warm greetings from the Bassington seniors. Then facing Bethany, Neville introduced them, "And this is Bethany, the love of my life."

Mrs Bassington quickly moved forward, gave Beth a great hug, and said, "Welcome, Dear. It is a great pleasure meeting you."

David Bassington said, "Hear, hear. Welcome, Bethany."

Standing in the doorway was a genteel young woman about Bethany's age. Mr Bassington turned and said, "My apologies, please may I introduce our daughter, Megan."

Megan pleasantly greeted them with a smile and a kiss on the cheek and then stood back and let her mother speak.

"Please, come inside. The footmen will take your luggage. I'm sure you are exhausted by your journey, particularly you, Eleanora, in your delicate state."

Eleanora Turner agreed and indicated she would appreciate a rest before dinner.

Jennifer Bassington turned to Bethany and politely said, "To avoid embarrassment, my Dear, is it acceptable if we call you Beth? We do not wish to embarrass you by appearing forward."

"By all means, Mrs Bassington, please call me Beth."

The Turners entered the fine house, glad of the warm welcome.

Mrs Jennings had fed the children, and Anne was upstairs readying herself for dinner at the Fox and Hound. Mr Stem waited for Anne in the kitchen. The Fintelton estate manager, a single man, was content being entertained by Mrs Jennings and the children. Sitting at the kitchen table, crunching some Turner's biscuits, he played a game of checkers with Simeon. William was giving him instructions at every second turn. Malcolm Stem enjoyed the family atmosphere, the warm cup of tea and the excellent biscuits.

It was nearly eight o'clock, and Mrs Jennings had previously given William and Simeon instructions that this was the last game. When Anne entered the kitchen, followed by Aggie, they all looked up and gasped in appreciation. She wore the most beautiful, pastel blue gown. A sheer overdress with full sleeves covered a blue silk dress with short puffed undersleeves and a deep, wide blue ribbon fastened by a gold buckle that matched her hair. It looked as if she was gliding on water.

"How do I look, family?"

Mrs Jennings said with tears in her eyes, "All grown up, little one. Now, Mr Stem, you will take particularly good care of this precious one tonight and bring her home safe."

In awe, William, Clementine and Simeon said, "Wow, you look beautiful, Anne!"

Aggie mentioned the debate over whether her hair should be in a bun or left out. Anne decided on a break with tradition and left it flowing over her shoulders. As it was a warm night, and it was only dinner with no dancing, the long hair left out would be acceptable.

Mr Stem said, "It is time, Milady."

Mrs Jennings and Aggie said, "Ooh!"

Anne smiled at everyone and then departed, followed by Mr Stem.

Emma and her mother were seated at the Fox and Hound dining room, hoping Anne would come before the good Reverend or Hugh. As Anne appeared at the dining room entrance, Emma waved. Anne smiled and made her way over, the waiter pulling out her chair in readiness.

Anne said, "Good evening, Emma. You do look beautiful tonight!"

Emma, dressed in a lovely crimson dress and with her hair tied in a bun, smiled and said, "Thank you, Anne. Please let me make the introduction. Miss Anne Turner, may I introduce my mother, the Countess of Fintelton, Lady Jane South."

Anne moved forward, curtsied, and said, "I am honoured to make your acquaintance, Lady Fintelton."

Lady Jane looked at Anne, "Good evening, Miss Turner. You are very pretty, and I like your dress very much. You should have your hair in a bun, but it is so beautiful I am glad you left it out. You look a picture tonight. Both you girls look wonderful; I wish I were forty years younger. Now I assume you two had met before as Emma recognised you at the entrance."

"My Lady, we met by chance this afternoon and took tea together. It was wonderful meeting Emma after Neville told me so much about her."

Lady Jane was astute and accepted the comment with a slight frown. Anne, being quite perceptive, noticed that mother's knowing look on her face.

"Then, if you know Neville, I expect you would know my son Robert?"

Both Emma and Anne breathed in as they were hoping Lady Jane would not make the connection. There was no avoiding an answer. Anne confirmed her acquaintance with Robert.

"Yes, my Lady, I have had that pleasure."

"Young lady, I will expect a full disclosure this evening, as Robert tells me nothing these days."

Emma was quick to spot the good Reverend and his wife at the door.

"Ah, Mother, here is Reverend Andrew Taggart and his wife, Laura. You will remember them; they have joined us at church in Petersfield for welcomes and farewells of two of our parish priests over the last few years."

Anne breathed in relief, thankful for Emma stepping in so quickly.

"Good evening, Reverend Andrew and Mrs Taggart. You will remember my mother, Lady Fintelton, and I understand you know Anne well."

Andrew Taggart was no fool, and he deduced the situation. Being still upset about his unfortunate comments last Sunday, he felt this might be an opportunity for redemption. Laura, Andrew's wife, came from an aristocratic family and was competent in these social circles.

Andrew bowed, "It is wonderful meeting again, my Lady. I think the last time was at the Reverend Martin Hendel's farewell, was it not? An excellent farewell. Now have you found a new minister yet for your living there?"

Laura Taggart followed her husband and curtsied, saying, "Good evening, my Lady, you are looking wonderful tonight."

"You too, my Dear Laura; it has been too long. Thank you for your kind compliment. I am far better than when we last met, and I take pleasure in this Guildford visit as part of our London trip. It has been two months since we visited St James's Square, and we need much restocking for the approaching winter. Christmas is coming, and we must make a start on that. Now, you present beautifully tonight, Laura – a gorgeous dress, if I may say so. Where pray, did you purchase this gown?"

"Hurst's, my Lady. It is in the High Street here. It is the same place where Anne had her dress made."

"I am surprised. I always buy from Mrs Spencer's in Piccadilly; they send someone across to 'Harting'. I had no idea that there was a good dressmaker here in Guildford."

Laura spoke again in support of Hurst's, "My Lady, they stock all the latest fashions and materials. Their work is quality."

Anne sat beside the countess, who put on her glasses, turned to Anne, and felt the material for quality.

"Yes, it is fine material indeed and well made. Emma, I am curious; we must visit this Hursts tomorrow morning, please?"

"Yes, Mother, our plan includes this for the morning. You will recall Anne's mother and father are the owners. They have a chain of Tailor's shops."

"I thought they were bakers!"

"That too, Mother. They have many business holdings."

Lady Jane, looking straight at Anne, thought about Emma's comment for a moment, then smiling, she said, "My, Anne, you are a pretty little thing, aren't you!"

Anne said, "Please, my Lady, not so much praise. It will overcome me. The honour of being your friend is ample."

"And that you shall be, Anne Turner. I am very impressed with you. Now, will you join me in reviewing the menu? What shall we order? I have always enjoyed staying at the Fox and Hound."

Anne sneaked a look at Emma, and they both raised their eyebrows at each other in delight. The evening had commenced on a far better note than either Anne or Emma expected. Laura Taggart assessed the situation and was pleased, as Anne deserved some recognition at last. She had been a star pupil at Reverend Taggart's school, with a gentle and beautiful personality. If she married into this family, they would be very fortunate indeed.

Lady Jane suddenly said, "Where is that Hugh? He is always late and usually makes a scene. We will go ahead without him."

They ordered their first two courses, and then Lady Jane asked Reverend Taggart for grace. Andrew gave a short and dignified grace, followed by all with a loud Amen.

Lady Jane then looked at Andrew and spoke. 'In answering your earlier question, Reverend Taggart, we presently have no minister. It seems Sir David's demands scare them off. He is getting crankier as he gets older and requests no sermon during the service. You see, he does not enjoy sermons about salvation or repentance. He thinks he is good enough. As you would understand, this upsets the new young ministers, and they fear his judgement. Also, because of the increased window tax, he has cut back on the living slightly, which again does not impress any new applicant."

"I see Lady Jane. How long now has it been since the last minister departed?"

"It must be nearly nine months. The bishop sends out a young fellow every so often, but they soon go. If you know anyone who fits the bill, please inform me. I would appreciate that."

"Certainly, my Lady. "

"Now tell me, Anne, how is it that you are a friend of Robert?"

"My Lady, this is now a long story, so I will economise where I can."

Lady Jane looked up in surprise, not expecting a long friendship but just an acquaintance.

"It all started several months ago when two of my brothers, William, and his elder brother Simeon, were sent home from school by Reverend Andrew one day. Being adventurous boys, they decided they would climb the ridge on the other side of the river Wey. As you know, that is part of the King's hunting forest."

Lady Jane and Emma both quietly listened while Anne revealed the whole story. Anne's perception told her that this lady was more adept than she let on. The countess would expect an accurate account and quickly deduce any prospect on the horizon for her son. She would have her informers. Emma was amazed that Anne was so open with her, worrying that her mother would not enjoy all this detail.

The further Anne delved into the story, the more Lady Jane seemed happily interested. As the account unfolded, Lady Jane asked several questions of clarification. The dinner courses came and went as they talked about various medical issues and places of interest.

"So, all of you visited Severndroog Castle for a picnic? I am jealous! I have asked Lord Fintelton to visit there for a long time, but he always finds an excuse. That must have been lovely."

"It was a wonderful day. We had two choices, either the seaside or the castle. My preference was the sea as I have never seen it. But Severndroog Castle was magnificent and closer, and Mr McPherson put on an incredible luncheon."

"Anne, it sounds like you have the best of friends." They both laughed.

Blushing, Anne said, "I have been most fortunate."

Once Anne had finished the story, Reverend Andrew asked if he may add a contribution if Lady Jane was agreeable.

"Certainly, Andrew!"

"My Lady! Sir Robert has honoured us by worshipping here last Sunday. Doctor Neville Bassington tells me that it is his opinion that through Robert's quick actions, he probably saved the lives of both William and Simeon Turner. We praise God for this."

Lady Jane was visibly moved and nodded her thanks.

Emma moved on with the conversation. "Mother, I am interested in viewing where Neville and Bethany will live tomorrow. Also, the building he has chosen for his practice."

"Yes, Emma, I agree, but I think I am more interested in this tailor, who we never knew about before. Now Anne, do they cater for both men and women or is it just women's fashion?"

"Both, my Lady. One side of the establishment caters for men, and the other caters for women. It is quite a large store."

"You will be taking us there tomorrow morning?"

"Yes, my Lady, then Emma and I thought after that we could have some tea, either here or at a coffee house close by the river."

"I understand your mother and father are away, so they won't have the pleasure of joining us. Such a pity. You do have servants looking after you, don't you?"

"Yes, my Lady, we have ample servants."

"Splendid, I look forward to meeting with you tomorrow morning, say about ten. That will give us time for what we need and then some tea. I think I am getting past my bedtime now and should go up."

As Lady Jane moved her chair, there was a horrendous crash outside the dining room entrance. Through the door came a large dishevelled man looking like a tramp. He stood there with his hair undone, smelling of scotch, and his shirt hanging out over his breeches. He had no coat, and his skin looked very pale indeed. It was Sir Hugh.

He clumsily stumbled into the dining room and grabbed a waiter, yelling at him for some scotch whisky. Then pushing that waiter away, he spied the table with Lady Jane's party, stumbled towards it and slumped into a chair.

The countess retook her seat.

Slowly looking up and giving a greeting wave, he said, "Ah, Mother, sorry I'm a bit late but here now!"

There was an embarrassing silence; then Lady Jane spoke up. "Hugh, let me introduce you. You will recall the Reverend Andrew Taggart and Mrs Laura Taggart."

Hugh stood, shook the Reverend's hand, took Mrs Taggart's hand, and kissed it. Then fell back into his chair.

Lady Jane commenced again, "Miss Anne Turner."

Sir Hugh looked up slowly, leaning over the table in Anne's direction, "Ah, the baker's daughter!"

Anne visibly moved backwards in terror as he eyed her over. She was immediately afraid of him. This man was disgusting, with the smell of whisky all over his clothes and being only half-dressed. Hugh stood again uneasily and looked around at Anne. Then he closed his eyes and fell straight back onto a gentleman sitting at a table behind them. Staggering onto his feet, Sir Hugh apologised but then vomited all over the man.

At that point, Mr Stem appeared; putting one of Sir Hugh's arms around his shoulder, he walked him off upstairs.

Lady Jane said clearly and calmly, "Thank you, Mr Stem."

Malcolm Stem nodded as he struggled with Hugh's weight, and they soon disappeared down the hallway.

Reverend and Mrs Taggard and Anne looked in disbelief that one of their highly honoured neighbours could behave in such an undignified manner. They all stood there in silence, watching. Emma was crying and had her face in her hands, ashamed of the display.

Anne rushed around and enclosed Emma in her arms with a gentle hug. "He is drunk, Emma. He will be better in the morning!"

Lady Jane was most impressed with this show of affection between Anne and Emma.

"Anne, Reverend and Mrs Taggart," Lady Jane talked as if this was a regular occurrence. "It has been a special evening, and I have enjoyed your company so much. I must apologise for my son, who is obviously under the weather. It seems he has bettered my prediction of him making a scene.

There, there. Now, Anne, we shall meet with you tomorrow morning. Reverend Taggart, if you would be so good as to see Anne safely home, please."

Andrew Taggart nodded, and Laura said, "It will be our pleasure, Lady Fintelton."

"Thank you. Good night, everyone. Now come, Emma!" Lady Jane put her arm around her daughter as they made off for their suite.

Later, as Emma assisted her mother into bed, Lady Jane said, "I'm sorry, Emma, that I did not give you a sister. I tried, but your father did not cooperate. He was too busy thinking about himself. I know how important a sister is. A confidant – someone who you love, trust and find comfort in."

"That's alright, Mother, I have you."

"That is very nice, Dear, but I'm getting older. I won't be with you much longer. You will need someone close to confide in."

"Mother, this is rather sad after such a pleasant evening. Let us talk about happy things."

"Emma, now listen! I am talking about happy things. This - Anne girl! If I could have provided you with a sister, she is what I would have wanted for you. Such a sweet little thing. Why if Robert would have her, I would agree in a shot!"

There was a silence as mother and daughter looked at each other. Lady Jane watched carefully for Emma's reaction.

"Why, Mother, I am all amazed! I thought you would want someone quite grand for Robert."

"I am becoming too old for that. I've seen so many unhappy marriages arranged by the gentry. I want you and Robert to be happy with your partners.

Your happiness means everything to me, Darling."

Emma could not quite believe what she was hearing. For the first time, she and her mother were talking intimately. The tears came down her face, and she hugged her mother.

"Thank you, Mother. I shall always love you!"

"And I will always love you, Darling. We should do these stops in country towns more often; they are quite entertaining!"

Emma burst out laughing and wiped her nose. Lady Jane had a naughty smile on her face.

"You know, Anne said to me, she has never seen the sea! Can you imagine that, Emma? They only live thirty miles from the sea. What has her father been doing?"

"From the size of the family, Mother, I think I know what he has been doing!"

"I think we must remedy Anne's situation, Emma. You shall invite this Anne Turner for a visit, and we shall overnight at the seaside. I would like a paddle in the sea again. What a wonderful evening this has been. From the moment I met that young lady, I liked her. It was as if she was family already. Do you like her, Emma?"

"Yes, Mother. She is a friend indeed!"

HMS Restless, Woolwich ...

The schooner raced up the coast towards Woolwich in a good fifteen knot southerly and demonstrated her capabilities. Robert was amazed at how fast she was without much sail trimming. He thought he might get another three or four knots out of her once he adjusted the sail settings.

Restless was a very agile and fast ship, but he was not keen on entering the Thames in darkness. He would hold off Margate for the night. When the wind grew in the morning, he would make the arduous trip up the river. Watching Captain Foster navigate *Providence* up the Thames taught him about the difficulties involved. The complexities of currents and wind shifts in confined spaces made navigation tricky.

Given this was his first voyage as Captain, he would ensure no mistakes, even if he lost six hours. Several other craft were also waiting for morning, so he set a good watch and went below. In his cabin, sitting at the chart table, he allowed himself the luxury of thinking about the events at Guildford. He assumed that all would be fine with Emma directing the evening. By now, Anne would have some friends at Fintelton.

Swanton, his servant, came into the cabin with a hot chocolate finding Robert with his head on the chart table, drifting off. The sergeant tapped him on the shoulder and guided him onto his bunk. He was soon in a deep sleep.

On receiving Robert's request for help, Horace Coombes immediately dispatched the best man for the job, Michael Swanton. He was a veteran from India who had seen his fair share of soldiering and was an expert in both concealment and killing, also totally trustworthy. Horace most liked him for his cooking – often whipping up an excellent meal for his men after a long raid. A letter of introduction sent by Horace explained that Swanton was included in the number of marines who would travel on *Restless*.

The Sergeant, who manoeuvred his men out of many a tight spot in India, was not convinced at all about this crew. From those met so far, he was unsure who could be trusted. They all seemed angry men, and uncovering the cause would take time. But time was short, so he must tread carefully. He bolted the cabin door and then also bolted shut the servant's room. Coming back into the captain's cabin, he placed a box about three feet from the cabin door and sat down on it. Leaning back against a pillar, he started doing some scrimshawing. On his way back from India, they encountered several British whalers where he purchased a small supply of whalebone. He found enjoyment in the hobby as it passed the time, and as most men knew, there was plenty of that in the army. No one would get near Captain South tonight. If they tried, they would receive a nasty surprise.

It was about three bells when Swanton suddenly opened his eyes. He must have drifted off to sleep and then, for some reason, woke up. Everything was quiet except for the wind in the sails and the sea running smoothly under the hull. Swanton rubbed his eyes in the weak candlelight and noticed the doorknob was slightly moving. Someone was on the other side, trying the lock.

He knew the door was firm as it was bolted from the inside. So, he quietly moved into his servants' quarters, where there was a peephole. Focusing his eyes, he could see nothing as the hallway was pitch dark. Someone had snuffed the candle. As his eyes adjusted, he could only faintly discern a figure or two trying the door.

The captain was correct; there were traitors in the crew. But who?

They would solve this only one way – a trap must be set. He would discuss this with the captain in the morning. For now, he would keep watch, just in case they forced the door. He sat back on his chair, making a bit more noise. The door handle did not move again that night.

London – Chandos Place ...

The Friday night dinner at the home of the Bassington's was a joyful occasion. Jonathon enjoyed David and Jennifer Bassington's company – they were intelligent, lively people who were wise and very caring. Jonathon was most appreciative of their concern for Eleanora.

It was after the second course that Eleanora excused herself and retired. The day in the carriage had been most tiring, and finding herself exhausted, she was soon fast asleep. Once dinner was finished, Jonathon excused himself, quietly moving upstairs to check on his wife. Neville stood behind him as they watched over her.

"I'm afraid she is slowly fading, Jonathon. I will do all I can, but there is only limited knowledge of this disease. We do not know what the complaint is – if we only had more understanding and better medicines. Although there is some good news, I think she will last longer than expected. Perhaps a year more if we are fortunate. Let us pray for more and be thankful for every day we have her."

The tears rolled down Jonathon Turner's face. "Thank you, Neville. It is very comforting having you with us."

Eleanora lay there in front of him, alive but asleep. Her beauty radiated out of her, even when she slept. He loved this woman more than anything in the world. She carried his child, and he regretted terribly the forceful action he committed against her. He could not dissociate his actions from the disease that now afflicted her. He would never forgive himself. God was now punishing him. But it affected Eleanora and others. Everyone would lose.

He must ask Andrew Taggart for some counselling. He wanted to fall on his knees and plead mercy. He felt helpless.

Looking straight ahead, he softly spoke, "Do you believe in God, Neville?"

Neville was not ready for this question. He thought about it for a minute, wondering if Jonathon was breaking down. "Yes. I do. When you look at the human body, how else could it have been created? When you cut yourself, the tissues heal themselves? It is so simple and yet so complex! I also think about that when I look at nature. There is just a never-ending display of creation all around us. Men have created this house with the gift of resources and the skills God has bestowed on us."

There was a short silence.

"Old Jeremy Stephens, bless his heart, warned me that I should not beat her. But I did not listen. I held the old ways. Women are our property, and we use them. Yes, there were good times together, but I always thought of myself as in control. It has only been in the last year, no, six months, that our marriage has been one of equals. I learned that we were partners.

Andrew Taggart's sermons suddenly became better. He credits this Reverend Charles Simeon fellow, whom he has been reading. Taggart's sermons taught me we were in a partnership, not a master-servant relationship. God is punishing me now for my indiscretions. And now I am losing my partner."

"You haven't lost her yet, Jonathon."

"That's true. Thank you, Neville, you have been very kind. Please excuse me. I would like time alone with her now."

Neville slowly stepped backwards and then turned and exited the room. Strolling downstairs, Neville pondered the situation, 'So I was right. He did beat her into submission. But he can't discern that his guilt has not caused her illness. While his guilt is unresolved, he will never understand his wife's illness.'

Neville found the others in the drawing-room talking about the wedding.

David Bassington asked, "How is she?"

"She sleeps peacefully and should show some improvement after a good night's rest."

Bethany was concerned, "She will get better, though, won't she?"

"We will see tomorrow. Perhaps when we go for our drive to Harley Street, she will join us?"

Beth was cheered by this, and they all started asking questions about the group of Surgeons that Neville was joining. They talked well into the night. Later, both Bethany, Jennifer and Megan excused themselves for bed.

Neville and his father sat gazing into the fire as it was the first chilly autumn night in London after a mild summer.

"Another scotch Neville?"

"Yes, thanks, Father."

"I must say you have found a wonderful girl for your wife."

"I'm glad you and mother like her. She is the most attractive and complete woman I have ever known. When we first met, we were at the Turner's house, and we walked together upstairs, checking on Simeon, who had broken his arm. That's when we first talked. It was as if I had known her my whole life, and we had so much in common. I knew then that this was the girl I would marry. It was a meeting of minds – it was not carnal but more spiritual. Strange that it happened so quickly. But it did."

"I'm glad."

"You told me once that when I met the right woman, I would know it! You were right! It was a feeling, something different and more exciting than anything I have ever felt before."

"It is called true love, or as the Greeks put it ', Agape'! "Something we cannot hold or see but something we feel with great intensity!"

"Does it last?"

David sat back and looked at his son. He reflected on his own life. There was so much he could relate but what he said must be short and meaningful.

"To start with, it does. Then the pressures of life become real and distract us. Life tests us in all sorts of ways. So efforts are needed to kindle your love, and you must continually work on it as a couple. You keep the trust relationship between yourself and your wife as sacred. Don't let anyone else inside that relationship except God. As you age, it changes again. It is an adventure that is ongoing. Yes, it does last, but you must work on it. Don't ever take your love for granted."

Neville took another sip of scotch and enjoyed the open fire. "Thanks."

"Will Mrs Turner last until the wedding?"

"Is it that obvious?"

"She is not a well woman, Neville. I would say there is a very significant underlying cause. I would also say she knows it."

Neville looked down into the dark rich liquid in his glass. His father would maintain confidentiality. He asked the question, so he deserved an answer.

"I have seen this complaint before. We do not know what causes it. There is no cure. It will have its way in time. It can be very aggressive, or it can linger for years. At first, I was afraid she would not last until now. But she surprised me and has rallied. The birth will be precarious. If she survives that, then I would not give her long, but as I say, we do not understand how each body will fight against this disease."

They both sat in silence for nearly five minutes, enjoying their company.

"If it gets worse and you need help with the wedding, send us a message, and we will be there. We can stay at the hotel and assist in any way needed. You don't know how people will react in such circumstances. Let's hope for the best."

"Thanks, Father."

"Time for bed."

The Turner Household, Guildford ...

William was a light sleeper. It was well after midnight when he heard a noise downstairs. Then it came again. It was like someone creeping around down below inside the house.

He pulled his covers up and whispered, "Hey, Sim? Do you hear that?"

No response, just a slight snore.

'That's not much help!' William thought.

He slowly and very quietly got out of bed. He tiptoed towards the stairs as softly as he could and peered down. There was no movement or noise. He stood there for nearly five minutes, then he heard it again, a soft footstep coming from the study area. William now knew there was someone down there. But why didn't Snups growl or bark? There was no noise at all from the dog.

William felt a shiver down his spine. Anne was sleeping on the floor below, and he must warn her. He crept downstairs. What about Mrs Jennings and Aggie? Why didn't they hear what was going on? Perhaps it was them doing something? Of course, that's why Snups didn't bark. Mrs Jennings must be checking the candles. He sighed a breath of relief. As William reached the first-floor landing, he noticed a dim glow coming from the study area below. It must be Mrs Jennings – he would go down and help her.

William went down the stairs full pelt, calling Mrs Jennings. He turned the corner and stopped in his tracks. In front of him was the older man he had seen in the afternoon. The man was now inside their house and staring down at William from about three feet away. Because the light was coming from behind him, William could not make out his face. Then suddenly, William saw white and then darkness. That was the last thing he remembered that night.

Out the back of the house, lying on the grass, Snups gave a last little whimper as the life drained out of his body into the earth.

Chapter 15

At Guildford …

William was a long way from the voice calling him. It was mother, and she sounded concerned. Poor mother was so unwell, and he saw less and less of her. 'William?' the calling came again. He tried calling out but found his voice would not respond. His legs were like lead. Should he sit up? Which way was up? With bubbles drifting up around him, it felt like he was underwater. Up above, he could see some light. As he floated up, the water became warmer. He needed breath! He tried calling out again, but nothing would come out. His head broke the surface, and he breathed in deeply. It was refreshing. Then, a violent flash of light in his eyes made him shut them tight.

Anne stirred in her sleep. Rolling over, she lay there in the warm bed dreaming about Robert. He must be in Portsmouth by now and on his new ship. How wonderful he must look in his new captain's uniform. She was smiling as she thought of herself in a beautiful dress, hat and ribbons floating in the breeze. Walking out on the pier, she waved to him as his ship passed. He returned the wave and then pointed behind her. His face was concerned as he yelled, 'Watch out!' What should she do? What was wrong?

Anne opened her eyes with a start. The extra covers were too hot, and she was sweating. Pulling them off, she heard a faint noise close to her. The door of her room creaked as it was slowly opened, letting in soft light.

"Is that you, Clemmie?" she called out.

The noise of footsteps, softly running along the hall, quietly disappeared down the stairs. A chill came over her as her mind started racing. It sounded like someone was in the house, and someone had left her door half open. She knew only the girls and herself were on this floor. The boys were on the floor above, but no sounds came from up there. Despite her fear, she decided – she must get up and investigate. It was not Mrs Jennings or Aggie, as they would have answered her call. She was convinced now a burglar was in the house.

Carefully rising from her bed and putting on her dressing gown, she crept forward silently and slowly opened the door. There was no one in the hallway. Nothing! No sounds, no movements. She checked the girls and found them all asleep. Tentatively moving into the hallway again, she could just make out the stairwell in the dull light. A faint glow from the floor below misted at the bottom of the rails. Anne decided someone was down there with a candle burning. It must be Mrs Jennings or Aggie up early. She peered down over the landing and called.

"Mrs Jennings? Aggie?"

There was no reply. Then the back door, outside the mudroom, banged shut with the sound of at least two people running off. The steps were heavy, as if they were carrying something. That was not normal. It must be burglars! Creeping down the stairs hoping they were all gone, she saw no one. Moving into the kitchen, she lit a candle and gasped. Mrs Jennings and Aggie were sitting in their nightgowns, bound, gagged and blindfolded.

Mrs Jennings's head was down on one side as if she was asleep. Aggie was awake, wrestling with the ropes and moaning as she chewed at the gag across her mouth.

Anne stood there in shock, taking in the scene. Snapping out of it, she rushed across, clawing at Aggie's ropes. She slipped the blindfold off easily, but the gag was a different proposition. They had packed Aggie's mouth with material, and a tight rope wound around her mouth and head held the gag fast. Anne was strong, but she was having difficulty finding any way of undoing the knot.

There was only one way; she must cut it. She opened the drawer where the knives were kept and found it empty. The burglars had littered the floor with kitchen utensils. She needed more light! Anne grabbed a candle near the warm stove and stuck the wick end in the embers, blowing on them. The candle came to life.

Now with more light, she found a knife. Putting it under the rope of Aggie's gag so that it would cut from the inside, she slowly started. The maid's eyes enlarged as Anne struggled with the task. Thankfully, the knife was sharp and cut cleanly through the rope. It finally fell, and Anne quickly pulled all the material out of Aggie's mouth.

Aggie coughed and spluttered for a full minute or two, taking deep breaths before she could talk. Her first words were, "Don't worry about me. Help Mrs Jennings." But Anne was already halfway through the rope binding Aggie's arms. She cut the rope and quickly unwound it, setting Aggie free.

They quickly worked on Mrs Jennings, who was unconscious. Anne grabbed the knife again and moved towards her. Aggie screamed, "No, it's a sailor's knot. Look, it is easy if you know how!" Aggie grabbed the rope and twisted it backwards, and then pulled. The knot fell apart.

"How did you know that?"

"My brother – he is in the navy!"

Anne quickly removed the gag from Mrs Jennings while Aggie undid the rope holding her on the chair. As they released her, the little lady slumped sideways and would have fallen heavily on the floor if not for Anne restraining her. They lay her down comfortably and then checked her breath.

"She is breathing!"

"Good, now get a pillow Aggie for her head and don't leave her while I check the rest of the house."

Anne was still not sure if any of the burglars were inside. She yelled up the stairs, "William, Simeon, come quickly! William, Simeon!"

She heard some movement from the boys' room and assumed they were both coming. She crept down the hallway and in through the doorway of the parlour. William lay on the ground, quite still and bleeding from the skull. He was unconscious.

"My Lord! Aggie, come quickly! Please come quick!"

She knelt beside him, checking his breath. Gently she rolled him over, calling, "William, William can you hear me? William, William!"

At first, there was no response; he lay there with his eyes closed. Then there was a flicker of eyelids, and his eyes opened.

"Yow! Yow! That hurts!" Then he passed out again.

Aggie peered down at him and saw the blood still oozing from his skull. "I'll get some cloth; we must stop that bleeding."

Anne could not talk; she was in shock. Her greatest fear of one of her family being fatally injured was happening. Would he live, or would he die? What could she do? She trembled in her helplessness.

"Please, Will, don't die! I love you so much! Please, God, help us!"

Deep down in his mind, William wrestled with the pain, which kept thumping his head like a large bass drum. Then it stopped for a while and then restarted. He shivered as his body became cold and then colder. He opened his eyes and took a huge breath. The light from the candle in his eyes dazed him, and all he could see was a bright glare. He shut his eyes tight again, dodging the light.

Then he felt a warm hand holding his. It must be mother, but the feeling was going away. He grasped it tight again and held on with all his might. He opened his eyes, but the bright light forced them shut again. The pain in his head increased, and suddenly he became cold.

"I'm cold!" he whispered, "I'm so cold."

Anne, who was close and holding his hand, heard the whisper. She suddenly realised he must be in shock.

"Aggie, blankets – quick, get blankets."

Simeon was soon there without her noticing. Quickly he blurted out, "He is in shock; turn him on his side. Here, let me help. Keep the pressure on the wound until it stops bleeding. I'll get help."

"But Sim, it is still dark outside, and they may be out there!"

"We can't wait, Anne. Jeb will be at the bakery by now. It's four am – he will be there. We must save William!"

"Yes, get help Sim. Please, a doctor if you can get one."

Simeon was gone. Searching for Snups, he flew out the back door and stumbled over his dog.

"Come on, Boy! You can keep me company."

Snups did not move. Simeon saw the dog's blood pooling beside him.

On his knees, Simeon screamed, "No, No, No! You bastards – you will suffer for this. We will find you, and heaven help you when my father hears about this."

Simeon found extra strength as he thought about these people who had violated their family home. Tears ran down his face as he paced even harder along an empty High Street. The pain inside him welled up so much that he screamed in agony at the loss of their dog. It was a cry both of pain and rage. Simeon would never forget this moment. Keeping his focus, he rushed on for help and made the bakery in a few minutes flat.

He was out of breath as he clasped hold of Jeb near some of the other workers loading the ovens. Jeb held his shoulders, astonished he was here so early in the morning.

Simeon was out of breath – he opened his mouth, but nothing would come out. He groaned in anger. Was he so weak that he could not speak?

Jeb knelt, moving his gentle hands down Simeon's arms, "What's wrong, Sim? Is something wrong at home?"

"Help, Jeb. They need help and a doctor. Snups is dead, and William is dying. Burglars. Help!" then the emotion got the better of Simeon, and he burst into tears.

Jeb Hiscock took the eight-year-old in his arms, lifted him in a hug as he stood, and gathered the surprised staff around him. "Aaron, you tend the ovens and get help from the other staff as they arrive. Rose, you take Simeon in a cart quickly back home, please. Take Jock with you for protection. I will bring the Doctor and then Constable Rawlins. Ralph, come with me. We will take that other cart. Simeon, you go home with Rose. Get a drink of water first, lad. You have done a great job, Sim. We will handle it now. Come on, Ralph. Let's go!"

With that, Jeb and Ralph Hands were off in the cart towards Doctor Sopwith's house on the road above the castle. It was not far, but Jeb was sure he would be asleep, so this would be a tug of war.

Robert tossed and turned in his sleep. He found himself on the quarter-deck navigating *Restless* down the canal past Guildford. On the embankment, Anne and Emma waved madly and beckoned. He could not make out what they were saying. *Restless* was flying along the canal, and they were left well behind. Then he heard, "Help us, Robert! Help!"

He sat up in a start, throwing the blanket off and taking a great breath.

Michael Swanton was still sitting on his box guarding the cabin door. At one stage, he nearly fell asleep but quickly resurfaced with a big yawn and a quiet walk around. As Robert woke, Swanton was sitting with his back to the captain's bunk. The quick movement as Robert woke with a start took him by surprise. He turned with a knife drawn, crouching into a defensive position in less than a second. The man was quicker than a big cat and looked as menacing.

"Sorry, Swanton! It must have been a bad dream or something!"

The servant relaxed and put his knife away. He stood up, stretched, and then checked the door.

"I will make you a coffee, Captain."

"Good man. No trouble last night then?"

"Not quite, Sir! Let me fetch your coffee first. I think we need a plan!"

Robert sat up straight, rubbing his head. He was still thinking about his dream. It must have been a nightmare. Right now, the situation here must be his focus. Emma would have everything under control in Guildford.

After Swanton briefed him on the night's events, Robert scratched his chin as he thought through the implications. A sailor forcing entry into the captain's cabin was attempted mutiny, a brazen action far more than he expected. The precautions taken were worthwhile, but Michael Swanton would need rest soon. He needed an extra servant sharing watches with Swanton until Horace and his men arrived. There was now no doubt the traitors were still on board and becoming more confident.

Woolwich would provide some safety, and arriving there must be their priority. A difficult task given the gusting winds and changing currents on the Thames. Complicating that was the issue of the traitors. He would need total concentration on the navigation, allowing him no time for detecting threats. Swanton must keep watch over him this morning. Once at Woolwich docks, he would visit Captain Connors of the frigate *Forceful*. He knew Connors as a trustworthy man.

It would be a risk, taking Connors into his confidence, but he felt there was no choice. He needed an extra servant now and someone who was not associated with the crew of *Restless*. His life might depend on it.

"Swanton, make breakfast for both of us, please. I will need you on deck with me this morning as we navigate the Thames. It will be tricky today with the tides and the gusting winds, and I must concentrate on that. You will watch my back. We shall both have some food and then get this ship into the safety of Woolwich. Have the Master at Arms issue you with two pistols! Once docked, we will visit Captain Connors on *Forceful*. We need a reinforcement!"

The Fox and Hound, Guildford …

Lady Jane's maid came into Emma's room and opened the curtains. Emma stirred, sitting up and rubbing her eyes as the maid placed a tray with a freshly baked croissant and warm tea.

"Good morning, Milady, it is a beautiful day outside, and your mother advises she will be ready for breakfast at nine o'clock."

"What time is it, Meg? Thank you for the tea!"

Meg was short for Margaret Lane, who had been Lady Jane's maid for several years.

"It's just past eight, Milady!"

Emma yawned, stretched, and admired the blue sky outside while she thought about the exciting plans for today. Meg slightly opened the window and allowed in some airflow. There was a light breeze from the south, and she could hear the robins and finches chirping in the hedge outside. Emma glanced out and was surprised by the number of people in the street. Certainly, Guildford was growing, and she understood why the Turner's businesses were so successful – the town was alive with people.

"Thank you, Meg. When you are finished helping Mother, perhaps you would give me a hand with my hair?"

"Certainly, Milady. There has been some excitement up the street. There was a burglary at the Turner residence last night. The parish constable and the doctor are there now. Wasn't it Anne Turner you dined with yesterday evening?"

Emma raised her eyes upon Meg quickly, with a worried expression.

"What happened, Meg?"

"I'm not sure, Milady. All I know is that the burglars killed the dog, and one of the boys was knocked out and has not regained consciousness yet."

"My goodness!"

Emma saw that this changed everything for the day ahead. She jumped out of bed and opened her travelling chest searching for a dress.

"May I help you, Milady?"

"No, no, Meg. You attend Lady Jane and tell her the situation. I shall join her as soon as I can. Also, would you please wake Sir Hugh and advise him of mother's arrangements for breakfast."

"From what I hear, Milady, Sir Hugh may not be up till late! Also, it may be safer if a valet attends Sir Hugh."

"Sorry, Meg, my mistake!" Emma forgot the staff would talk among themselves. Meg was wary of Sir Hugh's antics and was quite correct in suggesting an alternative.

"Yes, well, perhaps it would be better if you asked Mr Stem. He will wake him. Thank you, Meg."

"Yes, Milady."

Emma dressed in ten minutes. She took a sip of water and headed downstairs, leaving a message for her mother at reception. She quickly exited the hotel and moved up High Street through the crowd of shoppers now lining the streets.

At the Turner's house, it all appeared normal. She pulled the doorbell and waited. Aggie, the maid, opened the door and ushered her into the parlour, recognising Emma.

"Lady Emma, please come in. I will let Miss Anne know that you are here. Please excuse the mess, but we are still cleaning up after the burglary. The Parish Constable is here investigating. Perhaps they will find out who the burglars were!"

Emma noticed the Constable and another man, who probably was a watchman. Jeb Hiscock, the bakery manager, was also in the study.

"Thank you, Aggie. Where is Miss Anne?"

"She is in the kitchen having some breakfast; there has been no time until now."

"Would she mind if I joined her? I have not had breakfast, either!"

"Of course, Milady. I think she would welcome some support. Please follow me."

Emma avoided a formal meeting. She considered Anne a friend now and would assist her if she could. Following Aggie through, she found Anne sitting at the table with Marcia. They both looked up in surprise as Aggie showed Emma in.

Anne stood, "Lady Emma, I forgot our meeting this morning. There was a burglary here last night and some injuries, so I lost track of time. I am so sorry."

Emma saw that Anne was only just holding back her tears. She went around the table and hugged her. "Anne, I was so concerned when I heard about the burglary. I came straight away. It must have been very frightening. May I join you for breakfast, and please tell me about it and how we may help?"

"Certainly. Aggie, some breakfast for Lady Emma, please! Please join me, but would you prefer to eat in the parlour?"

"No, no, this is fine."

Marcia was curious about this new lady. Clutching a toy bear, she looked hard at Emma and felt she might be a friend. Marcia, dressed in a cute little smock with her long golden hair hanging down around her shoulders, stood beside Anne, watching Emma. Marcia looked dishevelled as Anne had not brushed her hair, but she still appeared cute. Emma smiled at her. The four-year-old needed no further encouragement, running around the table and standing beside Emma. She spoke up with wide-open big green eyes and a serious voice, "This is my bear! His name is Buster. Would you like to pat him?"

Emma was instantly taken with Marcia and said, "Who are you, little one? Yes, please show me your Buster."

"I'm Marcia. Who are you?"

"Why, I'm Emma!"

Marcia smiled and leaned against Emma's legs, passing over her Buster. Anne looked up from her breakfast and saw Marcia had already introduced herself.

"I'm sorry, Emma, I forgot the introductions. I am not thinking that well yet. Marcia, this is Lady Emma South from Fintelton Manor."

Marcia looked up and wondered what a manor was but did not say anything.

"Marcia, I think your hair needs brushing. Shall we brush it together? You have beautiful hair. How about you run upstairs and get your brush."

Marcia looked over at Anne. Anne nodded in agreement. Marcia smiled and rushed out of the kitchen in search of her brush. Aggie placed a lovely plate of fresh-cut fruit and a bowl of porridge in front of Emma.

"Thank you, Aggie. That looks divine. I'm famished!"

Anne, for once, was lost for words as she nibbled on a piece of toast. It was like a dream just sitting here in the kitchen with Robert's sister sitting opposite, sharing breakfast, and helping Marcia. Robert was right – Emma was a lady, but also, she was not scared of giving a helping hand. Anne found she had a growing admiration for this young lady – perhaps they would be friends in the future.

"Anne, our maid, told us that someone was injured. May I enquire?"

"It was William. It seems he was knocked unconscious. He must have been investigating what the noises were from the parlour. I found him on the floor when I searched the house. It was about four in the morning. I am not sure how long he was lying there. I thought he was dead at first."

Emma noticed as tears welled up in Anne's eyes and the apologetic half-smile as she wiped them dry.

"Anne, I am so sorry!" Emma realised how much this had affected Anne.

"I was so frightened for him, but then he moved, and Aggie and I bound his head wound. We put him in bed and waited for the Doctor. Jeb brought Doctor Sopwith soon after Sim raised the alarm."

Emma reached over and held Anne's hands, "How terrible. Has he recovered?"

"At first, he was struggling with it and not conscious. He was in shock, so we covered him in blankets and warmed him up. Then the doctor arrived and used some smelling salts. He groaned for quite a while as he could not tolerate any light in his eyes. He was in a lot of pain, but Doctor Sopwith is with him now, and he has given him some potions. He is resting comfortably. I am waiting for the doctor. I felt quite weak, so I came down for some breakfast."

"You poor thing, it must have been a terrible ordeal!"

"I must admit I was terrified. I am thankful William has a hard head!" Anne smiled for the first time since Emma arrived.

"There was a smile from him before I came downstairs. Clementine, Madeline, and Simeon are with Doctor Sopwith. I think our little William will live and fight another day." Anne managed a smile and then wiped more tears from her eyes.

Marcia burst into the kitchen with her brush.

"Emma, Emma, I found it. It was on the floor near the door. It is usually in my drawer. Can you brush me now?"

"Good for you! Yes, sit up here."

Emma hoisted Marcia up on her lap, head facing forward towards the table. Marcia loved having her hair brushed and gave Anne a gleaming smile. Emma arranged the hair and gently started the process. The lovely scene calmed Anne, and she happily thought about how she also talked with Robert in this kitchen.

"My, you have lovely hair, Marcia. Just like your big sister Anne."

"That's what Robert told me too. We played down at the river with Snups, and William, Simeon, and I conquered Robert's ship. I was a pirate."

"That must have been fun. Maybe we can have a game this afternoon. I like playing pirates."

Doctor Sopwith came into the kitchen and found Anne still finishing breakfast and Lady Emma South with Marcia on her knees, having her hair brushed.

Anne stood up, being a bit embarrassed and introduced them. "Doctor Sopwith, please may I introduce Lady Emma South."

Doctor Sopwith, clothed in his pyjamas and a dressing gown, stood there in an incomprehensible manner. It was obvious he was aware of class distinction. He was surprised to find Lady Emma South in the kitchen of the Turner household having breakfast. He regained his countenance straightening the dressing gown and giving a slight bow.

"Lady Emma, a pleasant surprise meeting you here. Please forgive my dress, however, it was an emergency early this morning, and there was no time to change. I have called on your father several times, and unfortunately, we have not had the pleasure of meeting in person. I trust your father is well."

"Anne and I are good friends, Doctor Sopwith, and yes, thank you, my father is in good health."

Doctor Sopwith swallowed, nodded and then addressed Anne.

"William is recovering well. I have checked him carefully. I am confident there is no brain injury. He seems alert, lucid and answers complex questions quickly. The head wound will heal today as he is young and healthy. I think you may find the biggest problem is keeping him in bed. I would recommend a few more hours of rest, but he must stay awake, please. I instructed him on this and arranged that Clementine and Simeon remain with him in shifts. His eyes are still a little sensitive, but I would expect that will subside in the next two hours or so. If it does not, please call me back. I have another potion here. Mix this in water in the afternoon well after lunch, say around three o'clock. The draft will lessen the pain from the headache.

After lunch, he should have a walk around the house for a while but quietly. Perhaps Aggie might keep an eye on him. Once he takes the potion, he will rest comfortably. He is a lucky little fellow. That blow could have been far worse. I will call back this evening and check on him again and on Mrs Jennings, although she seems wholly recovered now."

Anne was relieved and let out a great sigh, "Thank you, Doctor Sopwith. That is wonderful news. I thought he might be seriously injured. At first, when I found him, I thought he might have been dead. I was terrified."

"Anne, it may be good if you have a rest this morning as well. This burglary has been a bad experience. As this will be a busy day for you, try at least doing something relaxing."

"Perhaps tonight, Doctor, but we need the family home operating again for now. There is still the Constable, the repairs and the clean-up. Thank you for coming so quickly at such an early hour; we are very thankful."

"Ow." Marcia gave a little scream as the brush got stuck in a knot in her hair. Emma said, "Sorry, Marcia".

Doctor Sopwith looked at Emma and suggested, "Perhaps some water on the hair may help! It always helped when my mother did my sister's hair." He meant well, but he was slightly embarrassed at being so human and still in his pyjamas. For an instance, Doctor Sopwith looked at Emma and she at him, and then he regained his focus on Anne.

"Miss Anne, Simeon showed me the cast on his arm. I have never seen anything like it before. It is brilliant. He tells me it was Doctor Bassington who put in on?"

Anne was pleased with the query, "That's correct. I asked him about it, and he became aware of the procedure in France earlier this year. It is a new treatment. He calls it 'Plaster of Paris.'"

"So new that I have never heard of it before. I understand the Doctor will be returning here soon. I just wonder if you would ask if I could meet with him. I have not had the pleasure of being introduced yet. I am keen for some professional instruction on how this process is applied. Please pass him my good wishes. I must be off now. Time now that I dressed properly and had some breakfast."

Doctor Sopwith picked up his large black leather medical bag, acknowledging both ladies and gently shook Marcia's hand before making his way out of the kitchen. There was a short silence as Emma put some water on another knot in Marcia's hair and then brushed it out gently.

Emma looked up and saw Anne smiling at her. Given the good news from the doctor, she was recovering quickly.

"What, Anne?"

"I think Doctor Sopwith was quite cute in his pyjamas, and he may admire a certain young lady!"

"I can't imagine who that might be. Can you, Anne?"

"I think it might be Lady Emma South!"

"Really?" Emma blushed.

Anne continued, "My father always disliked Doctor Sopwith because he was an arrogant fellow. But today, I found him very pleasant indeed. How did you find him?"

"Very nice!" Emma blushed again.

For the first time, Anne caught Emma off guard but in a delightful way.

"I found him very charming indeed. He is far more genteel than I ever realised!"

"Who is genteel, my Dear?" came a loud enquiring voice as the Countess of Fintelton entered the kitchen.

Both girls stood up with a start, and Marcia fell onto the floor and said, "Ow!".

Lady Jane bent down and helped the little girl up. Marcia beamed up at Lady Jane, who smiled down at her.

"My Lady, this is Marcia, my youngest sister." Lady Jane bowed, and Marcia replied with a cute courtesy for a four-year-old.

"Aren't you beautiful, Marcia and such lovely hair!"

"Emma is brushing it for me. She is so gentle. I like Emma!"

"Mother, did you not receive my message?" Emma was as amazed as Anne was, greeting her mother here in the kitchen.

"Yes, but I also heard the news and felt Anne should have our support at this terrible time. My Dear, I am so sorry about what has happened. Now there must be something we can do. Hugh is chatting with the Parish Constable. Rawlings is his name, I believe, and your man Mr Hiscock. He seems a very pleasant fellow. The men can sort out the burglary. How is William?"

"He is recovering well, my Lady, and out of danger. Thank you for enquiring."

"Anne, I think William is a hero! It appears he disturbed the burglars at first before they attacked him. What a brave young man. He was probably protecting you and the other children!"

Anne took in a sharp breath as the thought occurred to her. William may have saved her life.

"The men can take care of all that. Now that fruit and toast look good, Anne. May I join you two, please? So much drama, I am famished!"

"Why Lady Fintelton, it would be an honour, but I am ashamed of serving you here in the kitchen. I......."

"Anne, being here is fine. I am just so glad that you were not harmed. Anyway, I cannot let you three girls have all the fun in the kitchen while I am stuck in that old hotel! Can I, Marcia?"

Marcia jumped for joy with these new friends and gave Lady Jane a big hug.

They all broke out laughing. Anne never expected to meet Robert's family in such an informal setting. Perhaps she might be welcome at Fintelton next July.

Lady Jane sat down at the table and watched Emma brushing Marcia's hair. The picture made her think about how Emma would make a fine mother. As Aggie passed Lady Jane a warm cup of tea, she turned and watched Anne as she and Emma talked and laughed. There was nothing false here; they were already getting on like sisters. Lady Jane smiled, thinking of when she first met the Earl and all the stupid things they did that no one would ever understand. Perhaps Robert and Anne had already started sharing times like that. She sat back in the chair, and as she sipped the warm tea, she thought, 'I like this girl, Anne. I find I like her more all the time.'

The McPherson Household, Greenwich ...

Thomas Turner and James McPherson returned from the brewery before lunch on Saturday, having spent three hours looking at the production systems. Thomas enjoyed James's company and found him friendly, possessing a good sense of humour, and well briefed on Thomas's role in Guildford.

During their discussion on introducing steam power into the Guildford brewery design, they agreed that external engineering skills were needed for the project. This led to other conversations about what should be raised with the engineers.

Marion finally found a gap in the conversation and advised Thomas that her father, Alexander Steele, and his sons would join the McPhersons for dinner this evening. Mrs McPherson had also invited Marion's mother, but Mr Steele had declined. Jennifer Steele's health had deteriorated significantly in the last weeks, and the doctors had now confined her in the convalescent home.

Marion and Thomas planned a visit on Sunday morning after church. Thomas was hesitant as Marion warned him that her behaviour was becoming increasingly violent, like a small angry child. Marion was determined, and Thomas would be pleased to escort her despite the mother's behaviour. After all, it was his future mother-in-law, so he wished for some form of a meeting if possible.

"From what I hear, the lady is not herself most of the time; she is quite a handful. Remember that it is the disease and not her. I believe she was a wonderful woman before her affliction." James knew more than this, but he thought he would allow Thomas the pleasure of finding out for himself. He hoped it would not scare the lad off.

Thomas was scratching his head. "I'll keep that in mind. Most people are not themselves when they are ill!"

Marion came into the dining room, "I saw you two were deep in conversation, so I took the opportunity of a discussion with my aunt. Tell me? How did the brewery visit go?"

"We have come up with some plans for improved systems, and James will have his engineers in Glasgow do some preliminary drawings for your uncle. A further meeting will be required when James returns in three or four weeks. So, I will be back probably before then. That gives plenty of time for another visit at Guildford if your schedule allows."

"I'll be down there like a shot. I have a couple of new dress orders for Hursts. That Mrs Smith is a wonder."

Thomas was quite surprised, as he was not aware that the tailor's shop in Guildford set such high standards. Beth and Anne always looked stunning in whatever they bought there, so perhaps it was the case.

"Is it the design of the clothes or the materials they use that makes the difference?"

"Thomas, you men are all the same. It is Mrs Smith. She has a great colour sense for buying both materials and dresses. Her book of designs is unique and covers all occasions. She treats you like a Queen, and nothing is too much trouble."

James chipped in, "Pity they don't do men's clothing then!"

"They do, James, they do. One side of the store is for women, and the other is for men. You must visit the next time you are in Guildford."

Thomas was thinking about the next meeting, "We could meet on Monday, October the third or the Tuesday, as I must be in Guildford the following week for Neville and Beth's wedding. Are you acquainted with Neville?"

"No, I have not had that pleasure."

Hamish McPherson came into the room with a note in his hand.

"Alexander Steele sends a note advising that Sir Robert South has berthed at Woolwich. Alexander has been working on his ship today and will bring him along tonight. He hopes this will not be inconvenient but feels it would be a pleasant addition as Thomas is here from Guildford. I have sent a response both to Alexander and Robert encouraging this."

Thomas was pleased Robert would attend. James was confused.

"Now, who is Sir Robert South?"

Thomas explained, "He is a friend of our family. It is a long story, but the week before you arrived, just before we left here for Guildford, Robert organised this wonderful picnic at Severndroog Castle that we all went on, including your mother and father. My sister and Robert are great friends."

James was keen to find out more, "Is there an understanding between your sister and Robert?"

Thomas felt the question was a bit blunt but answered, "Not as far as I know. But they are good friends. When they meet, their conversation is never-ending. They both have fine intellects."

"I see. This Robert sounds quite a character."

Marion excused herself as Mrs McPherson required her before dinner. Hamish poured Thomas and James a whisky each and then one for himself.

"Never too early for a good scotch!"

"Aye!" James looked at the glass with interest.

"Now, boys, what kind of efficiency will we see from these changes you suggest?"

The business conversation continued. The critical issue was engineering assistance, and they agreed on leaving early Monday for London. Hamish was keen for some engineering comments on their plans.

James said, "This calls for another drink."

It seemed an all-male affair with Alexander Steele and his three sons and Robert, James and Thomas at dinner. Hamish laboured at keeping the conversation interesting for the ladies. Still, it was a struggle and Marjorie and Marion withdrew soon after dinner, leaving the men with their port and cigars, talking about engineering.

"Now, Alexander, you say that you are installing two new canons on the bow of *Restless* over the next three days. Can it be done so quickly?" Hamish was surprised by the quick turnaround they expected.

"Yes, easily now that we have completed the other five frigates. There are only two canons, and we will install them on Monday."

James asked, "Robert, why are you having the canons installed on the bow of your ship. How will they help with a broadside?"

"They don't. These canons are stronger than what we traditionally use on the bow. They have greater range, and simply put, if we are chasing the enemy, we can sink them from behind. If we complete the installation on Monday, we will test them Tuesday once we are out of port."

Alexander looked concerned, "Won't you be testing them in the estuary here before going?"

"No, Sir. My orders require our departure for Portsmouth as soon as the guns are signed off as installed."

"It would be safer if we carried out the test before you departed. Any required adjustments can be made at Woolwich. The navy people don't understand how advanced these cannons are and the need for settling in."

"Sir, in that case, I suggest that you and your men travel with me on Tuesday when we leave port. We can test them off Margate, then make the adjustments, and I will drop you off there before heading south."

"If that is the only opportunity, Sir, it is settled. I will have my men ready."

James said casually, "Why the rush, Robert?"

"Orders!"

"So, where are you heading after Portsmouth?"

Robert thought this was a reasonably innocent question, but the detail of his next mission must remain secret. He felt it better if a wrong location was given rather than not saying anything. "The precise location must remain confidential, but I think we might be near Gibraltar!"

"A pleasant spot at this time of year."

Hamish McPherson changed the discussion, "So Robert, I hear you will be Neville's best man. We are excited about our invitation. Will your imminent voyage return in time for your best man duties?"

"Given good winds and a safe carriage ride, Sir, we will arrive on time. Especially for the bachelor party! Your acquaintances Admiral Sutherland and Captain Foster and their wives will also be attending."

"Good, Good."

Later in the evening, Robert asked Thomas for a few words about Neville's bachelor party. They withdrew into the entry hall away from the main conversation.

In a low voice, Robert asked Thomas if there was any further information about the McPhersons?

"They have a small fleet of merchant ships that operate out of Glasgow, called 'The Grey Line'. They bring in various goods but mostly grain."

Robert seemed more interested, "How is that done? Given the corn laws."

"I'm not sure; perhaps they have some exemption!"

Robert noticed Hamish coming over, "I thought we could rent the room that they have at the back of the Fox and Hound and organise some interesting entertainment."

Thomas smiled.

"I hope you boys will take pity on Neville as he is not as young as you two."

"Yes, Sir," Robert agreed, "But we must give him a suitable send-off. It may be his last chance, Sir."

"I remember my send-off with friends. I would be ashamed talking about it now. Better left unsaid."

"Mr McPherson, I must be on my way. Thank you, Sir, for your warm hospitality. Please pass my compliments to Mrs McPherson and Marion. We will meet again soon at Guildford, Sir. Perhaps a scotch together at the Fox and Hound in the afternoon before the wedding?"

"It would be a pleasure, Robert. Might I enquire if your parents will be attending?"

"I hope so. I believe Anne is meeting my sister this weekend. It may have already happened, and Neville, a long-term friend of the family, will invite my father and mother. May I introduce them, Sir, if you are agreeable."

"Very much so, Sir. Marjorie and I would be honoured."

"Excellent. Good night, Sir, and good night, Thomas."

At HMS Restless, Woolwich ...

Lieutenant Richard Small, the first mate of HMS *Restless*, saluted his captain as he came onboard. Small was a good ten years older than Robert, being in the navy since being a boy. Despite their age difference, Small maintained the proper respect that a Captain deserved. Small was on *Restless*, where the traitors almost murdered Captain Roderick Hughes.

While Robert previously discussed the voyage with Small and gained his view on the crew, he was careful that his orders remained confidential except for the installation of the canons and their return to Portsmouth. Robert's assessment of Small was that he appeared to be a reasonable officer so far. In time, he would decide if Small was trustworthy or not. At present, he felt uncomfortable, giving him his complete confidence.

"I hope the dinner went well, Sir?"

"Yes, Lieutenant Small, thank you, very well. All quiet here?"

"Not exactly, Captain. It appears Swanton caught a member of the crew leafing through the documents on your desk."

"A crew member was in my cabin?"

"Yes, Sir. Swanton was cooking his dinner and missed him entering. But he did keep checking the cabin and found Seaman Cobb at your desk. He is an able seaman on the foremast team."

"Right, that does it! Have Mr Trotter's report to me straight away and have the Master at Arms post his most trusted man as an armed sentry on my cabin door. Also, throw Cobb in the brig until I organise a court-martial. Breaking into the Captain's cabin and stealing information is a capital offence. I will talk with Swanton now. Thank you, Small."

"Cobb is already in the brig, Sir."

"Good work, Small."

The captain rushed below decks, nearly colliding with some crew members. While it was more spacious than the usual schooner, it was still reasonably cramped below decks. Robert noticed that all talking stopped as soon as the men saw him, and some had noticeable looks of anger on their faces. Could it be that there were more traitors on this ship than he thought!

Swanton was sitting in his servant's room as the captain entered.

In a low voice, "Swanton, what happened?"

"I caught this sailor rifling through the papers on your desk, Sir. I searched him, and it appears he did not steal anything, which makes me think he was looking for your orders."

"How long was he at my desk?"

"It must have been several minutes, Sir? I kept checking the room every five to ten minutes while cooking my dinner. Most of the time, I was guarding the door. Somehow, he knew that I was in my cabin and got in when I wasn't watching."

"So, he may have had up to ten minutes. Plenty of time for a quick read of the orders?"

"Yes, Sir. Sorry, Sir."

"No, Swanton, you did a good job. At least we have one of them. Tell me did he say anything when you caught him?"

"Nothing Sir, but we did not press him that hard. Thought I should wait for your instructions."

"Mr Swanton, coming into the captain's cabin and stealing information is a capital offence. Given there has already been one attempted break-in, we can assume his involvement. Once at sea on Tuesday, we will hang him high as an example."

"Yes, Sir, but it would be good if we extracted some information out of him before he hangs."

"I agree, Mr Swanton. Once that guard is on my door, I authorise your interrogation of the prisoner. I doubt he will talk, but it is worth a try. Please keep him alive for an enquiry and sentence on Tuesday morning. I'd hang him now, but we are in port. Better done at sea."

There was a knock at the door. The Master and the Master at Arms were waiting. Robert noticed the guard was in place outside the cabin door.

The Master at Arms reported, "Sir, a Lieutenant Wainbridge on deck from HMS *Forceful*, with a crew transfer. The new man is with him."

"Thank you, Mr Door, I'll deal with that in a moment, but first, I need both of you in here. Come in, gentlemen."

Swanton gave a short bow and grinned as he went out.

"Mr Trotters, you are the Master, and I believe that Cobb was a member of one of your sail teams. The foremast sail team, I am told. Locate Cobb's team captain and find out about him, please. Who were his friends? Go through his possessions and see if anything there links him to the traitors. Wake them up and grill them until you are thoroughly satisfied. Join me for breakfast and report back, please."

"Yes, Sir." The Master almost ran out of the cabin.

"Mr Door, you are the Master at Arms, and I am sorry we are not better acquainted. I have little time, and I will make some assumptions here. I believe there is another traitor on this ship. I think Cobb is probably one of them, but I'm not sure. Stealing information from the captain's desk is an act of treason with the penalty of death. Now Swanton is an ex-army man, an expert in killing. I have sent him down with orders that Cobb provides us with information. I'm sure you understand. It will not hurt the men to hear Cobb exercising his lungs. But Mr Door, make sure Swanton does not kill him, please. I am sure you will know when the man can take no more.

I want him alive and well for hanging on Tuesday. You will remind Swanton of this, Sir. I have already done so, but I must be sure he understands – sometimes, these men who use torture get a bit carried away. Do you understand me, Sir?"

"Fully, Captain. Leave it with me."

"Mr Door, just another thing. Post a guard on the brig. I do not want anyone near the brig or talking with him. Also, please make sure the guard on my door is changed every three hours. You may now send Lieutenant Wainbridge down."

"Yes. Sir."

"Dismissed."

"Aye, Aye, Sir."

Robert sat back in his chair and considered the situation. Whoever these traitors were, they desperately needed information on where this ship was travelling next. Why? Taking such a risk of being discovered in the captain's cabin seemed foolhardy, especially after being detected the previous night. These were desperate men, but why the urgency? A clever thief would wait for a good opportunity. Perhaps they thought that Swanton was also absent as the captain was ashore. But surely, a crew member would see them entering the captain's quarters – it is such a small vessel? Robert then realised it was possible that crew members did see him, and the beholders did nothing about it. Robert shivered. The cabins outside housed the officers. Lieutenant Small's was the next cabin. Surely not. If this revolt involved some of the officers, it might explain why the traitors took Captain Hughes by surprise.

Opening his sea chest, he checked the contents. He had carefully placed the general orders three layers below the top document. He noticed these papers were now ten layers below. So, they knew his orders. Thankfully, he kept his secret orders with him. He was sure the traitors now knew they would be heading back to Portsmouth.

If these people are Irish activists, perhaps there is a shipment of arms due, and they are seeking information on the ships in the area. As *Restless* was there recently, they correctly guessed she would be back. Perhaps a little bit of misinformation leaked may lessen the tension on board and slow things down!

There was a knock on the door. "Enter!"

A young Lieutenant, followed by an older man, obviously, a crewman, entered. "Lieutenant Wainbridge reporting, Sir. Captain Connors sends his compliments and this letter. The man you requested is Mr Bright, Sir. He will be available for as long as he is required."

"Thank you, Wainbridge. Please thank Captain Connors for me and advise him I shall be in contact at Portsmouth."

After the young Lieutenant left, Robert briefed Bright on his role. He was an Able Seaman about thirty years of age with a complexion that reflected many years in the navy. Robert was pleased to find the man quite courteous, and he spoke pleasantly when addressed.

"Bright – make sure you trust only Swanton and me! Our primary aim is survival. You will take shifts with Swanton guarding the door of my cabin each night. It is my opinion that there may be several traitors in this crew. For some reason, they are desperate to discover where we are heading. So, trouble could come at any time; however, I think it will happen during the night. Swanton should be back soon; he will brief you on accommodation and the daily program. Now I shall go on deck and meet the Officer of the Watch before turning in."

Climbing up onto the deck, Robert approached the First Lieutenant.

"Mr Small, things seem under control here. If the engineers settle the canons by Monday evening, we will be underway early Tuesday depending on the wind. I'm keen to be back at sea."

"I take it we return directly to Portsmouth, Captain?"

"Yes, that is correct. Portsmouth first, then let me say we shall see Gibraltar soon. But keep that confidential, please."

"Aye, Aye, Sir."

Robert thought, 'Let us see if either Swanton or Bright can pick that up as scuttle but in the next day or two!'

The Turner Household, Guildford ...

Jeb Hiscock and the builder attended the house repairs while Aggie and Mrs Jennings, who recovered quickly, were now cleaning the mess the burglars left behind. Every drawer in Mr Turner's desk was broken into, whether keyed locked or not. Constable Rawlins' opinion was that they were professionals from London, given how silently they entered.

"Miss Anne, would you like a rider sent, alerting Mr Turner of the burglary?"

"No, Jeb, I must not spoil their stay. They will hear when they arrive back on Thursday. Mother would be desperate and demand they return at once. We will be safe here. Did the locksmith make the repairs?"

"Yes! The locksmith has finished, and the carpenters strengthened the back-door area. The front door was not forced or touched. Sir Hugh talked for some time with Constable Rawlins before he went. He feels the burglars were looking for something but disturbed before they found anything. I am concerned it might be some of our recipes for bread and biscuits."

"It may be. I am not sure."

"But they did take the grandfather clock. Perhaps that's why you thought they were carrying something."

Anne shrugged without a reply.

"Miss Anne, I would like a guard here until your father returns. I would also like a guard posted at the bakery. They might try there next. I think Mr Turner would agree."

"Jeb, you are the manager. I will agree with your recommendations. I will feel far safer tonight if we have a guard on duty."

"This evening, I will join the guard for a while and then sleep at the bakery with Aaron. We will keep a watch there. By the way, I have buried Snups out the back."

"Thank you, Jeb. You have been very kind."

"I doubt they will be back, but best, we are careful. Please have the staff check all the locks tonight before retiring."

On the Road to London ...

Following their Guildford visit, Lady Jane South and Lady Emma continued their journey. As the miles went by, they recounted their adventure. Anne left the children in the care of the maids and accompanied them around Guildford for a couple of hours on Saturday afternoon. The ladies were particularly impressed with the seamstress, Mrs Smith, and spent some time going through her dress books and looking at the fine materials on display. Mrs Smith explained that as there was a chain of shops, they purchased materials from the wholesalers in London. Hursts ensured they kept up with the city's great stores.

Lady Jane thanked Anne for spending the afternoon with them at a most stressful time. She suggested that Mr Turner employ a butler if London visits became regular. Anne said that she would certainly mention this, given the burglary.

Emma continued reflecting on what caused the change in her mother. At first, she doubted her mother would spare Anne Turner any time, given she was a commoner. As far as she knew, Lady Jane rarely spoke with commoners. Her father was the same, if not worse. It was as if her mother had discarded her society rules, and visiting the Turners in the morning and taking breakfast in their kitchen was a miracle as far as she could see!

She was curious about what caused this change. As the coach slowly rumbled on, she built up the courage and asked, "Mother! May I ask you about our society."

"I thought you might after this weekend!"

"I have been brought up by you and father believing we were above the commoners. We have rarely even spoken with them. I presumed that you would not mingle with such people as the Turners?"

"You are correct, my Dear. That's how we brought you up, and that is what our society expects."

"Then have I been dreaming, or did you really have breakfast with Anne and myself in the Turner's kitchen and then welcome the chance of spending another two hours with Anne seeing Guildford?"

"You have not been dreaming at all. Perhaps we should restart our conversation of Friday evening before bed. When you suggested that we stop in Guildford, it may have looked simple, but you must credit me with some sense, my Dear. Emma, when you come up with a plan, I know you! There is always a good reason for it. And, of course, you suggested the plan the day after Robert was here. A mother does have some intuition. I am sure you will be just the same as me. There was a good reason for it wasn't there."

"Yes, Mother, and I think you may have deduced the reason."

"Perhaps, but that is not important. I will tell you the reason why. I was young once, as well. I had two older sisters and a brother, Rachael, Louisa, and John. Now John was the youngest, but he was a good five years older than I. They played as a group, and by the time I was five, they were off doing things and left me at home. My mother did not mind me playing with one of the servant's children, about the same age. Her name was Ruby. She and

I enjoyed the most wonderful childhood. I would sneak downstairs, and we would play for hours. We shared our dreams, talked about everything, and enjoyed childhood together. Then one day, Ruby was gone. I was inconsolable, and my mother spent a lot of time with me, helping me through those dark times."

"What happened to Ruby?"

"Ruby's mother, being in service, was not well off. The mother decided that Ruby would also enter service but with another family. I never saw her again."

"That is a pity, but what is the point?"

"Ruby was a commoner. Sometimes we shared breakfast in the kitchen downstairs long before my parents were out of bed. Quite often, we would be taken together on picnics in the company of Ruby's mother. I think those were the happiest days of my life. I will never forget them. Two years before Ruby left, my mother started a slow separation process. I was unaware of it then, but my governess started schooling me about the aristocracy and everything you have learnt about how we are superior. But you see, I had an education before that of reality."

"How did you know that, Mother?"

"I think Ruby was happier than I was. The hardships of life were a reality for her, but she could still smile, laugh and have fun. From about age thirteen, my mother took that away from me. My schooling from that age focused on one aim. The aim was that I would become a refined lady and marry a rich man who would provide me with a luxurious life."

"Surely that is normal for our class of people, Mother. We need money, so we can keep our estates running."

"That's exactly the point. It is a self-defeating purpose!"

"How can it be if we maintain our position?"

"Let me explain, Dear!" Lady Jane took a deep breath and gathered her thoughts.

"My father desperately searched for a suitable partner for me. A rich estate holder was the target. He felt that was his duty. I was young with no such ideas in mind and would have been happy marrying a farmer if I had found happiness and true love. But these ideals were not as important as the demands of the aristocracy. Once you marry outside the social circles, you are out. All contact is cut off. My mother was adamant this would not happen to her daughter. So, they found me a match."

"You mean you had an arranged marriage. You married someone you did not love?"

"That is mostly correct, but your father is unaware of that, and you should never tell him. You see, parents arrange most marriages in our society. There are a lot of unhappy women in our circles. That is why there are so many discrete affairs. The men have their quiet flings, and the women, to a lesser extent, get active while they are away."

"Mother, you didn't?"

"No, I didn't. We married late, and my energy levels would only cope with bringing up three children. But many ladies were married quite young and were easily seduced as they lacked experience in life. That usually led to other seductions and so on. I concentrated on my children, and I wasn't disappointed, but your father has entertained his different women at times."

Emma looked at her mother in astonishment. "How did you find this out?"

"Women talk about these things. Our networks are full of gossip, and there are other ways to find out. Discrete relationships are not without risk. Have a quiet discussion with Neville, and he will tell you about the risk of disease. I was never going to take that chance – for a woman, it would mean ruin. Men get away with it. I was fortunate that I didn't catch anything from your father."

"Mother, I have heard of discrete liaisons, but I have never even thought of the health issues. Not that I am considering any such thing, but I will talk with Neville about it. But surely you are happy, Mother?"

"I am happy with my lot in life, Emma, but I could have been as happy with a farmer, attorney or teacher. There is nothing special about the aristocracy. They are the same as the other classes, but they maintain this fiction about being superior. In some ways, they have the advantages of wealth, manners, and education. But even that is changing. You said that the Turners are bringing in huge amounts of money. Look at the Americans! Some say there will be more millionaires there one day than the population of Britain. Maybe and maybe not. The point is things are changing."

"So, you are saying that an aristocratic marriage is not important anymore?"

"Not at all. There are huge advantages financially if you marry into the aristocracy. If that is what you wish for, that is acceptable. But if you choose otherwise, we can manage that as well. Let me give you an example. For Fintelton, the entail is on the eldest son, and Hugh will get the lot. So, where does that leave you and Robert? There was no choice for Robert. We sent him away at thirteen to the navy to build a career for himself. That broke my heart."

Lady Jane stopped her conversation and dabbed a tear from her eye as she gazed out the carriage window.

"But if he had stayed here, what would have become of him? There was no future for him. Hugh will be the next Earl, and Robert would have depended on him for a living or been forced into the law or the church. That would have stifled Robert. He needed open air and adventure. Look at him now, already a captain.

What about you, Emma? What will become of you? Your father has put aside a dowry of ten thousand pounds so you will not starve. Do you desire some wealthy landholder somewhere in the south of England? Perhaps you will find someone."

"I am not sure. I always thought I would marry a rich Earl and live happily ever after. There must be many wealthy and available men in our society. I shall just keep mingling in our circles until the right one turns up, but you have made me think hard about the health issues. How awful!"

"Emma. I shall give you all the assistance I can, as it is time you were married, young lady."

"Thank you, Mother, but tell me why you accepted Anne so readily and took breakfast in her kitchen?"

"I will answer that by asking you a question? Why did you do the same?"

"I was concerned for her as she was a friend and a friend of Robert's, and he would never forgive me if I didn't help her. And I liked her. I could talk freely with her, and being with her and her family made me feel comfortable and happy. She is like a breath of fresh sea air. It was an exhilarating experience."

"Emma, don't you understand; it was the same for me! I have not always desired the high society of being upstairs. I have no desire to be estranged from Robert. I would welcome grandchildren."

She looked at her mother as if she was revealing a great secret. Then Emma looked out the window and thought about her mother's words. Life was strange, but her mother was right. Why should she not desire the happiness of her children?

"Mother. Father and Hugh will never accept her!"

"Why? Emma, we did! Why not them? We will work together on it. I think Robert may be smarter than any of us thought. I like this Anne girl very much!"

Emma happily snuggled up beside her mother. Lady Jane put her arm around Emma and gave her a warm hug.

"Mother, you said being upstairs was not always your desire. Was there someone else?"

"There was! But it never would have happened in those days. Would it?"

Chandos Place, London …

The Sunday night, Jonathan Turner did not sleep well. His mind kept telling him something was wrong at home. He tossed and turned until he could sleep no longer. Worried that he would disturb Eleanora, he got out of bed, put on a dressing gown and sat down in a chair in the large bedroom at Chandos Place. He took a glass of water and hoped that this would settle his nerves.

The trip had overtired him. He would sit here for a minute or two until his body settled down.

Eleanora woke at about six in the morning and found him fast asleep, a blanket around him in the chair opposite the bed. As the candle was burnt right down, she lit another and then brushed his brow. Jonathan woke.

"I couldn't sleep!"

"Thank you for not waking me. Best we get going now. Breakfast and then church."

Jonathan Turner stood up and stretched. He thought, 'This being in someone else's home unsettles me. I'm sure Anne has it all under control in Guildford. No time now for worry. Time for breakfast!'

At Greenwich ...

It was late Sunday morning, and the McPherson family were home from church. Hamish McPherson read James and Thomas's proposed plans while sitting at his study desk.

Jenkins entered the room through the open door, "Excuse me, Sir."

"Yes, Jenkins. "

"A rider arrived with a message, Sir."

Hamish looked up and took the message. Once Jenkins left the room, he opened the note and read it carefully.

"To Start

Burglary, Friday night at Turner's residence. Dog killed, so no alarm raised. Some property stolen, but no documents. One of the children, William, injured but safely recovering. Entry through back door – servants tied up. Police involved. Police think it was not about property but thieves looking for something.

Gentry from Fintelton Manor visited the family on Saturday.

Strawberry

Stop."

The message used the correct code. It was from Hamish's paid informer in Guildford. He sat back and contemplated if he should take any action. Did Jonathan know yet? Probably not. He thought, 'Thank goodness I did not leave any documents with Jonathan Turner.' They must discuss this soon after they arrive tomorrow. It was time Jonathan was made aware of what was going on.

Hamish leaned forward and took pen and paper in hand. He wrote a reply message:

"To Start

Find burglars and finalise this at once. Spare no expense. Advise when done.

Mulberry

Stop."

Sealing the message with wax, he called Jenkins. The butler appeared. He passed him the message and said, "Here. You know the procedure!"

Chapter 16

The Bassingtons decided on arriving for the wedding a week early, being available to assist if needed. David and Jennifer planned on hiring a coach and enjoying the sights of Guildford with Neville and Bethany before the big day.

Jennifer explained, "He has been in the navy so long, and we have hardly seen him for so many years. Now he has resigned, and with practices both in Guildford and Harley Street, it is a new chapter for us. Once they are married, time with Neville and Bethany will be a delightful luxury. David is also considering purchasing a country house as he feels a great attraction for Guildford."

Eleanora was thrilled that Neville's parents would provide them with support in their new married life.

"I hope you will spend time with Jonathan and me as well. The family often has an afternoon tea picnic beside the river on a Sunday, which has always proved popular with the children and guests. I do hope you can join us."

"That would be wonderful, Eleanora; it would be a welcome new experience for us."

HMS Restless ...

Alexander Steele stood slightly behind the captain on the quarter deck as the crew assembled. There was complete silence except for officers shouting orders and a steadily increasing southwesterly buffeting the limp sails as *Restless* stood into the wind. Although the First Officer briefed Alexander, he was uncomfortable being present at such a time. Today, the administration of naval law at sea was a frightening prospect for him.

Robert considered the words he would use carefully. The situation was critical. He must contain this crew before it became mutinous. The Admiral gave him specific orders, but it was one thing to issue orders and another to implement them. Discipline in the navy was often only maintained by brute force – a situation he would prefer to avoid himself. But now, it must be done, as the crew needed a demonstration that spying and mutiny would not be tolerated. Hopefully, for the crew members considering backing the traitors, a demonstration of strict discipline would make them think twice before following the rebels. There was no choice; he must make an example of Able Seaman Cobb.

Seeing every eye on him, he breathed in, steadying himself, then spoke in a strong, clear voice.

"Men of His Majesty's Ship *Restless*. A court of inquiry found Able Seaman Cobb guilty of treason and attempted stealing of confidential papers from the captain's cabin."

Robert took a deep breath and let the words sink in.

"The first charge is a capital offence. As Captain of HMS *Restless* and acting on the authority of His Majesty's Government, the guard detail will execute Seaman Cobb immediately from the yardarm."

A cry from Cobb echoed through the ship, "No, No, Captain, it is a mistake!"

"Silence the prisoner, Mr Small!" Robert felt quite sorry for the seaman as this was the harshest penalty military justice imposed. There was no choice given his orders from the Admiral. He was fully aware the crew contained mostly tough men who would not hesitate to take advantage if they felt their Captain was weak. In this situation, he must be as strong as iron.

Alexander Steele stood silently, watching them gag the prisoner, and then a noose dropped over his head and was fixed. With quick naval discipline, the seaman was hoisted by the neck high above the deck in clear view for all. He kicked and struggled for a few seconds, and then he lay limp as he lost consciousness. The silence on the deck where the crew stood shouted up at Robert. He looked down at them and could find not one eye meeting his.

The captain held the crew there in complete silence for five minutes. He wanted them, especially the traitors, aware of the penalty for any further treasonous actions. As an officer, Robert detested capital punishment. Now he was fighting for his life and, for the first time, understood how essential it was on a naval ship. Unfortunately, Robert knew this would not end until they weeded out the traitors. If not, he might be the one suffering their vengeance next. A chill ran down his back as he looked out at the expressionless faces of the men. His intuition told him that many would now be considering revenge.

Robert breathed deeply before speaking, "Officers and men of HMS *Restless*! Gentlemen, Able Seaman Cobb has paid the ultimate price for treason." Once again, he allowed a short silence as these words sank in. "Let me make this quite clear! This ship is in the service of His Majesty King

George the Fourth and his Government. We serve our King and Government without question. Your King expects this loyalty from you today. Any crew member who fails this duty may expect the same penalty as Able Seaman Cobb."

Once again, Robert paused to let the words sink in.

"I expect the total loyalty of every crew member that you serve our King and Country with honour. God save the King!"

The Officers and crew came to attention with a resounding shout, "God save the King!"

"Mr Small, please?"

The first lieutenant joined the captain on the poop deck.

"Leave the body up there until we finish our drill. Action stations please, Mr Small, and a practice broadside, each side in turn."

"Aye, Sir."

"You may proceed, Mr Small."

Small cupped his hands over his mouth and yelled out, "Hands to stations, All men to Stations. Prepare for action. Open the canon ports. Man, your canons!"

The crew dashed in all directions for their stations. While it looked like pandemonium, each crew member knew their position precisely.

"Mr Trotters, get your men aloft and make way! Have the helmsman bring her around downwind and raise the battle standard."

"Aye, Sir."

The ship was transforming into a battle state. There was yelling everywhere as the men opened cannon ports, priming and loading cannons and checking the cannon ropes. Slowly the officers barking out orders ceased. When all was ready, there was silence. The first lieutenant waited for the captain's order.

"Mr Small, you may proceed."

"Starboard team, Fire!"

The junior officer leading the starboard team was yelling as loudly as possible, "Fire!"

Restless rocked, absorbing the recoil. Smoke drifted up over the rails and passed over the deck.

Alexander Steele looked at Robert and saw him from his previous acquaintance in another light. He initially thought him a nice young man receiving an advantage by his birth. This demonstration now corrected his opinion of Robert. This Captain was made of iron and would take no-nonsense. He stood there without a movement as the whole process took place. This man would achieve his goals and tame this crew very quickly. Heaven help any man who disobeyed him. Sir Robert South knew precisely what he was doing and would achieve the required results no matter what stood in his way.

"Port team Fire!"

The ship rocked again in the other direction, and the smoke blew out in anger.

"Thank you, Mr Small, well done. The crew may return to duties. Please assemble the fore team for practice immediately. Once the hour passes, have the sailmaker ready seaman Cobb's body for a funeral. Following the testing of the canons with Mr Steele, I will lead the service."

"Aye, Sir."

The captain then politely beckoned Alexander Steele forward for the canon testing. Alexander nodded and made his way towards the bow.

"Mr Bright, bring my telescope please if you would. You will find it in my cabin."

McPherson Household, Greenwich ...

Jonathan perused the breakfast buffet eyeing what was available as Jenkins came in," Morning Jenkins – just surveying the offering. It all looks splendid."

"Thank you, Sir. Would you prefer tea or coffee, Mr Turner? Now or later? There is also juice available on the sideboard, Sir."

"I think I will start with juice and fruit, Jenkins, and leave the coffee for later – perhaps when the others are down. Now tell me, I am considering the employment of a butler. My business interests are expanding, and my family also, so the house seems regularly in chaos. It is all getting well beyond my housekeeper and her assistant. Pray, where does one find a good butler?"

Jonathan and Jenkins then spent several minutes discussing the attributes of a good butler and the appropriate house plan required.

"I shall keep that in mind when I look for another house. Thank you. Now for some breakfast."

Eleanora and Marjorie entered together at the end of the conversation.

"What will you keep in mind, Jonathan?" Eleanora enquired.

"Jenkins and I have discussed how a house works best with service staff. He gave me a few good pointers, which are most helpful."

Marjorie McPherson's eyes sparkled, and she spoke up, "Why, Jonathan, are you thinking of employing a butler?"

"Yes, the thought is becoming more attractive, but from my discussion with Jenkins, he has persuaded me that our house's design is unsuitable." Jonathan drank from his glass of juice and continued. "Given the renovations required would be most extensive with our existing house, I am now considering the alternative of either purchasing or leasing a more suitable residence. So, I am sure we will discuss various concepts during our trip home."

"Jonathan, I am surprised. But what would we do with our existing house?"

"Guildford is expanding, my Dear. I think we could rent it out quite easily."

Marjorie was becoming excited, "This is wonderful news, Jonathan. Now tell me all about what type of house you might prefer. I may be of some assistance!"

And so, the conversation continued over breakfast with the ladies suggesting numerous options for Jonathan's consideration. He was content as it allowed him time to enjoy a hearty breakfast.

Later in the morning, as the ladies embarked on a shopping trip for wedding presents, Jonathan and Hamish relished the freedom, allowing time for business discussion.

Hamish shared the first month's trading figures for the Epsom pub with his guest.

"Jonathan, the figures are strong. Look at how sales go up when there is a race meeting. If we build some more luxurious accommodation for the upper class, we might do very well indeed. But we will let it run for a year first and see how we go."

Jonathan agreed, "The sales are more than I expected! What are the margins, Hamish? How much are we making?"

Despite his business experience, Jonathan Turner was not gifted at interpreting financial statements and relied heavily on Anne for analysis and explanation. She would spot a trend or a mistake in seconds.

"If you look here, we are making a margin of around two hundred and forty-three per cent. So, in the first month, we cleared around eleven thousand pounds. Now don't forget that this does not take into account our capital and start-up costs which were around forty thousand pounds. By February or March next year, we should recover our capital investment. And remember, Jonathan, we are not trading with all our businesses yet. Once the fast carts are running, the revenue will increase again."

"This will be a good business, Hamish. I am encouraged indeed!"

"So, you should be Jonathan; this business will make a fortune for you and me in the next five years. But we will not stop at Epsom. I have found another site at Reading, but first, we should discuss your home at Guildford."

Jonathan was not expecting this and looked up from the figures straight at Hamish's face. "I was not aware you knew I might be looking for a new home?"

Hamish smiled, "I was not. It's about your existing place of residence."

"What about my home, Hamish?"

"Jonathan, as you know, I have extensive interests in Scotland and England, and market information is essential. Not only from a financial viewpoint but also from a community profile. I need background and current information on the community's current situation, keeping abreast of changes."

Jonathan was all ears, thinking this may resolve Anne and his concerns about the McPhersons.

"When I first discovered Guildford before we met, I engaged a person, who shall remain nameless for a good reason, to provide reliable local information. I needed this, so I had factual information assisting my decision making. Be assured everything reported on your business dealings was of good standing. Indeed, I reinforced the statement through my friendship with you and your family.

As your business interests expand, I suggest you employ similar methods. You cannot be everywhere at once. You will need help. Also, it is dog eat dog in business, so you need friends you can trust."

This revelation added up - it was what Jonathan expected. "I thought you had a contact in Guildford that fed information. You knew facts before they became knowledge here."

Hamish blushed, "I apologise if you thought I was spying on you. But it was all business, and it reinforced what I believed. I'm sure you have done your background checks on me. I think the business term is due diligence!"

Jonathan nodded in agreement.

"A message came yesterday concerning your home in Guildford. Another message has arrived since then. I deferred advising you until this morning as there is no damage done, and all are safe. If we had spoken earlier, Eleanora might have become alarmed unnecessarily!"

"What do you mean no damage done, Hamish?"

"On Friday night last or early on Saturday morning, little William discovered some burglars in the house. They broke in and tied and gagged the domestic staff before searching the house. William surprised them in the parlour, and they knocked him out with a head blow. He is alright! Doctor Sopwith was called and has visited several times to check on him. He is fine."

Jonathan was overly concerned, "William has a habit of walking around at night. I think he is a light sleeper. Thank goodness there is no long-term damage done to him!"

"It seems that William disturbed the burglars, who then panicked and did a rushed search of the house for whatever their target was. They searched the younger girls' rooms and entered Anne's room when she awoke and called out. They must have taken fright, ran, and escaped out the back door. However, there is one bit of bad news."

Jonathan, now alarmed, cried, "No, not Anne, please God!"

"No, she is fine, but they killed the dog, so he would not warn anyone. The children will be sad about this. They are all safe and well, and a guard has been placed on the house until you return. They are all safe, Jonathan! Anne is handling the situation well with the assistance of your new bakery manager, Jeb…."

"Hiscock."

"Hiscock, that's right! Eleanora's health is the most important thing, so you should continue with your plans, leaving tomorrow morning and stopping at Ewell again on the way home."

"My goodness, I had no idea. This news changes everything. I shall need a new house that is more secure!"

"Jonathan, there is more. If you would allow me five more minutes. As Eleanora is out with Marjorie, you have the time."

What else would Hamish say? The news of the burglary rattled Jonathan. He must advise Eleanora as soon as she returned.

"If it is not urgent, Hamish, it can wait. I must prepare an explanation of this for Eleanora."

"Jonathan, is that wise? She will only worry herself sick. Wait until the journey home. I'm sure Richard will break the news tomorrow when you reach Ewell. Why make her worry all that extra time. It will not help her health."

"Yes, I see, and you say they are all safe and well? "

"Yes, and your people have set up a guard for the house until you return. I have my contact there working in the background. Your family is safe!"

"Thank you, Hamish."

"Now, let me tell you another story. I think these details will explain the burglary."

Jonathan was interested and regained his focus.

"There is a lot of money involved in the brewing business. There are two types of investors, the aristocracy and the new entrepreneurs like you and me. I have learnt from bitter experience that competition is warlike. Developing a new chain of pubs is like declaring war on those already operating in the industry. So, there can be deep resentment and underhand activities that frustrate investment. There have been death threats against me and various destabilising attempts on my businesses. That is why I employ security staff and have a system of informers wherever I go. It may seem underhand, but it simply collects information to protect our business interests. Also, it protects against any threat to my safety!"

"You mean a murder attempt?"

"Yes, in Scotland, as we established pubs in one particular area, the population responded well as they found we sold a better beer at a lower price. The existing brewers feared our competition. Early one morning, they set our house on fire as we slept. It was then that I realised this was not a game but a war. For safety and the development of the business, we decided on relocating to Greenwich until the situation settled, which it has. The boys have remained relatively out of sight and ensure the business keeps a low profile while we still develop. However, the pub network in Scotland is nearly established and accepted. Hopefully, there will be no more dirty tricks. But down here in England, we will face a similar problem in time. The advantage of Greenwich is that there are more lawmakers down here, more protection."

"Do you think our relationship resulted in the burglary?"

"I don't just suspect it. I'm sure of it!"

"But why?"

"Jonathan, the brewing business involves the making of fortunes. Think about how many people drink good old English beer. Just about every man in England. The economic times are of no consequence; most men visit the pub every night. English beer is their second wife. Why do you think breweries are so large? It is a huge industry. The government love the tax we provide, swelling their coffers. The brewer does not complain as we pass this cost onto the customer. We still make our margins. But we are talking about fortunes. Why would someone making a fortune allow new entrants into their patch? Would you?"

"No, but I would not break the law. I understand what you are saying! I expect trouble when my new flour mill starts in February. There are already murmurings about how many it will put out of work. I think your idea about security is a sound one. But what were they looking for?"

"I think our business plans. They probably found the property deeds and drawings in your desk, but you will remember I returned the other documents here for safekeeping. They want information on where we will purchase or build pubs. Also, they are interested in how much beer we plan on selling."

"I see. And you say that these people think nothing of breaking the law?"

"Nothing! Large amounts of money attract some of the worst types."

"So, Hamish, your house here is secure?"

"Yes, that is one of Jenkins' duties. We have the dogs, you have seen them, but there are other measures. I am sorry that I did not brief you on this before. It may have saved you from this burglary. But it has occurred now and cannot be changed. Perhaps in good time, consider another house off High Street and better security. After all, Guy Fawkes night is coming up, and it will be another excuse for them."

"You are right; that night is growing worse. We have built a fence in front of the church, stopping the vandalism. Our Parish Constable and his watchmen are not much use. They don't have the resources they need for policing. I will think about a new house once we have all this capital expenditure out of the way. The cash flow from the new mill will be important. It is good news that the Epsom pub is doing so well. That will help."

"Jonathan, if I were you, I would rent a house at first. See if it is suitable. Plan for a quicker move and defer any major outlay on a purchase. If you ever need cash, let me know. We can arrange an advance. I have done very well and have ample reserves set aside. As business partners, we can assist each other."

"Thank you, Hamish, that is kind but not necessary. The bakery business in Guildford is thriving, and sales are still increasing. With improvements in productivity through new ovens and the new milling process, I expect profits will increase further. The business has blessed us. I am hopeful our joint ventures will show a similar profit."

"Jonathan, just a note for your diary. When you negotiate with the land-owners for more grain, let me know. Let's work together on these negotia-tions. Together we will have strong negotiating power. It's something these landowners will understand."

"I like that Hamish. When we meet again in two weeks, we will discuss this."

"When will you set up your tailor's shops in London, Jonathan? I hear Hurst's is doing well."

"Yes, that is true, but I only have two eyes, and they are both busy pres-ently. Hurst's will continue as it is for the time being. Perhaps another shop in 1828. You may be interested in investing. Let us wait until then. I must concentrate on successfully operating these other ventures first."

"That is what I like about you and Thomas, your focus. I wish my sons had it. They can go astray at times. Now, what about Eleanora? Will you tell her or wait until tomorrow?"

"I think you are right. Let Eleanora sleep well tonight. I will explain when we reach Ewell. She will be angry by the delay in being told, but everyone is safe, and we will be only a night away, so that may calm her. And now Hamish, I think I will have a quiet drink in the garden. There is much to consider!"

"Jonathan, you are correct. It becomes more and more complicated the more money that is involved. I'm sorry I held back from advising you, but I was keen that everyone had a relaxing time here. I apologise again."

"Thank you, Hamish. We understand each other far better now than half an hour ago."

Jonathan left the room and headed for the garden. Hamish sat back in his study chair. He thought, "If only I could tell you everything, Jonathan, but it is complicated and not the time yet. I hope my men in Guildford find these burglars first before the police."

Fintelton Manor, outside Petersfield ...

Sir Hugh South entered the dining room, joining his father. They dined alone as both Lady Jane and Lady Emma were now in London on one of their regular shopping trips. The autumn evening glow was fading quickly, and the servants commenced lighting the long table's candles. Outside, the western sun was diving below the horizon, sending up yellow and reddish rays painting the light clouds with a tinge of crimson.

The Earl welcomed his eldest son, "Good day in the fields, Hugh?"

Being in no mood for conversation, Hugh grunted back as he took a bottle from the drinks cabinet and poured himself a large scotch whisky. Slumping into a chair opposite his father, he took a thirsty gulp.

"It was hot out there today. Far hotter than it has been. I thought autumn was coming, but the hot days have come back. Summer is extending into autumn this year. I needed this drink!"

"How did the sowing go on the low fields?" the Earl persisted.

"Ours is all done, but some tenant farmers are dragging their feet. I will send men down tomorrow and give them some help. They were late harvesting and now late sowing. With labour prices up and their children taking employment in the city, they no longer manage well. Some may fail soon; perhaps we should retake their tenancies."

"Sounds like me, Hugh. Will you throw me off as well?"

"Father, I didn't mean that! You know what I mean. We need as many winter cereals as we can harvest before the spring sowing. That supplement is now quite important for our cash flow!"

"We have other income, Hugh, from the Indies. There are ten farms out there that you have never visited. They bring in a handsome income which could be improved. It is time you went out there and understood the business. Also, do not forget the estates in Scotland and Ireland. Why I have not visited there in years, you should go there."

"I have no interest in that plague-infested Jamaica. Let the attorneys look after them, and as far as Scotland and Ireland, perhaps one day I will visit. I am of more use being here, Father. If the tenant farmers let us down, we could lose a third of our income. Wheat farming does not change – it is just hard work, and some of these long-term tenancy farmers have grown too old. It is nature, Father! If we farmed it ourselves – we would make far more money."

As the next Earl of Fintelton, Hugh believed he understood the sources of the estate's income. He was an intelligent man and, from an early age, took an interest in the farming of cereals. The other estates were irrelevant to him, and he had no intention of changing his mind. There was no need for change while the corn laws kept prices up and tenant farmers maintained their production. But over the last few years, a consistent decrease in production continued.

The problem was better employment in the northern cities. The higher wages in the towns attracted the younger workers. The tenants now paid for labour, whereas their children's work was previously free. The Corn-laws kept the price of grain up and helped raise enough revenue for the tenant's subsistence. But now, with the labour costs, there was little left for paying their rents and feeding their families. They would cut back on hired help which in turn decreased their production. It was becoming an impossible life for the older tenants who had no alternative.

"We need a better solution than throwing them off their plots, Hugh. I have been friends with a lot of these men for years, and I will not throw them off."

"Father, we may have no choice if there is a bad harvest next spring, the tenant farmers may not afford their rents. Many of them are well behind now, and if next August they have a bad harvest, it will be difficult for them and us. Remember, Father, we must cover our costs and pay our taxes!"

The Earl was not impressed, "We have been through tough times before and survived; it will be the same again."

Hugh felt he should remind his father of their financial situation but held his tongue. It was no use! Steeped by tradition, his father had already made the decision.

He changed the subject, "Father, who are these people in Guildford that Mother and Emma welcome into our society?"

"I thought you joined them at dinner last Friday night."

"I was indisposed and retired early."

"Ah! I understand the young lady was a friend of Emma's. Not sure what the connection is, but your mother assured me they were quite respectable people. I'm sure we will hear more on their return."

"On the night of the dinner, someone broke into their house. In the morning, mother requested that I accompany her and check with the police to see if we could assist. The house was on the High Street and a decent size, with a raised ground floor and two upper levels. The burglars left the ground floor in quite a mess. Mother and Emma attended to the young lady, checking on her safety and took breakfast with her at the house. The father left the young lady in charge while he and his wife were in London."

The Earl looked up, "You mean the Countess and Emma took breakfast at their house on the High Street?"

"Yes, I thought it a bit peculiar, but there were servants, and mother and Emma remained long after I left. Doctor Sopwith was there also, and he advised me that Emma was a good friend of this young lady. But I have never heard of them before. I passed the kitchen where they were all taking breakfast, and Emma brushed a child's hair. I believe the young lady's name is Anne Turner. Sopwith said they are a respected family. The father is the chairman of the Parish Council at one of the churches there. That's right! – Taggart and his wife were at dinner."

"How did you know that if you had retired?"

"I dropped in on the gathering before giving my apologies."

Lord Fintelton sat back and thought about what Hugh told him. Confused, he tried recalling any connections named Turner. The only one the Earl remembered was that painter fellow recommended to him. He sold him a strange painting that he had never hung. He could not recall the acquaintance of any other Turners. Perhaps Emma made the acquaintance at finishing school or through the church. He was not sure. The Earl finished his main course of mutton and vegetables and asked Pike for tea. The butler brought him over a full cup.

"I'm finding it difficult remembering all these social connections. Your mother and Emma will tell us all about it when they return. If Taggart and his good wife were there, they must be respectable people. I think I will visit some of the tenant farmers tomorrow. Will you come with me? We can discuss with them why they are late sowing the crop."

"Thank you, Father, but I have some appointments in Petersfield. I will be interested in what you find out. Take Stem with you. He is quite aware of the problems and may make some valuable suggestions." Hugh would not waste his time, thinking, 'Not that they will take any notice, but worth a try.'

He took another swig of his scotch and watched his father finish dinner. Mulling over the event in Guildford, he wondered why his mother would be so bold and take breakfast in a commoner's house. It was just not done. Now that his head had cleared from his last binge, he felt far more robust than the mess he was in on the previous Saturday. He might pay Mayor Rupert Smith a visit in Guildford tomorrow for lunch, see if he could find out a little more about these Turners. The mayor would be well informed and might shed some light on these people. Also, he knew an inn with some fine wenches there in Guildford. That was far more enticing than talking with the mayor. 'Better do the mayor first, might need more time for the wenches later!'

"Father, I will join you at breakfast tomorrow morning, but I will be away overnight. I will return Thursday and have dinner with you."

The Earl was miles away, thinking about something else while enjoying his cup of tea.

Hugh sighed, understanding that his father was losing his hearing, "Pike, please remind father at dinner tomorrow night. I will be away, and I will be back on Thursday. After a few business appointments, I will also call on Doctor Sopwith."

"Thank you, Sir. I will remind your father."

The Turner Household, Guildford ...

Anne finished her Wednesday morning work at the bakery and was now sitting with William and Constable Rawlins at home, having a cup of tea.

Constable Rawlins was a tall, well-built middle-aged man with a friendly smile. Anne noticed the respect William gave him as he asked his questions.

" William, I am glad you are in good health. We were all anxious until Surgeon Sopwith gave us the all-clear. I take it there have been no after-effects from the blow?"

"What are after-effects?"

"Headaches, dizziness, memory loss – the usual things that come from a knock on the head."

"Not that I have felt. The headaches went on Sunday, and my eyes have not been affected by the light since then. I think I am fine. Can I still be a page boy at Bethany's wedding?"

Anne was about to reassure him when the Constable came in with a bit of a bluff, "It depends on how much you can tell us about the burglars. You are the only one who saw them. You may need protection. But I'm sure if you gave us a good description, we might let you be a pageboy."

William shrank back in fear and blurted out, "I can describe one of the robbers, but the other one who hit me came from behind, and I never saw him. I can't describe him. Does that mean I can't go to the wedding?"

Anne saw that the boy had missed the humour entirely and was now fearing he was in trouble, "William, Constable Rawlins is just funny. Of course, you will be a page boy at the wedding. It is alright – please tell him about the man you saw!"

"It was dark, but I would recognise the old man anywhere. His eyes were close together, and he had a long nose. I can draw it if it helps. His hair was curly brown with a few streaks of grey. He was about five feet, four inches tall, about twelve inches taller than me. He wore long grey working pants with a belt of rope-like what navy sailors wear, and his shirt was a soft flannel blue and worn – with some holes. He was old. I am not sure what age, but he was very sunburnt and weathered."

Constable Rawlins was writing as William spoke. He was amazed that a young child could give such an accurate description.

"Also, there was a big scar on the back of his neck in his hair. I think it was a scar, but perhaps it was a burn mark."

Anne looked up with a frown as soon as William said this. She, too, had seen this man!

"That's a good description, William. I think you may attend the wedding. Ha, Ha." Constable Rawlins was the only one laughing. However, William was most satisfied with the Constable's comment. "Now, the fact that this man carried a scar will make him stand out. This description helps a lot, William. Are you certain of this? Your description is detailed, so if it goes before a Magistrate, he will ask you how you could see so well in the dark?"

"I saw him twice in the days before. I noticed him watching the house. He was sitting across the road at the side of an alley. Then I saw him again as I followed him towards Abbot's Hospital. That's where he disappeared."

"I see."

Anne then remembered where she had seen this man. It came as a shock.

"Constable, I have seen this man today! While walking home from the bakery, he crossed High Street at the corn market near Tunstall Gate. He was only five steps in front of me. It was in a crowd, so he would not have noticed me. I remember because of his scar or burn mark on his neck. It is something that does stand out."

Constable Rawlins was silent, then asked, "How long since you came home?"

"About an hour."

The policeman's mind was racing. This sighting meant that the burglars were still here in town. Perhaps they were local lads, but he did not recall anyone with this mark on the back of the neck. But there were so many new people in Guildford. The place was growing too quickly for his liking.

"Miss Anne, I think I shall go now and have a look for this fellow in the corn market. Please keep the doors locked and keep William inside out of sight. I am not sure what is going on, but if William can identify this fellow, he may cause trouble. We should not let this happen. When is your father home?"

"Tomorrow – they stop at Ewell tonight on their way back from London."

"I will send a message by express. I would prefer if Mr Turner were home with you. I take it he will be visiting his brother's pub there?"

"Yes. They often discuss business."

"I will request they travel here directly, and you should expect their arrival late tonight. I will be back later this evening to assist the guard. The fact that this man and possibly the other burglar are still here in town is disturbing. Please keep the doors locked and not let anyone in before the housekeeper identifies them."

Anne was not comfortable with these arrangements.

"Surely, Constable, they would not try again. Why?"

"Not sure, Miss Anne, but they are still in town if you saw him less than an hour ago. Who knows what they are planning next! The good thing is, he doesn't know we have a description of him."

The Constable gathered up his book and equipment, excused himself and headed for the door.

McPherson Household, Greenwich …

Marion and Thomas's wedding arrangements were now well advanced, and the stay at Greenwich allowed both families some input. Eleanora resigned herself that Marjorie had completed the arrangements already, but she was thankful as she would have struggled to assist due to her poor health.

Before they travelled off for Guildford, words of thanks were passed on, "Thank you, Marjorie, for all the work you have put in. It will be a marvellous wedding, and I am so thankful for all your efforts. Please send a message as soon as you arrive for Beth's wedding. We will arrange a dinner and talk more then. And thank you so much for your hospitality."

"Now, Eleanora, you take care of yourself and that little one coming. We will be there a few days in advance."

The coach quickly entered the suburbs of London and headed for the Bassingtons, where they would pick up Bethany and Neville. Jonathan felt that it was time he advised Eleanora of the burglary.

"Eleanora, Hamish received a note yesterday advising there was a burglary at our house. All the children are unhurt, safe and well. It happened on Friday night, and since then, the police placed a guard at home, ensuring their safety."

Eleanora was stunned and was without words for a moment as she took in the news.

"You mean all this time we have been at the Bassingtons and McPhersons, Anne has been dealing with this, and we were unaware?"

"Yes, Hamish told me late yesterday afternoon, and we decided that it was better if you rested last night without worry. Today we make the first leg of our journey home. They will be safe until we arrive there tomorrow."

"No, Jonathan, we must arrive home today. You say they are all safe. But the burglars must have been in the house while the children were asleep. Poor Anne, how she must be suffering from all this. It must have occurred on the same night as the dinner. Jonathan, we must hurry home today. We cannot stay at Ewell; we must hurry on!"

"Let us see the time when we arrive in Ewell. It is a long way by carriage, and I am mindful of your condition Eleanora."

"Hang my condition, Jonathan! We must reach home today!"

At Guildford …

Sir Hugh South arrived at the mayor's office around eleven-thirty Wednesday morning. He stayed overnight at the White Rabbit in Petersfield, enjoying some entertainment. After twenty-five miles of a difficult road, the horse was exhausted, and Sir Hugh welcomed the sight of Guildford. Stabling his horse at the Fox and Hound, he made his way to the mayor's office. Rupert Smith welcomed the next Earl of Fintelton with open arms. It was to the mayor's advantage to have this young gentleman's society of noble birth.

"Mr Mayor, I understand this is short notice, but I wonder if you would join me for lunch at one o'clock at the Fox and Hound. I need your advice on some matters."

Rupert, never missing the opportunity of a free lunch and furthering his society, agreed at once. He would rearrange his appointments as Sir Hugh honoured him with his visit.

Sir Hugh made sure of a side table where they could talk freely at lunch. Rupert was disappointed, preferring a more prominent position, allowing his constituents a far better view. However, given Sir Hugh was paying, he did not object.

"Thank you, Rupert, for accepting my invitation; it has been some time since we last spoke. I have some business in Guildford and required advice on several matters, but before that, there is one family in town I am unfamiliar with."

"Certainly, Sir Hugh, how may I be of assistance."

"The Turner family. I believe Mr Turner is a baker, and the family live here in town. Are you acquainted with them and of their circumstances, please?"

"Certainly, Sir Hugh, but may I ask first why you require this information so I may provide the most appropriate detail?"

"Sir, the situation is delicate, and I would ask for your confidentiality and trust in this matter. My mother, the countess, has befriended them, and my father and I are unsure of their society. While we are sure the relationship is proper, my father and I thought you the best person for reference."

Rupert Smith sat back and thought about this intimate request. He was not aware of the Turner's acquaintance with Lady Fintelton. He recalled that a friend of Doctor Bassington, Sir Robert South, attended church with the family on one occasion, probably because of the son's close friendship with the doctor and not any acquaintance with the Earl's family. The society of the countess was a surprise. Being a politician, he immediately realised that he should be careful as Jonathan Turner was a man of significant influence in this town. The son of the Earl was, of course, influential in society but not that influential in business here, as their estate was outside Petersfield some distance from Guildford. The Fintelton Estate provided some local mills with grain – perhaps this was an area of interest to Sir Hugh.

"Sir Hugh. There are three things I can tell you quickly about the Turners. They are respectable people, and my son Richard has grown in the company of the two Turner boys, Simeon and William. Both are fine young fellows. The father, Jonathan Turner, has a large baking business in Guildford, also serving some outlying towns. Jonathan Turner is the chairman of our parish council. I am a member myself! I have never heard anything but favourable comments about him and his family. They also have other business interests which I shall elaborate on later."

"Other businesses? Not just a bakery?"

"Yes, and the bakery is a massive undertaking, employing many townsfolk."

"I see."

"You may be aware that Surgeon Neville Bassington and Bethany Turner, Jonathan's daughter, are engaged and will be married here the weekend after this."

"Yes, I am aware of Neville and the coming wedding."

"One of Neville Bassington's good friends, of course, is your brother Sir Robert. He has visited Guildford on several occasions with Neville. I believe he is the best man. I assume we will have the pleasure of you attending as well. Perhaps it is because of the friendship of Surgeon Bassington, who I believe is a friend of your family, that your mother has made the acquaintance."

"Yes, that is correct."

"Mr Turner is very entrepreneurial and is building a large new flour mill powered by steam. The town council is much behind this venture as it will be good for Guildford. Jonathan also has a business relationship with Mr Hamish McPherson, a brewer from London and Scotland. He has extensive interests in brewing throughout the country and is planning the building of a brewery here in Guildford. Mr Turner will be an investor in this, and his son Thomas will be the brewery manager."

Sir Hugh considered the information provided and tinkered with the suspicion that Robert may be more involved here than his family knew. Why was Robert not at sea and frequenting Guildford? Neville Bassington would marry a baker's daughter – a commoner! Why would he do that?

"Do these Turners have any relationship with the aristocracy, Sir?"

Rupert was annoyed at this question, thinking, 'Typical, they do not welcome any connection with we commoners!' Rupert was careful in what he said next.

"Sir Hugh. I believe Jonathan Turner is a self-made man like his father. I am not aware of any connections, but he did attend the Free School here for a few years, a privilege that I did not partake of myself. His wife comes from a family that also has business connections. I understand that Mr Hurst started as an apprentice tailor, took over the business in Woking, and opened other shops in nearby towns. The Turners inherited the business. They are hardworking and well-educated people who have had success in life. The family businesses are adjusting well to the change we all are experiencing."

"I see. And who is this Anne Turner that my mother has befriended?"

"Ah, Anne is a delightful girl. She is the second eldest daughter and now works part-time in her father's bakery business. She is most intelligent and a wiz with the figures. Her mother is with child and suffers from ill health, so Anne is taking on more and more of the management of the household."

Some of the pieces of this puzzle were coming together. Sir Hugh could only remember Anne vaguely, but he did recall her beautiful blue eyes and long goldish hair. He recalled the dinner, but his memory was blurred due to his inebriated state. The following morning, he saw her through the kitchen doorway. As Rupert said, she did appear an attractive girl. And his mother and sister were sitting with her. Most strange. Robert's several visits to Guildford must be the connection. This girl, Anne Turner, must be the reason. He must talk with Emma and find out precisely what the relationship was. He was hoping it was nothing serious.

"Thank you, Rupert. The information you have provided is most welcome and comprehensive."

"It is a pleasure, Sir Hugh. I take it you have received your invitation?"

Sir Hugh spluttered in surprise, "What invitation?"

"Of course, the wedding between Mr Neville Bassington and Miss Bethany Turner, Sir?"

"Yes, of course, excuse me for forgetting!" Hugh relaxed. Best if Rupert thought he was attending Neville's big day.

"It will be a magnificent occasion with so many guests coming from far and wide. Quite the social event of the year for Guildford, Sir!"

"Tell me, Rupert, who is on the guest list?"

Rupert thought this was a strange question but gave Sir Hugh many names and descriptions he recalled.

The waiter served their main courses. Rupert looked down in delight at the fine roast chicken meal set before him, a far better option than the sandwiches at his office. Sir Hugh was hungry as well but continued thinking about the guest list. He was surprised at the dignitaries attending. This Jonathan Turner fellow had significant friends and was building a large mill. What was Turner intending?

After taking a second mouthful of the chicken, he looked up at Rupert and agreed on the quality of the meal. Then he ventured a question, "Now Rupert tell me about Mr Turner's new mill. What does he intend with this?"

While thoroughly enjoying his meal, Rupert was far more comfortable discussing business, "Sir, let me explain."

Having gained the information, Hugh set off for Doctor Sopwith's house, requiring the doctor's opinion on some more personal business.

"Tell me, Doctor Sopwith, is there a problem?"

"Yes, I'm afraid there is. But it is treatable. Let me explain the use of this mercury ointment."

HMS Restless ...

Restless was making excellent time down the coast. Being mindful of his predicament, Robert drove the crew hard, leaving little opportunity for the traitors. He would relax once they reached the Solent. Horace Combes and his marines would be a welcome reinforcement and help sort out the crew.

Robert and Horace went back a long way. The South and Combes families moved in the same society, with both families having estates in several parts of England and Wales. They often holidayed together at their estates at Luccombe Village on the Isle of Wight. With rolling green hills, sandy beaches and exciting changes in the tide, it was an enchanted playground that few children in their society enjoyed. The Combes' two boys and a girl mirrored the South family. Emma put up with Charlotte Combes, as she was more interested in activities inside the house while Emma was off with the boys in the sunshine. For holidays, they endured each other. Hugh liked Harry Combes, and they were always playing tricks on the others. As a result, Horace, Robert and Emma allied to defend themselves against the practical jokers. Beautiful friendships developed that lasted years.

At nine-thirty in the evening, the ship was less than fifty miles from rounding Selsey Bill and then Spithead. With a black night, little moon and a heavy but broken cloud cover, Robert scanned the coast ahead for lighthouses. Kevin Trotters, the Master, was standing watch and carefully checking their position by dead reckoning. He seemed tense and was glad the captain joined him on the quarter-deck.

"Captain. The lights of Middleton-on-Sea off the starboard bow, Sir." Robert nodded, noticing the twinkling lights in the distance.

Trotters turned to the helmsman, "Two degrees port Mr Young, please. Not too near the coast at Selsey Bill, please. There is a bit of a point there."

"Aye, Master."

Robert moved slowly around the quarter deck, carefully noticing who was crewing the stations. If anything happened, he must know from where the danger would come. He then moved around the helm and stood behind Mr Trotters, murmuring with the Master without the helmsman hearing.

"Is anyone aloft, Mr Trotters?"

"Just one lookout Sir, in the foremast. I'll post two more as soon as we come into the estuary."

Captain South carefully noted the forty sailors on the main deck, standing ready. He usually would reduce sail early and find a sheltered area good for standing off at night. Tonight was different - he wanted this voyage over and Portsmouth harbour's safety. Without enough trustworthy men, he must somehow even up the odds. He needed reinforcements, and those would come after they anchored. The traitors were also aware of that, and Robert was highly alert, ready in case of an attack.

Mr Trotters moved back a step beside the captain. He also was alert keeping a close eye on the men on the main deck.

He quietly said, "Beg your pardon, Sir. It may be preferable if you stand in the mast's shadow there, Sir. With the moon breaking through the clouds at times, it may help."

Robert immediately knew what Trotters meant. He was clearly visible and an easy target by standing where he was, especially when the moon appeared. The captain was a more challenging target by moving over into the mast's shadow. He took two steps towards the mast.

"Thank you, Mr Trotters, a fine ......". As he spoke, a knife hurtled downwards, striking the deck exactly where Robert was previously standing. It came with such a force that it dug in deeply and shuddered before standing still.

Robert reacted instantly. He was under attack and must counter this threat immediately. Seeing the angle of the landing knife, he realised it must have come from the main tops.

"Trotters put men all around the deck so you may arrest anyone coming down. Call Mr Small and have all the young gentlemen assembled." With that, Robert threw off his coat, revealing his white shirt, jumped down onto the main deck, ran across, grabbed the shroud rigging and climbed upwards towards the main top in search of this assassin.

As he climbed, he thought, 'Damn this, I'm not remaining there as a target. Let me see who is up here!'

Robert could hear the officers shouting orders from below, but he focused his eyes on the rigging above. There was no one in sight, but he was still a long way from the tops. The pitching movement of the mast became more severe as he climbed higher. A big north-westerly gust belted into the sails, and the ship heeled right over. As she rolled, he found himself well outside the boundary of the vessel with only the choppy sea below. Looking up, he saw the flicker of a man steadying himself. He was hidden above the tops but looking straight down at him.

Robert stopped three-quarters of the way up the shrouds. The man quickly jumped onto the upper Jacobs ladder and started climbing for the crosstrees. Robert moved quickly and mounted the main top. The man disappeared behind the mast and rigging above. Scanning the rigging, Robert estimated the crosstrees were a further fifteen yards above. As the ship slightly changed course towards the Solent estuary, with one hand on the tops for balance and one tightly clasping the rigging, Robert peered up into the darkness, searching for the traitor.

Without warning, a knife shot down, out of the dark, piercing straight through his left hand. The knife pinned him to the tops floor, and Robert yelled in pain. Gritting his teeth, he reached over, grabbed the knife with his free hand and pulled it out, leaving a growing pool of blood. He fought against the pain, knowing he needed a clear mind as he instinctively planned his next move.

"Mr Small? Find a loaded musket and get up here straight away! Bring Swanton with you."

Robert ripped his shirt off, winding it around his bleeding hand. He put pressure on the wound, then sat there hoping the sailor would not come down, as he was presently defenceless. Robert could see a pair of eyes looking down at him from the top loft. He moved the bandaged hand around behind the mast hiding it from the man above.

After five long minutes, Small appeared over the loft's edge, and he heaved a musket and reloading pouch onto the floor. Swanton quickly followed him.

"He is up there, gentlemen. Now I want him alive, please. That traitor could solve this whole problem. How do we do it?"

Small said, 'We wait, Sir. We will be in port in two hours!"

"No, he would not be up there without an escape plan. We must secure him now. Why he could even jump when the ship heels, hoping he will clear the deck!"

"But surely no man would be so stupid!" Small was not keen at all on tackling the man.

"Not if he is Irish, Sir", Swanton mumbled.

"Small, what kind of a shot are you?"

"Not good, Sir!"

"Swanton, you are an army man; how about you?"

"I can hit a sparrow at one hundred yards, Sir."

"Good, wing him and put him out of action. Small, you climb up and arrest him."

"Up there, Sir?"

"Yes, up there! Swanton, move out on the yardarm, so you get a good shot. Secure yourself with some rope first. Small, get going up, Man!"

"I can't go any higher, Sir!"

"What do you mean? You are an officer, Sir. Get up there."

"Sorry, Sir. Scared of heights! I can't go any further!"

Robert looked at him and wondered if this was the truth or a trap. There was no time for a debate. He must climb up himself.

"Are you secure, Swanton?"

"Aye, Sir."

"Have you a shot?"

"Aye, Sir."

"Take it, Man."

The musket fired almost immediately. The blast was loud in Robert's ear, partly deafening him for a moment. Small was lying flat on the loft, shaking. Surprised by Small's cowardly behaviour, Robert concluded that the man must be experiencing a mental disorder or was unfit for his duties. He could not believe that his second in command was a traitor. No time for it now. He would deal with this later – if there were a later!

"Swanton, keep an eye on this damn officer, please. I don't trust him."

He jumped onto the rigging, climbing towards the crosstrees. Swanton reported a hit on the traitor's shoulder, but the man was still active. As he climbed, Robert called, "Reload Swanton!"

Up and up, Robert climbed, thinking, 'You bastard, knifing my hand and making me do this.' As he made his way up the rigging, his rage grew. Knowing he needed his mind calm, he suppressed it. The pain from his hand was immense and throbbed, but he ignored it.

At three feet under the loft, a sabre swung down at him in a flash of steel, missing by a whisker; then, another shot rang out from below. He heard a cry of pain and saw the sabre drop down past him, landing just beside Small. Thankfully, it fell without hurting anyone.

Robert pulled himself up onto the crosstrees. There sat an unknown sailor.

He sat with his back against the mast. His shoulder was a bloodied mess from the first shot, and the second shot partially blew off the hand on the other arm. He was losing blood fast. He said nothing but glared at Robert.

"Swanton, get up here. Small get some more men up here fast with bandages. Get going, Man, now!"

Small yelled down for the men and bandages.

Swanton hoisted himself onto the crosstrees. He saw Robert watching the traitor but not moving within arm's reach. The sailor was now unconscious from the loss of blood. Swanton yanked off the sailor's shirt and thrust it against the shoulder wound. He then removed his own shirt and bandaged the hand.

"Sir, I have not seen him before. He must have hidden somewhere. Perhaps he is the leader?"

"Whoever he is, we have met him now. By the way, good shooting Mr Swanton. You can be on my team anytime."

"If you don't mind me saying, Sir, that was pretty daring what you did. It matches anything I've seen in the army."

"Your support is most welcome, Swanton. Now climb back to the tops and send Small down, please. Our first Lieutenant, afraid of heights, is not of much use! Damn him! Do not let any of the men come up here. Just a rope we can secure from the yardarm. We will lower this one down. Get some help from Bright. I don't want an accident, and for no reason, he falls. This man will give us the information we need."

Swanton ducked back down the rigging. Robert sat back and looked at the sailor. He was wearing fresh clothes – this man was not part of the crew! Who was he? What was his escape plan? Surely, there was no escape from the ship. Then he thought, 'Unless there was a rescue boat nearby! Or perhaps once they killed the captain, someone would board *Restless*. My God!'

Robert screamed down at the quarter-deck, "Mr Small – Enemy in sight, Hands to stations."

Looking up in surprise, Trotters thought, "He must be joking, but why?"

Mr Small just stood there and did nothing.

Robert could see his call fell on deaf ears; he must get down there quickly. While he grabbed some rope and secured the unconscious sailor against the mast, he screamed at Trotters, "Mr Trotters, just don't stand there! Action Stations, man. I want all canons ready in the next two minutes."

Trotters suddenly realised that Captain South was aware of some danger ahead, and he hoped it wasn't what he was thinking. He screamed at the men for action stations, and the junior officers, in a panic, followed his orders, chasing their sailors into position. He glanced over at Mr Small, standing at the rail looking forward, scanning the dark. Then he noticed Small had a pistol tucked in under his coat.

A chill went down Trotter's spine. Surely the First Lieutenant could not be one of the conspirators? Trotters ordered the helmsman to bring the ship closer into the wind losing some speed; then he quietly asked the Midshipman standing beside him, "Mr Collins, not a word, please, get the Master at Arms as quick as you can. Make sure he brings a pistol."

Robert checked the sailor was secure and then stood up. As he scanned the sea in front of the ship, the moon came through a break in the clouds. As he suspected, he saw two cutters sailing towards their path in the distance. A large number of men loaded down each of the cutters. Robert now knew the plan. He leaned over and nearly lost his grip as he yelled, "Mr Trotters, hard a port, please."

"Aye, Captain. Helmsman, hard a port."

"Aye, Sir."

Trotter kept one eye on Small, who now seemed quite agitated and worried. Robert was halfway down the main shrouds when Midshipman Collins ran back onto the poop deck, bringing Mr Door, the Master at Arms. Small saw Door with a gun in his hand. He pulled out his pistol and shot Door in the chest. The Master at Arms fell, instantly dying on the quarter-deck, shot in the heart.

Robert was now just above deck level and jumped down. Running aft, he stopped in his tracks as Small pulled out another pistol. Robert saw the gun was not cocked, which gave him a two-second opportunity. Robert yelled out as loudly as he could, "Small, I order you. Drop that weapon, Lieutenant!"

Small smiled as he cocked the gun, "You're no longer in control, you bloody aristocrat!"

Robert knew he must keep him talking, "Where did you learn to shoot like that? You shot Door in the heart. He didn't have a chance."

"Wouldn't you like to know South? Wouldn't you like to know?"

He raised the pistol towards Robert, but a shot rang out from above before he could aim. The ball hit Small between the eyes, and the lower back of his skull exploded. He stood there for a second in disbelief and then fell back against the rail, ending in an expanding pool of blood and brains on the deck.

Robert breathed a sigh of relief. He was praying that Swanton was watching.

"You took your time, Mr Swanton," Robert yelled at his servant standing thirty-five yards above the deck with a musket in his arms.

From above, a very courteous reply came, "Reloading, Sir. You should have insulted his mother. That usually keeps them talking longer!"

Robert and Trotters looked at each other and started laughing in sheer nervous relief. There was a second for a deep breath before the realisation came back. It was not over yet.

"Trotters, who is Mr Door's assistant?"

"Mr Fulcher, Sir. A good man."

Robert looked at Trotters and understood what he meant. The captain decided that Trotters was a man he could trust. His recommendation was good enough for him now.

"Send for Mr Fulcher, please."

"Aye, Sir."

Midshipman Collins, who still stood there with his mouth open, rushed off for Fulcher.

"Master, bring her around ninety degrees to starboard, please. Get your sail teams aloft, Mr Trotters. We shall do some dancing."

"Aye, aye, Sir."

"Mr Fulcher is here, Sir."

"Good. Mr Fulcher! Now we have little time. You are now the Master at Arms. We may have more traitors onboard. I want the armoury opened and the officers and each of the young gentlemen given two loaded pistols. If they see anything untoward, tell them they may shoot the misbehaving men and then scream like hell. We will back them up. Now hurry, Fulcher. Go, Man!"

Fulcher swallowed, "Aye, Captain." And he was off.

"Mr Trotters, when I was above, I spied two longboats full of men about five hundred yards ahead of us. When we come behind them, we will give them a broadside. You may not see them, but that is of no consequence. The plan is we will scare the shit out of them. Load the starboard side with canon ball and the port side with grapeshot, please. Go to it, Man! I'll take control of the helmsman while you do this."

The Master was off instantly thinking, "Now this is what I like, a Captain who can fight and win!"

Robert watched the ship's bearing; it was now on its original course heading for Portsmouth. He gave it two minutes, putting them past the cutters. Once he was sure, he ordered, "Mr Young, come around eighty degrees to starboard."

"Aye, Captain."

The ship quickly responded as they were moving fast now with the wind increasing in strength. As *Restless* came onto the course, Robert allowed two minutes and then called the order, "Mr Trotters, you may fire now."

"Starboard canons, Fire!"

The young gentlemen bellowed out the order, "Fire!"

Restless jolted as the canons went off. The north-westerly pushed the smoke away from the ship. Once it cleared, the crew peered into the darkness, searching for movement or noise. There was silence.

"Mr Young, come back onto our course for Portsmouth, please. Mr Trotters, I will check first for any other cutters and then sail around them, then come back with the port side canons ready for any boats that appear hostile. I will inform you if a broadside is necessary. Mr Swanton, now you are down, would you please position yourself by the rail with a musket. Perhaps two or three muskets. Mr Fulcher, please arrange for Mr Swanton to have three loaded muskets and reloading supplies. Mr Collins and Mr Kent, you may assist Mr Swanton."

"Aye, Sir."

The ship fell silent as *Restless* ploughed on towards Portsmouth. As they forged ahead, there was no sign of any other boats. After a mile, Robert changed course by ninety degrees to starboard, coming around five hundred yards across the line he thought the cutters would be on. Then he changed course another starboard ninety degrees so he would come back towards them.

They were now running at about eight knots back along the coast. The clouds were thick above, and the sea was getting up with the stiff breeze. Trotters observed, "Hard to see them now, Sir!"

"I think we will see them, Mr Trotters and very soon, and I'm hoping we hear them before that. Now be ready when I give the order. Mr Young, I want a swift response."

They sailed on in silence for about twenty seconds when they heard a shot from beyond the starboard bow. A sailor near the bow fell backwards onto the deck.

"Hard a Starboard, Mr Young. Mr Trotters, you may fire the port canons as they bear."

"Port Canons, fire as you bear!"

"Fire!"

Two canons were fired immediately, and then three more in succession. Then the crew heard a pistol shot near the first port canon crew and then another. A junior officer started yelling, "Deserters, deserters!"

Four crew members dived over the ship's port side in quick succession.

"Mr Fulcher, take your men and find out what happened. Mr Swanton, I will come about, and you will have a clear shot from the bow. You know the penalty for desertion. Take no prisoners, please."

Swanton rushed off with Mr Collins and Mr Kent, carrying the muskets behind him.

"Master Trotters bring us about, back towards the deserters."

"Aye, Sir." Trotters gave the order, the helmsman madly swinging the helm. Trotters then started bellowing orders to the sail crews above.

While the ship was turning, Robert looked out over the stern. He could see in the distance the wreckage of one of the cutters with multiple bodies lying in the water. There was no sign of the other boat. Perhaps he was smart and headed seawards. They would land somewhere safe back along the coast. He was probably under sail and long gone.

Restless came about and quickly closed on the sailors swimming for their lives. They understood the sentence for mutiny, so it was escape or death. But it was too late. Swanton hit the first sailor at about two hundred yards. He dropped the musket for Mr Collins as Mr Kent passed another loaded musket. Aiming, he fired, hitting the next swimmer in the head. The ship was now far closer, and the swimmers were panicking. Swanton saw that one of them dived like a whale and went out of sight. He aimed and shot the third sailor at close range, and then *Restless* passed them with no sign of the fourth swimmer.

Swanton grabbed the reloaded first musket and ran aft. Resting the musket on the stern rail, he balanced it and waited. The traitor came up twenty yards from the stern, looking straight at Swanton. He saw the musket pointed at him and pleaded mercy. Swanton turned, and Captain South knew what he was asking! But he also remembered the dead sailor they shot at the bow of his ship.

"Execute him, please, Mr Swanton."

Wham went the musket.

"Done, Sir!"

"Mr Trotters, bring her about and pick up those dead sailors. I want identifications. Once they are loaded, we will commence a search for the other cutter; however, I think she will have her sail up and be long gone now."

"Aye, Sir, and may I suggest you go below Sir and have your hand washed and properly bandaged."

"Thank you, Master. In the excitement, I forgot about that. Carry On."

Swanton and Bright followed him into the captain's cabin. Crew members stood up and saluted as he went past. Robert gripping his wounded hand, noticed the respect and smiled.

Trotters, nudging Mr Young, said, "That was the gutsiest performance I have ever seen in the navy lad. Ever seen, I say! We've got a good one here by Jove."

"Aye, Master, a real good one; about time I say so, Master!"

The Turner Household, Guilford ...

Anne sat in a comfortable chair in the parlour. The house felt insecure now she was aware the burglars were still in town. Perhaps they were locals, and perhaps not? Knowing that her parents would be home tonight, she decided to read a good book until they arrived. It was now almost eleven, and she could hear Constable Rawlins and the guard talking out on the portico.

"Cricks, you maintain your watch here. I will check out the back. Keep your eyes open, man!"

Anne decided a few more candles might help so any potential intruder would know there were people still up and about. She sat back down in the chair, picked up her book, made herself comfortable and thumbed through the pages to her place. As Anne read slowly, her eyelids closed, and her head rolled over, resting on the wing of the chair. Soon she was fast asleep.

The wind was roaring through the rigging. It was nearly a gale, and it was a struggle for the crew above reefing the sails. The noise was incredible; Anne could see the men grappling with the sails high on the yards above. Ice cold water was washing right across the deck. Gripping the ropes at the mast, she looked up again, watching the men struggling. Then Robert was beside her, tying her tight against the mast so the waves could not wash her over the side.

A scream came from above as a man nearly fell from the yardarm rigging, the sail tearing and cracking as they flapped violently. Robert yelled, "Hang on, man, till the others reach you!" Then he lost his grip, falling straight down outside the ship's rail into the wild water of the violent storm. An enormous wave washed him up against the side. Robert ran, reaching for him before he was gone. Stretching his arm out as far as he could, he screamed, "Grab me, Man! Grab me......" The sailor grasped out...

"Anne, Anne? Wake up, child. You are dreaming!"

Anne woke with a start, and there was her mother. She opened her eyes wide, then a great smile came on their faces, and they hugged each other tightly. The relief was enormous. She was safe.

"Mother, thank God you are home!"

Chapter 17

William had run out of energy. Being his first day back at school, the afternoon lingered on slowly. Still recovering from the burglary ordeal, he appeared fit, but Mrs Taggart could see he was not one hundred per cent. Soon he complained of being tired, so she decided to walk him home before school ended. It was a bit early, but no harm in him having a part-day, and his house was close. She advised Reverend Taggart before the two of them set off.

"How are you feeling, William, after your first day back?"

"I'm a bit tired, and I usually have a rest around this time."

"That's a good idea. Once you have rested, you can take your dog for a walk and have some fun!" Mrs Taggart forgot that the burglars killed the dog during the robbery. "I'm sorry, William, I forgot about Snups. Perhaps when Simeon and the others come home, you can go for a play."

William made no reply. As they reached the house's front steps, he ran up the stairs and through the front door, nearly bumping into Mrs Jennings.

"William, I did not expect you home so early!"

Mrs Taggart followed the disappearing William up the front stairs.

"Ah, Mrs Jennings, I let William out early today, as he was becoming quite tired. I am sure he will fully recover soon. Now, how are you after that ordeal?"

"Ma'am, I was a bit overcome at the time but feeling well now. It was a bad thing, but we must move on. Thank you for letting us know William is home. I must be getting on now. Was there anyone else you require?'

"No, thank you, just letting you know he was home! I, too, must return now before school ends and assist Reverend Taggart. Good day, Mrs Jennings."

"Good day, and thank you, Ma'am!"

William jumped onto his bed and grabbed Snups's collar, hanging from his bedpost. Hugging the collar, he lay silently on the bed remembering the happy dog that was his best friend. As his eyes closed, William smiled, imagining Snups was licking his ear. Soon he was fast asleep.

Bethany came out of her mother's bedroom, where they were talking about the wedding plans. She heard Mrs Jennings call her, "What is it, Mrs Jennings?"

"Doctor Bassington is here, Miss. He is in the parlour."

Bethany hurried down the stairs and found a beaming Neville waiting for her.

"I have the advice from the attorney. The contract is settled, and the house will be ours by this Friday. I will move in on the weekend and set things up. What do you think of that?"

"Wonderful, Neville. May we go and see it now? It is so exciting! Just think of that, it will be our new home, and you will no longer be sleeping at the back of the medical practice anymore. Why not have dinner there on Saturday night?"

"Certainly, however, you will need a chaperone and a box for a seat. Perhaps Anne would be a chaperone? Mind you, I do not even have a table yet. I might find a big box, and we can have a picnic. Anyway, on Friday afternoon, I will pick up the keys!"

Bethany stood back and looked at Neville with some alarm, "Neville! In all our preparations we have not thought about after the wedding. I know we are going on a honeymoon, but we will need a bed and some furniture, crockery, and cutlery when we return. I should have thought of this!"

Neville smiled and reassured her, "There is a hotel nearby if we can't organise a bed. There is no rush. We should focus on the wedding and furnish the house as we need it."

Bethany was determined not to stay in a hotel at the end of their honeymoon. They would set about purchasing some furniture.

Coming from the kitchen, Anne heard Beth and Neville talking in the parlour. She ventured in, and Beth welcomed her with a quick question. "Anne! Would you be my chaperone on Saturday night, please, for dinner with Neville?"

After all was agreed and the plans decided, Anne checked on William and found him fast asleep on his bed, clutching Snups's collar.

She whispered, "Will, we all miss him too!"

She stroked his hair and covered him with a blanket.

Normality in the house was returning, and all welcomed it. Anne thought about how empty it was when she was alone without Beth and her parents. She enjoyed a busy house but not too exciting! 'Let me see what we can do about that dog?' Mr McPherson would have the details of where he purchased 'Boiler' and 'Red Socks'. She would acquire a puppy for the children if she could afford it, especially William. She took out pen, ink and paper.

At Portsmouth …

Robert quickly checked the time on the clock high on the façade of the two-storied building. He was due at fleet headquarters and mounted the stairs. His damaged hand throbbed from the physical activity, so as a precaution, he sought medical advice. The Surgeon advised the wound was clean and should remain infection-free, given regular rebandaging over the next few weeks.

He was concerned about fulfilling his role at the wedding.

"Will I be recovered in three weeks? I am the best man for Neville Bassington's wedding, and being free of bandages would be an advantage."

Surgeon Ludlam replied, "Yes, I am also attending the wedding. Neville and I are old friends. The recovery will depend on the healing process – it differs depending on the wound. Try washing the wound each night with salty water before renewing the bandage. Let the salt soak in for a while, and then dry it. You can always ask Neville for an opinion once you arrive in Guildford. I should be there on Friday afternoon and would be pleased to check it then."

"Thank you, Surgeon Ludlam, that is kind of you. By the way, what pray is your Christian name?"

"Reginald, Sir."

"Reginald, let us be on a first-name basis for the wedding. I take it you are attending the Stag night?"

"Yes, Sir. Neville sent me an invitation."

"I shall see you there."

Robert could not recall Reginald Ludlam on the guest list, but he knew that Neville was still sending invitations. Best he checked soon on how many Neville was inviting.

As Robert entered Commodore Richard Jacob's office, he rose from his desk and welcomed him. The reception was warm and well-meaning. "I say, South. That was quite a feat you pulled off. Well done. How is the hand?"

"No long-term damage, thankfully. The Surgeon assures me I will live if I keep the wound clean and bathed in saltwater for a couple of weeks."

"Good, Good. Now the Admiral is waiting. By the way, Admiral Crouch from the Admiralty is in there as well. I think they have more instructions for you. In you go, Sir."

Robert swallowed and strode towards the door. He knocked and heard, "Enter."

Opening the door, he found the two admirals standing by the window overlooking the harbour. Admiral Sutherland smiled and walked over, "Robert, welcome back. Let me introduce you. Admiral Sir Franklin Crouch, please meet Commander Sir Robert South."

Crouch walked over, slowly taking a good look at Robert, then he smiled and shook Robert's hand warmly.

"Commander South, I hear your last few days have been interesting. It appears picking up a couple of canons in Woolwich is not as straightforward as first thought. Eh, Ha Ha!"

"Not when the Irish are involved, Admiral. They have a different agenda, but we sorted them out."

"Well done, I say, Commander. Let us hope the crew is free of them now. I must admit I was surprised when I heard Lieutenant Small was a republican."

"I was too, Sir. I thought him a good officer until the pressure started. If not for the Master and my servant, I would not be here now."

"I look forward to your report, Commander, but by nine tomorrow morning, please. I'll brief you on that in a moment."

Admiral Sutherland noticed Robert's bandaged hand, "How's the hand, Robert?"

"It will recover, Sir. By the time of the wedding, should see it right."

"Good. Now Admiral Crouch has another task for you."

Robert, on hearing this became concerned. Unsure if he had found all the traitors yet, he was not keen on another mission. He braced himself, knowing he must comply willingly.

Admiral Crouch took a seat and waved the other two men towards chairs.

"Sir Robert, the Irish problem is growing. It will not go away. I forecast this issue will not resolve itself until we give them independence. But there are others, especially the Lords with landholdings in Ireland, who have a different view. With already two uprisings and a third building, we need far more intelligence on these activities. Especially gentlemen, for the Admiralty, which has the prime responsibility for policing our borders."

"I shall make the report my highest priority, Sir. You shall have it by the morning if that assists!"

"That would be good, Commander, but I need you with me in London for a presentation of your report. The gentlemen at the admiralty need first-hand knowledge and an opportunity for questions. It is Wednesday afternoon now. If we leave for London tomorrow, we will be ready for the following Monday. I will read your report during our trip. I trust you have an officer you may leave in command of *Restless*."

"Yes, Sir. The Master, Mr Trotters. He performed with distinction during our little action."

"It was no little action, Robert. You cleaned out about twenty of them for the loss of only two men. Mutiny is no small thing, and given the circumstances, it is miraculous you survived. You handled this well, Sir."

Admiral Crouch stood and agreed with Sutherland, "Commander, you have saved one of His Majesty's ships and protected her crew for the second time. The Navy needs young men like you and will not forget these acts of bravery. You have a promising career ahead. Now I will expect you at my coach at nine in the morning. Good day, Commander."

"Yes, Sir."

Robert saluted his senior flag officers, turned and set off for *Restless*. As he rushed along, he thought, "I hope this does not delay me for Neville's wedding."

The McPherson Household, Greenwich …

Hamish McPherson enjoyed a delightful bowl of fruit pieces as he sat at the breakfast table with Marjorie.

"Jenkins! The breakfast is superb. Just what we need for a healthy diet. Thank you for making the changes I requested. It is better than I expected."

Jenkins was visibly thankful and smiled as he said, "A pleasure, Sir."

Hamish finished off a plate of strawberries as he thought about the letter received from Anne Turner yesterday. Marjorie, when he explained the issue raised, was of two minds.

"Marjorie, after our discussion last night, I think the best approach would be a gift of a hound for the family. I saw how much young William enjoyed walking Red Socks and Boiler with Jenkins – he has a feeling for dogs, that boy! I am sure he is quite a melancholy little fellow now his dog is gone. The sooner the dog is replaced, the better. I'm surprised Jonathan has not acted already as it will also be a good guard dog for them."

"Surely if they want a guard dog, they would go for a Sheppard or a Doberman, Hamish?"

"I'm not sure they realise they need a guard dog, and the Vizsla is a fast hunting dog and very loving. They will smell a stranger at two hundred yards. That's why we have them. Beautiful dogs. William will be so pleased with one."

Jenkins re-entered the room with tea and coffee. Hamish took the opportunity.

"Jenkins, where did we purchase the Vizslas from?"

"Sir, I have all the details downstairs. When I heard about the Turner burglary and that the dog was lost, similar thoughts passed my mind, particularly about young William. Sir, I made enquiries as I knew how much William enjoyed our dogs. There are puppies available now."

"Good, Good, Thank you, Jenkins. Please procure one, and Thomas and James will take it down when they leave on Friday for Guildford. Marion will survive without Thomas for a week. I would enjoy being there when William sees the puppy, but the timing will not permit this with my London and Reading trip. The boys will have that pleasure. Perhaps I may stop there on the way back!"

Marjorie was not aware of the Reading trip, "Hamish, I know you will meet with the engineers in London, but why Reading as well?"

"Dear, I have completed some research on where the railway companies plan to lay tracks. Reading will be a central hub connecting London with the various southwest towns such as Bath, Bristol and Plymouth. It may even be a junction for the northern manufacturing towns. Mark my words, it will be a growth centre. That is why I want a pub there. My agents have identified several sites that require assessing before bringing in other investors like Jonathan Turner. Why not come, Dear – it will only be three or four days? You would enjoy the trip."

"What are you thinking, Hamish? Marion and I have far too much on with the wedding. I'm glad Thomas and James will be in Guildford. I will miss them, but it will free up Marion for wedding dress fittings. I left them alone as they were having so much fun. But there is still so much to be done!"

At Guildford ...

Constable Rawlings remained calm as Jonathan Turner raised his voice.

"You mean that despite the clear description my children provided of this older man, there is no further progress on locating him?"

"Mr Turner, we have done all we can with the limited resources here. Still, there is no trace of them. I would say that these chaps are highly professional and are keeping their heads down."

"So, we continue living in fear as these burglars freely roam the countryside?"

"I'm not so sure, Sir. There has been a detailed search with descriptions posted, and the burglars will know at least one of them is identified. I think they have moved on. Anyway, the Mayor has agreed that we keep up regular guard patrols past your house during the night. I would suggest you keep your guard on for the next week, and after that, we should talk again."

"I am not happy with this situation at all. I cannot have my family living in fear, Constable! Builder Robinson and his men will be here tomorrow, making some changes. Robinson will strengthen the ground floor doors and windows, increasing our security here at night. But thank you, Constable, for all your help. I am most thankful. Please stop in at the bakery tomorrow, and we will provide a fresh supply of bread and pastries for the watchmen's families in our appreciation."

"Why thank you, Mr Turner, the boys, will appreciate that. We will continue watching, but it is more likely these culprits are now gone."

With that, the Constable was off, and Jonathan, most frustrated at the lack of progress, was keen on sharing this information with his family. He entered the kitchen, appearing frustrated.

Eleanora, thinking about security, spoke up, "Perhaps Jonathan, we should acquire another dog quickly or maybe two as Hamish has."

"I know you all think I disliked the dog, but I had a soft spot for Snups! He was a good friend to the children, but he was not a guard dog. I agree, Eleanora! We should investigate purchasing a dog."

"Father, I took the liberty of contacting Mr McPherson to determine where he acquired his two vizslas. I expect we may receive a reply when Thomas returns on Sunday from Greenwich." Anne was sure Hamish McPherson would still have the information. "William loved their dogs, and they were such beautiful creatures. I think a new puppy would cheer him up no end."

"I hope Thomas has the details when he arrives. In the meantime, I will start making enquiries. Now Bethany, how are the preparations going for the big day?"

"Very well, Father. I have booked the rooms at the Fox and Hound, and we will accommodate the overflow at the Swan. The acceptances are returning, and you will be glad to hear that Robert South's family, the Earl and Countess of Fintelton, will be attending. They have a suite reserved at the Fox and Hound."

"I thought this would make you happy, Anne, but you seem upset that Sir Hugh, Robert's brother, is coming."

"It is that he is such a disagreeable man. He is about thirty, unmarried and has a reputation for drunkenness and womanising. He made a complete ass of himself at the dinner last Friday night. It was very disagreeable, I will not say any more, but I thought he was off the guest list?"

"We will keep an eye on him, Anne. He will not dare play up in our company. I think the Bassingtons insisted that the complete family be on the invitation. If David Bassington requests Sir Hugh's presence, he must have some good attributes!"

"Lady Jane and Emma are lovely people, so please don't judge the whole family because of the way I described Sir Hugh."

"I shall not. The meeting will be a great honour. It is not every day you meet an Earl and a Countess, and they have large land holdings near Petersfield, so they must produce much grain!"

At a Pub in Guildford ...

After finishing with Doctor Sopwith, Sir Hugh South headed off for his next engagement at an indiscrete hotel in Guildford. He reserved a room and then led two ladies with him up the stairs, each carrying three bottles of scotch whiskey. It was what Sir Hugh desired after a long day. Plenty of drink and some women for his lust. He found himself quite drunk when he woke in the morning with one of the ladies draped across his legs and the other fast asleep naked on the floor.

He rolled out of bed, and despite twice failing, he finally gained his feet and stood up before collecting the women's clothes. There was one thing that Sir Hugh could not stand: women in his room in the morning. He held no sympathy for them, especially after the price he paid for their company. Throwing their clothes and belongings out the bedroom door, he dragged them both, despite their protests, from the room into the hallway and laughed as he closed and locked the door. There were screams of disrespect and banging on the door for a short period and then silence as the women disappeared with their things.

After washing, he took a full breakfast in the dining room, gathered his horse from the stable, and set off early. During the ride, he kept dwelling on his conversation with Doctor Sopwith. The doctor's opinion was that Sir Hugh had contracted the 'Pox' and must use the mercury ointment morning and night for the next month. The Doctor was sure this would help, and he should soon feel some relief from the symptoms. Worth a try, he thought!

At Petersfield, he found himself not interested in the White Rabbit's attractions and continued onto Fintelton. As he slowly rode up the long drive, a strange relief came over him like a child finding its security in a mother's arms. Riding into the stables, a groom took his horse, and Hugh made his way into the house. Entering the back entrance of the manor, he climbed the stairs and noticed the butler in the drawing-room. Pike stopped when he saw him.

"Sir Hugh, I am glad you are home, your father has been taken ill, and I have sent for Doctor Sopwith. I do not expect him until the morning. Mr Barrett and Sally will stay with your father tonight – but I think it will be a long night. He has a fever and is raving!"

Sir Hugh frowned at the butler, "If he survives the night, I will see him in the morning. I am not well myself. Wake me if I am needed, but only if it is most desperate. Good night! Pike, organise a bottle of scotch for my room and have Sopwith see me once finished with my father?"

"Yes, Sir." The butler watched as Sir Hugh trudged up the stairs and into the hallway. Once he was out of sight, Pike raised his eyebrows and nodded. What would it be like working for this man if the Earl should pass away? He shuddered. Pike would prefer if the countess were home. Should he send a rider with a message? The rider would reach London by Friday evening before Lady Jane set off on Saturday. Yes, he would send a message.

'Harting', St James's Square, London ...

Robert was not fond of visiting London, mainly because of the congestion, air quality and fog. At least 'Harting' was a little oasis in the middle of a vast city. The home in St James's Square was most comfortable and convenient for family occasions, the best feature being its proximity to the Admiralty if he were ever posted there. The trouble was Robert was a country boy at heart and longed for the fields around Fintelton and the friendly atmosphere of Guildford.

Admiral Crouch resided in Mayfair and kindly delivered Robert to the front stairs of 'Harting'.

"Sir Robert, I am not sure of our meeting time, but I shall send a message here once I know, probably late this afternoon. It will be sometime on Monday. Please allow plenty of time for the traffic, as these men think only of themselves and their schedules. So please be on time. By the way, your report was well written, Sir. Just what I was after."

"Yes, Admiral, I will be there quickly. Is there anything you require emphasised at the meeting?"

"Yes, how desperate these republicans are! I am sure the admirals and the bureaucrats do not understand that we are fighting a small war here. It is my opinion that this will deteriorate. These men want political freedom from our crown. You know what happened in America. A similar situation is developing on our doorstep. I think the King and the government will take an uncompromising stand on this. I shall send you a message with the details. Please be ready."

"Yes, Sir, and thank you for the ride from Portsmouth."

"A pleasure, young man! A fine house, Sir!" With a wry smile, the Admiral then commented, "I should imagine you will sleep well tonight!"

"Very well, indeed, my Lord!"

The Admiral tapped the roof, and his carriage moved off, leaving Robert with his bag standing outside the family home in St James's Square.

Having only three hours of sleep since his meeting at fleet headquarters, Robert was worn out. It was four in the afternoon, and there were people everywhere. The bustle and intensity of London were both exciting and annoying. He turned and faced the four-story house and noticed the blinds were all open. 'Mother must be in town!' It was only then he recalled Emma's dinner with Anne. Time for some news and then a nap. He picked up his bag and briskly mounted the stairs, knocking on the front door.

The butler, Mr Matthew Staines, only recently appointed by the family after the retirement of the previous butler, Mr Dennis Hopton, answered the door.

"Good afternoon, Sir. May I help you?" The butler stood in the doorway, making sure he blocked any enquirer from moving through into the vestibule. Robert was meeting Staines for the first time and took a close look. He was middle-aged, about the early forties and a tall thin man with a firm face that would deter troublemakers. He was dressed impeccably in the family livery and appeared a no-nonsense personality type. His eyes cast across Robert in disdain as if saying, 'Who the devil are you calling on this household?'

"Ah, you must be Staines, the new butler. Let me introduce myself. I am Sir Robert South, youngest son of the Earl!"

The butler looked Robert up and down and did not change his expression. Robert detected that the butler was sceptical and was thinking through his next move.

"Sir. I have not had the pleasure. Lady Fintelton did not advise me of your coming. You will understand that I must check your claim as the countess advised that you are presently at sea off Portsmouth. My apologies, Sir. If you would please wait here, I will call upon the countess, who will verify your claim. Please take a seat on the portico. I will not be long, Sir."

As the front door was closed in Robert's face, he spoke, "I say...!"

Being weary, Robert was unprepared for this slight but took into consideration that the new butler was not familiar with his identity. He sighed, "There is always something!" After a long day on the road, he was not that concerned and slumped onto a seat at the small entrance placing his hat beside him. In other circumstances, he probably would have been ropeable about this, but he resigned himself, "Hopefully, this won't take long!"

After ten minutes, the door opened again, and the butler appeared, followed by Emma.

"Why, Robert, what a surprise – I never expected you here today."

"Hello, Emma. Neither did Staines! May I come into my own house now?" Robert eyed the butler.

Matthew Staines, offering assistance, moved to take Robert's bag. Robert, standing firm, held onto his case and walked past the butler with a grin on his face.

"Staines, I will be in my room on the first floor. If anyone calls, I am expecting a note from the Admiralty – please advise me when it comes. Now, Emma, will you accompany me upstairs? I must talk with you."

The butler stood back and nodded, "Yes, Sir."

Robert, becoming somewhat irate, turned and said, "It is 'Yes, Sir Robert' please? Remember that! Also, Staines, please have one of the maids bring up a bowl of warm water, some salt and some clean bandages."

"Yes, Sir Robert!" The butler replied without any change in expression and then remained silent as Robert led Emma upstairs. Robert carried his bag as the butler made no further attempt to assist him.

As they went up the stairs, Robert whispered, "He's playing a dangerous game!"

Emma said, very quietly, "Um! Yes, he is finding his way. Mother likes him. What do you need the warm water and salt for?"

"Washing the wound on my hand! Nothing serious."

As they reached the first-floor landing, "What room should I choose? The butler was not having the pleasure of allocating me a room in my own family's house!"

"Your old room will do – mother and I are the only others here."

"Good. Now tell me, how did the dinner with Anne go? What did you think of her?"

"It went better than expected; however, the plan did change slightly. Mother attended! Hugh made a late undignified entrance, and then there was the burglary at the Turner house! A quiet night overall!" Emma smiled and reassured him, "But don't worry, I like her!"

Robert looked at Emma in horror, mouth open, "It does not sound like our original plan? What happened?"

"Not now, let me tell you all about it but not here. You change, and we shall go for a walk in the square. Plenty of your clothes are in the cupboard. Mother will be so glad you are home. At dinner, I think you will be interested in her impressions of Anne!"

"Mother! Impressions of Anne! My goodness!"

At Guildford …

Jonathan Turner and Eleanora took the opportunity of a quiet cup of afternoon tea together while the girls were at Hursts for another fitting. Marcia was with Aggie and Mrs Jennings in the kitchen, and the boys played outside. For once, a tranquil quiet came over the household, and Jonathan relaxed. The London journey was over, and the Constable had thoroughly investigated the burglary. It was now opportune for quiet communion with his wife.

"Eleanora, you will recall as we journeyed home from London, we discussed having a butler and possibly renting a new home. I am in two minds about the matter and wanted your opinion on what we should do. I must say that after our recent trip I am not so keen on travel anymore. It has changed my views quite a bit. I would value your opinions on a butler and a new house."

Eleanora could see that Jonathan was unsure about the issues. Since London, she too wondered if it was necessary. The baby was due in February, and she was now visibly showing. She was troubled as her health was not improving. She feared that too much change, especially when a baby was due, could complicate matters more than solving any problem.

"Jonathan, thank you for asking. I have been very proud of you in the last few months. You have certainly been very controlled in your behaviour towards me, and I have appreciated this much. I feel far more at ease now than before.

My thoughts on these issues are that this is our home. With a baby coming and the state of my health, I think a delay for a year may be preferable. In a year, we may make a different decision!"

Jonathan missed the implications Eleanora suggested when mentioning her health. His mind, as usual, was on business.

"Eleanora, I have let things slip over the last two weeks. I agree with you. The butler and new house are not priorities currently. Robinson's men will make the adjustments we require for our needs. The most important thing for all of us is the business's success. I will concentrate on that."

"I would suggest the first thing you do, Jonathan, is rent or purchase those new offices. I need you out from under my feet here. This house will become far busier in the next three months!"

"It shall be done, my Dear."

At St James's Square, London ...

The message came a little before seven o'clock in the evening. Robert was dressing for dinner when Staines knocked on the door. "Come!" The butler opened the bedroom door and carefully entered.

"Excuse me, Sir Robert, the message has come from Admiral Crouch, Sir!"

The butler passed the message across, and Robert nodded. Staines took a few steps backward.

"Will that be all, Sir Robert?"

"Yes, thank you, Staines. I shall be down for dinner shortly. If there is a need for a reply, I shall advise you."

"Thank you, Sir." With that, Staines retreated from the room.

Robert felt satisfied with Staines's performance this time. He opened the message and frowned as he read. The Admiral regretted the meeting at the Admiralty would not take place until Tuesday next. However, Robert's attendance was required for a formal dinner tomorrow at the Admiral's house in Mayfair. A postscript said the dress would be a dinner suit, not a uniform.

"Damn!" Robert was frustrated by the delay. The stakes were high, and he was still uncertain whether Trotters would cope if the traitors tried any other tricks. There was no hope of him returning now before at least Thursday. Placing the letter on his dressing table, he thought about the implications. So, this was the life of a Captain. When you were on land, you might be away from your ship for some time. He must ensure the first lieutenant replacement was an officer capable of covering for him. Admiral Sutherland needed to replace Small with someone Robert would trust. Perhaps he should discuss this with Admiral Crouch at dinner tomorrow night.

On the road from Ewell ...

Around two in the afternoon on Saturday afternoon Thomas Turner and James McPherson's coach approached Guildford, and both were relieved to be near their destination. Setting off early from Ewell, they planned their arrival for mid-afternoon so the children could take the puppy for a walk.

"This farming country looks fertile, Thomas. You should have no shortage of grains here."

"It depends on our negotiations with the landholders. If they continue supporting the small mills, then we are in trouble. The negotiations for grain will be critical."

"Then, an incentive is needed. Reduce your margin and give the farmers a better price. Once the small mills are gone, you can slowly renegotiate the prices. You can achieve anything if you have a good strategy and plenty of time. Making too much profit is not the objective, plan for business continuity. The landholders will welcome this. Let them understand your plans – once they see a long-term future, they will be knocking on your door. "

"That's an interesting approach! We can afford some margin loss if it will favourably influence the landholders. Did you use this approach in Scotland?"

"We did in Edinburgh, but it was slightly different in Glasgow. The supply was more difficult, and we shipped it in – so the strategy was more bidding for contracts on the corn exchange."

Thomas had no idea about Scotland and wondered what it was like, "Do you enjoy living up there – it must be cold?"

"If you are born there, you don't know any different. Father had us schooled in England, which gave us an educational advantage but not our resistance to the cold. Yes – we found it hard on holidays when we went home, but now I'm living there, I don't mind. Anyway, there are other attractions!"

"What, you mean you've got a girl up there?"

"Aye, laddie! A wee lass of my liking! Glasgow is always a welcome sight."

"What is her name Jamie, my boy? "

"Why not come up and see?"

"Perhaps we might end the honeymoon there. That would be fun!"

"Why not! Come and stay, and we will show you the sights."

"Come on, tell me her name. I will keep it confidential!"

"There is a reason for my secrecy. You must give me your oath!"

"But I thought you would be proud of making it known?"

"My mother has busily arranged all my brothers' marriages, and I was damned sure she would not organise mine. So, I kept them guessing. As far as they know, I do not have a lassie. I thought I would break it gently to them when I was ready."

"I see. Then, James McPherson, you have my word. Shake on it?"

Thomas and James were developing a close friendship. They liked each other and had similar views. Thomas liked James because he hardly ever touched beer despite being a brewer. Thomas was of a similar mindset and found too much beer was not good for his system. They both leaned forward and shook hands and laughed.

Thomas then said, "The name?"

James blushed. It was the first time Thomas saw James overcome with emotion.

"Isla!" James's face beamed as he said her name.

"I think you must love this girl very much!"

James nodded and kept smiling as he turned and looked out the window. Thomas could see that he was still blushing and thought there must be quite a story here. But it was not the time for pressing his friend. There would be plenty of time in the future for this story.

Mr McPherson's carpenters had hastily constructed a wooden travelling box for the puppy. As they rounded the corner into High Street, the coach jolted on a rough cobble, and the puppy jumped in surprise. He sat up, opened his big brown eyes, and whimpered at Thomas.

Picking the puppy up, Thomas gently soothed him in a cuddle, saying, "Nearly home, boy. Just up the street now. I hope you're ready for some excitement." Putting its paws on Thomas's chest, the puppy licked him on the cheek.

"Affectionate little thing he is!" Thomas passed him over and then wiped his cheek with a handkerchief. "Here we are!" The coach pulled up outside the Turner's house, and all was quiet.

"That's good. The family are not expecting us. Usually, there is a welcoming committee outside and much merriment. We can sneak in with the puppy and surprise them."

Thomas hopped down and left the coachmen with the luggage. They both tip-toed up the stairs, carrying the puppy in its box. Thomas found the front door unlocked and carefully opened it. The two men went inside, James following Thomas as he approached the stairwell.

By coincidence, Mrs Jennings came out of the parlour at the same time and collided with James. She looked up and saw this unknown tall young man in a cape looking down at her; then she saw the back of another caped man climbing the stairs, box in hand. In her surprise, and not recognising either man, she panicked that the burglars were back and flew backwards, letting out an incredible scream of terror and then fainted on the ground.

Thomas saw her go down and rushed over, throwing his cape aside. James knelt beside the terrified woman speaking gently, reassuring her. Jonathan Turner sped from his study into the hallway and gasped at the sight. There were Thomas and James carefully sitting up a flustered Mrs Jennings. The puppy, scared by the commotion, jumped out of its box and dashed through Jonathan's legs and up the stairs looking for safety. At the top, it flew into Clementine's arms, shivering.

"You poor little thing!" Clementine cuddled it and slowly walked back down the stairs where the scene was unfolding.

"Why James and Thomas, we did not expect you until tomorrow."

"I gather that, Father!" Thomas said, looking down at Mrs Jennings, who was dusting herself off now, ashamed of her reaction.

James carefully picked up the things she was carrying and, with a smile, said, "Mrs Jennings, I am James McPherson, I am sorry about scaring you, but it was a surprise for the children! Thomas and I were delivering a puppy directly. We had no intention of scaring you; we are most sorry!" James passed the items he was holding to Anne and gave Mrs Jennings a comforting hug, "Now you are alright, Lass, aren't you?"

"Yes, Yes, Sir. I am still a little nervous after the burglary. I am sorry, Mr McPherson, I just reacted too quickly. I'm better now."

"Why my mother would have done the same, Mrs Jennings. Now come into the kitchen and sit down. I will make you a cup of tea!"

Thomas blurted out, "There's no need …." when Anne took his arm and stopped him from interfering.

"Thomas, just let it be. Let's all go into the kitchen and have a cup of tea."

Glancing around, James spied the kitchen door at the end of the hallway.

"Now come with me, Mrs Jennings, and we will make that tea."

Anne raised her eyebrows at Thomas, and the other family members followed them down the hallway. Thomas smiled and walked behind Clementine, who was still cuddling the puppy. Jonathan Turner breathed a sigh of relief that the burglars were not back. He quickly checked the front door was locked and then dashed up the stairs to check on Eleanora, who was sleeping peacefully. Relieved, he walked downstairs, and found Aggie making the tea. Marcia was on James's lap showing him her drawing, and the others were admiring the puppy, which Clementine was still cuddling.

"Sorry, Father, we planned to surprise the children, but Mrs Jennings discovered us at the wrong time. The puppy is a present from Mr and Mrs McPherson."

"You gave us a start, but no harm is done. Glad you are back, Thomas and welcome, James."

Anne suggested, "Perhaps Thomas, you could make the introductions?"

"I'm sorry, I forgot most of you had not met James. Let me introduce you. Please meet Mr James McPherson from Glasgow, Scotland, who has been my instructor in brewing. James, this is Anne, Clementine, Madeline, and Marcia. Of course, this is Mrs Jennings, who you now know well." The house-keeper gave a little giggle, "And this is Aggie, our maid. I assume the two boys, Simeon and William, are down by the river, and Bethany will be off with Neville somewhere."

Jonathan smiled, "Welcome, James. I shall thank your father for the puppy in my next letter. We were investigating a purchase, so this is most timely."

"That is our pleasure, Mr Turner. My father is hoping it will cheer up the children after the loss of your dog."

"He is too kind. Thank you, James. Now you will join us for dinner tonight, won't you? Mrs Turner will be most keen on your company. She is asleep upstairs at present."

"I hope so, Sir! Thomas has offered me a bed for a few days!"

At 'Harting', St James's Square, London ...

The rider came early Saturday morning as Lady Jane, Robert, and Emma took breakfast. The message requested Lady Jane's return directly as the Earl's health had deteriorated, and Pike had called the doctor. Lady Jane was stoic in these situations, given the Earl's previous record of serious illness. Thankfully, each time he recovered, but as he aged, each occurrence became worse.

"Robert, it seems we must leave you and venture home quickly. Your father is unwell, and Pike has sent word requesting our return."

"It must be serious if Pike has sent word. I will also come as soon as my business in London is complete." Robert re-read the message and was concerned – Pike always gave an accurate summary of the situation.

Lady Jane considered the travel ahead. "If we changed horses, say in Epsom or Guilford, we should make it through in one day. What do you suggest, Robert?"

"Mother, the roads between London and Guildford are reasonable, but from there, they deteriorate, and I would be alarmed if you were travelling them by night. Even if you left, now you would not arrive at Guildford until after dark. Change the horses at either Ewell or Epson. I would suggest Ewell as the connecting road to Guilford is better. Stay overnight at Guildford and leave at first light on Sunday morning for Fintelton. I know the situation is urgent, but it is quite dangerous in a coach at night. If you decide to continue from Guildford, I advise runners with torches ahead of the coach."

Emma, too, was thinking about the trip. "Mother, Robert is correct. We should stop at Guildford. That is more than enough for today. You know

Father – he always recovers!"

"I'm not sure, Darling. I have a bad feeling about this message. Pike does not normally send messages unless the situation is urgent. However, I understand your concerns, so we shall stop at Guildford."

She called the butler.

"Yes, Milady!"

"Staines, would you please arrange an express. Let the Fox and Hound at Guildford know that Lady Emma and I will require our family suite overnight and fresh horses in the morning. Please dispatch the rider soon; he should be there well before us."

"Yes, my Lady!"

Emma was thankful. She was concerned about a long country ride in the coach at night. "Robert, I would feel far safer if you accompanied us."

"You and Mother will be safe. The coach will reach Guildford soon after dark. Perhaps you would call on Anne? I wish I could come, but I am under orders, so I must attend the dinner tonight with the Admiral. Emma that is the navy; we must serve our masters and our country."

"You will come as soon as you can?"

"The meeting at the Admiralty is on Tuesday, so I should be there by Thursday night. I shall also stop in Guildford on Wednesday evening."

Lady Jane looked up as Robert said this and saw the smirk on Emma's face.

"Robert. We have already talked about this young lady, and from our meetings I find her most acceptable. Please remember, she is still young and impressionable. There is no need for haste until you are very sure of your feelings. Neville's wedding will provide an opportunity for a meeting with Anne's parents. Hopefully, your father will recover and attend, as well. But remember, this will not be easy. It will take some time before she is accepted. Are you sure this lady is the one you have set your heart on?"

Emma looked up. She was surprised by how openly her mother expressed these issues.

Robert put down his cup of coffee, straightened his back and faced his mother. He was determined that there should be no doubt in his mother's mind.

"She is the woman I love, mother. If I do not marry Anne, I will not marry at all!"

"Then, my boy, it seems you have your heart set on this young lady. I am glad for you, Robert. You will have my blessing and my support. I hope she knows what she is taking on! But now we must be off, Emma. That is enough breakfast! Let us be on our way."

After farewelling the coach, Robert came inside and asked Staines for another cup of coffee and toast. The day outside was fine and clear, with a light breeze blowing. Events were moving faster than he planned, with his mother now aware of his declaration of love for Anne. They would see her in Guildford tonight. He hoped this would encourage Anne. With her now having friends in his family, he gained confidence in the plan for Fintelton next July. As his mother said, the next challenge would be, 'I hope she knows what she is taking on!' He understood how unforgiving the upper class could be.

"Sir Robert?"

"Yes, Staines"

"Sir, while we are alone. If I might speak with you on a delicate matter?"

"Yes, certainly!"

"Sir, I must apologise for how I received you yesterday. It was my mistake not inviting you inside straight away. My caution was too zealous as I was unaware of your face and mindful of your mother and sister's protection. It was my mistake, Sir, and I apologise for any embarrassment I have caused."

"Staines, thank you for your kind thoughts. I am sure you were carrying out your job as expected, and I have no difficulties with that. But thank you for your kind words, and your apology is accepted. I hope that we will have a long and fruitful relationship. Now we shall let it rest at that."

"Thank you, Sir Robert. Your confidence in me is most appreciated. I have not had the pleasure of meeting Sir Hugh, so I will endeavour not to make the same mistake."

"Just one word of advice, Staines. Sir Hugh's approach is far harsher than mine. Be on guard as he will not be as forgiving as I am."

"As I have not met him, I am unsure how I might achieve this."

"Then you must find a way, Staines. It is in your interest. I suggest checking some of the family portraits in the stairwell."

"Thank you, Sir."

With that, the butler withdrew. Robert was quite impressed that he sought him out and apologised. The making of an apology was always a challenging task. His opinion of Staines improved.

Later that evening, Robert arrived at Grosvenor's Square. As requested, he was in dinner dress and a cape, top hat, and gloves, ensuring no embarrassment. It was an impressive house similar to 'Harting', four stories high with a small covered entrance at the front door protecting guests from the weather. There was a lower story, but with no visible access, Robert assumed there must be a lane behind the houses allowing tradespeople an entry.

Approaching the house, he noticed two other large coaches parked outside. As he neared the entrance, a gentleman in a suit moved into his path.

"Identity, please, Sir."

"Commander Sir Robert South, Sir, and who are you?"

"Colonel Scott, Sir Robert. Security."

Looking over Colonel Scott's shoulder, Robert saw several other men in the shadows, one in military uniform.

"May I proceed, Colonel?"

"Which ship do you command, Sir?"

"HMS *Restless!*"

"You may proceed, Sir!"

"Thank you."

Robert knocked with the entry knocker and waited for the butler. After a few minutes, the butler answered the door but said nothing. Robert then realised he must make the first move.

"Commander Sir Robert South for Admiral Crouch."

"This way, Sir Robert!"

The vestibule was polished marble with many large paintings of Royal Navy ships. The curtains were a thick blue and white velvet, and carefully placed candles gave the room a warm feel.

"Make I take your cape, hat and gloves, Sir?"

"Thank you."

The butler took the items and placed them in a small room at the side of the stairway leading to the first floor. Robert noticed another man watching him from inside the cloakroom.

"Admiral Crouch is expecting you, Sir. If you would follow me."

Robert followed and was led into a large dining room with a long, polished wood table with enough space for twenty guests. From the table setting, he noted there were only five places. Two large candelabras on the dining table provided a warm glow for the flower arrangements. Two massive chandeliers were hanging well above and provided magnificent lighting for the room. Several servants stood along each wall in naval uniforms. Admiral Crouch was standing with three other gentlemen nearby.

"Ah, Sir Robert, glad that you could join us at such short notice. Sorry about the security, but we can't take chances these days. Let me introduce my other guests."

Robert walked across with the Admiral, "Firstly, Lord Dawlting, may I introduce Commander Sir Robert South."

Robert quickly recognised the name and the esteemed company he joined for dinner. Scrambling for the correct etiquette, he stood at attention and gave a short bow. Moving forwards, the Earl held out his hand. Robert took the cue, and they firmly shook hands.

"Sir Cecil is the Earl of Dawlting and is now retained by the Admiralty Board as a consultant. Of late, he has been advising the Admiralty on the Irish situation."

"I have heard much about you, Robert. I understand the previous two weeks have been challenging?"

"Yes ……Lord Dawlting!"

"I enjoy meeting with our young navy captains. I remember my time at sea with great affection!"

Robert felt a little easier, knowing the Earl had a navy connection.

"Excellent, my Lord."

The Earl retook his seat, allowing further introductions by Admiral Crouch. The Admiral quietly mentioned, "Sir Cecil achieved the rank of commander in the Navy and then moved into a consular position. His career has been impressive. Now, you know Admiral Sutherland?"

"Certainly, Sir. Good evening, Admiral. I was wondering if you would be in London as well."

"And you too, Robert. How is that hand coming on?"

Robert lifted his left hand and revealed the bandage.

"Are you familiar with Surgeon Reginald Ludlam at Portsmouth?"

"Yes, I have met him."

"He gave me instruction on bandaging and bathing in saltwater. The wound is healing quickly. The treatment is proving very effective."

"Hm … I'll keep him in mind, Robert."

Admiral Crouch then introduced Mr Malcolm Smith from the Admiralty. Malcolm now held the position of Comptroller.

Malcolm came across, smiling and shook his hand, "Welcome, Sir Robert. We have not met since that dinner at the McPherson's in Greenwich. That was a fine evening, and I enjoyed your company then."

"Thank you, Malcolm. Much has transpired since we last met."

"Yes, and you are the one who has been having the exciting time, it appears!" looking at Robert's bandaged hand.

Admiral Crouch then offered Robert a seat, and the dinner began. Robert was surprised as he found the Earl good company indeed. There were no pretensions, and he was keen on making conversation.

During the first course, the Earl asked, "How is your father at Fintelton. It has been a long time since I have seen him. Lord Fintelton must be aging the same as myself. Would he be in his seventies now?"

"Yes. Father is in his early seventies. I have received news that he is quite ill, and I intend a rest stop there before arriving in Portsmouth. My mother and sister left London today urgently returning home. However, I am sure he will recover – these bouts have affected him before."

"That is most unfortunate. Please give your father my regards and best wishes for a speedy recovery."

Once they finished the main courses, as Robert expected, the reason for the dinner became obvious.

Admiral Crouch handed the conversation over to Lord Dawlting. "Robert, as you probably know, I served with the Royal Navy for some years, having two commands. I then moved into the Southern Department in the consular area, where I served in several posts, the last being in Ireland. Admiral Crouch has kindly requested my assistance consulting on the Irish problem."

Robert nodded that he was aware of what the Earl was explaining.

"We decided that rather than the full Board and other committee members receiving a presentation, we should first meet with you and fully understand what happened on your last voyage. From the report we have received, the circumstances are consistent with other events occurring. It appears that a pattern is emerging."

The Earl now captured Robert's attention, "Excuse me, my Lord, you mean there have been other traitors on ships?"

"Yes, many of the Irish have been press-ganged into navy service. The republicans easily convinced these men that revolution is the only way of achieving independence. There have been other incidents but none as dangerous as the previous incident on your ship when Irish boarders attacked Captain Hughes. To gain access with such precision, we are now sure there were collaborators amongst the crew. It appears a similar plan was in action for your return journey to Portsmouth. The more alarming fact is that these revolutionaries are working freely in England right under our noses!

Thanks to you, they suffered a significant defeat when you outsmarted them off Portsmouth. Well done, Robert – that was a heroic action. But it now confirms that we have a more significant problem than we first thought.

If it is not too much trouble, we would like your account from the start precisely describing what happened aboard your ship from when you first set foot on *Restless*. Admiral Crouch, if we could have a supply of coffee, please. I think this will take a while."

Robert noticed that Colonel Scott then joined the group with writing paper, ink and pen. Assuming he was taking notes for Lord Dawlting, Robert sat back, breathed in deeply and gathered his thoughts.

"Certainly, my Lord. I think I must begin after leaving Admiral Sutherland's office some weeks ago when I received my commission!"

Robert related the complete story for the next hour and fielded many questions from Lord Dawlting and the others. They were particularly intent on understanding relationships among the crew and how an officer could become a traitor.

"You mean you climbed up the rigging after this traitor? Why not send up an officer? A captain should remain on the quarter deck in control!"

"Sir, there was no time, and I wrongly assumed Small, the first officer was trustworthy. My assumption proved incorrect. However, I would have lost the ship if I had sent Small. Also, I was not keen on remaining a still target for this traitor, so I acted. It paid off by capturing the chap and flushing out Small. My great regret is that Mr Door lost his life."

"Yes, damn shame!" said Admiral Sutherland.

Admiral Crouch carried a grim face. "It is my opinion Robert that this rebellion is far from over. We have a small victory here, but I think they will try again. They want a navy ship for some reason. Perhaps it is for smuggling in arms, but you would think a smaller, low-key vessel would attract less attention?"

There was a short silence as they considered this question. Robert restarted the conversation by addressing Admiral Crouch.

"Sir, this is a new role for me, but I have thought about their aims. I saw the look in the eyes of these men as they died. They are proud and willing to die for their cause. They believe this is a war, and they will not consider it won until they gain independence. Their plan must be gaining assets that will allow inflicting as much damage on us as they can, gaining support for them in Ireland and their dream of independence."

The Earl interjected, "You are probably right, Robert. But they shall never achieve it! Ireland is part of the United Kingdom and will remain so!"

Malcolm Smith then gently replied, "Excuse me, my Lord. We certainly agree with what you said, but I am not sure that Robert's suggestion was such. I think, and correct me, Sir Robert, if I am wrong! You are saying that in the short term, if they acquired a navy ship, they would have canons at their disposal. They could inflict some terrible damage on any unsuspecting seaport area. Perhaps even sink ships. An action like this would draw attention and demonstrate their strength. A major victory for their quest. The republicans would score a public relations victory!"

Robert sat forward, "Precisely, Sir. If they have tried twice, whoever is in control has a specific plan, and they will try again. Admiral, I suggest you advise Captain Foster so he is forewarned. Who knows where they will strike next?"

The Earl sat up straight in his chair, considering Robert and his suggestion, "I understand now why Admiral Sutherland gave you this command. You are a good thinker, Robert. We need men like you."

"Thank you, my Lord."

Admiral Crouch said, "Gentlemen, I think we have heard enough for tonight. Thank you, Robert, for joining us. It has been a pleasure! I would also say, please keep this meeting confidential. We have kept a lid on these revolutionary tactics of the Irish. We do not want the public aware of what damage they are inflicting. It would not be helpful at this time."

Robert stood, then thanked his host and the others.

The Earl approached him as he was leaving, "Robert, my thanks for risking your life for your country. Your father will be in my prayers for a swift recovery. I have fond memories of Sir David. We spent some great times together over the years – you are probably not aware of how close we were. Please pass on my regards when you see him."

"I shall, Lord Dawlting. Thank you for your concern. It is much appreciated."

With that, Robert ventured down the stairs where the butler provided his hat, gloves and cape. Admiral Sutherland then appeared at his side.

"Interesting chap, the Earl. I will tell you a bit about him when we have time. But first, we must concentrate on your orders, Commander South. I am sure we will stop these Irish soon. Well done tonight. I will draft a message for Foster and have it away by Monday morning. He should receive it by the end of the week. I expect his first report will arrive by the time I return to Portsmouth. We shall have some more intelligence then.

Admiral Crouch and I have decided on an alternative strategy for the gentlemen at the Admiralty. There will not be a meeting on Tuesday. So, you may head off tomorrow – I'm sure you could do with a free day in Guildford."

The Admiral smiled as he shook his hand. Robert appreciated the cheerful encouragement that he always received from the Admiral.

"Good night, Admiral Sutherland."

He ventured outside, where he found his coach waiting. Colonel Scott stood holding the carriage door open. Before he entered, Robert said, "Thank you, Colonel!"

Colonel Scott smiled and gave him a wink as he gently closed the carriage door and waved the coach off.

During the ride home, Robert reflected on the meeting and the kind words from the Earl about his father. He was unaware of much of his father's history. As he considered the lengthy discussion that evening, Robert became concerned. Only Admiral Crouch appeared to consider this threat would escalate. Robert recalled the determination in the eyes of the Irish traitors. His opinion was that this struggle was only beginning and far from over.

At Guildford ...

Early Saturday evening before the sunset, Neville Bassington was sitting in the parlour of his new home in Guildford, located on a street up behind the ruins of Guildford Castle. The view from the front porch was panoramic, over the town and the forested hills across the river. However, the rooms were practically empty except for Neville's sea chest, his medical bag and several tea chests of different sizes.

A limited number of candles throughout the house provided enough light for entertaining this evening. A makeshift bed and some old drawers purchased at the markets were in his bedroom. His most extensive piece of furniture was his sea chest which would suffice as the table. Fortunately, the lid was flat. The furniture he and Beth purchased the previous day would not arrive for another week. So, he was without a table, chairs or parlour furniture. For chairs, he positioned several tea chests that held his belongings.

He glumly looked around the room, thinking, "Why did I invite Beth here with Anne. This dinner will be a disaster!"

Despite his gloom, he was happy. The house was now theirs, finally a home that did not rock at night. Fifteen years in the navy was enough – it was time for settling, and he was ready for a medical practice in a growing town. The girl he would marry was now the love of his life. They would make this house a happy home once they set it up. It was just a silly notion entertaining here tonight.

The knock came before he expected them. He jumped up and went through and opened the front door. There before him stood Bethany, Anne, Thomas and James McPherson. The girls each carried small bags of utensils and bread; the boys had baskets filled with all sorts of food. Also, a sling over Thomas's shoulder contained two bottles of champagne.

"Welcome, everyone!" Neville kissed Beth and ushered them all in. "Please excuse my sparsely furnished abode. Draw up a box and candle. Please make yourself comfortable."

"Not yet, Neville!" Thomas suggested, "Firstly, while the champagne is still cold, I think we should toast your new home."

"Here, here!" James backed up Thomas' comments, "Lighter bottles – easier carrying them home."

Everyone laughed, and Thomas and Neville worked on opening the champagne.

There was another knock on the door. James took over Neville's bottle as he answered the door knock. Neville wondered who could this be?

Standing in the low light was a young woman about Beth's age with a light brown cape over travelling clothes. Behind her, outside the front gate, was a medium-sized coach with two groomsmen. Her eyes sparkled in the candlelight as she looked at him from under the cape hood. As she pulled back the hood and said his name, he recognised her.

"Emma, what are you doing here?"

"We are travelling home and staying the night in Guildford. Mother is in bed at the Fox and Hound, so I thought I would catch up with Anne. I checked at her home, but they kindly informed me she was here. So here I am!"

"This is wonderful!" Neville wondered how Emma would cope with boxes on the floor for seating.

"May I enter, Neville?"

"Of course, of course, come in, Emma."

Neville stood back and helped her through the doorway.

"We haven't moved in yet. I mean, I have, but Bethany lives at home."

"I know, Neville. Please relax as I am your friend remember."

"Sorry, Emma, I am embarrassed at all these people coming when all I can offer is wooden boxes for seating and mugs for drinking."

"Suits me, Neville – it will be fun."

"Emma, you are here!" cried Anne in joy. "We did not expect you tonight. We are enjoying the first meal served at Beth and Neville's house. Please, James, another cup for Emma before we make the toast."

Emma quietly said, "Anne! Who is James?"

"Of course. James McPherson, may I present Lady Emma South of Fintelton Manor."

"A pleasure Lady Emma. Please accept this delicate glass of champagne for the toast." He handed her an old mug, and they both laughed.

"Now, everyone!" Thomas could wait no longer. "Lady Emma, I am Anne's brother Thomas. I am sure she will introduce us after the toast. Now everyone, to Bethany and Neville's new house, may they have a lifetime of happiness here and may all their troubles be little ones!"

And with that, everyone said, "Bethany and Neville's new house!" They drank the toast and made three cheers, and then conversations broke out all around, interrupted by another knock at the door.

Neville smiled, "Perhaps this is Robert!" Anne turned immediately and said, "Is Robert here? I will answer the door."

"No, Anne, I jest! I could not think who else it could be. Let me answer the door." He shuffled off again.

On opening the door, he found a well-dressed young gentleman standing there. He was younger than Neville and shorter but had a pleasant smile.

"Yes?" Neville was not sure who this could be.

"I beg your pardon, Doctor Bassington. My name is Doctor David Sopwith, I have a practice in Guildford, and I have desired a meeting with you. I heard that you purchased this house and that you have taken possession. I was on my way home. My house is close, in fact, only five houses along the street!" He pointed in the direction.

"As I was saying, just on my way home from a house call. I saw the candlelight, so I thought I should introduce myself and welcome you. I hope I am not disturbing your dinner? Please excuse my intrusion."

Neville stood back and said, "Why Doctor Sopwith, you are very welcome. Come in and draw up a box!"

Doctor Sopwith smiled but looked at Neville curiously as he entered, "Draw up a box?"

"Yes, sorry, I should explain. On taking possession of the house yesterday, I moved in, as I am tired of sleeping at the back of my practice. So, once the wedding is over, Bethany will move in."

"Of course!"

"The furniture does not arrive until next Friday, so we are short of chairs. Tonight, we sit on boxes and drink champagne out of mugs. Please excuse this vulgarity, but there is no alternative."

"Ah, I see. If I had known, I would have arrived with some flutes."

"No need. We are content! Now please call me Neville. We are all at ease tonight and relaxed. Please come and meet the others."

"Please call me David. I have been hoping another doctor would settle here with whom I might discuss professional matters. After waiting two years, I am encouraged by your arrival."

Neville realised David was genuine in what he said and was pleased to make the acquaintance of another young doctor in Guildford. He thought, 'God works in mysterious ways!'

As they entered the parlour, David Sopwith was surprised by Lady Emma South sitting on a box and drinking champagne out of a mug.

He immediately stopped and bowed, "Lady South, this is a pleasant surprise. I had no idea."

Emma rose and blushed a little but quickly regained her countenance. She was pleased he had joined them.

"Doctor Sopwith! I was unaware you were acquainted with Doctor Bassington."

Neville twigged straight away and chipped in, "Old friend of mine!"

David Sopwith opened his mouth, but Emma spoke first, "In that case, Doctor Sopwith, I demand you call me Emma tonight amongst our friends, and if I might, I will call you David?"

"Certainly, Emma!" David Sopwith, for the first time in many weeks, relaxed slightly. The work of a country doctor was endless, and he was close to exhaustion. He drew up a box and sat with Emma and Anne.

"Emma, I have been with your father for two days!"

Emma suddenly was all attention, "Is he alright, David?"

"Yes, he has pulled through, but it was close this time. He will need ongoing care. It was a slight stroke, and the left side of his face seems paralysed, but he can still talk, which is quite a miracle. He will be fine given care."

"Thank you, Doctor, I mean David. That is a great relief. I shall tell my mother in the morning, and she will be so grateful. Please understand that we would have travelled on tonight but decided against it."

"Good decision – the roads are in poor condition and not safe at night between here and Petersfield. I'm not sure what they use the money from the Turnpike on?"

The conversation was lively for some time, especially as everyone was helping serve the dinner. It was a great time of fellowship for this group of young people with much laughter and fun.

David noticed Neville's bed in the master bedroom. As he was exhausted, he decided on testing it. After having two mugs full of champagne, he was asleep as soon as his head rested on the pillow. The girls missing his company were looking for him and found him several minutes later.

Emma looked down on a peaceful David fast asleep on Neville's bed.

She ventured, "He is rather cute, isn't he!"

Anne looked at her and could see she had eyes for this young man, "Yes, he is, and a nice young man as well. I wonder?"

Emma, with bright eyes, mouthed, "I think he likes me!"

"Lady Emma South. I'm not sure what I can say about that."

"You may say whatever a sister would say, Anne!"

"I think he would be a good husband, but you may not see much of him. He seems always to be busy."

With glowing eyes, Emma replied, "I might just work on that!"

At Guildford on Sunday ...

The Turner family returned from church, the marriage banns between Doctor Neville Bassington and Miss Bethany Turner having been read for a second time. Less than two weeks before the wedding, planning reached a fever pitch. Conversations were excited about the forthcoming wedding and celebrations.

William was keen on returning home as he felt the new puppy required a walk. He was waiting for a break in the conversation so he could ask his father's permission.

As they approached the Turner house, there was an unexpected lull. William spoke up, "Father, may Simeon and I take the puppy for a walk, please?"

Jonathan Turner's thoughts were on other things, and he readily agreed, on the condition they were back in time for lunch at twelve-thirty. The boys raced ahead into the house, picking up the happily shaking dog and rushing upstairs for a change of clothes.

Eleanora commented with a smile, "Seems to have done the trick!"

Jonathan nodded in agreement, "I should have thought of it earlier! Thank you, Anne, for initiating this."

Anne smiled and walked happily back toward the house. She was wondering where Robert was and if he was safe. She dreamed every night about seeing him again, but she knew it would not be until the wedding.

Changing their clothes quickly, the boys, followed by the yelping puppy, rushed downstairs, through the mudroom and out the back door. The dog remaining without a name made it difficult to train him. The boys thought this was a priority as his constant sniffing became a nuisance.

"Come on, boy!" William yelled as the dog stopped to smell something along the path. They headed for their riverside playground, deeply breathing as they ran together down the street. The day was warm, and some of the leaves were already changing colour in the magic of autumn.

Madeline and Marcia were most upset that the boys had left them behind. They complained bitterly to their mother, who was worn out by the church service and the necessary greetings of friends. Eleanora looked at Anne, who soon worked out the message.

"Madeline and Marcia, if you come upstairs with me and change your clothes, we shall visit the river after lunch!"

There were some cheers from the girls, and they scampered up the stairs. Anne followed as she would also change her clothes.

The boys sat on the riverbank, watching the puppy smell everything. The dog's sense of smell was already impressive, showing he was born a true hound. Every so often, putting his head inside some brush, he would jump back and then forward again with his head down, as some insect frightened him.

Simeon said, "See how he smells everything? Why not call him 'Nose'? What do you think?"

William sat there and thought about the suggestion. He liked this name, but it was missing something.

"Sounds good, but why not 'Nosey'. It sounds friendlier?"

"Yeah, I like that, 'Nosey'.

William heard a yell from down the river beside the Millmead lock. Several men were peering down at the water, and more people were gathering there. The boys being curious, decided they would join the crowd.

"Come on, puppy Nosey," called Simeon.

The puppy looked up and bounded after them. As the boys reached the lock, more people were gathering and pointing. At first, they found their way blocked by the crowd. Simeon and William looked for another way to reach the edge. Several of the town's folk told them not to look and go away. So, they crossed the bridge and quietly weaved through the crowd on the other side.

William gasped as he saw the body of a man floating face upwards, his lifeless grey eyes looking at the sky. He recognised the body at once. It was the older man who watched his house and who he had confronted on the night of the burglary.

Simeon noticed the shock on William's face.

William shuddered! There was no doubt in his mind. It was him!

Chapter 18

Peering over the edge of the lock, the Parish Constable noted the body of a medium height middle-aged man floating face upwards.

"Well, well, well!" He looked around at the growing crowd in displeasure. In a firm, loud voice, he asked, "Please, ladies and gentlemen, stand back! Now, who discovered the body?"

William and Simeon watched as the lockkeeper and another older gentleman approached the Constable. Knowing their father would be expecting them for lunch, Simeon grabbed William and pulled him away. Nosey, revelling amongst the smell of so many people and dogs, was somewhat reluctant. Simeon picked up the puppy and carried him as they started toward home. The expression on William's face said it all.

"Was it one of the burglars, Will?"

"Yep!"

William was very quiet, and Simeon did not press him further. At lunch, after saying grace and into the main course, Simeon mentioned, "We were at the river, Father, and there was a crowd at the lock. We saw one of the burglars lying face up and dead in the water. William recognised him!"

Jonathan Turner stopped eating immediately and sat there, stunned, "Dead in the lock?"

"Yes, Father!"

"Was the Constable there?"

"Yes – he was interviewing the people who found the body."

Jonathan would have commented further but stopped. If one of the burglars was found dead, he assumed that the Constable would be calling soon. He wondered whether the man died naturally or someone murdered him. Perhaps it was old age.

"It was an older man, was it?"

"Yes. I think William is upset about the body!" Simeon was a kind boy and tried gentle words that would not stir William's anger.

"I was not scared!"

Eleanora intervened quickly, "Any of us would be upset seeing that. The Constable should not have let you that near."

Simeon explained, "We pushed through so we could see. That was before Constable Rawlins got there."

Jonathan Turner felt the rage stirring in his body. Eleanora quietly put her hand under the table and onto his thigh and gently rubbed him.

"It is unfortunate that someone has died. Let us as a family say a prayer for the dead person, whoever he might be."

William moved beside his mother and buried his face on her shoulder. Eleanora put her free arm around the boy. William whispered loud enough so Jonathan could hear, "It was the old man who burgled the house."

"Dear me! Let us pray. We thank you, Lord, for all you provide for us. We pray that the man who died was found by You and repented of his sin before his death. We also pray for the boys that they may be comforted from this terrible scene they witnessed. In Jesus, Our Lord and Saviour's Name, we pray. Amen."

All the family gave a loud Amen, especially Marcia, who loved saying an Amen at the end of family prayers. She sat there with a big smile on her face.

At Fintelton Manor ...

The countess rushed up the stairs, followed by Emma. The butler briefed them as they hurried into the Earl's room. The eastern wing bedrooms were larger than usual standard with French doors and large double-hung windows, making the rooms light and airy. The doors leading onto a small balcony were open, and Lord Fintelton was sitting on a sofa gazing out towards the horizon. One of the maids was preparing his next round of medicines left by Doctor Sopwith.

Lady Jane spoke as she entered the room. "David, I came as soon as I could. We overnighted at Guildford as it was too dangerous to travel at night. How are you, my Dear?"

The Earl did not move but continued staring out of the window. Sally, the maid, standing beside Lady Jane, spoke softly, "Doctor Sopwith thinks that the stroke affected Lord Fintelton's hearing or an infection may have caused it. He is currently slightly hard of hearing. If you stand in front of him, his Lordship will see you. He can talk, my Lady, but there is a slight paralysis. Also, there is a vision loss in his right eye, so you should stand on the left."

"Thank you, Sally." Lady Jane stood between the Earl and the view. She said again in a loud voice, "How are you, David?"

The Earl recognised her. He smiled, but only half the face moved, and he slurred his words, "Still here, Jane!"

She sat beside him, kissing him on the cheek. Emma knelt in front of him, gently holding his hands which were slightly shaking.

From behind, Sir Hugh's booming voice broke into the quiet scene. "Should be dead! You should have seen him Friday morning. I thought he was a goner, but he pulled through again. I think it was Doctor Sopwith who got him through. He arrived Friday morning early, so he must have set off from Guildford around midnight. Must have been a hell of a journey. He stayed all Friday and right through the night until about eleven on Saturday. He never slept a wink! He's a good doctor, that one. Father should be dead, but Sopwith got him through. Sally and Barrett have been with him ever since. Sopwith is coming back on Monday and will be here overnight!"

Sir Hugh sat down on a settee, quite content with his summary.

Lady Jane sat there, ignoring the rude parts of Sir Hugh's story. It happened before with her father and mother, who died of a stroke. Her husband's condition brought all the memories back, and a couple of tears came. Emma could see that her mother was becoming emotional and suggested, "Mother, father is safe now. Would you like a rest or perhaps freshen up and then come back? I will stay with him and talk with Sally."

"No, Dear, I will stay with your father for a while. You come back a little later. Sally looks tired, as well. See if one of the other maids may assist. I must think about the care arrangements; nothing may be the same again! Poor David! Poor thing."

Emma approached a silent Hugh and indicated that he should follow her. They left the Earl and Countess holding hands and looking out the doors over the estate farmlands they had shared for the last forty years.

Emma and Hugh moved outside the room and closed the door. Emma turned and faced Hugh.

"Now Hugh, quietly please – what did the doctor say about father?"

"Sorry, I should have spoken softer! Yes, well, he said he was surprised that father made it through Friday night, and it will be touch and go for the next few weeks. That is why he is coming back tomorrow. He's not sure how serious it is. I think he suspects something a bit more sinister than he told us."

Emma shuddered. She dreaded the thought of losing her father now. She was unmarried, and if she married, she wanted him there at the wedding. That was the problem of being a child of older parents – they might not be around for that long.

"Hugh, we must do everything we can and ensure his recovery! Tomorrow, we meet with the doctor and ask how we can help."

Sir Hugh looked at Emma and mumbled something unintelligible under his breath.

Emma could not understand what he was saying, "What!"

Hugh gave a low grunt which sounded like a yes, and then turned and walked away.

Doctor Sopwith's House …

"Thank you for offering me breakfast this morning David, but there was no need. It is most kind of you!"

The two friends walked up the street and stopped outside David Sopwith's house.

"The pleasure is all mine. I must apologise for falling asleep at dinner last night. I was at Fintelton Manor, Emma's home, treating the Earl for a stoke. I arrived there early on Friday morning and spent the night. There was no time for any sleep! Left mid-Saturday morning and was on my way home when I came past your residence and saw the candlelight."

"I'm glad you came in. Now tell me, how is Lord Fintelton?"

"It is hard to say. To start with, I calmed the Earl down and made sure the blood was flowing well, as best I could. He was quite cold, so I warmed him up and gave him some laudanum hoping it would decrease his anxiety. The draft seemed to assist, and it also helped the blood flow. Bleeding was a possibility, but I'm not sure what you think. I only use bleeding as a last resort. From what I could ascertain, there was no blockage in the brain, but you can never be sure. He was stable when I left, but there was some paralysis and blindness on the right side, so I will return on Monday and stay the night."

"I understand why you are returning if there is paralysis. The blindness should disappear quickly, but the paralysis may take some time. I have found that a couple of weeks' rest and then an increasing exercise program works well but only gradually. Please give them my best wishes."

"Certainly. My recommendations will be the same as your suggestion. Only time will tell us how bad the stroke was." David stopped talking as if he was thinking deeply, then commenced again, "I say, Neville! Are you busy over the next few days?"

"Only preparing for the wedding. But most of that is being done by Bethany and her mother. Why, what have you in mind?"

"I will be at Fintelton for two days. Might I ask that you take care of my patients while I am away, please? I will provide a list of their details. I must revisit the Earl. You never know with a stroke – they either slowly mend or go downhill fast."

"Why certainly, I am not overrun with patients yet."

"Thank you – that is a great relief. Come in for breakfast and then church. What will Taggart's latest masterpiece be this week? He's getting better, you know, there has been a significant improvement in the last six months. He has been using notes from a seminar he did with this Simeon chap from Oxford."

"I've only heard him a couple of times, but I like Taggart. He has a good mind and an air of goodwill about him."

"I say, Mrs Lane, Hello Mrs Lane?" David called the housekeeper as they went in the front door.

"Yes, Sir!"

"I'm back for a quick breakfast, and I have Doctor Bassington with me. Some breakfast for the good doctor as well, please."

"Yes, Doctor Sopwith."

At the local Church ...

The service was over, and Jonathan Turner surveyed the church taking note of who was there. It appeared packed, and many conversations began as people caught up with friends. As usual, there was a long queue before reaching Reverend Taggart as he enjoyed the company of his departing parishioners.

Jonathan looked sideways, and Rupert Smith caught his eye from the row across from him. Jonathan maneuvered out around the women and shook hands with Rupert.

"Jonathan, I had the strangest meeting the other day with Sir Hugh South from Fintelton Manor. I thought I should advise you on it privately. Perhaps tomorrow morning at my office, we can talk discretely there. I have no early appointments. We should also resolve the replacement on Parish Council for Jeremy Stephens. I have a few suggestions. I thought a united position before the annual vestry meeting would be most helpful."

"Yes, Rupert, I agree on both counts. I will call in at, say, nine in the morning. Would that be a good time?"

"Yes, Jonathan, excellent. Taggart must be doing a good job as the church is full this morning! He has prepared my Richard well for the Free School. When Simeon is ready, he will succeed there. I am not so sure about William – perhaps the army or navy?"

Jonathan took the suggestion on board and smiled, "I see William in the natural sciences. Perhaps an explorer or the navy would be good. Who knows, he may be another Cook! "

"Here, here! What a great man Cook was, but hopefully William will come home safer than Cook[23], Eh!"

Jonathan smiled.

Neville and Bethany were catching up with David Sopwith before exiting the church. David shook Reverend Taggart's hand and took a moment with him.

---

[23] Captain James Cook, 1728 – 1779, a famous British naval explorer, who among many discoveries achieved the first recorded European contact with the east coastline of Australia and the first recorded circumnavigation of New Zealand. Wikipedia

"Good morning, Reverend. I was very interested in your sermon this morning on grace. I am not sure I understand it at all. Might we discuss the subject together at some time?"

Reverend Taggart appreciated the comment as he, too, struggled with the subject.

"David, I think Martin Luther[24] wrestled for some time with it as well. Drop around and see me when you have a moment, and I will point you in the right direction."

David Sopwith's enquiring mind required an answer backed by evidence before he would accept anything. He nodded and called back as he moved on, "I shall do that, Reverend Taggart. I shall do that. Good morning!"

Andrew Taggart then greeted Neville and Bethany, who were following David Sopwith.

"The banns have been read three times. We are ready now. No objections so far, so it seems that in two weeks, you shall be married."

Neville grinned, "I can't wait for the day. We shall be away three weeks on the honeymoon Reverend. So, once we return, I hope you and Mrs Taggart will join us for dinner in our new house?"

"Certainly. Now I shall let you know when the rehearsal for the wedding will be, but it will not be this week coming, but probably the Tuesday after. Say three in the afternoon."

"We shall be there, Reverend." Bethany was keen for the day as well. For her, the time was now dragging as all the arrangements were complete.

"Good, good. Good day to you both."

In the afternoon, the family took a basket of biscuits and pastries for their normal picnic activities at the river. Thomas and James led the way with the younger children while the puppy ran all around them. William had recovered from his issues with the dead burglar, and Jonathan Turner was surprised they saw nothing of the parish constable during the weekend.

The day was unusually warm for the first day in October. The wind gently blew in from the south, bringing the English Channel's warm air. A cloudless sky and a warm sun were perfect for relaxation and enjoying the river and its green banks.

Neville breathed in the fresh country air and sat beside Bethany, "I am so glad that we will settle here! Guildford is such a beautiful spot, especially along the banks of the Wey. I could linger here forever."

Bethany smiled, "Perhaps this afternoon, but I fear there will be plenty keeping you away from the river in the coming weeks. Especially with the next two days looking after Doctor Sopwith's practice. What about your

---

[24] Martin Luther, 1483 – 1546, a German professor of theology and a central figure in the Reformation. Wikipedia

practice Neville?"

"That will be fine! Having a medical practice with only four clients, I think I can afford the time. Also, working with David may be a blessing in disguise. You recall my suggestion about hiring a surgeon who would work with me here. While I am away at Harley Street in London, he would cover for me. I am treating this work with David as an experiment. I hope it might lead to a joint practice with him, an excellent solution for when I am away. He has a sound mind, and he is open to new methods. He shares the same plan I am envisaging for my practice."

Bethany considered this as Neville continued, "Times are changing. I think the days of a one-person practice doing rounds are nearly over. Some doctors will forge on, but I am sure joint practices will become the norm over time. Practices of three or four doctors may become common in the future. The benefits of sharing knowledge and mutual support far outweigh the downsides."

"Is that why you set up rooms away from the house? I was wondering!"

"Yes – just preparing for the future. I'm sure it will work. I hope David will find the proposition attractive. The longer I have known him, the more I am impressed! Pity he is not married."

"I think Anne and Emma may have some plans for that!"

Neville looked at the riverbank where Anne was chasing the little ones around with a stick sword, screams of joy coming from the escaping children. Marcia was hiding behind James McPherson's legs clinging on with all her might as she was discovered and then tickled by Thomas and collapsing in a giggling heap in the grass.

"I should have known! Anne and Emma did seem very friendly with David last night before he fell asleep."

"I think Emma is interested."

"I am surprised! I thought she would have higher ambitions. That news raises my opinion of Emma greatly. They would make a good couple. However, we best keep that quiet!"

Jonathan Turner sat on the other side of the picnic basket from Eleanora, tasting some biscuits.

"These are tasty biscuits if I do say so myself. I wonder why we have not heard back from the navy yet. Perhaps I should visit them."

"Jonathan, do you think the issues with the burglary are over? I mean, now that the Constable found the old man?"

"Eleanora, he was probably not that old, as I am assuming he was about the same age as me."

"He was in his late forties then?"

"Yes, I would assume so."

"Surely, with him gone, the other must have moved on. Now one of the burglars is found, it would be dangerous to remain."

"I think you are right, my Dear. I think the danger is over. Let us relax and enjoy the afternoon. Would you like a biscuit or pastry?"

"Not yet, Jonathan. Look at the fun the children are having with James. He is a pleasant young man, very down to earth and like Hamish. Remember when Hamish saw you knocked out by William. I think Hamish was influenced favourably towards you by that incident, Jonathan."

"Do you think William's actions helped?"

"Most certainly, they did. The accident revealed you as being far more human than Hamish previously noticed. People enjoy your true character."

"He must have missed something because I consider beating that boy most of the time! He is continually in trouble or getting someone else into trouble."

"I'm sure your father said the same about you, Jonathan!"

Jonathan, being somewhat sceptical, was waiting for the next emergency. It did not take long. William spinning his sword, an unusually large stick, cracked James just above his left eyebrow and blood poured out.

"Ouch!"

William quickly said he was sorry. James retreated and joined the Turners. Noticing the look of disgust on his father's face, William promptly escaped and rejoined the game. Jonathan said nothing and let the game go on.

Eleanora could see that James was not sure of the size of the cut, "Sorry about William doing that, James. Let me have a look at the cut, please?"

James moved over beside Eleanora. She carefully removed the handkerchief covering the cut.

"We are becoming experts in treating these. William has a knack for catching unsuspecting players."

She dabbed the handkerchief on the blood and cleaned it up, instructing James that he keep the pressure on it.

"There is no harm done, Mrs Turner. I have suffered far worse from my brothers in earlier times. Boy's games sometimes get rough. William will be good with a sword one day."

"Mr Turner thinks he is bound for the navy."

James smiled. Then Neville arrived and took a closer look at the cut.

"Good thing it was not lower. You may have lost your eye. This scratch will need a couple of stitches, James and a bandage. Come with me, and I'll stitch you up at my surgery. We will be back in five minutes."

On their return, Anne smiled, "Now you look like a real pirate James!"

Eleanora decided it was a good time for afternoon tea and handed out biscuits and pastries while the curious children walked around James commenting on the bandage. James was uncomfortable being the centre of attention and started tickling Marcia. She twisted and turned and ended up in his lap.

"We will be sorry when you go tomorrow, James. Are you headed straight for Glasgow?"

"Yes, Thomas! It will be a journey of nearly two weeks."

"What is your role there?" Anne was interested in finding out what James did.

"This and that. Mostly brewing and the importation of grains."

"Why bring in grain when there are farms up there?"

"The farmers are not as productive as down here, and there is competition for the local supply. We can purchase at a lower price from the south of England. Our fleet of ships transports the grain and mostly lands it at Glasgow. When we complete the brewery in Guildford, we will ship it by barge from Woolwich to Guildford."

Anne understood this. She wondered what a young man whose parents lived in Greenwich would do alone in Glasgow.

"Do you live with your brothers up there?"

"No, my elder brother Douglas is married and has a wife and children, so they have a full life. I often see them and keep myself active when I'm not working. There is plenty to do, and I'm regularly meeting with my father in Greenwich."

"What about your other brothers?"

"Archie and Lachlan are both in Edinburgh with their families."

Anne was satisfied, and Eleanora passed her some biscuits and a pastry. The family sat back and talked for the rest of the afternoon, with the younger children often jumping up and running off and then returning. At about four-thirty, the family packed up and returned home.

As James stood, he swayed and nearly fell back down. Neville steadied him and asked, "Are you not well, James?"

"Just a bit giddy."

"Ah, probably the knock. Let's get you home and keep an eye on you overnight. Just in case!" Jonathan and Thomas walked either side of him, guarding against the giddiness returning.

Neville quietly spoke with Beth, "That's strange. I am surprised he is giddy."

On Monday morning, James left for the stables before light. He gave his farewells the night before, explaining he must be away early. Neville also rose early, wanting a final check on James's condition. Leaving home, Neville ventured directly to the stables.

Walking around the corner of the inn, he found James talking with a short, thick-set gentleman with a long coat. As he approached, the gentleman saw Neville coming, quickly spoke with James, turned and walked away. James looked up and welcomed Neville with a smile.

"James! All ready?"

"Yes. I need an early start. The distance is long today."

"Where will you change horses?"

"Henley-on-Thames, then on to Oxford."

"You will be tired tonight. How is that cut above the eye? Have you had any dizzy spells this morning?"

"No, right as rain. I am fully recovered but thank you, Neville, for your concern."

"Good. Might I enquire who that chap was you were talking with?"

"Ah," James paused as he thought, "A chap from the stables about the carriage. A slight repair was required yesterday before we set off. All set now!"

"Good! Shall we see you at the wedding?"

"I'm afraid not, Neville. I will not arrive in Glasgow until the Thursday before your wedding. I will return on one of our ships in November. I wish you and Beth the very best, of course."

"Thank you, James. Now just in case that cut causes you trouble, I brought you a jar of ointment. If it becomes sore, then you probably will have an infection. Just rub on this ointment morning and night, and it should heal."

"Thank you, Neville, it is much appreciated. Now I must be off as the coach is waiting. All the best."

James hopped up into the coach, closed the door behind him, and settled into the seat.

"Drive on!"

The coach slowly moved away up the lane and into High Street. James nodded as it rolled past, and Neville gave a small wave. He watched as it headed up the High Street and then approached a stable hand walking across in front of him.

"I say, boy! Who makes all the arrangements for coaches housed here?"

"That be Mr Jacks, Sir. There he is over there!"

Neville looked in the direction the boy was pointing and saw Mr Jacks across the courtyard. He was a tall thin man wearing a hotel uniform.

"Would he arrange all repairs for the coaches?"

"Yes, Sir, everything."

Neville thought perhaps he would confirm James's comment. He walked across and introduced himself.

"Mr Jacks, that coach that just left. The McPherson coach! Did it have any repairs yesterday?"

"Why no, Sir. It was in perfect condition. She was ready this morning, and a fine coach it was, Sir."

"Thank you, Mr Jacks."

Neville was somewhat surprised. The two stories were opposites. James's explanation did not ring true, and who was the man standing with him?

At the surgery, he found Constable Rawlins waiting. The Constable, walking backwards and forwards in front of the surgery door, appeared deep in thought.

"Ah, Doctor Bassington. Good morning, Sir!"

"Good morning, Constable! To what do I owe this pleasure?"

"Doctor, it appears Doctor Sopwith is off at Fintelton Manor, and you have the responsibility for his patients today and tomorrow. Doctor Sopwith often assists in our law enforcement work here at Guildford. We found a dead man in the canal yesterday, and I have stored his body at the undertakers. He is unknown in this town, but I am quite sure that he is one of the men who robbed Mr Turner's house. Would you please examine the body and confirm the cause of death and my suspicions! The Hundred Committee[25] meets this afternoon, and I must let them know."

"Certainly, Constable Rawlins, come into the surgery. I must fetch my bag, and then we are off."

Neville stopped, "You said suspicions! What do you suspect?"

"Doctor, I am no physician, but I know stab wounds when I see them."

"Stab wounds!"

At the Turner House …

Marcia burst into the boys' room and found William and Simeon still asleep. She knew Thomas would be at the bakery, but James' bed was also empty.

Marcia shook Simeon by the arm until one eye opened.

"Where is James?"

Simeon opened the other eye, rolled over and sat up in bed. He rubbed his eyes and then looked at Marcia again. She grew impatient.

"Where is he?"

"James has left for Scotland!"

Marcia stamped her foot and left the room. She ran down the stairs and went straight into Anne and Bethany's room.

"Anne, Thomas is at work, and James is in Scotland."

Anne opened her eyes and looked at Marcia.

"What are you doing up so early little one?"

"I wanted a wrestle with James. He's a good tickler!"

Anne pulled Marcia into bed with her and cuddled her. Then another hand suddenly tickled Marcia under her arm, and she screamed with laughter. Beth

---

[25] The Hundred Committee relates back to the Statute of Winchester of 1285 which revived the jurisdiction of local courts. A hundred is an administrative division that is geographically part of a larger region. Wikipedia.

tickled her again as she wriggled in Anne's arms.

"We have an energetic one here, don't we? Come on, we shall go downstairs, and you can have some breakfast and do a drawing."

Jonathan looked up from his breakfast as Bethany and Marcia entered.

"Morning, Father. You are up early! Are you going out?"

"Yes, I have business at the mill, then at the mayor's office at nine. After that, I will be home as there is much correspondence to answer. Thomas will be home later, as he and I must discuss several issues affecting the bakery and the mill. It will be a busy day."

"Father, I know you are busy, but please consider the need for another maid for mother. With all the work you do, my marriage in two weeks, and Anne working at the bakery, there will not be enough help. We need the maid soon, as mother's health is not improving!"

"You are right, Beth, and I will have Robinson's men here today working on the house. They will build the new storeroom and an additional maid's room. I will put it on my list for today."

Bethany nodded and then took care of Marcia as Jonathan Turner wiped his mouth and left for the bakery.

At the mill, all was quiet. Jonathan took the opportunity and did a quick walking tour before the engineers started for the day. The mill appeared finished. The engineers had fully installed the engine, and preparations for testing were underway. Jonathan smiled as this would be the result of two years' work and investment. Once this mill was operational, they would have an endless supply of low-cost flour for their bakery.

He next walked through the bulk store and then the bakery. At his desk, he commenced some planning, and as he delved deeper, he lost track of time.

Anne arrived and sat down at the next desk. "Morning, Father, I thought you were seeing the Mayor this morning? "

Hearing Anne's question, Jonathan realised he would be late. He saw on the clock that it was eight fifty-five, five minutes before he was due at the mayor's office.

"Thank you, Anne; I am nearly late. I must go."

Rushing, he put his coat on and thanked Anne again for reminding him and strode off up the High Street. On his way, he passed Neville.

"Morning, Jonathan!"

"Morning!"

"I say, could we talk? I have just examined the burglar's body!"

Jonathan stopped.

"Neville, I'm sorry, but I am late for a meeting. Perhaps I can call on you after lunch. Would that be convenient?"

"Better make it around four in the afternoon at my practice. I have a full day with David Sopwith's patients. Sorry about that."

Jonathan was out of time, so he agreed, bid him farewell, and marched towards the mayor's office.

Mayor Rupert Smith was waiting and offered him refreshment. Jonathan was craving a coffee and accepted the offer.

"Jonathan, as I mentioned at Church, I met Sir Hugh South for lunch last week. During our meeting, the questions he asked were very pointed! He inquired specifically about you and your family, business interests, and new mill."

"That is strange as we have no dealings with him!"

"Of course, I gave him a glowing report on your family and how the Council fully supports your new mill."

"Thank you, Rupert."

"Jonathan, I would be careful if I were you. He will become the next Earl of Fintelton and, with his large landholdings, will negotiate hard for a good grain price. He will also exert influence on his tenant farmers. I find the chap a bit hard to stomach. His reputation is not good. He is forthright and shows none of the manners of his father. So, if you are planning negotiations with Sir Hugh, you may find it hard going."

"I understand what you are saying, Rupert. Our aim is not to put anyone out of work or restrict competition. Certainly, with the sales growth, we are experiencing, there will be a requirement for more grain. Most of our grain comes from the west, but I would not be averse if the grain was available closer and at a reasonable price."

"Jonathan, at least he knows of your good standing in the community!"

"Thank you, Rupert. Now about this nomination for the Parish Council. I was wondering if we should approach that attorney, Mr Stewart. He is regularly at church, and people speak well of him. He would also add some skills that we do not have presently."

Rupert and Jonathan spent the next half hour talking about various candidates, and in the end, they agreed they should meet again with Reverend Taggart. Jonathan was glad when the meeting finished as the morning mail awaited him. He was expecting correspondence from the agents in London who were searching for his new Mill Manager.

The Turner Bakery ...

Standing by her desk, Anne tidied her hair while talking with Audrey Stern about more storage room. They were facing the rear of the building, and turning around, Anne found Robert on the other side of her desk, facing her with a broad smile.

"Got time for some lunch with an old friend?"

The whole world stopped for Anne; there in front of her stood a smiling Robert. She flew into his arms and hugged him so tight, making sure he was real.

Anne whispered, "Robert, Robert!"

He put his arms around her and hugged her tight. All the young women in the room stopped work and enviously watched. It was an emotional scene as Anne continued hugging Robert.

Her beautiful hair was under his chin, and he could smell the familiar sweet scent she used. Closing his eyes, he just breathed it in and enjoyed the moment. Then, opening his eyes, he felt the silent smiling watch from all corners of the room.

"I say, Anne, perhaps we should move along?" He gave a wink, and they all gave happy grins back.

"Where have you come from, Robert? I thought you were at sea!"

"The Admiralty required my presence in London, and I stopped here on my way back for a quick visit. Haven't much time as the coach leaves by four bells! Sorry I meant two o'clock. If we go to the Fox and Hound now, we can have lunch together."

"Yes – let's do that." Anne quickly organised her things and briefed Audrey on the next few jobs.

"Let's go!"

Robert said carefully, "Just one thing before we go. May I purchase a couple of tins of the biscuits, please? I will have a friend with me soon, an acquaintance of yours who is most partial and would enjoy a supply of Turner's biscuits."

Anne smiled and gathered three tins of biscuits in a brown hessian bag, "With the compliments of the Turner bakeries! Tell Horace not to eat them all at once!"

Not forgetting the office staff, Robert gave a friendly wave as they left.

Walking up High Street at its busiest time, they faded into the crowd. Although Robert was in uniform, he took off his navy hat, so they disappeared amongst the foot traffic.

"My father is in poor health, so I stop at Fintelton tonight. I made sure we left early this morning for enough time for this lunch. A lot is happening at present, so I wanted a few hours with you to talk about the things that matter."

"I am sorry about your father. Emma visited on Saturday night and told me. Robert, you have a bandage on your hand! What happened?"

"Just an incident onboard ship. It will be better by the time of the wedding. How are Neville and Bethany?"

"They are having an exciting time! The furniture for their house arrives on Friday. Neville will prefer a real bed to a straw mattress on the floor. Robert, there is so much to tell. I don't know where to start."

"How about at the beginning! Did dinner go well with Emma? I stayed with her at `Harting' in London. I understand the dinner changed from our original plan, but Emma said she likes you!"

"What is this `Harting' you mention? A hotel?"

"No. It is the family residence at St James's Square in London."

"Oh!"

Robert was so intent on talking he missed looking ahead. He bumped straight into a man walking quickly. Luckily the man saw him in advance and put his hands on Robert's shoulders, gently stopping him. Robert looked up in surprise!

"I'm sorry .... Neville!"

"Robert, what are you doing here?"

"I was passing through on my way back from London and thought I would make a quick stop."

"And spend some time with Anne, I see!"

Robert blushed and was short of words for a moment. Anne took up the conversation.

"We were going for some lunch, Neville. Will you join us?"

"I was having a break between patients and thinking about a quick lunch at the Dart coffee house. I know you both like the Fox and Hound, but the Dart serves a faster lunch. Why not dine together there, and then I will leave you alone. Probably be a good idea if I act as a chaperone. Ha, Ha!"

Robert saw his point at once. He always found himself so relaxed in Anne's company that he forgot their society's requirements.

"Good thinking Neville! Sorry Anne, I forgot about etiquette. Let's go with Neville and try a new place."

Anne smiled, took both their hands, and led the way across the street.

She laughed and said, "Gentlemen, I feel protected against the possibility of any vulgar rumours starting!"

The dining room of the Dart was quiet, allowing some intimate conversation. Neville was still puzzled over his meeting with James McPherson in the early morning and mentioned it.

"I will be seeing your father this afternoon Anne. Perhaps he knows who the man was."

Robert listened with more interest than Anne thought he should, "Is this the son of Hamish McPherson?"

"Yes, I found the fellow's company particularly amicable until this morning, when his story differed from the stable manager's."

"Perhaps he was confused!"

"But who was the man he was talking with, and why not introduce him?"

Anne thought about it and remembered her feelings when she first met the McPhersons in Greenwich. She had cleared her mind of these thoughts and would avoid returning there if possible.

"As far as I know, the McPhersons are upright, good citizens. Perhaps, we should not ask about them any further!"

"True," said Neville, "but I will discuss it with your father. He may know more. Now I must leave you two. It would probably be better if you escorted Anne home, Robert. That would look better!"

Robert agreed, and they made their separate ways onto the High Street.

As Neville went off towards his surgery, Robert asked, "Now Anne, have you become friends with Emma?"

"Of course, Robert. She is very dear to me, and I spent some time with your mother. I think she likes me. We did a tour of the town, and they spent a lot of time at Hursts."

"What is Hursts?"

"It's my parents' chain of Tailors and Dressmaking Stores! Neville's wedding suit is coming from there! I understood you would be wearing your navy uniform."

"Yes, I will be wearing my uniform, but I could use a new one for the wedding. Perhaps if I sent an old one to your home, you might arrange for this Tailor's shop to fit me out for the wedding?"

"Send it as soon as you reach Portsmouth. I am sure they will have it ready in time – but it may require a final fitting."

"So, you will join me at Fintelton next July?"

"Yes, I feel more confident about it now. Emma and I are planning a dinner party in Guildford. I think she has feelings for Doctor Sopwith."

"I am surprised." Robert thought about this for a few moments. "Good on her! It would be quite a move from our society and will not make the parents happy. Yet, I am encouraged that our plan worked well, except for the burglary. I was greatly worried when I heard about it. Ah, but look at the time. I must be off."

"But Robert, there is so much we need to discuss. I wish we had more time together!"

"The wedding is in two weeks, and I will be here most of that week. So, there will be plenty of time then. I'm afraid there are many more pressing issues now. I pray our plan for next July holds firm, Anne. We will visit the Isle of Wight, and you shall see the ocean. Time will pass quickly, and we shall be there before you know it!"

"The plans are firm, Robert, but it will be long before it happens. Please tell Emma I miss her company and give my regards to your mother. I hope your father is in good health when you arrive at Fintonten?"

"Fintelton! Don't worry; you will pick it up eventually." Robert smiled.

He took her hand and kissed her forehead, "I shall pass your regards on. I shall be back in less than two weeks, Anne!" With that, he was off back down High Street towards the Fox and Hound. She stood there watching as he walked away, disappearing amongst the crowd. Anne wondered if that was what it would be like being the wife of a ship's Captain! Sighing, she turned for home.

The Turner Household ...

William Turner was home from school and found the kitchen empty. He whispered, "Now's our chance for some biscuits!" Then he remembered that Sim was upstairs. The opportunity was too attractive, and he was hungry. Aggie would not serve afternoon tea for a half-hour yet, so he decided not to wait.

William tiptoed into the butler's pantry, made himself comfortable on a stool, and removed the biscuit tin lid. He took a biscuit and started munching it. The container was balanced on his lap when his father suddenly appeared around the corner.

The family rule was that no one was allowed in the butler's pantry except Mrs Jennings and Aggie. Some family members were allowed in during meal preparation if they were helping, but the helpers should eat nothing.

William looked up, and seeing his father, he dropped the tin of biscuits, spilling them onto the floor and ran. A hand with a grip of iron grabbed his arm, and an angry voice said, "Everyone in the family knows the rules. You should have waited until it was time. Now, boy, outside. You know the punishment."

Jonathan Turner kept his grip on the boy's arm and took him onto the back verandah. There he loosened his belt and commenced strapping the young lad on the legs. The rage overwhelmed Jonathan and rose through his body, and he started enjoying the young lad's screams. What should have been two or three straps of the legs turned into ten and then onwards. Blood poured down the child's legs as he screamed in pain. Jonathan Turner could not escape the memory of the boy peering into his bedroom as he slapped his wife into submission. His rage took over his body until a firm hand grabbed his arm from behind.

"Enough, Jonathan, Enough!" Neville Bassington fumed as he held Jonathan's arm with all his might.

Jonathan stopped and glanced into Neville's eyes. The man was in a trance, and Neville realised it was not the Johnathan that he knew. He was shaking and unaware of his surroundings, as if some demon was in control of his body.

William fell on the floor, crying and feeling his legs covered in strap cuts. He whimpered as he lay on the floor with Nosey carefully approaching and then licking William's face.

Neville shook Jonathan, breaking him out of the trance. Jonathan's eyes tried focusing, but he was still not seeing correctly. Then the focus returned, and the stiffness in Jonathan's body became relaxed. Seeing Neville facing him and gripping his arm, he seemed surprised. When he noticed the blood-stained belt he was holding, he dropped it on the floor.

Neville could see that Jonathan was under control again, and he loosened his grip.

"Where did you come from, Neville?"

"I finished with my last patient, so I thought I would walk up here and save you the trip. It seems just in time! Did you know what you were doing, Jonathan?"

"I was punishing William for stealing biscuits. He must learn there is a reason for the rules."

"Jonathan, turn around and look at what you have done to your son!"

Jonathan Turner stood there looking at Neville as if not understanding the words. Neville gently turned him around. Jonathan looked down and saw the boy lying whimpering on the verandah floor with blood pouring from the cuts on his legs. The doctor then knelt beside William and lifted him, taking him into the kitchen.

As he passed Jonathan, he said, "I will come and see you after I have bandaged William."

Neville sat the boy down on a stool, "Don't worry, Will; I am an expert at this. Plenty of practice from the navy. This salty water may hurt a bit as I bathe the cuts. That will mend them in no time."

William sat there, shaking. Once again, Neville saw one of Jonathan's children going into shock. This time by the hand of his father.

"Beth, Beth, bring a blanket!"

Jonathan Turner sat at his desk in his study. Mrs Jennings brought him a cup of tea, not saying a word as she delivered it. She was afraid of this man. Jonathan sat still, blankly gazing into space.

Neville Bassington realised for the first time that Jonathan was mentally sick. He must find the cause so he might cure Jonathan. A beating like this must never happen again. Beth quietly discussed it with him some time ago, but he thought little of it until now. Witnessing the treatment of the boy and the evil look on Jonathan's face confirmed there was something wrong.

He knocked on the study door and went in. Neville spoke as a doctor and not as a prospective son in law.

"Jonathan, what came over you, my friend?"

Jonathan sat there in silence and looked at his cup of tea. Then he looked up at Neville and said, "Close the door, Neville!"

Neville moved across and closed it. He then picked up a chair and sat down opposite Jonathan.

"This conversation is on a doctor and patient basis. I don't want you talking about it with my family."

"That may be difficult now that you have beaten William here in your home with them present!"

"You can use your discretion Neville, but this must remain mostly between you and me."

"Agreed!"

"My father was a strict disciplinarian. He kept us under control. Richard was beaten the most, but I received my fair share. Over the years, he beat us so much that I hated him and waited for my opportunity of revenge. The chance never came with him, but I found my opportunity at school.

There were several bullies at my school who all strived for dominance. Because I was a baker's son, a lower class of society, I was in line for much verbal abuse. From day one, it was continual. I was small and a target. It happened all too often. I loved the school but hated the bullies.

One day a big student twice my size abused me. He was not aware that I had worked as a manual labourer in the bakery since I was eight. I was as strong as an ox. I was also agile and could outfight anyone I met on the streets. Unfortunately, I also had a temper. On this day, it broke. I turned on this fellow, and he never knew what was coming. If not for the other boys pulling me off, I would have killed him. The problem was that once I started, I enjoyed it. It seems that I cannot stop once my rage ignites. I cannot control it." Tears formed in Jonathan's eyes.

He stopped for a moment, calming himself, and took a long breath. Neville knew more was coming.

"Since then, I have struggled with it all my life. There have been several incidents where I have beaten people to have my way. My worst grievance is that I have often beaten my wife, making her submit to my will. I am now ashamed of it, but I enjoyed it at the time. The rage takes over, and I am another person."

Jonathan stopped and gulped some tea. They both sat in silence.

Neville brushed the hair back out of his eyes, remembering he needed a haircut. He looked at Jonathan with his depressed posture and his sorrowful face. The man was sorry for his actions. At least he realised there was a problem. Finding a cure would take time. In the interim, Neville must put in place safeguards.

"Jonathan, you have a problem with the mind. It is not a separate thing 'your rage!' It is you. You decide on your actions, and speaking about this rage as if it is someone else has taken over your body is your imagination. You can overcome this. But I need time to decide on the best treatment.

You and I must agree on some changes that will protect your family. You must reside separately in a room of your own from now on. You will not sleep beside Eleanora until we cure your problem. If you attacked her and lost control, you might kill her. I am sorry, but I must protect your family against this happening.

Secondly, read a chapter of Proverbs every day, first thing in the morning. Think about the moral rules set out in that book. Think about the decisions you must make and the actions you should carry out in honouring these guiding principles. You may think they are outdated, but I can assure you they are as relevant now as when Solomon wrote them. Write them on your mind, and as you practice them, they will become a joy for you.

Also, each day you must repeatedly say, 'My rage is myself. I will control it!' You must say this several times a day. As often as you recall it."

Jonathan looked at him and nodded in agreement.

"But right now, Jonathan, you must apologise to William for what you have done. I will come with you!"

"But he broke the rules!"

"They are dammed stupid rules if they result in you giving your son a disability through a beating! We are only talking about a few biscuits!" Neville lost his temper and then restrained himself. "Jonathan, this is your son. Your flesh and blood. He is someone you should cherish. He is your family's future."

Jonathan looked up in pain and spoke in a low voice, "He will be the end of me, that boy. I will not apologise. His penalty matched his disobedience."

Neville could see that Jonathan held a deep resentment towards this child, which was illogical. Jonathan refused to understand how severely he had beaten his son. He covered the memory with a blanket in his mind and could no longer see it. Despite his lack of training for mental problems, Neville realised that Jonathan must understand now that others were aware of what he had done. There was no hiding the issue now – it was public.

Neville sat back in his chair, considering his next move. There was a danger here – if Jonathan's rage were let loose again without him knowing the implications, no one would stop him. He might kill the next person. Jonathan must be stopped now.

"Jonathan, I am worried that you may lose your temper again with William. If that happens, I will have no choice but to consult outside of this family, and much of the matter will become public. This revelation would not be good for your reputation Jonathan or your businesses. Now, I want an assurance from you that you will comply with what I have asked."

Jonathan Turner rubbed his eyes and sat up straight.

"I see you are giving me an ultimatum?"

"Yes, I am! Jonathan! We can cure your sickness together. You may no longer avoid the reality of the situation. Presently, you are a risk to your family and the public, and I cannot let that continue. If you refuse, I will have no choice other than to find an institution and admit you until you demonstrate you are free of this sickness. The process I have recommended must start straight away. Now let's go upstairs and see William. Now is when he needs his father, not tomorrow or the next day. This little boy needs his father now, just as much as you need him!"

Jonathan trembled and rubbed the tears out of his eyes. He stood up and followed Neville. He found Beth and Anne talking gently with a shaking William wrapped in a blanket.

Jonathan kneeled beside the bed, and the girls moved aside a little but not too far. They feared what he might do next. William backed along the bed away from him. He was petrified.

"William, I am very sorry for what I did!"

Beth and Anne looked up at Neville in utter amazement, but Neville put a finger up to his mouth.

Jonathan breathed in deeply, "I lost control, William. I am very sorry for this and ask your forgiveness. I shall never do this again."

A small voice murmured back, "Yes, Father."

"Thank you, William!"

With that, Jonathan stood up and left the room. Neville watched as Jonathan walked along the hallway and down the stairs.

Beth looked up at Neville, "I have never seen him apologise to anyone before! What did you say that achieved this?"

Neville came into the room and looked at William, warmly rugged in a blanket and yawning.

"Just settle William down now for a rest. He will be fine for a while. Then come downstairs, and I will speak with you both there."

William lay down but grunted as he moved his legs. Soon the need for sleep settled him, and the girls headed downstairs.

Neville explained the conversation with Jonathan without revealing all the details, "He has a condition of the mind that suppresses his control and ignites his rage. I have seen it in sea captains before and other people of authority. In Jonathan's case, it can become quite severe and violent. But I am sure it is curable, and he will be capable of controlling it in the future."

Beth and Anne could relate to Jonathan's behaviour over the years, which matched what Neville was saying.

"The problem is that left unchecked; the consequences could be fatal. It is quite severe in this case with William, but I am afraid of what would have resulted if I had not accidentally found and stopped him. William may have lost both his legs."

Neville explained his discussions with Jonathan and the safeguards he was putting in place. He also explained the importance of the household remaining stable and not agitating him.

"At this time, he will be full of remorse and needs support. We can cure him, I'm sure, but it will take a long time and a lot of love. Now I must go and brief your mother. Perhaps you girls could visit his study and reassure him of your love for him. I'm sure he is quite safe now."

Bethany and Anne looked at each other and gulped.

"Into the Lion's Den!" Beth smiled at Anne with unsure eyes.

Neville saw their reluctance, "He is now feeling very alone and scared about the future. Your love for him will mean everything."

Anne stood up and started walking downstairs, and Beth kissed Neville and followed.

Anne knocked and went in at the study door, finding Jonathan sitting, looking down at his trembling hands. She knelt in front of him. Jonathan continued staring at his hands.

"I have done a terrible thing, Anne, and I am very ashamed!"

Anne put her hands on his knees and then took hold of each of his hands.

Looking into his wet eyes, she said, "Father, remember when I did bad things, and you punished me. I knew I had done wrong; I knew you should punish me, and I cried so much because of my shame. But there was something more important. When the punishment was over, and I stood there crying and hurting, you would always gather me up in your arms and tell me how much you loved me. That's how I understood what real love was.

Father, you have a sickness, and it has caused some of these outbursts. But Neville knows he can cure this rage thing. You will get better."

The tears poured down Jonathan Turner's cheeks. Anne had never seen her father cry before. His shame overcame him.

"Father, we all love you. We forgive you. We want you cured, and we will help you get well. You are our father, and we are your children, and we love you so much."

Anne leaned forward and hugged her father tight. He, in turn, held her and wept as he had never before. Beth came in and joined, hugging them both.

"We love you so much, Father. We will help you become well!"

Chapter 19

After an early morning start from Fintelton Manor, the coach finally reached Portsmouth by mid-afternoon. Robert stopped at an Inn by the quayside and ordered a late lunch. He needed sustenance before joining his ship and checking the morale on board. While enjoying a well overdue meal, he pondered the crew members. If any traitors were left, they were probably keeping a low profile.

Having finished his lunch, he found an available naval cutter and quickly commandeered it.

As the crew raised the sail and cast off, Robert noticed several new arrivals anchored in the harbour, including a first-rate with a commodore's flag flying. He enjoyed the cold spray on his face and the feel of the stiff wind in his hair. Sailing between the ships, he spotted another first-rate, three second-rates and some frigates at anchor down the harbour. It seemed quite a fleet was in for replenishment.

Robert shaded his eyes and searched for HMS *Providence*. She was due in, but there was no sign of the frigate. He would meet with Captain Foster before the wedding and talk tactics for his upcoming mission. Hopefully, the frigate would be back in port before he left for Guildford.

The cutter headed around the rear of the first-rate. Robert saluted the officer of the watch, who peered down from the massive bulk of the ship, that towered above. A young officer he did not recognise returned his salute and smiled. Robert looked on and saw *Restless* about five hundred yards south. He was relieved on seeing his ship and impressed with the amount of work going on aboard. It appeared the Master followed his advice and kept them all busy.

Restless was a large schooner looking more like a small frigate with fore and main masts, square-rigged and a mizzen mast with a gaff-rigged spanker. She was built by the French and captured late in the previous century and with a refit only some five years ago. She looked fast and clean, the way a small fighting ship should be. Robert thought, "Ah, the French, they possessed great skills in designing a pretty ship that sailed well. Good thing their sailors were not as good as ours!"

As the cutter came alongside, he threw a rope, and a sailor pulled up his bag. Robert leapt across and scampered up her side, jumping onto the quarter deck.

"Mr Trotters, you have been keeping the men very productive. *Restless* is looking well-groomed!"

"Thank you, Captain. Welcome back, Sir."

"Glad I'm back! All quiet while I was away?"

"Not a peep out of them, Sir!" Trotters looked around and lowered his voice. "Mind you; we are in port, Sir. It may be different when we are back at sea."

Robert immediately knew what Trotters meant. He, too, was still unsure of the crew.

"Sir, I have word that Mr Small's replacement will arrive this afternoon. A Lieutenant Frederick Ham."

"That was quick. Where did you get word from?"

"It came from Commodore Jacobs at Fleet Headquarters."

Robert was disturbed by this as he expected some input into the selection process himself. But the Admiral must have sorted this out, with Jacobs ensuring a quick transfer. That would make sense, as the Admiral knowing of Robert's involvement in the wedding, would provide a capable First Officer who could keep tabs on the situation. He assumed the man was well experienced.

"Thank you, Trotters. Carry on!"

"Excuse me, Sir, but there is a Captain Horace Coombes in your cabin. He will be Captain of the Marines. Swanton is making him comfortable."

"Excellent Trotters, he is early. We will have a double number of marines on our next voyage. Coombes is a fine soldier. Just what we need."

"Aye, Sir." Trotters had a knowing grin on his face.

With that, the captain headed below. Pushing open the door, he found Horace sitting at his desk reading a report.

Captain Coombes rose, nearly knocking his head on the low cabin roof, "Ah Squire, good to see you!"

"And you too, Horace, you are a welcome sight, believe me!"

"I was reading your report, Squire. Jacobs arranged for a copy. You had a busy time during your first few weeks aboard!"

Robert smiled as Swanton came into the cabin.

"Welcome back, Captain. I'm glad there will be two of us entertaining Captain Coombes now, Sir. Not an easy task! Coffee Sir?"

Horace smiled, innocently saying, "Now then, Michael, I have behaved very well in the last two hours. Time for some navy coffee!"

Robert laughed as he saw the close relationship between Horace Coombes and his Sergeant.

Swanton raised his eyebrows, "Coffee, Sir?"

"Yes, thanks, Swanton. Horace, your Sergeant Swanton is a one-person army! He saved my life last week, and I will be eternally thankful for his assistance. Where did you find him?"

"In the Army, we train them well, Squire. Taught him everything he knows, Ha Ha. But I think his agility must have come from his parents. Ha, Ha."

"He has served with distinction here. Ah, I see you have brought the crossbows!"

"Thought we might get some practice in before our next hunt, Squire."

"Strange thought indeed! These may prove most useful if an attack by stealth is required. Have you read the report? Swanton, close that cabin door, please!"

Swanton moved across the cabin like a cat, had a good look outside and closed the door. He nodded at Robert, indicating that there was no one outside. He then disappeared into his servants' room and prepared the coffee.

"Horace, I am alive, thank God! They damned well nearly took me out. These Irish traitors are very good at what they do. They must have a strong network that produces the number of men I was up against last week. After the wedding, we are heading back into their territory. I'm afraid there is no guarantee the crew is free of them yet!"

Horace's big grin faded as the conversation took a serious turn. He sat back down at the desk. "I understand, Robert; these bastards have killed some of my good friends. We'll sort them out. But on a lighter note, did you come via Guildford by chance?"

"Why, yes, I did!"

"And did you bring any of those biscuits, Captain?"

"A tin especially for you, Horace. We shall have some with our coffee." Robert placed a medium-sized tin of Turner's biscuits on the desk.

"That cheers me up no end. It is bad enough that I am stuck on this small ship, but some of those biscuits will go a long way towards making the seas smooth. Best biscuits I have ever tasted."

Robert smiled, "I took the liberty of ordering a dozen tins before leaving. Anne will have them ready at the wedding next week."

The mention of Anne jigged Robert's memory, "Swanton, while I think of it, pull out my second uniform please and wrap it up. I must send it to Guildford for a fitting."

Horace licked his lips as he removed a biscuit from a tin. The smile broadened right across his big face, "Fine girl, that one, Squire. Any news there yet?"

Robert knew that Horace was fishing for information, "Next year Horace. We have a conquest first. When are your marines coming?"

Horace snapped back into work mode, "They will arrive at the same time as we return from the wedding. Monday afternoon, I expect. Lieutenant White is leading them down here. He and a couple of sergeants. They are good men, well trained and can fight like tigers. They won't take any nonsense from these Irish traitors! Mark my words Squire, they are fighting men through and through."

Robert sat down at his desk and picked up a biscuit. Having his old school chum, Horace here lifted his spirits no end. Swanton placed the hot brewed coffee on the desk. They sat back and enjoyed the sweet taste and crisp biscuits.

"Swanton, try some of these biscuits, lad. We need the recipe!"

Michael Swanton accepted the invitation, took the biscuit, and retreated into the servant's quarters.

"Your command, eh, Robert. Not bad at your age!"

They looked at each other and laughed.

"Not bad at all, Horace!"

Laughing, they had a toast with the coffee. Swanton, who watched from the servant's door, began appreciating how close these two were. He heard they were at school together but knew little of their story yet. He liked the banter that Sir Horace brought with him. There was nothing as good as the Army sense of humour.

At Guildford ...

Jonathan Turner felt some confidence today as he had slept well. The support from his wife and daughters would help him carry on. He would beat this problem, and he found a new respect for Doctor Neville Bassington, a man now aware of his secret, who did not judge him but offered help. For most of his life, Jonathan's guilt suppressed any desire to change his behaviour. He felt a sense of relief now that the secret was out. He must be cured and would comply with Neville's instructions. He was pleased that this man would soon be his son-in-law.

Opening a letter from his agents in London, he read the engineer's details they had found and recommended for the position. Mr Terrance Spencer was a middle-aged engineer who was experienced in developing steam power for various applications. Spencer wanted a quieter life in the country, seeking an escape from the crowded city and a better place for his wife and children. The man sounded ideal, and from the description of his character and personality, it appeared he would fit in well at Guildford. Jonathan set about writing and confirming with the agents his appointment.

Thomas Turner entered, "Would you share a cup of morning tea with me, Father? We must discuss a few matters, so shall I see Aggie, and have it brought in here?"

"Yes, Thomas, that would be good!"

Jonathan continued with his mail, noting a letter from the Admiralty. He opened the letter and read:

The Admiralty
Office of the Comptroller
September 1826

Dear Mr Turner

Thank you for supplying samples of your biscuits for testing aboard His Majesty's ships. This testing has found the biscuits nutritious, tasty and capable of long-term storage.

I am pleased to advise you that the Admiralty now provides a preliminary order for your biscuits as per the specifications attached. We intend a broader and longer duration of testing amongst the fleet.

The order is for 1000 tins of biscuits required for delivery at Portsmouth's navy stores by 16 February 1827.

The contract is enclosed, and I will attend your offices in Guildford for contract discussions on Tuesday, 17 October 1826. I would ask for a full tour of your baking facility and a detailed inspection of the biscuit production facility at that time.

I will be staying at the Fox & Hound in the High Street and ask that you be available at ten in the morning to tour your facilities for myself and the other members of my party.

I look forward to meeting with you.

Yours faithfully
Mr Malcolm Smith
Comptroller

Thomas came back into the room and sat near his father's desk.

"Have a look at this letter Thomas!"

Thomas took the letter and smiled as he read it through.

"This is what we have been hoping for, Father. Congratulations on this new order."

"Thank you, Thomas; we have been fortunate in our connections."

Jonathan and Thomas then spent some time discussing the changes required for the biscuit production. Their discussion noted their falling grain stocks and the increase in grain required to meet the contract conditions.

"Before we commence operations at the mill, we need to forecast our production targets for next year. Perhaps Hamish McPherson can provide what his pubs will require. I will write and ask him for the figures."

"Father, I think he will be here earlier. James told me he was visiting Reading this week and would come here on his return home either Thursday or Friday. So, we may discuss this tomorrow or the next day."

"Why was he in Reading?"

"I'm not sure, but I would assume it would be for a new Pub!"

"Makes sense. We will have two opportunities, either this Friday or at the wedding. Now, which landholders should we target for grain purchases?"

Fintelton Manor, outside Petersfield ...

Dr Sopwith stayed an additional day assessing if Lord Fintelton's health was improving from his prescribed treatment. It also gave him the opportunity of bleeding him each day, reducing his blood pressure. He was worried about further clotting and the chances of complications.

The Earl was responding well and regaining some colour. The paralysis was less apparent, giving the doctor hope the attack was less sinister than it first appeared. The other reason for his stay was Sir Hugh's disease was manifesting, displaying severe flu-type symptoms. He remained in bed all Tuesday and complained of a complete lack of energy. He slept most of the day and then on and off during the night.

Lady Jane was beside herself, and Emma spent much time looking after her mother. On Tuesday evening, only Emma and Doctor Sopwith appeared for dinner. David Sopwith was glad of the opportunity.

"Thank you, Pike. Please pass Mrs Wapples my compliments. The meal was delicious!"

"Thank you, Lady Emma. I shall pass this on. Would you or Doctor Sopwith care for coffee and port?"

"A tea, please, Pike."

"And you, Doctor Sopwith?"

"A coffee and port would be very nice, thank you."

The butler nodded and set off on his mission.

"Lady Emma, I must say how sorry I am that your father and brother are in such poor spirits."

Emma looked hard at Doctor Sopwith and then smiled. This young gentleman's polite conversation attracted her. She was now sure many failed to appreciate his generous manner; despite their friendly meeting the previous Saturday night, David Sopwith claimed no advantage or privileges.

"Come now, David; we are safe. You may call me Emma now that Pike is out of the room. I think I should be thanking you for your splendid care of my father and brother. Father appears much improved, but please, what is wrong with Hugh?"

"He is suffering from a disease I am afraid may never be cured. I dare not explain further. Patient confidentiality demands I say no more."

Emma was quite dumbfounded by this comment. She was not aware that Hugh carried a disease. This news immediately caused her more concern. Her father's illness was worry enough over the past days, but now he showed signs of recovery; she felt more relaxed. This news about Hugh rekindled her fears.

David saw the expression change on her face and regretted telling her Hugh's condition.

"David, can you not tell me more? I am his sister. He is not married, so I am his closest relative besides our parents. But they are in no position to assist him at their age."

David looked down at the table and considered her question. He realised her claim for the information was legitimate. Indeed, if Sir Hugh's condition deteriorated, he may soon require nursing. But how might he gently explain this without frightening Emma?

"Emma, there is truth in what you say ..."

"Your coffee, Sir!" The butler appeared and put down a cup of coffee and a glass of port in front of him. David raised his eyes, startled that the butler noticed the anxiety on his face.

Pike was a good judge of character. Having served the family for many years, he perceived the intimacy of the Doctor's comment.

"Doctor Sopwith, you may rely on my discretion. May I suggest you re-position yourself beside Lady Emma, Sir? This way, you will require only a softer voice!"

David agreed with the suggestion. He marvelled at a butler with such understanding and quickly moved to a new position beside Emma.

"Thank you, Pike. You are very kind and wise."

A thin glimmer of a smile came upon the butler's face as he served Lady Emma's tea. He then withdrew.

David Sopwith recommenced the discussion, "Emma, as I was saying, there is truth in what you say. Explaining this is both difficult and requires delicacy. But let me try."

"Take your time David. My brother's condition is a great concern for me, and I can assure you of my confidentiality."

David breathed in and swallowed, as he would not find this easy.

"Are you familiar with your brother's pursuits?"

"Yes, he enjoys farming and riding. He is out in the fields all day. He also likes travelling."

"I mean his more intimate pursuits?"

"I know he likes drinking and sometimes flirts with ladies."

"I'm afraid, Emma, it is more than that. I am sorry, but there is no easy way to explain this. He often keeps the company of ladies of ill repute!"

Emma sat back and looked in disgust at David.

"How can you suggest such a thing?"

"He told me so! Unfortunately, this has been occurring for the last fifteen years. I have only been treating him for two years, but he has closely related the length of time he has followed such pursuits. Hugh has suffered from the disease for nearly twelve years. There have been several outbreaks, each worse, and some of the doctors consulted have provided ineffective advice. He is now treated with a mercury ointment to slow the disease but not cure it. There is no known cure."

Emma, horrified, would not hear any more of this. She needed air.

"Shall we take our refreshments out onto the balcony? It is such a beautiful evening!"

She stood up, rushed over and flung the balcony doors open. At the balcony rail, she stood there, gazing out toward the horizon in the evening twilight.

David sat there, unsure what she expected of him. He was terrified of damaging the relationship now established with Emma. Her realisation of Hugh's condition would not be easy. He sat there for a few minutes as she stood looking in the direction of the sea.

She put both her hands on the balcony rail and then put her head back and took a good deep breath. Turning, she called through the balcony doors, "David, please come out here? I would like you with me so we may continue our discussion!"

He rose and walked through quietly and suddenly saw the breathtaking panorama in front of him. Something, due to his workload, that was not apparent before. He placed his hands on the rail and enjoyed God's creation.

She turned towards him and said, "I wasn't telling the truth. My notion was that I should not sacrifice the South family's good name, but I was wrong. Yes, I know about his indiscretions. I was too proud and withheld it. You are the one who is being truthful, David, and you have acted far better than I. My apologies, but I found it hard to acknowledge the truth. You will now tell me he has contracted this pox from a loose woman. Is that right?"

David would rather avoid speaking further on this subject, but he knew Emma would not be satisfied until all details were revealed, "Yes, that is most of it."

She shuddered, "And how bad is it?"

He spoke very softly, "Difficult to say. It is a strange thing that comes and goes. But he is in what they call the secondary stage. In time he will become disfigured and then die. His life expectancy may be years. I have no way of telling, but the symptoms have deteriorated much faster than I thought in the past few weeks. He may be quite alright next week. As I say, it is a strange disease, and it ebbs and flows. There is no known cure, and it will eventually have its way with him."

"No! Please, God, help him!" she whimpered.

Emma stood there in silence beside David as they both gazed at the view but not taking it in. Then she quietly started sobbing.

"First, it was father and now Hugh. Mother is old, and she will go soon. Robert is always away. I will be on my own soon. I am so alone, David!"

She started shaking and then sobbing uncontrollably. Her tears fell on the balcony rail and onto his hand. He turned and took her in his arms, and she put her arms around him, hugging him hard as if she was clinging to life.

He whispered down in her ear, "Emma, you will never be alone. I will always be here for you."

She heard what he said and hugged him harder still. She wanted his arms around her forever.

Lady Jane looked down on the balcony. From the Earl's bedroom with the full-length windowed doors, she had a clear view of the large balcony below. She smiled and shed a tear herself as she saw them embracing.

Dr Bassington's Surgery, Guildford ...

The rider arrived at the surgery mid-morning on Wednesday as Neville enjoyed his morning tea. He paid the rider his dues and took the note inside. It read:

My Dear Doctor Bassington

My apologies, yet I am delayed here at Fintelton. Another family member has fallen ill. There is more work than first estimated.
I will return by Thursday evening and speak with you then.
Thank you for your care of my patients. I am indebted to you.

Your friend
David Sopwith

Neville smiled as he read the note. He thought, 'I am in his debt! He does not understand how much I have enjoyed my time with his patients. It is I who is in his debt. I must tell him this when he returns.'

Bethany and Mrs Turner sat in Hurts' rooms watching William's final fitting for his page boys' uniform. The young man was all smiles as he carefully slipped on the pants over his bandaged legs. Then his white shirt and black tie, followed by the light blue vest, went on.

For William, this was an exciting time, his first experience of wearing formal clothes. As he gazed in the mirror, his mother and sister checked the fittings were correct. They rearranged his clothes, checking from different angles, ensuring a perfect fit. Once complete, he received a pat on the back, making him proud of himself.

Across the hallway, Anne and Clementine tried on their bridesmaid's dresses for the final time. This fitting was the third, and no amount of adjustments would make them upset as they admired the beautiful dresses.

After finishing with William's fitting, Bethany returned to the seamstress's salon and admired the two bridesmaids checking every detail.

"My, my! How will I ever look as beautiful as you two on the day? You both look radiant. Clementine, you are so beautiful in that dress. You look all grown up."

Clementine blushed and said, "Thank you, Beth, but I will never match your beauty!"

"In my eyes, you always will, and you too, Anne!"

Anne turned and giggled, "If we could all find partners, perhaps we could all marry on the same day!"

"It would save your father a lot of money!" Mrs Eleanora Turner laughed as she brought the handsome page boy across the hall and into the fitting room.

They all said, "Wow, William, look at you!"

William dived behind his mother's dress and peered out at them with a big smile.

Mrs Smith pinned a couple of places on the dresses and said, "All done, ladies. It appears we will be ready on time. You may pick up the clothes on Monday morning, and I will stand at the back of the Church and admire the wedding parade. It should be magnificent. When will the young gentlemen be arriving for their suits?"

"We hope early next week, perhaps Tuesday. But Sir Robert may be a bit late – it depends when he leaves his ship!"

HMS Restless, Portsmouth …

"Horace, we are short of space despite *Restless* being larger than your normal schooner. So, you will sleep in my cabin, and Lieutenant White will take the small port side cabin outside this one. Lieutenant Ham, when he arrives, will have the starboard cabin across from White.

I will have the carpenter make up a bed for you this afternoon. I say, Swanton! Would you please have Dodds come up here and measure Captain Coombes for a bed? I don't want his feet sticking over the end of the bunk! Ha, Ha!"

"Aye, Captain."

With that, Robert left for the headquarters of the Commander in Chief ashore. He was keen for a full briefing from Commodore Jacobs on Ham, as the rapid selection by the Admiral had unsettled him. Given the previous antics of his first lieutenant, Robert was being cautious.

At Jacob's office, the clerk advised Robert that the Commodore was out and would return in half an hour. Robert passed his wrapped uniform to the young Petty Officer with the delivery address details and a few shillings.

"Jessop, please have this sent today."

The Commodore's servant placed the package on his desk and then provided Robert with a coffee and offered him a chair on the outside balcony, with a spectacular harbour vista. Robert enjoyed a clear view of the first-rate this side of *Restless* but could only make out the stern of his ship. He noted a cutter heading for the first-rate, and then it turned behind the stern and headed for *Restless*. It must be taking Lieutenant Ham out to the ship.

'Damn! Can't be helped; probably better he received this information about Ham from Jacobs first.' With a few spare minutes while he waited, Robert commenced planning how he would exercise the men until Monday afternoon next or perhaps Tuesday morning. To ensure he was in Guildford for the week, he should leave by midday Tuesday. Surely Ham could handle that! Swanton and Bright would guard Ham's back while he was away. That would work!

"Commander South, Commodore Jacobs will see you now."

"Thank you, Jessop."

Robert picked up his half-full cup of coffee and brought it in from the balcony. The servant took it from him, but before he withdrew, a loud shout came from the office, "Keep your cup, Commander, and Jessop, please bring me a pot of coffee and a cup."

Robert took his cup back and walked into the Commodore's office. Putting it down on the desk, he shook hands with Jacobs.

"Welcome back, Commander. Sorry, I was out, but with this Red Squadron in port for replenishment, it is non-stop. Also, the Admiral won't be back until after the wedding in Guildford. He has left me in charge."

"Thank you for seeing me, Commodore. I will be quick, Sir. I was curious about Lieutenant Ham, as I understand the Admiral has appointed him as my first Lieutenant. I wondered if you would give me a rundown on his background?"

"Ah, I see. I was aware you wished input into the selection, but Admiral

Sutherland required someone on your ship quickly. I think you will be out of port as soon as the wedding is over!"

"Why do you say that, Sir!"

"Captain Foster failed to rendezvous with the packet. There is no sign at all of him at his designated port. The packet Captain carried out a two-day search and found nothing. We may know more when you return next Monday."

"The Admiral will still be attending the wedding, Sir?"

"Yes, definitely, but not Foster and his wife. I sent another packet out last Monday and expected their return this Friday. We will know more then. Now about Lieutenant Ham."

"Yes, Sir."

"Ham has served well for twenty-five years in the Navy and has made his way up from seaman. No mean feat. He is highly qualified and, by all rights, should be a Captain by now. But as you know, ship numbers are decreasing with the budget cutbacks. His record is spotless, and you can trust him. The Admiral wanted someone with no Irish connections. Ham grew up in the midlands and spent most of his service in the Americas and French patrols. He will be a great asset. Ham is competent and intelligent. The main problem will be that he is a bit older than you at forty, so take this into account in your relationship with him. From what we know, there is no chip on his shoulder. He has earned his promotion."

That was enough for Robert. He now understood why he was not consulted and respected the decision. He was thankful for this carefully selected crew addition.

"Thank you, Sir. Now my men need further training and canon practice. I would like to embark this afternoon and return early Tuesday morning if that is acceptable, Sir."

"Good idea, Captain! Keep them busy! Ham will keep a good watch while you are away. There will be a briefing with the Admiral the following Tuesday afternoon. Shall we say three o'clock? If you leave Guildford on that day, you will need an early start. Give Neville my best wishes."

"Thank you, Sir. With this crew, I will train them till they drop!"

"I agree."

With that, Robert took his leave, and within five minutes he was aboard his cutter heading for *Restless*. The southerly was gaining in strength, and if this continued, it should provide some good training for his crew. He expected the Irish sea would present far more challenging conditions than this.

As he climbed aboard *Restless*, he was met by a piping party with the Officers ready for him. Lieutenant Ham greeted him with a salute.

Robert returned his salute and asked, "Lieutenant Ham, I presume?"

"Yes, Sir! It is a pleasure and honour gaining a posting onboard your ship."

"Thank you, Mr Ham. Please have the Master and Master-at-Arms, and your good self join me in my cabin. You may dismiss the pipe party and have Lieutenant Brinkley replace you as Officer of the Watch."

"Aye, Sir."

With that, Robert went below and found Horace still reading his report. The carpenter and his mate were well underway, making up Horace's bed. Captain Coombes looked up.

"Ah, Robert! A few questions about your report."

"Later, Horace. I have a meeting coming which involves you. Get ready!"

"Here?"

Robert nodded, and there was a knock at the door. Horace sat up straight. "Enter."

Lieutenant Ham, Warrant Officer Trotters and Senior Petty Officer Fulcher came into the cabin. Robert dismissed the carpenters for the duration of the meeting.

"Thank you for coming, Gentlemen. Firstly, let me welcome Lieutenant Ham on board. He comes with a glowing report of excellent navy service. I am very pleased he is with us."

"Thank you, Sir!" Ham said with a smile.

"Now, as you know, there were some difficulties with traitors when we last sailed. We still don't know if any remain. If they do, I want them flushed out, so we maintain our vigilance, please. I would prefer the marines on board, but the need for training is more urgent. I am not expecting any trouble, but we must be ready for anything. In terms of protection, Captain Coombes and Mr Fulcher will keep an eye on things.

Now, Fulcher, you will immediately report to me if you see any funny business. No hesitation, you hear?"

"Yes, Sir. "

"This is our last chance, Gentlemen! Let's sort out this crew before we commence our next mission. Understood?"

There was a resounding, "Aye, Aye, Sir!"

"Now we are off for some training. Mr Ham, take us to sea and drive the men as hard as possible. It would be good if we were clear of Spithead and into the channel by six this evening."

"Aye, Sir."

With that, Ham, Trotters and Fulcher almost ran out of the room. Robert could hear the commands yelled everywhere and the rapid manning of stations. Within five minutes, the capstan party were raising the anchor, and sails were unfurling. Robert felt life flowing into his ship again, and he revelled in the feeling.

He saw Horace putting on a coat, "What were the questions?"

"I think they can wait. Time, I saw this whole crew in action. See if I can spot some Irish boys!"

At Guildford ...

David Sopwith saw the familiar outskirts of Guildford come into view, confirming he was nearly home. Both the Earl and Sir Hugh showed signs of improvement, and the increasing confidence between Emma and himself was heartening. On Wednesday evening, after Lady Jane retired, he and Emma talked long into the night. David found her company charming. The attraction between them was increasing, and he would have stayed for another day had she asked.

He thought back on what passed between them this morning as he left. He farewelled Lord Fintelton and the Countess in the Earl's bedroom, where Sir David continued making a steady but slow recovery. Emma joined him at the coach. They were careful that no signs of intimacy were apparent. He understood that servants talked, and at this stage, it was better if their friendship remained their secret.

On the steps, just far enough out of earshot of the servants, Emma said her farewell.

"Dr Sopwith, I cannot thank you enough for your help during this crisis. I am so glad my father is recovering. When shall we see you again?"

"I will call next Tuesday again and stay the night if that is not inconvenient. I must leave on Wednesday morning as Neville and Bethany will be married on the Saturday following. I understand you will be there."

"I will."

"I would advise against your father attending in his current condition. Perhaps your mother could attend, but she may prefer remaining at home with the Earl. Sir Hugh's condition may prevent his attending; however, he may improve quickly. It is a strange condition. Will you remain in Guildford for a few days?"

She smiled and moved closer and spoke softly, "David, Anne is organising a dinner party at her house. I would stay for that if you were to attend!"

"It would be my pleasure if it is held in the dining room and not the kitchen." They both laughed.

"Perhaps my brother, Robert, will be there as well. You would enjoy meeting him."

"I will meet him at the wedding!"

"Yes, that is true. Anne and I shall arrange the details and advise you. I will be staying with her. Thank you again, David!"

She moved a step away from the carriage and said, "Goodbye, Doctor

Sopwith."

"Goodbye, Lady Emma."

She gave him hope that she would accept his question when the time was right. He, a simple doctor in a country town, had been her admirer for some time but always thought she would never accept his company. How wrong he was. She asked no questions about his family or connections, and even more pleasing, her intimacy was for love and not position. She was a rare jewel, this Emma. He was amazed at the stark difference between Emma and her brother Hugh.

At four in the afternoon, David was passing Neville Bassington's surgery. He decided on a visit, hoping to catch Neville. The coachmen would deliver his bags home.

This was his first visit to the surgery, and he found the waiting room light and airy, which impressed him. His surgery was at home, and the thought of opening a standalone surgery was a long-term aim until now. But here it was.

"Would Doctor Bassington be in, please?"

The nurse sitting at the desk was a local Guildford girl and recognised him at once, "Certainly Doctor Sopwith. Just a moment, and I will let him know you are here."

She left the desk, went down the hallway, knocked on the first door, and entered. She kept her word and returned, asking Doctor Sopwith to follow her.

She showed David into a surgery room where Neville bent over William Turner's legs, dressing some of the cuts. Bethany Turner was standing on the other side of the bench on which William lay.

"David, welcome back."

"Thank you, Neville."

Beth kissed him on the cheek, "Welcome back, David. May I have Neville back now? There are still some preparations needed for the wedding!"

David Sopwith stood back and remembered the wedding was Saturday week. He shuddered – his Fintelton visit would have kept Neville from the wedding preparations.

"Bethany, I am sorry. I forgot. My apologies, please. I shall leave him alone now. I have been very selfish!"

Beth gave a tense David a hug, "No, David, he loved it. It has kept him busy while we completed the final dress fittings."

William's eyes lit up, and he excitedly said, "Doctor Sopwith, I have a page boy's uniform and will wear it at the wedding!"

David moved closer, noticing what Neville was doing, "Good for you, William. I shall sit in the aisle and give you a wink when you go past."

William thought this was very good and smiled like a boy who was passed a slice of cake with a strawberry on top.

Neville finished the right leg and then took the old bandages off the left leg.

David could not believe what he saw. There were seven or eight deep long cuts on the boy's leg. He had suffered a savage beating. He opened his mouth, but Neville cut in, "It is under control, David. I will explain in a minute."

There was a story, and David was curious about how William had suffered this beating. As Neville spoke quietly with William, Bethany drew him aside and gave a quick explanation. David's concern grew as he heard the details.

"I was not there, David, so I will let Neville give you more details. However, we think we now have a bad situation in hand. Thank goodness."

Nodding in agreement, David re-joined Neville and asked, "Did you use salt water for bathing the wounds."

"Yes. I started on Monday night. It's amazing how fast it works and stops any sign of infection, thank goodness. William, you will recover quite well, and I think there will not be too many scars there in a few months. Let us wait and see."

Neville finished the bandaging and then sent Bethany and William on their way.

"Neville, how did it go?"

"Better than I expected. I must admit I enjoyed the work. The navy work is different. I think you develop a better relationship with the country people."

"Yes, it is gratifying when you can make a difference but depressing when you find there is nothing you can do for them. I have enjoyed my two years here, but I missed collaborating with other surgeons in London. It is something we must discuss soon."

"I had intended the same thing!"

"Let me go first as I raised it."

"Go on then, David."

"Neville, in Guildford, the requests for my services come either at once or very sparsely. When patients call for me, I find the demand for my services erupts. I may not sleep for nearly three days. But then there may be only one or two patients for a week. I find it very hard coping as a doctor on my own."

"I see!"

"I wondered if you would consider joining your practice with mine, and we would support each other. We are both young and keen on learning. I also see that this would benefit you while you visit London. In time a third surgeon working with us would be a possibility."

Neville broke into a broad smile, "This is extraordinary, as I have been planning the same thing. Would you be agreeable if we established a joint practice in this surgery? There are five spare rooms. I purchased hastily and took what I could get. But in time, I think we could use all the rooms."

Neville's reply overjoyed David. They shook hands on the agreement.

"Now, David, while I am away on my honeymoon, if you would care for my patients, that would make a great start. There are three of them plus the Turner family."

"Such a large practice, Neville. I am not sure that I will cope!"

"David, it will build up! I have sufficient funds behind me for a few years, so with the growth in Guildford, it won't take long."

"I agree. My patient numbers climbed from zero to over a hundred within three months, so I'm sure your practice will too. Now Neville! I must update you on what has transpired at Fintelton Manor. The Earl is recovering, but I am afraid he will suffer another stroke soon. But what I am more concerned about is Sir Hugh. Being in the navy, you must have seen a bit of the pox? Do you know of a treatment besides mercury?"

At the Turner Household ...

A knock came on the front door as the family were preparing for dinner. Aggie paid the rider and went in search of Mr Turner. Jonathan and Neville were finishing a session in the study as Aggie knocked and delivered the message. This week's sessions proved productive; however, Neville was worried about his looming departure on the honeymoon. Jonathan required regular attention, so he must find a replacement.

Given his new agreement with David, Neville thought he might have an answer for his absence if Jonathan would accept David Sopwith. The meetings would be twice a week and concentrate more on Jonathan's physical health. Neville would continue the psychological sessions again once he returned.

At the table, Jonathan placed the message in front of him and inspected his dinner serving. Eleanora, sensing that the note might be important, questioned him.

"Jonathan, don't keep us all in suspense. Who is the message from?"

"Sorry, I should have shared it straight away. Hamish McPherson writes that he will be in Guildford tomorrow and asks if he could join us at dinner."

Eleanora's eyes lit up, and there was a sense of excitement among the women at the table.

"Wonderful, Jonathan! He will be aware of the progress of Marion and Thomas's wedding. I hope Marjorie briefed him well!"

Thomas's interest also rose, hearing himself mentioned, "I would like an update. Father, may I join your meeting with Mr McPherson as there are several issues we require his advice on?"

"Which issues, Thomas?"

"When James was here, he suggested how we might negotiate corn contracts with the landholders. I thought it would be helpful to hear Mr McPherson's suggestions."

"Certainly, this would fit in with the other discussion points."

Neville sat forward and said, "I was waiting till after dinner, but given it is news time, I should announce that I have agreed with Dr Sopwith today to run a joint practice from my surgery building almost immediately."

"Neville, that is wonderful. David will cover your patients while you are away!" Beth kissed Neville, confident the arrangements were coming together well for their wedding.

Jonathan sat back and contemplated this. His acquaintance with Dr Sopwith was scant. He did not care for him replacing Neville; however, Eleanora and Anne had only praise for the young man.

"Will that mean he will replace you for my sessions?"

"Yes, Jonathan, it is important that you keep having these sessions for some time. But Doctor Sopwith will concentrate on your physical health only."

Jonathan frowned. He led the family in grace and then eagerly commenced his meal.

At the mention of James McPherson and his advice on grain negotiations, Neville remembered the strange conversation of the Monday morning.

"Thomas, I'm glad you mentioned James, as I meant to tell you of a conversation with him before he left town Monday morning."

Neville related the story in full as the others listened intently.

Thomas questioned, "You say Mr Jacks was unaware of any repairs. Perhaps James brought in someone else?"

"I thought of that, but Mr Jacks said the coach arrived in excellent condition!"

"I wonder who the man was?" Thomas found the comments contradictory as well.

Jonathan Turner took in the details but said nothing. Perhaps it was Hamish's informer. There were other possibilities, so probably in time, this would be solved. However, he was glad Neville had mentioned it.

In the morning, Anne finished her work at the bakery and returned home, finding a letter for her from Lady Emma South. On opening the letter, she smiled as she read.

"My Dearest Anne

Since returning from Guildford, I find I miss your company very much. I am alone here apart from my parents and my brother, Sir Hugh. I found our time in Guildford full of fun, and it is hard to remember a better time than the dinner party last Saturday evening. It reminded me so much of my best childhood memories."

Anne thought, 'You were charming as well.'
The letter continued:

> *"You will have heard that my father, Lord Fintelton, suffered a spell the week before last while mother and I were in London. Doctor Sopwith spent much time with him while we were away and saw him into recovery. He is a dedicated doctor, and my brother Hugh cannot speak highly enough of him.*
>
> *Father is making a remarkable recovery, thanks to Doctor Sopwith's care. If this continues, he may attend the wedding, but perhaps not the reception. At present, we are taking one day at a time.*
>
> *I cannot recall a happier time when we celebrated in Bethany and Neville's new house. Sitting on boxes and sipping champagne out of mugs was delightful and made me realise what a snob I have become. I owe you so much, Anne, for introducing real happiness into my life again. I am sure you are now having a wonderful time with Beth seeing the new furniture arrive."*

Anne said, "I forgot. I must go down there and see."
The letter continued:

> *"Doctor Sopwith has revisited my father, providing me with the opportunity of becoming better acquainted. I discussed the possibility of a dinner party in Guildford, and he readily agreed. He was excited by the idea. I am encouraged by the prospect that he may hold genuine feelings for me.*
>
> *We must discuss plans for the dinner when we see each other at the wedding. I thought I should write and confirm the plans for our trip. I will arrive in Guildford next Thursday and hope we might dine together. At this time, I am not sure if Mother and Father will be attending. I do hope they both come, as I would like the pleasure of introducing you to my father.*
>
> *I am most excited about revisiting Guildford. You have brought such joy into my life. Thank you so much.*
>
> *Until then, Dearest friend*

> *Love*
> *Emma."*

Anne wiped a tear from her eye as she looked up from the letter. She rushed upstairs and into her room, where she found Bethany sorting out the clothes she would pack for her honeymoon.

"Beth, I thought you were managing the arrival of furniture at your house?"

"I was, but it is all there now, and it is wonderful. I needed some lunch and then a few minutes of sorting clothes out. I have been so busy I haven't started packing. Would you join me at the house this afternoon and help me position the furniture?"

"Yes, that would be so much fun. Beth, you must read this letter."

Anne's excitement was contagious, and Bethany was curious.

"Beth – this is a private letter – but I must show you. You must keep it confidential, especially from Neville, please?"

"Certainly, Anne, but what can it be? You seem a bit overcome."

"You will see when you read it."

"Lovely, it is from Emma!" She read on.

"Her father is unwell, and she speaks highly of Doctor Sopwith!"

"Yes, yes, but see what comes next."

Bethany concentrated on the remainder of the letter, and as she read, her smile grew. She looked up at Anne.

"Anne, it may be that David Sopwith cares for her. He must have secretly admired her for some time. That is wonderful!"

"Beth, may we use your house for the dinner party? I know you will be away, but I will guarantee we take good care."

"No, Anne. That would be scandalous! I think you need a venue where you have chaperones, and it is visible. You must always remember your reputation, young lady. What would Robert think if he heard?"

"I'm hoping he may still be here and attend."

"I would suggest you have it at home. Mother and father would gladly accommodate it. Why not?"

"It would disturb mother, and father is depressing at times!"

"I would suggest that they adjourn early, then you will have a lovely time. It will be quite reputable and far more relaxed for all."

"You don't mind if Emma stays in our room and uses your bed?"

"Anne, I leave the Saturday after next and never return. The room is yours then, and you may have your friend there anytime you wish."

Anne suddenly realised her sister would be moving forever. Of course, there would be room for Emma. She hugged Bethany and said, "I will miss you, Beth. I missed you so much while you were at Woking. Perhaps it has prepared me for this. But I will miss you so much!"

The Fox and Hound Hotel, Guildford …

After settling into the Fox and Hound Hotel, Hamish McPherson enjoyed a late afternoon stroll up the High Street with the Turner residence ahead. It was now early October, and the evenings were becoming decidedly cooler. He enjoyed the low temperature as it reminded him of Scotland, the land of his birth.

He missed the beautiful lakes and mountains, the vast landscapes, his sons and families, and so many of his friends they had left behind. Being in Guildford was a nice change from Greenwich, allowing him some time in a peaceful environment where he could relax. He relished the tranquillity.

As he approached Jonathan's house, he picked out Simeon and William playing on the front portico with the puppy. He smiled and thought, 'It has done the trick. The boys are smiling and laughing.'

The young boys peered at the approaching man as he walked up the stairs. William recognised him immediately and, running over, welcomed him.

"Hello, Mr McPherson. Thank you so much for sending us Nosey. He is hopeless at catching a ball, but he is learning."

"Hello, William, Hello, Simeon. Hello, Nosey! How are you all?" He patted the shaking dog, who was wagging his tail madly.

Hamish sat down on the long bench against the front wall, "Show me how you are training him."

Simeon grabbed the ball, "Mr McPherson, we first let him smell the ball, then say fetch. Then I throw it a few feet hoping he will grab it. But he just looks at it!"

"You are not giving him an incentive! William, please ask the housekeeper for a few small bits of cut-up bacon. Tiny bits about fingernail size."

William looked at Mr McPherson and then smiled as if he had solved the riddle. He darted through the front door towards the kitchen. As he went past, Hamish noticed the significant bandaging on his legs.

Hamish asked Simeon, "Appears as if William has been in the wars?"

Simeon considered his question. This man was now a close friend of his father, so it should be allowable if he confided in him.

"It is very private, but William was naughty, and father caught him eating biscuits in the butler's pantry. He knows the rule and should have waited for afternoon tea. So, William got a strapping."

Hamish rubbed his chin, "It appears more than a strapping!"

Simeon rubbed the dog's ears and mumbled, "Father got carried away as usual. But Neville stopped him and is teaching him how to control his rage."

"My, my!" Hamish was a man of great perception and refrained from making it a big issue.

William returned with a half dozen small bits of bacon. Hamish got off the chair and sat on the floor with the boys, "Let me see. Now put a bit on one of your fingers and let the dog smell it but not eat it. He will grab at it but whip it away before his tongue licks it up."

William nodded that he understood and carefully put a piece of bacon on his index finger and called Nosey. The dog came over at once, licking his lips as he could smell the bacon. He sniffed it on William's finger, and then Hamish quickly pulled the finger away from Nosey's tongue.

"Good, now just put the bacon bit on the ball and throw it, but not too far, just a few steps away. Then call, 'Fetch.'"

Nosey watched with interest as William transferred the bacon. The dog tilted his head and gave a little bark.

"Fetch boy!" William threw the ball gently towards the other end of the balcony. Nosey jumped after it and grabbed the ball before it went halfway. He found the bacon and gobbled it up.

They all cheered. Nosey, for the first time, chased the ball. Hamish grinned and was glad it worked.

"Now do that a few more times with the rest of the bacon, and he will remember the first step. The next step is training him to bring it back. That's a bit harder. See if you can figure that out? If you can't, I shall explain it after dinner."

Eleanora Turner came through the front door and found Hamish McPherson on the floor with the boys and the puppy. She thought if only Jonathan would do things like this, he might become a happier person.

"Hello, Hamish. We were expecting you! It is so good you are here!"

Following dinner, Thomas, Jonathan and Hamish were finishing their conversation about the corn negotiations. Hamish explained how he and James negotiated in Scotland.

Thomas, listening carefully to his explanation, asked, "So it is a game of bluff?"

"Thomas, bluffs are acceptable, but you also must be fair. It is bad business if the supplier and his family starve because you are paying too little. Suppliers given a good price will support you in the future. Mark my words."

Thomas sat back and nodded his agreement.

"Thomas, if you would excuse us, please. I must talk with your father privately."

Thomas jumped up and said, "Of course, Mr McPherson. If I don't see you in the morning, I will look forward to seeing you in Greenwich."

"Good night, Thomas."

Thomas quietly walked out of the room and closed the door.

"Jonathan, I am glad we have met tonight. I have some good news for you. The Pub in Epsom continues to increase in profitability. The results are far better than expected. By next May, we will be completely debt-free. It is a better investment than I ever imagined. When all these men gamble, they purchase a lot of drink."

Hamish passed Jonathan the new figures.

Jonathan smiled, "This is good news, indeed."

"Oliver is doing a good job up there. If this continues, and I expect it will, we should pay him a bonus at Christmas."

"Agreed!"

"Eleanora is looking well. Her health seems to have improved since we last saw her!"

"Yes. Neville Bassington is a good Doctor. He sees her weekly and has been recommending a diet that has helped. I have firm hopes for her long-term health."

"Where did Neville get his experience from?"

Jonathan explained Neville's background and training and that he now had the family all eating fruit every day.

"Interesting! I understand he has rooms in London."

"Yes, he will start practising two days a fortnight after returning from the honeymoon. He is interested in the healing of bones."

"Your family will gain a valuable addition. Now tell me about William!"

Jonathan suddenly felt nervous; the same feeling of fear had arisen when Hamish warned him about Eleanora in Greenwich.

"What about William, Hamish?"

"I understood he was having nightmares about the burglary!"

Jonathan relaxed.

"He was concerned for some time, but he seems over that now. It must have been the puppy that did the trick. Constable Rawlins and I have been more concerned than the family members. I am sure you know that one of the burglars was found dead in a lock, down on the river. It was the older gentleman."

"Jonathan, as I told you, I have some informers here. They have let me know that you will not be bothered by these men again."

Remembering Neville's comments at dinner last night, Jonathan became uncomfortable. He was unsure what Hamish was alluding to, so he felt he must ask.

"How would they know that Hamish?"

"As I told you in Greenwich, Jonathan, this is a tricky business. My friends were far more active than your parish constable. Those burglars will never worry you again!"

"The other burglar did he escape?"

"I'm not sure, Jonathan. All I know is that my contacts have assured me that you will never be bothered again by them."

"I think I have heard enough on that subject!"

"That is probably for the best! Now, Jonathan, I return from Reading, where I have found a new pub site. I am looking for investors. This proposition will be different from Epsom, where you and I are the owners. This investment will require between four and six investors. Are you interested? The return will be substantial but not as fast as Epsom. Already numerous coach routes use Reading as a staging post. The attraction is that Reading will be a railway hub. The time for establishing an investment there is now while the building prices are low. The town has a secure future as a transport centre. Perhaps in time, we may have three or four Pubs there."

"I am interested, Hamish. When will this happen?"

"Probably towards September next year. I have identified the site, and the attorneys are negotiating. It is close enough for delivery of your bread, biscuits and pastries. I will supply the beer, and once the Guildford Brewery is open, the beer will come from here. When the railway connects Guildford with Reading, the travel time will be a fraction of the coach trip."

"Sounds better all the time, Hamish. Thank you for considering me."

"Now Jonathan, this Neville that your daughter Bethany is marrying. He sounds like a fine young Doctor. I understand you are receiving treatment from him. Make sure you do what he asks Jonathan! Your health and your family's health are of utmost importance. You are a good business partner. We will achieve much together yet. Let Neville assist you! He will be a great help."

Jonathan Turner sat back and agreed with Hamish. He wondered how Hamish could be so familiar with his family life. Then again, he seemed genuine in his care. What harm could there be in that?

Chapter 20

The floorboards creaked as cold northerly gusts buffeted the house. Autumn was well underway, with a sudden drop in temperature and rain squalls blowing across the town. Bethany sat in the back of an open carriage jostling south towards the coast. She surrounded the Reverend Upton's children against the wind and rain with her cape. But it was no use, the gale was drenching them, and the temperature was still dropping.

A cry came from behind the coach, "Wait, Beth, wait! I must come with you." It was Robert, his wet hair plastered his head, and a blue cape flew out behind him as he scrambled towards the coach. The coachman cracked his whip, and the horses broke into a canter. As the coach pulled away, Bethany turned and screamed, "Run, man, run, they won't wait!" Robert doubled his efforts and drew near. She could see the pained expression on his face. Gripping the seat, Bethany turned and reached out over the rear of the carriage. She nearly touched his hand, but then he fell.

Looking up from the mud with the rain pelting down harder, she saw the look of desperation in his eyes. "Stop!" she cried, "Stop the coach. Stop!" She sat up in fright and pushed the blankets off.

"What is it, Beth?" the soft voice of Anne from the other bed suddenly broke into her dream. Bethany sat there for a moment rubbing her eyes. Anne sat up, brushing her long hair away from her face, and giggled.

"You were dreaming, weren't you? I warned you about the blankets. It is only mid-autumn; it will warm up again soon. Too early for winter yet."

Bethany heard a rain squall pelting the side of the house, and raindrops tapped against the windowpane. She folded her arms together around her chest and shivered. Rubbing her eyes, she blinked as she gazed across at Anne.

"You're right, I was dreaming, but it felt real. Why does the mind do that? I was terrified!"

The house was still except for the noise of the gale outside. There was only a faint hint of the dawn light through the window, and the room remained dark. The heavy overcast conditions outside and the strong wind made it chilly, and Beth pulled the blanket up around her.

"Come on, Beth, let us go down and get a cup of tea. Thomas will have left hot water on the stove."

The girls slid out of their beds, lit a candle and pulled on their night cloaks. They tip-toed past their mothers' room and went down into the kitchen, where the stove made it warm and cosy.

Sipping their tea, Anne asked, "Tell me about your dream? Was it the wedding?"

"No, I was in a coach protecting Reverend Upton's children from the rain. Then I saw Robert running behind chasing the coach!"

Anne sat there for a moment, then blurted out, "Robert? Perhaps it is because he is not here yet!"

"Anne, don't fret. I'm sure he will be here soon!"

Anne sighed and looked at the oven fire through a vent above the fire chamber.

"I have been considering what it would be like being the wife of a naval Captain. You may not see your husband for years. Then he may return with one leg missing or some injury like that. I'm not sure I like that idea."

Bethany was amazed; she thought Anne was madly in love with Robert. But here was a girl who was considering a long way ahead. She was planning far more than Beth had ever considered. She must have inherited this from her father or perhaps grandfather Henry. They were both planners and profited from it. Possibly Anne would be better off in business rather than being a wife at home.

"I'm sure he will be here soon!"

HMS Restless …

Robert worked the crew hard, sailing *Restless* as far as Plymouth, then heading back towards Portsmouth into some changing weather. They were twenty miles south of Weymouth when the full force of the gale hit. Taking down sail and reefing, the crew fought hard, keeping the ship from floundering. The waves became enormous, and spray came horizontally, driven hard by the wind, stinging the crew's faces as they worked frantically.

Robert stood holding a safety line from the mizzen mast and kept an eye on his crew struggling high above where the sails were ready to burst. He could hear the shouting of men as they wrestled against the elements high up in the rigging. As the wind rose even further, it was becoming dangerous having men above decks, let alone being in the rigging so far above the ship.

"Lieutenant Ham! Get them down as soon as you can. I don't want any man lost overboard in this weather!"

"Aye, Sir."

Ham lifted the megaphone, pointing it upwards and shouting orders. Slowly as men finished furling, they descended, sopping wet and shivering. Each headed below for the protection of the cabin and hopefully some warmth from hot drinks.

Swanton appeared beside his Captain with a cup of steaming coffee.

"Thank you, Swanton. Blast this weather! I should be near Guildford by now."

Horace Coombes, who was gripping on for dear life, stood on the other side of the mast. He turned and yelled, "Lovely day for it, Squire. We will be halfway across the channel towards France within a couple of hours!"

Robert smiled as he noticed Horace's colour. The face was white, or perhaps he detected a little green!

"You are correct, Horace. I will maintain this course so we can gain ground up the channel. In this weather, long tacks are best if possible. Every time I come about, I must send the men back up. If we can stay on this tack for an hour or two, we can turn and head straight back for Portsmouth."

Horace looked at him with a grin, "It's far easier on land with horses! They may complain, but you can go directly against the wind."

Robert thought about Horace's comment as the wind howled through the rigging. If they could harness steam engines, then a ship could do the same and not be at the mercy of the wind.

"Mr Ham, how many lookouts have we above?"

"Not any, Sir. I considered it was too dangerous."

"You're probably right, Mr Ham, but I don't want a collision with another ship in the channel. Put one up the main, with a lifeline and change him every hour. Inform me of any other craft, especially ones in trouble."

"Aye, Sir."

Robert yelled at the quartermaster, "Mr Young, please ease her off about three points south. She'll run a bit gentler as the lookout goes up."

"Aye, Sir."

Holding his lifeline rope tight, Robert watched as the lookout scrambled up the rigging. He hoped the gale would be short-lived. Otherwise, he would be late arriving at the wedding if he arrived there at all! Reginald Ludlam would be aware and explain his delay. Thomas would stand in as best man – yes, that would work! Still, he felt guilty about not making it on time. There was no time for thoughts of the wedding; his first concern now must be for the safety of his ship. The weather he could not control, the ship he would!

At Guildford …

David and Jennifer Bassington and their daughter Megan arrived in Guild-ford on Tuesday evening and lodged at the Fox and Hound. They kindly picked up Marion Steele from Greenwich for the trip. Marion found Megan a pleasant travelling companion, and they spent the hours in the coach talking about their lives. The Turners hosted Marion with them until the McPher-sons arrived on Friday.

A note arrived for Jonathan and Eleanora Turner from Fintelton Manor, stating that the Earl was still too frail and must provide his apologies; however, Lady Fintelton would be attending with her daughter Lady Emma. She advised that Sir Hugh would watch his father and remain at Fintelton. Anne was much relieved that Sir Hugh was not coming – she imagined the consequences if there were any unwelcome displays from Sir Hugh during the week. Bethany and Anne were pleased Lady Emma would come in advance and join them for today's Wednesday afternoon tea.

"Anne, perhaps you would visit the Fox and Hound and ascertain if Emma has arrived by lunch. Let her know about the afternoon tea. I have invited Megan Bassington, as well. Marion, you will enjoy some time with her at Hursts this morning, so please remind her of the afternoon tea. Mrs Jennings and Aggie should have everything ready here by half-past two. Marion, while you are at Hursts, would you please enquire of Mrs Smith if the ribbons for the pews are ready. Please ask if one of the tailors might deliver them here."

Anne looked up and gave an understanding smile as Bethany read aloud from her list. The wedding was only three days away, and Beth seemed stressed. Making matters worse, their mother remained in bed again and was not well at all.

"There are so many tasks! I never realised the amount of organisation required for a wedding!"

Marion was thinking aloud as they took breakfast together, "I am so glad Mrs McPherson is helping with mine. I should never have coped with all this."

Anne realised, probably for the first time, that Marion's mother was placed in care over two years ago. Since then, until Marion resided with the McPhersons, she coped at home by herself. "It must have been hard losing your mother like that?"

"Yes. At first, I was so depressed I visited my mother nearly every day, but she did not recognise me. I was unprepared for what happened as my father and brothers fought over mother's care. No one was running the house, and the servants were hopeless. Mrs McPherson visited one day and found the house in such a state, and me attempting some progress on the cleaning. It was then that they approached my father and asked if I could move in with them. He was unhappy about it, but he knew I needed a mother's influence more than being in a house full of arguing men."

Bethany asked, "But who ran the house? Surely, there would have been no mistress when you left?"

"Yes, Father then realised the home needed a housekeeper. It is much better now, but I am better out of it. Your mother has done a wonderful job here!"

Bethany and Anne just sighed. Their mother's failing health continued, and they were now making the daily household decisions, with a guilty feeling creeping in. The subject was delicate, and their mother took offence if it appeared she was not in control anymore.

Anne sighed, "I will be glad when our mother's baby arrives. Perhaps she will gain more strength after that!"

Bethany changed the subject, "Megan Bassington seems a lovely young woman! She is just back from New York. Her father trains her as a journalist in his business. Imagine being sent to America for job training. Why we would be lucky if we visited Hursts in Woking!"

"You will always be welcome at the McPhersons in Greenwich while I am there. I'm also sure that after I marry Thomas and move here, then the McPhersons will still wish for visits."

"Thank you, Marion. That is kind."

Beth thought about this and mentioned, "I think the Bassingtons would be happy entertaining any of us! If Neville's practice is a success in London, we may even acquire a London house, and you might all visit me there. What a time we could have together touring London."

"What a wonderful idea. One day when we are all married, we should do that." Anne thought about the new friends she now shared and how they all enjoyed each other's company. Would Megan Bassington also be a friend? She was not sure – perhaps she would learn more today. Then she thought about Emma.

"If we visited London, perhaps Emma would entertain us at her London house. I wonder if it is large. Robert says it is in St James's Square. Where is that in London, Beth?"

Bethany frowned, 'I'm not sure!' She then brought the focus back onto the day's events, "Girls, the future will be exciting, but first we must face today. Best if we get on with it!"

Anne was keen not to miss the opportunity with Neville's sister, "Marion, what time will you meet Megan this morning? I might join you at Hursts!"

"That would be lovely! We are meeting at the hotel at ten this morning. We should be at Hursts by ten-fifteen."

"If I leave for work now, I should have most of it finished by ten. I will join you there." Lack of time for social engagements now convinced Anne that training a bookkeeper at the bakery was an urgent priority. Audrey Stern was progressing well, and now was the time for speeding up her training. If Audrey took over most of the figures, Anne would have far more flexibility in managing her bakery work and social activities.

At Fintelton Manor …

Ensuring her arrival at Guildford by lunch, Emma left the Manor early in the morning. This afternoon, she would meet with Anne and perhaps dine tonight with David Sopwith. She sent David a note advising of her arrival.

Emma said her farewells the previous night. Her father missed what she was saying, and her mother issued all kinds of instructions for the suite at Guildford. The early departure avoided her sorting out any further issues. The plan worked well, and the coach now approached the halfway mark of the trip. Travelling allowed her reflection time which she craved, as life became more complicated at the manor.

She prayed for her father's health, concerned about Hugh becoming the Earl. She would rather ask her father's permission about entertaining David Sopwith than plead with her brother for approval. Managing Hugh would be tricky and might even put her inheritance at risk. She loved her father dearly and would not want him suffering, but who could control his health? His life was blessed with good health and longevity despite his continuing turns. She prayed that good health would return. Lady Jane was no longer capable of managing her husband's disabilities on her own. Extra maids must be employed, strengthening the staff caring for her parents. The Estate's finances would cover the costs. She and her mother would address this.

Emma sighed as she watched the green country roll past.

Why was life so complicated? The class system made it too difficult for everyone, but it was the reality of this world. If only David were from the aristocracy. She needed more information on his background. Perhaps she could find something making him more acceptable. Robert was right; the class system was a hindrance.

The coach pulled up outside the Fox and Hound around eleven-thirty. Emma saw a party of three well-dressed women arriving at the hotel's front door. As she peered harder, she recognised Anne Turner and Marion Steele. Emma was cheered by this. But who was the other young lady? She was well-groomed, and her dress was particularly smart. Then she realised it was Neville's sister, Megan Bassington. Not having seen her since February last year, before she left London for New York, she was impressed by her transformation. Megan would be a great addition. She always found her company very enlightening.

As the coach stopped, Anne spied Emma peering out of the open window with a great smile and a wave.

"Marion and Megan, look, it is Emma. What perfect timing!"

The three girls waved excitedly and rushed over beside the newly arrived coach. Emma flew through the coach door and into Anne's arms.

"Anne, I have missed you so much. You too, Marion and Megan. Why, Megan, we had not met since February last year. You are so grown up, and look at those lovely clothes."

"You are too kind, Emma. I was fortunate to bring home a new set of outfits from New York. However, my father was not pleased as my tour there was aimed at teaching me journalism. But we girls must have nice clothes!"

They all giggled and made suitable comments about Megan's outfit.

"We have visited Hursts, and Mrs Smith has noted Megan's dress and arranged a further viewing for some other outfits. It may be that we can keep up with New York in Guildford by having Megan here! Marion and Megan will help you unpack Emma and then accompany you up the High Street this afternoon."

"That will be splendid. Perhaps we might have a small lunch soon – I have not eaten since leaving Fintelton! No morning tea at all."

At the mention of food, Megan joined the conversation saying, "I'm famished too. We must visit the dining room. The coachmen will look after the luggage. Emma, you may tell me about Robert's activities. Why we have not met since that ball we attended together in London in February last year. What a time that was!"

Anne watched as the three girls made their way into the hotel. Raising her umbrella as another squall made its appearance, she turned and walked toward home. She realised there was much she did not know about Robert. How involved was he with this girl Megan? Of course, he must know her – Neville and Robert had been friends for years. She must put this out of her mind. But where was Robert?

At the Turner Household ...

William insisted on having his page boy uniform on again. Eleanora Turner decided to use the opportunity, so Simeon and William became more familiar with the outfits. The boys were about the same height, as William was growing quicker than Simeon.

"My, you boys look handsome. It will be such a wonderful bridal party with one of you on each side of Madeline. I am sure everyone who attends will admire you. Now then go and change before the guests arrive for afternoon tea."

Simeon was off in a hurry, rushing away upstairs. William lingered and held his mother's hand, indicating a question on his mind.

"William? What about changing your clothes?"

Her youngest son's perception matched Anne's, if not more so. Eleanora was aware that William was far more perceptive than other children of his age. Despite his never-ending energy and continual desire for active pursuits, Eleanora knew William's thought processes would rival any of her other children. She knew a challenging question was coming when he was deep in thought.

Over the last six months from observation, it registered with him that his mother's health was failing. He noticed she was sleeping longer and longer. Terrified of his father's brutality, he was thankful that no further beatings eventuated. Surprisingly, his father apologised for the last beating. William thought nothing of it as he knew his father would never control his rage.

"Mother, do you think that father will beat me again?"

"I don't think so, William. He now knows that he should not. Any punishments from now on, and let us hope there are none, will be verbal only. He has promised us."

William doubted this as he only saw anger when his father was with him. It was as if there was no love at all but only hate. He avoided his father at all costs. There was no trust between them.

Eleanora said, "I know your father has mistreated you, and I have too at times. He has become a new man over the last three months, and I think he is changing for the better."

"But it was only last week that he whipped my legs so badly, Mother. I could not stand up. If it were not for Doctor Neville, I think he would have whipped my legs off. And if he attacks you again, it may be the same, but he might kill you!"

"Your father would never do that!"

"Mother, why do you sleep all the time and still look tired?"

"I am sick, William, and when you are sick, you get tired. It is true it is happening more often, but nothing will stop me from seeing your sister Beth married and the birth of this new baby. Perhaps another brother for you, William. How would you like that?"

She sat down and held him close. William thought about what she said. He hated seeing his mother tired all the time. He wanted his happy mother back, who would laugh and play with him.

"Mother, will you get well again?"

Eleanora took a weak breath. She was wrestling with this question and hoping for a happy ending. Unfortunately, she knew in her heart there would be no happy ending for her.

"I'm not sure, William. I am trying so hard, but sometimes even when we try our hardest, it doesn't work. We all must die at some stage. Look at good old Doctor Jeremy Stephens. He was a kind, good man, but the Lord took him home. Why, if Robert had not saved you and Simeon from that stag, who knows what would have happened. We must accept that our Lord takes us home when he knows it is the right time. It is a natural thing. Usually, we do not understand this and perhaps never will. But sometimes, we must accept what is happening."

"Please don't die, Mother. Who will protect me from father then? He will kill me!"

"Now, now, William, I have already told you your father will never hurt you again. And you can always talk with me whether I am dead or alive. Just pray to our Lord Jesus and say, 'I would like a talk with my mother again,' and he will let you talk with me. As you grow older, you will understand this. Our Lord will protect you!"

"Really?"

"Yes, I will always be with you. You can always talk with me, and I will talk back."

William looked up and smiled at her.

"Thank you, Mother. I already talk with you in my dreams."

"I know, Darling, and I dream about you too!"

William looked straight at her face and could see how weary she was, but she was trying so hard to be brave. It was then that he knew his mother would soon be gone. But he must be brave for her also.

"Thank you, Mother."

He softly walked out of the room and then rushed upstairs.

Eleanora steadied herself, knowing the disease was spreading throughout her body. Rising each morning was becoming more difficult. If only she could last long enough for the birth.

She prayed for healing and the protection of her family.

In the kitchen, Anne and Beth were assisting Mrs Jennings and Aggie with the afternoon tea.

"Bethany! It is time Father employed an additional maid. This madness cannot go on where he thinks two staff members are enough for this family. When the new baby comes, it will be chaos. You and I must talk with him before the wedding. We must!"

Bethany looked up from the decorated plates she was arranging cakes on, nodding in agreement. "This evening, when the children are in bed, we will talk with him."

Anne was also mindful of the stress a new baby would cause in the house. Mother would never care for a baby in her present condition. Despite her father's mental health, he must face this decision.

Fintelton Manor, outside Petersfield ...

Lord Fintelton made steady progress in recovering from his stroke, surprising everyone! On his last visit, the doctor was astounded at how quickly the paralysis disappeared and most of the other symptoms. Doctor Sopwith concluded that the stroke was not as significant as first thought.

The servants were relieved now that the Earl was up and about. Caring for him was now less of a burden. The butler noticed how the staff had struggled with the extra duties. He intended a conversation with Lady South about a nurse for the Earl. He was sure there would be a relapse soon, and it might not work out as well the next time.

As Lady Jane took breakfast, the butler moved forward, "Ahem. My Lady, a word if I may."

"Yes, Pike, what is it?"

"My Lady, we are all pleased that His Lordship has made a good recovery. In fact, with his health improving, we may take him into the garden soon. I'm sure he would enjoy some sunshine."

"Yes, that would be good, but only in the sheltered area. If the Earl feels confident, then, by all means, try. Some sunshine will do him good!"

"Yes, my Lady. His recovery has been almost Biblical; however, I think we must consider the future. We both know that these occurrences have happened too often, and a recurrence is likely. The next time may be far more serious, and at Lord Fintelton's age, his dexterity will slowly decline. I would suggest that you allow the housekeeper, Mrs Walsh, to commence recruiting a nurse or a highly skilled maid. Preparations need to be put in place for the Earl's final years."

Lady Jane stopped eating breakfast, putting down her knife and fork. Her previous consideration of such an eventuality suggested the same initiative. Doctor Sopwith also had made similar suggestions. The countess was a lady of duty. She always felt it was her responsibility to care for her husband personally. This last stroke revealed she was no longer capable of these physical duties. It was time for action.

"Pike.......... Thank you for your suggestion. I think you are correct. It is now time we made inquiries. However, I shall review any chosen applicant, please. I will discuss this with Sir Hugh, so he understands the situation."

Pike quickly realised the implications of involving Sir Hugh. Knowing how little he cared for his father, he recognised the son's ambition and his disappointment on the Earl's rapid recovery. Discussing this decision with Sir Hugh would be a mistake indeed.

"My Lady, if I may offer some advice. You are the Countess, and the decision is yours, alone! I am not sure that Sir Hugh will show a great amount of compassion in such a discussion. His general demeanour has not been that helpful during the present crisis."

Lady Jane was quite wise, and she too noticed Hugh's lack of empathy. She excused Hugh based on his infirmities. The suggestion from Pike was arousing suspicion about her son's goodwill towards his father. Sir Hugh might well make the whole process more difficult. As her husband aged, Hugh would wield more power until he finally became the new Earl. If she confided in Hugh, he might feel this strengthened his position. It would be better if she made the decision herself. It was final then!

"Yes, Pike. Thank you for the advice. You may proceed."

"Thank you, my Lady."

Pike stepped back, breathing a sigh of relief. The Earl surviving as long as possible was far preferable for more reasons than one. The thought of Sir Hugh ruling the roost was unthinkable.

Sir Hugh entered the breakfast room and plonked himself down opposite his mother. For the first time in a week, his sleep had refreshed him. Following Doctor Sopwith's instructions, he felt some energy in his body. More importantly than this, his appetite had returned.

"Mother, father seems considerably improved. The staff will be quite capable of caring for him over the next few days. I shall join you in Guildford for the wedding. Father will be more comfortable if I am with you. He is always concerned for your protection."

"That is kind of you, Hugh. Mr Stem is also accompanying me. He has business in Guildford. I shall let you make the arrangements with him. Now I set off tomorrow morning after breakfast, so please be ready by then?"

"Certainly, Mother."

Hugh smiled. The invitation was for the family, so it would be difficult for the hosts to refuse him entry. It would allow him a meeting with this Turner gentleman and possibly his daughter. Who knew, there may be some attractive young ladies present!

At Guildford ...

The Reverend Andrew Taggart organised the wedding rehearsal for five pm on Wednesday evening. Sitting at his study desk, he considered his address for the bride and groom. Having known Bethany since she was a child, there was an emotional attachment here, and it must be a splendid address. At this stage of his preparations, he was still unsure which of the talks he would use. He thought perhaps a walk along the street would help. So, he closed his books, found his hat and stepped out.

It was a bright sunny Wednesday afternoon. The gale was abating quickly, much like the weather in this part of the country. On some days, there were three seasons in one day. He paced it out along the side of the street, enjoying the fresh air and the warmth of the sun on his shoulders.

Walking towards the Free School, he spied William Turner sitting on a bench with his dog Nosey. Taking the opportunity, he walked along until reaching the seat and sat down beside the boy.

"Hello William, did you enjoy school today?"

"Yes, Reverend, but I left early so I could try on my page's uniform again. It is special and has beautiful bright blue colours."

"I'm sure you will look very handsome, William. Not long now till Saturday. Will you attend the rehearsal this afternoon?"

"Yes, Reverend."

Andrew noticed that William wore a deep look of concentration on his face. William rubbed Nosey's ears as the dog put its head between his legs. There was a slight pause in the conversation. The Reverend leaned back against the bench and knew the boy would ask a question.

"Reverend Taggart, will my mother talk with me after she dies?"

Andrew sat forward and looked sideways at William. "Why would you ask this, William?"

"I was talking with mother this morning, and she was trying hard not to say she was dying, but I can see she is. She looks more and more tired every day, and she is asleep most of the time."

"I see."

Andrew Taggart felt ashamed that he was not aware of the recent developments in Eleanora Turner's health, given all the preparations going on for Beth's wedding. The comments from William brought it all back. If she looked tired and more so each day, there was certainly something wrong. But how would he answer this question from this little man wrestling with an issue far greater than he could comprehend?

"William, where do you receive your wisdom from?"

"What is wisdom, Reverend Taggart?"

"Ah, well, it is the answers or explanations you receive when you want something explained. Like you are asking me now. But mostly, you would ask someone in your family, wouldn't you?"

"Yes, my mother. She always gives me a good answer. Bethany and Anne do too."

"They have the answers because they must have found their wisdom from somewhere else. Where do you think they found their wisdom?"

William cheered up a bit as he thought he knew the answer, "From their parents!"

"Yes, that's right, but it is much more than this. When you use a hammer, and you hit your thumb, what do you first think of?"

"I go, Yeow! Because it hurts."

"So, the next time you use the hammer, what don't you do?"

"Yes – not hit my thumb because it hurts."

"So that is a lesson about where you discover wisdom from."

William looked up at Reverend Taggart with a smile and said, "I see it comes from our lessons."

"That's right, and where do we get the best lessons about how we should live?"

William thought hard but could not think of the answer. So, he shrugged his shoulders.

"We get our best lessons from the Bible each Sunday. The Bible tells us how God wants us to live."

"But how does that affect my mother?"

"Your mother has been beside you every day of your life. So, since you were born, she has protected and cared for you. You have received lots of wisdom from your mother. Whispering in your ear as a baby, helping you stand up and learning to walk, visiting the river so you can catch butterflies, bandaging up your bruises and cuts. She has given you all this wisdom that is in your memory."

William sat there, silently thinking about what the Reverend said. He saw it was true – his mother had taught him so much.

"Now, when your mother passes on, and we hope that will not be for a long time yet, then you will have all these memories and words of wisdom in your mind. Your mother will be with you always. But while your mother is still here, keep looking at her and remember her beautiful face. When you are lonely, pray to the Lord Jesus and ask for his help remembering your mother. In that way, she will always be with you for your whole life."

William sat there, thinking about what the Reverend said. He remembered mother baking a cake with him and all the girls laughing when it came out of the oven flat, but mother gave him a big hug and said, "What a good first cake, let's eat some, shall we?"

He knew he had so many memories of what his mother told him that he would never forget her in so many ways. She would always be with him. William turned and asked, "Do you remember your mother and speak with her?"

"Yes, I do, William. Quite often!"

William lifted his eyes and looked Reverend Andrew straight in the face. Andrew felt as if William was examining him, seeing if he was telling the truth. William broke into a big smile, and with that, he was off with Nosey running and jumping behind him. Andrew Taggart watched him run off and then pulled his handkerchief out and wiped his eyes. He gave thanks, "Thank you, Lord, for my mother, and thank you, Mother, for all you taught me!"

Standing up, he continued his walk in the bright sunshine with new vigour in his step.

HMS Restless ...
The gale died as quickly as it had started. *Restless* was now nearly ninety miles across the channel and no longer being tossed around by the seas. Robert saw some glimpses of blue sky on the north horizon. In the south, the sky was still dark but receding.

"Master. The weather we have been waiting for!"

"Aye, Sir."

"Bring her about Mr Ham. Set a course for Portsmouth."

Mr Ham nodded and then yelled, "All hands above."

The rigging became alive as men climbed upwards, finding their yard positions high above.

Lieutenant Ham was also keen on returning to port and decided on what sail setting would speed them on their way, "Mr Young, bring her about. Mr Trotters, put out the top gallants, please. Let's make the most of the breeze we have."

Horace was standing by the quarterdeck rail, and Robert joined him. Horace suggested, "I thought we were joining the married couple on their honeymoon in France. Is that the French coast over there?"

"We are well over halfway. That is St Anne, not France. We should make port late tonight if the wind holds. Cross your fingers."

Horace laughed. He held no ambitions for the navy as he detested how the weather could slow operations down. Now seeing it firsthand reinforced the frustrations a sailor's life held. He preferred his life of marching and attacking at his choosing. This navy life was an alien world.

"You can have the sea, Captain. I prefer land advances."

Robert smiled, "I think the Spanish would agree with you there, Horace!" They both chuckled. Robert then advised the First Lieutenant.

"I am going below Mr Ham; she is yours."

"Aye, Captain."

"Horace, will you join me in my cabin for some coffee."

"Only if you include some of Turner's biscuits, Sir."

"I think I can arrange that!"

Fintelton, the Thursday before Bethany and Neville's wedding ...
HMS *Restless* quietly entered Portsmouth harbour after midnight on the Thursday morning, after a swift trip across the channel with a firm but gusting northerly blowing. The moderate weather allowed navigation carefully into the harbour late that night.

Horace and Robert left *Restless* and set out for Fintelton at three in the morning. By mid-morning, they arrived. Robert found his father sitting in the garden, bright and chirpy. Pike, the butler, had explained that Lady Jane, Lady Emma, and Sir Hugh were all in Guildford for the wedding and that the staff were keeping a careful watch over the Earl.

Robert, somewhat disturbed that Hugh had not remained with his father, went out into the garden and sat down beside the Earl.

"How are you, Father?"

At first, Sir David did not hear the greeting from his son. He just sat there, enjoying the garden and relaxing in the sunshine.

"Father, it is Robert. How are you?" Robert raised his voice and was almost speaking in his father's ear. The Earl heard him this time and turned with a smile.

"Ah, Robert, you are back from the sea. Someone to have dinner with me. All the others left for Guildford. You will not see them. Gone off to some fellow's wedding. Marrying a commoner, you know – a bad business."

Robert frowned. Yes, this was father back to his usual self. He disapproved of mixing with commoners if he could avoid it. He was not above visiting his tenant farmers, but that was a working relationship. There were matters of more importance on which Robert required answers. How was his father recovering from the stroke? Was he still capable of managing the estate? Not having much time before Horace finished changing the horses, he must find answers quickly as they would soon be on their way again.

"Father, how are the Estate's finances going? Have we done well in the harvests?"

"I leave all that with Stem now. Hugh says the harvest is down, but I am not sure. He says the tenants are getting old and cannot produce enough. Hugh should be out there helping them."

"What about the plantations in the Indies?"

"I have suggested several times that Hugh visit and understand those businesses. But he is not interested. A visit will be necessary soon; who knows what is happening in Jamaica?"

"But surely the agents have written reports? Surely there are records of progress?"

"Not sure, my boy. Anyway, do not worry. That will be Hugh's problem. When I am gone, the lawyers in London have the papers. There will be a nice little nest egg for both you and Emma and an income for your mother, so she is independent. The attorneys manage the investments. Hugh will take over the Estate and the investments in the Indies. He will realise soon it is his responsibility."

"Father, who are the attorneys in London? Do they manage the business with the investments in the Indies?"

"Yes, always have. I wanted someone interested, who keep tabs on them, Manifold and Stout Attorneys. You remember Michael Manifold, a neighbour at St James's Square, nice fellow, completely trustworthy. Letters come from them regularly. I pass them on to Hugh. He takes care of it now."

"But Father, did not Michael Manifold die a couple of years ago?"

"No, no, couldn't have. I receive letters from them now and again. Check with Hugh. No, Michael will be still at St James's Square."

"Father, when was the last time you were at St James's Square?"

"Can't recall, son. Why the roses are looking good this year, aren't they? That gardener is doing a fine job. Mrs Walsh has a big bunch brought into my bedroom every few days. All sorts of colours. I do enjoy them, Robert. Do you like flowers, son?"

"Yes, Father."

Robert was sure his father would be safe for the next day while the family attended the wedding in Guildford, but he was disturbed that Hugh was not at home with him. As the next Earl, he should be here, certainly while his father was recovering. Who knew what could happen next? There was nothing he could do about it now. He wrestled with staying by his father's side, but his duty was with Neville and the requirements for the best man. They must head off. He would fulfil his commitment.

His father reclined quietly in the garden, smelling the sweet scents of the extensive rose garden that adjoined the manor. Sadly, Robert could see his father was losing perception of what was happening around him. He was still mentally agile but only at times. The determination and memory that he previously had were gone, but Robert smiled as he thought of the comment about the commoners. Good thing his father was not born a commoner! He would not have coped!

Walking back inside, he joined the butler at the large open doorways leading onto the drawing-room.

"Pike, how do you find him now?"

"He is a sick man, Sir. He may not survive the next attack. Sir Robert, excuse me, but may I speak freely?"

"Why, yes, Pike, you and I have been friends all my life. I would value your comments."

"Sir. I find this difficult, but I must advise you. Sir Hugh is openly saying now he would be glad if your father was gone."

Robert turned to Pike in surprise, "Openly!"

"Yes, Sir. It is only Mr Stem who is managing the Estate. As you will understand, I talk with the staff. It seems the Earl has not been managing the Estate for the last five years, and the money is becoming tight. Lady Jane and

Lady Emma know nothing of this. Sir Hugh drinks and womanises wherever he goes, and he outlays much on these vulgar pursuits. Thank goodness he does not gamble. That would certainly be the ruin of the estate. Sometimes the staff must wait for their wages as there is not enough money. Sir, if you would have a word with Sir Hugh, this might help."

"Pike, I had no idea that the situation was so bad. I shall make enquiries at once. You and I know that no one can tell Sir Hugh anything. Yet, I will try."

"Thank you, Sir."

"Pike, Sir Horace and I leave now for Guildford. I will not wish my father goodbye as he will be disappointed. I am perplexed why Hugh did not remain. But your comments explain a lot. As the next Earl, he should be here with his father. I shall return after the wedding and visit again. Now I must be off."

"Yes, Sir. I hope the wedding goes well! ... Sir Robert?"

"Yes, Pike – what is it?"

"I know you are worried about your father. I will ensure his safety. You need not worry about this while you are at the wedding. I shall ensure he has the best of care."

"Thank you, Pike. Knowing you are here is of great comfort!"

With that, Robert rushed through the Manor and towards the stables. Horace was waiting with two freshly mounted horses.

"I got old Jenny ready for you, Robert. A sailor needs a dear old horse that will not cause him much trouble. Ha, Ha, Ha!"

Robert smiled at Horace's humour. He mounted his horse, and they were off. The estate's affairs were of concern but must remain secondary at present. He could see that his father's health had been significantly declining since they met last. With his mission in the Irish sea soon beginning, he may be far away and uncontactable when events took place. He must consult Emma on this and have her make enquiries. She would be in London far sooner than he. Perhaps they could take Anne with them on their next shopping trip. He relaxed a little as he thought about Anne. What a better place this world was because of his love for her.

The Wedding at Guildford ...

Eleanora Turner woke early on Saturday morning and sat up in bed. She could feel the baby gently moving inside her, and for once, she was not in pain. Her health improved in the last two days, and today Eleanora felt alive and well. The big day was here when she would marry off her eldest daughter.

Knowing that her life would be different after this day, she hopped out of bed and dressed. No more would Beth be on call as she would have a husband and there would be children. Now it would be Beth who needed help. She shuddered about the future. 'Think positive. I will enjoy today!'

A slight knock came at the door, and it slowly opened. Jonathan appeared with two cups of tea and some buttered rolls.

"I thought I heard you wake. I was down making myself a cup of tea, so I returned downstairs and made you one. May I share a cup of tea with you, my Dear?"

"Certainly, Jonathan. Come in and sit down."

Jonathan placed the teas on the bedside table and drew up a chair. Sitting, he sipped his tea before taking a bite out of one of the rolls.

"I was thinking about our wedding, so long ago now, and all the children we have. Another one is on the way! Today we marry off the first before we finish the birthing of our children. It is a strange feeling but a good one."

"I know Jonathan, and I was thinking the same thing. It is sad in a way, but we should enjoy the positives. We will have a new son-in-law, and the Bassingtons will have a new daughter-in-law. I do hope they have a lovely honeymoon. I will miss Beth terribly."

"Now, Eleanora, it was you who said that we should remain positive!"

"Yes, yes!" Eleanora sipped her tea and then looked at Jonathan and said, "And how are you, Mr Turner? Are you a calmer man today?"

"Yes, I am Eleanora. I am very content here with you. Quite content."

A knock came on the door, and Eleanora said, "Yes?"

Simeon and William ran in and asked if they could put on their page uniforms.

"Not for a little while, boys, but you may go down for some breakfast with Mrs Jennings."

The two boys darted off.

"They are excited, aren't they, Jonathan?"

"Yes, yes, it would appear so!"

Bethany was the first awake in the girls' bedroom and sat there in her bed, thinking about the day ahead. Today her title would change from a Miss to a Mrs, and her new name would be Bassington. She would no longer be a Turner. The name change unsettled her, but she knew it was the tradition she wanted. Then the current issues of making sure all the arrangements were made took over much of her thought.

Looking out the window at the town of Guildford surrounding her, she thought about it being her friend for the last twenty years. What would the future bring? She then realised there was no time for dreaming and focused on the list of jobs still waiting for this morning.

Anne rolled over at the sound of Beth sitting up in bed and asked her, "It is the big day. Are you ready?"

Bethany considered the question and replied, "Probably not ready, but ready as I ever will be!"

Anne smiled at this and sat back in bed, thankful that Robert had finally arrived in time, "I wonder how the party for Neville went last night."

Then she suddenly thought of Robert's final fitting for his new uniform. Panicking, she looked at Beth, "The uniform. I forgot Robert's new uniform!"

"It is fine, Anne. I have organised it all with Mrs Smith. She will visit the Fox and Hound early and finish it there. However, he may not appreciate Mrs Smith waking him early after a late night! Teach him about arriving late, won't it?"

The girls laughed, which brought Clementine, Madeline and Marcia into their room, and the games began.

The Fox and Hound, Guildford ...

It was a busy night at the Fox and Hound, but all was now quiet. The company of young men successfully found their rooms despite the influence of an unusually large amount of alcohol taken on board. The night's activities were pleasant and well behaved until Sir Hugh South gate crashed late in the evening. Making matters worse, Sir Hugh was considerably drunk and brought a whore with him.

"So Bassington, here is a little present for you, a pretty madam for your pleasure. I knocked her off a few times this afternoon, priming her ready for you. Will be much more fun than that baker's daughter you have lined up. Ha, Ha, Ha. Here take her out the back and give her a thumping!"

Neville glared at Hugh, resisting taking offence at the vulgarity of his comments. Robert held him back and quietly said, "Don't worry, Neville, he is drunk. We will get rid of him." Thankfully, Thomas was nearly asleep and missed the comments.

Sir Hugh could see the displeasure on Neville's face and was enjoying it, "Come on, Nev boy, be a man and take her out the back. Maybe you are not up to it. Maybe all those years in the navy have changed your preferences? Ha, Ha, Ha!"

Neville had heard enough. In all his years in the navy, he had never suffered such revolting suggestions as this. The rage exploded in his body and consumed him as he stood and then ran towards Hugh. He would knock his head off. Of course, this was what Sir Hugh was aiming for, as he knew Neville was no fighter and would be a pushover if the baiting worked.

Now Sir Hugh was not a small man and stood nearly six feet tall with a muscular build. He was strong and could hold his own in a fight, but he never saw the punch from Horace coming. Captain Horace Coombes, who stood three inches taller than Sir Hugh, was combat trained and an expert at killing. He was incensed that an aristocrat, such as Sir Hugh, could have such vulgar manners at a friend's stag party. Horace had met Neville through Robert and knew that Nev lacked the fighting skills needed with a thug like Sir Hugh, even a drunk Sir Hugh. So, he quietly stood up behind Sir Hugh after the first insult and waited for his opportunity. It came soon enough as Sir Hugh was intent on creating a situation.

Horace darted in front of Sir Hugh and stood like a wall between the vulgar man and Neville. As Sir Hugh lifted his drunken eyes, unsure of what was blocking his view, the lights went out. He never reacted before Horace's great fist blasted his left eye socket. It was like an iron bar hitting a melon. Sir Hugh fell like a lump of clay, putting his disruptive behaviour at an end very soon after it had started. With that, the unwilling whore fled out of the room, wailing.

Horace walked forward, stepped over Sir Hugh's motionless body, sat beside Robert, and grunted like a bull.

Robert, who watched the entire incident with great interest, glanced over at him and said, "Nicely done, Horace! Why I didn't even have time to blink!"

Neville stood looking down at Sir Hugh, unconscious on the ground with a swelling left cheek.

David Sopwith standing up beside Neville, inquired, "Sir, what is your diagnosis of this ugly chap on the floor?"

Neville shook his head and, in a loud voice said, "David and my fellow friends, I would say it is a plain case, mostly found in commoners, of the vulgarities and results in a severe swelling in the left cheek and a very nasty headache in the morning!"

A loud cheering of, "Here, here!" was then heard, and the party continued late into the night with many sea shanties and toasts.

Now it was morning, and there was no movement from the men's rooms and probably would not be for another couple of hours yet. A gentle knock came on Robert's door. He rolled over with the alertness that any sea captain has and answered the door. Outside, he found Mrs Smith and her assistant with his uniform ready for the fitting. Robert attempted a smile, but it was a tired face that was not working well. He ushered them into his room, where Horace was still fast asleep in the other bed.

"Don't mind Horace; he had a rather busy time at Neville's party last night. Now let us proceed with the fitting, please."

Mrs Smith's assistant looked at the enormous man in the other bed, and all she could say was, "Ooooh!"

The local Church, Guildford ...

The Reverend Andrew Taggart sat at his desk and looked up with a smile. He had made his final decision on his address. Glad this task was complete, the Reverend checked the time. Soon, he must be at the church and check that all was ready with the verger. This service would be the largest for Guildford during his time as Rector.

"My! What a wonderful day it will be!"

He then prayed, "Lord, let this service glorify you today and let me be your obedient servant. I pray in Jesus, our Lord and Saviour's name. Amen."

Feeling he needed further steadying after this, he poured himself a glass of sherry and sat back with a content look on his face as he sipped it.

The Turners had scheduled the wedding for two-thirty that day, and there was enormous interest from the townspeople, who knew Jonathan Turner and his family well. For a hundred yards, in the direction the bride's carriage would come, bystanders lined the street waiting for a glimpse. It was almost like a celebration day for the town.

As Eleanora Turner stood at the church entrance, waiting for her daughter's arrival, she grasped the Reverend's hands in hers, "Andrew, I am so pleased that this wedding should bring such joy to our town. I am overwhelmed by their kind wishes."

As the bridal coach approached, there was an outpouring of cheering and waving from the crowd. At the church, the crowd was deeper, and the commotion grew as Jonathan Turner helped his daughter down onto the pavement.

Bethany turned and waved, which resulted in an almighty roar of good wishes from the joyous crowd. Andrew Taggart watched in disbelief that there could be so many wishing the young couple well. It was like a Royal wedding in miniature. The guests inside were left with no doubt that the bride had arrived. Excitement grew in the expectation of the bride's entrance.

"It may be good if you take your seat now, Eleanora. Laura will take you down. I will remain here and arrange the bridal party before we commence."

"Thank you, Andrew." Eleanora took one last look at her radiant daughter being led up the steps by Jonathan. She hurried off with Laura Taggart towards the front row with tears in her eyes. Laura kindly agreed to sit with them in case Mrs Turner lost energy.

The Reverend Andrew Taggart checked that all was right with the bridal party, gave Jonathan Turner a shake of the hand, and then proceeded down the centre aisle and approached the groomsmen.

As the bridesmaids organised the bride's dress before the actual procession started, there was a growing excitement inside the church. Andrew Taggart came over, "Neville, it is time! "

The groom stood up with his groomsmen. Robert could see that Neville's healthy complexion was changing into a whitish colour. He stopped talking and seemed in a bit of a trance. Robert quickly realised Neville was freezing up. Settling down the groom was now his priority. Moving slightly closer, he spoke softly.

"This is the moment you have been waiting for, Nev. It will all go well. You need not worry; I am here with you for support."

Neville stood there, and Robert noticed the trembling. Robert had previously placed a glass of water behind the lectern in case of any issues. Knowing Neville well, he was not expecting difficulties. Still, others advised him to prepare for anything, including the groom running out of the church at the last moment.

He asked Thomas for the glass of water.

"Have a good drink, Neville."

Neville made a raspy reply, "Yes, thank you."

Robert knew he needed more than water, "Remember when you looked into her eyes on the stairs at the Turner's house. Remember how it changed your life, Nev! She is coming now, and together, you will start a new journey. This wedding will be the best thing you have ever done in your life. This girl will complete you."

"It will? Are you sure I am not making a mistake?"

"I am sure, Nev. You and Bethany are made for each other. You are her warrior, and you will protect her for the rest of your life. Nev, she will protect you in every situation. This marriage is good. You have always desired this. Be strong, my friend and celebrate this woman giving herself freely to you. Neville, this is true love."

Robert could see the colour coming back into Neville's face as the tears rolled down. Robert, being the close friend he was, could see they were no longer tears of terror but tears of joy. Slowly a smile came onto Neville's face, and he started shaking his hands, relaxing them.

"At a boy Nev! Today is yours and Beth's day. I am so privileged to share it with you."

Neville gasped and finally found his voice again.

"I don't know what came over me then. I lost it all, didn't I?"

"No, it is just stress. The same as before we go into battle, it does funny things."

Neville carefully dried his eyes so that the congregation would not see. "Robert, thank you for being my friend. You will never know how much it means. You are an inspiration. Thank you."

Neville held out his hand and shook hands with Robert. "You inspire me as well, my friend!"

Andrew Taggart watched the bridal arrangements in the vestibule, keeping one eye on this and the other on the groomsmen. He could see that suddenly for no reason, the groom was paralysed by fear. This type of incident often happened, and it was the best man that calmed everything down. He could not remember a groom changing body colour to a bloodless white before.

He noticed how Robert just calmly talked Neville through the process and brought him back down into a calm state again.

Andrew was relieved, 'Thank you, Lord, for Robert! He understands what is required. I need another sherry!'

Andrew was in a sweat and wiped his brow as the verger gave him the signal that all was ready. He nodded, appearing relatively calm, stepping forward and addressing the congregation.

"Welcome, Ladies and Gentlemen. Would you all please stand!"

The organist commenced the anthem requested by the bride and groom. The guests stood, all eyes turned towards the church entrance, as the proud page boys, William and Simeon, flanking the flower girls Madeline and Marcia, led the procession. Emma, watching the conversation between Neville and Robert, looked straight at Robert. She was acquainted with Neville as a friend for nearly ten years now and detected the stiffness in his stance. She understood from his body movements that he was freezing up in fear. She saw the conversation between Robert and Neville and understood what was happening. When she saw the Reverend wipe his brow, it confirmed that Neville had faltered but had now regained his confidence.

When the groomsmen turned and faced the bridal procession coming down the church's centre aisle, Emma looked directly at Robert and smiled with a knowing look. Robert looked first at the bridal procession but then saw Emma smiling at him. She was aware of the crisis and its resolution, now giving her approval of a job well done. Robert gave her a happy wink and looked back at the procession. Emma, watching the page boys and flower girls pass by, thought about her brother. 'That is Robert. He can cope with anything. Why can't Hugh be like that?'

As Clementine moved gracefully down the aisle behind the page boys and flower girls, Robert found himself entranced. Clementine appeared to drift just above the floor, slowly down the aisle, as her beautiful gown of light blue silk complemented the girlish curls that dangled around her sparkling eyes. She was a picture of sophisticated beauty only surpassed by Anne as she followed, gleaming in her dress that shimmered in the light shining down from the high side windows of the church. If anything resembled angels, he thought that Clementine and Anne must be the closest he would ever see.

Robert looked closer at Anne and noticed her beautiful golden hair curled in a bun. She looked dazzling, like Clementine, but more so in Robert's eyes. His heart burst with love for her as she carefully walked down the aisle, almost afraid to lift her eyes. She smiled at several people near the aisle as she neared the groomsmen. Then she looked up, and her eyes met Roberts. He nearly shed a tear as he saw her dazzling beauty utterly open to him. With a smile, she quickly looked away as she took her position beside Clementine.

Robert visibly steadied himself as he refocused on the task at hand. He noticed Neville looking down the aisle with his mouth open.

"Nev, I think you should smile, old boy. The open mouth is not the best pose!"

Neville checked himself as well, as the beauty of these young women overcame him. Then his eyes met Bethany's eyes, and he broke into the happiest smile Robert would ever see from him.

"That's the boy!" Robert encouraged him.

Lady Jane South was amazed by the dazzling beauty of the bridesmaids and then the bride. The meeting of eyes between Anne and Robert was not unnoticed. Their faces told her that his attachment was far more serious than she had thought. She was happy for him as she could not imagine a lovelier young lady than Anne for her son. She sighed, 'I'm glad I am here at this wedding.' It confirmed her views on so many things that, in the past, were sacred to her class. It was not that society was changing, but young people were discovering a changing world with broadening views. In many ways, she was pleased with the undercurrents of change.

She looked across the aisle at Eleanora Turner, a beautiful woman and a mother today so proud and happy for her daughter's future happiness. She would develop a friendship with her and discover more about the mother of her possible future daughter in law.

Bethany and her father now approached the end of the aisle. Neville and Bethany could not keep their eyes off each other. It was a match made in heaven; they were so in love. Jonathan Turner stood behind his daughter as instructed by Andrew Taggart.

Reverend Taggart waited as the bridesmaids arranged the bride's train. The two bridesmaids then stood beside Bethany, and everything was ready. The page boys and flower girls sat down with the Turners in the front row. When all was quiet, the Reverend commenced.

"Welcome again, everyone. Would you please be seated? I always find this helpful before we commence the service.

We are here today to join this couple, Neville Winston Bassington and Bethany Charlotte Eleanora Turner, in Holy Matrimony. Neville and Bethany and their families have asked me to say how honoured they are that you are here celebrating with them today. They have also asked me to welcome Lady Jane South, Countess of Fintelton and her son Sir Hugh who celebrate with us today."

There was respectful clapping and a quick pause as Reverend Andrew Taggart opened his prayer book.

"We have come together here in the sight of God, and in the presence of this congregation, to join this man and this woman in holy matrimony, which is an honourable state of life, instituted from the beginning by God himself, signifying to us the spiritual union that is between Christ and his church.[26]

The service continued.

……. Therefore, if anyone can show any just cause why they may not lawfully be joined together, let him speak now, or hereafter remain silent."

There was silence. Sir Hugh moved slightly beside his mother; however, Lady Jane took his hand and quietly said, "Shush!"

After a good silence, the Reverend said, "Who gives this woman to be married to this man?"

Jonathan Turner came forward and gently took his daughter's hand, kissed it, and then placed it in Neville's hand. He then withdrew and sat beside his wife. She looked at him with tears in her eyes and said, "Well done, Jonathan."

He was overcome with emotion for one of the first times in his life, and could not speak but managed a soft smile with a twitch in his cheek.

William peered at his father and mother sitting there together, looking at each other in a very loving way and wondered how this same man could have beaten her just six months earlier. How could this be? He could not understand emotions. Perhaps his brother-in-law would explain this.

The time arrived for Andrew Taggart's public message during the ceremony, and he addressed the couple.

"Neville and Bethany,

I am so pleased that you found each other. What a wonderful couple we have before us today. Don't you agree with me, everybody?"

He encouraged the congregation, and they started clapping. There was a tremendous uplifting response and a round of applause from the congregation, which lasted nearly two minutes. The couple was moved by this and turned and said thank you as the people clapped and some shouted, "Hooray!"

Andrew continued, "It seems our whole town has come together offering their heartfelt congratulations. I feel this is most appropriate, especially as we welcome a new surgeon into our town and community.

There are just two things I will say today.

Families of the Bassingtons and the Turners, what you are witnessing today is the creation of a new family. You all become in-laws to this family but always remember that it is no longer your family. Neville and Bethany are now a new family, a union of two people under God's blessing, which is Holy and must never be violated.

Neville and Bethany will set up a new home in Guildford. They will have children and bring these children up under their guidance. It will be the responsibility of each of their families to assist them as best they can. But hear my words. It is not the place any more of the Bassingtons or the Turners

---

[26] An Australian Prayer Book for use together with The Book of Common Prayer, 1662.

to direct them in what they do. Neville and Bethany are a new family unit blessed by God and will flourish in their way.

Secondly, let me encourage this wonderful couple with a few words on persistence in a relationship. Neville and Bethany, at present, you both are feeling so much in love that you would wonder what could ever go wrong with your relationship. But I am sure you will recall the vows that will follow. 'For better or for worse!' Yes, there will be times ahead when you will not feel as you are today. As you age, there will be challenges, and it may become harder in time!

................." Andrew continued for a few minutes with a compelling message before finishing.

"Now, May the Lord bless you both with long lives and health. Amen"

The service continued, and on the fourteenth of October eighteen hundred and twenty-six, Neville Winston Bassington married Bethany Charlotte Eleanora Turner and enjoyed a magnificent wedding followed by a reception at the Fox and Hound, which would be remembered by all who attended with great affection.

Chapter 21

As the sun peeked over the eastern horizon, the Reverend Andrew Taggart slowly dragged himself out of bed, quickly washed and dressed, and headed downstairs for breakfast. He was encouraged with his officiating over the wedding service yesterday, especially the renewed contact with the South family from Fintelton Manor.

"Never hurts having friends in high places!" he murmured.

Finishing breakfast, he took his sermon notes and walked across and in through the arched main entrance of the church. Walking through the vestibule and towards the pews, he noticed a tall man silently reflecting while sitting in the back pew. As he walked closer, the man seemed somewhat familiar. He recognised him as Sir Hugh South.

Andrew stopped. This morning's preparations for the early service were waiting, and he was not expecting anyone in the church at this hour. Reverend Taggart recalled that Sir Hugh escorted Lady Jane at the wedding yesterday, but Sir Hugh was strangely absent during the reception. He wondered if there was some misunderstanding. On reflection, Andrew recalled the black shiner around Sir Hugh's left eye as Hugh sat in church yesterday. It startled him at the time; however, he had quickly put it out of his mind. Perhaps the celebration at the stag party on Friday night was a bit rowdier than he was aware.

Sir Hugh remained sitting there quietly, looking straight ahead. Andrew gathered himself and then walked forward and sat beside Hugh, leaving a respectful distance. He sat there for a while, allowing Sir Hugh the first move.

They sat there together for a full five minutes before Sir Hugh looked sideways, "Good morning, Reverend Taggart."

Andrew looked at the tired creased face of a man who had not slept. Sir Hugh still carried the shiner on his left eye socket. It looked painful. Despite his dishevelled appearance, Hugh looked calm, and it was clear he was in control of his emotions.

"I was baptised in this church some thirty years ago, Rector!"

"I'm afraid that was a bit before my time, Hugh!" Andrew took the liberty of a first name basis as he was in church, and Sir Hugh needed a confidential discussion.

"Yes, it was a long time ago!"

Then there was another period of a few minutes of silence.

"I did not see you at the reception last night, Hugh. Were you unwell?"

"Yes, I was unwell, but that was not my reason. You see, the hosts did not personally invite me to the church or the reception! My Father has suffered some ill health lately. My Father requested I escort my mother, Lady Jane."

"Ah, I'm sorry about your father, but I'm sure the bride and groom would have welcomed your attendance at the reception?"

"I'm afraid not, Rector. I'm afraid not!"

Andrew could see that this young man had much on his mind. He considered finding a more convenient time with Sir Hugh that allowed more flexibility for a discussion of his worries. It was always a busy time preparing for a church service. Despite this, Andrew felt there might be something more important here that required careful attention. Perhaps it was more important than preparing for the next service.

"I dined at the Fox and Hound by myself last night. There was nobody else there. Everyone booked into the hotel was at the reception. I was staying in my mother's suite. By the time I finished dinner, I was becoming a bit lonely and thought perhaps I might attend the reception. I found a six-foot army Captain built of iron blocking the entrance. I deferred, having made the acquaintance of this chap the previous night."

Hugh pointed at his left eye. "I withdrew rather quickly!"

'Ah!' thought Andrew, 'This is where the shiner came from!'

Sir Hugh sat back and took a deep breath, "So, I grabbed a couple of bottles of whisky and found a whore. I took them into the hotel suite for some fun. But when I sat down in the suite and recognised this was the room of my mother and sister, a strange sensation came over me. I felt uncomfortable with what I was doing. You see, I listened carefully yesterday. Your message struck a chord with me. I am not religious, do not believe in God, and am not interested in being saved, but your descriptions of families and how sacred they are has affected me. I have been thinking about your words ever since."

"And what have you found from your consideration of this subject, Hugh?"

Sir Hugh sat there for a while, looking down at his feet. He struggled within himself for the words but found they would not come. Andrew then saw the emotion on his face. Hugh looked up and then looked down again. Taking a deep breath, he said in a low tone, "I have nothing! I am nothing!"

Andrew allowed Sir Hugh some recovery time from what he said. He knew well that when a man recognised which way his life was travelling, it was a critical decision point. It may be a turning point, just so slight, that eventually, it may bring a ship back on course, but it required the most delicate care.

"I would be interested in how you realised this, Hugh?"

Hugh looked up, "I have been sitting here most of the night, Rector, thinking about what I have achieved that is of worth. Every time I come up with something, I realise that it is not something of worth but something I have either been given or taken. In terms of self-worth, I find my name on the score page has nothing against it."

"Hugh, if I may, I think I may be of some help, but I will not push you in a direction you are not comfortable with."

Sir Hugh raised his head. He rubbed his swollen eyes and peered into Andrew's face.

"Reverend Taggart, you are the only person in this world that I would have confidence in trusting. You may speak as freely as you wish, as I have run out of ideas."

Andrew was staggered by this comment and the honour Sir Hugh gave him in his trust. He sat back, giving careful thought to his next words. These words would be critical in this young man's life.

"Hugh, I'm not sure you are aware, but I was born an aristocrat! Yes, estates, money and prospects. I made a choice and gave it all up. Now I am not saying you should do the same. It is just something I did, and I took a chance. Some would say I took a step in faith."

Hugh continued looking at his feet with his head slightly tilted towards Reverend Taggart, indicating he was listening.

"I'm not sure if it was a step in faith – I have always found the notion of guidance rather vague! Sometimes you must go with your gut. I'm sure you will identify with that. But since then, I have learned that the only things in life that you value are the things that require you to sacrifice. Let me give you an example. I have always enjoyed fishing. To become a clergyman, I sacrificed that hobby and a way of life. But my career as a clergyman has been most rewarding. Last year I took two weeks' vacation, so Laura and I went further west and found a small cottage beside a running brook. The owner delightfully situated the place, and I could walk out on a bank near the house and throw in a line. It was pure joy.

I valued this time very much, but I realised then that my sacrifices were worth it. You see, fishing was most enjoyable, but it did not compare with the blessings I have received from my ministry. I will not bore you with the details, but I am a satisfied man."

Hugh looked at him and said, "I don't understand."

"I sacrificed the aristocratic life for a minister's life. Being a minister of religion involves sacrifice every day. I have gained blessings a hundred times more than what might have been if I had not taken that step in faith. I found a loving wife, children, a happy lifestyle, and friends from every parish I served. Friends like you!"

Hugh smiled, "You count me as a friend?"

"Of course, I do. You are a good friend!"

Hugh considered this for a moment, "You are a very content man, Rector. I do not have any contentment in my life."

Andrew was careful that the words of his next response were specific.

"Hugh, please think hard about this question before you answer it. I mean, answer carefully. The answer from you must be truthful, and I shall keep the answer you give in total confidence forever."

Sir Hugh nodded, "If you so wish!"

"Hugh, just tell me one thing. Do you like yourself as a person?"

Hugh sat up straight and looked up. He gazed ahead for several seconds and then turned towards the Reverend with a pained look. Hugh then looked away. He wrestled with this question in his mind. He stood up and walked back and forth, occasionally looking at the Reverend. Andrew could see the stress this reality check was causing him. Sir Hugh sat down again.

"I need a truthful answer, Hugh?"

Hugh stood up and walked away into the vestibule as if he was leaving but then stopped and returned, "I must confront this, must I not?"

"Yes, you must confront it."

"Then, I do not need to answer."

"On the contrary, one of the most important things you do in your life is to answer this question!"

He sat down beside Andrew, and looking straight ahead, he said, "I hate myself!"

Andrew lost no time once he heard this answer.

"Hugh, you have now been honest with yourself about where you are truly at in your life. You are not the first, and you shall certainly not be the last to find yourself in this position. Hugh, you can turn this around. If you desire this, I will help you. But it will not happen overnight. There will be no miracles. Have you the desire for change, Hugh? Do you desire self-esteem?"

"More than anything else, Rector!"

"You have made the first step in the right direction, Hugh! You wish for a better life with yourself and others. There is a simple first step. I would ask that you think of yourself and others this week in a different way. Do unto others as you would have them do unto you. Think about that this week.

Now enjoy this day. Revisit your foundations, Hugh. Take your mother and sister home and enjoy their company and your father's company for a week, then come back and see me, and we will talk further. While you are at home this week, consider what you do not like about yourself and how you might change that. We should talk again, say Monday week. By the way, you are welcome at church this morning if you wish."

Hugh stood up and towered above Andrew Taggart, sitting on the pew.

"Is this something I can achieve, Rector?"

"Yes, Hugh! You have decided on your path, and you must determinedly follow it. I have full confidence that you will achieve your goal. Go and have a wash and some breakfast, son! You will feel better for it."

Sir Hugh South waited for Andrew Taggart as he stood. Then he shook his hand and slowly walked out of the church. Andrew Taggart watched him go. Then he turned and rushed into the vestry. Opening the vestry door, he thought, 'Now, where was I!'

At the Fox and Hound …

Lady Jane and Lady Emma South found a clean-shaven and well-dressed Sir Hugh finishing breakfast alone at a large table in the dining room. Admiral Sir Tristram and Lady Amanda Sutherland and Sir Robert appeared and walked together. Robert led them over, and they joined the party, Robert sitting beside Hugh ensuring a position where he might control any embarrassing outbursts from his brother.

In a clear voice, Hugh immediately said, "Robert, my apologies for my unpardonable behaviour on Friday night. It was disgusting, and I am ashamed of myself. This behaviour will never happen again, and I beg your forgiveness."

The conversation at the table fell silent.

Robert, taken by surprise, was astounded at this change in his brother. After looking at Hugh with an open mouth, he recovered his composure rubbing his chin, "Thank you, Hugh, apology accepted. It may be better if you also find Neville and make amends with him. But I appreciate what you have said. Thank you."

"I will apologise as soon as I meet with him today. I will seek an opportunity as I now understand how badly I have behaved."

Robert watched Hugh as he made this comment and was surprised as he found Hugh quite genuine.

The conversation at the table recommenced as the waiters served breakfast. Lady Jane gazing across at Emma lifted her eyebrows. Robert made use of the opportunity of discussing a few issues about the estate with Hugh, particularly while he appeared approachable.

The party was finishing breakfast when Admiral Sutherland took Robert aside.

"Sir Robert, if I may have a word, please?"

They both stood and moved out of hearing distance.

"Robert, I know you have a few duties here yet with this wedding, but I need you back at Portsmouth as soon as possible. I was expecting Foster here, but he has not arrived. He gave me a commitment he would be back in time for Neville's wedding. You know Foster, he is a stickler for timing, and he does not miss a beat.

I have grave fears, Robert! Foster has not been heard of since he set sail for the Irish Sea. It may be a coincidence, but I am starting to fear the worst. There should be some news as soon as I get back, but if not, then we have a problem on our hands. I will need you up in the Irish Sea. We must either find him or discover his fate. Sorting out what has happened to Foster must now be done before you embark on your mission.

Please clear your commitments here in the next day and a half, then make sure you are back in Portsmouth by Wednesday night at the latest. The briefing will be Thursday morning. I should have more information by then. I expect you at sea Thursday afternoon and heading north-west, Sir! I shall advise Lieutenant Ham that *Restless* must be ready."

Robert nodded, "He may have encountered the same gale I experienced delaying my arrival. However, there would still have been time for his arrival here. I hope he has not suffered the same fate as Captain Hughes."

Robert paused and said, "I will find him, Sir!"

"Good. Now keep this confidential. It was a fine wedding, and you did well as best man. I shall invite you and Neville for dinner at Portsmouth early next year once we solve these problems. Hopefully, Foster can join us as well."

"I'm sure he will, Sir!"

"I wish I was as certain as you, Robert. Off you go and see that lass of yours."

"Thank you, Sir."

Later in his room, Admiral Sutherland shared with his wife, "Amanda, I hate being an Admiral, sending off young Captains who may never return. It gives me nightmares. I would rather be at sea myself again."

"Tristan, you have had your turn, Dear! The younger men are quite capable! They are in no doubt about what they are taking on. It is the navy way. By using your experience, you can assist Captains like Robert. May God go with them!"

"Amen! Now let us load the coach, my Dear. Portsmouth awaits, and I am keen on returning. There must be news by now."

At the Turner Household ...

The Turners entertained several wedding guests, including Lady Fintelton and her daughter Lady Emma for luncheon. Eleanora Turner sent off a note early in the morning kindly inviting Sir Hugh. A message returned thanking them for the kind invitation and stating that Sir Hugh would accompany Lady Jane. Eleanora, who was unaware of what had transpired at the stag night, was being hospitable and greeted Sir Hugh warmly.

Anne made sure her mother invited Robert and Sir Horace Coombes. Mrs Jennings, being excited about Sir Horace returning, made sure there was a ready supply of Turner biscuits. Because Aggie and Mrs Jennings worked in the kitchen, Anne arranged for three of her office staff to wait tables during lunch.

As the guests arrived, Eleanora and Jonathan welcomed them and issued them into the parlour. Jennifer and Megan Bassington, keen on assisting, managed the distribution of drinks and proved a capable team. As Jennifer and Megan handed out the glasses, cheerful conversation was all around as the guest became familiar with each other.

Sir Hugh remained by the fireplace and was interested in talking with Thomas about the new brewery that would be built in Guildford. Anne was delighted when Robert and Horace arrived, rushing over and giving Robert a hug and kiss on the cheek. Ensuring parity, she gave an awkward Horace the same welcome. Horace was a bit overcome and blushed from the show of affection from Anne.

As Horace viewed the room, his eyes met with Sir Hugh South. They both looked at each other uncomfortably, with Horace's gaze fixed on him. Sir Hugh put down his glass and joined Horace. He extended his hand, saying, "Sir Horace, I must apologise for Friday night!"

Horace considered Hugh's gesture, but he clasped and shook the hand when he heard Sir Hugh's words.

"Thank you, Sir, but I believe you should direct any apology to Neville. I accept and welcome your apology. Might I add there was no hostility on my part? I was protecting a friend."

"Point taken, Sir Horace, and the shame of this situation must be all mine. I shall apologise as soon as an opportunity arises with Neville."

Captain Coombes was quite surprised by this show of humility by Sir Hugh, which differed considerably from the previous behaviour of the Earl's son. The captain was not one for holding grudges and was pleased the tension was now gone from the situation. Changing the subject, he opened a topic close to his heart, "Sir, have you tasted any of these Turner biscuits? They are tasty and to my liking!"

Sir Hugh was not presently interested in eating biscuits but welcomed the diversion, "No, Sir Horace, I have not had that pleasure."

"Sir, join me in a few; they are damned good!"

The captain passed a plate of biscuits across, not before capturing one himself.

Mrs Jennings formally rang the gong for lunch, and the various parties moved into the dining room. With the number of guests, it was a bit of a squeeze, but this only made the company more joyful. Anne made sure she took Robert's arm as they proceeded into lunch, and they followed the countess, who was enjoying this different level of society with their similar manners but less space.

Robert was finally relaxing now the wedding events were over. "What a marvellous wedding, Anne. I must admit I enjoyed every part of it. You swept me away in admiration when I saw you in that beautiful bridesmaid's dress. It appeared as if you were floating on air."

Anne was thrilled, "That was the plan. We were unsure if it would work, but the silk finishes did the trick. Mrs Smith at Hursts is so clever."

Robert sat between his mother and Anne and was pleased with his position. It allowed gentle talk with his mother and the opportunity for discussion between the three of them.

"Mother, I am so glad you have made Anne's acquaintance. I'm sure you have found what a delightful young person she is!"

"Yes, Robert! I understand Emma finds it quite refreshing that so many pleasant young ladies are in such proximity. Emma enjoys Anne's company immensely and, of course, Bethany, Marion, and Megan. It has lifted her spirit no end!"

Emma, who sat directly opposite Anne, replied, "Mother, I am so glad, and I agree with you entirely. I thought I might invite Anne with us on our next London trip. I would welcome her assistance in all the shopping we must do, and I'm sure Mr Turner could spare her from the office for a week." Emma turned and looked at Jonathan Turner, who sat there stunned.

"I'm sure Mr Turner could spare her. I agree with you, Emma. Anne, will you join us on our next shopping adventure?" Lady Jane was quite determined in her pleasant invitation.

As Anne heard the generous invitation, she was amazed that it would come so early. She was a little overcome by the generosity that the countess offered her. In hope, she glanced at her father, who gave her a worried frown but nodded in agreement.

"My father agrees with this invitation, my Lady, so it gives me great pleasure to accept you. But this is such generosity; I am overwhelmed."

Anne was unaware of Robert's detailed discussions concerning her with his mother. Lady Jane, who had already accepted the match, was now concentrating on possible wedding dates and in the not too distant future.

Pleased with Anne's lovely response, Lady Jane sat back in some relief, "Not at all, Anne. You are a beautiful young lady, and London will welcome you. I hope we may have the pleasure of Megan and Marion visiting us while you are with us?"

The other two girls readily agreed, and some excited young ladies spent the next half hour talking about what they might achieve in London, especially from St James's Square.

Robert remained quiet but smiled, "Thank you, Mother!"

Lady Jane looked at Robert's bandaged hand and saw how tired but happy he was here in the company of these people. She moved closer and whispered in his ear, "Robert, you have found the happiness I always wanted for you here! Just make sure you come back safe from your exploits, my Dear."

Jonathan Turner sat between his wife and Megan Bassington. He was interested in what she told him of the development of bakery shops in New York, which had him thinking of innovations. Beside Megan sat Sir Hugh, who was keen on engaging Jonathan Turner in conversation. When the opportunity arose, he caught Jonathan's eye, "Mr Turner, I would enjoy hearing about your new mill. I hear there is considerable interest in the town about it!"

"Please, Sir Hugh, call me Jonathan? It would be my pleasure. Is there any special point of interest you have?"

"Yes, Sir. If you would enlighten me on why you are building such a large mill when we have plenty of existing mills in the area?"

"I see! The story is that Turner's bakery has developed into a large business. We have the largest market share in Guildford and surrounding towns, and we use substantial amounts of flour from the mills up and down the Wey and connecting streams. Over the past two years, the market has increased, and our demand for flour has grown. The small mills that operate in the Guildford area have charged us a premium for this increased demand. Consequently, our margins have dropped, making the small mills a handsome profit.

By having a mill of our own, that is not dependent on waterpower, we can produce flour far more quickly and at half the price of the existing mills. You would understand they continue using a technology that has existed for centuries and have not recognised the steam engine's productivity. By using steam power, we can completely change the production process."

"But surely, Sir, the use of coal would result in a higher cost? The coal must be shipped in by barge, but the mills use waterpower which is free?"

"That is true, Sir Hugh. But think of it this way! A mill such as, let us say we use the Hetting Mill as an example, might produce twenty or thirty bags of flour a day. We will be generous and say fifty bags a day, for example. The river flows at one speed which is only a few knots, and might marginally increase through channelling, as some mills do! In our new steam-powered mill, we will produce around four hundred bags of flour a day. This production will increase as we refine the systems. We are unsure yet, but the forecast for our mill is between six hundred and eight hundred bags a day. The productivity difference easily covers the cost of coal and our development costs. It will allow a decrease in the retail price of bread, and we will remain profitable."

Sir Hugh sat there with his mouth open and then asked, "You say four hundred bags of flour a day? That is amazing. How will the other mills compete, Mr Turner?"

"I'm afraid they won't, Sir Hugh unless they build their own steam-powered mills. It is the change our world is embracing, and the users of the new technology will survive, and the mills that remain unchanged will cease. I am afraid it is inevitable!"

Megan Bassington added, "Sir Hugh, I have recently returned from New York. There is progress in the baking industry over there unknown in our businesses here in England. I think Mr Turner is heading in the right direction. I have encouraged him and feel sure a New York visit would be invaluable."

Having met Megan Bassington only this morning, Sir Hugh was surprised she should share her opinions so freely. He must say something in reply and finally spoke, "I am sorry, Miss Bassington, but I am unaware of what you are saying. What kind of developments are happening among our American friends?"

"There is consolidation in the American milling market. The small mills are closing, and larger mills using various technologies are taking over. The American industry is making progress, where new technology is being applied. Improvements in ovens and other finishing processes allow for a greater variety of products. All these changes will come here. I think Mr Turner is quite visionary in experimenting with a steam mill."

Sir Hugh nodded in reply and sat back and sipped a cup of tea. While he was pursuing his leisure activities over the last fifteen years, he neglected the changes around him at his peril. Thankfully, his mind was still sound, and from today onwards, Hugh was making some significant changes in his life. Now, he was concerned about a change that would directly affect the local grain market. If the Turner mill swallowed up all the other surrounding mills, this would create a great danger. It may leave his grain from the next harvest unsold – this would be a disaster for the estate. Better that they switched early and established contracts and good business relationships with this Turner chap now before the market consolidated.

Sir Hugh decided on action, "Mr Turner, and thank you, Miss Bassington, for your insights. I will be leaving England soon for the Indies, where my father has some plantations. He has requested I become familiar with the operation of these estates. Before leaving England, perhaps we might discuss the trading of grain. We are not presently one of your suppliers, but that does not preclude us from negotiating for the future, Sir. Given I am in town this

Sunday, there is no difficulty with my remaining overnight and meeting with you and your advisors tomorrow. Would that be convenient?"

Jonathan Turner welcomed this suggestion.

"Certainly, Sir. Let us say ten thirty tomorrow morning at the bakery. I will first give you a tour of the bakery operation and the new mill. I think you will find it interesting."

"Done, Sir. I thank you, and I will be there at ten-thirty."

Megan Bassington, who was listening with interest, was keen to join the tour.

"Excuse me, Mr Turner?"

"Yes, Megan!"

"Perhaps, if possible, might I attend this tour as well? An understanding of the bakery and mill operations would be most informative. I would depart soon after that with no wish of interfering with your negotiations, gentlemen!"

"I'm sure Sir Hugh would welcome you joining us. We will meet at ten-thirty in the morning. The Bakery Manager, Mr Hiscock, will meet you at the entrance."

"Thank you, Mr Turner. That is most kind of you."

Sir Hugh nodded his agreement but was displeased that this young woman would be joining them. However, he felt dutybound to agree, given Mr Turner had accepted her strange request. He wondered at her interest. After all, she was a woman, and what role did women have in business? He thought it most disturbing, but he would refrain from voicing his objection in the interest of good manners.

The lunch was finishing when through the front door entered Neville and Bethany Bassington and Doctor David Sopwith. Neville beamed with a great grin and started talking almost immediately.

"Hello, everyone, we have finished handing over the medical practice, and David is fully prepared for the next two months. So, we will commence the honeymoon tomorrow morning relaxed and ready for an adventure."

There were loud comments of acclamation and good wishes following Neville's announcement. Hamish and Marjorie McPherson congratulated the young couple, saying that it would be a grand success if Marion and Thomas's wedding could be half as good as this one. The four of them talked at length as the other guests rose from their places, starting individual conversations. The guests enjoyed each other's company, and no one was leaving.

Neville came across and asked Jonathan Turner, "Mr Turner, we thought that if the usual family afternoon tea at the river occurs, we will join you for a couple of hours if that was agreeable."

"Certainly, Neville. I should let everyone know. Excuse me, everyone, for those who are staying on till tomorrow. The family usually visits the banks of the Wey, relaxing on a Sunday afternoon. If anyone is interested, please come and join us. The young people will bring down some light refreshments."

There was a general acceptance of the invitation, and various people volunteered their help. Anne quickly grabbed Robert's hand and led him to the kitchen, where Mrs Jennings was already busy preparing picnic supplies.

"How may I help? What may I carry?" Robert asked.

"This basket of bread rolls and biscuits, Robert. I will bring the basket with the tablecloths, knives and butter. The boys can bring the drinks. Let us go."

Sir Hugh waited for his opportunity and carefully manoeuvred around beside Neville Bassington. Neville turned and found Sir Hugh facing him. The smile disappeared off Neville's face. Shocked at seeing him in the Turner house, he kept calm and said, "Good afternoon, Sir Hugh!"

"Neville, I must apologise for my offensive behaviour on Friday night. I have no one else to blame except myself. I feel great shame about the whole incident. The comments were degrading and vulgar, and I apologise from the bottom of my heart. I would ask for your forgiveness and friendship."

Neville was astonished, having known Hugh for many years as a selfish, arrogant brat who approved of no one except himself. Was this the same man?

"Yes, Sir Hugh, I accept your apology most willingly and may I say you have always had my friendship, and this shall continue. I was upset at your comments. However, I understand you were under the weather, and I am relieved by your words. I accept your apology unconditionally, and we shall hear no more about it. Thank you, Sir Hugh."

Sir Horace Coombes, who was close by, came over and patted Sir Hugh on the back, "Hugh, it takes a good man who is prepared to make a public apology like that. I am greatly impressed by you, Sir."

"I am far from a good man, Horace, but I desire some improvement in the future!"

"You are making a good fist of it now. Come man, and you can help me carry some drinks. Perhaps we can find a cart."

Lady Jane South witnessed all these happenings in the Turner family home. Looking around, she thought there must be something special here. She was amazed at the change that came over her firstborn son. It was as if a Damascus Road conversion took place. She was not aware of Hugh speaking well of people since he was a small lad, and yet at present, he was making friends and offering help. What had come over her son? She was not complaining, but she must talk with her eldest son when the opportunity arose.

David Sopwith approached, "Lady Fintelton, the river is a slight distance. May I offer you transport in my carriage?"

"You keep a carriage, do you, Doctor! Yes, I would appreciate that."

"I must warn you, Milady, that I have invited other passengers being your daughter Lady Emma, Miss Megan Bassington and Mrs Eleanora Turner. I hope that is acceptable?"

"Certainly, Doctor, I will enjoy attending a Turner family picnic. I have heard much about them and that one must keep a special eye on young William, who becomes greatly excited."

Neville chipped in, "Ah yes, Milady, we shall make sure you are protected."

Anne and Robert walked down the High Street carrying their baskets and continually chattering, catching up on time lost.

"What kept you, Robert? I was so worried you would miss the wedding. At one stage, Beth was having nightmares about it. On Wednesday night, during the gale, she stacked on the blankets and woke after a terrible dream in the morning. But I knew you would get here. I'm so glad we are together."

"The same gale drove my ship halfway across the channel. Once back in port, we rode all night, and despite the delay, we arrived safely. My damaged hand did not help either."

"I'm sorry, I should have remembered your hand before passing that basket! How is it healing?"

"It is nearly healed. In another week, I will not need the bandage."

"Good. I don't want you back at sea injured. Where will the next mission take you?"

"Sorry, I must keep it confidential. Secrecy is vital."

"Robert, I do not want you in danger. You must take care!"

"I am taking care! Now I am the captain, the younger officers take most of the risks. The captain remains on board. One day when I am in command of a first-rate ship, you will join me as we sail the seas."

Anne considered his comment, "You mean a ship's Captain may take his wife with him?"

"Yes – it has become quite common. Not into battle but on longer cruises with less danger."

"I should love that – but I have never seen the sea. I should be so afraid."

"I thought, while you are at Fintelton next year, we would visit our estate on the Isle of Wight for a few days. We would travel by boat and see a great deal of the seaside. You will see the sea."

"Robert, that would be heavenly. We would need chaperones, of course."

"I think my mother and father would be available. They have time now."

Anne's mind was awash with dreams of the seaside and the adventures they could have. Sailing in a boat would be another new adventure she had never experienced.

"Robert, I sometimes think this is all a dream, and it cannot be true. And the London trip; I am so fortunate with the invitation from your mother.

Emma and I will have such a wonderful time."

"Anne, be careful of London. It is full of scoundrels. I do not like the idea of you being there without me. London is a dangerous place!"

"I shall be safe, Robert. I will be with your mother. Perhaps even your father will come."

"It is a possibility as he is making a good recovery."

"I was so afraid the night of the dinner when I met your mother. I was petrified and expecting a difficult night, but your mother is very understanding, Robert. I like her very much!"

"You are as surprised as I am. I think you will enjoy St James's Square and Fintelton estate when we visit. Fintelton is a fine estate but requires more care. We are fortunate Mr Stem is the estate manager. He is a good man!"

"Mr Stem asked that if I ever visited Fintelton, he would value some tutelage on accounting. Would you mind if I spent some time with him?"

"No. Not at all. I think that would be helpful. Anne, I tell you this in confidence, and it must go no further. Pike, our butler, who I have known all my life, told me on Friday that he has fears Hugh is not managing the estate's finances well. I will talk with Emma and request she makes some enquiries over the coming months. As she is not skilled in finance, she may ask you as a close friend for advice. Would you mind doing this?"

"Certainly. But surely the estate is managed well? I am not sure if I have the expertise advising on an estate of that size."

"I am not asking for advice but an explanation of the figures. I am worried that the cash may be running out. I would not wish my mother and father to be destitute. Please keep this confidential as my mother is not aware yet."

"Robert, you told me the same last time, but she knows far more than you think."

"I am not aware that she knows about this. Please, Anne?"

"How could I refuse such a handsome young man!" Anne put her arm through his, and they continued chatting while walking down the High Street towards the river.

The picnic was most enjoyable until around four-thirty when the breeze turned cold, and some of the party preferred the warmth of their lodgings. The countess proved a favourite with the children and told them various stories about the country, also fascinating Megan Bassington. Her only country experience was visiting the Souths with Neville at Cowes for short holidays. Lady Jane kept a close eye out for William. When he came running across at her with a branch spinning around his head, she stood up and, in a loud motherly voice, called out, "Drop that branch, William!" The lad stopped in his tracks, dropping the branch and then sheepishly joined the other children sitting at Lady Jane's feet. Jonathan Turner was very impressed with the way

Lady Jane handled William and saw another quality in her that he admired.

As the Turner family finally arrived home that Sunday afternoon, Eleanora Turner found she was exhausted. After requesting that Mrs Jennings keep a small supper for her, she retired for a rest. The regular household routine commenced with feeding and washing children before bedtime. Thomas and Marion joined the family for dinner, and Robert promised he would arrive at eight.

The other wedding guests remaining in Guildford either dined privately or joined at the Fox and Hound.

At the Fox and Hound ...

Eager for a conversation with Lady Fintelton, David Bassington, seated beside her, enquired, "My Lady, I hear that Lord Fintelton has not been well. Please may I inquire, how is his recovery progressing?".

"Thank you for enquiring, Mr Bassington. He has made a remarkable recovery, and the close attention he received from Doctor Sopwith has made all the difference. The doctor was very attentive and spent much time at Fintelton in the past three weeks. We are most appreciative."

"That is wonderful, my Lady."

"Yes, without this recovery, I would not have attended the wedding. It has been a very enriching experience. I am now so grateful for the invitation."

David Sopwith was sitting directly opposite David Bassington and was talking with Lady Emma.

"Now that Neville will be away, my workload will increase again, so it may not be possible for me to spend as much time at Fintelton looking after your father."

"Why David, that will be a disappointment, however, I will be here with Anne soon, and you will recall we discussed a possible dinner. So, I will send an invitation when the arrangements are complete. I think Anne may be quite engaged tonight with Robert. She must make the best of the opportunity while he is here."

"From their behaviour during the weekend, it appears they are close. I would not be surprised if there were an announcement soon."

"I hope so, as I think Robert and Anne would make an excellent couple, don't you?"

"Yes, but she must carefully consider the prospect of him being away much of the time, given he is a navy man. The profession is safer now that the French are peaceful, but there are still risks. She may become lonely, depending on where they settle. Perhaps they would set up a home in Guildford, close to family. That may work well."

"Yes. Living in Guildford may be a good move for Anne, but perhaps she may want otherwise. I have not discussed it with her. However, I would welcome her as a sister-in-law. Her conversation is lively, indeed."

"What about yourself, Lady Emma, if you married and moved from Fintelton, where would you live?"

"Why David, that is a very forward question. I am quite flushed thinking about it. It would depend on the man I married."

"Perhaps if I could put it more gently. Suppose an eligible young gentleman in Guildford made an offer! Then would you consider living in Guildford in more modest circumstances? From my visits with the Earl, you are familiar with a comfortable lifestyle. I wondered what your expectations might be."

"You forget my life in London, Sir! The circumstances at St James's Square are not so grand as at Fintelton. I also think that other considerations may come into the matter. It would depend on how much I loved this unknown eligible young gentleman!"

"My apologies Lady Emma, I had no wish of embarrassing you, and I am unfamiliar with your life in London."

Emma smiled at David and wondered if she should give a direct answer on this or not. Etiquette demanded she may not be open with him until he declared his love. He alluded to it, but no proposal came. Should she encourage him? Her mother was across the table, and she had no wish of embarrassing her.

She gently said, "I think I can cope with most things, David, but perhaps we should discuss this again soon. We shall meet at the dinner Anne and I are arranging." She moved her hand under the table, took his hand, and gave it a little squeeze.

Doctor Sopwith's eyes brightened considerably, but David Bassington cut the conversation short when he asked from across the table, "Doctor Sopwith, I understand you trained at the same medical school as Neville. Were you there at the same time?"

"No, Sir, Neville was there a good four years before me. I have only been practising for five years. Three in Belfast and two years here. I am five years younger than Neville."

"Ah, I had romantic ideas that you and Neville may have trained together! In Belfast then, are you of Irish origins, Sir?"

"No, Sir, I was born in London and grew up there, but my mother inherited two Irish estates before marrying my father. He came from an engineering background and had a foundry in the west of London. They made all kinds of things. Please do not ask me what they made as I had no interest in it. I always found anatomy more interesting, so I trained as a Surgeon. So, Neville and I have similar interests, and I feel I can learn much from being in practice with him."

"If you lived in London, why did you practice in Belfast?"

"My father moved the family there when I was twelve. After my schooling in Belfast, I attended university in England and studied the arts. I soon found my interest was in medicine, and within a year, the medical school accepted my application. The family remained in Belfast for about five years as my father's business served the shipbuilding industry. It also allowed time for the management of the estates mother inherited. It proved a very profitable time for the family."

Lady Jane joined the conversation, being quite surprised that Doctor Sopwith's family were landholders.

"Tell me, Doctor Sopwith, where are your mother's estates in Ireland?"

"One is near Cookstown, and the other is near Coleraine. I am not sure of the details, Lady Jane, as I have no interest in the estates! But I believe one is ten thousand acres and the other twenty-five thousand acres."

There was a sudden silence in the room as everyone digested the size of the estates.

Emma said, "Those are rather large estates, David, I mean Doctor Sopwith."

"I would not know Lady Emma. I'm not sure just how large an acre is."

"Thank you, Doctor Sopwith. Now, Megan, your father informs me that you intend to depart for New York. I understand you are much attracted to the city."

"Yes, my Lady. It is such an exciting country, and there is so much freedom. I will be writing articles for my father, who may publish them. There is a lot of interest in the British aristocracy from the Americans. They are always hungry for the latest news. Despite our two countries' differences, there are still great links between the two which I believe will continue. I think my future lies there."

"I am surprised, Megan. You are very adventurous, but I know very little of the American colonies or, should I say the Union."

"Sir Hugh, I believe you have estates in the Indies?" David Bassington was keen on hearing about the South's interests overseas.

"Yes, we have two sugar plantations in the Indies and eight cotton farms. I will visit them soon as it is time I checked on their production. My father has encouraged me often, and I think the time is right."

Lady Jane and Emma looked up when they heard Hugh mention a visit. Hugh's intention came as a surprise as he had never previously shown any interest in the plantations. They both wondered what brought about this change.

"Sir, it may take you more than two months. Pray, are the plantations lucrative?

"We have received a steady cash flow over many years, but I will be more knowledgeable on this subject on my return, Sir."

At the Turner Household ...

Slowly members of the family were excusing themselves and retiring for the night. Jonathan Turner worked in his study. Marion said good night and retired. After seeing her up the stairs, Thomas returned and indicated he would also retire.

Robert and Anne found themselves alone in the parlour.

Anne enjoyed sitting and watching the fire content after the excitement of the wedding and all that followed.

"What are you smiling about, Robert? Tell me so I can share it with you."

"I was thinking about how refreshing it is here with you. It is relaxing not worrying about a ship or what is needed next. I have found being a Captain is far more demanding than I imagined. There are tremendous responsibilities. Being here is like a dream. Every night, Anne, I wish I was with you, but realising that I must wait so long. Now I am here with you alone; it is very pleasant."

"What is pleasant about it?"

"Everything. I am content sitting beside you; it is like being in heaven! But a cup of tea would add more pleasure!"

"Really! Come on, and we will make some tea."

They found the kettle still hot in the kitchen, and Anne brewed some tea. As they returned, Robert stopped at the entrance to the parlour and studied the floor.

"So, this is where the burglar knocked William out and where you found him?"

"Yes. It was one of the most distressing moments of my life."

"Have they found the burglars yet?"

"Yes – one of them turned up dead in a lock at the river. The Constable thinks the other burglar must have long gone by now. Father has improved the house's security, so we all feel safe. But it was quite terrifying at the time."

She shuddered and moved closer. Tossing her hair over her shoulders, she took Robert's injured hand in hers, "Tell me more about what you think of me when you are far away?"

He felt the excitement in his body as she came close. He knew he must be careful here, or his desires would take over his actions.

He whispered in her ear, "I love you, Anne Turner!"

She pulled herself back from him and looked him in the eyes. She could see he was still smiling, but he was serious. This time he was saying what was on his heart.

She moved forward and let him gently kiss her on the lips. She wanted more but was aware of her father in the adjoining room.

"I love you too, Robert!"

He kissed her gently again and then sat back on the couch, contented, "We can go no further than this at present, Anne. Perhaps we could announce something after Fintelton next year."

Anne was far from convinced, but she felt she must abide by what Robert said. After all, he was several years older than her and must know better. But if they loved each other, why could they not become engaged now? Of course, the family! Robert's family may not accept her. Why was it always the family when there were aristocratic connections?

"Why can't we become engaged, Robert? Do you feel your family will not accept me? You will not be the Earl, so why would this matter if we make a life together?"

"I think my mother and sister will readily accept you now. Did you see how my mother relished talking with the children today? I'm sure she would love grandchildren."

"We can provide that pleasure for her, Robert!"

"I want that too, my Dearest Anne, but my next mission may be quite dangerous."

"What danger, Robert?"

He said quietly, "This next mission - already many men have died. There will be many more in the coming months. I am unsure what the outcome will be. We must wait. I will not marry you and make you a widow."

Anne looked at him, alarmed, "Please don't go. There is no need! I need you here where we can be together. You can find a job on the estate. We can find another way. Robert, please, I don't want you in danger. I don't want to lose you!"

"You will never lose me! I will always love you!"

He sat back, thinking about how he could explain, "Anne, there is no job free of danger. As a navy man, I must accept this and follow my orders. We will plan our future together once this mission is over and we have met at Fintelton next July. The time will quickly pass, and I will write and perhaps attend the wedding."

"But you told me you loved me. I love you with all my heart, Robert. I understand that you are a navy man, and there will always be another mission. We both have futures we can combine for our advantage, Darling! So, why not become engaged? At least that would give me some sort of commitment from you. At present, I am left on the shelf with nothing."

Looking back over his life, Robert's only commitments were honouring his family and his pledge of loyalty to his King and country. Always, he found commitment hard. For him, it was one hundred per cent or nothing. There was nothing in between. He felt the sweat on his brow as Anne pleaded with him.

He saw the begging in her eyes. He knew he would not see her again for many months, and it was unfair that he declared his love for her without any engagement. But Robert was not only a man of action but also prudent. He realised that he might lose the woman he adored if he left without committing. Robert weighed up both sides of the problem and found he preferred what Anne suggested. If his family disagreed, then hang them. He would suffer the consequences. He may end up a sick old captain on half-pay. Maybe not.

The Admiral himself advised him to see his lass and get what was needed finished. He wavered. If only he could talk with Neville, he needed guidance. But Robert knew he wanted this wonderful girl in his life forever. It was only fair that he gave her some assurance.

She placed her head on his chest and put her arms around him, "I want you with me forever, Robert. I will not live without your love, no matter where you are."

Robert made his decision. He slid down onto his knee and sat her up on the couch in front of him. She looked down at him in surprise.

"What are you doing, Robert?"

"Something I should have done long before now. Anne Turner, would you do me the honour of becoming my wife. Of course, next year – I cannot do it before then. After Fintelton. Please, Anne?"

"Yes, Robert, yes! With all my heart!" They both stood up and kissed.

At that point, Jonathan Turner emerged from his study, yawning, and stood there watching this beautiful young couple kissing.

"Robert, you will need a good explanation for this."

"Yes, Sir. I have proposed! I have asked your daughter Anne to become my wife, and she has accepted, Sir!"

"That is a good explanation, Robert! I assume it is real from the compassion I am witnessing in front of me?"

Anne was crying for joy. She rushed and hugged and kissed her father. Jonathan smiled and said, "It appears I have given my permission, Robert. Congratulations! I am sure we will enjoy each other's company. Now tell me, Sir, is this engagement public or not?"

Robert looked down into Anne's happy teary eyes as she released Jonathan, hugged Robert again, and said, "I think it would be better public, Sir. I am not sure I could hold the secret much longer than tonight. I will advise my family at Fintelton tomorrow night. I would not ask Anne to withhold this secret from her friends more than a day."

"Sounds a good plan, Robert. Rest assured, nothing will be mentioned by our family until after tomorrow, allowing you time with your family."

"Thank you, Mr Turner. I appreciate that. Dearest Anne, you have made me the happiest man in England tonight. I feel complete now we have become engaged. Do you feel relieved?"

"Thank you, Robert. I am now complete, as well. We shall marry in the end. I will wait for you!"

"I will come back. I promise. There is nothing in the world that matters more. Now it has been a long weekend. I must go, and you must retire. I will be away early and write and tell of the meeting with my family."

With that, they walked hand in hand along the hallway. Anne would not let him go, but Robert withdrew his hand, kissed her gently again and made his way across the entrance and down the front steps. She watched him walk down the street and out of sight. Closing the front door, she turned and found her father standing near.

"He is a gentleman, indeed, Anne."

"Yes, Father, he is. Sometimes I wish he were not so gentlemanly."

"Be careful what you wish for Anne. It may come true."

Chapter 22

At the Turner Bakery, Guildford ...

The planned Monday tour for Sir Hugh South and Megan Bassington finished in the bakery offices.

"The bakery is far larger than I thought, Mr Turner, and impressive. Your idea for a biscuit production line in the adjoining building is also innovative. When will the process commence?"

"I am meeting with the Admiralty gentlemen tomorrow. We will sign the preliminary order contract for one thousand tins of biscuits to be delivered over six months. If we satisfy their requirements, I expect further orders to follow."

"So once again, you will have demand for additional grains?"

"Yes, a new supply from your estate would be quite helpful."

Sir Hugh had thought long and hard about how he should negotiate with the Turners. Both Jonathan and Thomas Turner appeared quite sharp, and yet in the negotiations, he found them fair, providing a price higher than his other buyers.

"Mr Turner, I am surprised you offer such a reasonable price for our grain. I expected you to drive a hard bargain and push the price down."

"We understand that each estate must maintain its margins. We are in the business of creating partnerships that will last, Sir Hugh. If we pay a fair margin, then our suppliers become loyal. We will still achieve our margin with our productivity efficiencies. So, it is a successful situation for all, Sir. I hope you will sign with us."

"Mr Turner, I will discuss the contract at Fintelton this week, including an explanation of your plans for the new mill. I'm sure that my father will take heed of my advice. I will also discuss this with the tenant farmers before the end of the week. I will advise you of the outcome next Monday when I return here. I am sure the majority will agree."

"This is good news indeed, Sir Hugh. Will you join us in a whisky?"

Sir Hugh hesitated and said, "I shall join you, Sir, but may I have water instead of whisky. I am working on my health and staying off the spirits."

"Certainly, Sir. Let us toast our future partnership!"

For Jonathan and Thomas Turner, it was a good outcome. They secured a new supply at a slightly higher price than preferred, but it was a long-term investment. In ten years, when all the small mills were gone, they would reduce the price paid for grain. It was also possible the government might repeal the corn laws by then, and the cost would fall further. European corn would be far cheaper if they regained access to the Corn Exchange. Jonathan felt their long-term plan was sound. The next step was the commissioning of the mill.

Sir Hugh was pleased with the contract as it promised extra income for the next harvest, improving their financial position significantly. He set off in high spirits.

At Fintelton Manor ...

The two officers parted company before the Petersfield turnpike. Having travelled the road many times, Horace would avoid the turnpike fee by riding west and then back into the town on a pathway. He would take an early lunch there and rest his horse.

Taking the opportunity of a discussion before they parted, Robert confided in Horace about his engagement to Anne. Horace welcomed the news, slapping his friend's back. On mentioning the issue of parental approval, Horace shrugged his shoulders.

"They set you free in the navy, Robert. They cannot have it both ways. You will certainly be welcome on my estate at any time!"

"Thank you, Horace. Tonight may prove difficult! Best be off, and I will join you tomorrow in Portsmouth."

Horace understanding the difficulties of class distinction, wished him luck. He took his leave and galloped off along a westward farm path. Robert knew of a shortcut in the opposite direction and watched as his friend disappeared around a bend.

By the time he reached Fintelton, it was after two in the afternoon. His father had retired for a nap, and Robert was not expecting his mother, Lady Emma, and Sir Hugh before late afternoon.

The butler welcomed Robert and enquired about the wedding.

"It was a great success, Pike. Now how is my father? Is he improving?"

"Yes, Sir, he is up and about by himself now. He stood up alone on Sunday morning and has been shuffling about the manor. The recovery is remarkable. I am hopeful of his full recovery by the time Doctor Sopwith arrives on Friday afternoon. The Doctor will spend the Saturday and Sunday here."

"I am glad, Pike. I have been concerned for my father as I would like him to live for some time yet. I know I am often away, but this is still my home, and I hope to call here much in the future. Now, given your previous advice, I think I shall take the opportunity of visiting Mr Stem. During the next few months, Lady Emma will make some enquiries, and from this information, we may correct the issues you advised me of."

"Very good, Sir. May I also ask a further question, Sir, if it is not inconvenient?"

Robert wondered what revelation he would hear now. He would indulge Pike as he knew the butler held the best intentions towards the family.

"I would welcome any question you ask, Pike!"

"Sir, would I be correct in assuming that there may be a romantic attachment between Lady Emma and Doctor Sopwith? I have noticed they spend much time together when he visits."

Given Robert's duties at the wedding and his quest for time with Anne, he was unaware of any attachment. Neither Emma nor Anne had commented on this. He did recall that David and Emma often spoke at the reception and danced together. Then he recalled David Sopwith attended the dinner with Lady Jane and Emma at the Fox and Hound last night. Perhaps there was truth in this.

"Pike, not that I am aware of; however, I would not be surprised. I shall add this to my list of enquiries, and we shall speak privately again before I leave for Portsmouth tomorrow."

"Thank you, Sir."

"Now, I must see Mr Stem."

"I believe he is in the north fields, Sir, with one of the tenant farmers."

Robert arranged a fresh mount from the stables, and he cantered off in the direction that the butler indicated. Within ten minutes, he found Mr Stem walking the fence line of a newly ploughed field some way from the Manor house. As a tenant farmer left on his cart, Robert gave the farmer a wave and approached Mr Stem.

"Mr Stem, good day!"

"Sir Robert, I have not seen you for some time. You look well, Sir."

"I am well, Mr Stem! I have come on a mission. I make enquiries from you that I would like kept confidential."

"Certainly, Sir."

"How are the finances of the estate? I am worried about the financial situation!"

"The estate books are in my office, Sir. We can work through them together if that is a help!

"Thank you, but I do not require the books at present, Mr Stem. I need your assessment of how the estate is running."

"Sir, you know that the Earl has been reducing his involvement for nearly five years now. Sir Hugh has taken over many of the management tasks."

"No, I did not know that!"

"It is your father's health, Sir. The Doctor may explain this better. His mind has lost its edge, and he cannot remember things. He is well into his seventies now, and we should expect this. It is not his fault, Sir!"

"Well said, Mr Stem."

"Sir Hugh is not that interested in the Estate. At his request, I take on much of the management." Stem paused as if gathering a breath. "Sir, may I speak openly without fear of reprimand?"

"That is my intention, Mr Stem."

"Sir, You and your brother are quite different. Might I say one is the black sheep, and you are the white sheep? We would all prefer you as the next Earl. Unfortunately, Sir Hugh has his faults, and this leads him astray."

"You mean the drinking and womanising?"

"Yes, Sir. It may be that we only see him one day a week. He travels from town to town during the other days, searching for whisky and new women. I am afraid, Sir, the alcohol has enslaved him. With the Earl suffering in his health and Sir Hugh absent, often I must make decisions without their approval. Also, Sir Hugh and your father differ in their ideas about running the estate. There are often disagreements between them."

"And the finances, Mr Stem?"

"They are steadily decreasing, Sir. The estate harvest output has not changed, but Sir Hugh advises less money is available. A better price for grain and some productivity improvements are needed. The tenant farmers are ageing and require assistance. The estate has the potential for increased grain production, but his Lordship will not hear of it, insisting the methods he used thirty years ago are still better. Sir Hugh feels he must respect his father's wishes."

"I see!"

"Sir Hugh should be given some credit, Sir. He has recognised the problems, and I have advised him how he may overcome them. He is frustrated as the Earl will not hear of the changes required. Perhaps if Sir Hugh had a better relationship with his father, we could make more progress."

"I see. Thank you, Mr Stem. By the way, are you familiar with the income from the estates in the Indies?"

"No, Sir. I believe the London Attorneys handle these. They also look after the lands in the north of England and Ireland. I could not advise you on that. Your father holds all the information."

"Thank you again, Mr Stem. I will be back in contact with you. Lady Emma will require the books at some stage – for a few days only."

"Certainly, Sir."

Pike's fears were well-founded, and Robert was afraid no one was effectively managing his father's estate. He must talk with his sister tonight. Emma would be concerned, and although she would be tired, he could count on her for help. The need for action was urgent, and a plan must be made. The danger was that Hugh, the heir, may not agree with anything they proposed.

Lady Jane and Emma arrived around four in the afternoon and Sir Hugh at about six. The family was assembled for once, and the Earl would have company tonight. Robert decided he should make his announcement after dinner rather than earlier. This way, the complete family would be there and feeling content after a good meal.

Pike organised dinner for seven as his Lordship preferred eating earlier these days. Once assembled in the dining room, they all took their traditional places, and the Earl said grace.

"My, it is good you are all home again tonight. It cheers me up no end!"

They all agreed as it may be some time before Robert was free from his next mission. As the footmen served the first course, Lady Jane gave the Earl full accounts of the wedding and other events in Guildford. Sir Hugh was unusually well mannered and quiet.

Lady Jane recalled, "It was delightful sitting with the Turner children and watching them play by the river. They are such sweet children, particularly Marcia. She stole my heart! She has the beauty of her mother, that one!"

Lord Fintelton was interested in the news, and he recalled, "You said that this Mrs Turner was quite a beauty, my Dear."

"Yes, she is a wonderful lady and is full of sophisticated conversation. I will further the acquaintance if the opportunity arises. Unfortunately, she suffers dreadfully from her present confinement, and this will continue until at least February when the child is due."

In a concerned voice, the Earl said, "Let us hope the delivery is smooth and both mother and baby remain well. Many mothers pass away at childbirth with great sorrow for the family. I am thankful that you, Lady Jane, were spared this."

Robert changed his plan. With this pleasant discussion taking place, the time was right. These would be a few momentous minutes in his life. Better make the announcement now as the earlier done, the more time for defending his decision if required.

"Mother and Father, Brother and Sister, I have some good news for you, which is particularly opportune as we are all here together."

Emma looked up from her food with a look of surprised expectation on her face. She thought, 'Surely, he hasn't! She did not expect that news until next year. It must be a naval issue?'

Robert looked at Emma's worried expression, "It is good news, Emma. Don't fret!"

The family were now greatly interested, expecting some great news about the navy.

"Mother and Father, last night I asked Miss Anne Turner to be my wife. I am pleased to say she has accepted."

Lady Jane stood up, rushed around the table, and hugged Robert, "Wonderful, Robert! You could not have picked a more beautiful partner for your wife. I am so pleased for you. She will make a worthy addition to this family."

Emma also rose, coming around the table, "Robert, you will be giving me the sister I always wanted. Having Anne as a sister-in-law will add much joy as we travel together soon. I am speechless – it is so wonderful."

The Earl and Sir Hugh sat there while Lady Jane and Emma spoke with Robert. Then Sir Hugh stood and quietly walked around, putting his hand out with a big smile. They shook hands, "Congratulations, old boy, from what I have seen of her, she will be a fine partner for you. I wish you all the best."

It was clear that Sir Hugh was genuine in his intentions, which surprised Robert, Lady Jane and Emma. Robert was thrilled with the unexpected support he was receiving.

Lord Fintelton sat quietly, outnumbered at the end of the table, watching all this. He then said, "I am not familiar with this young Lady, Robert, but I understand you have your own life now that you are a Captain of a navy ship. I wish you all the best, my boy. But at some stage, I must meet this girl you are proposing as a member of our family. After all, she will be the mother of my grandchildren, so I should become acquainted."

"Thank you, Father. You certainly will meet her, and I think you will find her one of the most wonderful young ladies you have ever met. You will be very proud of her, Sir."

"I'm sure I will, my boy. I'm sure I will. Now when will the wedding be held?"

"Next year Father. We plan on you being in excellent health before the wedding takes place. My wish is that our complete family is at the wedding. Hugh, I would like you as one of the groomsmen. I will also be calling on Neville and perhaps Horace, as well."

"Ah yes, young Bassington, fine fellow. You know he has joined in partnership with Doctor Sopwith, Robert. They will make a strong team."

"Yes, Father, I think they will!"

Robert looked at his mother with relief on his face. She came and gave him another hug and whispered in his ear, "Peer pressure can be a good thing at times, Robert." Lady Jane almost broke out into a little laugh but held it back. Emma's face was also beaming, given that they carried the day.

Later that evening, as Lady Jane wished her husband good night, the Earl questioned his wife, "I refrained from embarrassing myself or Robert tonight, but who is this young Turner lady? Why I have never heard of the Turner name before?"

"Dear, she is the sweetest little thing I have ever met, and do not worry, finding out about her name is unnecessary, as she will go under the name of South once they are married. So, sleep well, my Dear, knowing Robert has made a wise choice."

"Capital, capital!" said Lord Fintelton and kissed his wife goodnight.

At Guildford …

Before the McPhersons left for Greenwich, Jonathan took the opportunity of meeting with Hamish. It was their first opportunity given the activities of the wedding.

"Jonathan, you will be pleased with your share of the first quarter's profits from the Epsom pub. I expect Reading will be even more successful. The first five years' performance may not be as quick as Epsom's, but it will perform well in time. Will you be joining me in this investment? It will be sound as the building purchased stands near the proposed railway station. Once the railway commences, it will turn into a gold mine."

"Yes, Hamish, count me in. Please have your attorneys send me the documents. I will have Anne review the figures, and our attorneys forward the investment sum by the end of the month."

"Jonathan, what would you do without Anne? It is wonderful news about her engagement, but you need her in your business. She is a wizard with figures. Such a good mind for someone so young."

"I am hoping they will settle in Guildford. After all, Robert will be away most of the time, and it will be close for her mother."

"Let us hope our investments expand, and you can provide them with ample servants so she may remain a part of the business. Did the meeting with the Ministry go well? How is our friend Malcolm?"

"Malcolm was in good spirits and enjoyed his tour. We have signed the contract, and the pilot plant will be operating by December. There will be a strain on our cash flow as the Admiralty are a slow payer, but it is a profitable venture, so we have planned for the delay. "

"Good, Jonathan, a wise move. Take my advice, Jeb Hiscock should be left in charge of the bakery and put another in charge of the biscuit factory. This venture will need a new level of experience. Let Jeb concentrate on your core business. He will have his hands full developing the cart runs and the integration of the new mill."

"With the Mill commencing trials this week, we will start supplying bread to your pubs as soon as the grain arrives for the mill."

As Jonathan approached the mill the following day, he found Thomas and Stanley Percival preparing the boiler and crusher for another test. The final testing process had commenced two weeks ago and had progressed well, except for the quality of flour produced. Thomas was sure the problem was the engine coupling with the milling stone. While the grade of the flour made was more refined than that coming from other mills, Jonathan required it finer. Thomas and Stanley replaced the milling stone with an iron constructed crusher mechanism. As far as they knew, this crusher was a first for flour milling. They would see today if it worked.

On entering the mill, Jonathan acknowledged the men working on the project with a wave. The noise from the boiler was building as the pressure increased. Shirtless sweating men were quickly shovelling coal and building the furnace's fire. Thomas was above, checking all the couplings in the gear assembly.

"Good morning, Stanley. Are we ready?"

"Yes, Mr Turner. The boiler pressure is correct. After a final check of the couplings, we shall all stand clear and release the safety locks. Hopefully, we will see history today, Sir. We think it is the first steam-powered mill in Surrey since the Albion Mills!"

Jonathan nodded, "Let us proceed then!"

He watched Thomas as he descended the ladder from the gears and coupling area overhead.

Thomas explained, "We are using fifty bags of wheat grain this morning and testing it as a production line. We should stand beside the collection hoppers."

Several large hoppers were in place, ready for the milled flour. Jonathan looked at the residue on the hopper and saw the previously milled consistency. The noise levels were high, so he shouted at Thomas, "We will soon know!"

Thomas smiled and crossed his fingers.

Mr Percival sounded a horn, and the workers stood clear. Then he released the safety locks, and the mill's steam engine came to life, turning the huge iron crusher. Men on the platform above emptied sacks of wheat into the pipe that fed the crushing area. The noise rose even higher as the mill commenced.

Jonathan waited nervously. So far, the investment in the mill was around forty thousand pounds, a significant investment for a single investor. A small fortune for most men, but investment in new technology required vast amounts of cash for a mill of this size. If it failed, he was bankrupt. The tension rose as they waited on the results.

The first pour of flour appeared from the crusher. Thomas and Jonathan patiently waited. Stanley Percival could wait no longer, picking up a sample with the cup of his hand. He rubbed the flour and then looked up and smiled.

Jonathan loudly cautioned, "Not yet – let the bulk of a few bags go through, then check the consistency at a higher production rate."

The flour flow continued, and as the first hopper was nearly full, a man shifted it aside by pushing a second hopper into place. Now the pouring was at full speed, and Jonathan walked forward and scooped flour into his hand.

He closely inspected the yellowish powder, and from his experience of years of baking, he knew they had achieved their goal. The flour was more refined than anything he had seen. The mill was a success. No one would now replicate their products unless they sourced flour as fine as this. Better still, as far as they knew, they were the only ones producing flour of this quality.

Jonathan looked up and smiled at Thomas, who also tested the flour. Thomas had a great grin on his face. Jonathan grasped Stanley Percival's hand and shook it. It was a huge relief that two years of development would now result in income flow.

"We have succeeded, gentlemen! Congratulations. Now Thomas, find Jeb and show him the new flour. There is no time to be lost; we must test this flour in baking. Test our recipes. Show Sophia as well, Thomas; she is good at creating new baking products. We probably need a new baking kitchen where we can develop new recipes. Congratulations everyone! Thomas, hand out free bread for all the employees today – as much as they require to celebrate our success!"

With that, Jonathan happily acknowledged all his men and left the mill. This success would be a turning point for his business. They would now have unlimited quantities of higher quality, low-cost flour available. How they would exploit this advantage was now the question. The links with Hamish McPherson would help, but they also must move forward carefully.

Anne looked up as Jonathan Turner came back from the mill. "How did it go, Father?"

"It worked, Anne, it worked!" Jonathan was almost beside himself with joy.

She stood and shook her father's hand, then gave him a big hug, "So we are on target with our plans then?"

"Yes, it would appear so! But where do we start?"

"At the beginning, Father, but first, do you have time for a walk?"

"A walk! But why now? I am somewhat distracted by our success today!"

"Yes, Father, a walk. It is important, and we must discuss it."

An enquiring look sprang onto Jonathan's face. She said softly, "In private, Father!"

"Yes, certainly, let us go for a walk!"

Jonathan grabbed his coat, and Anne led him out of the bakery towards the river bank. It was mid-morning with few people along the riverside.

"Now, Anne, what is on your mind?"

"Father, firstly, you know we discussed offices for the business. We need offices soon. We cannot continue confidential talks in front of the general office staff. You and I run the business now, and we need more privacy. You will understand after I have explained."

"I have thought about that – we can build new offices soon. It will free up space for the biscuit process, that now becomes a priority. But in terms of running the business, what about Thomas? He is involved as well."

"Yes, Father, our plans should involve Thomas, but he is also leaving and becoming a brewer for the McPhersons. Who will be doing the engineering design work then? We will need someone."

"Correct, I hope the new Mill Manager, Mr Spencer, can fit into this when he comes."

"No, Father, he will be an employee and do his job. Thomas is family and has an incentive to improve and expand the business! How will we replace this?"

"I see. I'm not sure yet. But we will find a solution!"

Anne stopped beside a weeping willow tree and checked that they were alone. Her father noticed her looking both ways, "What is wrong, Anne?"

"Father, we need complete privacy on this matter. I have finished a review of all our finances and projections for the next year. Here is the analysis."

Handing it over, Anne pointed out the headings of various columns and the different lines of the calculations. Jonathan looked at the figures. "This looks very impressive, Anne, but what does it mean?"

Anne sighed as she knew her father was a good businessman, but understanding figures was not his strong point.

"Father, it means that if I have projected all our cash inflows against all our cash outflows, then we run completely out of money next September!"

Jonathan looked back at the figures with a confused look on his face.

"How can that be Anne? We have over one hundred thousand pounds in the bank!"

"Yes, Father, but with your commitments with Mr McPherson and our own internal capital needs, the costs keep mounting. You must talk with me before you make any further commitments!"

Jonathan Turner stood there looking back and forwards between the figures and Anne. Was she correct, or was this a ploy? Why would she do that? It was her fortune, as well as the family's, that was at risk.

"Let us find a seat somewhere, and you can explain the figures."

"Across the river Father, in the park. There are seats there. But don't say much as there will be people moving past us. I will explain, but quietly, so no one overhears us. The cash flow from the new commitments does not provide sufficient funds to offset the capital outlays. The only way to offset these is by using bakery funds which are not free cash flow. We have no option but to use finance, which I would avoid at all costs as it puts our future in the hands of the banks."

"What is free cash flow, Anne?"

"For the bakery, it is the money left over once we have paid all our costs."

Jonathan Turner stood there, thinking as the river ran slowly downstream. This daughter of his was like William. She was far more mature than her age. She was showing the experience of a well-trained business owner and more so. She knew more about his business than he did. He had no idea he was in trouble financially, which led him to another problem. What would he do once she was married and having children?

Anne edged forward, but Jonathan stopped her, "Anne, I am sure you are correct, and you will explain the issues to me while we talk. It may be prudent if Thomas does not see this yet. He may reveal this to Hamish accidentally. That would not be helpful at present. You and I will change the plans and ensure we have sufficient cash."

"I agree, Father. But Thomas must know at some point. But perhaps not now."

"Anne, what will I do without you once you are married?"

Anne looked at her father in surprise and considered what must be said next. She must encourage her father as confidence in a crisis was essential.

"Father, I will never leave the business until the day I die!"

"But Anne, what about Robert and your engagement? He will expect a wife who will support him from home. That is what our community expects!"

"And so, I shall, Father. But he will understand I am a woman of property, and I am not dependent on him. I will take his name and have his children, but I will never give up my business interests. I love doing this. It has been my life, and I will not let it fail. I will be with you, Father, at your side until you are ready for me and any other members of the family you wish as your replacements. You will want to rest someday, and I will be there for you!"

Jonathan Turner looked at his daughter in disbelief at this radical suggestion. A woman managing in business, this was not done. A woman's place was in the home raising children, instructing the hired help. What was Anne thinking?

"Anne, this is very radical. Will Robert understand?"

"Father, Neville requires of you a daily reading from Proverbs, does he not? Read Proverbs Chapter thirty-one. That is what a good wife does. That is the biblical expectation of a Christian wife. That expectation is my ideal and does not preclude me from running a business!"

"True, Daughter, but it will be so difficult for you to be a property owner in our society. You will be looked down on by men."

"Yes, I will, Father, but not by Robert. We have discussed this, and he understands change is coming. I have also talked with Megan Bassington, and I am encouraged by what is happening in America. We will need a company formed and allocate equity to family members. The banks have advised me they prefer that structure. Hamish McPherson has this in place for his sons."

Jonathan took a step back. His daughter's knowledge was far more advanced than he ever imagined! She was already an integral part of their business management. He knew he would not cope without her. The news that she would continue with him was a great relief.

"Daughter, you are already running much of the business. I am very thankful for your support. Your suggestion of a company structure is something I do not understand but let us develop it. If it helps keep the business safe for your younger brothers and sisters, I am for it. I will find a way and give you more control. We will run this together, Anne, and we will succeed."

"Thank you, Father. I love working with you. You have taught me so much. I do have another question for you. May I train Audrey Stern on the books, Father! I trust her completely, and she has the ability and would be willing. I need more time to review figures and checking the contracts. I am worried about the contracts you have signed with the McPhersons!"

"Yes, Anne, you may. I will need you more than ever in the next twelve months. I only hope that Robert understands. His parents certainly will not."

"Robert and I will settle that, Father. At present, we must focus on our cash flow forecast."

"Agreed, Anne. Now, where was that seat you pointed out? But just one other question? What about Clementine? It is time she commenced in the business."

"She will assist Audrey, Father. I have already discussed it with them both. Clemmie is unsure of herself, but Audrey will bring the best out in her."

Jonathan smiled. He should have known Anne would be one step ahead of him.

She led her father across the river, where they enjoyed each other's company as they discussed strategy for several hours.

At Richard Turner's Pub, Ewell ...

The letter from the shipping line confirmed the booking for Richard, his wife Sarah, and their daughter Katherine. Their destination of Grahamstown, South Africa, was now a reality. He rushed into the kitchen, where his wife made morning tea sandwiches for the hotel guests.

"Sarah, it has come! The letter with our passage has come. We are going in February!"

Sarah Turner shuddered. She was far from convinced farming in Africa was a sensible idea at their age, but she had dutifully followed her husband in his ventures. She looked at the letter and then passed it back, saying nothing.

"Sarah, are you not happy about our good fortune in gaining land in Africa?"

She nodded and said, "You know my concerns, Richard. I may never see my sons again!"

"Not so, Sarah. We will return in five years with a barrel of money for investing in a far larger pub. This journey will be a good move for us. Also, Katherine will see the world courtesy of His Majesty's government."

"I'm happy for Katherine, Richard, but it is hard leaving one's home when there seems no need!"

Richard was familiar with his wife's doubts but would not yield. In his opinion, if they would ever succeed, this was the opportunity. The plans were complete, and soon they would sail overseas. The prospect of a grand adventure excited him. It would make their fortune.

Richard was the optimist of the family. Sarah always dwelt on reality and kept the family stable. Together they had mastered every situation they faced. But this was different. Richard proposed relocating thousands of miles away from their home country. This time she might let him go alone!

"Harry manages the pub here, and Oliver is doing well in Epsom. Jonathan will care for them if there is any need. I must write today and advise him we depart from Southampton. I wonder if they will come and farewell the ship."

With that, Richard dashed off to his study. He pulled out pen, ink and paper and started a letter.

Mr Jonathan Turner
High Street
Guildford

Dear Jonathan
I am writing today advising of the excellent news we have received from His Majesty's Government. My family is granted passage to Port Elizabeth in South Africa at the government's expense. We leave from Southampton on Wednesday the twenty-eighth of February 1827.

As we discussed at our last meeting Jonathan, you will mentor Oliver and Harry, ensuring their development in the management of pubs. Sarah and I are most thankful for this. I am confident Oliver has everything in hand at the pub in Epsom. I understand you and Hamish McPherson will mentor him in the years ahead. I pray you will show the same interest in Harry for my pub at Ewell. A review of the accounts each month would be very encouraging for our youngest son.

The personal effects we require will travel with us, and the livestock will follow soon after with the same shipping line. It seems that all our plans are falling into place. I am content with our decision and will advise you further in the coming months.

We will join you in Guildford for Christmas. Our arrival will be on the twenty-fourth of December around mid-afternoon. We shall remain with you until the twenty-seventh of December, when we must return home. I am not sure if Harry and Oliver will join us. We will work towards solving this.

I also received your note advising of the engagement of Anne and Sir Robert South. We are so pleased for Anne and pass her our congratulations. Katherine is most excited for Anne and is longing for our Christmas visit.

Please write and tell me when you will visit next.

Your loving brother
Richard Turner.

At the Turner Household, Guildford …

Jonathan Turner read the letter in disbelief. He nodded his head and said aloud, "Foolish! This move is far too soon, Richard!" Jonathan knew Richard was essential in mentoring both Oliver and Harry. Oliver was only three months into his appointment as manager at Epsom. Despite his success so far, there were still many changes Hamish required. The stability that Richard provided in implementing these changes was invaluable. Harry was inexperienced at managing a pub, and Richard ignored this and embarked on his adventure.

With the confronting issues Anne raised about their business cash flow, the prospect of caring for Richard's sons was unsettling Jonathan. His brother claimed he would return in five years. Jonathan thought it would probably be ten years if they were lucky. He required an alternative plan.

The Church School, Guildford …

Mid-afternoon, the Reverend Andrew Taggart decided the children would go home early today. He justified his decision by knowing that they would be well behaved when the children arrived home as their energy levels would be lower.

"Now, children! We have finished school today, so we will say the Lord's prayer, and then I would ask that you all quietly walk home." The children readily agreed.

Simeon and William walked together, looking for things of interest in the shop windows. Madeline was on the other side of the street with friends, and they giggled about the day's events.

The Turner boys were unaware that Richard Smith and Caleb Elliot were sitting outside the Free School further up the street. Now a Free School student, Richard carried a heavy burden of expected achievement given his family's investment in his education. His father aspired Richard would enter politics and perhaps sit in the national parliament. Mayor Rupert Smith's ambition to become a parliament member seemed distant, so his hopes were now firmly pinned on his son.

Caleb's father required assistance in the blacksmith's shop, so rather than attending the Free School, Caleb took on an apprenticeship under his father. The two boys remained good friends despite their embarking on different paths. Richard, who was lazy and slow, struggled at school and gained few friends, so he cherished any time sitting and talking with his friend Caleb.

The timing of the meeting between the two boys and the Turner children was pure chance. There was bad blood between the boys, as Caleb suspected William of knocking out his two front teeth. Caleb, seeing them approaching, pointed them out to Richard. They would not let an opportunity such as this pass by.

Since his apprenticeship and the long work hours, Caleb's personality had changed, becoming an angry young man. Richard was easily persuaded, being scant on moral principles, and some dirty work sounded like fun. They moved quickly up the street into an alleyway and waited for their opportunity.

Admiring a model sailing boat in the shop window, Simeon was wholly immersed in his discussion with William. His fortune was only a few shillings, but he was keen on acquiring the model.

"I bet it would sail well at the river. We could sail it along the bank. William, will you lend me your three shillings so I have enough to buy it?"

"I like the model Sim, but I think three shillings is a lot of money. I only get an allowance of sixpence a week. It takes a long time to save that money. I will lend you one shilling."

"If you wanted the boat, I would lend you the three shillings. I would do it for you, Will! Come on, you don't spend it on anything, and I will pay you back. I promise!"

"If you pay me back, you must pay me back three shillings and sixpence, Sim."

"But that's not fair, William! I am your brother so we should help each other. Mother always says we should look after each other!"

As they walked past the alley, Richard pounced with an empty wooden box, which he crashed down on William's head. Caleb grabbed Simeon and pushed him against the wall. It only took two punches from Caleb, and Simeon doubled over on the footpath and wailed for help. William was inside the box, which Richard kept kicking, some of the kicks finding their mark on William's thighs and stomach.

Fortunately, some women heard Simeon's cries for help and came running, yelling. Richard and Caleb, ignoring it was early afternoon, suddenly realised the attention they were attracting. People were running toward them and warning them off. Richard saw his father watching from the other side of the road with his mouth open. The boys withdrew as fast as they could down the street, away from the disturbance they had caused.

William pulled himself out of the broken box and saw Richard and Caleb running away along the High Street. He picked up a stone from the road and hurled it with all his might at the two boys. Unfortunately, it hit Richard on the top of the head, deflected and smashed a window panel. Richard fell flat on the footpath with blood pouring from his head.

Simeon, who watched as he lay on the ground, said, "Nice shot, Will!"

One of the ladies who frightened the hooligans off gave Simeon a hand up. As she brushed him down, she complained, "Those ruffians were too afraid to face the music. They were cowards; they just ran off. Now, are you boys all right?"

Along the street, Richard took out a handkerchief, pushed it against his head and quickly limped off. Caleb was already long gone. Surprisingly William was not injured at all except for a few bruises. Simeon was still doubled over and slowly moving into an upright position. He took in a few big breaths and then stood up.

The ladies advised William and Simeon that an explanation would be advisable for the storekeeper. The boys walked over and stood beside Mr Higgins, the shop owner, peering in disbelief at his shattered glass window. Madeline ran back and joined them. She took over the negotiations.

"Mr Higgins, we are so sorry about the window, but it was an accident. My brothers were attacked by vandals just over the street here. They fought them off, and William threw a stone after them, which hit one of them on the head but also hit your window. We are so sorry, but it was an accident."

"You are the Turner children, aren't you? You will need to pay for this. The new glass will cost me nine shillings. Now I want that money by tomorrow. If I don't see that money, I will speak to your father."

Simeon said, "Yes, Mr Higgins, we will have the money for you tomorrow morning. You know where we live if you need us. We are very sorry. May we help you clean up?"

"That is very good of your children, but I don't want you getting cut by the glass. Now off you go. I will expect you tomorrow with the money."

Further up the street, Mayor Rupert Smith sat down on the seat outside the Free School, thinking about what he had witnessed. His son and Caleb Elliot had attacked two innocent children. He knew Caleb was a bad influence, but surely Richard knew better. Thank goodness the attack had not seriously injured anyone. Tonight, he and Marjorie would have a long talk with Richard. Rupert was sure this was not the proper behaviour of a private schoolboy.

The three Turner children came away from the shop and crossed the road, heading home.

Simeon complained, "William, I hope you are happy. We owe Mr Higgins nine shillings, and we don't have the boat. Why did you throw that stone? If father finds out about this, you should hide. He will be furious."

William cringed, thinking about the threat of a beating. Then he thought about the money.

"Sim, you have four shillings, and I have three. We only need another two shillings. Madeline, how many shillings do you have?"

"None! I spent it on a sweetmeat."

"You're not allowed, sweetmeats!"

Madeline became agitated, "William, don't tell Father! I don't want a beating!"

"If you don't want a beating, help me persuade Anne. She will have two shillings."

Madeline was not keen on being part of this, but she also understood the penalty for breaking the rules.

"Alright, but Father must not hear of it!"

They all agreed on keeping it a secret. When they arrived home, Madeline sweetly asked Anne if she could see her upstairs in their bedroom.

The boys were hidden in the bedroom, under the beds. As Anne came in, Madeline closed the door, and the boys slid out and stood.

Anne said, "What's this?"

Sim answered, "Anne, there has been an accident. William threw a stone and broke Mr Higgins' shop front window."

Anne looked at William with some disgust and said, "William, you know you have been told not to throw stones."

Madeline interjected, "It is a bit more complicated than that." She explained the whole situation.

"I see, and is Richard all right?"

"Yes, his father was just across the street and saw the whole thing. He did not help Richard at all but just watched. Richard ran away."

William pleaded, "Please, Anne, would you give me two shillings? We can't tell Father; otherwise, we will all get into trouble, and none of us wants that."

Anne looked at the three frightened little faces and took pity on them.

"I think I have two shillings somewhere! But you must pay it back. It's all I have in the world. You must pay me back."

"Yes, yes!" the three of them cried out. "We will pay it back."

Simeon then said, "Of course, William, I can lend you four shillings, but you must pay me back four shillings and sixpence!"

Dinner at the Turner Household ...

Jonathan Turner pushed back on his chair and stood. He announced that brother Richard's family would visit for Christmas and remain a few days. Clementine was incredibly excited, as she was good friends with her cousin Katherine, and they shared fond memories of previous gatherings when the children all went on outings.

When Jonathan also announced that Uncle Richard would settle for five years in South Africa with his wife and daughter, there was a sudden silence.

Anne was shocked. "Why? Why go to Africa when he has an excellent business in Ewell? It is dangerous out there!"

Clementine joined in, "What will Katherine do? It is so far away. There is no society, just cannibals and wild animals!"

"Uncle Richard seeks a better life for his family. His application has been successful, and the government has allocated a large allotment of land near a place called Grahamstown. He will establish a sheep and cattle farm there."

"Will this be a profitable venture, Father?" Anne asked.

"Uncle Richard is of that opinion."

"I can understand wool, father, but not cattle. Surely there cannot be a meat trade?"

"There is, but you are correct, Anne. He will commence with far more sheep than cattle."

Clementine feared for her cousin Katherine, "Please, Father, might Katherine stay here with us? She may stay in my room with Madeline and me. She would be no problem. It would be far safer than living in Africa."

Eleanora also agreed, "Jon, I agree with Clemmie. If Richard wishes for this risky adventure and Sarah is willing, then let them go, but let us save Katherine from this awful wild place. She is a wonderful girl and would fit in here so well. Please speak with Richard and ask that she might stay with us."

The others then all joined the pleading. It appeared that Jonathan must save Katherine from the wilds of Africa.

"Eleanora, it is not my decision! Richard is in control of his own family. The best I can do is assist him as he requests!"

"But Jonathan, he is your brother, and he will respect your opinion."

Jonathan Turner was not convinced and feared damaging his relationship with his brother. Anne then mentioned it might be helpful having Katherine in the household with another baby coming.

Jonathan wavered, seeing some merit in the proposal. He agreed, indicating a mild discussion with Uncle Richard might be possible, and then changed the subject.

"As you all know, Thomas will marry Marion on the eighteenth of next month. We will all attend the wedding. Mr McPherson has arranged a rental house for us near the church where they will be married. Your mother and I are keen that we arrive well before the wedding. We will be leaving the week before, and Mrs Jennings and Aggie will also attend."

Many conversations among the family broke out, but Jonathan raised his hand.

"I have made enquiries for another maid and would hope for an appointment very soon."

Anne and Clementine smiled at each other in relief. Their Father had answered their prayers.

"The new maid will attend to your mother and complete other duties as required. She will also join us in Greenwich. As the wedding date is drawing near, we must all begin packing for the journey. This occasion will be a great event for the family, so your mother will be discussing with you any new items of clothing required."

The girls readily identified with this comment and quickly talked about their requirements.

Eleanora asked, "Jonathan, where will Thomas and Marion live until the brewery company builds their house?"

"Thomas discussed this with me, advising the brewery house will not be ready for at least a year. Until then, I will rent a house for them."

Anne gave her father a stern look, as this was the first that she knew of another expense against the cash flow.

Jonathan continued with a smile, "Something special happened today! We tested the new mill, and Thomas, you may explain the result."

Thomas stood up and puffed out his chest with a big smile, "The mill worked as we planned. The test produced the finest flour I have ever seen. We think we can now produce the best flour in England. Let's not tell anybody yet, but the mill crushed fifty bags of grain in two hours. Now, if you take the local mills, they only crush around twenty bags of grain a day. Our productivity advantage is now massive. We will have an endless supply of the best flour in England."

Jonathan then said, "This is such a momentous occasion; it deserves a celebration with champagne."

Mrs Jennings brought in two bottles of champagne, and Thomas opened them, everyone cheering at the popping of the corks.

William and Simeon called out, "May we celebrate, Father?"

"Yes, my children, you shall all have a small glass. So shall Mrs Jennings and Aggie."

There was much delight as the glasses were poured full of the bubbly liquid. Then Jonathan stood and proposed a toast.

"To the Turner Flour Mill. Long may she produce!"

William took a sip and put his glass down. He watched everyone cheering and the much jovial talk. As his father consumed more champagne, he noticed the more relaxed he became. William stood and approached his father.

"Father, would you give me sixpence, please?"

Jonathan, feeling quite light-headed, noticed William's approach and heard his question. He looked down his nose at William and then smiled, "Certainly, William!"

Chapter 23

HMS Restless, East Coast of Rathlin Island, entrance to the Irish Sea ...

Coming on deck from his cabin, Robert noticed the sky was darkening in the west, the temperature falling quickly, and an increasing south-westerly drove a misty rain across the ship. After ten days of sailing higher into the Irish sea and following the proposed search route, there was no sign of Foster's frigate. Robert now questioned in his mind the search plan being followed.

At the Portsmouth briefing, Commander Jacobs sketched out the proposed track set for Foster. Sailing straight up through the Irish sea, he would round the top of Ireland and patrol the western coast for two weeks. Admiral Sutherland was doubtful that Foster ever reached the west coast, as there was no communication from his proposed home base of Donegal. It appeared that his ship vanished without a trace.

Robert and Horace Coombes sat together at dinner and mulled over the charts. The search plan they had devised together yielded no results. Information was sparse, and their Irish contacts proved unhelpful at best. Thousands of places to hide a ship dotted the coast of Ireland. Surely some kind of information would leak out soon. But from where? At this stage, it appeared like a dead end.

Robert looked up from the map. "Horace, this is not working for us! We need some information from the Irish side. Our contacts in Ireland are giving us nothing. We need an informer. Any suggestions?"

The ship shuddered as the gale bearing down from the west increased its intensity. Lieutenant Ham entered the captain's cabin with dripping oilskins.

"Sir, I have reduced sail and may do so again until this gale is over. Any further instructions?"

"No, Lieutenant. I will be on deck soon but continue reducing sail."

"Aye, Sir!"

And with that, he was gone.

Robert was satisfied with Lieutenant Ham. He was competent, and his decisions were sound and quickly implemented. Having a reliable man as First Officer made all the difference and allowed Robert planning time. But with no reliable information at hand, the starting point was unclear. Someone had captured the ship, and whoever took *Providence* their organisation was now deep in hiding. They would be aware the navy was searching for them and would have covered their tracks.

Horace scratched his head. "Look, the army has units all over Ireland, but the population resents us. If nationalists have overrun the ship, the local population will protect them. The army is not our answer; they are too disliked, and anyway, we want this information undercover, so we have the benefit of surprise."

"If we can't use the army, then who?"

Horace grinned. "I thought the navy had spies that the government used?"

"Yes, they are mainly people with influence who move in high circles and have sub-networks that delve deeper into the population. I am not sure the admiralty would give us access. Anyway, Horace, it would take a week before we arrived at Portsmouth!"

"Pity. It may give us a lead!"

They both stopped talking and looked back down at the charts. It was a needle in a haystack; who would have information about a ship stolen in the Irish sea? Even the slightest bit of information might give them a clue.

As the current process yielded nothing, Robert decided why not start from the beginning? He considered again how and where information would emerge from the source. If there was a mutiny or the ship had been boarded, the traitors would have the frigate hidden at an unknown dock somewhere in Ireland not visible from the sea. To maintain secrecy, they would be keeping a close eye on the dockworkers, who must be aware of the ship. Ireland had much trade with Scotland and England. Perhaps a dock worker or a sailor arriving in Scotland would speak freely in a pub. They were looking in the wrong place! The ship was well hidden where they would never find it. But sailors and dock workers travelled and enjoyed a yarn in a pub. Perhaps the pubs might be far more fruitful.

"Horace, let us say that *Providence* was taken and hidden somewhere in Ireland. There must be a lot of people who know about it. A ship the size of a frigate is hard to conceal! "

"Probably, but where would we find them?"

"We know that the Irish talk wildly when tipsy and are often drunk. So, where do people go for a drink if you are associated with the docks or ships?"

"In the bars beside the docks!"

"Yes, I had the same thought! Where would you watch if the navy was making undercover inquiries if you were the traitors? In Irish port bars?"

"Yes. In Irish pubs near the docks! it could be very dangerous venturing in there alone."

"Agreed. But sailors travel Horace. Where does trade take them?"

"Most trade on the East Coast of Ireland would be with Scotland first and then England."

"Right, and in which bars would we find Irish sailors?"

"Irish pubs."

"Are you keen on frequenting Irish pubs, Horace?"

"Don't mind it as long as they are not in Ireland. I think you may be onto something!"

"We are wasting our time searching at sea. We need some subversives in the pubs collecting information. I will write a despatch tonight advising our new plan. We will turn for Douglas straight away and send the despatch. Then we are heading for Glasgow."

"Why pick Glasgow?"

"Captain Foster headed for Donegal. The Admiral directed that this would be his staging port. I have no evidence for this, but somehow, I would say the Irish knew about his home port. We know there were traitors on *Restless*, so it is not unreasonable that there were traitors on *Providence*. It is most likely they used a similar attack as *Restless* encountered. This time it worked. I would also assume the attack came within the Donegal estuary. When you look at the charts, the estuary there silts up to narrow the channel. Perfect for an attack or ambush!"

Horace rechecked the chart looking at the Donegal estuary. "The channel becomes very narrow. All they would need is a chain across, and she would be dead in the water and an easy boarding target! The population there would be difficult as well. Very nationalist! Sutherland made a mistake – they should have used Derry. Better port with more support."

There was something in what Horace said that made Robert feel uneasy. He scratched his head but could not come to grips with a question lurking for him far deeper within his mind. He regained his train of thought.

"Horace! Where is the closest large Scottish port from Donegal?"

Hamish studied the chart quickly, "Glasgow!"

"I agree. So, there is a high probability of scuttlebutt in the Irish pubs at the docks there. That is the biggest Scottish port for trade with Ireland. So, start practising your Irish accent as we are going on an Irish pub crawl in the beautiful city of Glasgow."

"I don't mind green beer! But I thought the Admiral's subversives would do this?"

"We can't wait that long. I'm sure Foster and his crew would agree."

"So, we are the subversives! I should have known. Swanton some of those biscuits, please!"

"Horace, you and I will stop shaving in the next few days. We must look dishevelled when we visit Glasgow. Swanton will provide some old sailor's clothes, so we look authentic."

Robert still had in the back of his mind that something was missing. There was a nagging feeling that he missed some crucial bit of information. At present, Robert must work with the information available. He put on his oilskins and boots and tramped back onto the quarter deck.

"Mr Ham, set a course for Douglas, please. We must be there by tomorrow evening. Plot a course and come about as soon as you can. Get the men aloft and make the ship fly. We are short of time!"

Ham looked at his Captain and wondered about this sudden change in plan. He replied, "Aye, Captain."

He and the Master quickly looked at the chart behind the helmsman and agreed on a course. The First Officer then started bellowing orders out. Men scrambled up the rigging onto the yards. Within five minutes, *Restless* was coming around onto a southerly course and running smoothly with the wind.

Robert watched with appreciation as Lieutenant Ham trimmed the sails pressing the schooner hard without endangering the ship in the gale. As the sails set, she responded with vigour; all the crew enjoyed the feeling of acceleration as *Restless* flew towards the south. It was an experience any seaman would enjoy.

As he thought about the despatch required for Admiral Sutherland, Anne suddenly came into his mind. A letter was long overdue. He was unsure how long this mission would last. Writing letters home was not his best skill, particularly to the woman who was now vitally interested in his safety. He advised the officers he was going below decks and set off ready to pen a letter.

At the Turner Bakery in Guildford ...

On Saturday morning, Anne watched over Audrey's shoulder as she worked on the figures. With a quick eye for detail, Anne promptly pointed out any of Audrey's mistakes. Anne was a firm believer in learning from mistakes, and Audrey proved a fast learner.

"Audrey! Mr Turner and I must talk, so I will leave you for a few minutes."

She moved over and sat beside her father.

"Father, have you decided on where we shall rent offices yet? Vacating this area will allow the setup of the biscuit factory. Time is critical."

As Jonathan finished his discussion with Anne, he noted the time, "Anne, I must go now. Your Mother will be expecting me. We can talk about the offices tonight."

He and Eleanora would interview a new maid this afternoon, recommended by the Agency. A Mrs Ethel Nibley applied, and her references were faultless. Jonathan cleared his desk and quietly left the busy office.

Johnathan was heartened by the bustling crowds. The High Street was full of carts, buskers and tradespeople selling their goods from makeshift stalls, much to the dislike of the shopkeepers. The town council had agreed to encourage all types of commerce for Guildford's financial development, a strategy that Jonathan was entirely behind. The more people in town, the more business!

As he approached the Guildhall, Jonathan saw Mayor Rupert Smith standing at the entrance. Jonathan waved and then walked over and greeted him.

"Rupert, I bid you a good day. The town is thriving! The policy you have put in motion is working well. There appears to be a growing number of traders present."

"Good day, Jonathan. Yes, it is very satisfying. But Constable Rawlins tells me that petty crime is rising. I think we are attracting some of the London vagrants. I'm not sure how we combat this."

"Rising crime is unwelcome. I suggest we work towards a full-time professional police force as they are establishing in London. The Parish Constable tries his best, but it is a voluntary position, and Rawlins must also earn a living. Perhaps the Council would consider this in next year's budget."

"It would mean tax rises, Jonathan. Would our property owners support this?"

"Rupert, I would, as the importance of law and order cannot be underestimated. Remember Fawkes[27] night is coming and the problems that creates. Some of these vagrants will cause trouble for sure. Have you talked with Constable Rawlins about this?"

"Yes, he is enlisting more watchmen for the night, but it is not that easy as many men are more worried about protecting their homes than the town's High Street."

"The landholders must also assist and supply some of their tenant farmers for the night. These men are law-abiding and can do with the extra money. I'm sure that Patrick Easton would send men from the Manor. There are various other landholders that we should approach. George Pently and Malcolm Jessop would assist. I will also ask some of my workers if they are available. The larger our watchmen force, the less trouble the Fawkes rabble will cause.

---

[27] Guy Fawkes (1570 – 1606) a member of a group of provincial English Catholics who planned the failed Gunpowder Plot of 1605. The plotters stored gunpowder in an undercroft below the House of Lords, Fawkes being placed in charge of the stockpile. The failure of the plot is celebrated each year in the UK since 5 November 1605 as Guy Fawkes Night. Wikipedia.

Why not let them set up their bonfire on the outskirts of town and then block their way. Don't let them into our streets. If we had fifty watchmen for the night, they would not dare!"

Rupert considered what Jonathan was saying. He knew the Guildford budget was tight, but if there were infrastructure damage, it would be some time before the Guild could repair it. Perhaps Jonathan was right; block them out of the town. The cost of the watchmen would be minimal against repairing burnt buildings.

"Perhaps you are right, Jonathan. I will discuss it at Council. I may need your assistance with a few councillors before the meeting. However, I am not keen on involving the recusants. Should we be so bold, Jonathan?"

"Rupert, Catholic emancipation is coming. They are people like us who must earn a living and desire a quiet and secure life. We must let go of our old fears. Why should they be barred from commerce? We need them. I have no problem dealing with the Catholics. I have no problem with being their friends."

"Jonathan, be careful. Emancipation may take longer than you think. I would tread carefully if I were you. Now, there was one other matter I would like your advice on and given we both have the time, could you spare me a few minutes?"

"Yes, Rupert, but I must be gone in twenty minutes as we are interviewing a new maid this afternoon. "

"Twenty minutes will be more than enough. Come in, my friend."

Jonathan and Rupert went into the Guildhall and sat at a table near the rear. The room was empty, so it was private.

"Jonathan, I am worried about my son Richard. As you know, he now attends the Free School, but he struggles. He has no friends and has become lazy. Also, he associates with the blacksmith's son Caleb Elliot who leads him astray. Pray, do you think Richard should be at the Free School, or should he be indentured?"

Not seeing this coming, Jonathan wondered how best he should answer the question without volunteering his help. Formerly, the Reverend Andrew Taggart briefed him on Richard's bully tactics and how the church school needed to discipline him. Perhaps Richard was a bit slow for the Free School because of his comfortable life at home. His mother pampered him, but he knew how proud Rupert was of his son. He would not want this belief destroyed.

Before Jonathan could answer, Rupert continued, "I was walking in the High Street yesterday and saw Richard and Caleb attack some passers-by for no real reason. He did not see me witness the attack, but I was ashamed of him. It was not the behaviour expected of a Free School student. Since then, I have been thinking of pulling him out of school and having him apprenticed.

Why spend the money on him if he has no ambition."

Jonathan was alarmed by what may follow! Rupert would ask that Richard be indentured at his bakery. That was the last thing Jonathan wanted, given his knowledge of the boy, not that he would tell Rupert that.

"Rupert. I think you act in haste. Richard is a fine young man and needs time. Perhaps the Free School is not the school for him. You are a man of means. Why not consider a school further from home. A spell at boarding school may encourage his initiative. Consider this! He has the advantage of a loving mother at home who does everything for him. He might become more independent and resilient if you removed him from this.

Also, some of the more distinguished boarding schools would put him among the best. He would gain valuable contacts there for the future. Why he may even consider politics."

Jonathan could see that Rupert was sitting taller by the minute as he praised his son. The father certainly had aspirations for the boy, but it would not happen while he remained pampered at home in Guildford.

"That is the answer. Richard is a fine boy. He will succeed, I am sure!"

"Why, Jonathan, this is a grand idea. I shall make enquiries at once. Why did I not think of this? Thank you, Jonathan. Now you mentioned an interview. I hope the new maid is acceptable. Please give Eleanora my regards. Good day Jonathan."

As Jonathan walked from the Guild Hall, he thought, 'Poor Richard, it will be sink or swim now, but I would not want him working for me!'

At the house, Jonathan found a young woman standing on the portico. She was well dressed in a dark blue working dress and a modest hat. Her brown hair was tied in a bun. He noticed she was quite attractive.

"Excuse me, Miss, may I be of assistance? I am Jonathan Turner, the owner of this house."

"Ah, Mr Turner, I am Mrs Ethel Nibley. I have come for the interview!"

"Welcome, Mrs Nibley. Come inside, and I will find my wife. We were expecting you!"

Jonathan seated Mrs Nibley in the parlour and then asked Aggie for some tea. He then went upstairs and found Eleanora.

"Eleanora, the applicant for the new maid's position, is down in the parlour. Are you ready for the interview?"

"Yes, I have been waiting for you! Jonathan, I am not convinced that we need this maid? My health has improved considerably in the last few weeks. I'm not sure about this!"

"Eleanora, this will make your life far easier, and it is Neville's recommendation as well. Imagine how hard it will be with the new baby coming. It is for the best, my Dear. Let us do the interview, please?"

– 466 –

"As you say, Jonathan."

They went down together, and Jonathan introduced Eleanora.

"Mrs Nibley, let me introduce my wife, Mrs Eleanora Turner. The position is for Mrs Turner's lady's maid. So, she will ask most of the questions."

"Good day, Mrs Turner."

Eleanora looked at Ethel Nibley and saw a younger woman than herself, perhaps thirty years in age and well-groomed. She was impressed with Ethel's presentation and warmth.

"Mrs Nibley, welcome. It is good of you to come. Now, if I may, I would like your references, please."

"Certainly, Mrs Turner." Ethel passed them across.

Eleanora expected several references but found only one. It was from the Jessop Estate near Camberley, where Ethel had worked for the last five years. The reference was excellent, and it stated that Ethel moved of her own accord, the Jessops being sorry she was leaving.

Eleanora passed the reference over and Jonathan, who was sipping a cup of tea, commenced reading.

"Mrs Nibley, you have left of your own accord from the Jessops. Your reference is excellent; however, may I ask why you decided on a move?"

"Yes, Mrs Turner. That is very understandable. May I say that I was content in my previous position, but Guildford has much on offer for me. It is a lovely place, and my mother is a resident here on Portsmouth Road, just out of town. She is a seamstress and has a small business which helps provide a living."

"Mrs Nibley, I assume you have a husband; what does he do?"

"He was in the army Ma'am, but he died six years ago. He battled with consumption for some years and finally succumbed. So, I was a widow left with a young daughter. I required an income, so I entered service. The attraction here is that my daughter resides with my mother. If I gained employment in Guildford, I thought I might see her once a week."

"I am sorry about your husband, Mrs Nibley. What rank was he?"

"He was a Lieutenant in the infantry. The Army stationed him at Sandhurst before he became ill."

Jonathan Turner changing the subject, said, "Mrs Nibley, are you comfortable with the duties and the conditions the Agency advised?"

"They are what I expected, Mr Turner. The one thing I would ask is that when it is convenient each week if I might see my daughter for a few hours?"

Eleanora said, "We would encourage that, Mrs Nibley. We have several children, and we understand the importance of being with them. Don't you agree, Jonathan?"

"Yes. Indeed!"

Mrs Nibley then added, "I understand the duties. They are similar to those in my previous position, and there would be no difficulties filling any other duties required. I assume you have a butler?"

"That is appreciated, Mrs Nibley, but we do not have a butler. However, we are making enquiries, and we shall keep that in mind. Now you understand that it is a live-in position, and the hours are quite long most days, but it is a happy home."

"Yes, Mrs Turner, I understand from the agency that your family is highly esteemed in the community, so I would be pleased to work here."

Jonathan opened his mouth as Eleanora said, "Mrs Nibley, I think we are most happy with you and may we know when you are available. You have no objection to us calling you Ethel?"

"Certainly, Mrs Turner, I prefer Ethel rather than Mrs Nibley! I am available from tomorrow!"

Jonathan was amazed. Before they came down, Eleanora seemed against the proposal; now, she was pleased with the young lady. He smiled and let her continue.

"Good, I will have the maid prepare your room for tomorrow. We will welcome you then, Ethel. There is one thing I must mention. My son Thomas will be married in mid-November. The family will visit London for two weeks. We would expect you to accompany us. As you can see, I am well advanced in my confinement, and will need assistance. We have rented a fine house for the time in London. I hope that is acceptable."

"That will be quite acceptable, Mrs Turner. Thank you both for offering me the position."

With that, Jonathan wished Ethel farewell at the door. As he returned, he decided not to comment and smiled about Eleanora's change of mind. Eleanora spoke first, "I know what you are thinking, Jonathan, but I noted her good manners and fine speech, and I thought this would also assist the children, so why not? Why keep interviewing when you find a good servant the first time? The Agency did a good job. Poor woman losing her husband and then finances, forcing her into service!"

"Yes, Dear."

Jonathan agreed with the decision. Ethel Nibley appeared perfect for the position.

"My Dear, this is a note for Hamish McPherson organising a meeting in Reading later next week. I will take the opportunity of visiting grain merchants there to ascertain what supplies are available."

"How long will you be gone, Jonathan?"

"I shall leave on Wednesday and return on Saturday. It will only be three nights away, and Ethel will be with you and the other servants. You will be fine, especially as your health is improving."

Upstairs at the Turner House ...
Anne sat on her bed reading a letter from Lady Emma South:

Fintelton Manor
East Harting
Sussex

Miss Anne Turner
High Street
Guildford
Surrey

My Dearest Anne

As we discussed some time ago, my mother and I intend on a shopping trip to London on November the tenth and remain there for the week. As Thomas will be married on the Saturday of this stay, I will stay in London until after the wedding.

I was very thankful for the wedding invitation for myself and my parents, and as you will know, I have accepted and will enjoy being with you again.

My mother requests you join us as we travel and stay with us at St James's Square until Marion requires you for wedding duties. These arrangements should allow us ample time for shopping in London and enjoying the company of Megan Bassington. I contacted Marion by letter, but she fears she will be much engaged in marriage preparations. But perhaps she may stay one night.

We will leave Fintelton on November the tenth and stay overnight at Guildford. On the eleventh, we will rise early and drive through to Epsom for the Saturday stopover, and then on to London on Sunday. With the improving health of my father, he will join us on the journey. Sir Hugh will remain at Fintelton, as there is much on his list at present.

We are excited about the prospect of you being a member of our party and ask that you join us on November the eleventh. Our carriage will arrive at your residence at around eight in the morning. Having you with us will add great pleasure to the trip.

If these arrangements are acceptable, please send a note and advise so.

Your Dearest friend
Emma South.

Anne was thrilled the invitation had arrived. The trip to London with friends would be so exciting, and it fitted in so well with Thomas's wedding. There was a section in the invitation that was a bit confronting. The Earl would also be travelling with them. Meeting the Earl for the first time in his coach might be difficult. Anne hoped it was a large coach; otherwise, it may be quite a close introduction.

She rushed downstairs with the letter in hand.

"Mother, the invitation from Lady Jane and Lady Emma has arrived. I will be in London at St James's Square for a week. It is like a dream - it will be wonderful!"

Eleanora took the letter and read it.

"My, this is an elegant invitation, Anne. You are fortunate indeed. It seems the Earl has accepted you even before meeting him. This news is good, indeed. Now you must check first with Marion when you are required. Perhaps you should write before you accept?"

"Yes, Mother, the plan with Marion is already made, and I need to attend her on Wednesday afternoon. I will write to Marion as you ask, but I will also send a note accepting Emma's kind invitation. I must put the family of my future husband first. At St James's Square, I will be close enough if Marion requires me. It is an easy distance, and I always planned to arrive on Wednesday. I shall write to Emma today with my acceptance."

"Your father expected you would travel with us, Anne, so it would be wise if you advised him of your plans."

"Yes, we will need a plan for the business needs while away."

At Fintelton Manor …

Doctor David Sopwith was eager to arrive at Fintelton for his visit, checking on the Earl's recovery. Given Neville's honeymoon, the employment of a replacement doctor was organised at some expense, with David hoping no emergencies occurred during his absence. He was already missing Neville and was nervous about leaving his patients for the weekend. His coach stopped at Petersfield, allowing for a good lunch, and approached the Fintelton Manor estate gates early Friday afternoon.

A single rider came into view as the coach progressed along the drive. Doctor Sopwith soon recognised the rider as Sir Hugh South, leaving the estate on some mission. As their paths crossed, Sir Hugh brought his horse alongside the coach.

"Doctor Sopwith, you have come for my father. Very good of you. You will find him improving and in far better health. He is up and about."

"This is good news indeed, Sir Hugh. The countess has kindly invited me for the night. I hope I will see you at dinner, Sir?"

"Unfortunately, not, Doctor. I have some business in Petersfield tonight! Then Guildford on Sunday and will call on you for my appointment Monday morning. I have business with Mr Jonathan Turner – the estate has signed contracts for grain at his new mill."

"I understand this may be a very prudent decision Sir Hugh. The Turners are changing the history of milling, it would appear. Steam power is changing our world."

"Yes, Doctor, and I would not want Fintelton Manor left behind in the ship's wake. We must move with the times. I bid you a good day, Doctor."

"Good day, Sir Hugh!"

The heir of Fintelton dug his spurs into the horse, with the mare cantering off. David Sopwith noticing Sir Hugh's slightly improved complexion thought it a good sign. Perhaps he conquered his urge for scotch for some days. David knew he would find out on Monday. Hopefully, his business in Petersfield would not lead him back into his old habits.

"Drive on!"

Pike, the butler and two footmen waited on the front steps as the arrival committee.

"Good afternoon, Pike."

"Good afternoon, Doctor Sopwith. Lady Jane is expecting you. I assume you will meet with his Lordship this afternoon before dinner?"

"Yes, Pike. I have brought some equipment with me as well as my bags. I will assess the Earl's recovery this afternoon if you would place my medical bag where he is now. The rest of the luggage and equipment may be deposited in my room, please."

"Very good, Sir. Charles, Peter, please take care of the doctor's luggage and equipment. Driver, follow the driveway around the Manor, please, and you will find the stables. The groom is expecting you. If you would follow me, please, Doctor."

They proceeded through the large double entrance doors of the old estate house. Each time he came, David Sopwith noticed some new ornate item. Of course, his interest in this house had heightened knowing that Lady Emma appreciated his company. He hoped this was not because of his family estates in Ireland – but of course, she would not be aware of these facts. David believed that any future decision Lady Emma made in their relationship should not be influenced by his wealth or lack of it.

Pike led Doctor Sopwith into the drawing-room with its large glass panelled doors overlooking the estate. The Earl was sitting on a beautiful leather couch and appeared rested.

Lady Jane stood from her seat and was most welcoming, "Welcome, Doctor Sopwith. It is generous of you to come so far! Look here at his Lordship. Does he not look most improved?"

The Earl turned to see who his wife addressed. As his eyes opened wider, they adjusted, and he recognised the doctor.

"Doctor Sopwith, my apologies. My eyes take some time to transition these days. Now I see you. Thank you for returning. My health is much improved since the last time we met."

"That is excellent news, my Lord. If I may discuss the symptoms, you are now experiencing, with you this afternoon. Then tomorrow morning, we will carry out some tests assessing your health. The results of these tests will help with future examinations. I am sure your family is keen that you have a few more years of good health."

"That will depend on our good Lord. I am thankful for each day!"

Lady Jane asked, "Doctor, would you care for some tea?"

"Thank you, Lady Jane, that would be most refreshing after the journey."

Doctor Sopwith spent the next hour talking with Lord Fintelton about every symptom he could relate. When finished, he reread his notes, checking they were correct. He thanked the Earl and watched as the servants carefully led the old gentleman upstairs to dress in time for the dinner gong.

"Dinner will be at seven, Doctor. Charles here will show you to your room."

As the footman led Doctor Sopwith up the stairs, Emma appeared on the landing.

"Doctor Sopwith, welcome!"

"Ah, Lady Emma, Charles is showing me the way."

Emma followed them, "Thank you, Charles, that will be all."

"I hope you are ready for some cards tonight, Doctor Sopwith? Mother and Father will join us for a short time, but I am afraid they will retire early after dinner. Sir Hugh is in Petersfield, so that it will be you and me."

"Good, Lady Emma, that shall be entertaining!"

In Petersfield ...

Saturday morning, Sir Hugh woke to find the room a mess and a completely nude woman asleep beside him in the bed. A half-empty whiskey bottle leaked onto the sheets. His head ached. Seeing several empty bottles on the floor, he realised why!

Gently, he pulled the covers over the sleeping woman. He could not recall last night but noticed she was young and quite attractive. Sitting there, he watched and considered this young woman's situation in life. This girl was someone's daughter. Some woman laboured through nine months of confinement and delivered this child into a life of poverty. Her parents probably sold her to a madame, who now offered her body out for profit. She would probably die of the pox.

As he watched her chest move up and down, he thought she was no different to him. He was miserable, so he drank a lot! He had the pox, and he would die of it! He might be an aristocrat, but he shared a bed with her! What was it that Reverend Taggart said? 'Do you like yourself, Hugh?' No, he found his life useless and hated himself. He could not last a week without scotch and women.

Deep within his mind, there was a longing for something different. He was unsure of where this search would end. Was it that he was afraid of what he would find? He slipped out of bed, washed his face and did a quick body wash removing the whisky. Pulling on his clothes, he left a few pound notes on the bedsheets. "Good luck, darling!" He said softly and left the room.

Sir Hugh headed off for Guildford. He was unsure why but he knew he must keep moving. Monday morning, there were appointments, so he might as well arrive there early.

At Fintelton Manor ...

David Sopwith was fast asleep when the footman entered his room and opened the curtains. The light flashed in, bringing the room to life. It was a large bedroom on the first floor of the manor house. The windows looked down over the gardens at the side of the building.

He rose and admired the beautiful estate running down a shallow valley to the south. Newly ploughed fields stretched as far as the woods, which lined a stream at the bottom of the valley. He admired Emma walking with a basket in the gardens beside the house. She must have risen early and was cutting flowers.

He then remembered the dinner last night. The Earl and Lady Jane were good company. They talked about the wedding, Robert and Anne's engagement, and Neville Bassington's medical experience. He tried as best he could to contribute, but his lack of knowledge of these people hampered his discussion.

"David, tell us more about yourself." Lady Jane requested. "You mentioned at our dinner, the night after the wedding, that your family has estates in Ireland. Tell us about your family."

"There is not that much to tell Lady Jane. My mother was a girl from Hampshire who married an English army officer, a lieutenant Lacey. His father had estates in Ireland. I believe they were in the family for generations. The marriage produced no children. After his death, she married again to an engineer, a Mr Sopwith, and they had three children, two sons and one daughter. I was the younger son.

When Lieutenant Lacey's father died, it appears that his father willed the inheritance to the eldest male offspring of the family. The Laceys only had one child, and he was dead, so my brother inherited the estates. That's about it."

"Pity that you should miss out, Doctor Sopwith, but that is the way of entailments. So, you have set up your practice in Guildford. Do you think it will prosper?"

"I think so, Lady Jane, as it was quite difficult being absent this weekend. I have employed another Doctor who has guaranteed care for my patients if anything should arise. Let us hope nothing does. Joining forces with Neville will be a blessing. I am run off my feet with my existing patients. Also, my Guildford clientele pays their bills on time which is even better."

The Earl liked the sound of this, "Nothing like good cash flow, Doctor!"

"Yes, my Lord."

Emma was quiet during the dinner and only added a few comments. She seemed distracted. David felt that the open communication that existed between them might have disappeared. Only after the Earl and Countess retired could they freely talk.

"Lady Emma, I feel you are distant tonight. I hope I have not offended you in any way?"

"David, please call me Emma now my parents have retired. No, you have been a perfect gentleman. I always enjoy your visits. Perhaps a little too much!"

"Is that not a good thing, Emma?"

"David, this is hard for me to say, and I cannot explain it all. You will need to give me time. There is so much happening with our family at present, and I feel confused and overwhelmed. I need space and time! Please, if you would understand this, it would help?"

"Certainly, Emma, please forgive me if I pressure you on anything? If there are other issues, please give them the priority they deserve. I agree that time is required when difficult issues face us."

"Thank you, David! When you were here last, I told you of a dinner that Anne and I were organising. I'm afraid we must postpone this now, as there is no time before Thomas Turner's wedding and my London trip with Mother. Please accept my apologies for this. With Father's sickness, the issues with Sir Hugh and other matters, the situation overcame me. I feel I may have led you on, and it is my fault."

"Not at all, Emma. I understand the emotion that stressful situations can create. Whatever you said will always be kept in confidence."

"Thank you, David, you are such a kind gentleman!"

"Emma, I will not pry, but if there is anything I may be of assistance with, please call on me?"

"Not at the moment, David."

He wondered if he knew why this young lady who previously displayed no hesitation in accepting his advances was now turning away from him. He was disappointed at this polite rebuff. It must be because of his station in life. He would not marry a woman who was not content with the offer of himself and the living from his medical practice. It now appeared the step down for Emma may be too far.

"Tell me, Emma, please, and I shall not question you again. I would like to understand your thoughts on this! You are a member of an important family and reside in a large estate house. Your lifestyle is comfortable, indeed. Emma, these issues you mention, might one be the consideration of the loss of position and lifestyle?"

Emma immediately knew what he was asking. Was it because her station was above him in life? Emma had thought this through, and it was of no consequence for her. The major problem was that from her discussions with Robert, she was now aware of the perilous state of her family's estate. If she and David became attached, he would be obliged to assist the estate and its financial difficulties. She would not burden him with this. If their relationship was to continue, it must be as equals. Currently, she was unaware if her family would prosper or decline in the future. Her purpose in the coming months would be to assist Robert and find solutions.

"It is not status or lifestyle, David. There are other problems that you are unaware of that our family must solve. It is better that you are not involved in this. It would help if you trusted me, as I hope the family will soon solve these issues. I just beg that you give me time. Can we not remain good friends? I do enjoy your friendship so much."

He must do her the honour of accepting her explanation for now. Good manners demanded this. But David Sopwith felt most grieved that it appeared the possibility of a romantic attachment with Emma, whom he adored, was becoming unlikely.

"I will be your friend Emma whenever you need me. Let me know when these issues you talk about are solved. Tomorrow, after fully examining your father, I must be on my way. I am worried about the doctor I have employed in Guildford, and I do not wish to intrude."

"Why David, you are more than welcome here tomorrow night." Emma noticed that while David remained very courteous, it was as if the tenderness had disappeared from his voice. Should her family duty come first or her love for this young man? She felt very vulnerable and pressured.

"The tests will only take an hour. If I leave after that, I should make Guildford before dark."

Emma looked at him in surprise. It seemed men must have a definite and immediate answer to everything; otherwise, they became resentful. She wondered if she should confide in him all the issues – he may stay on, and they could be together. No, she could not drag him into these issues. It would not be proper to divulge the family details. Emma was most disappointed with his change in attitude. The tears flowed down her cheeks, and she lost her calm.

She blurted out angrily, "David, my mother and father invited you for two days, and when I ask for understanding and time to think, you leave. Why can't you understand that I need time?"

Emma stood up and rushed out of the room, slamming the door as hard as possible. She made her point, but he was confused and sat there with his mouth open. Indeed, he was doing the gentlemanly thing! He agreed with her and would not rush her. It was preferable if he left now so she would not be distracted by him. But this sudden anger and outburst, what did that mean? For him, the conversation of last night left him confused and disappointed.

Quickly dressing, he went down for breakfast and found himself alone in the dining room. Pike served him a good breakfast and asked, "Now, Doctor Sopwith, where would you like your equipment set up?"

"Ah, thank you, Pike. In the drawing-room where the Earl was yesterday. If that is convenient?"

"Yes, Sir."

The Earl made his appearance around ten in the morning and sat down beside the Doctor.

"This morning, my Lord, we commence some tests that will provide us with a baseline reading for the coming months. We will compare back as we do future tests, tracking your improvement." Lord Fintelton readily agreed.

"Firstly, please breathe as hard as you can into this tube. You will see it connects to this glass cylinder with a ball inside. This instrument will give me an indication of your lung condition. All you must do is blow as hard as you can into the tube. Do you understand this?"

"Yes, Doctor."

The tests continued with David writing copious notes about each test. Finally, David completed the examination, and his instruments were quickly packed up and loaded into the coach.

Lady Jane came out from the parlour as David was packing.

"Doctor Sopwith, Lady Emma tells me you are leaving us this morning. I was looking forwards to your company at dinner again. Are you sure you must leave?"

"Lady Jane, your invitation was truly kind, but I am worried about the surgeon I hired in Guildford and some of my patients. Please forgive me, it must seem rude, and I apologise. But I must go."

The mistress of this house for the last forty years was no fool and understood what the underlying problem might be. She would not interfere but felt that it might be a good idea if Doctor Sopwith departed after farewelling Lady Emma.

"Doctor, I am sad that you are leaving, but I expect you will soon return, checking on the Earl."

"Yes, his health seems remarkably improved, but if you feel it declines in any way, please contact me. Even the slightest symptoms may be serious."

"You can be assured, Doctor, I will contact you immediately. Now Emma is in the garden; you must say goodbye, please. Before you leave!"

David was reticent. He made his farewell last night and had no wish that he inflamed the situation. However, he must not offend the family.

"Certainly, Lady Jane, now which way should I go?"

"Down this hallway here and out on the terrace. I think Emma is arranging some flowers."

"Thank you."

David walked slowly down the hall as if he were facing an executioner. He realised his bedside manner was aloof, but this was because he concentrated on the medical issues and wanted the best for his patients. He had few romantic skills. His best experience conversing with females was fighting with his younger sister some years ago.

Emma was standing at a table on the terrace, cutting flowers and arranging them in a vase.

David approached her slowly, saying, "I thought I would come out and say goodbye. I mean until we meet again in Guildford. I have completed the tests on your father, and he is remarkably recovered. So, I thought I would come and say goodbye, Emma."

Emma did not look up but just said, "Goodbye!"

David thought that she would at least turn around and face him. She must still harbour anger.

"Emma, I am sorry if anything I said last night upset you. It was not my intention."

"You are not sorry! You are leaving!"

"Emma, you asked me for time. You said there were other issues. I should withdraw and give you the time needed. I will always be your friend, Emma!"

She said nothing, and there was a short silence. David then felt awkward standing there.

"Goodbye, Emma."

As he turned and walked, she said, "Doctor Sopwith, may I remind you it is Lady Emma!"

He stopped but did not turn around. David was most hurt and could not understand what had caused this. It was no use now. He continued walking, back through the hall and out the front of the house down the steps where Pike was waiting beside the coach, holding the door open.

"Thank you, Pike."

David got into the coach and slumped down on the seat. Pike did not close the coach door!

"Sir, if I may say something, please?"

"All right, Pike, you are certainly my senior in age, so out with-it man. I have no objection to hearing from you." David was somewhat frustrated and sounded impatient.

"Sir, I would not wish to be presumptuous. I say this as a friend. I have served this family for over forty years, from well before Lady Emma was born. I have assisted closely in her upbringing from birth to the present day. There is not a mean bone in her body Sir."

"Really!"

"Yes, Sir, I have seen the two of you together and served you. I have noted the attachment. It is genuine, Sir. It needs time. Do not become confused, Sir. The attachment is real."

David was about to snap back with a smart answer but restrained himself. He calmed his anger and thought for a few seconds about what this wise old butler was saying. Suddenly he relaxed and smiled at Pike.

"I have overreacted, haven't I Pike?"

"I would not be sure, Sir, but time is a great healer and solves many problems."

"Thank you, Pike."

David looked at Pike and understood the wisdom the years had implanted in this man. A man worth taking into your confidence. David smiled and shook his hand.

"I must be on my way, Pike. Take care of them, please. Especially Emma!"

"I shall, Sir!"

With that, Pike gently closed the coach door.

David tapped the coach's ceiling, and the driver cracked his whip, the coach starting down the driveway. Pike watched the coach slowly move away from the house. He turned and walked up the front stairs, along the hallway and peered out onto the terrace where Lady Jane stood hugging a sobbing Emma.

Thomas thought, 'Ah yes, …. young love!'

High Street, Guildford …

William and Simeon finishing their Saturday chores, bolted along the street and peered into the shop window. There sat the sailing boat in all its glory. It was a beautiful model of a gaff-rigged fishing vessel made with precision and looked quite seaworthy.

The boys already had picked a spot where they would launch the boat, a quiet pool a little way upriver where the flow was weak. If enough wind came up, she would sail across quickly, and one of them would turn her on the other side and point it back. Nosey rubbed his head against their thighs, looking for a pat. The boys ignored him as they chatted excitedly about their boat.

"If we go halves Sim, it will only be nine weeks before we can afford it!"

Simeon was a bit more pessimistic. "That is ages away. Someone else might buy it by then. If you had not broken that window, we would be sailing it by now. I wonder if there is some other way we can find the money."

"When we have finished paying back Anne, perhaps she would consider giving us the money." William was a born optimist. He knew Anne put her money in the Guildford bank. She was wise and would be rich one day.

"If we ask father or mother, they will probably suggest it as a Christmas present."

"It will be Christmas before we can save the money anyway. Somehow, we must stop anyone else from buying it."

Then as they watched, the store owner reached into the window and took hold of the little fishing vessel. Smiling at the boys, who stood there with their mouths open, he took the boat and placed it on the counter. A well-dressed man passed over nine shillings and then walked out of the shop and down the High Street with the boat in his arms.

The boys watched as the man carried their dreams away into the distance!

William was annoyed and walked into the shop, followed by Simeon.

He puffed up his chest and said in a loud voice, "Excuse me, Mr Shop Owner!"

The man behind the counter looked up, "Sorry about the boat, boys! I saw you outside, admiring it. But that chap had the money. That is only fair! "

"Do you have any others in the store?"

"Not like that one, but the man who made that boat is making another, and it will be here in January. Come back then! I'm sure it will be as good as the last one."

The disappointed boys both said, "Thank you, Sir."

Coming out of the shop, they saw Anne on her way home from the bakery. They rushed across and told her what had happened.

"That is a pity, William and Simeon. If you don't have the money, best if you wait for the next boat."

"Anne, what if we built a boat? It might cost less, and we could build it now."

"That's a great idea, Simeon, but do you know how to build a boat?"

"No. But how would I learn?"

Anne thought about this and then had an idea.

"What about the Institute. There may be a book there about boat building. What a pity Robert is not here – he would love helping you with this!"

William chirped up, "No, he would be kissing you, Anne, and forget about us. We must build it ourselves."

Anne blushed, "Robert likes you two. I'm sure he would help, but you are right; he is not here. I have a few spare minutes now. Why don't we go and ask Mr Sharples at the Institute about boat building? They will have books on it down there. Simeon, you are a good reader. You can learn from a book!"

"I'm a good reader too, Anne! I can learn!"

"I'm sure your reading is getting better, William. This exercise will also help your reading. Because I am rushed for time, we must go now. Mother is expecting me in a half-hour. I will leave you two there, so please behave. Is that an agreement?"

The boys nodded.

"Let's go!"

William then said, "What is the Institute?"

"It is a place where they have all kinds of books about doing different things. Some of the poor people go there and learn how to read and write. Then they are given courses in skills that will find them a job. It can be busy at times. We have employed some people from there in the bakery."

Anne enjoyed helping her little brothers, especially when they were learning new skills. She even thought this might be a project that would keep them out of trouble for some time.

Arriving at the Institute, Anne introduced the boys.

"Mr Sharples, these are my brothers, Simeon and William. They are interested in building a model sailing boat. Do you have any books on this?"

"Good day Miss Anne. Hello Simeon and William. Let me have a look!"

Mr Sharples led off. William and Simeon were amazed at the number of bookcases filling the room. Mr Sharples picked up a small book he called the index and found boat building.

"Ah-ha. Now models, let me see! Oh, Dear! Now let me see. No, no models, just real boats.!"

Anne said, "That is fine, Mr Sharples. A real boat is just bigger than a model. It will give them an idea. Are there any plans?"

"Why yes, there are plans for all sorts of boats. I will let you boys take all this, and you can sit at the table over there and choose the boat design that interests you. My, my, there are a lot! Here Simeon, put them in this box and take them over."

William piped up, "Mr Sharples, are there any for me?"

"You may share with Simeon, William."

Anne helped them shift the plans onto the table, where they sat down and started leafing through different drawings.

"Now I must be going, boys, so make sure you behave."

There was no response from the boys; they were 'Ooh-ing and Ah-ing!' at the different plans.

Anne suddenly realised that a new world was opening for them. The different boat plans entranced Simeon and William. On her way out, she asked Mr Sharples, "They are expected home for lunch at twelve-thirty. Would you please send them home then?"

"Certainly, Miss Anne. They seem interested in what they are doing!"

"Yes. Young minds finding out new things!"

"Miss Anne! While you are here, I kept this book aside for you. I know how you have borrowed many books on accounting."

Anne took the book from Mr Sharples. "Thank you. What is it about?"

"Companies and their structures. It also tells a bit about the South Sea's Bubble."

"I'm interested in companies, Mr Sharples?"

"Read and find out more, Miss Anne!"

"I will. Thank you, Mr Sharples."

Anne took one last look at the boys. She saw William excited as he made comments about all the boat plans in front of them. Simeon was sitting there looking at the bookcases. It was as if he was mesmerised by the collection of books that was in front of him. Being perceptive, Anne could see that Sim had found a new place of interest that would open all kinds of opportunities for him.

Anne rushed off along North Street and up the lane beside the wool factory to High Street. Turning up the street and passing the church, she could see the Turner home in the distance. The coach Anne expected outside her house was not there. Perhaps the doctor had walked, and she rushed harder towards home.

Entering the kitchen, she found Mrs Jennings quietly preparing lunch.

"Is Doctor Sopwith here examining mother?"

Mrs Jennings looked up and advised that the Doctor left a note late Thursday, putting the appointment back to Monday.

"Your mother must have forgotten or become confused!"

"I see. I will discuss it with mother upstairs."

Anne turned and walked along the hallway and up the stairs. She knocked gently on the door and entered. Her mother was lying on the bed, wide awake and looking at the ceiling. She turned her head as Anne came in and smiled at her daughter.

As she approached the bed, Anne said, "A penny for your thoughts, Mother?"

"I was thinking about you, Anne. I am so pleased that you found Robert. He will be a wonderful husband. I wish I could be here and see your children. But alas, my health is failing."

"Mother, don't be like that. You will see all my children born. You will be there, always giving me advice."

"Yes, I will, darling, but it will be spiritual advice. My time on this earth is almost finished. I am becoming tired, Anne. I cannot fight it any longer."

She closed her eyes and shuddered a bit. Anne held her hand, leant down and whispered in her ear, "You must fight on Mother. For the sake of the baby. I will help you. We will all help you. It will be all right."

They sat there together, Anne holding her hand and Eleanora with her eyes closed, relaxing in the company of her young, strong daughter. Anne did not mention the confusion over the appointment time. Anyway, she would see Doctor Sopwith on Sunday at church and ask how Emma was.

Eleanora spoke, "You are an inspiration, Anne. I'm not sure where you get it from, but you are unique. I have never seen such a pretty young daughter who is competent in running the family's affairs. And you are so gentle with us all – never a harsh word. Forgive me for when I have been unkind."

"You have never been unkind to me, Mother! You are the best mother any girl could have!"

Anne felt her mother squeeze her hand and slowly release it as she drifted off to sleep. Anne looked down on the tired face that was now relaxed, enjoying the wonderful place where she could be nurtured and refreshed by her sleep. Neville told her that rest was the best cure for all diseases. She now understood what he meant. Anne saw her mother almost frantic at times with whatever this disease was. Then she would sleep and wake back in control again.

Ethel came in and nodded. The new maid was a blessing. She was calm and competent, but most of all, gentle and quiet. She was perfect for this family. Anne whispered, "She is asleep now. I will sit with her for a while." Ethel smiled and nodded back. She came over and gently covered Eleanora so she would be warm. Then slowly tip-toed out and closed the door.

Anne sat there for fifteen minutes, gently holding her mother's hand and watching her. She spent some minutes remembering all the good times they had shared. From picnics to piano lessons, they enjoyed so much fun. Life was something that did not stop. People change a little bit every day. Could the clock be slowed or even rewound? She wanted life as it was now, but she knew life moved on every second, and there was no stopping it. Then she thought of Robert and how she would change for him. She wanted him as he was but knew he would change over time as well. Changes he may never have thought of yet!

Time would not remain still. Just as the muddy water that flowed down the River Wey came and went, never to be seen again, she and her family would pass on. God only allowed each one of us a certain time on this earth. It was our responsibility, and we must use this gift wisely. Life was a precious commodity. She looked down on her mother and acknowledged the truth that she would die and soon. Anne decided that she would make that time as comfortable as she could for her mother. Robert would understand and wait – she must be beside her mother until the end.

At Greenwich ...

Hamish McPherson opened the letter on his desk. He smiled as he saw it was from Jonathan, letting him know he would join him in Reading on Wednesday evening. Hamish welcomed this news as he was excited by the location of the new pub and keen for Jonathan and the other investors to inspect the building. He sometimes thought he was more in the real estate business than the pub business. If you bought a suitable property, you were sure of a substantial gain at sale in ten to twenty years.

Hamish McPherson decided against disclosing his sizeable investment in a company building a railway from London to Reading. There would be no risk with the Reading pub if this investment fulfilled expectations. He was so convinced that Reading would be a growth centre; that another deposit was already in process for a second Reading pub site. Hamish was sure the town would support four or five of his pubs in time.

Reading a report put together for him by his attorneys in London, Hamish recalled his bitter experience in property investment. He left nothing to chance these days, ensuring he used the best advisors he could afford. Nearly going bankrupt in Scotland some thirty years ago, it was only by good fortune and not good business management that a new investor bailed him out. In his optimism for his business and ambition, he overcommitted himself, and the banks threatened foreclosure. Scottish banks' reputations for being risk-averse were infamous, and they would call in debt if a business even sneezed.

One night around ten pm, there was a knock on the door, and a mysterious person entered the lobby of the McPherson's newly acquired house in Glasgow. The gentleman delivered a package for Hamish. He would not give his name or who he represented. He stated that the letter attached would explain everything.

The timing of this encounter was uncanny, as the banks that day had advised Hamish that they would foreclose on one of his best pubs in a week if he did not meet certain loan payments. The package which Hamish received that evening contained a letter and ten thousand pounds cash. The letter was mysterious and read:

Hamilton & Associates
Locked Bag
George Street Post Office
Glasgow

Mr Hamish McPherson
McPherson Breweries
Glasgow
Scotland

Dear Mr McPherson

Thank you for receiving this letter from our courier. Our dealings with you must remain confidential.

Hamilton & Associates have reviewed your business activities and propose an investment in your company. We seek no equity using shares or participation in your business but the furnishing of information and services. The attached finance with this letter is a down payment for these services.

If you are interested in this proposal, our Mr Michael Jones will discuss this matter in detail with you on Monday, June the fifteenth, 1794, at the above address. If you would visit the Glasgow Post Office, they will hold an envelope for you. The envelope's contents will provide the address and more information about the meeting. Mr Jones expects you at eleven in the morning on Monday.

If you decide not to proceed, please return the contents of this package to our above address?

Yours sincerely
Mr Harrold Pinkerton Mumford
Senior Partner

While Hamish was conservative, his business dealings now placed him in a dangerously overextended position. Given his wife and four young children must be supported and his difficult cash position, this letter appeared as a lifeline. The timing was an extraordinary coincidence. So, he decided on a meeting with Mr Michael Jones.

At the meeting, Mr Jones explained what was required. Hamish readily agreed and signed a declaration. He then advised that Hamish was dealing with the British government, which required contacts in Scotland capable of providing high-level information. The remuneration would be considerable. Mr Jones placed a contract in front of Hamish that allowed him to access twenty-five thousand pounds annually. Hamish readily agreed and signed both the contract and the confidentiality agreement.

It was a little over a year since Hamish's brother had died from the consumption, and Mr Jones notified Hamish that mysteriously his brother's estate contained a shipping line. Hamish was surprised as he had never heard of this company, and secondly, his brother suffered from seasickness just thinking about the sea. Nevertheless, the Executors of the estate were releasing the assets of the shipping business to Mr McPherson and asked that Hamish carefully develop the business. At a subsequent meeting with Mr Jones, he informed Hamish that regular cargo would be provided so that the shipping line would succeed. Once again, this was the subject of a confidentiality agreement.

So, in twelve short months, the McPherson Brewing Company was saved from the jaws of bankruptcy and became a secure company with a strong balance sheet. Hamish McPherson soon found himself mixing in prestigious circles where he made many high-level contacts in business and government.

As he read the report on Jonathan Turner's business interests and future financial stability, he saw a parallel with himself some thirty years ago. It was slightly different as Hamish was sure Jonathan Turner was unaware of his overcommitment. Should Hamish bail Jonathan out, or should he provide advice to assist him?

Hamish felt an obligation that Jonathan be alerted to his perilous position. He would be surprised if Jonathan were aware, as it took Hamish's advisers two months to put together this report. But the McPhersons desired the marriage of Thomas and Marion and their future success. Hamish was sure Marjorie would never forgive him if the ceremony did not occur. The coming meeting in Reading would be a convenient opportunity for a discussion of finances.

He murmured, "Poor Jonathan!"

Chapter 24

The Turner Household, Guildford ...

Ethel answered the door where a rider stood with a message. She knew Anne was home from church and found her in the parlour talking with Thomas and Mr Turner.

"What is it, Ethel?"

"A message for you, Miss Anne."

Anne took the message, moved across the room and opened it.

Fintelton Manor
East Harting
Sussex

Miss Anne Turner
High Street
Guildford

Dear Anne

Please, would it be possible if I stayed with you for a day or two? I must talk with you, as I am confused about some personal matters and need your advice. You are now one of my closest friends, and I would value the time with you immensely.

I will source a room at the Fox and Hound; however, if it is not inconvenient, I would prefer to be with you and your wonderful family, if that is possible. I shall arrive late on Monday afternoon.

Until then.

Your Dearest Friend
Emma.

P.S. I will bring my maid, Jane, ensuring no gossip. Would there be a place for her, please?
Please, Please, Please.

Emma was calling for help. Anne's perception of Emma was a confident, outgoing person, lacking nothing and knowing where her life was going. The message seemed so out of character for Emma. There must be something seriously wrong. Of course, she could stay. There was a spare bed in Anne's room. They could talk all night in private. Anne hoped she possessed the wisdom needed for this situation.

"Father, I have a letter from Lady Emma South asking if she might stay on Monday night till Wednesday this week coming. Would this be acceptable, please? Emma would stay in my room and her maid in the other bed in Ethel's room. It is only for two nights. She must be home soon as our London trip commences on Saturday."

Jonathan raised his eyes toward Anne with a worried look on his face.

"I'm not sure our rooms are equal to the standards at Fintelton Manor. Will she find our accommodation acceptable?"

"Perhaps the maid may find it difficult, but Emma will put up with anything. She is very accommodating in her demands."

"One of the nights, Ethel might stay with her mother and spend time with her daughter. It would be acceptable to us. I shall advise your mother. After all, Emma is your future sister-in-law!"

"Thank you, Father."

Simeon and William, with their model boat plans in mind, asked their father if they might use some of the spare wood in a pile behind the house.

"It will be a small raft Father with a sail on it. We want to sail it across the river Wey. I will be on one side of the river and William on the other. When it reaches the far side, William will turn it around and send it back."

Jonathan Turner thought about the wood. It was all leftovers from Robinson's builders. Wood that was either an offcut or not used in the house renovation.

"Only the old wood, boys. The new wood may be of some use!"

Eleanora entered the room and hearing the conversation protested, "Jonathan, you will never use any of that wood. Let them have the lot!" She was pleased the boys were showing initiative, embarking on a project that required the development of new skills.

"Jonathan, why don't you help them with it?"

The suggestion did not enthuse Jonathan. He had no intention of wasting his time with the boys on some hair-brained project.

"No, just the old wood. That is my final decision. And I do not want you boys in the river either. Neither of you can swim!"

Simeon and William agreed readily and were excused. They quickly exited the back door and gathered some wood, moving it onto the back veranda.

They sorted the wood selecting pieces with merit.

"We will need some twine, Will. Where can we get that?"

"Whatever you do, do not ask father. He will beat us! But I have seen Mrs Taggart use twine at the school. Perhaps she will give us some."

"First, how much do we need? We can arrange the wood in the pattern of the raft. Remember, we want it small, so only use the little bits."

Keeping in mind the plan they examined at the Institute, the boys enjoyed deciding which pieces would fit. Various friendly arguments broke out as different pieces of wood were checked against design positions.

Nosey sat on the veranda, watching them with his tail sometimes wagging. He found these human antics somewhat confusing. Waiting for a piece of wood thrown for him from the veranda, he soon gave up hope and enjoyed a late morning nap in the sun.

After lunch, the boys finally agreed on the design. As the time for the family riverside visit was near, they packed the wood in two neat piles at the far end of the veranda. This way, they avoid the displeasure of their father – a risk they feared greatly.

Ethel was concerned the afternoon was too chilly for Mrs Turner. She bundled up some warm clothes in a bag in case the weather changed quickly. None of the children except William had much energy for today's pirate game and enjoyed being with their parents and watching the barges passing on the river. Jonathan opened the basket of biscuits early as he was hopeful of returning home soon.

Anne was sitting a little way from the group around her mother when Doctor David Sopwith passed. Stopping, he greeted Mr and Mrs Turner and then saw Anne a bit further away. Walking over, he addressed her.

"Miss Anne, good day! Have you heard from Neville and Bethany since they left?"

"No, Doctor Sopwith. Nothing yet, but we do expect them at Thomas's wedding."

"I see! Miss Anne, may I join you for a moment? I have some questions on my mind, and I think you may be of assistance."

"Certainly, Doctor. I will try, but please forgive me if I am of little help."

"I think you will be of great help, Miss Anne!"

"Doctor Sopwith, if we sit here together this Sunday afternoon, I would be far more comfortable if we were on a first-name basis. You understand that it is for relaxation when the family comes down here. Would that be acceptable?"

"Certainly, Emma, I mean, Anne!" He sat down beside her at a reasonable distance displaying good manners.

Anne smiled, "David, I think I know who is on your mind."

His frown became a half-smile, "Yes, you probably do!"

He sat there for a moment, viewing the river. The sun peeked out from behind a cloud, and the temperature immediately rose a few degrees. Everyone was surprised as the afternoon turned beautiful and more people ventured down to the riverbank, enjoying the tranquillity. David carefully looked around, ensuring no one was within earshot.

"Anne! You are a close friend of Emma South. Tell me, do you think that Emma may have feelings for me? I am sorry, I may have put that a bit too directly! My parents and brother died some time ago, and my sister is in Ireland at our family home. I see little of her except when I take a few months off and travel, which is rare. I think the lack of family has found me becoming too direct. I am afraid some people misinterpret it as being haughty. So, I apologise if I was too direct."

"What is your sister's name, David?"

"Victoria."

"That is a lovely name! If your parents and brother are dead, who looks after her?"

"There are servants and trustees. She is eighteen, so she is an adult and can look after herself. I expected her engaged by now, but I think the tragedy of losing our parents and brother has been hard for her."

"I dare say it would be very hard!"

"So, the question Anne. Have I any hope with Emma?"

"David, I will try to assist as you have told me your circumstances, and they are unfortunate, indeed. I assume you ask me as you have no other friends familiar with Emma who you can talk with?"

"That is correct, Anne. I am sorry if I have presumed too much."

"Not at all, David. You honour me with your friendship. My opinion would be that Lady Emma values your friendship highly!"

"Would this be the extent of the relationship?"

"It would, David! That is until you make it more?"

David Sopwith sat back and thought about this. Anne could see the concerned look on his face.

He lowered his voice and explained. "I did. I made my affection for Emma clear in a conversation with her on Friday evening. The conversation ended in an argument, with her crying, running from the room and slamming the door. I was quite distraught as she sternly asked that I should address her as Lady Emma in the future. I find that I am totally at a loss understanding her!"

On hearing this statement from David, Anne was amazed, as she thought Emma was more than fond of him.

"David, may I say I am astonished hearing this. There must be some misunderstanding?"

This question surprised David. The words were on his lips when William and Simeon interrupted.

"Anne, do you think our raft will sail across the river?" William was right beside them, followed by Simeon. The boys jolted David and Anne out of their deep conversation.

"William! I was not aware you were there. You surprised me."

David Sopwith looked around for the raft and questioned, "I don't see a raft, William."

The boys needed no further invitation and blurted out the whole story. He listened with interest.

"When I was a boy, I built model boats. I did it for years with my brother Frederick. We found it such good fun. It is not that hard if you have the right materials."

"We have some wood, Doctor Sopwith, but no twine!"

"What do you need twine for?"

"To tie the wood together."

"I thought you wanted a boat, not a raft?"

"We do!"

"So why not start with a boat?"

"We don't know how! Anne took us into the Institute, but there were only plans, no instructions."

"I see."

David Sopwith thought about this as he looked at the keen expressions on the two boys' faces.

"I have some free time on a Saturday afternoon. How about I teach you two how to build a boat? It will take a lot of Saturdays, but it will be worth it. We could start next Saturday. First, we must decide on a plan at the Institute and then work out what materials we need. Mind you, I am talking about a boat about two feet long-only, not a real boat."

"Yes, Doctor, Yes! Would you come with us and see the wood we have for the boat?"

"Certainly. Perhaps one afternoon this week after I have finished with patients."

The boys cheered, rushing off, telling their parents what the Doctor promised.

"That was kind of you, David. There is no need."

"Anne, I am on my own. I have the time and would enjoy the company, and making model boats is fun!"

Anne thought about this comment. Here was a young man who had lost his parents and brother, his sister was in Ireland, and he was all alone. He was so keen for some company that he would give up time building boats with her young brothers. She found a genuinely good man in him, probably keen on having a family. Why then would Emma spurn him? Perhaps it was the thought of not marrying a nobleman. But Anne was sure Emma would give all that up for love. She wanted the same kind of life that David wanted. Anne understood David's confusion.

"David, I would not give up on Emma yet. It will be a difficult decision for her. It will take time."

"That's what she said yesterday. I agreed and did not press her, but she was most annoyed. I was so convinced that she had feelings for me that I invited my sister from Ireland in the belief she should meet her. She will come at Christmas. Now I think I may have been premature. But I shall enjoy Victoria's company."

"Might I meet Victoria as well, David? I would like that very much. Perhaps you and Victoria would join our family on Christmas day. I am sure Neville and Beth will be there. Think it over. But you and Victoria would be very welcome."

"Your invitation is kind, and if your parents are agreeable, we would certainly attend. It is also a relief as I wondered how I could fill Victoria's day given it seems there will be no attachment with Emma."

"As I said, David, that may be a misunderstanding. Do not give up on Emma yet! Who knows, she may enjoy model boat building?"

They both laughed and continued talking about David's sister.

At Guildford ...

The Monday morning was fresh and crisp, with patches of blue sky appearing regularly between the rain clouds. Sir Hugh climbed out of bed and breakfasted by nine, keen on making his appointment with Doctor Sopwith at ten. After enjoying two nights of drinking scotch whisky and entertaining loose women, Sir Hugh wore bags under his eyes and felt worn out. He presented at the doctor's surgery in poor shape.

While sitting through the examination, he explained his dilemma between the aim of regaining some moral standing and his failure over the previous two days. He listened in silence as Doctor Sopwith gave his medical assessment and advice.

"Sir Hugh, I must be frank with you. Your behaviour is now your worst enemy. Alcohol and sexual relations will lower your resistance and encourage the spread of the disease within your body. Your reform must be ongoing, and it will be a great struggle. But you must abide by it. If you do not, the complications will come far faster than you realise.

I understand you have been using mercury ointment, but there are no signs of improvement. You must use it more often, perhaps twice a day. Sir Hugh, this is most important! If the disease progresses, there is no turning back. It will certainly kill you, and there will be deformity and misery before you go. I cannot emphasise enough the importance now of abstinence and treatment."

With two jars of ointment in his bag, Sir Hugh left for his next appointment at Turner's bakery. There, he delivered signed agreements for the spring harvest from Fintelton Manor and fifteen of his tenants.

"Mr Turner, I will be leaving for the Indies sooner than expected. The Estate Manager, Mr Malcolm Stem, will have authority during my absence. The authorisation will also require my sister, Lady Emma South's agreement. A safeguard for our estate that I am sure you will understand. Mr Stem is a fine man and has the good of both the family and the estate at heart. Come harvest time; I suggest your collection man deal with Mr Stem and my sister. We will meet again after my return from the Indies."

Sir Hugh shook hands with both Jonathan Turner and Thomas and made off for his next appointment. He trudged up the street, leading his horse and entered Reverend Taggart's church.

"Reverend Taggart, I decided last Sunday after being with you that I would reform my life and change. In my mind, I have made a commitment, but I struggle, Reverend Taggart! I failed and fell back into my old ways on Friday and Saturday nights. I do the things I will regret! I seek pleasure in the things that will destroy me!

I am sure that I am dependent on alcohol. The women are of no consequence, but they provide comfort in my lonely existence. I crave fellowship, Reverend, but I am not a good partner.

I feel that I am losing the battle."

Andrew Taggart was encouraged by Sir Hugh's honest assessment. He recognised that while Sir Hugh resisted help, he would continue struggling with his addictions.

"Sir Hugh, please take note of what I say! While we are on this earth, there will always be battles. Some you will win, and others you will lose. I would encourage you as there is help at hand. From a spiritual perspective, the battle is won. Your Saviour will assist your willpower. Let me show you some verses."

Sir Hugh begrudgingly listened and read as Reverend Taggart selected the appropriate verses about victory in the Gospel.

Sir Hugh sat back and shook his head. In the past two weeks, he tried several times talking with God, but there was no answer. Why should he persevere when he did not believe?

"This is all hogwash, Reverend! Why should I believe this? It is fairy tales and non-sensical. Religion is not for me. I must win the battle myself and be free of these curses that plague me. I thank you for your kind advice which I have found helpful. I also value your friendship Reverend. You are my only friend at this time, and I will never forget you."

"Hugh, take these pages with you. I have written down some notes and verses that may assist. There may come a time when you find comfort in reading these pages. I would value it if you did!"

"You are a fine man, Andrew Taggart. Thank you for your friendship and understanding. I know I am not an easy man. I will take the notes, but I can provide no promises."

Sir Hugh shook Andrew's hand and packed the notes in his bag before leaving the church. He mounted his horse, leaned back in the saddle, and, breathing in deeply, took a final view of the town and rode down the High Street.

At the Turner Bakery, Guildford ...

Jonathan Turner, Thomas and Anne sat around a table working through Sir Hugh's contracts. The contracts had solved part of the problem for them. The difficult question was from where they would source the additional grain. Jonathan's visit to reading was now taking on more importance.

Anne finalised the figures late in the day, and Jonathan sat back, reviewing the report. They talked through the issues together, and all breathed a sigh of relief. Despite the extra costs of increasing production, the plan was more than affordable if sales achieved expectations, leaving a healthy amount of free cash for future development.

"Enough for today! I need more time on these figures tonight. Anne, I believe you may have a guest waiting for you. Thomas, please check with your mother about your bridal house. The furniture should have arrived now. We shall talk about the plan again tomorrow."

Anne and Thomas agreed. Anne asked Jonathan one further question.

"Father, we have not yet included the cost of the new biscuit production line. The set-up will incur costs and is urgent. Perhaps we should consider selling both the recipe and the contract? The sale would improve our cash flow in the short term."

"It is possible, Anne, but not at present. We would require proof of success. That would come after we gain a full order from the navy. There is much goodwill involved in this contract, and it is prudent we continue with it for at least the first order. But this is an option if the bank becomes difficult."

Anne, not convinced, understood her father's explanation. She nodded and excused herself. She was off home in search of Emma.

Jonathan sat back in his chair. He was grateful for her comments. She was quick at finding innovative ways of managing their business challenges, even faster than Thomas. The thought of selling the biscuit recipe had merit. He would keep it in mind, but now he was exhausted after today's planning session. Realising it was time for a changing of the guard, he pondered if

Anne was ready. Perhaps the experience of a few more years would not hurt before he gave her control. What about Thomas? He may return in time. The one thing Jonathan was becoming sure of – the transition must come within the next five years.

Thomas, who heard Anne's suggestion, walked over and sat beside Jonathan.

"Father, what Anne is saying makes sense. But if you do sell the biscuit recipe, would you consider giving it to me? I think I could make it into a viable business in the coming years. I mention this, so you have it in your mind for future reference."

Jonathan Turner was surprised by this comment from Thomas. He was embarking on a career in brewing, yet he would make this suggestion. Perhaps his decision on a new career was wavering!

The Turner House, High Street Guildford …

Emma arrived early on Monday afternoon while Anne was still in conference with her father and Thomas at the bakery. Ethel answered the door and ushered Emma into the drawing-room where Mrs Turner was reading.

Eleanora stood and received Emma, "Welcome, Lady Emma. I hope your trip was pleasant."

"Thank you, Mrs Turner. Please call me, Emma. Thank you for agreeing at short notice. The trip was most comfortable but long as usual, so I find your company most refreshing."

"Emma, I hope your maid will understand that our accommodation is limited. We will do our best to make her as comfortable as possible. Has she visited Guildford before?"

"Jane will be quite content, Mrs Turner. My heartfelt thanks for accepting her. Before entering service, she was brought up in Basingstoke and visited Guildford several times. She is a lovely, pleasant person and very attentive. The other servants will warm to her quickly. She is happy sharing and will assist with other duties if required."

Eleanora was pleased with this outcome, as another pair of hands always helped. She did not enquire about the purpose of Emma's trip as she understood from Anne that it was confidential.

"I must say you look very sophisticated, Emma, in that lovely brown travelling outfit. It is so nice seeing young ladies so well dressed."

"Thank you, Ma'am, but I must compliment you and your daughters' lovely dresses. They dress as well as any of the young ladies in London. At the wedding, Clementine was beautiful, and I would not be surprised if she did not rival Anne in looks in the not too distant future."

"Yes, she is certainly blooming. We are thankful for how she is developing in many ways. I hope we never become pretentious about these things, but it is pleasing!"

"Mrs Turner, I think most people would be envious of your wonderful family."

"You are too kind, Emma. We have our problems, just the same as any other family. We probably hide it well, but there are always daily problems to overcome. Will you have some tea with me?"

"Yes, thank you, Mrs Turner. Let me ask Jane. I will call her in, please, so she may meet you if that is convenient?"

"Just before you do, Emma, there was one issue we might discuss while Anne is not here. I hope you do not mind me asking, but I am sure your parents may have preferred an equal match for Robert. How will your family adjust to Anne? Will it be difficult for her? You have seen them together, and they are both determined, young people. Perhaps they underestimate the issues. As you know, we cannot ignore our county's class system."

Emma sat back and thought about this. "Mrs Turner, I originally had precisely the same thought. I understand your concern, but I would reassure you that I think my parents are more worried about me than Robert. Robert is the younger son; he will not benefit from the inheritance. Sir Hugh will be the next Earl of Fintelton, and he is a healthy young man."

Emma stopped there and suddenly realised that Sir Hugh was far from healthy, but she would not allude to this at present.

"My parents have made it quite clear that Robert must make his way in the world. The navy became his career at a young age for that precise reason. Mother was concerned that he should have a career, and as Robert is an adventurer, the navy seemed a sensible choice. He does not expect anything from my parents and would not expect any interference in his marriage plans. However, I will say that Robert has been very mindful of this and has always kept his parents informed. He loves mother and father dearly and wishes their blessing on the union, which I am sure they will provide. Some in our circles may indiscreetly criticise the match, but there will be nothing but support from our family."

"Thank you, Emma, that is most reassuring. I must apologise if I have embarrassed you with this question. However, as you know, I am not in good health, and I have reflected on how we may assist this young couple. I was keen on inviting your family here for dinner, but I was unsure if this would be appropriate. I am more confident now!"

"Mrs Turner, I am sure an invitation would honour them. My father's health improves by the day, so sometime in the next three months would be fine. I know that Thomas's wedding is soon, and I will be attending. So perhaps after that. Mrs Turner, if you agree, it would be my pleasure to assist with this venture."

"Thank you, Emma. I will probably do that. Now let us call in Jane."

Later that evening, as the girls were preparing for bed and Jane was nearly finished hanging up Lady Emma's clothes, they talked.

"Jane, that will be all for today. Thank you. I will call you after breakfast – no need before then."

"Yes, Milady. Good night. Good night, Miss Anne."

"Good night, Jane. I hope your accommodation will be comfortable."

"Thank you, Milady. It is more than adequate."

With that, Jane was gone, and they were free for the rest of the night.

"Does it concern you having a servant hovering over your shoulders all the time?" Anne noted how much attention Jane took on every facet of Emma's dressing and undressing.

"Yes, it can be tiresome; however, it can be quite an advantage when you must change several times a day for different functions at Fintelton. You will find out one day as an Admiral's wife. My advice would be if you can afford it, do not refuse it. Jane is also helpful with fashion ideas."

"Then she would enjoy meeting Mrs Smith at Hursts."

"I am glad you mention Hursts. Your mother has suggested a shopping trip tomorrow morning. She is taking Clementine, Madeline and Marcia with us. I thought I should take Jane, as well. It will be fun, and Jane will be interested."

Anne sat straight up and laughed, "Mother never told me about this. I am jealous. I must find a way!"

"Perhaps she imagined you would spend much time shopping in London next week?"

"You are correct; there are some forecasts that must be finished tomorrow before Father's Reading trip. We have been planning for next year, and it is a bit of a challenge. At first, the cash flow looked weak, but then it became far stronger as we tested different levels of production and sales forecasts. It has taken much of last week. Probably it would be best if I remained at work."

Emma was interested as she had never heard of testing cash flow before. Perhaps with Robert's list of enquiries for their attorneys in London, this may be something she should know about in advance.

'What is testing cash flow, Anne? I have never heard of it, and now that I am becoming more involved in the running of the estate, perhaps I should know."

"I'm sure Sir Hugh does this for the estate, Emma!"

"I'm not so sure if Hugh knows what cash flow is, except for buying scotch!"

"I will show you tomorrow if you are interested. It can be quite laborious. Varying plans are prepared for next year, ensuring we have enough cash flow for any eventuality."

"My goodness Anne, this is complicated. You are far more skilled than I realised. I have never heard of a woman so involved in a business before."

"There are some! It is just that the banks and the government do not like women having property and investments. It is a man thing; they feel women are inferior and should remain at home. Men may have more physical power than we, but we can quickly outsmart them."

"I would agree with that. It is like this entailment process for estates. It is all based on men. Even if there are no male offspring in the family, they search for the closest male cousin. It is so discriminating, and there is no valid reason for it besides outdated traditions. You could be comfortably enjoying life one minute, and then an unknown cousin might inherit the lot and throw you out of your home into poverty. It is so cruel."

"Here, here, Lady Emma South, Member for Fintelton. You shall emancipate English women through parliament. I shall vote for you if you stand, and I had the vote."

"Who me? I don't like parliament!"

"I understand, Emma; neither do I."

"But Anne, is there a benefit for you in business?"

"I have been working for Father since I was thirteen, and in that time, I have saved over three thousand pounds and inherited some investments from my grandparents. Poor Robert is not aware of what a determined little girl he is entangled with."

They both rolled on their beds, laughing as they imagined Sir Robert South saluting them both in the future.

"But Emma, tell me what is bothering you. Let me see if I may assist!"

Emma rolled over and looked Anne in the face, "Little future sister-in-law, I am eager for your advice, but please keep it confidential for the time being."

The humour now disappeared from Emma's voice, and she became serious. She sat up on her bed and hugged her knees.

"Where should I start? It is not easy."

"Calm yourself and take your time. But do not be too slow because if you find me snoring, you will know I have lost the plot!"

Emma laughed, "I'm not sure I have the total plot, but it is complicated and needs careful explanation."

Emma sat back on her bed, leaning against the bedhead. As she thought, Emma looked at her hands which she held together as if she was wringing them in pain. Then she looked up at Anne with her beautiful light brown eyes widely open. Anne appreciated her beauty, 'You are a beautiful young girl, Emma. If only you knew how attractive you are!'

Emma started, "David called on my father – medical check-up - last Friday afternoon and was to stay until Sunday. I think we both were anticipating time together and some freedom in developing our relationship. But Robert previously made me aware of the estate's difficulties, which weighed heavily on my mind. David was eager, and I was in two minds, somewhat burdened by Robert's message.

Friday dinner was most enjoyable until we were alone playing cards. I think the estate issues may have dulled my personality on that night, and David noticed. I was thinking about these issues and kept them from him, as I felt it unfair that he too should be burdened with them. I explained that I would need time to sort them out.

He said he understood and started talking about how he would give me time. But I felt he was disappointed and would have proposed that night."

Anne looked up, "Really! Did he?"

"No, he did not, but he made out how he was doing the gentlemanly thing by giving me time and not putting any pressure on me. We drifted apart during the conversation. Then he decided he should leave in the morning. I was so disappointed as the invitation from my mother was for Friday and Saturday nights, and he had accepted. He was very gentle and polite, but I felt threatened. I was unsure what to do." A tear ran down Emma's cheek.

"I thought he was acting like a child wanting everything his way, but I was probably wrong. Anyway, I unleashed my temper on him, and I raised my voice and told him to grow up and stomped out of the room.

Looking back at it, I am not proud of what I did, but he was so strange in his actions. He attempted an apology on the Saturday morning before he left. I was not having any of it. I was still angry. I do not usually become angry, but I felt he pushed me into his timing. I needed more time. The other issues are most pressing. But I wanted him to stay and be with me. I was so confused by it all. Perhaps I should have confided in him. I'm just not sure, and the only other person I can discuss this with is Robert, so given he is out of contact, I wanted you, Anne, as you are now my closest friend."

"Emma, let us see if we can solve your dilemma. Let me ask you a question. If David, let us assume, was not invited for the Saturday and Sunday and arrived on Friday unannounced. I am sure he would have been welcome. But if he then proposed, what would your answer have been?"

There was alarm in Emma's voice, "But that's not fair. He did come on Friday, and we talked in the evening. That's what happened!"

Anne calmly smiled and explained, "No, we must establish what your feelings were for him before the frightful incident on Friday night."

Emma blushed as she thought about it. Then she said, "Of course, I would have said yes! But I would have liked some roses in advance." They giggled.

"So, you do have feelings for him. Perhaps, may I say deep feelings for him?"

"Perhaps, you might say just as deep feelings as you have for Robert!"

"In that case, the issue is simple. You must find David and fall into his arms and say Yes!"

Anne jumped out of bed and walked towards the door calling for Jane. Emma jumped in front of Anne and held her hand over Anne's mouth, "What are you doing, Anne?"

With a smile on her face, Anne turned around, ran back and jumped in under the covers of her bed, leaving her nose protruding over the sheet. Emma watched and returned, as well.

"The fact of the matter is Emma. You are madly in love with David Sopwith, and you have had a misunderstanding with him. Now you want advice on how you may solve it. I would advise you to contact him and let him know you still love him!"

"I have not told him I love him as yet!"

"I think he may have a good idea about that."

"But what about all the other issues pressing on my mind? I can't drop them and do what David wants."

"I have the same problem with Robert, and he will someday understand that I am a key member of the management team of the Turner businesses. But I will always see him whenever there is an opportunity. I will work around it. You can do the same?"

"I'm not sure I know how!"

"Emma, how many men have you ever known that you feel the same way about as you do with David?"

"None."

"I think he is worth your love then. But now he thinks you don't care for him at all."

"Do you think so?"

"Yes, I do!"

"But how should I tell him."

"If I were you, I would write him a sweet letter saying how it was all a big misunderstanding, and you regret how you reacted, and you would be pleased if he called on you on his next visit. That should be ample as you want some time for these other matters. Who knows, he may be of assistance."

"But I must not burden him. I can't drag him into these matters."

"Emma, this is the love of your life. David is the man you will live with until you die! If you cannot be open with him now, then how will you ever do it in the future? If you love him, you must take that step in faith and give him your trust. He will probably surprise you with joy. I respect David Sopwith's intelligence highly."

Emma sat there on her bed, knowing she had chosen the best of her friends as her confidant. She marvelled at how Anne straightforwardly explained the issues that she was confronting. Now she understood her feelings on these matters, she breathed out and relaxed.

"Thank you, Anne!"

"Hold on, Emma, no relaxing for you just yet. Still a bit of stress tonight!"

Anne opened her desk and picked up paper, pen and ink.

"Sister, write the letter tonight while you know what you feel. There is no better time than now. He is probably pining for you."

"But, but...."

"Now, Emma!"

Anne was not the kind of girl you disobeyed. Emma stood up and accepted the pen.

"You are right. I do love David so much!"

At the Turner Bakery, Guildford ...

Thomas looked around the bakery where he spent the last eleven years of his life. It was a second home with so many memories. The training of the new staff appointments was complete, and now it was time for his transition into the brewery business. It seemed strange, as if he were trading one life for another. Suddenly he was unsure of his decision.

"Thomas, thank you for training the new team. It was a great help. I'm sure I will consult with you often during your transition."

Jonathan Turner still struggled with Thomas' decision and was now relieved that a well-trained management team was ready before Thomas moved on. Jeb Hiscock was a fine bakery manager, and Peter Hammer, Aaron Hall, Rose Bell, and Sophia Stanton proved excellent support as bakers. Also, the new stable manager, Robert Baxter, was changing some of the stable's systems, making them a far more modern organisation. Jonathan Turner was comfortable, now satisfied they would cope.

"Father, I was reminiscing my history here and questioning if leaving was a mistake. Probably, just pre-marriage nerves. Come tomorrow; I am sure my thoughts will be different."

Thomas was undergoing a huge transition, and Jonathan could make it no easier. He had rented a house and furnished it for Thomas and Marion once they returned from the honeymoon. Eleanora chose a maid to support Marion until she decided what staff she needed. They had spared no expense, and Jonathan would consult Hamish on Wednesday night in Reading about any other assistance matters.

"Thomas, you know that there is always a place here for you. If you do not enjoy the brewing industry, we can always fit you back into baking. When Anne arranges the company, I will ensure you receive your fair share of the equity. However, I thought you might be ready for a change of hours. Especially with a new wife!"

"Thanks, Father, the change will do me good. Let us see how it goes. But for now, it is full speed ahead."

"Good boy Thomas! Now Anne is finishing up, and I have her reports. Why don't you accompany her home? The start of your packing is overdue. You will be off on Thursday, and I'm sure your mother wants some time with you before you go."

"Thanks, Father, I will do that!"

Thomas joined Anne and suggested they walk together.

"That would be nice, Thomas! It may be our last chance!"

The last few days were mild, and there were few signs of autumn. A cold north-westerly swept down from the Atlantic across Britain and into Guildford. Anne shivered as she walked up the High Street without the protection of a coat. She snuggled up against Thomas for warmth. It would be a cold night and a foretaste of probably an icy winter. Perhaps they would see snow this year for Christmas.

Thomas smiled as Anne pressed close beside him. He put his arm around her and said, "Let me warm you up, little sister."

As they walked up the front stairs of the house, Thomas stopped under the covered area of the entrance and looked around at his boyhood home. This situation held great affection for him. Anne saw a wrap left on a chair near the front door, pulled it around her, and sat.

"It's our place of security, Thomas!"

Thomas agreed, "Yes, it has been for my whole life. It will be strange leaving it."

Anne knew Thomas was struggling. She hoped she could help him here.

"I was thinking the same thing the other day. Now I am engaged. I am not sure where I will be living in the future. Hopefully, somewhere close by the business where I can visit home often. This place means so much. Beth told me it is easier after you have been away for a while, but it is my home."

Thomas sat down on the chair beside her.

"Anne, it is different for a boy than for a girl. You will always be close with both mother and father and probably never be that close with your husband's parents. A man must make his way in the world. I must find new territory and explore new fields, so this will be my final. Whatever happens, it will never be the same for me again. Still, being in Guildford would be a blessing, but it may not. I'm not sure Marion will adapt, and perhaps a move away from Guildford for me would be better. We will see. It is a funny feeling, but I know that I will never be coming home again."

"I will always be your sister Thomas. You can count on me!"

"I know Anne, and I thank you for that. Who knows where we will all end up? It's time I started packing before I become melancholy!"

An excited Emma came through the doorway, greeting Anne, "Come and see all the new clothes purchased, Anne. Quick before your father gets home and finds out."

"Yes. Quick! Let me see!"

The girls rushed inside. Thomas sat there for a few moments. He gazed down the street at the church where he first attended school. Then up the street to the houses where he played with his childhood friends. Out across the valley and down at the river Wey, where the family spent so many happy picnics. He thought it would be nice if Marion were here, sitting with him and sharing his dreams. Perhaps that was it. He missed the comfort of his bride to be. He was incomplete without her, and he noticed it more each day. It was time for packing.

HMS Restless, Irish Sea ...

The northerly was almost reaching a gale as they pressed on towards Port Glasgow. Horace Coombes' face was now sporting a growing beard, as did Robert's, and they each enjoyed a bit of banter over the other's healthy growth. If there were more time, the beards would become more authentic, but the change now would suffice.

Restless had overnighted in Douglas two days ago and now was fighting her way against the north-westerly up the Firth of Clyde towards Dunoon. The gale slowed them down considerably; however, Robert was impressed with how well Lieutenant Ham managed the adverse conditions and gained every bit of way he could achieve. Once they passed Dunoon, they should have smooth running into Port Glasgow with the current weather.

"Sir Horace? Would you join me in my cabin, please?"

"Certainly, Captain."

"Lieutenant Ham, I am going below. Once you round Gourock, head for the navy wharf at Port Glasgow. Bring her in and report to the harbour master, please. As we planned, Captain Coombes and I will remain below."

"Aye, Sir."

Ham was a sound officer, contained in his speech and acting quickly on whatever the Captain required. Robert was confident he would control the ship until he and Horace completed their reconnoitre into the seaport pubs of Glasgow.

It was just after two pm; they would stay below, so no searching eye watching the ship secured a close look at the Captain or the Captain of Marines sporting well-growing beards. Swanton offered him the clothes requisitioned for the sortie as he sat in his cabin. Sir Horace frowned at the dirty looking garments catching Swanton's attention with a stern face.

"Swanton, you have not completed the washing lately, have you?"

"I beg your pardon, Sir. Yours is done daily!"

"Good man. I just don't fancy these rags you are giving us. Some dirty coats as well, please?"

"Easily done, Sir!" With this, Swanton reached around behind the door into his quarters and grabbed two old torn coats.

"I say, Swanton, we are not derelicts but ex-sailor men looking for a job."

"I'll mend the tears, Sir."

"Thank you."

While this was going on, Robert was deep in thought. In the back of his mind, there was a worry about something they had missed.

"Horace, we both think that *Providence* is hidden somewhere in Ireland. I'm not sure that we are correct on this."

Horace turned away from the clothes he was holding and looked at Robert. "It seems logical that the Irish would hide a stolen British ship somewhere safe in Ireland. Possibly some hidden inlet. Somewhere the locals are so onside with the rebellion that no one will reveal its location!"

"Yes, but what about the captured crew?"

"They would probably ask for volunteers for the new crew and kill the rest. That type of persuasion finds many volunteers. We know these traitors are savages after what happened with Captain Hughes. I would be surprised if Captain Foster is still alive!"

"I'm not so sure about that. The nationalist will force as much information from Foster as they can. The reason they want that ship aligns with the information Foster might provide. Now Horace, who else hates the English as much as the Irish?"

"The Scottish!"

"That's right. So why could we not find *Providence*?"

There was a silence as Horace thought this through. He suddenly reached for the charts.

"I see. You think she is in Scotland somewhere. A place we would not readily think about until we exhausted all our options in Ireland! That will buy the traitors time for whatever they are planning. You also think these Scottish people will side with the Irish?"

"That's spot-on, Horace! Some of the Scottish would welcome the Irish. They think we will be searching in Ireland for the next few months. So, a better place for concealing the ship is not in Ireland. England is heavily populated! The Welsh would more likely support the English! So why not Scotland, where there are so many remote hiding places?"

Horace looked at the chart of the Scottish west coast, "I hope you are right,

Robert. It is still a needle in a haystack. It could be anywhere!"

"Yes, it may be, but I think they are carefully planning this exercise with a short timetable. The republicans will realise they have a limited time for recruiting and training a crew before we discover them. Perhaps they already have a crew, but I doubt it.

Sooner or later, someone will notice an English frigate sitting in a sound somewhere. If they planned this ahead of time, which I am sure they did, they would have a base somewhere in a very uninhabited part of Scotland. Or perhaps a town they can take over for a few months without anyone knowing. It would be very remote, small, anti-English, with few people and a deep passage. Calm waters – I would say in a fjord or a long bay sheltered from the Irish sea!"

Horace smiled, "Robert, old chum, you should have been a detective!"

"I did think about it at one stage, but it seemed too much hard work. The navy had better benefits."

They both chuckled at this as they looked at the charts of Scotland around Glasgow.

"The other thing is, if they need men for a crew, they will be looking now. It may be that they have finished recruiting, so our questions must be more about a passage home and paying our way as crew members!"

"Our line of questions will be about a passage home?"

"Yes, and some heavy drinking for loosening tongues. Just one reliable clue may be enough. We will be sailors eager for Christmas at home."

Horace grinned, "I don't speak Irish – can't get that accent. I may pull off a faint Scottish accent, but that's probably all."

"I wasn't planning on that. I thought if we were half-drunk, it would not matter what accent we had. Most of the time, all you need to do is grunt. We will be the dregs they are looking to recruit.

Our cover story will be Christmas in Belfast. We need crew places on a freight packet going that way. If they ask about our experience, we say we were paid off from the navy after the war and then served on an Indiaman, 'The Duchess', out of Bristol until mid-year. We worked on the farm harvests the last few months, saving for a passage home but would prefer a packet needing seamen. That should do. What do you think?"

Horace scratched his head, "Where's home if they ask us?"

"Gweedore, man. Me father owns the pub at Gweedore! That will do. They will not know it, as it is as far away in the nationalist territory as can be. But it is authentic, and by the time they discover it is a cover, we will be long gone. Now remember Horace, you are Mick Ryan with no family. I'm Michael O'Flaherty."

"Sounds good."

"Now we each take a sugar bag full of dirty clothes and find some accommodation for the night. The pub owner or the man behind the bar will either give us some scuttlebutt or point us in the right direction. The network will talk, and someone will approach us. Firstly, we start looking for accommodation."

Horace was a man's man and stood a good six feet four inches. This moving into the seaman's accommodation was not his ideal environment. "Now, Robert, there is a limit. I am not sharing a bed with a sailor. You know in some of these places they rent two in a bed. That is not me, and I am not going into the general bunk room either. If they break our cover, they will knife us in ten seconds."

"You miss the point, Horace! We only appear as if we are staying there. We drop our bags in the room, talk with the sailors and see what eventuates. Once we gain their confidence, the message will travel, and hopefully, there will be contact."

"Understood, Captain, but this is not my expertise. You can do the talking. I always knew it would be an interesting assignment with you!"

About six in the evening, after dark, Robert and Horace went on deck in disguise and carrying their sugar bags of clothes. The ship's boat lay aft, ready for them. Lieutenant Ham remained on the quarter deck as they dropped down into the gig. Hugging the shoreline, the crew rowed in silence up the Clyde towards the merchant docks. Robert felt the cold of the night seeping through his light clothes. He quickly put on his coat, but it too was made of flimsy material, and the cold soon seeped through. He shivered, thinking, 'The sooner we find a warm pub, the better.'

They climbed up onto the merchant dock. It was dark, ideal for the two sailors mounting the end of the pier unseen. From here, they both walked in the shadows past various freight packets, either being loaded or waiting for freight in the morning. There was little foot traffic on the street. Robert noticed the dull candle glow in the windows of various establishments. He wanted the cheapest accommodation available. The recruiters would be working there searching for desperate sailors.

After passing by several establishments and being propositioned by some working girls, they turned into a darker street further away from the docks. Here, there was a decrepit looking building that offered rooms for the night and public accommodation. Robert was interested. "This looks promising – Mick!"

Horace nodded and thought, 'Oh No!'.

They ventured in.

At Guildford ...

Thomas was returning home with a new suit from Hurst's and noticed the twilight settling and the temperature dropping. A man carrying a large package walked towards him from the other side of the street. Then he recognised David Sopwith.

"Hello David, what brings you here?'

"Good evening, Thomas. I have a package for Simeon and William."

"May I deliver it for you?"

"Probably not, as I should discuss it with the boys."

"In that case, please come on in, and we shall find them!"

"How fare the preparations for the wedding, Thomas?"

"Nearly finished. I have been packing today, and this is my new suit for the wedding. Pity you are not attending. I'm sure the boys and girls will miss you."

"I'm sorry I can't be there, as someone must care for the patients. There is some consolation in that Neville and Bethany will attend."

"Come on, let's find these boys for you."

Thomas and David climbed the stairs, moved across the portico, and in through the front door. Ethel was descending from Mrs Turner's room, and Thomas asked where the boys were. She informed him they were on the back veranda with their boat building materials.

"Good. Thank you, Ethel. David, you know the way, just through the kitchen and the mudroom. I take it; you do not need my assistance in navigating. I must put this suit upstairs."

"Yes, thank you, Thomas, I know the way! I'll see you before you leave!"

David walked down the hall, carefully ensuring the large package did not scratch the walls or knock anything over. He opened the kitchen door gently, backed through, turned, and faced Lady Emma South. He almost jumped backwards in shock on seeing her.

Emma sat at the kitchen table, Marcia on her knee holding her toy bear while her hair was brushed. Emma looked in disbelief as she saw David awkwardly standing there, shifting from foot to foot, holding his enormous parcel. She tried speaking, but her mouth was open, and nothing came out.

David recovered first, "Lady Emma, no one told me you would be here. My apologies for barging in. I was delivering some wood for Simeon and William. You see, we commence with a keel and a stepped mast, and I have the wood here and some more for the hull."

Emma was still surprised until Marcia put her finger in Emma's mouth, saying, "Mother always tells me I should close my mouth!"

"Ooh!" said Emma and closed her mouth. "I was just washing Marcia's hair!"

"Washing!"

"No, I mean, brushing! My, you have surprised me, Doctor Sopwith!" She blushed.

David regained his countenance and felt he should not disturb Emma any longer. "Please excuse me, Lady Emma. I am visiting the boys. We are working on a joint project. They are on the back veranda, I believe?"

"I believe so, Doctor. Out there on the back veranda!"

He stood there looking at her in a part trance, thinking how lovely she was! She admired him, wishing they had never argued!

Then he said, "Best go now. Bye Marcia."

David moved through the kitchen, but as he juggled his parcel out into the mudroom, he knocked a loaf of bread off the kitchen bench. Mrs Jennings, who was close by, picked it up, saving David from bending down with the parcel in his hands.

"Thank you, Mrs Jennings. I was just going onto the veranda!"

Aggie, preparing vegetables for dinner, came in from the scullery room, wondering what the commotion was. She found Mrs Jennings with the loaf in her hand and Doctor Sopwith looking quite uncomfortable.

"Yes, Doctor Sopwith, so you were. I have it now. Off you go!"

With that, David disappeared onto the veranda and talked with the boys. Mrs Jennings said, "These boys are all the same!"

Emma continued combing Marcia's hair as the child told her a story about 'Buster'. Thinking about David, she felt herself becoming tense. David's appearance here took her by surprise. Suddenly, she recalled the letter written last night. He did not mention it, so perhaps he had not been home yet, or he was being thoughtful and not mentioning it. 'My goodness,' she thought, 'What if he has received the letter and I said nothing? What must he think of me?'

Anne came into the kitchen, asking Mrs Jennings if she could help with the dinner preparations.

"I think you could take over with that one! Lady Emma has been very attentive to Marcia until Doctor Sopwith came. Now she seems a bit distracted."

Anne said in surprise, "Doctor Sopwith!"

Aggie pointed, "Yes, he is on the veranda with the boys."

Anne peeked through the mudroom door and saw Doctor Sopwith kneeling on the floor arranging pieces of wood, with William leaning on his shoulder and Simeon in front of him questioning each move.

Anne quietly said, "Emma, come and see this."

Marcia jumped down, "Me too!"

She ran to Anne putting her arms around her legs, and peered out the door.

Emma came over and carefully glanced out. The boys and David were deep in conversation and were unaware of the audience. It was a picture that neither Emma nor Anne would ever forget. Anne found it difficult to remember her father ever interacting with the boys like that. Yet here was this man, a recent family friend, doing the things a father should do. It was a lovely scene.

Emma watched as David and the boys exchanged comments and moved bits of wood into different positions, agreeing on the correct place for each. They were a team creating something out of scraps of wood. Poor Hugh, her brother, never experienced this type of interest from her father. Perhaps his future may have been different if his father had shown such affection.

The girls came back into the kitchen. There was silence as they thought about the scene they had witnessed.

Anne suggested, "Will you ask him if he received the letter?"

Emma was surprised, "I couldn't do that. It would be rude. Should I?"

"Of course, you should!"

Marcia asked Anne, "What letter!"

"A letter for Doctor Sopwith which Lady Emma sent this morning!"

"I'll ask him!" Marcia would do anything for Emma. Before they could stop her, she darted out onto the back veranda, rushed around in front of the boys and Doctor Sopwith and said in a loud voice, "Doctor Sopwith, have you received the letter from Emma?"

The boys and David stopped talking, and all looked up.

"What letter Marcia?" David said with a quizzical look on his face. Simeon and William just looked at Marcia and then looked back down at the pieces of wood.

"Thank you, Marcia. I shall probably find it when I arrive home. I'll be going in a minute."

"Thank you, Doctor. I will tell her."

"Thank you, Marcia."

Marcia ran back into the kitchen with a grin on her face, "He thinks it may arrive at home!"

The girls were not annoyed with the little one as she was so keen. "Thank you, Marcia."

Emma looked across at Anne and said, "I think I owe David an explanation!"

Anne smiled and nodded. Her smile encouraged Emma.

Sauntering out onto the back veranda, Emma leaned against the rail and watched as the boys and David finished up. They packed away the wood bits and quickly talked about what they would do on Saturday afternoon. David could see her there, waiting for him.

Once they finished packing, Anne called the two boys in for dinner. David turned, "I'm sorry about intruding, but I was not aware you were here. If I had known, I would not have disturbed you."

"Thank you, David, and you are not intruding. I am glad you are here!"

"Really?"

David Sopwith looked at her and wondered if this was the same girl he argued with on the weekend. The gentle, soft-spoken girl he was in love with was there again in front of him. She had reappeared as if it was a miracle.

"I have written a letter." Emma looked down and blushed.

"I think someone just told me about that, but I have not been home, so it is unseen as yet."

"It is an apology for my behaviour on Friday night."

"There is no need for an apology Lady Emma. It is I who should apologise. I forgot my place. Forgive me, please?"

"David, please call me Emma and secondly, let us accept each other's apologies."

David was relieved by this comment and continued gazing at Emma, taking in the sight he missed so much. She looked at him and moved closer, almost where he could lean over and touch her.

She smiled at him and put her hand in his. His world suddenly became blurred, but he could see her in front of him. He decided there and then that he would not let this opportunity pass again.

Softly he said, "I love you, Emma."

Emma smiled, "I know, David."

He leaned over and very lightly kissed her on the lips. She returned the kiss.

Thomas, running into the kitchen, said, "Is David Sopwith still here? I must ask him something!" Not noticing the tension in the kitchen, he ran out onto the back veranda. Opening his mouth to speak, he stopped upon seeing David kissing Emma.

Without saying a word, he turned around, rushing back through the kitchen, saying, "It can wait! It can wait!" and disappeared down the hallway.

Anne looked at Mrs Jennings, and Aggie looked at Anne. They broke out in happy laughter. Tears started rolling down Anne's cheeks. Mrs Jennings said, "There, there!" and took Anne in her arms. There was nothing like a gentle hug as she shed tears of joy.

Marcia darted out of the kitchen after Thomas. All they could hear was Marcia crying out after him, "What can wait? What can wait?"

Chapter 25

The weather in Reading was windy with some light rain, but that in no way stopped the busy town with numerous merchants trading livestock in the marketplace. Jonathan Turner reflected on the building that Hamish McPherson purchased for the new Reading pub. The position appeared highly desirable, situated on the High Street near the town's northern entry. The proposed railway station site was close by and offered the prospect of growing business and passing traffic.

Jonathan was surprised by the traffic noise and the traders' banter on the High Street. He raised his voice, "You are sure about the railway station site, Hamish, aren't you?"

"Yes, Jonathan! Based on the site approval, I have invested a small sum in the railway that will link London, Bath and Bristol. I understand the Reading Guild is working with the Government on plans for the station. We should see it built within five years. In the meantime, it allows plenty of time for experimenting with our existing business in this busy town."

"It certainly is busy, Hamish! There are people everywhere!"

"Jonathan, it is the excitement of the railroads that is driving everything. The Government has mooted a connection to the midlands and various new lines southwards! There is also a company proposing a line as far as Cornwall."

"I see. Is Reading famous for anything else Hamish, other than being a stopover?"

"Yes, Jonathan. Reading, being centrally located, is a hub for all the farming activity here. Bristol is connected by canal with the Kennet river, giving the linen manufacturing industry easy access to the east and west coasts. There is already some brewing activity going on. That is why our investment was timely before the building prices increased."

Jonathan Turner looked around and could see why Hamish was so keen on this site. Activity usually bred more activity. Jonathan agreed with Hamish's thoughts that this would be a growth centre. The earlier they got in, the better.

"I think your hunch is right, Hamish. Reading is another town where we can't lose a penny. My initial assessment is favourable. I think it is a wise choice!"

Hamish shouted back as a loud coach, followed by several rickety carts, passed. "Come down inside my office Jonathan. I will show you the plans; then we can walk through the building. This pub will be our best yet! We will need a good operating company running it."

Jonathan nodded and followed Hamish. He liked Hamish's business model for pubs. It involved establishing a profitable business and then selecting a functional group to run the pub long term. There were numerous groups interested but few with the capital required. The Epsom pub was an excellent example of this. Jonathan was already enjoying great returns, and this would only increase.

Hamish and Jonathan were booked into the same hotel, allowing more time for discussion if needed. It would also enable exploring Thomas' housing arrangements after the wedding.

As they indulged in the second course of dinner, Hamish said, "Jonathan, your business is flourishing, and I know you have committed significant capital into our new pubs. I remember my early years of business when cash was always a problem. As a friend, I felt I might warn you about the dangers of being overcommitted."

Having worked on the cash flow plan over the last few weeks, Jonathan was ready for this.

"Yes, Hamish. I had similar concerns around a month ago. Anne and I have completed our budget and cash flow plans for next year. Costs were up, but factoring in the use of your grains gave us an acceptable margin. We will introduce the new mill slowly, so we are overlooked by our competition. Rather than flood the local market with our new low-cost flour, we will seek out markets further afield, such as London. If our predicted sales are too optimistic, it won't be a concern as we have spare cash that will tide us through."

"Anne must have worked hard on this, Jonathan. It is not an easy analysis."

"She has an intimate knowledge of our business model. She will continue as a director in the business after she is married."

"A sound idea Jonathan."

Hamish was quite impressed that Jonathan's planning was so advanced. However, he suspected it was Anne who alerted Jonathan. The girl had a natural flair for business. He knew only of a few such women. They seemed born with natural skills and became outstanding managers. The difference here was that Anne was so young!

"Mind you, Jonathan, Robert may have other expectations."

"I think we can manage that! After all, he will be away most of the time in the navy. It makes sense that she will be close by."

"On another subject, Jonathan, I thought I should warn you there is some protest footwork taking place in parliament about brewing and alehouses. I thought I should brief you in case you are worried about the issues."

"What are the issues, Hamish?"

"The licencing process may become harder as a new Act is[28] proposed for an annual licensing meeting. My sources tell me it won't pass in 1827 but could come in 1828. That's why I am moving quickly on some of these pubs. Some opportunities will develop for us from this!"

The two men remained in a deep conversation for some time. As Jonathan was about to clarify the arrangements for Thomas, Hamish stood up. A lady approached their table.

"Good evening, Mrs Stubbington." Hamish beamed as he saw a most attractive middle-aged woman join them, "I have been watching out for you! Won't you join us, please?"

Hamish introduced Jonathan, "Mrs Janet Stubbington, please may I introduce my friend and business associate, Mr Jonathan Turner from Guildford."

"Ah, Mr Turner, delighted." She held out her hand, and Jonathan took it in his.

"It is a pleasure, Mrs Stubbington. Please join us!"

"Jonathan, please call me Janet. Hamish has told me so much about you and that steam-powered flour mill you have built."

"Is that so? We are encouraged by the substantial efficiencies achieved! Now tell me, Janet, how do you know Hamish?"

"Let me explain, Jonathan!" Hamish was keen to elaborate.

"Frank Stubbington was a self-made man such as you. He had butcheries, a lot of them!"

Janet nodded in agreement.

"Frank also enjoyed the fox hunt, and a couple of years ago, unfortunately, he was thrown from his horse and died. The accident left Janet with a couple of young sons and all these butcheries."

Here, Janet added, "I was not familiar with the operation of butcheries except that they sold meat. Hamish being a close friend of Franks, suggested that he assist!"

"That's correct, so we sold all the butchery shops, raising quite a hefty sum, and now Janet is a mid-size investor in McPherson Breweries and realising a very healthy income from it."

"I am very thankful for Hamish assisting me in a time of deep distress. Like you, I have ventured down here to inspect this new site that Hamish is developing. We will be joint investors!"

---

[28] The Alehouse Act 1828 which was soon followed by the Beerhouse Act 1830. Wikipedia.

"Yes, yes, I hope we will often meet at the investor meetings Mrs Stubbing-ton, I mean Janet!"

This unannounced addition stopped any discussion about Thomas. Jonathan sat back and listened while Hamish and Janet reminisced. Jonathan's curiosity was aroused, and he wondered if Hamish appeared too attentive with Janet Stubbington. He gave it no further thought, and his mind jogged him about the grain producers he would meet with tomorrow. Three major producers and a couple of small farmers were available for contract discussions with him at the hotel. Hamish volunteered his assistance with the process – so the morning would be a full one.

"Jonathan, we will meet at the wedding of Marion Steele and your son Thomas. Marion is a dear child, and Hamish and Marjorie have invited me. I am so glad that Marion has found such a good young man in Thomas. She is such a lovely girl!"

"Yes, my wife and I are excited as well. Thomas has left for Greenwich, and we will also leave on the weekend. It will be a hectic time. I hope we see some more of you during the week. My wife and Marjorie have completed most of the organisation, so I am not even sure who is on the guest list."

"You are like my Frank. He was only interested in business affairs. Jonathan, you must forget your work and enjoy the wedding."

"I will, Janet. As soon as we complete the grain meetings tomorrow, I will return home, probably first thing Friday morning."

The conversation then veered away, remembering old times with Frank, and Jonathan felt a little out of it. He finished his after-dinner scotch and excused himself.

Later in the evening, having familiarised himself with the grain contracts and finishing his nightly reading of Proverbs, he thought about Thomas's situation. By securing a rental on the house in Guildford, he knew Thomas and Marion would have a decent home for the next twelve months. He still was unsure when the company house would be available. Hamish should have returned by now! Jonathan decided to walk along the hall to his room and check with him.

Putting on his dressing-gown, he strolled down the hall. As he was about to knock, he heard a woman's giggle from inside the room. Jonathan held back and quietly listened for a few seconds. A woman was inside Hamish's room, and then he heard Hamish laugh. Jonathan quickly retreated, passing another gentleman in the hallway who he assumed was a guest, and quickly closed his door. He stood there and thought, "Perhaps Hamish may have a bit more than an investor in Janet Stubbington!"

Checking the time, he saw it was eleven-thirty. He was tired and needed sleep. As he lay in his bed, his mind would not slow down. What was he doing here in Reading? Why was he involved in brewing when he owned a healthy and growing business in Guildford? He must calm himself.

He was already heavily invested in the brewing business. He was committed. There was no turning back now, and Jonathan knew the McPhersons represented his future. They had taken him over. Anne was right again! What did the pub contracts say? He should have spent more time reading them. He was not even sure of the extent of his liability. Thank goodness she was reviewing them.

Jonathan lay there on his bed and sank into a deep depression. His day was long, and now he was in a dark place. Rolling over, Jonathan thought about the whole situation. Closing his eyes, he drifted off into a safe place where he was with Eleanora, young again, walking beside the river Wey and thinking about all the future held for them. They walked together, laughing in a warm place as he drifted off into a deep sleep.

St James's Square ...

Lord Fintelton slept for the last part of the trip. After spending the night at the McPherson's new pub in Epsom, the coach travelled towards London. Anne enjoyed meeting cousin Oliver again, who seemed entirely in control of the new business he managed. As the coach passed through the outskirts of London, Anne watched as the buildings became more clustered together and taller. She was surprised at the filthy streets and the rags people wore. The sun was now setting earlier as it was late autumn, and the light was fading quickly at four-thirty in the afternoon. This twilight made the drive through the crowded streets even more depressing. Anne recalled how Robert hated the congestion of London. She had wondered at his comments but now understood.

Emma leaned over and said, "Nearly there!" They were both glad, needing a stretch after the confinement of the coach. There was also the excitement that would occur in the next few days, which made them both impatient for their arrival.

Anne was highly emotional before the coach arrived at High Street on Saturday morning. She knew the Earl's first impression of her must be the best she could contrive. Her costume and makeup must be perfect. She spent much time grooming and employed her mother's assistance with a full inspection to ensure the job was complete.

The Earl sat on the far side of the large coach, enjoying the view from the window. As the coach stopped at the Turner's house, Emma hopped down and hugged her friend Anne. The footman placed some special steps below the coach door, which allowed Lord Fintelton to descend with some assistance.

Emma made the introductions between the Earl, Anne and Mr and Mrs Turner. The Earl was most polite and welcomed the acquaintance.

"Ah, Mr Turner, Good Day, Sir! At last, we meet. I must apologise for my ill health, preventing my attendance at your daughter's wedding. It gives us great pleasure that Anne, our future daughter in law, joins us for the trip. We will ensure, Sir, that she arrives safely for your son Thomas's wedding. I think Emma has planned a full programme for the week."

Emma and Anne talked excitedly as the fathers conversed.

Jonathan Turner gave a short bow, "Lord Fintelton, we are overwhelmed by yours and Lady Jane's generosity by including her in your party. Certainly, the London trip and the wedding will be most exciting, and we pray your trip is safe."

"Thank you, Mr Turner. As we aim for Epsom today, we should be on our way. The coachmen have stowed Anne's trunk, so we must be off."

The Earl turned from Jonathan looking for the girls and found himself gazing directly into the light blue eyes of Anne Turner. Her golden hair was perfectly groomed, with waving hair over her shoulders in the gentle breeze and her costume was rich in pastel blues and whites. He could not recall such a beautiful picture in some time. The old Earl stood there without a word until Lady Jane called, "David, will you not welcome Anne?"

"Good day, Miss Anne Turner. Come, my Dear, we must board and be on our way!"

With that, he held her hand as she climbed up into the carriage, followed by Emma. The girls sat together, both full of excitement, ready for the trip. Lord Fintelton climbed aboard and moved across, taking his seat. He tapped the coach ceiling as the Turner family waved their goodbyes.

Lady Jane noticed her husband considering Anne for the first ten minutes of the trip with a pleasant smile. She leaned over and quietly said, "Dear, now you know!"

He glanced back at her and said, "Capital, my Dear, Capital."

Anne enjoyed the trip, having several long conversations with the Earl. She now felt more confident as there seemed to be no difficulties and felt readily accepted as an equal.

As the coach entered St James's Square and pulled up outside an enormous house with at least four if not five floors, Anne peered out, thinking how this house was so much grander than the McPherson's house in Greenwich.

"It has been in the family for several generations and needs quite a lot of upkeep. I hope you approve of it?"

"Emma, it is like a fairy tale. It is magnificent. Thank you so much for bringing me here."

Emma smiled and thought, 'How different it is for me, as I think this is normal while it is a fairy tale for Anne. It will be an exciting time for her.'

The servants' carriage pulled up just as they were alighting, and Anne noticed that all the servants descended the downstairs staircase. Emma directed the family up the front stairs where the butler, Mr Staines, waited for them.

"Welcome back, my Lord and Lady. I hope your journey was pleasant?"

"Excellent, Staines. Glad I'm back. Now is that scotch waiting for me in the study?"

"Yes, My Lord!"

With that, the Earl was in through the front door and made a rush for his study. Lady Jane quickly followed him, ensuring he did not overindulge. Emma made the introduction between Anne and the butler.

"Staines! Let me introduce Miss Anne Turner, a dear friend who will stay the week. She will have Robert's old room beside mine on the first floor. When Jane is available, you may send her up."

The butler nodded and turned and looked down his nose at Anne and said, "Miss Turner, I will show you the way if you would follow me."

"Thank you, Staines."

Emma spoke again, but this time in a firmer voice, "Staines, you are probably not aware, so I should be fair and advise you straight away. Miss Anne and my brother Robert are engaged. The engagement is very recent. The marriage will be next year. Due to the proximity of the marriage, I think from now on in this house, the appropriate address will be Lady Anne!"

The butler swallowed but with no change in expression and said, "Thank you, Milady. I was unaware. Congratulations, Lady Anne. If you follow me, I will have pleasure in showing you the way."

Emma raised her eyebrows at Anne as they walked together. Anne smiled, and Emma recognised it would be a significant transition. They would have fun managing this together.

As Anne entered her room, she was surprised by its beauty. Several candles created a pleasant glow, and some antique French doors leading onto a small balcony overlooking St James's Square gave a splendid view. The lampposts twinkling through the windows supplemented by candlelight from various buildings around the square made a dazzling display from the balcony.

The family had lavishly furnished the room with a large double bed and several beautiful pieces of furniture. The colours of the wallpaper reflected the candlelight everywhere, so the room almost shone like daylight. Heavy curtains with soft, see-through sheers draped beside the French doors and a deep soft mauve rug adorned the floor. The room's beauty overcame Anne. As Emma came in, she said in appreciation, "It is beautiful, Emma. I did not expect this. It is like living in a palace."

"Enjoy it, as it is all yours for this week. Now I have requested Jane attend you first as dinner will be at half-past seven. I am next door if you need me. When you are ready, we shall go down together."

"That is kind of you to share, Jane, but there is no need!"

"Yes, there is. You must understand how this all works, Anne. We will share Jane this week. She will help you with everything. Make sure you use her – she also has good taste in selecting clothing, particularly evening wear. If you are short of anything, we can pick it up tomorrow when we go shopping. It will be convenient as my mother has advised me that we are all invited for dinner tomorrow night. Admiral Crouch is an old friend of my father and wanted the pleasure of his company while he was in town. When he heard that mother, you and I were here also, he insisted that we join the party."

"Must we, Emma? I'm not ready for London society yet. I don't feel confident!"

"It will only be a couple of old men catching up on good times, and you will meet Admiral Crouch's wife, Kate. She is a lovely lady – you will enjoy her company, Anne! I'm quite sure they will attend your wedding, so it is a good opportunity for making a new friendship."

Anne sat down on the bed, appearing a little more confident. "As long as you are beside me, Emma, I will feel invincible. But please, don't leave me alone."

"We will be like glue!"

As Anne sat considering the dinner, two footmen came in with her trunk. Jane appeared and said, "Milady, let's unpack your trunk, shall we?"

Anne nodded and smiled at Emma as she slipped away into the next room.

HMS Restless …

Restless was sailing purposefully around the bottom of Kintyre, making for the open sea. The wind gusted between ten to twenty knots from the west, with light rain falling. The crew were thankful for a respite from the gale of the previous week.

The Glasgow expedition started very slowly, with no results on the first night. Robert and Horace remained in their accommodation overnight. Horace was relieved as they rented a room together, which spared him the indignity of sharing a bed with a sailor. Quite amused by Horace's complaints, Robert said they would make great tales for the years to come.

On the second night, a small man with a heavy Irish accent approached them at a seedy bar in the back streets of Port Glasgow. He was looking for recruits for a ship destined for a return trip to Boston. Robert convinced him of their interest, and they engaged in the arduous talk of remuneration and signing on. As the evening went on, they poured more and more whisky into the little gentleman. He did not complain one bit except that he would only drink Islay whisky, which he had recently discovered. By the early morning hours, the Irishman displayed his fondness for singing but was still doing well at keeping his information guarded closely. At about three in the morning, his guard fell.

The more he drank, the more he accepted Robert and Horace's story. Some poor Irish boys wanting a way home. Keen on impressing his new friends, the little chap found solace in letting some information slip that might encourage their revolutionary leanings. He lowered his voice and informed them some weeks ago that the Republicans had secured a large ship refitting for the Boston run. A crew with experience of the Atlantic was required, particularly for running into the coast of Ireland. The crew would train here in Glasgow, but a boat would sail them to the ship when the time was right.

"And where is she moored, Ian?"

"It is a secret, my friend! But for another song and a couple of rounds of Islay scotch, I will tell you about an outlying island bay sheltered from the Irish sea where anyone can hide a ship."

Some anti-Irish Glasgow boys bounded in, looking for a fight and cutting off the flow of information. After that, things became a bit heated. By this time, the small Irish chap thought he was Saint Pat and decided on a single-handed charge against the Scots. Robert and Horace promptly retreated through a side door but unfortunately found several Scots boys looking for deserters outside the bar. Horace sorted out the scuffle quickly, with Robert only having a slight altercation with a large but dumb Scotsman with good aim. The English officers, sporting many bruises, disappeared into the foggy darkness of the early hours of the morning. They were much relieved on reaching *Restless*.

"So, Horace, what have we got?" Robert sat at the table in his cabin, reviewing his notes on what the small Irish man told them.

"Some rather bad bruising, my friend. Pass over that bottle." Horace took another glass of scotch, put it down and rubbed his sore spots.

"I meant intelligence, Horace!"

"Ah, Oow!" Horace jumped as he rubbed a rather delicate chest muscle.

"The little man said on an outlying island and hidden in a bay. Now let's see. That means the hills on either side of the bay would be reasonably high, and the bay sheltered from the Atlantic. It would also be remote."

'You're not relying on that Irish dwarf's words, are you? We are back where we started. I thought we might have got a lead."

"Hold on, Horace! Now that I recall what Ian said again, he didn't say sheltered from the Atlantic, did he? He said they sheltered from the Irish Sea. So, we were right. *Providence* is somewhere in Scotland!"

"Yes, he did say the Irish sea, Squire. But I would not rely on him! There are over a hundred bays like that in Scotland!"

"But there is more information than that. We know the ship is out there, and someone has taken her. My hunch is that little Irishman knows much more about it than he was letting on. But what do we know of him?"

"Not much Robert, except Ian, was his name, and he was recruiting and wanted payment in Scotch whisky for the privilege." Horace was not impressed at all and doubted his veracity.

They both sat there, thinking about the little man. Nothing was indicating from where he had come. Robert rechecked his notes.

"Whisky! He wanted whisky Horace. Whisky all the time! He could take in an incredible amount, and it did not affect him. But what kind of whisky did he want?" Robert suddenly sat up straight.

"He said he only wanted Isle of Islay whisky!"

"Yes, but there was more. Ian said he had only recently discovered it, and he wouldn't touch anything else!"

"That's right."

"Islay Horace, Islay. He must have been there recently. That must be where *Providence* is?"

They sat there, looking at each other in silence.

Then Horace said, "I think you might be onto something with that. It is more than a coincidence. I think you've cracked it!"

Robert grabbed a map of the area and blurted out, "Quick, look at this chart. Laggan Bay! If you go further past Port Charlotte,[29] you find Loch Indaal, a nice sheltered, hidden bay with very few people around. These traitors are smart. But maybe not smart enough. First, we must find out if the ship is there. Horace, if we can enter Loch Gruinart up here, I will have a job for your marines."

He pointed at the top end of the island on the chart. "You can take a small force of say ten men across the island. Find a high spot where you can scout Loch Indaal. See if *Providence* is there. I want you in fatigues so you blend in with the country. What do you say?"

"Now that's the work I like, Sir. Count me in! But we don't need ten men! That would slow us down. Two men will do, myself and Sergeant Wait. He's like a cat, same as Swanton and fast."

"Good man! I will keep well off the coast until twilight. By which time we will be in position. Now sunset will be around six in the evening, which should help. We'll move in slowly past Ardnave point and find a drop-off point as close in as we can. The high tide overnight should help. A hike across

---

[29] Port Charlotte was named around 1828 so the writer apologises for using poetic licence here, however it gives a better location description for the story.

by morning should be possible, depending on how high the terrain is. Then back either for an evening pick up or the next morning. From what I can see, it's only about three miles across. It depends on how far you can take the dingy up the loch. From this chart, it appears there are some sandbanks with a sort of tidal channel. If you can reach here at the base of the high ground, then the hike may only be two miles before there is a view of Loch Indaal."

The plan convinced Horace. He liked the idea of having his feet on dry soil again and enjoying some action. Every one of the marines would volunteer, keen for some land action.

"Get me there, and we can do it in a day. Early morning, say two am and pick us up in the evening. That would be better. The army travels faster on land than you think. The less time we are ashore, the better. We will stay undercover during the daylight, probably at our vantage point."

They agreed on the plans and checked the details as *Restless* left the Mull of Kintyre in her wake. Robert went on deck, briefed Lieutenant Ham and then set a course well out of sight of land. They would head back into the northern end of Islay after nightfall. Robert knew how good these republicans were. They would be watching, so nothing must be left to chance. This intelligence was critical in planning the next stage of the operation.

Horace and Wait were changing into fatigues that blended in with the countryside. Horace preferred marching into a town in uniform, but he and Robert agreed they must be invisible, so there was no chance of prior warning reaching the republicans.

Horace noticed the worried look on his face.

"Don't worry, Captain; this is Wait's and my speciality. No one will see us! Make sure you're back early after dark. Wait doesn't like his dinner too late."

"Done, Horace! Now get your things ready, and then some sleep. I will chart a course for a drop-off tonight. With this wind, we will easily make it on time. Off you go and prepare your plan with Sargent Wait. I will wake you at two am."

Horace grinned, "Aye, Sir!"

"I just hope we are right, and *Providence* is in that bay!"

At Guildford, the Turner Household …
Late on the Friday afternoon, as the light was fading, Jonathan Turner arrived home from Reading with good news about the grain contracts. He hoped that most of the packing for the trip was now complete. Leaving for London on Monday was a two-day trip, arriving on Tuesday, allowing some settling in before the wedding rehearsal on Thursday.

Jonathan entered through the front door and found the parlour empty. He found Ethel, Mrs Jennings and Aggie in conversation in the kitchen.

"Welcome Home, Mr Turner. Mrs Turner will be glad you are home."

"Thank you, Ethel. Is she not in good health?"

"Sir, I meant that Mrs Turner has missed you and will welcome your return. There has been so much packing for the trip. She is exhausted and is sleeping upstairs. Yes, Sir, she is in good health."

Jonathan breathed a sigh of relief, "I am glad. I know this trip will not be easy for her, but she must not miss the privilege of seeing her son married. Now I will go upstairs and see her."

With that, Jonathan backed out of the kitchen. As he went, he was pleased that Ethel understood Eleanora's care needs. He was relying more on Ethel than he expected. Their decision to recruit her was sound.

He crept into the bedroom and watched his wife sleep. The breathing was light, and Eleanora looked relaxed. Having been away for three days, he took the opportunity to sit back and let the world's cares disappear. His home was where he should be. Jonathan thought about the several nights at Reading where his mind tempted his celibacy again, but he had held true. He was relieved and found a certain amount of strength in it. 'What a funny thing', he thought. Standing up, he quietly moved out of the room.

Clementine saw him and followed.

"Father, welcome home."

"Thank you, Clementine."

"Father, will there be enough room for us in the carriage? Where will everyone sit? As we are all going and the servants! I wonder how we will fit everyone in one carriage?"

"That is a good question, Clementine, and I will give you a good answer. We will be taking three carriages. The first will be for your mother, myself and Marcia and Aggie. The second will be for Mrs Jennings, who will look after you, Madeline, Simeon and William. The third carriage will be for Ethel and her daughter and all the remaining luggage and equipment we will need to set up the house for a week in Greenwich. If you feel too many are in your carriage, I am quite happy if you choose Ethel's carriage."

"Why are we taking Ethel's daughter, Father?"

"Clementine, Ethel has taken good care of your mother over the last few weeks. As thanks for that, your mother and I thought Ethel might enjoy her daughter coming. They only meet once a week, so it is an opportunity for Rosalind to be with her mother. She can help in the kitchen with Mrs Jennings."

"How do you know her daughter's name?"

"I asked Ethel!"

"I shall wait until Monday morning when I meet Rosalind and tell you."

"Does that answer all your questions, Clementine?"

"Yes, Father. Dr Sopwith is here! He is on the back veranda with Simeon and William."

"I see! I shall join them."

Clementine followed her father through the house.

"Ah, Doctor Sopwith, I see you and the boys are hard at work!"

Doctor Sopwith was deep in conversation with Simeon and William as they poured over the sailing boat plans. They were discussing which wood to select for the frame.

"Mr Turner. Welcome home from Reading, Sir. I trust the trip went well?"

"Yes, very well, Doctor. All our forward orders for grain are now complete. Now we wait on a bumper spring harvest."

"It is some way off, Sir, so I hope you have plenty of grain in store?"

"Yes, we do. The bread supply in Guildford is secure until next spring. And may I ask how the plans for the boat are developing?"

William could not resist, "Father, Father come and have a look. She will be a beautiful boat."

Jonathan walked over and looked at the plan, "There is much detail in this, Doctor. Do the children understand it?"

"I thought the same, Sir, but I find they both grasp the detail quickly. They are both intelligent boys and quick at learning. We shall start making parts tomorrow afternoon. By the way, Mr Turner, I think I advised that I would not be at the wedding at Greenwich. My circumstances now allow my attendance. I have advised Mr and Mrs McPherson that I will be there. I thought I should let you know."

"This is good news indeed, Doctor. The boys will miss the boat building, but I am sure you and they will catch up when we all return."

"Mr Turner, there is one issue of concern. Sailing a boat requires water. In all probability, the river! But I find that both William and Simeon cannot swim. If one fell in, then it may be a disaster. May I suggest that when we return from the wedding, it may be prudent if I give them swimming lessons? Are you a swimmer, Sir?"

"No, I never had that opportunity."

"Would you join us? It is the best exercise!"

"I'm not sure, Doctor. I have never desired that ability, but it may be useful. I will think about it."

"I suggest we use the Gentlemen's club, roman baths. I am a member, and the water is heated so that it will be pleasant. I know you are a member as well, so please join us. It will improve your health, Sir."

"Doctor Sopwith, how can I not but obey if you prescribe it? We shall set a time as soon as we return. I'm sure the boys will quickly learn; however, I must warn you, I am not a quick learner. I may test your patience."

"Thank you, Mr Turner. I will value your presence with us."

"Father, you will learn to swim with us! We shall have fun. But I'm sure the water will be cold!" Simeon was quite excited about the prospect, which enthused William as well.

Doctor Sopwith encouraged the boys, "It will be warm fellows. The baths are heated, and you will find the water most refreshing. Our first lesson will be about floating. It is easy once you know how."

Jonathan Turner was amazed by the change he found in this young man. It was possible that he initially misjudged him. Jonathan was impressed by the friendship that David Sopwith offered his family. He enjoyed Doctor Sopwith's company.

"Doctor, will you stay on for dinner? We would be glad of your company." The boys cheered in agreement.

"Thank you, Sir, but I have three farmers coming in fairly early tomorrow morning for minor surgery. They have little time to waste, so I must prepare tonight and be ready for them. Perhaps another time. But thank you for your kind offer. It is much appreciated."

St James's Square ...

Anne was glad she had purchased several new dresses for the trip. The outlay of nearly fifteen pounds came from her savings, but she thought it a good investment if anything like this ever eventuated again. She wished Robert was here. Not having heard from him in over three weeks, Anne became concerned, and her heart ached for him. She tried not to fret as Robert could look after himself, but she knew long-distance relationships were always challenging.

"We must leave in a few minutes, Anne. You are beautiful. I have not seen that dress before!" Anne watched as Emma walked around her, admiring the latest acquisition. The dress, one of the current fashions with pink and white satins, short sleeves and ruffles, was enough to keep her warm but gave a sophisticated look. She was a picture with her hair in a bun and a light necklace.

Jane stood back so Lady Emma could take a closer look, "It is a beautiful dress, Milady, isn't it?"

"Yes, Jane, we shall visit Hursts soon. Mrs Smith is very clever in her designs. Would you mind putting on my necklace, please?"

"Thank you, Emma. I had a couple of dresses made in case such an occasion arose, and I was also preparing for the wedding. But of course, we must care not to outshine the bride on her big day, so I have something straightforward ready."

"I agree. I thought about that also and will have something made this week. We will be busy tomorrow at the dressmaker's. It is such fun being in

London and seeing the fashions."

With a cheeky grin, Emma continued, "David will need a very profitable medical practice given my liking for new dresses. I hope he has some money saved up!" They both giggled.

"Anne, as Jane is finishing here, I might request her back for a few final touches if that is acceptable."

"Certainly, Emma, I am ready, so I will wander down and wait for everyone there."

Anne gently closed the door of her room and moved off down the stairway. She was still amazed at the splendour of this house. The deep coloured mahogany lined the walls, with portraits of family members going back centuries. There was quite a history here, including pictures of royalty, and Anne wondered what the connections were.

As she reached the bottom of the stairs, the butler greeted her. "You will find the Earl and Lady Jane in the drawing-room, Milady."

"Thank you, Staines. I appreciate your kindness. Now, which room is the drawing-room?"

"Let me show you, Milady."

The butler led Anne through the hall towards the front door but turned left as they neared it. He opened the door for her, and she entered a beautifully decorated room with large comfortable chairs and light tables. A fire roared on the far side of the room, and lush carpets and relaxing seats beckoned. Lady Jane and the Earl sat on a couch facing the fire, not hearing her as she entered. Anne walked softly up around the sofa and greeted them.

"Good evening, my Lord and Lady Jane. This drawing room is beautiful."

An admiring Lord Fintelton stood, "Anne, you become more beautiful every time I see you. No wonder you have snatched Robert's heart."

"Thank you, my Lord."

Lady Jane joined in, "Now I'm sure that is a new dress from Hursts. That Mrs Smith is a gem. You look beautiful, my Dear. Now, as soon as Emma is here, we must be off. The carriage is waiting outside. Admiral Crouch's residence is not far from here."

"Thank you, Lady Jane. May I ask what the connection between the Earl and Admiral Crouch is?"

The Earl replied, "Yes, you may, and a good idea at that! My parents were friends of Frank's parents. We both attended the same boarding school; however, he was a good five years younger than I. Then at university, I was one of his mentors. We have kept in contact ever since. Over the years, we have quite often visited each other's estates and shot together. But being a navy man, the opportunities were taken when he was at home. Lady Jane developed a strong friendship with Lady Katherine Crouch, and they met far more often than we boys. They are very nice people. But you may find the Admiral a bit gruff at first. I think navy men develop this as they reach a higher rank. You know, being in control and all that. But Kate is a gem, just like you, my Dear."

"Thank you, my Lord. Robert did mention he has met Admiral Crouch. I was wondering who he was?"

"My Dear, Admiral Crouch is the First Lord of the Admiralty. He controls the British Navy!"

"In that case, I had best behave myself tonight then. Robert would not want me making any mistakes. I will rely on your help if he asks me any curly questions."

Lady Jane could detect that Anne was a little tense. She tried calming her, "Don't worry, Dear, I will be with you all night and make sure you are safe. His Lordship will keep an eye on you as well. We did promise your father that. I believe the Admiral has invited a few other close friends tonight so that it will be an opportunity for you in a simple format. Not only will you be safe, but you will have a most enjoyable time."

Emma joined them, looking a picture she received praise from her parents on her pretty new dress. The butler then assisted the party into the carriage. The Earl tapped the roof, and they were off.

Anne noticed several military men outside the Admiral's house receiving the guests. Other men in suits were not guests but security standing near the front door. As the coach pulled up outside the entrance, a man in uniform opened the door, and another man in a suit welcomed them.

"Lord and Lady Fintelton, welcome. I am Colonel Jonathan Scott of His Majesty's Guards and Chief of Security for the Admiralty. I am pleased to welcome you and your party tonight. Please, these young ladies with you, I assume they are your daughter Lady Emma and Sir Robert's fiancée, Miss Anne Turner. Would I be correct in that?"

The Earl stood up straight as best he could, "Yes, thank you, Colonel, you are correct. You know my son, Sir?"

"I have had that pleasure, Sir. Sir Horace Coombes is a good friend of mine as well. Please pass on my congratulations to Sir Robert, Sir."

"Good. Capital, Capital! If you would show us in, we would appreciate that."

The Colonel smiled and looked carefully at each of them, then indicated the way. A butler opened the front door and welcomed them into the vestibule. Taking their coats, he handed them to a footman for care. Anne noticed another suited man inside the cloakroom watching.

The butler quietly said, "Sorry, Lord Fintelton, about the security, but since the Admiral became First Sea Lord, the protocol requirements for security has increased. Whenever he entertains, security vets the guests. Please follow me upstairs."

The butler gave the party his full attention as he led them up the stairs onto the first floor. Anne noticed how the decor of the building had a definite navy theme, with blues and whites predominating the colour scheme, portraits of high-ranking navy officers and paintings of ships in action. There were hundreds of candles throughout the entry room, up the stairs and onto the first-floor balcony. It was a magnificent sight, and its brilliance overcame Anne.

Emma took her arm, "What a beautiful room and staircase. These navy men decorate well."

"It is magnificent, Emma. I have never seen anything like it!"

"Remember it is only lots of candles and simple people. We shall both remain calm and enjoy the company. I think the men outnumber us tonight, so we shall stay together."

The party entered the room, and Admiral Crouch darted across and shook the Earl's hand warmly.

"David, I am heartened that you are here. I heard of your ill health and was concerned. Welcome, my good friend."

"Ah Frank, glad I'm here and well! I thought you would be retired by now; you are only five years younger than me. You look in good health, Sir!"

"I am in good health, it has been a blessing, but I step down next year. I will tell you about that later. Now please introduce your party. Ah, Lady Jane, you look as young as ever. I believe you visited with Kate last month. She is here tonight, so you must catch up."

The Earl waited as Admiral Crouch and Lady Jane talked and then introduced the girls.

Anne took in a deep breath as the admiral turned.

"Admiral Crouch, may I introduce my daughter Lady Emma who I believe you have met before, and Miss Anne Turner, my son Robert's fiancée and, of course, he is in your service, Sir."

Admiral Crouch smiled at both the girls. "Emma and Anne, thank you for attending tonight. I am pleased that you are here. You will be a little outnumbered by the gentlemen, but I shall make sure we care for you. May I compliment you both on your beauty! The room brightens up immensely with your presence. Now, Emma, I think you joined Lady Jane when you visited Kate last month, did you not?"

"Yes, Admiral. It was a lovely luncheon."

"Good. Kate is most fond of you and your mother. I think that when I retire next year, we shall see much more of your family. We plan on visiting Fintelton."

"I am thrilled by this. You will be very welcome, Admiral."

While they chatted, Anne spotted Admiral Sir Tristan and Lady Amanda Sutherland nearby, and they smiled at her. She smiled back but turned back quickly as Admiral Crouch addressed her.

"Now, Miss Turner, I understand you are engaged to Sir Robert South? This news is wonderful. I know Robert well, and he is on an important mission for us presently. You are very welcome tonight."

"Thank you, Admiral. You are very kind."

The Admiral stood back and regarded Anne, moved by her beauty. He coughed slightly, "Now, let me introduce another of Robert's friends. Come Emma and Anne and meet some of the Admirals."

He waved his hand, gesturing they walked beside him. They moved forward across the room where a group of gentlemen were talking. One was Mr Malcolm Smith, who Anne knew from the dinner at the McPhersons in Greenwich. The other two she did not recognise, and the Admiral introduced them.

"Lady Emma South and Miss Anne Turner, may I introduce the Earl of Dawlting, Sir Cecil Fowey. My Lord, Emma is the daughter of Lord Fintelton and Anne is engaged to Sir Robert South, Commander of HMS *Restless*."

Both Anne and Emma gave a curtsey and waited on the Earl.

"Wonderful meeting both of you, young ladies. I fear we old men here tonight outnumber our younger guests, but we shall ensure that we entertain you. Now please may I introduce my wife, Hannah? Ah, I fear Admiral Bird much entertains her at present, perhaps during or after dinner. Anne, I believe you are sitting beside me. Perhaps I might walk with you into the dining room?"

Anne blushed but maintained her countenance, "Certainly, my Lord, I would be most honoured."

The dinner gong rang, and Admiral Crouch announced, "Good! Dinner, my friends, let us go in!"

Lord Dawlting held out his arm for Anne and led her off, quickly followed by Admiral Crouch, who escorted Emma. A kind and generous lady, Amanda Sutherland smiled at Anne and lifted her eyebrows as she passed them. Anne contained herself well, despite almost shedding laughing tears as she felt like a princess led by a prince.

Once all the guests were seated, Admiral Crouch stood up, welcomed the party and said the grace. The staff then served dinner as various conversations started. Anne noticed the regimental style of organisation that flowed flawlessly as the evening progressed. She also saw Colonel Scott in the background, carefully watching everything happening.

The Earl was a serious but entertaining conversationalist, and Anne enjoyed his company.

"So, you will marry Robert. Pray, Anne, when will this happen?"

Anne wished for the appearance of a lady of society but decided she lacked these skills and took Emma's advice speaking freely with the Earl.

"My Lord, we have not set a date yet, but we hope later next year. Robert has a new commission, and he will not be free before next June, so we must wait till then."

"Do you know what a gallant gentleman you are marrying Anne?"

"I know he is the kindest man I have ever met, and when we are together, there seems no end to our conversation. He has a quick mind and is patient with me as we speak. My family have found him very kind, and my younger brothers and sisters adore him. I love him so much. We will be happy together."

Anne told the Earl how Robert rescued her younger brothers from the wild stag on the hills overlooking Guildford. She recalled the talk between Sir Horace, Robert and herself in the kitchen tasting biscuits and Horace engineering some tea and pastries from Mrs Jennings. The picnic held at Severndroog Castle, which Admiral and Mrs Sutherland attended as well, and their game of cricket played on a beautiful sunny afternoon.

The Earl turned and gazed at her. He enjoyed the freshness of this young lady's conversation with no airs or graces, just the pure joy of life dancing from her lips. He could see the love in her eyes as they talked about this young man. Lord Dawlting was envious of youth long gone and the beautiful feelings it brought out.

"I think you love this young man very much, Anne!"

"I do, my Lord."

"I am pleased about that. Robert deserves a fine young bride, such as yourself. I'm not aware if you know much about his naval service, but he has distinguished himself twice. The first time, he was instrumental in saving his ship and capturing a Spanish vessel through courageous leadership. The King knighted him on that occasion for services to his country. On the second time, and I cannot say much, he saved his ship again while being wounded in action. His actions will not go unnoticed in the future. He is a gallant fellow and has a promising career in front of him."

"I think so, too, Lord Dawlting!"

"Well said, young lady, well said," and the Earl chuckled. He liked this young lady very much. She had something different about her, not seen by him for a long time. She was a breath of fresh air. The other guests looked up and wondered what the humour had been.

Admiral Crouch enquired with a friendly voice, "Lord Dawlting, are you to include us in your humour?"

"I was just telling Anne what a fine fellow Robert South was, and she replied, 'I think so, too!' I should have known that! Well said." He laughed again.

Admiral Crouch spoke again, "Anne, may I introduce my wife, Katherine? I'm sorry there was no time before dinner. She is keen on making your acquaintance and will meet with you and Emma after dinner."

"Lady Katherine. It is a pleasure to meet you, Ma'am."

Lady Katherine smiled across the table and said, "I am so glad Robert has found you, Anne. He deserves such a beauty as you. We must talk after dinner – you will understand that we navy wives must remain close!"

The Earl agreed with Lady Katherine, "Here, here, Kate. Well said." He laughed again.

"Lord Dawlting, I hope I am not presumptuous, but may I ask if you are an Admiral?"

"No, no, Anne. After I gained the rank of Commander in the Navy, I then moved into the Home Office. I presently advise the Navy on various matters. Admiral Crouch and Sir David and I go back a long way. You are good company, Miss Anne Turner. Please accept my best wishes for your wedding."

"Thank you, Lord Dawlting."

The Earl looked up and addressed Lord Fintelton, who was sitting further along on the opposite side of the table.

"Bless you, my Lord and Lady Jane, for bringing Anne and Emma along tonight. They are most handsome young ladies, and they have cheered me up no end. I am glad you are well, David. You and the Countess will honour Hannah and me if we are so fortunate to be included on Robert and Anne's wedding guest list, please?"

"I am glad my health allows me here, Cecil and assure you that you and your lovely wife will be on the guestlist, Sir unless you are unavoidably detained due to foreign affairs business. I understand how busy you are!"

"Capital, Capital, David. We shall look forward to the occasion. Next year, there will be more time as I will be joining Frank and standing down. We must have a schoolboy reunion and keep in contact. Some more wine here, please!"

The Earl then turned his attention to the other guest beside him and gave Anne the chance to catch up with Malcolm Smith sitting on her other side. He enquired after her family and was interested in the coming wedding of Marion and Thomas. Also, Anne shared a few words across the table with Mrs Sutherland.

Emma, sitting further down the table, was amazed at how Anne fitted in as if she belonged in this company always. She checked herself, knowing this was beneath her. Emma realised she should be glad for her future sister-in-law that she excelled here tonight. The thought was passing Emma's mind about what society she would enter when she married David Sopwith, whose class was that of a local country Doctor. Emma struggled with this ongoing issue. Love was more important than society, and she would make it so even if it were not. She could not imagine the future now without David.

Admiral Sutherland sitting beside Emma noticed how she seemed deep in thought and far away from the evening.

"Now Emma, meeting you tonight, Robert's sister, is most fortunate. He has mentioned you on several occasions. I understand your family is very close."

Miles away in her thoughts, Emma quickly refocused on the Admiral, responding, "Pardon me, Admiral, but I was miles away in my thoughts. Yes, Robert is very attentive and often seeks opportunities to attend family gatherings. He is a fine brother, one who will listen at any time. We miss him while he is at sea."

"Hopefully, he will be home soon. I expect a dispatch from him on my return."

"That is good news, indeed! Are you aware of where his ship is?"

"Unfortunately, not! He has been out of contact for the last few weeks, but we have a regular reporting system where he will send me updates by dispatch. The dispatch packet is due on Thursday. I'm sure all is going well. When are we to see you with a young fellow like Anne, Lady Emma?"

"I hope so in time Admiral."

"No one in particular on the horizon as yet?"

"I would be not true if I said there was no one, but it is early days. Perhaps by the end of the year. We shall see, but I am not in a great hurry. I enjoy my life at Fintelton, and the forthcoming marriage of Robert and Anne will keep the family busy. I think they are planning for the new year."

"I will keep that in mind when I decide on postings for next year. It would be good for Robert to have some leave for his wedding. I hope Anne understands how often a navy Captain is away?"

"I think she is learning quickly. She is an amazing girl. You understand that she is intimately involved in managing her father's businesses. She is very gifted with figures."

"I was not aware of that, although I have had a high opinion of her intelligence from the first time I met her at Greenwich. She will be a match for Robert. Anne will keep him on his toes. Where do you think they will settle?"

"I believe, Guildford. My brother Hugh is the heir, so Robert must make his own future. As Anne is much involved in her father's business, I think they will stay close so she may continue with that work. Fintelton will also be near, that being another advantage."

"Sounds a good plan. Now how is your father's health? I heard he had not been well."

Emma explained the health issues and was pleased as Admiral Sutherland introduced his wife. She warmed quickly to Amanda, and they continued a good conversation over dinner.

"If the ladies will adjourn with Lady Crouch, we men will have some port!"

As Anne followed Lady Jane and the other women into the drawing-room, she thought, 'So this is the society that Robert moves in.' She was unsure if she was ready for this yet and then wondered where Robert was and what he was doing. A sudden chill came over Anne as if a bitterly cold wind passed across her. She sensed he was in danger – she shuddered!

Emma noticed Anne's shudder. She put her arm around her and asked, "Are you cold, Anne?"

"No, not at all! I was thinking of Robert and felt a cold chill. I hope he is alright!"

"I'm sure he is! Admiral Sutherland told me he expects him in port either the week coming or the next. That is good news, is it not?"

"Yes, it is. That is good news, indeed!" But as Anne smiled and stayed strong, she remained unsettled about Robert. Underneath her confident, happy exterior, she prayed for his safety.

HMS Restless ...

Lieutenant Ham and the Master, Kevin Trotters, agreed on the course required for the mission's next stage. As they proceeded slowly into Loch Gruinart for the recovery of Captain Coombes and Sergeant Wait from their reconnaissance mission, Lieutenant Ham approached the captain, who was standing on the port side of the quarter-deck.

"Captain, we have plotted the course you requested. Would you inspect the chart, please?"

"Yes, Lieutenant."

Robert walked over to the chart table behind the helmsman. The three men traced the plotted course the captain requested. Given that they were now slowly moving towards the mouth of the loch, Trotters arranged a cover over the chart table so that observers would see no light from the shore. They must not be detected entering the bay.

Robert commented on the charted course, "This will allow us out tonight, out of sight of land, and then at Laggan Bay early tomorrow night."

"Yes, Sir. It gives us time for some easy tacks past Port Charlotte if needed. We should be outside the Loch around eight o'clock tomorrow night if this wind holds. It will be pitch dark by then."

"Good, now the recovery of Captain Coombes. The other cutter is on standby?"

"Yes, Sir. We will have both whalers in the water in the next few minutes. I have requested two additional armed marines in each boat for the pickup, Sir.

We should be at the rendezvous point in half an hour."

"Let us hope Coombes is there on time. I'm not keen on remaining here long. Once you pick him up, put up as much sail as you need, Ham. Let's move out of here quickly, please. No lights on deck until we are well out to sea. Carry on!"

Robert walked along the port side and watched as the crew organised the whalers for transfer over the side. The men worked in silence and were well disciplined in what they did. From the teamwork amongst the crew, it now appeared the traitors were all gone. He hoped that was the case, but he was not sure. Best not take any chances. He would brief Swanton with a backup plan just in case.

It was now around nine o'clock and pitch dark. The wind blew steadily in from the northwest at around fifteen knots, with regular rain squalls dousing *Restless* and keeping the decks wet. It would keep those ashore indoors tonight. Only the foolhardy or hard men would be out. He prayed they were all inside in their warm beds. Another rain squall came racing through, pelting the deck. Robert's mind drifted for a minute towards home and Anne. Where was she now, and what was she thinking? He missed her terribly and longed for their reunion. Perhaps there would be time for a visit down to the coast. How could anyone not have seen the sea? He was amazed by this.

"Whalers away, Sir."

Robert kicked himself. He allowed himself the luxury of drifting off in the middle of a critical operation. Immediately he refocused on all that was happening around him. The tension hit his body as if a plank hit him. Would Horace have found *Providence*?

"Thank you, Mr Ham."

They stood together on the port side, watching as the cutter delicately went into the darkness. The critical moment had come! In a matter of minutes, Robert would know if they were going into battle or not. Suddenly he was eager – he strained his eyes, searching for the whalers, but they were gone in the darkness. It was now a waiting game. All was quiet on the deck.

Ham watched two sailors on the port side, taking soundings. Quietly he checked the reported depth and then confirmed the ship's speed in knots. Ham and Trotters standing at the chart table, discussed how long till they brought her about. The plan was for a run up the Loch several hundred yards while the teams on the whalers checked depth. They would then turn and tow the whalers as they ran out of the Loch.

As the mouth of the Loch was in sight, Robert saw one of the whalers sprinting back towards them. Coming alongside, a midshipman jumped across and spoke with Lieutenant Ham. Ham then reported.

"Midshipman Collins reports that the Loch is too shallow for *Restless*, Sir."

"Thank you, Mr Ham. We shall patrol around the entrance then. Carry on."

Ham lost no time. "Mr Trotters have your men climb above, quietly, please! Make sure they understand no shouting."

"Aye, Sir."

Trotters scrambled along the main deck area and had words with all the sailors waiting for orders. Then in one move, they were off climbing towards their yard stations high above. The crew achieved the whole operation in complete silence.

They cruised for another seven minutes, then Ham moved behind the helmsman and quietly ordered *Restless* brought about slowly. Robert watched as his schooner turned one-hundred-and-eighty-degrees and commenced running out of the Loch. Trotters and Ham then worked together, finding the best tack for the outward journey.

Robert peered out from the ship's stern, checking if Horace was there. He could see a thin shape about two hundred yards behind them. Then he heard a faint yell, "Slow down, you navy bastards!"

It was Horace. Robert quickly moved over beside Ham and quietly ordered, "A slow full three-sixty turn Mr Ham. The cutter and ship's boat are behind us."

Lieutenant Ham looked up in surprise as he scoured the sea in the wrong direction.

"Aye, Sir. Mr Trotters, full three-sixty degree turn, please. Slowly."

That's what Robert liked about Ham. No questions asked. He responded immediately and then managed the new situation. Wondering how the cutter was behind them, Ham asked, "Perhaps the tide was stronger than we estimated, Sir?"

"No, I think you and Trotters were exactly right in your navigation Mr Ham. It's just that we are dealing with the army here. They are not used to dead reckoning. But we have them now – that's the important thing. Get them on board, please."

Lieutenant Ham was satisfied with the response from the captain. He was sure they were in the correct position, and wanted confirmation, given the boats were well behind them when he expected them ahead.

Within five minutes, Robert saw Horace's blackened body heave over the side, and then a big smile framed his face.

"She's there, Sir! Your hunch was dead right. Just down by Port Charlotte. Time for our battle plans."

"Good work, Captain. Good work. Let's get you below. You also Wait. Good work!"

Robert smiled. For the first time, he was ahead of the traitors. Now, Robert could surprise them. He prayed he would be in time for Foster and his men.

St James's Square …

It had been a late night at Admiral Couch's house, and the South home at St James's Square was quiet at ten the following day. Anne dressed and went down for breakfast, joining Emma. They were both excited about the shopping trip which would follow. The girls, thankful for the privacy, compared notes on the previous evening.

"Anne, you did so well last night. You must give me some pointers on making conversation. How do you find such a range of talking points? I was tongue-tied most of the evening. Imagine another Earl being there and all those Admirals. It seems Admiral Crouch has some important friends."

"When the Admiral introduced me, I was a bit overcome. For a few seconds, I was without words. Fortunately, the adrenaline kicked in, and the conversation flowed. I think the guest list would be handy before any other dinners. I was dumbfounded. I must have looked very out of place!"

"No, no, you were fine. I think we both carried it off. It would have been easier if Robert was with us."

"Yes, I was thinking the same thing. Shame on him for not being there and protecting us!"

They both giggled at this thought.

"I wonder where he is."

"Wherever it is, you can be sure he is in trouble. He always ends up in the hotspots. You heard about the smugglers in Spain he caught."

"No!" Anne was alarmed.

Emma told Anne as much as she knew about the incident and explained that was why the King knighted Robert. The Government had not advertised the occasion for diplomatic reasons, and it was kept quiet, but the family was pleased.

The Earl came into breakfast, took his seat, and greeted the girls.

"A wonderful night last night. Good that Cecil was there!"

Anne asked, "My Lord, how did you meet Lord Dawlting?"

"He was at boarding school with Frank and me. We are all old school buddies. A bit hard keeping up with Cecil, though. He was always off somewhere. I wouldn't have been surprised if he had entered politics and become Prime Minister. We all have our foibles, but he handles them quite well."

The girls looked at each other and smiled.

Emma spoke up, "Perhaps next time Father, you might warn us on who the other guests will be."

"No need, Emma; you girls did very well indeed last night. I think everyone was impressed."

Staines came in with some mail for the Earl and a note for Emma. Sir David checked the mail and found a letter with the Fintelton seal.

"Ah, here is a letter from Hugh. That is strange as he usually does not write much at all. Must be important."

Sir David opened the letter and read it aloud.

Fintelton Manor
East Harting
Sussex

The Right Honourable
The Earl of Fintelton
Harting House
St James's Square
St James's
London

Dear Father,
I hope your stay in London provides a pleasant change and this letter finds you enjoying a relaxing time.

I felt compelled that I should write a short note letting you know of some recent decisions I have made. As you know, I have been concerned about the decreasing income from the tenant farmers and the effect on the estate's future. I understand your concerns about these tenants' tenure, and I will lobby no further for any change on these tenancies.

We have signed grain contracts with Mr Jonathan Turner for the Spring harvest at a fair price. Mr Stem, our Estate Manager, has been briefed on this and will ensure the grain is harvested and made ready for the Turner Mill. I suggest that you provide Emma with an authorisation in addition to Mr Stem on this process. Mr Stem has copies of the signed contracts and will welcome Emma's assistance. He will also deal with the tenant farmer contracts.

May I also encourage discussions with Mr Stem about the sheep and ensure he arranges the shearing is complete before the end of autumn. Mr Stem is aware of the process of selling the wool. Let him do the negotiations and achieve the highest price.

There should be enough money for the estate expenses with the grain and the wool but little for any capital investments.

That being the case, I will now explore the other sources of income from our overseas estates. You have requested me to visit the Indies on several occasions and become familiar with our plantations there. With that in mind, I will be on a ship bound for Jamaica by the time you receive this letter. I write this letter from the deck of the good ship

'Frogmore', which sets sail tonight via Ireland, New York and then onto Jamaica.

On arrival in Kingston, I will call on the Governor and ensure all my documentation is correct before contacting our agents. I will set up a home at the largest plantation near Kingston and visit the others from there. After establishing income details and gaining some understanding of the workings of these plantations, I will contact the agents and commission valuations of each of the properties. I estimate this will take at least three months.

Once I return home, I will stay for a few weeks before visiting our estates in the north and Ireland. I am now concerned that I understand little of these estates and what contribution they are making.

I have estimated the complete Jamaican trip to take at least six months, if not more. The New York leg alone will be three or four weeks depending on the weather, and then three weeks onto Jamaica. I will write regularly informing you of my progress and what I find over there.

Would you please pass on my farewell to mother and Emma and my good wishes to Robert and Anne?

Your son
Hugh.

"I am surprised — Hugh sails for Jamaica. At last, he has taken notice of my advice. I think Hugh may be changing his ways. The next letter will tell us more."

Anne noticed that Emma had folded her letter and held it under the table.

"Father, we are off shopping. Perhaps you would advise Mother we will return for afternoon tea."

The Earl, hard of hearing and in a world of his own, continued reading his mail.

Emma sighed, "Staines, let Lady Jane know, please?"

"Certainly, Milady. Afternoon tea will be ready around four."

"Many thanks, Staines."

Emma smiled, and the girls were quickly off, making themselves ready before boarding the carriage. Once on their way, Emma passed Anne the letter.

"David Sopwith has written advising that he is now attending Thomas and Marion's wedding. He looks forward to my company. He will be staying with your family while here in London."

Anne looked up from the letter with a smile, "Perhaps you will marry David before I wed Robert, Emma?"

"Perhaps!"

Emma appeared distracted, "Now, Anne, I have not advised you, but we must attend a meeting before shopping at the attorney's offices, Manifold and Stout. I would ask that you join me as I will require your support. Robert requested I send the original of this letter to the Attorneys and seek a response from a Mr Michael Manifold. Robert believes that Mr Manifold is deceased, but evidently, our father believes he is alive and running the firm. I have made a booking for ten-thirty, so we shall see if Mr Manifold is still with us. We are running a little late, but I am sure they won't mind."

At the Attorney's office, a receptionist showed Emma and Anne into a large office, and a tall, middle-aged man in a dark suit introduced himself as Mr Evan Finchley.

"Welcome, Lady Emma. Would you please introduce your friend?"

"Certainly, Mr Finchley, this is Miss Anne Turner, my brother's fiancée. She is also a good friend of the family. You may speak freely in Miss Turner's presence."

Anne was amazed at the access Emma was allowing her. She was undecided if she was prepared for this access yet.

"Mr Finchley, I am enquiring about my brother's letter. I believe you would have received it some weeks ago. Due to his naval commitments, he authorised that I discuss the response with you. I have a copy of the original letter with me. I would appreciate it if you would discuss the response with me now?"

"Yes, Lady Emma, I have been expecting you and here is the response."

Mr Finchley passed across an envelope containing several pages. Emma read through the pages quickly.

Mr Finchley continued, "It is most detailed. Let me summarise. Firstly, let me say I think the Earl's dealings with us may indicate some health problems. We notified him about the passing of Mr Michael Manifold some three years ago; however, he continues addressing Mr Manifold in his letters. We are also concerned that he has not visited our offices for some five years.

Perhaps you would advise him of the changes. I am now the senior partner and have taken care of all his work since the demise of Mr Manifold.

Concerning the estates in Jamaica, Mr Manifold advised him that the cash flow from the estates commenced decreasing significantly some five years ago. From our understanding of the contracts, the income remitted here is far smaller than the contract stipulates. I have detailed the discrepancies in our response.

I would note that I and Mr Manifold, until his demise, have each month consistently sent your father letters for the last five years, notifying him of these issues but received no reply despite several reminder letters each year.

We believe the manager in the Indies may be skimming money off the surface and possibly defrauding the estate. However, without directions, we have not acted on this. It may be that you would search your father's records for our letters. I will have copies written and delivered if the originals are missing."

Emma took a deep breath, swallowed and then asked, "Please, did you contact my brother, Sir Hugh, seeking his assistance?"

"Yes, we did try by mail and messenger several times, but there was no reply. It seems he spends little time at the estate. At one point, I sent a junior attorney and stationed him in Petersfield for a week. He called at the manor each day. Unfortunately, when Sir Hugh finally appeared, he was intoxicated and incapable of making sense of anything. I am sorry we must advise you of this, but I am glad someone is looking into the situation.

By the way, we managed your father's investments for some years, and I advise that these are all sound and have grown well. The management has been prudent, and they remain substantial. I have attached a list for you."

Mr Finchley handed over a document detailing the investments.

"Thank you, Mr Finchley. The document is most helpful. By the way, my brother Hugh has recently embarked for Jamaica, intending an inspection of the plantations. Would you have any advice for him?"

"Lady Emma, given what I have previously explained, it is most unfortunate he missed the opportunity of meeting with us before departing. Jamaica is a frontier town, and His Majesty's navy must often enforce the Governor's authority. My advice would be that he tread very carefully. Who knows what is afoot over there! He should employ the services of a security assistant. I'm sure the Governor's aides will be of assistance once contacted."

"I shall write and inform Sir Hugh of the situation. Mr Finchley, I also understand that there is an estate in Scotland and one in Ireland. Are you familiar with these, and would you know who manages these estates?"

Mr Finchley looked at Emma as if she could not be serious. "Certainly, we are aware of them as we hold the titles here in this office. However, as for the management of the estates, our understanding was that the Earl took full responsibility. We hold no instructions for the management of the estates."

"I see. Thank you, Mr Finchley."

"Lady Emma, may I write and gather urgently the information you require from the estate managers?"

"Yes, that would be most helpful. I shall study the documents you have provided today with my brother Robert and be back in contact. Perhaps when available, you would advise me by letter about the details of the estates in Scotland and Ireland?"

"Certainly, Lady Emma. I am glad that you and your brother are now taking an interest in the management of the estate. There is much work needed!"

"Mr Finchley, just one further issue, please. In the list of the investments, I notice there are trust funds for my mother, my brother and myself. These amounts appear substantial. At what point in time would these trusts be released?"

"Lady Emma, as you are aware, the estate is entailed for the eldest son, being Sir Hugh. Your father, in his wisdom, wished a portion of his estate be made available for his wife and children who would not benefit from the entailment. The creation of the trusts is outside the reach of the entailment."

"I see, but when do the trusts become available?"

"This depends on the trust deed and your father's will. As you would understand, as an executor, I am not at liberty to discuss the will's details without direct instructions from your father. However, I may discuss the management of the trust. The trustees are your father, myself and the late Mr Manifold. Your father never replaced Mr Manifold despite our repeated requests.

The Trustees must comply with the trust deed, which gives explicit instructions that on his death, that is your father's death, or the marriage of either of the children, the funds held for that beneficiary will be released. Hence the answer is Lady Emma; the funds will be immediately available either at your father's death or your marriage."

"Thank you, Mr Finchley. It appears that my father took great care when he set up the trust structure."

"Yes, Milady. Some years ago, he was concerned that the entailment would leave your mother, your brother and yourself with nothing. So, he requested that we set up a structure where all his dependants would benefit in the event of his death. Indeed, he is a wise man, and we have used this structure now for several of our other clients."

"Thank you, Mr Finchley. Your advice has been most reassuring!"

"That is my pleasure, Lady Emma."

"Goodbye, Mr Finchley."

"Good day, Lady Emma, Miss Turner. It has been my pleasure."

The young ladies were assisted into the coach and set off for the shopping district. Anne being uncomfortable with the detail of her knowledge of the family's personal information, requested clarification from Emma.

"Emma, I value your friendship greatly, but should you be revealing so much of your family's financial affairs? Robert and I are only recently engaged. I am uncomfortable given such access."

"Anne, was it not you who advised me that I should take David into my confidence? I am putting my trust in you as you will soon be a member of this family, and it is best you understand the difficulties the family faces."

"I am honoured, Emma."

"I need your help, Anne! I am a baby about business, but you have far more experience than me. Robert spent time with me before he left for Portsmouth. He was aware of Hugh's activities and advised me that Father and Hugh were mismanaging the estate's affairs. He was correct. Mr Finchley has confirmed this, and Hugh has left without thorough preparations. I'm not sure when Robert will return. I need help, Anne! Will you help me, please?"

"Of course, I will, Emma, with all my heart."

"Good then, in that case, I think with the kind news received from Mr Finchley this morning about my trust, I feel somewhat relieved. I think we deserve a morning cup of tea together in the best shopping area in London!"

Anne also was ready for morning tea, "Where pray is this shopping area?"

"Piccadilly, of course!"

Chapter 26

At Greenwich ...

Marion became desperate as she watched her mother eating from a bowl of grapes but giving no signs of recognition. Small tears rolled down her cheeks as her mother, Jennifer Steele, drifted further away after weeks of gentle encouragement and many visits. Time was now short.

"I will be married next Saturday, Mother. Do you understand you are attending the wedding?"

Her mother made no response. Thomas could see that Marion was exhausted and that no answer would ever come. He edged forward and said, "It is time we left Marion. She seems content. Now is the best time; shall we go?"

"No, Thomas, I must make her understand. I must! It is so close now!"

A nurse standing near put her hand gently on Marion's shoulder and comforted her.

"Marion, it is the disease. She cannot understand anymore. She is like a child and does what she wants. It is perhaps best if you left now and came back next week."

Marion looked up with tears in her eyes and nodded in agreement. She slowly stood up, and as she backed away, Jennifer threw the entire bowl of grapes, hitting her on the chest. With stains all over the front of her blouse, she staggered backwards, breaking into tears. The nurse rushed in and restrained Jennifer from any further action.

Jennifer Steele laughed and then started screaming, "Go away. Leave me alone. I do not know you. I do not know any of you. Get out of my home. Leave me alone!"

Marion fell into Thomas's arms, crying bitterly. She longed for her mother's recognition, but she knew in her heart that it was hopeless. Her mother was gone. She was in a mindless world where she recognised no one. It was a tragedy for the family. Even Alexander Steele's sons now concluded she was better cared for in the asylum.

Thomas guided Marion out and assisted her into the carriage during a gap in the gentle rain. The Sunday morning proved busy, firstly attending the Greenwich church, where they took the opportunity of talking with Archdeacon Rufus and Mrs Felicity Handle over morning tea. Thomas and Marion were pleased to confirm the timing of the wedding rehearsal for five pm on Thursday evening. Next, they visited the asylum and spent nearly an hour with Mrs Steele. It was time for a retreat into the security of the McPherson home, where Marion could regather her spirits after this very emotive meeting with her mother.

"Come, Marion. A good lunch will help you settle your nerves. You have done as much as anyone could, Darling. No one doubts your devotion to your mother!" Thomas called out, "Drive on, please!"

Marion tearily looked out the coach window, knowing her dreams of recognition from her mother were in vain. She was unsure if she was happy or sad. One thing she did know was that next Saturday would be the most important day in her life, and she needed her emotions under control. If her mother attended, it would be chaos. Marion realised it was time for a decision. Jennifer Steele was unfit for any social gathering, and Marion must drop her demand that her mother attends the wedding.

Thomas was right. A good lunch would help!

Hamish McPherson arrived home on Sunday afternoon, spending the evening greeting family and Thomas, who came from Guildford the previous day. Hamish was comfortable with the wedding plans and briefed Thomas on his meetings with Jonathan in Reading.

Now he was back beside Marion; Thomas found himself quite cheery. As a couple, they seemed stronger together and found confidence for the week ahead. The invitation from James to visit Glasgow at the end of the honeymoon was exciting, and Hamish agreed this would be a good business opportunity for Thomas. Thomas could tour James's Glasgow brewery by mixing a little business with pleasure. He mused that perhaps he and Marjorie might join them for a few days in Scotland and discuss some business matters with James.

Marion and Thomas were keen on the idea and set about planning with Marjorie McPherson the timing of the meeting. It would be a great opportunity before Hamish fully involved Thomas in building the brewery. James owned a large house in Glasgow that would accommodate them all. Hamish and Marjorie were excited about the plan, and Marjorie commenced drafting a letter giving the details of their visit. She was sure James would welcome their company.

At dinner, Marion mentioned, "Now Thomas, I will visit Emma South and Anne in London at St James's Square on Tuesday. We will spend the time shopping; it will be a lovely day! I shall be back in time for dinner in the evening. I am sorry about leaving you all alone for the day. Lady Emma arranged the meeting well in advance, and I must honour it. After all, one does not receive invitations like that too often!"

Thomas smiled in agreement as Marjorie spoke up, "I think it is right that Lady Emma invites you. Anne will soon be your sister-in-law, and you have the acquaintance of Lady Emma, so it would be rude if they issued no invitation!"

"Mrs McPherson, I don't desire the invitation for social standing. I appreciate your thoughts which are most commendable in our society. Rather I accept the invitation because Anne, Emma and I are friends. I hope Megan Bassington will also be there. We shall be a happy party as we tour the shops."

Marjorie thought about Marion's comment and felt a tinge of criticism. She realised Marion required some education on the realities of their society, but in a kind way.

"I see, my Dear! Your belief in friendship is most worthy, and I hope it is fulfilled. My thoughts were on the advantages of having a friend such as Lady Emma South, the daughter of an Earl. She may introduce you and Thomas into higher society, perhaps even royalty in the future. You never know what can happen in our circles now. If you only knew how Hamish and I have struggled for acceptance with the English. Why coming from Scotland is not an advantage at all! It has been no easy road. You must take every advantage of the acquaintance in this world. That is the path to follow in English society."

There was a short silence, and Thomas smiled at Marjorie, showing his agreement. Marion suddenly understood that Marjorie was offended. She rushed across and knelt beside Marjorie's chair.

"Mrs McPherson, I would never criticise you. You must forgive me. I misunderstood what you meant. I hear what you say, and I will do as you ask. Please forgive me if I have offended you in any way."

Marjorie, now overcome by the genuineness of the apology, lifted the girl and hugged her.

"My Dear, I only crave what is best for you and Thomas. Life can be hard, and you will need every advantage within your reach. Lady Emma is a good acquaintance for you."

Thomas added, "Anne will be too. She will marry Robert, and he will progress in the navy."

"Yes, yes, in the navy. But Robert will not inherit the title. Lady Emma is better positioned, and that is where the advantage will come from." Marjorie was clear where her attention should be directed.

"Ah!" Thomas said and looked down, feeling somewhat insulted. Marion put her hand under the table and rubbed his thigh. She leaned over closer and whispered in his ear, "We can talk about this later. Change the subject!"

Thomas was not slow on the uptake and immediately engaged Mr McPherson in conversation.

"Mr McPherson? Do you have any reference material on brewing that I might read? It would be helpful in preparation for the new year, especially as I will be working full time on the new brewery once I return. Also, if you have the time, might we review the building plans?"

"Certainly, Thomas, good idea. We can visit the brewery together on Tuesday and spend the day there while Marion is away. What do you say?"

"Yes. That would be most helpful. Thank you, Sir."

Hamish smiled and continued with his dinner. An awkward five-minute lapse followed until Marjorie broke the silence, "Marion, the Turners arrive on Tuesday evening at their house in Greenwich. They will be here for dinner on Wednesday night. I hope you and Thomas have no plans as I would request that you both attend!"

"Thank you, Aunty. The dinner will be a wonderful opportunity before the wedding. Thank you for organising this. I assume my father and brothers are coming?"

"Yes, Alexander and the boys."

The mention of the dinner restarted the conversation. It appeared Marjorie had no wish for the difficulties to continue.

Later, when Marion and Thomas were alone in the drawing-room, they talked.

"I think she is insulted by not being invited. There is nothing I can do, as it is a gathering of Emma's friends. I am fortunate to be invited. She becomes upset so easily these days. I understand she is ageing, and everything must suit her. I yearn for our marriage Thomas and the freedom of our own home. After all, she is not my mother. I sometimes think that she feels she has power over me. I appreciate all she has done, but I want my own home."

"Marion, do not forget the amount of work Mrs McPherson has put in over the last few months organising this wedding. She has taken the place of your mother and done a wonderful job. We are in her debt. It will only be another week. We must finish here on good terms and show our appreciation as they have been kind indeed. My employment depends upon it so we must try hard. Do not worry! Soon you shall be mistress of your own house in Guildford."

Marion leaned over and kissed Thomas gently, "Come up to my bedroom tonight, Darling? I want you so much!"

"Not until after the wedding ceremony, my Dear! We will be thankful for it as I come from a very fertile line. Just think, you may be pregnant within three months. Within a few years, we shall have a family."

Marion hugged him, "As long as we can keep making love forever!"

Thomas agreed with this, "That would be nice! Perhaps I could come up with you tonight for a few minutes. But just a few minutes."

"Good boy Thomas!" Marion had a naughty but loveable look on her face.

At Guildford …

On Monday morning, three coaches parked at the front of the Turner household. Before the Turner's finished the loading, Clementine met Rosalind Nibley, Ethel's daughter, who arrived early with an old brown case containing her clothes.

Ethel left Rosalind with Clementine while she attended to the other servants ensuring the packing was complete.

"Where do you attend school?" Clementine was curious about this girl. The carriage Rosalind and Ethel were allocated offered more space than the one assigned for Clementine. Perhaps if the girl was friendly, their carriage might be preferable. She liked Ethel and found her a very fair and honest person. Perhaps her daughter was the same!

"The free church school at the local church. It is only free in the mornings, so I help with the sewing at my grandmother's in the afternoons."

"You sew!"

"Yes, everyone sews! Don't they?" Rosalind was surprised by Clementine's question.

"No one has ever taught me sewing! I struggle along by myself. Mother has been ill for over a year now, and there has never been anyone with the time!"

Rosalind thought about Clementine's confession. Perhaps this girl was honest with her. She was timid about saying too much; after all, this was the daughter of her mother's employer.

Clementine was interested but still not convinced. Rosalind appeared to be a nice girl, and she spoke and dressed well, like her mother. The dress and coat she wore were pretty.

Clementine, who was never afraid of voicing her opinion, posed a question, "Rosalind, if I came in your carriage, would you teach me some sewing?"

Rosalind, at first, thought it might be a trap. Who would attempt sewing in a moving coach? Then she saw the pleading glance on Clementine's face and realised she was asking her for more than sewing. Clementine was asking for friendship.

"Yes, I would. But it may be a little bumpy!"

Clementine smiled, "We can talk about sewing and practice in Ewell or Greenwich. It will be fun! How old are you?"

Rosalind, who was tentative but excited at joining her mother this morning, felt slightly less tense as the gesture of friendship was made. She smiled and replied, "I am thirteen. My birthday was on the second, the Thursday before last. That is a pretty dress you are wearing!"

"Thank you!" Clementine thought she might enjoy talking with Rosalind!

Jonathan Turner joined them at the third carriage, "Now Clementine, have you decided on which coach you will travel in?"

"Yes, Father. I will ride with Rosalind and Mrs Nibley. Rosalind and I will be sewing!"

Jonathan stood there, seeing both girls' wide, begging eyes pleading with him. He could see no harm in this.

"Very well!"

He tipped his hat and checked with Ethel and Aggie as the coachmen loaded the final chest. The group of three carriages was soon on their way.

Late that evening at the pub in Ewell, Jonathan and his brother Richard took the opportunity of talking privately.

"Eleanora looks well, Jonathan! Is she on some new powder or found a new cure?"

"It is a funny thing, Richard. Some days she is good, and others, you would swear she was at death's door. When it occurs, it is not comforting, but then she regains her strength. I am not sure how the baby survives, but it happens. It is pleasing that she appears so well after such a long day on the coach."

"Let's hope this continues."

"Amen, Brother! Now, where are you at with your plans for South Africa?"

"All the paperwork is complete, and the land transfers into my name are complete. I have confirmed the transport of the livestock, and they will follow two weeks after we leave in February. The time with you at Christmas will be a welcome break. Oliver and Harry will come too, as they have found replacements. Katherine will come with us, of course."

"The preparations appear complete! You have left wills with an attorney?"

"Yes, I took your advice and used Mr Wood in Guildford, and you, Oliver and Hary are the executors. Otherwise, all is complete. I will keep working with Oliver and Harry in the pubs until February; then, we embark from Southampton."

"Richard, you recall our discussion that once you are established, William might join you?"

"Jonathan, the boy is only six years old!"

"Nearly seven now! I find him most vexing, Richard. You know of my temper! I fear that I will injure the boy in the future. Some months ago, I lost control and strapped him. The results might have been far worse if not for our doctor arriving and restraining me. It was most embarrassing. My rage was so consuming I was unaware of what I was doing. It seems that William and

I grate on each other. I must find a solution."

"I am not sure South Africa is the best solution. Why not a boarding school in England? That's what other parents do!"

"Yes, they do, but the child returns home regularly for holidays. I need him far away for some time. I will have him accompanied when I send him. I understand the trip is long, so I will wait till you establish yourself. Let me know when you are ready. I must do this, Richard, and keep both William and myself safe. For the time being, let us keep this confidential between ourselves."

Richard considered Jonathan's expression. He mused that Jonathan's proposal was in jest when first suggested. He now saw the determination in his face. Sending his flesh and blood so far away at such an early age was criminal! A boy belonged at home with his mother at least until twelve. What effect would it have on William? He feared for the boy's wellbeing, wondering what state of mind his brother was in, punishing him like this. Surely, Eleanora would never agree?

"For the time being, but you must promise me, Jonathan, that you discuss this fully with Eleanora before you set out on this course. I will not take the blame here. It is your decision and yours alone!"

"You have my word on that!"

"Good, now let's have another scotch."

"Just one other thing, Richard. Eleanora is concerned about Katherine being transported overseas at her stage of life. With marriages occurring and new connections in our family, there will be opportunities here if she remains in England. Would you and Sarah consider her residing with us? Both the girls and Eleanora have suggested this. I am for it as well. For a boy, it is different but a tender girl of her age, Richard. Would you discuss it with Sarah and let us know? We are concerned for her."

Richard put his hand down from the scotch bottle and tapped his fingers on his glass. He found Jonathan a complex mystery. On the one hand, he thought nothing of casting his son aside, and on the other, he showed much compassion for Katherine. The prospect of Katherine living in South Africa worried him as well. The significance was that Sarah, too, might remain in England if her daughter did not come. There was a strong bond between mother and daughter.

"I will discuss it with her. But I warn you that Sarah would find it hard to separate from her daughter. She may even decide to stay with one of the boys rather than leave Katherine. I would like Sarah with me in Africa, particularly if William is coming later. I will consider it, Jonathan and discuss it with Sarah. Now, what about that drink."

The butler opened the drawing-room door and announced, "My Lady, Miss Megan Bassington!"

"Megan, welcome, Dear! We were not expecting you until tomorrow."

"My sincerest apologies Lady Jane, my father's commitments today and tomorrow only allowed the one opportunity when I might commandeer the coach. As it was this afternoon, I took the liberty of assuming accommodation overnight and arrived early. My apologies again, but I am eager to join Emma, Anne, and Marion tomorrow for shopping. My chest remains in the coach as I was unsure if the accommodation would be available."

"That is quite acceptable, Megan, as we have plenty of room here. You are very welcome. Emma will have Staines take care of the luggage. Now come in and join us, and I will ring for tea."

Emma arranged a room as Lady Jane and Anne welcomed Megan. The discussion then focused on Neville and Bethany's honeymoon.

"Now tell me, Anne, when do Neville and Bethany return?"

"My Lady, I believe they will arrive any day and be in Greenwich for the wedding this Saturday coming."

"I hope they stay on for a few days. Their stories will be fascinating. We shall have dinner and hear all about their travels on the continent. Such a romantic start!"

"I think, my Lady, they will be here until the Wednesday next, and Robert also so that it may be possible. I am sure the McPhersons would be delighted in making the acquaintance of His Lordship and yourself. Perhaps they may attend as well?" Anne was keen that Marjorie McPherson was fully aware of her engagement. She found Marjorie's matchmaking most disagreeable. This would end it.

Lady Jane was quick on the uptake, "Now Anne, are they the brewing family? We have not had the pleasure, but I would welcome it. I shall write today and invite everyone for Tuesday evening. I'm sure Lord Fintelton will discuss at length with your father the quality of the estate's grain."

"You are too kind, my Lady. I am sure your kind invitation will overjoy the McPhersons!"

From her long experience in society, Lady Jane was not without sources of information. She was also eager to further her own daughter's happiness if possible.

"Now I have heard that Dr Sopwith will attend the wedding and reside with your family Anne. I thought I might invite the young Doctor as well. He has shown so much care for the Earl. I would only do this if you, Emma, are not ill at ease with such a request. I know you and the Doctor parted not on the best terms when he last visited Fintelton."

Emma sat there tensely, not answering at first. She wondered if her mother was fishing for anything further that had transpired between the couple. Despite their intimate meeting while Emma stayed with the Turners, there was no proposal yet. Seeing Emma's possible embarrassment, Anne defended her, "That would be lovely, Lady Jane. Doctor Sopwith is such a nice young man, and I'm sure Emma would love having him attend!"

After giving Anne a slight glare, Emma quietly replied, "That would be agreeable, Mother. I should welcome the chance of making Doctor Sopwith's acquaintance again."

Megan Bassington, being a journalist, was quite alert and saw the look Emma gave Anne. Megan wondered if there was an understanding. She inquired, "Who is this, Doctor Sopwith?"

"Why Megan, he is your brother's partner in the medical practice at Guildford."

"Of course! My apologies Anne, now I recall. Neville did tell me about him."

Megan looked over at Emma, who was now blushing.

"I was unaware you were acquainted with Dr Sopwith, Emma."

"Only because he is our family doctor, Megan."

Anne joined in, "Doctor Sopwith has a sister in Ireland arriving for Christmas. We have invited them for Christmas lunch so we might meet her, and perhaps she might attend church with us and come for a walk in the afternoon."

Emma looked up. "Now it is I who has forgotten. I do not recall this, Anne."

"You will recall him helping William and Simeon with a model boat. The three of them are having such fun. I have never seen Doctor Sopwith smile so much. During one of our family outings at the river, he happened upon us and told me about his sister and that she was travelling from Ireland. So, I thought they should not spend Christmas alone. I invited David and Victoria for Christmas."

Lady Jane carefully listened, "That is very kind of you, Anne. I'm sure the doctor and his sister will be most grateful for that."

Megan added, "I'm surprised he did not visit his estates in Ireland rather than have his sister travel alone over here."

There was a short silence as Lady Jane, Emma, and Anne digested this comment.

Lady Jane enquired, "Megan, what do you mean, his estates?"

"I thought you were all aware that his parents and brother died. He only has his sister left."

"Yes, but we thought that his sister inherited the estates?" Lady Jane was quite specific.

Megan looked at them and then smiled. "No, not at all! I see! He is a quiet one! Neville explained that David Sopwith is a good six years older than his sister. When his brother and parents died, he inherited two large Irish estates and a considerable fortune as well. He is the Trustee and guardian of his sister, who lives at the larger estate with an appointed guardian. I understand that the sister also inherited a fortune. He is not desirous of many people knowing about this so I may have spoken out of turn. Perhaps we should keep this in confidence, please. But now I have, as you would say, 'spilled the beans!' He is one of the richest men in England. For my brother's sake, would you all keep this confidential?"

"Certainly, Megan." Lady Jane replied with a slight smile on her face.

Emma sat there in disbelief. Her expectations were that if David proposed, she would live in reduced circumstances as a country doctor's wife. She would suffer much so they could make their life together. When David asked her father for her hand in marriage, her main concern was what issues he would raise! But now, with this information, a new perspective came into view for her future life.

Anne looked at Emma and smiled, then started giggling. Emma looked at Anne, blushed and laughed as well. Megan looked at them both and wondered why they were giggling. Lady Jane could not resist having a little smile on her face for some time after the conversation ended.

HMS Restless …

The strong north-westerly whipped up the seas, with white caps stretching into the darkness. The weather was perfect, and *Restless* remained unnoticed as she slowly tacked her way into the bay. At one in the morning, Robert was content with their progress. With small particles of ice now forming on the rigging, the conditions meant even the hardiest would seek shelter tonight. The tricky part would be at the head of the bay, where it was more sheltered. Here long tacks close to the wind should allow sufficient headway. Once near Port Charlotte, a track along the far side of the loch may keep them undetected. If they could find *Providence* and take her, the getaway would be easy with this north-westerly.

"Horace, are the men ready?"

"Yes, Sir. Ready and willing!"

"Camouflage on?"

"Aye, but I would rather have them in their uniforms, Sir."

"This is where we learn from the Americans, Horace. The red uniform stands out like a red rag to a bull. The aim is a surprise, so we must be almost on them before commencing the action."

"Sounds easy, Robert, but it will be a close thing, especially if *Providence* is well manned, which I expect she will be."

"I, too, expect the ship will have sentries, but we may employ whatever force needed. The Admiral insisted we may kill them all if required. We show no mercy here. We go in and take that ship quickly. The capture will be a lesson that we will retaliate if they murder our people."

"Aye, Sir. But what if they have not killed the crew. Should we not show some mercy. Otherwise, we will be no better than them. If they surrender, Sir, we must take prisoners. We must have some honour."

"We have our orders, Horace. Our priority is winning the ship back first. Once we have prisoners, then we will decide on their fate. Now about the first attack, Swanton is an excellent shot, so I think we should take him with us in our boat. If you and I handle the crossbows, he can assist us once the alarm goes up."

"Why the crossbows?"

"They provide the perfect shooting system in a stealthy attack. The crossbows make no noise, and if we hit them in the right place, they will not make a noise except for the body dropping on the deck. I would be surprised if the night watch were more than four men and an officer. First, we take these men out with the crossbows and then the marines storm the ship. We position the two whalers alongside *Providence*, and our gig, say fifty yards off the ship, where we can gain a good aim. We take out the sentries silently, and our men swarm aboard. Then we go in with our gig, followed by Ham in *Restless*. The rest of the crew will then board and finish off the job."

Horace thought about this carefully, with his hand rubbing over his chin.

"So, we load the whalers with men and have them alongside *Providence* as we pick off the frigate's security detail."

"Yes. The marines could climb the sides and position themselves below the rail before we use our crossbows if that is preferable, but it must be silent!"

"That's better! I was worried the break between knocking out the sentries and when we come aboard may be long enough for them to regroup."

"Yes, I thought about this too. We must attack with complete surprise. We give them no chance of regrouping. Once *Restless* is alongside, we will easily outnumber them."

Lieutenant Ham approached, "Lights of Port Charlotte on the starboard, Sir, but there is no sign of *Providence*."

"That is good, Mr Ham. That means they can't see us. I would guess that the frigate will be between half a mile to a mile past Port Charlotte. We will see her when we are closer. Now you have the plan clear in your mind?"

"Yes, Sir, stand-off downwind at about five hundred yards. Let your gig and the other two whalers go in first. Once you are on board, we come in fast, then board. If there is an attack from the shore, we use a broadside and subdue them."

"Good. Now Mr Ham, shorten the tacks and keep wide from Port Charlotte. Then check every man is blackened. I do not want any reflections tonight. Once you have checked the men, lower the boats, ready for loading. Very quietly, please!"

Ham rushed off, relaying his orders into action. The men were all moving boldly, fuelled by a shot of rum and their newfound confidence in their Captain. They were eager for action. Robert could feel the high morale and the excitement on their faces, and he knew they supported him. They would win this action.

Horace moved beside him and said, "I can't see the ship. I hope she is still there."

"She will be there! Give it ten more minutes as we slip past Port Charlotte. Then she will be in sight. My wish is the original crew is still on board and locked below. We will need the extra hands to man *Providence*. The crew on *Restless* is barely enough to operate both ships."

"I wouldn't count on them all being there."

"What else would they have done with them?"

"Either recruited them or killed them!"

Robert did not answer this. He preferred his first thought. He paced the deck repeatedly as they quietly tacked the ship up against the north-westerly. Swanton came out with Robert's cape and two hot cups of chocolate. The night became colder as the spray flew across the deck, driven by the wind, turning to ice. The hot chocolate gave them a bit of warmth.

"Thank you, Michael. See if the cook can rustle up the same for the men. We still have time."

"Already done, Sir. Just give the order."

Robert smiled, "Hot Chocolate for the men, please, Mr Swanton!"

With that, Swanton nodded and was off. Robert could soon see the men taking delight in the sweet, warm drink as the icy spray whirled around them and through the rigging.

A dull shout came from the lookout above, "Ship ahead!"

"I knew she would still be there. Here we go, Horace! Good luck. We either bring this off, or we die together, eh!"

"Let's take them apart, Sir!"

"Good man. Into the gig then."

The wind and chop were knocking the whalers around severely, but they settled as men climbed down, taking their positions. Once loaded, they were cast off and drifted astern until the long towing ropes tightened. Once in place, Lieutenant Ham completed the tacks slowly so the whalers could maintain their position.

Ham brought *Restless* onto the five-hundred-yard mark with precision, then turned into the wind, this being the signal for releasing the whalers. It was bitterly cold, and the men enjoyed the warming effect of the physical exercise pulling towards *Providence*. As Robert expected, the wind was dropping as they neared the lee side of the captured ship. The water was calming, allowing them to better aim with their crossbows.

The patchy cloud cover meant each time the moon broke through, Robert could clearly see the enemy camp in the distance. He moved closer, "Horace, we must move fast – I don't like how easily they can see us from the shore."

The Irish had set up camp around three low buildings surrounded by twenty or so tents. Several carts were apparent, but it appeared the buildings might be stables lodging horses and equipment. There were ten whalers and various other small boats moored against the shore. Robert was surprised by the camp's size – a substantial force lay there, and an unknown number stationed on the ship. Robert reflected that the rebellion appeared far more organised than Admiral Crouch may be aware. Thankfully, no movement or light appeared around the camp. They must be asleep!

Horace was also considering the camp.

"There may be well over a hundred of them, Sir. If they come at us from the shore, we are in for a fight."

Robert nodded as he quickly assessed the camp, "Ham has orders for grapeshot if they try anything like that. Disregard the shore for now. Let's take the ship!"

The gig that Robert and Horace were in edged ahead of the other whalers and moved directly towards the captured frigate. At two hundred yards, Robert started picking out the detail. At least two men, perhaps four, patrolled around the ship. They must be sentries. He could not make out any lookouts up the masts. The news was good, as it appeared they were not expecting company.

At one hundred yards out, they could see four sentries. A low glow came from the Captain's cabin at the stern, where more sentries might be sheltering from the icy cold wind. Probably at this time of night, they were fortifying themselves with a bit of rum or scotch. Robert hoped they were drinking lots of the stuff and were stupidly drunk.

Horace put down his telescope, "There is something funny about the deck. It seems piled high with cargo."

Robert was surprised by this. He lifted his telescope and saw large piles covered with tarpaulins along the deck.

"Must be some supplies for Ireland. Anyway, it will give us more cover as we get on deck! "

Robert signalled for the other two whalers, each with twenty marines on board, to move alongside the ship. One whaler would go around upwind and the other downwind. Once they were in position and had a few men halfway up the side, Robert and Horace would let loose with the crossbows.

The whalers edged in slowly, not showing any sudden movement. The wind blew harder, white caps running down the frigate's side as she pulled hard on the anchor chain.

"They are in place!"

Robert's gig was now less than fifty yards from the ship with a clear view of the four sentries. Each sentry held a musket and used oilskins for protection against the cold. They looked awkward as they stamped around the deck, keeping warm. Then an almighty gust of wind and rain came through, followed by a light falling of snow. The snowfall kept increasing, but it was light. The falling snow attracted the sentries' attention.

Robert murmured, "Perfect, they are watching the snowfall."

One of the sentries called out, and four more sentries came on deck but without their muskets. They started dancing around, grasping at the snowflakes falling everywhere.

Horace quietly said as he let loose the first arrow, "Goodnight, Buddy!" Robert followed quickly and watched as the arrows streaked across the water at their targets. The sentries at the ship's bow never knew what hit them, with each arrow penetrating their skulls. The short, deadly shafts struck without noise, undetected by the dancing men at the stern end of the ship, shouting about the snow.

The next two arrows were ready within ten seconds, and Horace aimed first. Robert noticed one of the sentries calling out towards the bow. He aimed at this man, quickly following Horace, letting the arrow free. The arrow hit the man in the side of his back near the heart. He went down wailing but was soon quiet. Horace's arrow hit the rearmost sentry once again in the head.

The four remaining sentries turned in horror as the two men fell. Horace quickly let another arrow loose and hit a sentry who was peering down in horror at a dead man. It was unclear where the arrow hit the man, but Horace was sure it fell below head level. Robert was aiming when the remaining three sentries ducked below the railings.

Robert yelled at Swanton, "Pick them off!" Swanton could see one face peering out from a gap under the ship's rail below the rigging. Swanton squeezed the trigger, firing the musket with a wham, and the sentry's face was blown apart. A marine handed the sergeant another loaded musket. He quickly aimed and fired, dropping a sentry running for the hatch. That left one sentry unhurt. To date, there was no returning fire that suited the attack well. Horace cupping his hands, yelled, "Marines on board." Instantly the marines responded, pouring over the rails onto the deck and swarming around the last remaining sentry. There was a shot, quickly followed by several more shots.

"Quick men, get us alongside!"

The sailors pulled hard, and the cutter lurched forward towards *Providence*. Robert turned towards the tents on the shoreline and could see frantic movement commencing. The musket fire would have woken the heaviest sleeper, which meant danger.

As they reached the frigate, Robert noticed *Restless* coming near but passing between *Providence* and the enemy camp. He flinched from the noise of a broadside strafing the shoreline. Ham must have seen the swarm of men gathering into boats. Quickly positioning the schooner, he hit the shoreline with a broadside of twelve canons. It was deadly accurate, Robert noticing several of the whalers sunk or damaged and men dragging others back ashore. While some whalers continued, many men were now running towards the buildings.

Followed by Horace, Robert quickly swung himself onto the deck. Lieutenant White approached, shouting, "All clear on deck, Sir." Robert noticed the corpses of several men. He also saw one marine down badly injured from a gunshot wound. Robert called, "Mr White is that man, alright?"

"Wounded arm, Captain. We have applied a tourniquet. He will survive."

"Good. Did you find out anything from the sentry who was still alive?"

"No, Sir, he refused."

"Swanton, see what you can get out of him. Quickly man!"

"Aye, Sir."

As Robert heard screaming from the prisoner, he commanded White, "Get a squad and load a canon with grapeshot, then blast those boats approaching."

"Aye, Sir!"

"There are men below, Sir. In the hold!" Swanton did not smile as he spoke. Robert saw that blood covered Swanton's hands.

"Horace, I want a search party down there straight away. Make sure they watch out for any traps. See if they can find anyone."

Horace screamed, "Sergeant, Wait, lead the search party below. Quickly man, as we have little time. We must be out of this bay before light."

Robert looked around, assessing the situation. Then a cannon boomed off, and grapeshot cut through the boats approaching. The cannon blast sunk two, and one limped around back toward shore.

"Good shot, men. That gives us a bit more time!" He knew there would be no more reinforcements before *Restless* came alongside. They could not wait. Time was critical.

"Mr Trotters, get the men you have up the mainmast, prepare the mainsail and the main topsail. Then assemble the marines around the capstan and get that anchor up! We are still within musket range. They may have canons on the shoreline. Let me know when you are ready. We will help with the capstan."

"Aye, Aye, Sir." Trotters loved action and a Captain who was in the thick of it.

The first thing Horace did was check under the tarpaulins. He found large piles of firewood covered the deck — tons of it.

"Look at this, Robert – piles of firewood!"

"The Bastards! They were preparing *Providence* as a fire ship. They would set our fleet on fire, a public relations nightmare! Once at sea, it all goes over the side."

Wham! A cannon blast came from the shore. It sounded like a six-pound carronade. Then a ball flew well above the deck, pounding into the sea fifty yards beyond the ship.

"Damn," said Robert. "They have at least one canon. I hope Lieutenant Ham heard that." He strained his eyes, looking for *Restless*, but there was no sign of her. The darkness and the sea spray were more intense, and the snow became heavier.

Wham. Another cannon fired further down the shoreline, but this ball fell two hundred yards away. A spout of water towered into the air as the ball dug in angrily.

Horace laughed as he saw the inaccuracy of the shot, "They haven't a clue!"

Wham! This time a larger cannon fired, the ball hitting the water just behind the stern, creating a colossal waterspout. The smile had disappeared from Horace's face as he yelled, "Marines, get this capstan going. We are getting the hell out of here!"

Yells of agreement greeted Horace's order, with Robert and Trotters joining twenty men pushing the capstan around hard. At first, the capstan moved slowly, and then the pace increased. Robert felt the anchor let go. He grabbed Trotters and dragged him back beside the helm.

"Trotters, get that mainsail out quickly if you can."

Trotters screamed at his men above, "Let go, mainsail."

Instantly the mainsail appeared, and Robert turned the helm as the wind filled the sail, and *Providence* edged around, turning downwind. The anchor was coming in too slowly, but the Marines were gaining pace.

Wham! Wham! Two more shots from the shore, but this time the frigate took a hit on the starboard bowsprit. Splinters flew everywhere, one unlucky marine struck by a two-foot splinter in his thigh. The man went down on his back, gasping in pain.

Robert yelled, "Get him below. Everyone keep your heads down."

Trotters yelled, "Away, Topsail."

As another sail fell and burst open, filled by the strong north-westerly wind, immediately Robert felt her gaining speed, perhaps three knots now. Then an almighty roar came from beside them as *Restless* passed their starboard side, tacking back up the bay and let a full broadside off at the bank. Once again, Ham used grapeshot with devastating effect. The guns on the shore lay quiet, almost afraid that there would be another broadside. Robert saw many bodies lying among the canon mounts ashore.

"Sir, we have found survivors of the crew below. We think one is Captain Foster. It is not a pretty sight, Sir."

Robert responded, "Thank you, Sergeant Wait! Trotters, get a few more sails up if you can on the foremast. I must go below for a moment."

"Aye, Sir."

"Horace, get that anchor up out of the water!"

Horace grimaced as the sweat poured down his face.

As he went below, he heard Trotters yelling out, "Foresail, let go." Once again, he felt the increase in the way as *Providence* headed towards the sea.

Deep in the hull, a group of more than twenty-five men lay in miserable conditions. Further along the hull, five dead sailors were heaped in a pile. The survivors were chained together and lay in their faeces. The smell was horrible, and the men seemed like lifeless skeletons, but Robert could see they were moving.

Robert and another sailor moved among them with a pail of water, giving them a fresh drink. They sucked desperately at the water. One sailor croaked in a weary, faint voice, "Sir, Sir?"

Robert went down on one knee, recognising Marsden, one of his gun crew captains, when he served on *Providence*. He put his ear close and said, "How are you, Marsden?".

"Sir, they murdered all the officers except the captain!" He gasped for air. "The rest of the crew joined up with the traitors or were shot. They have been starving us. We knew you would come, Sir! We knew our Robbie would come!"

He patted the sailor on the shoulder and gave him a drink. The man coughed as he gulped the water down. Then Robert stood up and addressed them.

"Gentlemen, I am surprised to find you looking so well. You will be pleased to know that His Majesty's Ship *Restless* has retaken HMS *Providence*, and we sail for Portsmouth at once. You will be taken above, cleaned up and fed." There was a soft cheer and coughing from the men who could hardly raise their heads. It was a pitiful sight. It was apparent that the Irish were starving them.

"Gentlemen, my name is Commander Sir Robert South. I am taking acting command of this ship on behalf of Captain Foster. Please follow this order – from now on, no one Jack Tar of this crew shall die! You shall have the best of care."

Lieutenant White noticed the reflection of candlelight in a tear running down Sir Robert's cheek as he said these last few words.

'Huntley', Greenwich …

On Tuesday evening, the Turners arrived at Greenwich and settled into their large home rented for the next week and a half. The boys rushed inside and faced a rather large man dressed in livery who blocked their path, "And who might you be?"

William spoke up as Simeon was still thinking about the big man's uniform.

"I am William Turner, and this is my brother Simeon Turner. We will be staying here."

In a booming voice, the large man addressed them. "Young Turner gentlemen, I am glad we have met. Welcome to 'Huntley', which is the name of this house. My name is Mr Charles Boot, and I am the Butler. You may call me Mr Boot! I control all the servants in the house, including those who have accompanied you. Now I assume you, young gentlemen, are exploring the residence. I would ask that you stroll, please and not knock anything over. Please note that the house furnishings have been readied for your family and will not be disturbed. Your bedroom is number five on the first floor. We will have a more detailed discussion later – now on your way, gentlemen, quietly, please."

The boys, with their mouths open, nodded in awe. They decided they should not trifle with Mr Charles Boot. Quietly they walked away towards the staircase.

"He is a big man, isn't he?" Simeon whispered.

"Yes, I think we better keep on his right side. He looks like he could hand out a real beating!"

As the boys stood before the staircase, they were surprised at how large the house was. There were eight bedrooms on the first floor and two on the ground floor. They knew the house had a second floor, but the staircase finished on the first floor. Once out of sight of Mr Boot, the boys rushed upstairs and found bedroom number five. It was large with three beds, a closet and plenty of chairs and a sofa. There was a fine view out the windows onto the park across the street.

Having seen their bedroom, they continued their exploration. William thought, 'I wonder if there is a lookout platform on the roof?'

Miss Mary Troath kindly directed the Turner staff in through the back entrance, with Clementine accompanying Ethel and Rosalind as they entered the downstairs area. Having finished introductions with the family upstairs, the butler now stood at the head of the servants' dining table. There were a couple of extra footmen in livery, three maids and an assistant cook for Mrs Jennings.

Mr Boot found Ethel and kindly asked if she could gather the staff around the table. Clementine was still talking with Rosalind when Mr Boot commenced his briefing in a booming but kind voice. She looked up in fright.

"Welcome everybody to 'Huntley'. The house is rented out for special occasions while families visit Greenwich. It has been in the Huntley family for generations, and they use it occasionally. However, mostly it is rented out. We welcome the Turner family from Guildford, and their staff, here for the next week and a half.

During your stay, please address me as Mr Boot. Our acting Housekeeper will be Mrs Ethel Nibley, from Guildford, and I will be talking with her after this meeting. Mrs Jennings, I understand you will be head cook. Mrs Smythe, our cook, will be your assistant during your stay here.

Now the dinner for tonight will be served at seven-thirty as requested by Mrs Turner. Staff will meet here at five-thirty for their dinner. Staff dinner will finish at six o'clock, after which the ladies will be expecting their maid's assistance. I will assign the footmen's duties later. Please be punctual as we commence our programme this evening.

Mrs Nibley, Mrs Turner advised me of one daughter staying with you, not two? Your daughter is welcome in the kitchen but must remain either downstairs or in the servants' rooms on the second floor. If you would explain, please? Now, who is this other young lady with you?"

"This is Miss Clementine Turner, Mr Boot."

"I must apologise, Miss Turner. I thought you would be upstairs."

"I travelled with Rosalind on the coach. We are friends. I would ask if Rosalind could visit me upstairs at times as she is helping me with my sewing?"

"We shall arrange that, Miss Turner. Please, Mary will take you upstairs. Your bedroom is number six beside your brother's room. Thank you, Miss Turner."

Clementine felt obliged and followed the maid, Mary, and waved goodbye to Rosalind as she walked towards the stairs.

Eleanora Turner feeling quite tired after the long trip, stood at the foot of the staircase, glad she need not climb them. Their bedroom was on the ground floor, carefully positioned at the rear of the house, away from the main rooms. Jonathan would use an adjoining room to not disturb her in the evenings. To assist Eleanora's rest, Jonathan, thinking ahead, requested details of Nanny Jones from the McPhersons. He was impressed with her care for William on their previous visit. Nanny Jones appeared from downstairs.

"Good day, Mr and Mrs Turner. I am Nanny Jones. I am sure William has told you about me. We spent much time together at the McPhersons."

Eleanora said, "It is a pleasure, Miss Jones. You will have a few more this time. William, Simeon, Clementine, Madeline and Marcia. They are a handful, so please make us aware if you need help. My lady's maid, Mrs Ethel Nibley, who will be acting as Housekeeper here, has brought her daughter, Rosalind. She may act as your assistant if required."

"I would much appreciate that, Mrs Turner."

"Also, our daughter Clementine is nearly fourteen and now out of school. She may assist with the childminding also. The main requirement is dressing them, ready for the wedding by about two in the afternoon. The coaches will depart for the church then. Please, you will attend as well, keeping an eye on them. It will be a grand occasion."

"It will be a pleasure, Mrs Turner. Now I will just go and meet with the Butler, Mr Boot, and find my room and unpack. I'm sure the children are exploring the house at present. It is a grand house!"

"Yes, far grander than our house in Guildford."

'Harting' House, St James Square, London ...

After Megan Bassington arrived on Monday afternoon, Anne found that she made a point of dominating Emma's time. Anne decided not to interfere. Relief came in the evening when, at dinner, Megan spent much time talking with the Earl and Lady Jane about her time in New York. They were very interested in how the relationship between the American colonies and Great Britain was thawing. This discussion allowed Emma and Anne the opportunity for a conversation of their own.

"Anne, why did you not tell me David was a man of means?"

"Because I was unaware! I know he loves you very much and was hurt and confused when you dismissed him from Fintelton. Perhaps, it is better that I did not know, and you also presumed he was not a man of means."

"Yes, perhaps it is. I would take David without any fortune. We are of a common understanding now."

"Has he proposed?"

Before she answered, Emma, thought about that question, "He has told me he loves me, but he has not proposed yet."

"That is nearly a proposal, but I agree you need the real thing before he asks your father. I demanded that of Robert, and he did it with flying colours. I wonder where Robert is."

Anne felt a cold chill down her back again and imagined Robert was in danger. She became unsettled and shivered.

Emma noticed the worried look. "Anne, the Admiral told me he expected Robert home soon. Who knows it could be today? Perhaps he will make the wedding."

"I doubt that. There has been no letter in two weeks. Some action must be happening! The Earl said it was an important mission. I hope it is not so important that it leads him into danger."

"We shall see in time."

"Emma, now that we know David is coming, do you think he will propose this time?"

"I hope so. I would like it announced rather than a secret we two must keep."

"I will see him probably on Wednesday when I join my family. Perhaps I could give him a hint or two."

Anne gave a naughty little laugh, and Emma's face broke into a wide smile.

"If you feel you know him well enough, please do. I would appreciate it. All we need is somewhere we can meet."

"He knows your family. I am sure he could visit you. There is nothing improper in that. You might engineer a time alone with him. If not, as he is staying with my family, I think you should stay with us overnight after the wedding. This way, you will see him before he departs."

And so, the conversation went for some time until all had retired on Monday night.

Marion Steele arrived in time for morning tea on Tuesday, finding the girls most talkative and ready for their shopping adventure.

"How has your stay been, Anne? It was so kind of Lady Jane to invite you. I understand your family will be arriving this afternoon. Would you share my coach back to Greenwich?"

"Thank you, Marion, but I will remain here till Wednesday afternoon, as we have some plans for Wednesday morning. I will be at Greenwich mid-afternoon Wednesday. I understand the house is not far from yours, so if I may, I will bring my bridesmaid dress across later that afternoon. I will be there before Thursday, as we agreed, so that I may attend the rehearsal."

Anne felt a little criticised by Marion. She was unsure if Marion was upset because she was not at Greenwich with her family or if she was jealous of her friendship with Emma.

Both Emma and Megan asked, "Please, Marion, may we join you at the rehearsal?"

"Yes, I don't see why not. It would be a great honour. Mrs McPherson would only let me have two bridesmaids as she was not keen on a large bridal party. If I had known of your interest, you would have been bridesmaids as well. But I am sure you will enjoy the wedding."

Emma was curious about the stress of a wedding, "Marion, it must be a busy time? I hope we have not made it more difficult for you."

"It is quite stressful with all the organisation, but it is lovely having a break.

I mean a complete break – away from Thomas, the family, and the house. It is nice being here with you girls so we can chatter. I find there are so many pressing things each day, and it will not stop after the wedding. There are so many thank you letters to be written, and so on."

"You will have the challenge of living with a husband." Anne smiled, "I'm sure you will whip Thomas into shape over time."

"The first thing needed is stopping his waking so early. His timeclock seems stuck on three in the morning. He is always up early."

The girls looked at each other and began giggling. Marion blushed and said, "Whenever I come down and take breakfast, I always find he has been and gone off some time ago. No, we have not done it yet! Thomas is very insistent on waiting until after the wedding!"

Emma said, "A splendid fellow indeed!"

There was a short silence, and then they all burst into laughter.

The girls filled the day with fun, shopping, lunch, and more shopping. They all found the arcades extensive, with Emma and Megan still looking at hats while Anne and Marion found some afternoon tea. Anne took the opportunity and gently broached the subject that Marion was displeased with her in the morning.

After taking a sip of tea, "Marion, forgive me for asking this but are you a little angry with me today?"

Marion sat up straight and looked Anne in the face. She was not aware of being so obvious. Since making her comment in the morning, she had thought better of it.

"No, not at all. I am sure you have important tasks here with Emma. But I must admit I was a little put out as you are one of my bridesmaids. I thought you might stay with me for the week rather than at the Souths. But perhaps I was a little selfish?"

Anne felt that she could now speak freely to Marion. There was a problem, and she must address it.

"I understand what you are saying, Marion. If not for the invitation from Lady Jane, I would have joined you at Greenwich. Emma and Lady Jane were keen that I attend here, and since I am Robert's fiancée, I felt I should not decline. The wedding will be wonderful, and I will be with you late tomorrow afternoon. You indicated you did not need me until the rehearsal tomorrow, so I apologise if you needed me before this."

Anne could see Marion sitting there, thinking deeply about her response. Anne felt she had made it clear to Marion that while she honoured her friendship and from Saturday would be her sister-in-law, she also had responsibilities to Robert's family. It seemed Marion understood this as well.

"Anne, I am sorry, and I have been selfish. You must also be on good terms with your future family. I am still coming to terms with all these relation-ships. Let us put this behind us. I am sorry if I caused you any grief. We shall have such a wonderful time in the next few days. You must see my going away outfit. I love it. I hope Thomas does."

"I'm sure he will!"

Portsmouth ...

Commodore Jacobs dashed into Admiral Sutherland's office with a smile, "Admiral, two ships are coming into port – unexpected ships!"

"What do you mean 'unexpected' Jacobs?"

"It appears that one is *Restless*, and the other is *Providence!*"

The Admiral opened his mouth in amazement, "You mean........."

"Yes, Sir. It is Captain South, and he has found *Providence* and brought her home!"

"My Lord! This news is wonderful."

The Admiral moved quickly and peered out his window at the busy port. Sure enough, *Providence* was coming in under full sail, and *Restless* followed at a respectful distance.

The Admiral clapped his hands together, "This is wonderful news. I must notify the Admiralty at once. No. No, first I must meet them and find out what happened. Jacobs, arrange my gig. We shall meet them. By Jove, this is great news!"

Robert stood behind the rail on the poop deck. Beside him sat Captain Foster, wrapped in blankets and enjoying the fresh air.

Leaning down, Robert said, "Good entering our home port again, Sir."

Foster had suffered terribly during his capture, and he was recovering slowly. His captors tortured him violently for information, leaving him with only one hand and three fingers. Robert appreciated this man had suffered enough and endeavoured to lift his spirits by seating him beside himself as his ship returned successfully to Port.

"Captain Foster! May I have your permission to bring *Providence* in?"

"Bring her in, Robert!" Foster coughed after speaking. He had little breath and was only just regaining his voice.

"Mr Trotters, please bring down the jibs, staysails, topgallants, and topsails. We will proceed under the courses and spanker."

"Aye, Sir."

The frigate glided sweetly into port like a sophisticated lady entering a room followed by her attentive consort, *Restless*. They made a stunning sight, and quite a few sailors and officers either lifted their caps or waved as they passed their sister ships in the Blue Fleet.

"Captain Coombes, once the anchor is down, have your marines form up a guard of honour. I expect the Admiral won't be long before coming aboard."

"Aye, Sir."

Trotters yelled out the order, "Anchor Away."

The anchor dropped, and *Providence* swung around into the wind.

The few crew up the masts were working hard furling sails. It was mayhem for several minutes, but then order returned, and the men came down on the deck.

Robert requested all the men assemble and addressed them.

"Gentlemen, it has been an honour serving with you. We have brought HMS *Providence* home with her Captain and some crew. You have served honourably in the service of your King and country. Once we have received our guests and they are gone, the Purser, who seems slightly recovered from his captivity, will issue three extra rum rations. Well done, men, on a successful mission."

Trotters yelled out, "Three cheers for Captain South and Captain Foster."

The crew cheered heartily, followed by much back-slapping and laughing on a successful mission as they milled around waiting for their guests.

"Admiral's gig is approaching, Sir!" Swanton advised Robert.

"Organise a few men, and please bring Captain Foster down from the poop deck. I'm sure the Admiral will speak with him."

"Aye, Sir."

Admiral Sutherland scampered up the ship's side, and the crew greeted him with the customary piping aboard and an honour guard of marines. Unable to keep the smile off his face, he saluted the guard and then rushed across, grabbing Robert's hand and shaking it.

"Congratulations, Commander South. Your arrival is the best present I have received in a long time."

"Thank you, Sir!"

"And Foster, welcome home Captain."

Captain Foster tried standing, but he was too weak and emotional for speech.

"Calm yourself, old friend. We will take good care of you now. God knows how much you have suffered under those traitors! We will arrange transfer of yourself and your men ashore quickly."

The Admiral looked around the ship and saw Sir Horace. He walked over and shook his hand.

"Thank you, Horace, for a job well done."

"I think you will enjoy Robert's report, Sir Tristan."

"You are jolly right there, Horace. I will take in every word. Well done, all of you! Come and dine with me tonight when you have finished here, Commander South and Captain Coombes. I will expect you at seven, Sir. In the meantime, I will have Jacobs arrange the transfers of the injured. I will also send a quick letter off notifying the Admiralty of this deed."

The Admiral then walked back across, lowering his voice, "I knew you could do it, Robert! But I must admit I have been worried sick for the last two weeks. I expect you will be off to the wedding and see that lass of yours. I will arrange your leave. Should be plenty of time if you leave in the morning. We will talk at dinner. Well done again."

The Admiral noticed *Restless* dropping anchor beside *Providence*.

"Give me a megaphone, please."

Megaphone in hand, he moved against the ship's rail and waved at Lieutenant Ham, "Good work, Lieutenant Ham!"

"Thank you, Sir," Ham shouted back across the water and saluted.

With that, the Admiral and Commander Jacobs descended back into their gig and sailed ashore.

The Wedding at Greenwich ...

Alexander Steele stood in the church's vestibule as Anne arranged Marion's train. The sight of his daughter reminded him so much of Jennifer that it was uncanny. She was the image of the woman he married some thirty years ago. His daughter was so beautiful and with the promise of many years of happiness ahead.

Marion looked up at him and noticed the tears in his eyes. She gave him a little hug and said, "Thank you for being my Father. I love you so much. I just wish mother could be here."

Alexander struggled with the answer. He was between two places, the joy of seeing his little girl all grown up and marrying the man she loved and the memories of all the happiness his wife and he had enjoyed over so many years. When he thought of Jennifer, he was angry. 'How could God be so cruel, letting Jennifer suffer this way? What was the point of faith when misery like this occurred?' His feelings were mixed, but he would not let this spoil the day. He smiled down at his daughter and said, "I am as proud as any father could be with my only daughter. If she were well, remember that your mother would also celebrate and find so much joy in this special day for you. Live this day as if she were here, Marion. That's what she would have wanted."

Marion looked up at him and smiled, "I know that, and I will, Father!"

Anne finished with the train, and Marion's other bridesmaid, Nicole Stephens, an old friend from school, assisted in straightening out Marion's dress.

"Girls, are we ready?" Archdeacon Handle always checked everything was ready with the bridal party before leaving the vestibule and joining the groom at the front of the congregation.

Anne looked at Marion, who nodded in agreement and said, "Yes, Archdeacon."

"I will join Thomas. Once I am sure he is ready, I will signal the organist. The verger will then open the doors, and after he plays a few bars, please commence down the aisle, Nicole."

Everyone agreed, and the Archdeacon set off. The church was packed. Marjorie invited far more guests than the Turners expected, and there was no shortage of people sitting on either side of the centre aisle. Once Anne counted Nicole taking eight steps, it was her turn to step out. She took her first step and then, lifting her eyes, saw a mountain of faces watching her and smiling as she followed.

Anne found the first three steps nerve-racking, gaining her confidence when a few familiar faces appeared and smiled. Halfway down the aisle, a navy man was sitting beside the aisle but facing forward. He turned, and a familiar broad smiling face appeared. Anne stopped in her tracks as she saw it was Robert. All she wanted was Robert's arms around her, but she held herself back from running toward him. Tears of joy came from her eyes, making her look more radiant as she regained her step. He reached out and touched her hand as she passed, and their eyes met in a bond so strong that no one else would ever understand.

William sitting beside his mother, poked his head around, peering up the aisle for Anne.

Recognising Robert, he shouted, "It's Robert!"

Eleanora said, "Shush, William!" But as soon as she heard William's call, it filled her with even more happiness. Today her first married daughter was sitting behind her, her first son was waiting for his bride coming down the aisle, and her second daughter, the bridesmaid, was engaged to a wonderful young man who sneaked in unannounced. Johnathan noticed the tears in her eyes as she smiled. He passed her his handkerchief, which she accepted. Dabbing her eyes, she found the words would not come; such was her emotion. Eleanora quietly thanked her God for all the blessings she was receiving.

Waiting now for some time, Thomas commenced trembling. His best man Jeb Hiscock passed him a small bottle, "Here, have a swig of this!"

Thomas took the bottle but did not drink. He murmured from the side of his mouth, "I'm not sure I can do this, Jeb!"

"Yes, you can! This girl coming is the one you have always wanted. This marriage is what you have always planned. Take a swig first and feel the fire."

Thomas fumbled with the bottle and finally removed the cork. He took a good-sized swig of the scotch whiskey, surprising Archdeacon Rufus Handle. Passing the small bottle back to Jeb, he felt the burning liquid flow into his stomach, giving a warm sensation inside.

"Now, Thomas, turn around and smile at Marion."

With that instruction, Thomas slowly turned, noticing most of the congregation were watching the bride approach. Gaining some composure, he looked down the aisle and focused on Marion's beautiful smile as she followed the bridesmaids toward him. She was his princess coming to meet him in all her beauty. Not prepared for such a sight, Thomas was dumbfounded by her radiance as she moved with grace up the aisle. She floated along the floor in a magnificent white wedding gown with a beautiful smile and her eyes fixed on him.

Jeb leaned over and whispered in Thomas's ear, "Now start thinking about tonight!"

Thomas turned around and smiled. Then he turned back and thought, 'Yes, the time has nearly come.' He now was feeling a lot stronger.

Archdeacon Handle moved across and asked Jeb, "Is he all right?"

"He's fine."

The Archdeacon was relieved. He knew the ones with a best man were usually under control. It was the grooms without a best man who became the problem children. Rufus breathed more comfortably as he watched Thomas almost glow with pleasure as his bride came closer and closer.

Rufus Handle was aware of the disappointment Marion was experiencing because her mother was not attending. His discussions with the bride's father revealed Alexander blamed God for his misery. He thought, 'People usually blamed God for letting things happen. But in this case, it was just the unfortunate situation that Jennifer fell ill from this disease – whatever it was!' Rufus saw much suffering by people of all ages, mostly at their bedside, as they drifted out of life. He often wondered if medical science was making any headway at all.

Carefully watching as Marion and her father approached, he noticed Alexander's smile lacked the bride's joy. The father was putting on a brave face, but Rufus could see the pain of being without his wife. He suspected this might be the case.

Once the bride and groom were facing him at the end of the aisle, he commenced the service.

With a great smile on his face, he said, "Dearly beloved, we gather here today to join this man and this woman in Holy Matrimony."

Rufus could see that many women in the congregation were already dabbing their eyes. He even noticed Reverend Andrew Taggart using a handkerchief as the service continued.

At the appropriate time, Rufus gave his address. He understood that he should recognise Marion's mother, and he would do his best.

"Thomas and Marion! I will not speak long, but there are a few things of importance that I would like to say. This occasion is a serious time when you make Holy vows to each other and enter a marriage relationship between you both and God the Father."

Rufus continued with a couple of points before addressing the absence of Jennifer.

"But there will often be hard times.

Today, we are all mindful that Jennifer, Marion's mother, cannot be here with us. On this earth, her mind is somewhere else. Unfortunately, this is the effect of the disease that afflicts her. We all know how much Marion, her daughter, and Alexander, her husband, wished she could be here.

Though you are hurting, let us be of good cheer and remember she is in God's care. God does not desert his children!"

He paused for a few seconds letting this comment sink in.

"God keeps them in his wonderful care. After all, we all know how much He loves each one of us. He gave up his only Son for each of us on the cross so that we could have life everlasting. What greater sacrifice could He have made for you and me? He cares for Jennifer in the most intimate way, and I am sure that He is with her now, and she is with us in spirit, full of praise on this beautiful day.

So, let your hearts not be troubled but be thankful for His grace and His care for Jennifer on this glorious occasion!"

Soon he ended his message and continued with the service.

Alexander Steele that day listened carefully. As the service progressed, he was mindful of his response in this situation. Yes, he blamed God, a God he was not sure even existed, for Jennifer's sickness. He was bitter because of the hard decisions forced upon him. He was drifting away from his children in his angry state and had forgotten his blessings. But life had blessed Jennifer and him with four beautiful children who loved their mother so much. Was this wrong? He was still unsure. Yet he realised he should be thankful. Was it right that he should feel happiness?

During the prayers in the service, he spoke with this unknown God, 'God, I am not sure if you are there. I am sorry, God, I blamed you for Jennifer's suffering. Surely someone was to blame, and I needed a focus. I now know that I was wrong. Thank you for caring for my wife. Thank you for this wonderful wedding today for Marion.' With this, Alexander found he could let go of his grudge against God. He then felt a tremendous emotional relief in his body, something he had never experienced before. Slowly his muscles relaxed, and the tension in his body decreased. He felt he could rejoin life again. Faintly a smile came on his tearful face as he saw his daughter Marion make her solemn but joyous promises to her husband Thomas and joined with him in creating a new family.

Mark Steele, Alexander and Jennifer's eldest son, noticed his father's tears and put his arm around his father, hugging him.

On that day, Miss Marion Steele became Mrs Marion Turner, witnessed by some five hundred guests. The celebration continued late that evening until the bride and groom made their exit, waving from the carriage after saying their goodbyes.

Thomas moved a little closer, "At last!". He kissed her passionately for some time.

Anne Turner and Sir Robert South clung together, and every so often, she kissed him again. William and Simeon Turner tugged Robert's sleave and pestered him with questions. "Did you sink any pirate ships, Robert?"

"Lots of them, and one exploded, sending all the pirates into Davey Jones's locker!"

"Who is Davey Jones?"

"I'll tell you tomorrow! I'm busy now!"

Megan Bassington and Emma South talked with David Sopwith. David inquired, "Lady Emma, I have received a letter from your mother, Lady Jane, including an invitation for dinner on Tuesday night at St James's Square. I have accepted and hope you will also be there."

"I will be! I am glad you are here, David. You will enjoy seeing St James's Square. I will be spending some nights before that with the Turners. Perhaps you would escort me to dinner?"

"It would be an honour, Emma." David broke into a broad grin and could not take his eyes off her.

Megan excitedly said, "I will also be there, and Neville and Bethany. It will be quite an occasion."

Megan found that David and Emma seemed distant, so she excused herself and approached Lady Jane.

"My Lady! Do you think there might be an understanding between Emma and David?"

Lady Jane softly made a friendly reply, "I do hope so!"

Moving closer, she said quietly, "Who knows, Megan, what Lord Fintelton might announce on Tuesday night at dinner?"

Eleanora Turner walked with her husband, "Thank you, Jonathan, for bringing me here! And all the money you have spent on this. It has been one of the most wonderful occasions in my life."

She took his hands gently and, in a contented voice, said, "I can go now, Jonathan and I will be happy!"

Jonathan understood that Eleanora was telling him for the first time she knew she was dying. He struggled with his answer, and the tears welled up in his eyes, "Hold on, Eleanora, my Dear. For the baby and me!"

He clasped her hands and drew her to him, "I am so sorry for all the misery I have given you. I am changing and trying my best now."

Gently she whispered, "Jonathan, you have changed! I love you so much. Let us take these last few steps together, shall we?"

Jonathan nodded but could not speak.

William Turner followed his parents and took comfort, seeing them holding hands. He pondered, 'Perhaps I am safe', not having seen this before. I hope they hold hands forever!'

For William, it was a long day, and he was tired! He saw Aggie standing near the coach. William ran over and put his hand in hers. "I'm tired, Aggie. May I go in the coach with you?"

Aggie hugged William and kept him close. She helped him into the coach. Sitting beside him, Aggie let him fall across her lap and raised his feet on the seat. After she had covered him with a wrap, he was asleep in no time. She stroked his hair gently and whispered down, "Sleep well, precious little one. Find all the rest you can. There is a lot ahead of you in life!"

www.ingramcontent.com/pod-product-compliance
Lightning Source LLC
Chambersburg PA
CBHW020243030726
47499CB00001B/33